*The Killing Frost*

# THE KILLING FROST

Thomas Hayden

St. Martin's Press
New York

Library of Congress Cataloging-in-Publication Data

Hayden, Thomas, 1928–1989.
    The killing frost / Thomas Hayden.
      p.  cm.
    ISBN 0-312-07010-1
    1. Ireland—History—Sinn Fein Rebellion, 1916—Fiction.
I. Title.
PR6058.A977K5   1992
823′.914—dc20

91-36427
CIP

First published in Great Britain by Random Century Group.

First U.S. Edition: March 1992
10 9 8 7 6 5 4 3 2 1

This is the state of man: to-day he puts forth
The tender leaves of hopes; to-morrow blossoms,
And bears his blushing honours thick upon him;
The third day comes a frost, a killing frost;
And, when he thinks, good easy man, full surely
His greatness is a-ripening, nips his root,
And then he falls, as I do.

William Shakespeare
*Henry VIII*

Failure or success seem to have been allotted to men by their stars. But they retain the power of wriggling, of fighting with their star or against it, and in the whole universe the only really interesting movement is this wriggle.

EM Forster
'Our Diversions'

# The Return

# I

Alexander Carew put the flask to his mouth and let the last of the brandy trickle over his tongue. When he had drained the flask he placed it on top of the locker beside him and lay down again on the narrow berth. The tiny cabin was unheated and he felt frozen to the marrow. From below, the rhythmical pounding of engines beat steadily up through the decks; he could feel the vibrations throbbing against his spine.

Two hours before, when the ship had cleared the harbour of Holyhead, the noise had seemed unbearable. Now it merely irritated. Like the cold, it was just one more discomfort that had to be endured. He stared vacantly up at the lances of pale gold slanting through the thick glass of the porthole above his head. Several times he had felt impelled to get up and go down the corridor to the bar and relax there with a whiskey and soda. Each time he had resisted the temptation. There was always the possibility of meeting someone he knew, someone whose offer of a drink he could not refuse without being discourteous. All the time he would be waiting apprehensively for the conversation to dry up; for the long awkward silence; for the first hesitant mention of Valerie's name. . . . Then the usual mumbled, maudlin expression of condolence would follow and after that the questions would begin and his wounds would start to bleed all over again.

I'm safe here, he reassured himself, closing his eyes, feeling himself swaying gently with the easy roll of the ship, feeling the warmth of the brandy thawing the chill from his body, safe. . . . He began to breathe easily and deeply. It occurred to him that this was the first time in a long while he had permitted himself the luxury of resting like this during the daylight hours.

'A few more minutes,' he whispered, yielding to the lethargic sensation stealing over his body. 'Just a little while longer . . .' He slept.

3

He was striding down a dim-lit, deserted street that seemed to stretch away into infinity. It was raining steadily and beyond the flickering gas-lamps, the buildings rose, tall and dark, like the sheer blank walls of a canyon. Not one window displayed light – it was as if the entire city had been abandoned. In the desolate silence, the hasty beat of his footsteps raised sharp clear echoes above the hiss of the falling rain. Panic intensified with each rapid step. Valerie was waiting – waiting with dwindling hope and mounting despair. He could only hope and pray he was not too late. He drove forward against the slanting rain, castigating himself for squandering all those precious hours; experiencing remorse for his callous indifference to her frantic appeal for help. 'I delayed too long,' he moaned to himself, 'too long.'

He came to a standstill beneath a massive stone structure which reared up into the rain-swept darkness. The ground-floor windows were ablaze with light. He stood for a moment, watching the shadows moving behind the cream embroidered drapes, listening to the animated chatter and the occasional burst of laughter from within. Could Valerie still be here? He mounted a long flight of steps, trying to keep hope alive, and into a large hall floored in chequered marble. His heels clicked sharply against it as he strode towards the door. He twisted the handle, pushed inward and stood, blinking against the brilliant light.

He was at the edge of an immense luxurious ballroom. It was crammed with people. They stood in groups, talking, laughing, drinking. It seemed to be a reception of some kind. The gentlemen were in evening dress and the ladies wore long splendent gowns and white elbow-length gloves. Here and there a tiara caught the light from the chandeliers and flashed like a heliograph. He hesitated for a moment, painfully conscious of his wet clothes and dark, dripping hair, then closed the door and walked forward. Heads turned towards him; he could hear whispered comments in his wake. By the time he reached the far end of the ballroom the talking and the laughter had died away. He turned to face them in the sudden hush. Suddenly, as if acting on a signal, everyone turned away and started to talk and laugh again. He closed his eyes in despair. Too late, too late. . . .

The boisterous group in front of him were separating. For a few brief seconds he could see the other end of the room. His heart leaped. A woman stood alone by the door. She was attired for the street: grey coat, fur hat, hands enclosed in a muff. Distance blurred the features, but he knew it was Valerie. He stepped forward, weak with relief. He wriggled through the crowd. Progress was slow and he had to restrain himself from forcing his way through.

4

He could see Valerie clearly now – could see her turning her head slowly from side to side as her eyes searched the crowd. He wanted to call out – wanted to raise a hand to attract her attention. But the sense of urgency he had felt only a minute ago was receding. Somehow the motivation for it all eluded him. He forced his mind to think back. Then he remembered. Someone had been waiting. . . .

When he opened his eyes it was with a feeling of utter weariness as though he had travelled a great distance. The ballroom was deserted and the first grey light of day filtered through the drapes covering the windows. The only evidence of life having existed here lay about his feet–a broken wine-glass, a crumpled fan, a lorgnette that had been crushed underfoot and ground into the carpet. In the faint cold light of early morning the room had a dreary, dishevelled look. He stood, numb with shock and dismay, until the spectral greyness faded into the bright gold of day. Then he buried his face in his hands and wept.

The sudden blast of the ship's siren jerked him awake. He lay, stunned and dazed by the hollow roar drumming against his ears. It ceased abruptly. In the sudden silence the shrieks of seagulls, muted by the thick glass of the porthole, scrabbled at his fuddled senses. He remained still, staring blankly up at where the flat, hard light of late evening burnished the grey steel plates overhead. Tiny beads of moisture clung to his eyelashes. He could taste the salt of tears on the tip of his tongue.

He struggled upright, wincing at the movement of his chilled cramped legs, then moved stiffly off the bunk and stood, swaying a little, feeling the heavy heart-beat of the engines throbbing under his benumbed feet. His mouth was arid and sour from the brandy; he could feel his face grimy and sticky where the tears had dried and caked. Looking down, he saw that his uniform was creased and rumpled. He straightened the tunic, and slid the palms of his hands over it in a vain attempt to smooth out the crinkles. Suddenly he was overcome by a feeling of fury at his appearance. He twisted the tap on the small hand-basin and, bending down, formed a cup with his hands and let it fill with water. Then he buried his face in it, enjoying the icy tingling freshness. It cleared his sluggish senses.

He dabbed at his face with the towel, and turned to the small rectangular mirror. He stood before it, adjusting his tie, sweeping back a few stray hairs with the palm of his hand. The long, narrow face stared solemnly back at him. Deep lines of exhaustion were etched into the grey skin; the eyes were flat and stoical. He remembered Sinclair's languid drawl coming through the half-open door.

5

'Alec Carew? Oh dear . . . how can I best describe him? Ever see a tree that had been struck by lightning? That's Carew. Burnt out. Look into his eyes sometime. Eerie experience. . . .'

Tonight, he told himself, they will celebrate my transfer to Ireland with sighs of relief. They will sit back and relax before the fire and allow their pent-up feelings to flow out over the whiskies and gins. He could imagine Sinclair leaning back in a chair with a glass in one hand and a cigar in the other, gazing reflectively at the ceiling, drawling in that affected lazy accent of his, 'Personally I couldn't abide the cove. Too morbid . . . too introverted . . . Good riddance, that's what I say . . .'

He glanced at his watch; they were not due in for another half-hour. Curious, he reached for his greatcoat and cap. He welcomed the opportunity to get out on deck; the cabin had suddenly assumed the cramped oppressiveness of a prison cell.

He closed the door and walked down the corridor. A man came towards him from the other end, and swerved into the bar. For an instant the noise of tipsy laughter and drunken good-fellowship was trapped between the swing of a door. He twisted away from it and mounted the steps.

He came out on deck to see the ship gliding slowly into fog. He pulled the collar of his greatcoat up about his ears and, hands deep in pockets, sauntered up the deck towards the bow. He was relieved to find it deserted; the bitter cold and the sight of fog had driven everyone to shelter. Visibility was reduced to a few feet. He picked his way along the wet and slippery deck, back and forth between barrier and bow, like a sentry on his lonely beat.

The dream came drifting back. Remorse, he told himself bitterly, what's the use of feeling it now? If only I had felt like this when I read the letter . . . even the slightest touch of compassion. . . . He winced, remembering how he had gloated over the lines of self-reproach, the appeal for forgiveness, the frantic cry for help. The threat of suicide he had dismissed as feigned hysteria.

He reached the bow and turned about, seeing himself once again in that musty-smelling cab, staring out at the grey drizzly London streets jogging past, indifferent to the presence of the portly police constable sitting beside him. This is a mistake, he had kept repeating to himself, some kind of ghastly mistake. He had maintained the delusion right up to the moment when the sheet had been drawn back from the white rigid face and the voice had inquired gently, 'Can you identify the lady, sir?'

He flinched at the memory and tried to push it from his mind. Think of something else, an inner voice urged, anything.

Then another voice spoke, cold, stern, merciless. *Murderer!*

I killed her, he told himself fiercely, killed her as surely as if my own hands had sent her plunging down into the muddy waters of the Thames. He halted at the barrier and stood staring into the fog. It pressed against his face like a wet heavy blanket. He felt exhausted–worn-out by lack of sleep and the constant conflict within. An eyelid began to twitch; there was a crawling sensation about the shoulder blades. He took his hands out of his pockets and gripped the top of the waist-high barrier, nerves on edge.

The ship's siren gave a sudden blast of warning, jolting him out of his reverie. His head jerked up in alarm.

'Jesus!' He staggered back, heart leaping in terror.

An old man stood gaping at him. The face was narrow and gaunt with high prominent cheekbones. The wild fixed stare and the slack open mouth gave an impression of mental instability. Tall and thin, in an overcoat too big for him, he stood clasping a brown paper parcel to his chest.

Carew swallowed hard, feeling a mixture of shame and anger at his own violent reaction. He spun on his heel and strode quickly back up the deck. He came to an abrupt halt ten seconds later, heart pounding. He held himself rigid, digging his fingernails into the palms of his hands. He took several deep breaths then turned and walked slowly back towards the barrier. All he could see was a short stretch of deck disappearing into fog. He rested both hands on top of the barrier and leaned over, listening intently, trying to catch the sound of footsteps. But he could hear nothing, only the slow muffled thump of engines beating up from the bowels of the ship.

The craving for a cigarette came back and he reached into his pocket for his cigarette case. Then he remembered he had smoked the last one. Nevertheless he took it out and opened it, and read once again the delicate copperplate inscription inside.

> *To Alec,*
> *with love and devotion,*
> *from Valerie.*

'Devotion,' he murmured to himself, but this time the old feeling of bitterness was absent. There was no more pain in remembering. He leaned forward, resting both elbows on the rail, the cigarette case sandwiched between his joined hands, and gazed reflectively down at the heaving blue-green water. Acheron, he mused. He was separated from that other world by this stream of sorrow. It will be a permanent

7

separation he solemnly vowed to himself. I never want to see England again. He had left so many bitter and painful memories behind. If the powers that be ordered him back, he would resign his commission – retire to Carewscourt.

He turned the cigarette case over in his hands. Her gift to him on their second wedding anniversary. It was like an umbilical cord holding him firmly to the past, tugging away at him with memories. He glided his thumb back and forth over the smooth gold surface for nearly a minute, then tossed it away. He watched it spin out into the greyness and vanish. He sighed. '*Factum est*,' he whispered, and straightening up, walked away towards the bow.

The fog was less dense now; light was beginning to filter through. He stood watching it dissolve into shreds, peeling away like sleep from the eyes. Then suddenly they were in the clear and he blinked against the brightness. Under his feet he could feel the engines coming slowly to life and starting to pound again. The deck began to roll slightly as the ship picked up speed. A half-mile away lay the port and the huddled houses of the town and beyond, sharply outlined against the pale evening sky, the long purple sweep of the Wicklow Hills.


## II


The light was fading. In Dublin Castle, Major Calder switched on the green-shaded desk lamp and resumed reading the despatch from the War Office. It was more like a reprimand. He flinched at certain phrases as though he were being rapped over the knuckles: 'lamentable paucity of information . . . underestimate the seriousness of the situation . . . more initiative and less reliance on . . .' He could feel his anger mounting; it abated a little when he came to the footnote.

'Your request for an assistant has been sanctioned. Captain Alexander Carew will arrive May 3rd. Please make necessary arrangements.'

The Major grunted and reached for his pipe and tobacco pouch. For almost a year now he had been pestering Whitehall for an experienced Intelligence officer – preferably an Irishman or someone with an understanding of the country and its people. The response never varied; always the matter was under careful consideration.

He began to fill the pipe. If I had not decided to bypass the usual channels, he told himself, nothing would have been done. Asking Reggie Sinclair to intercede had been the only alternative. Pipe in mouth, he applied the match flame to the bowl. After giving several puffs, he lay back in the chair. Only three weeks since I wrote to Sinclair, he thought with satisfaction, always knew he had influence.

He watched the grey clouds of tobacco smoke spiralling upwards towards the ceiling. This was the time of evening he enjoyed most, when work was at an end and he could take his ease, smoking the pipe. But for once he could not relax. The critical tone of the despatch disturbed him. Obviously Sinclair had gone over someone's head; had possibly persuaded some politician friend of his to bring pressure to bear. He bit on the mouthpiece. He realised now, with the wisdom of afterthought, that he had blundered badly. He had acted on impulse, out of sheer frustration. It had not occurred to him that his action might be construed as treachery by his former colleagues. God knows, he thought with concern, I never wanted to cause dissension—not now of all times.

A highly confidential report had come in about the formation of a subcommittee under the control of the Committee of Imperial Defence. It was to meet and discuss how best to combat the growing menace of German espionage in Britain. Already three agents had been arrested, but this was just the tip of the iceberg. Enough evidence was now in hand to show that over the past few years German Intelligence had built up and established an extensive and effective spy-ring. That it could do so with impunity was due to inadequate laws and the ineffectiveness of British Intelligence as a whole. Military Intelligence in particular, the Major knew, was way behind that of France and Germany. It was a situation which filled him with dismay and foreboding.

He sat for a while sucking at the pipe, delaying the moment when he would have to file away the heap of documents and records that lay on the desk before him. It was a task he disliked, but regulations were strict: anything of no further use, however innocuous, had to be destroyed by him personally before leaving. He began to assemble the papers first. Ironic to think that once he had complained of having nothing to do. He opened the top file; he had read this dossier at least six times over the past few months, but still he wanted to go through it again to refresh his memory.

MYLES BURKE
Date of description: 20th March 1867.

*Height*: 6ft 2ins
*Visage*: Long. High, prominent cheek-bones
*Hair*: Black
*Eyes*: Dark blue
*Complexion*: Pale
*Other distinguishing marks*: Long horizontal scar above right hip. (Result of bullet wound: Battle of Fredericksburg, December 1862.)

The above was born in the village of Turlough, 3 miles north-east of Castlebar, Co. Mayo, March 1842. Family emigrated to Canada, 1847.

*Note*: Wholesale emigration from Ireland took place during and after Famine years, 1845–1850.

The Burke family moved from Quebec and crossed border into United States of America sometime in 1849. (Above information supplied by prisoner under interrogation.)

Served with distinction in Union Army (Irish Brigade) during American Civil War. Participated in battles: Bull Run, Fair Oaks, Antietam, Fredericksburg. Wounded at Fredericksburg. Decorated and promoted to Captain, February 1863. Believed to have become a sworn member of the Irish Republican Brotherhood whilst still a commissioned officer. (Oath probably administered by James Stephens, the Fenian Commander-in-chief.)

Arrived in Ireland (1866) with other Irish-American officers to participate in Fenian uprising. Following the defeat of rebel force at Tallaght, Co. Dublin, Burke was captured after a brief skirmish with troops in the Dublin mountains.

*Note*: At Burke's trial, a murder charge against him had to be dropped for lack of evidence. He is believed to have shot and killed Private William McKay of the 92nd Highlanders whilst breaking through a military picquet about two miles east of Tallaght village.

Tried before a Special Commission (19th April, 1867) and sentenced to fifteen years' penal servitude. Served twelve years of sentence in Pentonville Prison, London, and then released but not allowed to return to Ireland or settle in Great Britain until the completion of the term of imprisonment to which he had originally been sentenced. Sailed for Rotterdam (29th April, 1879). Burke remained in Holland for about two years, then moved to Belgium. He left Belgium early in 1882 and settled in Paris where he obtained a position as tutor of English.

In March 1889, Burke crossed from Calais to Dover with a party of Fenian officers led by Garret Lysaght. Their intention was to destroy with explosives the gates of Pentonville Prison and release the Fenian prisoners. (Mostly those who had been involved in the dynamite campaign in London some years previous.) The complete details of the proposed operation had already been supplied to Scotland Yard by the British Secret Service. (See their agent's report, CBS/HO 7673/S.)

The SS agent (posing as a Fenian officer) was able to procure the addresses of the lodgings of Lysaght and his party together with the names and addresses of sympathisers involved in the operation. On receipt of this information, police launched simultaneous raids all over central London. Numerous arrests were made without much resistance being made.

Burke's lodging at 43 Wynyatt St, EC1, was raided by a small party of police under the command of Detective-Inspector Butterworth. In the scuffle that ensued, Burke shot and wounded Inspector Butterworth before being overpowered.

Burke's trial took place at the Old Bailey, 21st May, 1889. (Transcript of trial attached.) He was indicted with the following: (i) the shooting and attempted murder of Detective-Inspector Butterworth; (ii) conspiring and attempting to cause explosions at an occupied public building, thereby endangering life; (iii) being a member of a proscribed organisation. Accused pleaded guilty to all three charges. Sentenced to life imprisonment, 24th May 1889.

In the reports which followed this bleak summary, what impressed Calder most was the man's tenacity and apparent indestructibility. Burke had survived the Famine when half his family (and God knew how many others) had not. He had survived the terrible Atlantic crossing in the fever-infected hold of one of the coffin ships engaged in the emigrant trade. When the ancient brig set out carrying her cargo of three hundred and fifty ragged, half-starved souls, many were sick and some had the fever. Typhus. The captain of a British merchantman later stated that he was able to follow the course of many of the emigrant ships by the corpses floating in the water. Later, Burke and his remaining family were to discover that they had fled from poverty and hunger in Ireland only to find it in the slums and shanty towns of the New World. His father, like most of the emigrants, was without skill or trade. To exist, he like they fought and scrambled for the most menial and filthiest of jobs. Despondent, home-sick, some of them drank themselves into oblivion with cheap, rot-gut whiskey. As Myles Burke grew up, he learned to fear the effects of drink on the wreck of a man that had been his father.

As soon as he could, he left for Boston, where he worked – when he could, for work was scarce and labour plentiful – and taught himself to read and write. It was there, in Boston that he fell under the spell of Garret Lysaght. A native of Limerick, Lysaght was the sole survivor of his family; and when the heart-lacerating grief was over, there remained nothing but a deep burning hatred for England. As he described to Myles Burke the scenes on the Limerick docks – food and livestock being taken on board bound for England and a long line of red-coated British soldiers guarding them, forcing back the howling, hunger-crazed mob with the point of a bayonet – the two young men made their decision firmly and irrevocably: to dedicate their lives to the cause of Irish freedom. Their determination never wavered or dissipated as they grew into full manhood. Rather it intensified with the passage of time.

In the ten years which followed the Famine, more than two million Irish had crossed the Atlantic, settling in or passing through the great cities on the Eastern seaboard of North America. Nearly all had fled from poverty and oppression; a mere handful were political refugees who had come to create a revolutionary organisation among the large Irish population. When approached, Garret Lysaght and Myles Burke enrolled immediately. A sister organisation, the Irish Revolutionary Brotherhood, had been established in Ireland. The American Fenians were to provide any future rebel army in the field with trained officers and arms. There was no problem in procuring arms; practical military experience was more difficult to find. The opportunity to obtain some came with the outbreak of Civil War.

After the first shots had been fought at Fort Sumter, Garret Lysaght and Myles Burke responded to the call for volunteers and enlisted in the Irish Brigade. They gained promotion and experience during those first, fierce engagements of the war: Bull Run, Fair Oaks, Antietam. . . . And then, the bloodiest of all, Fredericksburg.

At Fredericksburg, Burnside's army had to traverse a half-mile of open ground under heavy rifle and artillery fire before reaching the Confederate positions on Marye's Heights. Attack after attack was beaten back with fearful slaughter. The rebel position was almost impregnable. Nevertheless orders were given for one more attack – marye's Heights had to be taken at all costs.

Shoulder to shoulder, the long lines of Federal infantry advanced, stumbling over the bodies of the dead and wounded from the previous attacks. The Confederate artillery opened fire; spherical shot tore wide bloody gaps in the blue-coated ranks. On they came to where the Confederate infantry waited with levelled rifles behind a low stone wall which ran along the foot of Marye's Heights. As the Federals came within range, they opened fire.

The two leading waves disintegrated under a furious hail of bullets; three more volleys wiped out the two waves following. Still they came, advancing doggedly into the murderous fire of the Springfields, falling by the hundred before the low stone wall. The survivors, shocked and dazed, fell back in disorder, or sought protection behind the bodies of their fallen comrades.

The firing died away. The thick grey smoke of battle dissolved slowly in the cold December air, revealing the scene of conflict in all its horror. Powder-grimed, combat-weary Confederate troops slumped over their heated rifles against their stone barricade, gazing dully out at the carnage in front of them.

The only survivors of that last charge were Captain Garret Lysaght and his second-in-command, Lieutenant Myles Burke. Although both were badly wounded, they managed to crawl back to the Federal lines, carrying the colours with them. After a brief stay in a field hospital, they were both transferred to a hospital in Washington. After the bloody defeat of Fredericksburg, the North badly needed something to restore morale, and found it in Lysaght and Burke. They were both decorated by President Lincoln.

During the years of the Civil War, the Fenian movement made spectacular progress, and now numbered nearly two hundred thousand. Its sister organisation in Ireland had grown more slowly, largely because of the Catholic Church which condemned it as an oath-bound militant body. Nevertheless, it did grow and, from America, officers with military experience arrived in large numbers to train the future rebel army. Arms began to filter through.

By 1865, most Fenians felt that the time was ripe for insurrection; but they lacked resolute leadership and it wasn't until the beginning of 1867 that a group of senior officers, including in their number Garret Lysaght and Myles Burke, sailed for Ireland with the intention of starting the long-awaited rebellion. But much valuable time had been lost. The British authorities were by now fully alert and ready for any outbreak. The rising, when it did take place, was sporadic and too widely dispersed. It fizzled out in a series of minor skirmishes under atrocious conditions. Lysaght and Burke were both captured and tried. They were each sentenced to fifteen years' penal servitude.

Lysaght had escaped from Portland prison; Burke had served out twelve years of his sentence before his release; he was not permitted to reside in Ireland or England until the term of his sentence was complete. He had settled in Paris, where he had obtained a position as a tutor of English. Until, from New York, came news of Lysaght's plan; a group was being formed to attack Pentonville Prison and release the Fenian prisoners there. The scheme was to blow with petards the outer and inner gates, thus giving immediate access to the office between the two in which the cell keys were stored at night. It was an audacious undertaking – but doomed from the start. One of Lysaght's chosen men was a British agent.

Late in January 1889, Lysaght and his men sailed from New York to France; in March, half the party crossed from Calais to Dover; the rest followed two days later. Lodgings had been arranged for them in various houses within a mile or two of Pentonville Prison; it did not take the authorities long to find out where. They acted without delay. In the early hours of an April morning, raids took place all over central London. They were a complete success – or almost. A detective was shot and wounded; and Garret Lysaght eluded them. Once again, he was free, while his disciple, Myles Burke, had been sentenced and was now serving a life-imprisonment.

Since then, the Major reflected wryly, Garret Lysaght had used the pen as a weapon; and with altogether more success. While Burke was rotting in prison, Lysaght was in New York creating mischief. Whenever Anglophobia among the American Irish showed signs of flagging, he was there to whip it up again; he inflamed the emotions and the fears of American isolationists and put political pressure on members of the Senate – and now the growing tension between Britain and Germany was providing him with an excellent opportunity. In the event of an Anglo-German war, he wrote, the freedom of Ireland could be achieved only by the defeat of Britain. He set out to weight the scales against Britain from the start. 'Just hot air . . .' the new British Ambassador reassured the Consul General in New York. But Lysaght, in the Consul General's opinion, was far more dangerous than any number of German agents; his worst fears were confirmed when Lysaght was reported seen in the company of the German Military Attaché.

Calder felt cold and uncomfortable; he pulled open the lower drawer of his desk and produced a half-empty bottle of whiskey and a tumbler. He filled the glass to the brim and sat back in his chair. Whitehall had the impression that conspiracies were happening all over Ireland. He was harassed by insistent demands for information. And he had none to give – not even the name and address of one IRB man. The entire resources of the Dublin Metropolitan Police and the Royal Irish

14

Constabulary were at his disposal, and yet the special file he had opened months ago was still empty.

He reached for the bottle and poured for himself another liberal measure. The whiskey was making him morose: a faint feeling of resentment began to stir in him. He found himself dwelling on the wording of the despatch from the War Office . . . 'lamentable paucity of information . . . more initiative . . .' He swallowed a mouthful of whiskey and thought bitterly: They consider me to be the same as my predecessor – incompetent, indifferent, content with twiddling my thumbs while the police Special Branch do all the work. He had been obliged to rely on the police for information and advice. The Royal Irish Constabulary not only dealt with ordinary crime, they also maintained a close watch all over Ireland for any signs of subversive activity – not even the remotest village escaped surveillance. And yet, for the first time in sixty years, the reports reaching Dublin Castle contained nothing of a political nature. The explanation, as the Deputy Inspector General had pointed out, was that the old injustices which had been the cause of rebellions had disappeared. The country had never been so prosperous. And now, with Home Rule about to be realised, the last obstacle in the way of a permanent peace between Great Britain and Ireland would be removed. These factors, he had emphasised, plus the opposition of the Catholic Church, had eliminated the Irish Republican Brotherhood more effectively than the police or military could ever have done.

Working on the assumption that the Irish Republican Brotherhood was still in existence and active, Calder had devised a scheme which he hoped would lure some members of that organisation out into the open, so they could be observed and identified. The idea had suggested itself one morning after he received a cable from the War Office requesting information concerning the theft of dynamite from a quarry in Cork. Regan, the Deputy Inspector General, had been his usual confident, reassuring self.

'No cause for alarm, Major. The explosives were stolen for poaching purposes. We caught the culprits. Swine – they must have killed half the fish in the Blackwater!' He had sat there twirling the waxed end of his moustache, a puckish look in his eye. 'Only poachers, Major Calder. Nothing more sinister than that. No cloak-and-dagger stuff – no IRB involvement. Your people in London, Major, are becoming more and more obsessed with something which no longer exists. Oh, I daresay – ' he forestalled the Major's objection with an upraised hand – 'I daresay there are a few IRB men remaining, the leaders – the Supreme Council.

15

But they have been rendered ineffective. Of what use is a headquarters' staff without an army to command?'

Calder did not share the DIG's confidence. His job was to flush out any remaining revolutionary activity that might assist the Germans, and he had been stung by the constant rebukes from Whitehall that he was not doing that job. The solution, when he thought of it, seemed brilliant in its simplicity and it appealed to the fisherman in him. A decoy: that's what he would do, find a decoy to lure the rebels out into the open – just as he might lure a trout from the cool depths of a summer stream. Myles Burke had been the obvious choice.

The Major tapped the ashes from his pipe and refilled it with fresh tobacco. Burke had been released from prison that morning. He had been issued with boat and train tickets, five pounds gratuity, had been escorted to Euston and put on the mail-train for Holyhead. By now, the Major told himself, he should be coming ashore at Kingstown.

The Major picked up a photograph. It had been taken at his request for identification purposes in Pentonville less than three weeks ago. The long gaunt face, the hollow cheeks, the thin strands of white hair brushed flat across the high forehead. But it was the expression on the face that the Major found disturbing, the wide frightened eyes and the slack open mouth. It made him wonder if all his efforts had been in vain. Burke would not have been the first man to have lost his sanity in prison.

Calder slouched over the desk, smoking his pipe, and gazing at the photograph. Burke looked far older than sixty-seven. Calder shook his head and thought, Sixty-seven years – and thirty-two of them spent in prison. Again he felt a little dart of compassion. 'You poor old bastard,' he murmured. 'Better for you if you had died at Fredericksburg.'

III

Myles Burke pressed back against the ship's rail as the turbulent luggage-laden crowd jostled and pushed past him towards the gangway. He tried to steady himself against the continuous buffeting by gripping the rail with his left hand. His right hand clutched a crumpled brown paper parcel to his chest; several times it was almost torn from his grasp. The clamour – the feverish activity, fretted his nerves. He felt an

16

immense weariness and an intense desire to rest somewhere in peace. For an instant he found himself almost wishing for the desolate silence of the prison cell. He stood there waiting for the rush to subside, a tall, seared, dishevelled figure in a dark-grey overcoat that hung loosely on his frame. Long strands of white hair lay untidily across the high narrow forehead and the eyes stared out from the grey furrowed face in fright and bewilderment.

A hoarse, tipsy voice bawled, 'Aye, would yeh look at bloody Methuselah!' and the drunken fraternity from the bar swayed before him. A thick-set man with a bowler perched on the back of his head thrust a flushed sottish face forward.

'Wassamatter?' he inquired with a look of mock concern on his face.

He leaned away from the man's whiskey-tainted breath – away from the grinning faces. They clustered round him while the unheeding crowd struggled past. He knew what they had in mind: a little horse-play – preferably with someone too old and feeble to resist. His heart began to thump painfully as the man with the bowler pressed against him.

'Please . . .' he croaked appealingly.

'Ah leave him be, Durkin, before he dies of fright,' one of the group said. He sighed with relief as the man called Durkin took one step back – then watched with apprehension as the man stood facing him, grinning mischievously, rooting in the pocket of his overcoat for something. He produced what looked like a whistle and placed it between his lips. It was a curious little thing: a tiny cylinder of candy-striped paper lay on the tip. Myles braced himself for the shrill blast as the man's cheeks ballooned. Instead the whistle emitted a squeak and the paper swiftly unrolled and darted towards his face like a lizard's tongue.

'Jesus!' He reared up like a startled horse. His cry of terror was immediately drowned by loud guffaws. Durkin threw back his head and roared with laughter, displaying several gold teeth.

Then they were gone, staggering arm-in-arm through the crowd, bawling out a song picked up in some London music hall.

> Not too tall, not too small,
> Not too thick nor thin.
> She should go out where
> She should go out,
> And in where she should
> Go in . . .

He turned and sagged against the rail. The rapid beat of his heart terrified him. He could feel the cold sweat of fear on his forehead. He had a vision of himself sliding sideways to the deck, clutching his chest, dying under the indifferent eyes of strangers without having stepped ashore. Sweet merciful Jesus, his mind pleaded, don't let it happen. Not now – not after all I've been through . . . His free hand gripped the rail. His mouth was dry and tasted of chalk. He waited – waited for the pounding in his chest to ease, afraid to move, indifferent to the crowd pushing past behind him. He could see them hurriedly moving down the gangway, scurrying across the dock and through the sheds to the waiting train beyond. I'm going to miss it if I don't move now, he told himself with a feeling of panic. His legs were still trembling from the shock and he was unwilling to put them to the test.

He gazed out over sheds and pier, over the curve of shoreline to the Martello Tower on the distant point. Already it was being blotted out by the incoming fog. He could feel the first icy tendrils nipping his cheeks. He moved away slowly towards the gangway, holding on to the rail with his left hand, clutching the paper parcel to his chest with his right.

He stepped cautiously down the steep gangway. He could hear groans of impatience from behind. Further back, someone yelled: 'For God's sake, get a bloody move on!' They swarmed past him as he hobbled painfully across towards the sheds. The boots he wore were too heavy and too big and his ankles were sore and raw from the continuous chafing.

The train was packed. He stood, bewildered by the bustle and noise. Porters hurriedly trundled loaded trolleys down towards the mail-van. The rapid passage of iron wheels over stone made a frightful din. He moved down the platform searching for an empty third-class compartment. He found one – the last compartment in the last carriage. It looked empty; he could not see anyone near the windows. He turned the handle and climbed in, banging the door shut after him.

There was a startled movement in the far corner. A man twisted round on the seat with an annoyed expression on his face while his female companion gave a little cry of dismay.

He sat down and placed the paper parcel on his lap and stared out of the window. He was painfully aware of having interrupted lovemaking; he could sense their resentment at his sudden intrusion. In some carriage further down they were singing.

Oh, isn't it singular,
Awfully, very peculiar.
That new cousin I found
Cost me over five pound,
Oh, isn't it singular . . .

Was that the sort of song they preferred nowadays? He could not understand a word of it. He watched the fog swirling over the sheds and across the platform, dissolving into moisture against the glass. A newspaper seller came out of the greyness.

'*Evenin' Mail* . . . Final . . . *Evenin' Mail*. . . .' He held a copy up to the window.

DYNAMITE FACTORY BLOWN UP NEAR GENOA.
HONEYMOON ACCIDENT.
THE BUDGET: CHANCELLOR'S STATEMENT.

He shook his head and the man walked away. He was unmoved by the events of this modern age – the disasters, the scandals, the political upheavals. For twenty years he had been secluded from the world outside. Once again he had to pick up the thread – from now on he would have to learn how to exist by his own endeavours.

But I'm sixty-seven, he thought with despair. Instinctively he reached into his pocket and drew out a handful of money. The five gold pieces in the palm of his hand gleamed dully in the failing light. Five sovereigns, he thought dismally. For how long will they last? He leaned his head against the cold glass of the window and closed his eyes. He tried not to think of the future.

There was a furtive, rustling movement down at the far end of the seat. He could hear the man's hoarse whisper and the woman's giggle of protest. They think I've fallen asleep, he thought. A faint feeling of envy stirred in his brain. Never had he known the softness of a woman; never had he allowed himself time for the pursuit of a little happiness. Long ago, he had forsaken all to follow Garret Lysaght.

The years fell away and he could see himself standing in the small cramped cabin of that other ship with the rest, staring at the tall, black-bearded, frock-coated figure standing at the head of the table with glass upraised.

'To Ireland free!' The strident voice with its harsh Boston accent echoed and re-echoed in his brain.

They had responded to the toast. Everyone had been in a jubilant mood. The long Atlantic voyage was coming to an end and Ireland lay

19

just over the horizon. The success of their venture had seemed so certain.

He shifted uneasily on the seat, disturbed by memories. How confident all of them had been. He could feel only anger now when he remembered how he had deluded himself with dreams of glory. He had visualised himself leading charge after victorious charge against the red-coated squares; seeing them crumble and fall under the fury of his attack. He had thought: how glorious it would be to die leading a charge like that. He opened his eyes to find the compartment in darkness. Outside, the fog covered the windows like a curtain.

He had been too experienced a soldier to dismiss completely the possibility of defeat, but he had never expected the rebellion to collapse so quickly and so ignominiously. And capture had not meant the martyr's death he had wished for. Instead it had led to imprisonment; to humiliation and degradation. It had led to this – sitting in the dark, old and unwanted, with all he possessed on his lap, listening to the frantic squirmy movements at the other end of the compartment.

Suddenly he was overcome by a rush of fury at the sounds they were making. To be disregarded like this – as if his sensibilities were of no account. He twisted round as the woman began to whimper.

'God blast the pair of ye!' he shouted. 'Find someplace else to fornicate!' In the shocked silence he could hear his own laboured breathing. He was surprised and as startled as they were. For the first time in twenty years he had given vent to his anger. The lights flickered on and he turned his face to the window, not wanting to witness their shame.

'I'm sorry,' he mumbled hoarsely. 'I had no right . . .' He made a sweeping movement with his hand. 'Pay me no heed . . . no heed . . .'

The carriage gave a sudden lurch, and began to move. He pressed his face against the glass as the train picked up speed. In the distance a light flashed off and on through the murk. Lighthouse, he thought. Kingstown Pier. . . .

In 1867, they had stood side by side on the pier in the grey dawn light, manacled hand and foot, shivering inside their thin convict uniforms. They faced the harbour: behind them and on both sides, soldiers with fixed bayonets stood on guard. They waited, mute and miserable, for the arrival of the ship that was to take them to England and prison.

A seagull rose lazily from the water and circled over the harbour. As one man, all eight prisoners lifted their heads and watched it, envying it its freedom. It swept around once more before gliding out into the morning mist.

The little Cork boy on his right gave a deep sigh. He wanted to say something comforting – something that would ease his agony of spirit. But his own physical agony was far greater. The leg-irons were too small; he could feel them cutting deeply into the flesh. To move his legs even a fraction caused intense pain. He gritted his teeth to prevent himself from crying out. The torment and the knowledge of what lay ahead was beginning to affect his reasoning. He found himself estimating the distance from where they stood to the edge of the pier. He thought wildly, If I were to pass the word along the line . . . Linked as they were together, even the reluctant ones would be dragged forward. It would be all over in seconds, he told himself, if I were to give the order.

In his mind's eye he could see eight grey-clad figures stumbling forward, plunging over the edge before anyone could stop them. Death would come quick, for all of us, he told himself, weighed down as we are.

The moan of a ship's siren cut across his thoughts. It came from along way off, and the little Cork boy began to weep.

'Oh, Myles,' he gasped, 'Myles.'

'Easy, lad, easy,' he whispered, 'don't let them see your tears.'

An officer paraded before them. For one so tall he took short deliberate steps as he walked slowly along the line, looking at each man's face with a mixture of contempt and distaste. As he reached the end of the line, he spun smartly around on his heel and walked back again. Again the short deliberate step; again the cold contemptuous stare. He came to an abrupt halt in front of the first man, turned, and repeated the performance. He was midway down the line when Joe Furlong broke the silence.

'Yeh know, Myles,' he said in a loud voice, jabbing him in the ribs with his elbow, 'at Sandhurst, they insert a cork between the cheeks of yer arse to prevent yeh from takin' too long a step!'

The entire line exploded into laughter. He could hear some of the soldiers behind him tittering furiously. His own laugh dwindled to a whimper. The pain from his tightly manacled legs was almost unbearable.

The officer stood before them, shaking with rage. 'Rebel scum!' he sputtered. 'Facking Irish pigs!'

Joe Furlong uttered a feigned shriek of horror. 'Oh la – such language! If me poor oul mother only knew the company I was mixin' with.'

★

21

He found himself shaking with silent mirth. That Joe Furlong – had there ever been another like him? Never had he known such an incurable optimist. He too had been sentenced to fifteen years' penal servitude, but not once had he given in to despair. Even in the prison van taking them to Kingstown he had joked all the way. Joe had maintained his good humour all through those first dreadful years in Pentonville. His cell had been next to Joe's. He remembered the times when he had sat after the lights had gone out, sick with despair, hands torn and raw from picking oakum. Then Joe would call out, his voice coming faintly through the thick stone wall. 'Myles . . . Myles Burke. Stick it out, oul son. Keep the oul heart up.' It had been a black day for all of them when Joe had been transferred to Portland Prison.

From then on they had been forced to work beyond their capacity. One angina sufferer was compelled to wield a pickaxe; another man made to pick oakum long after his fingers had been broken by a heavy stone. He could remember yet another who, although suffering from a severe eye complaint, had been forced to sew mail-bags. He was blinded as a result. And there had been the ones who simply broke under the strain.

The little Cork boy ran amok one day in the prison yard and attacked a guard with a shovel. It had taken three strong men to hold him down. He died years later in an asylum.

And Fouvargue. . . .

He stirred uneasily on the seat and began to pluck at the string of the parcel on his lap. He had been right behind Fouvargue when it happened. They were being escorted to their cells on the top floor after exercise, when Fouvargue suddenly broke from the warders and dived headfirst over the rail. Even now after so many years, he could still hear the horrible cracking sound as Fouvargue's skull struck the flagstones sixty feet below.

The gloom of fog and darkness suddenly swept away from the windows as the train rolled in under the bright lights of the station. He did not move or turn his head away from the window after the train had come to a standstill, but waited. Then he raised himself awkwardly from the seat and, holding the parcel under his arm, opened the door and stepped down on to the platform.

He remained standing, rooted to the spot by fear. Several yards away, the man called Durkin and his companions sang and swayed together, as people swerved to avoid them. Durkin turned as a young woman hurried past and swept a broad hand up against her bottom.

'How's the heart, darling?' he yelled.

She squealed like a rabbit and fled. Durkin and his friends staggered about the platform laughing uproariously. Myles hobbled over to the wall and waited for an opportunity to slip past unseen, but there did not seem to be much chance of that. He watched a timid little man and his wife being subjected to ridicule as they scuttled by. The platform was almost deserted. My turn next, he thought despairingly and closed his eyes. He waited for the cry of recognition, the triumphant howls. His mouth was dry with fear and he could feel his heart beginning to thump painfully.

'Out of my way!' a voice rapped. He opened his eyes to see a tall man striding past. He had the appearance of a labourer. A cement-crusted army haversack hung from his shoulder. He marched straight through the group, roughly elbowing aside any who happened to be in his way. Durkin received a thrust which sent him staggering.

'Lout!' he shouted after the retreating figure.

The man halted and whirled round. He stared steadily at the four men. He wore a weather-stained cap on the side of his head, the peak almost covering one eye. He had the face of a pugilist. The nose was broken and twisted to one side. His voice was harsh.

'Which one of you bastards called me that?'

Durkin took two steps forward, then stood with legs wide apart. His friends rallied around in support.

'I did,' he answered defiantly.

The man drooped one shoulder and let the haversack slide to the ground. Then he raised his fist and walked slowly back towards Durkin.

Myles did not hesitate. He sidled forward against the wall, thankful for the diversion. Out of the corner of his eye he saw the man grab Durkin by the coat collar, saw the fist draw back, heard the thud and cry of pain as he tottered towards the barrier. The last of the crowd were hastening through, casting nervous glances over their shoulders at the scuffle going on up the platform. Myles surrendered his ticket and followed them.

A tall, portly man in a tweed overcoat leaned casually against the wall at the top of the steps leading to the street. He was like a bored spectator at a parade. With legs crossed and homburg tilted up to the hairline, he watched the crowd with flat, indifferent eyes as they passed by. Hand on rail, Myles took the steps slowly and cautiously. He knew the man's eyes were on him. He was aware of a familiar sensation at the nape of his neck – the same feeling he always experienced whenever the tiny aperture in his cell door was opened silently at night as the warder peeked in.

I wonder who he's waiting for? he asked himself. The nonchalant pose did not fool him. He had been tracked too many times down too many streets in the past not to recognise a detective when he saw one.

He pushed open the station door and walked out into the fog-draped street. Again he was surrounded by bustle and noise. People were clambering into cabs while flustered swearing cabbies were loading the tops with luggage. Whips cracked. One by one the cabs moved away into the murk. Newsboys shouted excitedly, frantically trying to dispose of their remaining newspapers among the dwindling crowd. He walked down towards a waiting cab which stood under a street-lamp. The cabby was about to close the door when he saw him approaching. He pulled it open again then spoke to someone inside. 'Another fare, sir. I'm sure you won't mind sharing the cab.'

Myles waited expectantly in the shadows. There was a movement in the interior, then a head appeared in the open window. He immediately recognised the face under the officer's cap. My high-strung friend from the boat-deck, he thought.

The English accent was cold and precise. 'I most certainly do mind!' he snapped and pulled the door shut. The cabby turned to Myles and made a face.

'Bastard,' he muttered and climbed up to his seat.

Myles stood and watched as the cab pulled away from the kerb. It turned a corner, heading west towards the city centre. He stood for a few moments on the now deserted pavement, undecided what to do. The cabs were all gone. If he headed west he would eventually reach the poorer streets beyond Christ Church Cathedral. Lodgings for the night, he thought, someplace not too expensive. And something to eat . . . hot soup, thick slices of bread . . . His stomach ached for want of food. His last meal had been at Euston station ten hours ago. He stepped off the pavement and hobbled slowly and painfully across the road.


IV


The orderly rapped lightly on the door and opened it. 'Captain Carew, sir,' he announced and stepped aside.

24

Carew strode in. He came to attention in front of the desk and saluted. The orderly withdrew, closing the door behind him. Major Calder stared up with blank, puzzled eyes, his mind fuddled from too much whiskey.

'Captain. . . ?'

'Carew, sir. War Office.'

Several seconds passed before the Major understood and rose clumsily to his feet.

'Good lord!' he exclaimed in a slurred voice. 'I was not expecting you for another four days.'

Carew gave a weary sigh. 'I apologise if I have caused any inconvenience.'

The Major gave a vague wave of the hand. 'Not at all, not at all. . . .' He tried not to let the annoyance he felt show on his face. To be caught off guard like this! He was acutely conscious of his open tunic and the empty whiskey bottle at his elbow. He sat down heavily and gestured towards a chair against the wall.

'Take a chair an' sit down,' he said, belching slightly.

Carew sat down, his cap on his lap. He did not remove his greatcoat. The fire, he noticed, had been allowed to die and the room was as cold as his cabin had been.

He said, 'I've taken a room in a hotel nearby. I'll stay there until my quarters are ready.'

The Major gave an absent nod as he tried to collect his thoughts and think of something to say. 'I, er . . .' he began, 'asked for an Irishman, or someone who knows the country well.'

Carew nodded. 'I know, sir. That's why they picked me. Although I was born in England, I was brought to Ireland as a boy to live with my uncle after my father died. Carewscourt – that's just outside the village of Carewstown in County Mayo. It's about twenty miles south of Castlebar. Are you familiar with that part of the country?'

''Fraid not,' the Major replied thickly. 'Know it fairly well further west, though. Damn good fishin' country.' He was unable to articulate properly and decided to let the man facing him do most of the talking. It would give him time to sober up.

'Tell me about yourself,' he said and picked up the phone. He dialled the orderly and asked for coffee and sandwiches.

'Well,' Carew began, keeping his voice even, 'I left Ireland after getting a BA at Trinity and entered Sandhurst. From there, I was gazetted as a second-lieutenant to the 16th Lancers after qualifying with honours. I also received a special certificate of merit in military law, topography, reconnaissance and riding.'

The 16th Lancers, the Major thought, scowling. He had been snubbed by some of that crowd when they discovered he was a ranker. 'You would have been stationed at the South Cavalry Barracks in Aldershot, then?' he said.

'Only for a short while,' Carew replied. 'Six weeks to be exact. When the war broke out in South Africa we were shipped out without delay. That was the time when White was falling back on Ladysmith.' He felt a little pain in remembering. It had also been the time when he had married Valerie. They had married in haste – on impulse. He had just received his embarkation orders.

The Major sat upright in the chair, holding himself rigid, trying to keep his mind clear. He stared at Carew with suspicion. He had arrived four days earlier than expected. Why? To see things as they really were before I had a chance to prepare? What if he should send off a report to Whitehall tonight? He winced. He knew how he must look. Drunk, dishevelled – the picture of incompetence.

There was a tap on the door as it opened, and the orderly walked in bearing a loaded tray. He placed it on the desk in front of the Major and withdrew.

'Cream and sugar, Captain?'

Carew held up a protesting hand. 'Nothing for me, thank you.'

The Major drank his coffee black – two full cups in rapid succession. Then he reached for the sandwiches and devoured them ravenously. His displayed an uncouthness which Carew found refreshingly different from the well-mannered behaviour of his former colleagues in Whitehall.

The Major filled a third cup and swallowed the contents in one gulp. Then he picked up his pipe and tobacco pouch. 'Did you see much action in South Africa, Captain?' he asked.

'A little. I was assigned to one of the Rifle Associations as an instructor. They were volunteers,' he explained as the Major raised a querying eyebrow, 'who had been formed in the British Colonies to defend their territories against Boer incursions. Good fighters, but without any discipline.'

'How long were you with them?' the Major asked, holding a lighted match over the bowl of the pipe.

'Three months or so,' Carew answered. 'Then I was wounded in the arm. Couldn't move it after they had extracted the bullet. The surgeon thought the nerves had been damaged. After a while they sent me back home for further treatment. Fortunately the condition of my arm was not as serious as first suspected. The arm was inclined to stiffen of course, but that was remedied by constant muscular exercises.'

26

He put his hand in the pocket of his greatcoat and took out a small, hard, rubber ball. He squeezed it tightly several times. 'You'll be seeing me doing this quite often,' he said with a wry smile. 'Necessary I'm afraid. Keeps the muscles in tone.'

Major Calder, pipe in mouth, gave a slight shrug. 'Not much of a handicap.'

'I suppose not. Nevertheless it was sufficient to end my career as a cavalry officer – or an infantry one for that matter. And I wanted to stay in the army. I decided to sit the entrance examination for Staff College. It was a hard grind, but I managed to pass, qualifying in French and German.'

'What branch of Intelligence were you in?'

'Foreign Military Intelligence section.'

'Then you would have been under Reggie Sinclair?'

'Yes.'

'Capable fellow, Reggie.'

Carew watched the broad, fleshy face for traces of cynicism, but he saw only open gruff honesty. His instincts told him that this middle-aged Scot with his untidy appearance and ruffled sandy-grey hair was a man he could trust. How I prefer his brusqueness and straightforwardness to Sinclair's duplicity, he thought. Two days ago at his leave-taking, Sinclair had shaken his hand, his mouth twisting in a malicious grin.

'Good luck, ol' boy. You'll need it, with Jock Calder over you. A blusterer – but he rants and raves merely to conceal his feelings of inferiority. A ranker, you know.'

The Major relaxed back in the chair, smoking his pipe. He had recovered his composure and the alcoholic haze that had clouded his mind was beginning to dissipate.

He said offhandedly, 'I suppose they fully informed you of the situation here?'

The feigned nonchalance did not fool Carew; he could see the look of apprehension in his eyes. Calder was fishing for information. He remembered the DMI's parting words to him before he left for Ireland.

'Calder is incompetent, but we intend to let him stay in command until the time comes when you think you are ready to take over.'

Carew hesitated for a second or two before replying, 'Yes, of course.'

The Major remained silent until he was sure Carew was not going to say anything more, then said in the same casual tone, 'I'm afraid it's going to be sheer drudgery for you during the coming weeks, Captain. I have some important things to attend to and I shall have to leave all the paper work for you.' He indicated the filing cabinets with the stem of his pipe. 'You should have seen the state of those files when I took over. Everything jumbled up or mislaid. My predecessor was content to let Special Branch do all the intelligence work, while he spent most of his time either playing polo in the Phoenix Park or escorting debutantes to the Castle Balls.'

He's trying to defend himself now, thought Carew. Trying to cover up his own inefficiency by blaming everything and everybody.

'I had a hell of a job trying to get things reorganised. And the amount of time it took – time that should have been spent on more important things.'

Carew was aware of an immense weariness creeping over him. It had been a long day – the longest day he had ever known. It seemed to him that he had covered a vast distance in time. I'm not the same man, he told himself, who set out from London this morning. Somewhere along the way a transformation had taken place. His gaze drifted from the Major to the window behind him. Grey fog billowed up against the glass.

'Are you all right, Captain?'

He was suddenly aware that the Major had ended his discourse and was staring at him with a look of concern on his face.

'You look quite pale,' he said.

Carew sighed. 'Just tired. I've been travelling since early morning.'

The Major leaned back in his chair. 'You're going to find Dublin a dreary place compared to London.'

'I was never a one for the hectic life, I'm afraid,' he said with a shake of the head. 'I'm glad to be back in Ireland. I'm looking forward to seeing Carewscourt again. And my Uncle Walter. Fierce old warrior. Crimean War veteran, you know. Bit of a martinet, really. I was always very fond of him.' He lapsed into silence, staring down at the carpet with a thin smile, reminiscing.

The silence lasted for nearly half a minute until it was broken by the Major's embarrassed cough. 'And, er . . . your father,' he prompted. 'Was he a military man too?'

Carew shook his head. 'Oh no. He was a clergyman. We Carews, you know, have a long tradition of service. It was always either the church or the army, though most of them preferred the latter. Still, they made their mark, whether it was for God or the Crown. There were at least two bishops and there was a Cornet Carew who served Queen Anne under Marlborough.'

Landed gentry, the Major thought sourly.

28

'. . . then there was Colonel Richard Carew who came to Ireland with Cromwell. It was he who founded the Irish branch of the family. Granted lands in Mayo for services rendered.'

The Major bit on the mouthpiece of the pipe. He might have been a young man again sitting in isolation in the mess, listening to the haughty English accents about him. He remembered how their conversation always managed to come around to one particular subject – lineage. Did they contrive to talk about that only in my presence? he wondered. To humiliate me? To remind me of my lowly status? Calder shrugged in resignation. After all, he told himself, Carew's a stranger here and knows no one.

'Come down for a few drinks and I'll introduce you to the others,' he said. 'Do you play billiards? We could have a game.'

Carew shook his head. 'No, no, thank you. Another time, perhaps. I am rather tired,' he added.

The Major smiled to hide his disappointment. 'The entire day in bed and you'll be a new man after,' he assured him. A thought occurred to him. 'Tell you what,' he said. 'Two friends and myself are going to the Punchestown Races at the week-end.' He gave an embarrassed grin. 'We're bringing three very charming ladies with us. Would you care to come along? There will be no difficulty finding another female companion for yourself.'

Carew lowered his head. 'I would rather not,' he said in a low voice.

To a bachelor like the Major there could be only one explanation for his refusal. He said, 'It never occurred to me that you might be married. Are you?'

Carew raised his head and looked at him. 'My wife is dead,' he answered curtly.

'Oh.' The Major's face reddened. 'I'm sorry.'

Carew rose and extended a hand.

'I'm afraid I've detained you for long enough, sir,' he said. 'Please accept my apologies for coming at an inconvenient time . . .'

The Major remained at his desk after Carew had gone, contemplating. Had there been some sort of tragedy there? he wondered. The army never changed, he told himself bitterly. If you have someone on your hands who is likely to cause trouble, have him transferred – let someone else have the worry. He heaved a sigh and straightened up in the chair. He was quite sober now and could feel the coldness of the room. He began to clear the desk. He pushed the tray to one side and put the tumbler back in the lower drawer. He picked up the empty whiskey bottle and smiled to himself, remembering Carew's parting words

29

about coming at an inconvenient time. Was he being sarcastic? He dropped the bottle into the wastepaper basket. The file on Myles Burke lay open on the desk before him. He turned over a few pages. It was of no further use to him. He had read through it so many times he knew it all by heart. He would return it to Dublin Castle in the morning. Every Friday he had a conference with several police officials to review the Intelligence returns for the week. But tomorrow will be special, he told himself. Tomorrow I'll interview the detective tailing Burke. I will issue instructions – exercise my authority.

He stood up and began to button his tunic. All that was needed now was patience and a little luck. He picked up the file and turned away from the desk. Then he saw the pale grey fog outside the window. He walked over and peered out in dismay. He could not see a thing. Pressing his face against the glass, he swore softly to himself. How could the detective manage to keep Burke in sight in weather like this? And if Burke should become aware he was being followed, he could easily evade the man who was stalking him.

He turned away from the window, overcome by rage and frustration. It seemed to him that all his schemes were destined to fail. Six weeks of careful preparation, and now this had to happen. He walked in despair towards the door. I'll go down now to the others, he told himself savagely, and drink myself into a bloody stupor!

He was about to open the door when he remembered that Burke was sixty-seven years of age. Immediately his mind conjured up a vision of a tall stooped figure shuffling along through the streets, legs weakened by age and from long years of confinement. The picture was reassuring; so much so that he began to laugh gently to himself. Why, he had worked himself up over nothing. The detective would have no difficulty in following Burke – no difficulty at all.


V


Clutching the soggy brown paper parcel to his chest, Myles Burke hobbled painfully on through the fog. He was cold, wet and hungry, and his ankles were raw. Somewhere ahead he would find all the comfort his body craved for in some cheap lodging-house in one of the poorer streets near the cathedral. He continued heading west towards the oldest part of the city.

A bell tolled. He counted the slow ponderous strokes. Ten o'clock. It might have been midnight, for the streets were almost deserted. It was dark along here; no lights shone from the windows. This was the commercial section of the city and the banks and offices had long since closed. He picked his way with care from street-lamp to street-lamp.

A distant glow filtered through the wet veil of fog. Fascinated, he moved towards it, pressing the paper parcel against his chest. As he drew nearer the glow began to weaken and dissolve: it was only a reflection, magnified and distorted by the fog, of a large number of coloured lights decorating a glass canopy above the entrance of a place of entertainment.

Stronger light shone out from the interior, lighting up the pathway and part of the road. It was like an oasis of gaiety and splendour in a desert of gloom. He came to a stop underneath the canopy. A pretty young woman smiled coyly at him from a large photograph which occupied most of the space between the two doors. Beneath was a caption.

GERTIE MILLAR
Queen of Song

And alongside a gaudy playbill.

TWO JESTERS FROM CHESTER
(Monarchs of Mirth)
MARVO THE MAGICIAN
RICARDO AND HIS TANGO DANCERS

He could remember when music-halls had been seedy, bawdy dens of depravity. He peered through one of the glass-panelled doors. Things had obviously changed. Plush red carpet, apricot-coloured walls, gilt-edged mirrors . . . The foyer looked so warm and snug he was tempted to push open the door and walk in. He moved away with reluctance, and looked back with regret.

Then he saw him. A man was standing under the canopy studying the playbill – a tall portly man in a tweed overcoat and with a homburg set squarely on his head. Myles recognised him immediately: he had seen him at the railway station less than an hour ago. He remembered how he had stood at the top of the steps scrutinising everyone as they passed by. The man was a detective, he was certain of that, and had obviously been waiting for someone.

31

Then the thought occurred to him. Waiting for me?

He could feel a cold chill of fear spreading from the pit of his stomach. He backed away, turned and stumbled forward as fast as he could, until he collapsed against a wall, exhausted, chest heaving. Fighting for breath, he told himself he had nothing to fear, but when he heard footsteps approaching he sidled away into the darkness.

He groped his way along the wall like a blind man. Then his fingers clawed at space. A doorway. He backed into it and slumped against the closed door.

Click, click, click. The man was wearing steel tips on his shoes. A sharp metallic note rang out with each footfall. He pressed the paper parcel to his face to muffle the sound of his harsh breathing as the man passed the doorway with the slow measured tread of a policeman. He remained motionless, listening to the footsteps fading away. After his breathing had returned to normal, Myles emerged from the doorway and moved off.

He picked his way with care through the foggy darkness. Reason told him that he was acting under the influence of an overactive imagination, but an instinctive sense of danger told him otherwise. He trusted that more than the logical deductions of the mind. He tried to make himself as inconspicuous as possible – hugging the wall and the deeper shadows, putting down each foot slowly and carefully like a tightrope walker. Every few seconds he stopped and listened before moving on. Twenty years of prison life had dulled his senses; now they were awakening and becoming active again.

A bell rang out the quarter-hour; it sounded very near. Christ Church Cathedral, he told himself. He judged it to be about fifty yards ahead of him. He had his bearings now. The street-lamp he was approaching marked the entrance to Fishamble Street which led down to the quays. That would be the route he would take – down into the narrow ill-lit streets where one had a better chance of eluding one's shadower. He disliked this main thoroughfare with its long line of office buildings and lack of cover.

The bright globe of the electric street-lamp seemed to expand slowly with each forward step he took. It was like a balloon filling with gas. Under its harsh glare the fog dissolved into thin wavering strands. Just outside the arc of light, half in shadow, the detective stood motionless.

Myles came to an abrupt halt and flattened himself against a wall. He felt a sudden urge to go back, but he feared the slightest movement or sound would betray his presence. He waited and watched, thankful for the cloak of fog.

32

The detective appeared to be listening intently. With his rigid body and craned neck he looked like the conductor of an orchestra searching for a discordant note. He retained the pose for nearly a minute, before moving about inside the small circle of light. He was clearly undecided as to which direction to take. Please, God, Myles implored silently, don't let him come back towards me.

Suddenly the man strode away, heading west. Myles waited for several seconds, then moved forward with thumping heart into the glare of the street-lamp. For an instant he felt naked and exposed; a momentary touch of panic made him move a little faster. He turned the corner; the street before him wound downhill into the darkness. He took the steep slope cautiously, keeping close to the fronts of the houses, groping his way down.

The street was narrow and sinuous, like most of the streets that lay about the cathedral. This was the oldest part of the city – the old Viking settlement. Here in the silent darkness he could feel the past closing about him like the fog. He was suddenly conscious of walking in the footprints of ancient Nordic warriors – Sitric Silkenbeard, Olaf Cuaran, Magnus Barefoot. His fingers felt old crumbling brick. Somewhere along here Handel had first performed his *Messiah*. His mind was beginning to ramble. He felt lightheaded from fatigue and hunger. For a few seconds he lost control of his legs and staggered drunkenly down the slope, before his knees struck the dustbin.

It hit the ground with a thud and the lid spun out on to the roadway bouncing and clattering noisily downhill over the cobbles. The din made him wince; it seemed to go on and on.

He remained still, shocked and dazed, listening with trepidation. How far had the noise travelled? He staggered down the hill, hastily and unheedingly. Twice he almost fell. When he reached the bottom he had to pause to catch his breath.

Then he heard it – the sound of steel tips striking stone. No measured tread this time: the dark narrow street echoed to the beat of quick-moving feet. The bloodhound had picked up the scent again. He uttered a groan and trudged wearily across the road and turned the corner. He wrinkled up his nose at the sour smell of river-mud. Here on the quays the small huckster shops were still open for business. Greenish gas-light shone out from the windows and mingled with the glow from the street-lamps, the combined light dividing the foggish darkness into segments up along the broken pavement. There was no place where he could hide. He felt more exposed now than when he had been on the main thoroughfare. He could hear the click, click, click a

33

little way behind him. The man had resumed his leisurely pace. He could feel anger gathering inside him. Why in God's name is he following me? I'm no ticket-of-leave man.

Reason it out, his mind counselled, reason it out.

He had been a political prisoner, therefore the man following him had to be a political detective, from G Division of the Dublin Metropolitan Police, but why Dublin Castle should want to have him followed baffled him. He could think of no logical explanation. Unless . . . He shook his head at the thought. It was too improbable, yet he was unable to dismiss it.

What if the Irish Republican Brotherhood was still in existence? What if some of his old comrades were still alive and engaged in revolutionary activities? The more he thought about it the less improbable it seemed. After all, he had been absent from Ireland for forty-two years and was completely ignorant of the political situation. He had assumed that the cause he had fought for had gradually died out over the years, but he might have been wrong. Hope began to flicker.

Although he had heard nothing from anyone all those years he was in prison, that did not mean to say the old idealism was dead. Perhaps they hoped he would lead them to the revolutionary heart of Ireland. The notion that he was being used as a decoy made him smile. Did the men at the Castle think he had been kept in touch all these years? No, he was too old, too long absent. The comrades probably thought he was dead. Indeed, you might as well be dead once you were in prison, for all anybody cared. The sound of the detective's footsteps interrupted his train of thought.

Damn you, you flat-footed swine! Why don't you go away and leave me alone! He swept the moisture away from his eyes with an angry gesture. He was going away from the district of the cheap lodging-houses; somewhere up ahead lay the brewery and beyond that the suburbs. He groaned aloud. He was on the verge of collapse, yet he forced himself on. Sooner or later the detective would have to give up, but what if he did not? Anger swelled up within him.

'Then he can follow me till I damn well drop!' he snarled.

He passed under a street-lamp and shuffled on towards the next, twenty yards away. As he came towards it he could see a figure taking shape under the greenish gas-glare. A straw boater came into view. At first he thought it was a man. Then he saw the boa wound around the throat. A woman lolled against the lamp-standard smoking a cigarette. As he emerged from the fog she straightened up and threw the cigarette

34

away. She walked to the middle of the footpath and stood with her hands on her hips, barring his way.

He came into the light. She made a wry face and moved aside. ' 'Night grandad,' she said, giving him a roguish wink as he went past.

He shook his head in commiseration as darkness enveloped him. Poor bitch, she must be in dire straits if she has to solicit on a night like this. Then the thought struck him. Would she accost the man coming up behind? His heart fluttered with excitement – this could be the chance he had been waiting for. O God, he prayed fervently, let her detain him for just a minute or two so I can get away.

'Hello, sweetheart.'

He forced himself to move as fast as he could from the voices behind him. He could hear the man's bellow of annoyance. 'Get away from me, ye 'hure!'

A shriek of outrage followed. 'Here, don't you push me, ye bloody ill-mannered cur! Why you. . . !'

The sounds of a scuffle made him look back. The detective had his back up against the lamp-standard, frantically trying to keep the woman at bay as she clawed at his face.

He did not linger a second longer. He turned around and hobbled painfully up the footpath, desperately searching for somewhere to hide. An open halldoor of a tenement would have done, but this section of the quays was non-residential. There was nothing along here, only dark silent warehouses. He drove his exhausted, protesting body onwards.

He could see a dull glow in the distance. It was probably light from a shop window. He staggered towards it. It looked like a public-house – and it was separated from the adjoining building by a narrow laneway. Did it lead to anywhere? Or was it a cul-de-sac? He did not care – it offered refuge. He was doubtful of reaching it even though it was less than ten yards away: he felt drained of energy. Nevertheless he forced himself to make one last effort.

He deliberately pitched himself forward into a stumbling agonising jog-trot. His heart thumped violently – he could feel the blood pounding in his ears. Somehow he managed to reach the mouth of the laneway and turn the corner. The heavy boots slithered over the wet greasy cobbles.

His legs finally crumpled and he fell against the wall of the public-house and slid to the ground. He lay on his side, gasping for breath. The thumping of his heart terrified him. He thought despairingly: Is this the way it's going to end? Dying in some filthy laneway? He was dazed by the fall and there was a faint tapping sound in his ears. He shook his head to clear it, but it went on and on, becoming louder every second. It was the sound of running feet. Steel-tipped shoes beat furiously against the pavement. Click, click, click, click . . . He raised himself up, trying not to panic. Somehow he had managed to retain his grip on the paper parcel: it had burst in parts and pieces of woollen underwear peeked out. He stood on weak wobbly legs like a new-born colt, his right hand pressed against the wall for support. He could see a flight of steps leading up to the side entrance of the pub about five yards away. He staggered towards them, his shoulder brushing against the wall. Nightmares were often like this: the sounds of approaching danger, the frantic efforts to escape, the feeling that one's feet were weighted with lead. He mounted the steps with effort, the rapid beat of quick-moving feet in his ears, and pushed in the door.

A barman was hunched over a newspaper spread out on the counter. He did not bother to look up as Myles staggered in, panting for breath. He closed the door behind him and turned his head towards the window – just in time to see a shadow fleeting across the frosted glass. The detective had gone. He leaned his head back against the wall, breathing in a mixture of smells: stale tobacco smoke, beer, sawdust. He heaved a sigh of relief. Sanctuary.

A hand grasped his shoulder and shook him awake. He looked up in a daze. The barman – or was he the proprietor – was standing over him with an angry look on his face. 'This is not a bloody hotel,' he rasped. 'If ye want someplace to rest,' he indicated the door with a backward jerk of the thumb, 'find it elsewhere!'

Myles stiffened with indignation. 'Bring me a drink.'

'What sort of drink?'

'What sort?' He had not taken alcohol in twenty years. His last drink had been with Garret Lysaght in Paris. 'Absinthe.'

'*What?*'

'I mean brandy.'

'Brandy!' The man glanced at the crumpled torn parcel on the seat and gave a derisive snort. 'Mebbe ye would prefer a glass of champagne.'

Myles rooted furiously in his pocket, took out a sovereign and slapped it down on the table. 'A *large* brandy!'

He glared at the retreating back, trying to control his anger. I've taken enough, he told himself. First those drunken swine on the boat, then that damned detective, now this bastard.

The man came back with a glass of brandy on a tray. He had a pronounced limp. He set down the brandy on the table and began to dole out the change, counting under his breath. 'Thirteen, fourteen and six, fifteen . . .' Silver and copper coins lay scattered over the table. Myles selected a shilling – the price of a night's shelter – and tossed it on to the tray.

'For your trouble,' he said curtly. He did it contemptuously, as if he were throwing alms to a beggar. The man glared at him, face twitching. Then he twisted away and stumped back over the sawdust sprinkled floor.

Myles sighed and picked up the glass. It had been a foolish gesture and one which he could ill afford. Nevertheless he was conscious of a feeling of satisfaction. He had been humiliated once again, but this time he had retaliated. He took a tiny sip of the brandy; he could feel it trickling down inside him like liquid fire. He took another sip, and leaning back looked around him.

There were scarcely any customers at this end of the bar. Besides himself, there were only two men dozing at a table near the front door and another perched on a high stool at the counter. The barman stood inside the counter scowling down at the newspaper. Perhaps the news is not to his liking, Myles thought, or else he's still smarting from the insult. There was a half-open door beyond the counter; light from a landing above showed stairs leading to rooms overhead.

A low hum of conversation drifted from the other end of the counter. Myles turned his head towards it. He could barely make out groups of figures huddled around the tables. The light was dim. Had the gas-jets been lowered deliberately? he wondered. There was a furtive atmosphere about that part of the bar; it gave the impression that criminal plots were being hatched.

He sipped his brandy contentedly. He felt at ease here among the riff-raff and the down-and-outs. It was rather like being in prison again. He took another sip. The brandy was creating a warm glow inside him; it eased the sharp pangs of hunger in his belly. He felt relaxed and a little drowsy. He thought of the detective prowling the upper quays, peering into doorways baffled, angry. Myles smiled to himself. He'll have to invent a damn good excuse for his superior, he thought.

After twenty years of abstinence, the little he had consumed was making him drunk. It was a strange but pleasant sensation. Only now did he feel truly liberated. The years of isolation, the long years of living in the enforced silence, were over. He wanted to celebrate his new-found freedom in laughter and song. He thought of the detective and how he had outwitted him. He couldn't stop laughing. His eyes were streaming. He was on the point of hysteria.

Suddenly the door was pushed violently open. It was like having cold water dashed in his face. Myles sobered up immediately, senses alert. But it was only a scarecrow of a man who stood on the threshold, hesitating.

Myles watched him with mild interest, slightly puzzled by his behaviour. Perhaps, he thought, he has been thrown out of here in the past. Even a pub as low as this must have its undesirables. His eyes followed the man as he walked falteringly towards the counter. He came to a halt a little away from it and called out in a soft voice, 'Flurry . . .'

The bar-man moved away from his newspaper with reluctance, and stopped as he recognised the man. 'Whacker!'

'Ah, now, now, Flurry,' the man protested. 'Just a glass, just a glass.' He held up a coin for inspection.

Flurry seemed to debate whether he should serve the man or not. Then he filled a glass and placed it on the counter. The man surrendered the coin.

'Thanks, Flurry oul son.' Grinning, the man turned to Myles.

Myles winced. The left side of his face was hideously disfigured. From eyebrow to chin, the flesh was deeply scarred and puckered. The left eye was missing. Some surgeon had mercifully hidden the empty socket by sewing the eyelid to the mangled flesh of the cheek. It gave him a lop-sided look. But if one half of the face was stiff and dead, the other half was mobile and alive. The remaining eye was wide and alert; it surveyed Myles for a moment then swivelled away to the table.

'Hey, boss,' he exclaimed, 'does all that money belong to yew?' He leaned forward, hand shielding the side of his mouth. 'Put it away quick,' he whispered hoarsely. 'There are a few fellas here that'd slit yer gizzard for the price of a ball o'malt!'

Myles picked up the coins a few at a time and transferred them to his pocket. Whacker watched his movements with interest. When the table had finally been cleared of money he gave a heavy sigh.

'Wasn't it fortunate for yew,' he remarked, 'that yeh sat down at this particular table? With an honest man,' he added.

Myles nodded and reached for his glass. He swallowed the last of the brandy, and picking up the parcel, rose to his feet.

Whacker gave a cry of dismay. 'Yer not goin'?'

'Have to, I'm afraid.'

Whacker jumped to his feet and laid a restraining hand on his shoulder.

'But yeh can't see yer hand in front of yer face out there,' he protested.

38

'Oh, I'll be all right, I assure you,' Myles said.

'Best wait till the fog clears,' Whacker declared firmly forcing Myles back down on his seat. He sat down himself, picked up his glass and emptied it at one gulp. He gave a little belch and shook his finger at Myles as though he were admonishing a child. 'It's for yer own good. What if yeh met with an accident. Sure, I'd never forgive meself.'

'But the fog is not as bad as all that.'

'It's bad enough.'

Myles gave a shrug of resignation and lay back, closing his eyes, but he could not relax. There was a long silence before Whacker asked anxiously, 'Are yeh goin' to have another drink?'

Myles opened his eyes. He gave a deep sigh. 'Oh, I suppose so . . .' and watched the man staring ruefully at his empty glass. He asked with reluctance: 'Will you join me?'

The man rubbed his hands together vigorously. ' 'Tis a fierce, cold, damp night. Brandy, now, would take the chill out of a fella's bones.'

Whacker twisted round towards the counter and called out, 'Two brandies if yeh please, *Mister* Lynch.'

Myles fumbled in his pocket as Flurry came limping towards them bearing the brandy-filled glasses on a tray.

'The gentleman is payin',' Whacker said promptly.

'I know bloody well *you're* not!' Flurry growled. 'That'll be one shilling and tuppence.'

Myles counted out the money with despair. Each penny spent meant one step nearer the gutter. Flurry waited patiently.

Whacker swallowed a mouthful of brandy and gave a long gasp of pleasure. 'Ahhh . . . that's the stuff to give the troops.' He thrust his hand inside his jacket and took out a few grimy papers; he selected a crumpled, cracked photograph and handed it to Myles.

Myles leaned towards the light, looking at the faded sepia-tinted photograph of a uniformed figure with a pith helmet under his arm.

'That was me, boss, that was me,' Whacker said in a breaking voice. 'Before they floured the husk and sent me home to hawk me brow . . .'

Myles stared at the full unblemished face – at the two eyes staring proudly at the camera. He gave it back in silence, unable to think of anything to say.

Whacker put it back inside his jacket. A tear ran down one side of his face. 'Do yeh know,' he snivelled, 'I used to stride through the Liberties in me red tunic? All spit and polish and soldiery snap, with me pill-box on the side of me poll and me swagger-cane under me oxter. An' now looka me. Without a deuce in me pocket.' He opened his jacket wide, exposing a torn filthy shirt. 'Not even enough clothes to dust a bloody fiddle!' He grabbed the glass and tossed back the remainder of the brandy, and, without a pause, called for two more.

Myles gave an involuntary yap of alarm. He picked up his glass and drank the brandy in short quick gulps while his other hand groped the seat beside him for his parcel. He told himself furiously, I'll be damned if I'm going to squander any more money on this old sponger! He put down the empty glass.

Whacker stretched out a hand and grabbed him by the sleeve. 'I hope,' he said with concern in his voice, 'me behaviour didn't cause yeh any distress?'

'Not at all, not at all . . .' Myles replied, trying to disengage himself.

'It's just that,' the man explained with an apologetic smile, 'I get these little fits of depression now and then.'

He retained his grip on the sleeve; he did not let go until Flurry was standing over them and depositing glasses of brandy on the table. Myles gave a groan of despair and put a reluctant hand into his pocket.

Flurry picked up the empty glasses that lay about the table. He said offhandedly, 'That'll be one and . . . sixpence.'

Myles paused in the act of withdrawing his hand. 'It was only one and tuppence last time,' he complained.

'Oh.' Flurry gazed reflectively down at the glasses on the table and then nodded. 'Yer right – one and tuppence.'

'I'm not *that* drunk,' Myles snapped – and immediately thought, but drunk enough. Not once in twenty years had he dared to talk to anyone like that.

Flurry's face turned a deep red. 'A mistake,' he explained roughly. 'A slight lapse of memory.'

Whacker drew back his head a little, his eye wide with feigned horror. 'God forgive yeh!' he exclaimed in a shocked voice. He jumped to his feet and began to perform a little dance, singing in a cracked nasal voice.

> Did yeh ever hear the music
> In a tripe shop?
> An' the ham-bone dancin'
> On the dish.
> The sausages tryin' to do
> The cake-walk,
> An' the pig-cheeks roarin'
> Out "Police!"

Myles winced at the raucous laughter; he looked on sourly as the man sat down and picked up his glass and began to sing again.

> I was drunk las' night,
> I was drunk the night before.
> I don't care if I'm drunk
> For evermore . . .

> The more I drink,
> The merrier I will be.
> I belong to a drinkin' famileee . . .

Myles began to add up in his mind the amount of money he had spent over the past half-hour. Anger and frustration made him squirm on the seat. He could have lived for nearly a week on that. He picked up the glass and sipped the brandy. The very thought of what was going to happen to him when all the money was gone filled him with dread. The One-Eyed man ended the song on a high note and raised his glass in a toast to Myles before tossing off his drink. Myles studied him with envy. The man was destitute like himself. The difference between them was that he was much younger and knew how to survive better than Myles could.

Then the door was pushed open and the detective walked in.

Myles hunched up instinctively and watched him with beating heart as he walked slowly to the counter. He had an air of authority about him – there was no mistaking the fact that he was a detective. Flurry was obviously aware of it. Myles noticed how quickly he responded to the man's request for a drink. The man who was sitting alone at the counter took one sidelong glance at the newcomer and hastily swallowed his whiskey and walked out. Myles felt a sudden urge to do likewise; his hand felt for the parcel beside him. At that moment the detective turned round, a pint of porter in his hand, and began to look about him.

The publican was staring apprehensively at him. Flurry gave a sickly smile. 'Bad oul night, sir,' he said with forced pleasantry. The detective gave a non-committal grunt and took another swig.

Flurry lowered his head and busied himself with the washing of a large number of tumblers and glasses. It was a task which could have waited till morning, but he needed to do something to occupy his mind – something to help disguise his nervousness. He began to stack them upside down on the counter to dry. His hands shook.

Over the past few weeks, a Dublin evening newspaper had been demanding police surveillance of certain public-houses which were hot-beds of vice and crime. The paper had made an oblique reference to his own pub – it had referred to it as an 'iniquitous pot-house on Usher's quay, frequented mostly by the criminal classes'. It had also alleged that certain rooms on the premises were being let for immoral purposes. The paper had no positive proof of course, although it had tried to obtain some. A reporter had walked in one night seeking information; later he had been lured into the laneway outside and badly beaten up for his trouble. It had been a warning to every other newspaperman in the city – and one which they had obviously heeded, for he had not been investigated since. Not till now, he thought with consternation.

The detective looked down at the half-open door beyond the counter. 'Tell me,' he asked casually, 'is there a lounge upstairs?'

Flurry gave him a startled look. 'No, no . . .' he answered quickly.

The detective gave a grunt of satisfaction.

Flurry swirled the remaining tumbler around the basin of tepid sudsy water and placed it with the others: more than two dozen were now arrayed, three abreast, on the counter. He dried his hands with the dishcloth. The detective's inquiry about upstairs had completely unnerved him. He took out his watch and looked at it. It was fifteen minutes to closing time, but it was too risky to wait that long. He made his mind up – he would close now. He picked up a tray and limped down towards the lower end of the bar. He moved from table to table, picking up empty glasses and tumblers and placing them on the tray. He raised his voice. 'Time, now, time . . . ye've five minutes to drink up and go home!' He deliberately ignored the astonished upturned faces as he limped back towards the counter: here a customer was allowed to drink into the early hours under dimmed lights and behind shuttered windows.

Behind the counter again, he began to rinse the tumblers and glasses he had collected: he placed them one after another on the counter with the others. The detective lay hunched over the counter idly looking on. From the shadows opposite, Whacker called out for brandies.

'No more drink,' Flurry shouted back. 'It's gone the hour.' And then, to impress the detective, added, 'Ye know the law.'

The One-Eyed man gave a shrug of resignation and stood up; swaying a little, he extended a hand to Myles. 'Lave it there, me oul segocia . . .'

Myles stretched out his hand reluctantly. The man gripped it and began to pump it up and down slowly.

'One dacent oul skin,' he said solemnly. 'The heart o'the rowl . . .
the salt of the earth . . . a gentleman . . . a scholar . . . a prince . . .' He
lifted his head and stared open-mouthed at the ceiling as if trying to
think of a further compliment. He remained like that for several
seconds; then, closing his eye and moving his head slowly from side to
side, began to sing.

> Ol'pal, ol'gal, yew lef'me all alone.
> Ol'pal, ol'gal, I'm jus' a rollin' stone . . .

Still holding Myles's hand, he leaned back at a precarious angle. Myles
felt himself being dragged along the seat into the glare of the gas-light.

> Shadows they come stealin'
> Through the weary night.
> Yew'll always find me kneelin'
> In the candle light . . .

Flurry raised an exasperated face from what he was doing and
bawled: 'Enough of that, now! Finish yer drink and go home!' He
grabbed the tray, came from behind the counter and limped over to the
table. He jabbed a thick forefinger against Whacker's chest. 'Yet get
yerself outa here fast,' he hissed venomously, 'or by Christ I'll boot ye
out!' He swept the glasses from the table on to the tray and hobbled over
to where a little old man was sleeping serenely beside the door. He
picked up the man's empty pint glass. 'Come on, you,' he said roughly,
'it's past the time.'

But the man continued to sleep on, his face hidden by the bowler hat.

Flurry kicked at his booted foot. 'Are ye deaf?' he rasped.

The bowler lifted and two woebegone eyes peered up at him from
under the brim. 'Ah piss off!' the man croaked wearily and went back to
sleep.

Flurry gave a little leap of fury and nearly dropped the tray. He
swung his arm round in a grabbing motion – then Whacker began to
sing again.

> Oh we all come into the world with nuttin',
> With no clothes to wear . . .

Flurry twisted round to see him dancing nimbly on his toes up and
down the bar. He was holding out both sides of his overbig jacket by the
pocket-flaps to give the impression of a skirt. Loud applause broke out
as Whacker ended his song and dance. Hands clapped, feet stamped,
there were several shrill whistles. The detective glared at Flurry – who

43

suddenly lost his nerve. He grabbed a pint tumbler and began to pound it against the counter top. 'Shut up the lot of ye!' he yelled. 'Clear out, out, out. . . !' Then the tumbler shattered.

Flurry stared in stupefaction at his cut and bleeding hand. He raised it to his open-mouthed face and began to turn it this way and that as though he was not sure if it belonged to him or not. A dart of pain made him wince. He grabbed the dishcloth and wound it tightly round his hand as the One-Eyed man acknowledged the applause with a little bow. Flurry came from behind the counter and stumped furiously towards him.

Whacker threw his arms wide and announced loudly, 'An' now for me next act – '

Flurry lunged. He caught him by the collar of his jacket and lifted him then rammed him against the wall. 'Listen, ye scrawny little melt,' he roared. 'Get the hell outa here before I bloody well wipe the floor with ye!'

Myles stood with the parcel under his arm, ready to depart through the side door. He swayed a little from the effects of the brandy. It was a strange experience being drunk; he felt a different person altogether. Alcohol had dissolved the old feeling of fear and timidity. He forgot about the detective and stepped out from the shadows and laid a restraining hand on Flurry's arm. 'You have no right,' he declared harshly, 'to treat the man like that!'

Flurry threw off the hand angrily and twisted round. 'No interference from ye!' he snarled. 'Get out – and take Balor of the Evil Eye here along with ye!'

Whacker gave a shriek of outrage. 'What's that? What's that yeh called me, yeh hoppy bastard?' He struggled out of Flurry's grip and made a wild swipe at him with his fist. Flurry tottered back, surprised by the sudden onslaught. But he recovered quickly. 'Bloody little parasite!' he choked. 'Comin' in here, cadgin' brandy – '

'Brandy!' Whacker echoed. 'D'yeh call that watery slop yew sell, brandy?' He darted forward and thrust his disfigured face up into Flurry's. 'I call it cat's piss!' he yelled.

Flurry struck out savagely with his blood-stained, cloth-wrapped fist. The blow glanced off Whacker's shoulder and sent him backwards, spinning like a top. Flurry made a futile swipe and almost fell, hampered by his stiff arthritic leg. 'I'll knock yer bloody head off!' he bellowed in frustrated rage.

Myles found himself hemmed in, but he was too drunk to care; even the fracas going on in front of him had an air of unreality about it. An

44

elbow poked him in the ribs and a voice bawled in his ear, 'What the hell are yeh dancin' around for, Whacker? Go in and finish the bastard!'

Goaded, Whacker pranced forward, weaving and ducking. It was the opportunity Flurry had been waiting for. He drew back his arm and swung with all his might. The cloth-bound fist struck Whacker's forehead and sent him flying backwards. There was a frantic scramble to get out of the way. One man was not fast enough. Whacker's body struck him, bounced and whirled, then went plunging headlong down towards the lower end of the bar. He threw out an arm to save himself. It skimmed over the counter top, sweeping before it the stacked glasses and tumblers Flurry had left to dry.

Flurry's hysterical scream was drowned by the noise of breaking glass and splintering wood as Whacker collided with a table and several chairs. Then there was silence.

No one moved for several seconds. Then the detective walked forward from the counter. Bending down, he gripped Whacker by the lapels of his torn jacket and hauled him to his feet.

Flurry gripped the detective by the sleeve. 'There musta been twenty pounds' worth of damage done here tonight,' he said, trying to keep his voice under control. He pointed a shaking finger at Whacker. 'And that little scut,' he snarled, 'is goin' to pay!'

Whacker guffawed. 'Twenty pounds! Sure, I'm not a man of substance like yerself.'

'Then ye'll pay in another way!' Flurry roared. 'Six months-hard!' He tapped the detective authoritatively on the shoulder. 'I want this man arrested and charged,' he said sternly.

The detective looked at him with dismay. He had walked in here thinking he would be taken for just another customer. It came as a shock to realise that his identity had been apparent from the very beginning.

Flurry scowled. 'Ye've all been enjoyin' yerselves tonight, haven't ye?' he said sarcastically. 'Well, now the lot of ye can go down to the police station with the detective here and give evidence.' Immediately everyone began to disperse. Myles was nearly thrown off balance as the crowd pushed past him towards the door. A minute later he was standing alone, a dazed spectator as Whacker struggled to free himself from the detective's firm hold.

'I'm not goin' to any bloody police station,' he fumed. 'If yeh have to arrest someone, let it be that 'hure-master standin' behind yeh!'

'Shut yer lyin' mouth!' Flurry shouted, raising his fist and taking a step towards him. The detective tried to warn him off and at the same time tried to maintain his grip on Whacker. Then Flurry and the One-Eyed man started to scream abuse at each other.

Myles backed away towards the side door. The detective swung his head round towards him. . . .

Later, when he paused to rest under an archway leading into a narrow slum street, he remembered the expression of helplessness and despair on the detective's face before he closed the door. The round popping eyes; the gaping mouth . . . He reminded him of a goldfish he used to keep in his flat in Paris years ago. He tittered.

The feeling of wild mirth he had been trying to suppress all night surged up. He started to laugh . . . and laugh. He could not stop. He slumped to his knees clutching the parcel to his chest, hearing the sound of his laughter echoing and re-echoing down the length of the archway.

# Book One

# Chapter One

## I

The train crawled between the flat green fertile fields of east Mayo, heading north-west. Gerry Troy's buttocks ached from the constant sitting. He shifted on the seat to relieve the numbness. The monotonous clackety-clack of the wheels and the heat of the mid-day sun shining through the windows had induced a deep slumber on the other occupants of the carriage.

He looked down at the four people sleeping at the other end of the carriage. Two mountainy men and their wives. Their clothes reeked of peat-smoke. The men were dressed in homespun tweeds the colour of oatmeal and the women wore russet shawls and bright red skirts. They clearly did not belong to this fertile plain, but to the inhospitable western regions beyond Lough Carra where the Partry Mountains reared up above the wild barren boglands.

He turned his head away and stretched his cramped legs. His foot kicked against the leg of the sleeping man sprawled on the seat opposite. The man grunted, but did not wake. My dour, silent fellow passenger from Dublin, Gerry thought. The man had slept for most of the long journey.

Gerry studied him. He guessed him to be about thirty years of age, although it was difficult to determine exactly. Privation and brutal toil could quickly age a man. The man was a labourer; he could tell from the weather-stained cap and clothes and the cement-crusted army haversack on the seat beside him. But it was the face that interested him. Rugged and wind-burned, with a broken nose that was twisted a little to one side, it told of innumerable brawls on building-sites and in low public houses. He had been in a fight quite recently, for his knuckles were grazed and swollen.

Gerry turned his head to the window. His eyes, so long accustomed to the dusty drabness of city streets, found the countryside fresh and colourful. Emerald green fields, criss-crossed by hedges in full bloom,

49

stretched away to the Partry Mountains rising stark and blue against the western sky. And Sullivan and the others, he told himself, thought I was mad coming here.

He smiled, remembering Sullivan's astounded face when he told him.

'Carewstown?' he had asked open-mouthed. 'Where the hell is that?'

'It's a little village in Mayo about twenty miles south of Castlebar.'

It was during lunch hour and they had been standing at the window of the deserted classroom which overlooked the dingy tenements of Whitefriar Street.

'Why in the name of all that's holy,' Sullivan had asked in amazement, 'do you want to bury yourself alive in an out-of-the-way kip like that? I can understand a countryman wanting to leave here, but you're city born and bred – you won't be able to stand the loneliness. Jesus, after a few months they'll be bringing you home in a strait jacket!'

Sullivan and the other teachers had tried to persuade him to change his mind, but he had been adamant. 'I simply want to teach in an environment different from this,' he had explained to each one of them. 'I'm fed up trying to drum a little learning into the heads of a crowd of indifferent ragamuffins from the slums of York Street and Mercer Street.'

It had been a feeble excuse for wanting to leave, but he had not been at liberty to tell them the real reason. That was a secret shared between himself and Fintan Butler. He stared thoughtfully out of the window.

Until he met Fintan Butler, Gerry Troy had been drifting through life, rudderless. His career had been chosen for him. His father had insisted that he become a school-teacher like himself. He had acquiesced, because there were few openings in Limerick City for a man of good education. He had gladly taken the train to Dublin for the Teachers' Training College.

He had disliked the college from the start. The food had been unpalatable and he had been averse to sleeping in the long draughty dormitory with twenty others. Eventually he had settled down, studying hard, not only at the college but also at the university for a BA. His progress had been moderate – moderate because he had lacked enthusiasm for his intended profession. Often he wished for something to happen to give him the impetus he so desperately needed.

One evening he travelled by tram from Drumcondra to Sackville Street. The city had been in a festive mood: King Edward VII and Queen Alexandra were due to arrive on the morrow. He had walked down Westmoreland Street and into College Green, enjoying the carnival atmosphere. The main streets had been a riot of colour: Union Jacks and red, white and blue bunting everywhere. Dublin had been proclaiming its loyalty.

After a while he became bored with it all and had gone into the Empire Music Hall for light relief. To his dismay he found himself having to watch further demonstrations of loyalty. Each succeeding act had been more jingoistic than the one before. Much to his surprise the audience had been enjoying it all – thunderous applause at the end of each act.

Nevertheless he remained in his seat during the interval, telling himself that the last half would be different. Then the lights had dimmed and the curtains had parted and John Bull walked out from the wings. He groaned as the man, a baritone, sang something about the sun never setting on the jolly old Empire.

Gerry had been on the point of leaving when a man jumped to his feet four rows away and started shouting at the singer. His action had obviously been a signal for others to do likewise: more shouted protests could be heard coming from different parts of the house. Missiles were thrown at the stage. A startled and confused John Bull staggered back as an egg broke against his red, white and blue vest.

The lights were turned on and several ushers came rushing down the aisles. Scuffles broke out. Women in the audience started to scream. The man who had started it all was dragged out, still shouting.

He was to see the man an hour later in a modest little restaurant in Capel Street, sitting in a corner smoking a cigarette over a cup of coffee. Gerry sat down opposite him.

He smiled, remembering the look of apprehension on Fintan Butler's face. He must have thought I was a policeman.

'That was quite a performance you gave tonight. Far better than the one on the stage.'

The tense look slowly faded from the man's eyes. He smiled. 'I'm only sorry I was not there for the finale. It must have been interesting.'

'There was no finale, thanks to you. Tell me, do you do that kind of thing often?'

Still smiling, the man shook his head. 'No – only on special occasions.' He was a man of about thirty; tall and thin with a pale, sensitive face. The black hair and the falcon nose revealed his Norman ancestry. Then the smile vanished and the well modulated voice became bitter. 'The whole city has gone mad over this visit of King Edward. My God, it makes me sick to see Irishmen and Irishwomen

51

behaving in that way. Have they no pride, no memories? Sixty years ago the population of this country was halved by famine. And what's left is being steadily reduced by emigration because the young people have no future and no hope. Ireland is bleeding to death – and the cause of it all is England. And here they are, cheering like mad and waving their Union Jacks.'

He ceased abruptly and gave an apologetic smile. 'Forgive me . . . but some of us felt we had to make some sort of protest.'

It had been the beginning of a deep friendship between himself and Fintan. From then on they met several times a week, mostly at week-ends. Fintan had a small business called Kincora School Supplies which he ran from a tiny office in Thomas Street. He was a bachelor and both his parents were dead. He occupied a room in a house in Stamer Street off the South Circular Road. He was the only lodger. The landlady and her sister, two elderly spinsters, lived in the rooms underneath. Gerry remembered how they had curtseyed with old world charm when Fintan introduced him. Fintan had laughed gently when he closed the door of his room.

'Those two downstairs are true-blue Unionists. It's a good thing they don't pry, else they would have hysterics if they saw my art collection.'

On the walls were portraits of Irish patriots – Wolfe Tone, Lord Edward Fitzgerald, Robert Emmet. Above the mantelpiece was a framed drawing of King Brian Boru on horseback, sword in one hand, crucifix in the other, addressing his army prior to battle.

'A vivid drawing that, Fintan.'

'Yes.' Fintan nodded his head in agreement. 'Miriam Durkin presented me with that. It was she who did the illustrations for my book.'

'You wrote a book?'

Again Fintan nodded. 'For Irish boys. Their impressionable minds have been too much influenced by the works of G A Henty. Thanks to him they now know all about Richard the Lionheart and Clive of India, but nothing of our own Irish heroes.'

He took a book from the shelf and autographed it before presenting it with a self-conscious smile. 'Just a small token.'

He had stood before him, waiting for his criticism as he turned the pages. The title of the book was *The Sword and the Cross* and underneath, in brackets *(The Life and Times of King Brian Boru)*. There were six full-page illustrations. A smaller version of the drawing above the mantelpiece was reproduced on the frontispiece.

'It looks very good. I shall treasure it always, Fintan.'

52

'I'm so glad you like it. I'm writing a new one about Finn and the Fianna.'

'I'm sure it will be a success.'

'Thank you. But one wishes for a more personal contact. That's why I envy you. As a teacher, you will have the opportunity of moulding the minds and characters of the boys under you. If you are a *true* Irishman, you will preserve them from the perversions they are being subjected to in the classrooms. Look here . . .'

Taking another book from the shelf, Fintan held it up for inspection. 'This is the standard Reader currently in use in our national schools. Just listen to some of the contents. *The Field of Agincourt, Grace Darling, The Death of Nelson*, Tennyson's *Charge of the Light Brigade*. Poets: Wordsworth, Keats, Shelley . . . My God – Shelley. A mocker of Christianity – the man who wrote *The Necessity for Atheism*!' He flung the book into the wastepaper basket. 'You see. This is how the children of Ireland – the descendants of kings – are being educated, as if they had no history or cultural heritage of their own!' He began to pace the room, his voice shaking with emotion. 'My God, it makes me furious just to think about it. Here we are, one of the oldest nations on earth. Once our missionaries went forth to preach the Gospel in Britain and the European continent. Their influence was felt from the North Sea to the Mediterranean, and from the Bay of Biscay to the banks of the Elbe. They became the teachers of whole nations, the counsellors of kings and emperors. Ireland's Golden Age! The whole island was devoted to piety and learning, while on the other side of the Irish Sea the *Sassenach* was painting himself blue with woad and worshipping the sun!' He gave a sardonic laugh. 'And they boast of their glorious past, of their Empire on which the sun never sets. Bah! Plunderers of the earth! Barbarians! They have destroyed eastern civilisations more ancient and more cultured than their own in their mad quest for territory and treasure. Parasites! Growing fat and insolent on the sweat of millions of their subjects, black, brown and white.' He came to a halt and pointed a quivering finger. 'It's men like you who can determine the fate of this country. You *Gearóid*, will have the ear of the young. Teach them to have racial pride. Tell them about our own glorious past before ever the *Sassenach* set foot on these shores and laid his red thieving hands on our lands. Teach them to play Irish games like hurling and to spurn those alien games like soccer and cricket.'

A caravan slid into view, then another, two more. . . . Ragged, barefoot children scampered alongside. Tinkers on the move, heading

53

northwards towards Castlebar. Gerry wanted to record the event. He reached into the pocket of his overcoat on the seat beside him and pulled out his diary. He never let a day pass without making some entry, no matter how trivial. What seemed unimportant now could be of interest to some historian of the future. He did not write for his own amusement but for posterity. He wanted to be the Samuel Pepys of his age. He told himself that when the history of this period came to be written, his diaries would be a source of valuable information.

Friday, 30th April, 1909.
I shall be in Carewstown shortly. I wonder what sort of place it is and what the people are like? I am curious about the school manager, Father Devlin. What kind of man is he? His letter was courteous enough. Writes with a firm hand. Hope he's not the Jansenistic type of priest, the sort that tries to make everyone conform to his own rules. Was it because of him three teachers resigned over the past two years? Or did they leave because they could not stand – to use Sullivan's phrase – the 'Godawful loneliness'?

Ah well, *che sarà, sarà*. More than likely I will have to struggle against provincial small-mindedness and apathy, not to mention loneliness. However, I am not easily deterred. I am young and healthy and a born optimist into the bargain. Nevertheless I ask myself, will I change Carewstown or will Carewstown change me?

He put the fountain pen back in his breast pocket and lay back turning over the pages. He came to the preface he had written sixteen months before.

The idea of starting a diary occurred to me one night about two weeks ago. Fintan Butler had just come back from America and had invited me to tea in his room in Stamer Street. Two friends of his were there. Elderly men. One was a Mr Kinsella who lives in Macken Street near Ringsend. Worried-looking little man with a straggling grey moustache. Father of a large family. Eldest son a priest. (St Catherine's, Meath St.) Scrivener in a solicitor's office – and not a well-paid one judging by his appearance. Sat in a corner for most of the night without saying a word. Noticed him biting his nails a few times. Fintan told me afterwards that he was a reformed dipsomaniac. That's why he locked up the whiskey. Although a strict teetotaller himself, he keeps a bottle for guests.

The other man, Mr Furlong, was much different. Talked a lot. Language quite coarse, though. Observed Fintan frowning every time he heard the Holy Name being used profanely. (Fintan once studied for the priesthood.) Interesting old josser nevertheless. Old Fenian. Was sentenced to fifteen years' penal servitude for his part in the abortive '67 rebellion. Was with Garret Lysaght in Portland Prison. Became very excited when Fintan told him he had spent some time with Lysaght in America.

Listening to them, I thought how fortunate I am to know such men. Joe Furlong for instance. He is a link with the past; he knew the legendary Garret Lysaght and the other leaders in the Fenian movement.

And as for Fintan . . . A statesman in the making! He will be a great man someday. If his dream of an independent Irish Republic is realised, he will undoubtedly be its first President.

Then I thought what a tragedy it would be if these times should go unrecorded. There and then I decided that I would try and do what Pepys had done for the Restoration period.

In this diary I shall try to emulate him. I shall try to be as objective as he was when he recorded what he saw, felt and heard. Therefore, if my pen-portraits should appear to be cruel at times, it is because I do not wish to romanticise but to paint people as I see them, warts and all. This, then, is my diary. I dedicate it to you, the Historians and Biographers of the twenty-first century.

Much had happened to him since writing that. He idly turned over the pages, pausing now and then to read.

19th November, 1908.

Fintan invited me to tea. Cold, frosty night. We sat before the fire eating muffins. Later, relaxing in two easy chairs, Fintan asked me if I had ever heard of an organisation called the Irish Republican Brotherhood. Told him I had heard my father talking about it many years ago. 'As dead as the dodo, now,' I added.

Fintan looked at me strangely, then said, 'Not quite. True, it frittered away over the years, but it never died. Now it has been infused with a new vitality. Younger men are taking over. There is a steady flow of funds from Clan-na-Gael in America.'

'How do you know all this?' I asked.

His reply startled me. 'I am a co-opted member of the Supreme Council.'

He began to inform me about the IRB, but I must confess I did not pay much attention to what he was saying. I just sat there asking myself how I could have been so mistaken about Fintan.

I knew he was a fervent nationalist. I knew he was striving for an independent sovereign state, but I always thought he wanted to bring that about by constitutional agitation. Now here he was openly admitting to being a member of a conspiratorial organisation whose policy has always been one of armed revolt.

Was that the reason why Fintan left the seminary? Or was he expelled?

The IRB is an oath-binding revolutionary organisation, and as such is open to condemnation by the Irish Catholic hierarchy.

Gerry turned the page.

20th November, 1908.

This night Fintan asked me to become a member of the IRB. 'We do not recruit indiscriminately,' he told me. 'We pick only men we know and trust; men with influence in cultural, athletic and social circles. Our aim is to have at least one such man in every small town and village in Ireland.' Told him I would need time to consider his request.

10th December, 1908.

My confessor refused me absolution when I told him I was contemplating joining the IRB. Told me I was deliberately putting myself outside the laws of God and man.

13th December, 1908.

Another night without sleep. I lie on my bed, wrestling with my conscience. My Church has always been my comfort and strength. Must I abandon it now to follow Fintan?

30th December, 1908.

Fintan administered the oath to me tonight in his room. No third party present.

The train was slowing down. The engine gave a long ear-piercing screech of warning. At the other end of the carriage one of the men awoke with a startled snort, muttered a curse and rudely shook the others out of their slumber. They gathered their belongings hastily as the train came to a halt. There was a rush for the door. Gerry turned sideways on the seat, legs drawn in, as they scrambled past. The last to leave, a big burly man, stumbled over the outstretched legs of the sleeping man opposite. The man gave a grunt and awoke. He looked about him dazedly for a few seconds, then pushed himself upright on the seat. Gerry closed the diary and put it back in the pocket of his overcoat. Fintan's reaction would be one of horror if he knew I kept a diary, he told himself. Resting his hands on his knees, he stared out of the window.

'There are no IRB men in east Mayo,' Fintan told him. 'You will have the honour of starting the first circle. Get to know the people of Carewstown. Find out what the political views are of the men in the village and the district around. Then start to recruit. But for God's sake be circumspect! Investigate thoroughly each man's background before approaching him.'

There was a shrill blast of a whistle as the train began to move. He watched the tiny station sliding past. The train gathered speed. School-teacher by day, he thought, and IRB organiser by night. He would be leading a double life. He wondered if he was equal to the task. He hated deception.

The land was changing colour. Lush green grass was giving way to brown barren bogland. A group came into view. A man was cutting turf, tossing the sods over his shoulder. Nearby his wife and two children were collecting them for drying.

'Ah, sweet Christ!'

Gerry started. The man opposite had spoken on impulse. His face revealed his sudden embarrassment; the expression looked strangely out of place on the pugilistic features. He gave a backward jerk of the thumb.

'Seein' those people workin' on the bog,' he explained roughly, 'brought back memories.'

He put his hand in the pocket of his jacket, pulled out a packet of cigarettes and lit one. He wore a weather-stained cap on the side of his head, the peak almost covering one eye. Red stubble covered his cheeks and jaws. Gerry thought he was about to relapse again into a sullen silence when he said, gazing reflectively out of the window, 'We were like that once – my father and mother, my brothers and sisters, slavin' away on the bog. Not just for fuel, but drainin' and seedin' it, makin' it grow food.'

'It must have been a precarious existence,' Gerry said.

The man nodded. 'Aye, it was. But we managed. When my father came to this district first, he rented a cottage and twenty acres of land for two pounds a year from Walter Carew of the Big House. Two acres of poor rocky land and eighteen acres of what was mostly cutaway bog. The lot combined wouldn't have fed a snipe! But my father met the challenge. He cleared the two acres of rock with pick and crowbar and fertilised the soil until there was grass enough to feed a cow. After he had fenced it off, he began to inch out into the bog, reclaimin' it bit by bit. By the time he got married he had drained and cultivated more than eight acres of what had been useless land. Gallagher the Bogman they called him. It was a name he wore with pride.'

57

'Gallagher . . .' Gerry pondered over the name. 'An uncommon name for this part of the country.'

'My father came from Donegal,' the man said slowly. 'He was a mountainy man.' He took a deep pull of the cigarette. 'The English Lord who owned the land my father lived on wanted the mountains for a particular strain of deer he was bringin' over from Scotland. So that they could romp and breed undisturbed, he had every human bein' driven off at bayonet point. More than two hundred people, men, women and children, had to take to the road. It was a cold wet autumn and the workhouse was full, so they had to sleep out in the open. Many died from hunger and exposure.' He dropped the butt of the cigarette to the floor and ground it underfoot. 'My father took the road south into Connacht. When he reached Carewstown he decided to stay. He had twelve gold sovereigns in a purse tied around his neck – the savin's of a lifetime.'

Silence fell between them. At last Gerry said, 'What sort of place is Carewstown? What are the people like? I'm the new school-teacher,' he added.

The man shrugged. 'I've been away for ten years. Places change, people change.'

'I've been corresponding with the school manager, Father Devlin. Was he parish priest in your time? If he was, I would be grateful if you could tell me anything about him.'

The man stared at him in silence. His eyes narrowed and features hardened. He turned his head away and gazed dourly out of the window.

'So,' he murmured after a while, 'Devlin still rules the roost, does he?' He stared out of the window for a few minutes, lost in thought. Then he turned his face to Gerry again.

'So you want to know about Father Devlin, do you?' he asked in a harsh voice. 'Well, I'll tell you, if you're spineless, if you're the sort that jumps when another cracks the whip, then you and him will get along famously. But if you're not, if you're a man with gumption, then God help you!'

They were the only passengers to alight at the small station. The porter, a small man with a wizened face and beady alert eyes, stared at them with open curiosity. He stretched out his hand to Gerry for the ticket, inspecting him from head to foot as he did so. Then he focused his attention on the other man. He cocked his head sideways like a bird and stared up into his face. Then he gave a little gasp.

'Cross of Christ!' he exclaimed with awe. 'It's Con Gallagher!'

The tall man grinned. 'Ye have a good memory for faces, Mickeen Gavan.'

'Faith, then,' the porter replied, 'it would be hard to forget the likes of yours. As ugly as sin – and more so now with that nose of yours squashed against yer face. Tell me now, was it some jealous husband did that to ye?'

The grin slowly faded from Gallagher's face. 'No, Mickeen,' he answered grimly, 'that was done by one of the bastards who put the torch to my house ten years ago.'

The porter clicked his tongue. 'A bad business, that.'

'Did Walter Carew sell the land we lived on?' Gallagher asked.

'Aye, he did,' the porter answered. 'Oul Walter fell on hard times. Sold all the land around. Now there's only the demesne left. And the village. He can still live in style on the rents he gets from Carewstown.'

'Who did he sell our land to?'

The porter gave a humourless laugh. 'Need ye ask?'

'Bull O'Malley?'

'The same,' the porter replied. 'As hungry as ever for even the smallest patch of cutaway bog.' He opened the low wooden gate and allowed them to pass through, before walking out into the middle of the narrow dusty road to stare after them.

They were an odd-looking pair. One tall, with his coarse work-stained clothes. The other low-sized but powerfully built, dressed in navy-blue serge with his overcoat draped over his arm and weighed down by a bulging suit-case. The porter stroked his chin thoughtfully.

'Begob, Gallagher,' he murmured to himself, 'there'll be quite a few people who won't be glad to see ye back in Carewstown.'


II


Gerry transferred the heavy suit-case to his left hand. He felt uncomfortably hot and tired. Sweat trickled down from under his new straw hat and down inside his high stiff collar.

'How far away are we from Carewstown?' he asked.

'About two miles,' Gallagher answered.

Gerry sighed and glanced down at his dust-smeared shoes and clothes. Again he looked back, hoping to see a cart or some sort of vehicle coming up from behind, but the road was deserted. Not one person had they encountered from the time they had left the railway station a half-hour ago. He gave a weary shake of the head.

They trudged along between high hedges. There was a gap to the right a little further up, filled by a gate and a low stone wall. As they came level with the gate, a dog came bounding and barking from a large farm-house situated about thirty yards back from the road. It thrust its head between the bars and growled at them with bared teeth. Startled, Gerry jumped back. Gallagher stooped to pick up a stone and flung it at the dog. Both men laughed as the animal went racing back towards the farm-house, yelping.

'That's Bull O'Malley's place,' Gallagher said. 'The dog is like its master – all spit and snarl but damn the bit else!' He stood in the middle of the road, looking on. The house was much bigger since he saw it last: a new wing and an outhouse had been added. O'Malley, he thought, has become more prosperous during the years I've been away.

Gerry stood waiting a few yards further up the road, his suit-case on the ground beside him. He felt hot and tired and a little irritable.

'I don't think it's a good idea to stand under this sun for too long,' he said. Gallagher nodded and they pressed on. The sun was at its height. Gerry could not breathe, encased as he was in a tight-fitting dark suit and high hard collar. He unbuttoned his jacket; his white linen shirt was soaked and stained with sweat, and his new shoes were pinching. He began to limp. Every few minutes he had to switch the heavy suit case from one hand to the other.

He envied the man beside him. Gallagher walked with loose easy strides, hands in trouser pockets. His collarless shirt was open to the navel and his haversack dangled from his shoulder. Gerry cleared his throat. His mouth was dry and gritty from the dust of the road.

He said hoarsely, 'Are you going into Carewstown?'

'No,' Gallagher answered. 'I'm goin' to the house where I was born,' adding bitterly, 'That is, what's left of it.'

Gerry remembered Gallagher's remark to the porter at the railway station. 'One of the bastards who put the torch to my house . . .' His original conception of Carewstown as a sleepy hamlet was beginning to change. He also recalled Gallagher's cynical remarks about Father Devlin. What was Father Devlin like? What were the people of Carewstown like? He wanted to know before he entered Carewstown, before he presented himself to Father Devlin.

They continued until they came to a rutted track branching off to the left. It fell away down a slope, curved to the right, and disappeared between high banks of wild yellow furze.

60

Gallagher came to a standstill at the top of the track. 'This is where I leave you,' he said and pointed. 'Carewstown lies about a mile up ahead, just beyond the Big House there.'

In the distance, away to the right and high above the quivering heat haze, a massive structure stood, stark and bleak against the bright blue of the sky. It rested on a hill – the only piece of elevated ground for miles around.

Gerry took off his straw hat to fan his perspiring face. He screwed up his eyes against the glare. 'So that's the Big House?'

Gallagher nodded. 'Aye, that's Carewscourt. Where our lord and master, Walter Carew, lives.' He turned and looked at Gerry. 'Christ, man,' he exclaimed, 'you look like a boiled lobster!'

Gerry gave an exhausted sigh. 'I feel like one.'

He did not want to go into Carewstown looking like this: travel weary – physically and mentally exhausted. He looked at the track curving out of sight.

'Can I get to Carewstown by that way?' he asked.

Gallagher nodded. 'Yes, but it takes longer.'

'No matter. I just want to find a quiet spot where I can rest awhile. Someplace where I can wash and brush myself down. Is there a river or stream?'

'There's a spring near where I used to live,' Gallagher said, picking up the suit-case. 'Come on.'

Gerry took off his jacket and limped after him. His new shoes were pinching more than ever and there was a burning sensation on the soles of his feet. He could feel blisters forming.

They started along the track. It was about fifty feet below the level of the road and it wound in and out between high banks of sweet-smelling furze. They were out of the glare of the sun now and the air was a little cooler. Gerry felt thankful for that at least. He lagged behind Gallagher who ambled along swinging the bulging suit-case from his hand as though it had no weight at all. After they had travelled for about a quarter of a mile, the bank of furze to the left of the track petered out. Suddenly they were on the edge of the bog.

It stretched away to a distant river sparkling in the sun. A light breeze soughed across the flat barren waste. Gerry gave a gasp of pleasure as it penetrated his shirt, cooling his sweat-covered body. It made the going a little easier. There were deep cuttings along the edge of the track where the local people had dug for fuel, but further out it was virgin bog, brown-coloured with green patches here and there and speckled by white clumps of bog cotton. It steamed in the heat; it had absorbed the rains of centuries like a sponge.

The track ran straight ahead between the bog and rising bracken-covered ground, which rose gently eastwards in the direction of the Carewstown road. On the fertile upper slopes, a few sheep grazed. Gerry could see a cottage in the distance, on a hump of ground about eight yards back from the track, and overshadowed by a large rock. He stopped and shaded his eyes with his hand. He could see more clearly now. It was just a roofless shell. Gallagher's place, he thought. It had to be; he could not see any other house in the distance beyond.

Gallagher was way ahead of him now, but as he came near to the cottage his pace slackened.

Gerry watched him walk slowly up the slope. When he came to the cottage, he put the suit-case and haversack down beside the doorway and stood looking into the ruin with his arms above his head, both hands pressed against the lintel. He remained like that for almost a minute, then stooped low and entered.

Gerry hobbled on past. This was a moment when a man should be left alone with his memories. A little further on he found the spring Gallagher had told him of. Several large moss-covered stones circled it. He placed his overcoat and jacket down on a clump of heather nearby with his straw hat on top. He sank to his hunkers and, cupping his hands together, lowered them into the water. He drank slowly, enjoying the cold, pure taste. Having slaked his thirst, he stood up and removed his collar and shirt. Soaking his handkerchief in the water, he washed the sweat from his face and body.

Ten minutes later, as he was fastening his collar, he heard the crunch of gravel behind him. He turned his head to see Gallagher walking towards him carrying a fire-blackened billy-can. His face was expressionless. He knelt on one knee before the spring and lowered the billy-can into it.

'Feelin' better?' he inquired without lifting his head.

'Like a new man,' Gerry replied.

Gallagher stood up. The billy-can was full to the brim. 'You'll have to drink your tea black,' he said. 'I've no milk.'

Gerry laughed. 'I gave up drinking tea with milk for the seven weeks of Lent. Now I can't break the habit.'

Gallagher gave a grunt and walked away. Gerry followed him, his shoes in his hand; he had taken them off to give his tortured feet relief.

Gallagher had a small fire going in front of the cottage. He placed the billy-can on it and rummaged in his haversack. Gerry sat down with his back against the wall. Gallagher spread some of the contents of the haversack on the grass: a chipped enamel mug, a knife and spoon,

62

butter wrapped in thick grease-proof paper, the remains of a loaf of bread. . . . He sliced the bread into two chunks and unwrapped the greaseproof paper. The butter had melted in the heat and was almost liquid. The water in the billy-can bubbled. Gallagher took out a glass jar from the haversack and unscrewed the top; it was quarter full of tea and sugar mixed. He emptied the lot into the billy-can and stirred it with the spoon.

Gerry looked on as Gallagher poured the tea into the mug and the glass jar. He handed the mug to Gerry together with one of the chunks of bread. Gerry accepted both with thanks. Gallagher picked up his jar of tea and bread and sat down beside him. The two of them ate and drank slowly in silence, staring at the barrenness in front of them. The shrill cry of a curlew pierced the stillness. Gerry chewed the bread into mush: it was stale and hard. He washed it down with one long gulp of tea and put the empty mug down beside him.

'That land out there, was that yours?'

Gallagher sat with his legs drawn up under him, elbows resting on knees. He stared grim-faced at the scene before him.

'Yes,' he replied bitterly. 'That was the land my father sweated and slaved over for more than twenty years. He made it fertile. A whole family existed on what that land yielded. Now look at it! Sweet Christ – just look at it!' He gripped the jar tightly, anger swelling up inside him. The land on the other side of the track was covered with waist-high grass and weeds. Further out, the soft peaty soil had become water-logged; he could see the gleam of water where pools had formed. The drains his father had cut had long since crumbled and fallen in. He put down the jar beside him and lit a cigarette. He inhaled deeply and let the tobacco smoke ooze out between his lips. He spat out a shred of tobacco.

'We may have had full bellies,' he said, 'but our pockets were always empty. Every penny we earned had to go for rent to Walter Carew of the Big House. There was never any money to spare – not even for a doctor when my mother took sick. If she had got medical attention at the proper time she would have lived. That's why my brother Farley hated this place and the way we had to scrape for a livin'. After my father died, he went to Cork City and got a job there. When he had enough money saved, he sailed to America. He landed in New York, worked, saved money and then sent the passage fare home for Sean and Norah. Stacia went out after them the followin' year, and Brigid the year after that.' He paused. 'Then I was on my own. I could have gone to America with Brigid, but I preferred to stay here. I loved this place, you see, the same way my father did. I never wanted to leave. And I liked bein' my own boss. I was the youngest and had always been under the thumb of my parents and the rest of the family. Now with everyone gone I was free to go and do as I pleased. Durin' the day I worked in the fields and tended the cow. At night I'd wander off to some neighbour's house for a game of cards or maybe go to a dance at the crossroads. For the first time I had money in my pocket. There was a market for vegetables and turf in Carewstown. I supplied both, usin' Johnny Boyle's donkey and cart to carry them in.

'Johnny was my nearest neighbour and the best friend I ever had. He was a widower, and lived without chick or child in a little cottage further up the track, about half a mile from here.

'Johnny had only two pleasures in life – playin' the fiddle and drinkin' whiskey. He always kept a gallon jar of poteen handy. He made it himself. Sometimes the two of us would get roarin' drunk.' He flicked the butt of his cigarette away with his forefinger.

'Then one day the old parish priest, Father Lanigan, died. A new one came to take his place – Father Devlin. He was a powerfully built man over six feet tall, with a voice that could be heard from one end of Mayo to the other. He was not long installed when he made a tour of his new parish with his curate, Father Nolan. I was milkin' the cow when the pair of them drove up in a pony and trap.

'Father Devlin was friendly enough. Asked me how many acres I had and how was I managin' on my own; did I go to Mass regularly and so on. I answered his questions politely and they drove off.

'The followin' Sunday, Father Devlin told us from the pulpit that he intended to make his parish a shinin' example for every other parish in the country. It would be a place, he told us, where wickedness and lewdness would not be allowed to flourish. A place where the law would be respected. He warned all of us he would not tolerate interference from any of his parishioners in the performance of his duties. He lectured us about dishonesty – on not payin' our lawful dues. He told us there was a certain merchant in Carewstown who was owed a lot of money and was not gettin' it. To withhold payment for goods received was a mortal sin, he warned us, and a person who refused to honour his debts would not be granted absolution.

'We all knew who the merchant was he was talkin' about. Phil Costello. He was the gombeen man. In a bad year, if the crops failed, Phil Costello would let you have Indian meal on credit. A bag contained sixteen stone of meal and cost a shillin' a stone. Costello charged a shillin' a week interest on each bag. He would charge sixpence a week interest on a sack of flour which cost twelve shillin's. There was a sayin' in Carewstown: "What doesn't go to Walter Carew goes to Phil Costello."

'After that sermon, Phil Costello was loud in his praise for Father Devlin. Told everyone he intended supportin' the good Father in anythin' he choose to do. And the rest of them, the men with money – the publicans, the merchants and the big farmers – were not slow followin' Costello's example. They found it was to their advantage to be on friendly terms with Father Devlin. He became their champion. They showed their appreciation by donatin' large sums of money to the church.

'Once Devlin knew he had these men behind him, he rode roughshod over the rest of us. There were certain books, he told us one Sunday mornin', that could corrupt. If anyone had in their possession novels by authors like Emile Zola or Thomas Hardy or books by socialist writers such as Karl Marx, then they were to bring them to him at once. When no books were delivered to the presbytery, he organised a committee – he called it a vigilance committee – to collect them from every house in the parish. They came to my house. Five of them, three men and two women. The youngest was about fifty. I knew them all – the worst bunch of hypocritical craw-thumpers in the village of Carewstown! When they asked for whatever books I had in the house, I chased them away with a pitchfork!

'Unfortunately no one else did the same. It would have been our answer to Father Devlin that we were not a crowd of sheep willin' to submit to his bullyin'. Instead they surrendered what books they had. The committee brought them along to Father Devlin – a whole cartful.

'Devlin found somethin' wrong with nearly every one of them – even the most harmless love stories, which he called "impure literature". He had a bonfire made of the lot in the middle of Carewstown while the whole village looked on.

'After that, there was no stoppin' Father Devlin. He put an end to the crossroad dancin'. Said they were the cause of immorality, as afterwards the couples wandered off into the fields and the dark wayside places where temptation lurked. To make sure his orders were obeyed, he patrolled the roads at night, sometimes with his curate or one or two members of the vigilance committee carryin' lanterns. Several times he came across couples courtin' in the ditches and cut the backsides off them with his blackthorn!

'As time went on, life became unbearable for the young people of the parish. It was like a prison to them. They had no place to go, nothin' to do. Many of the girls and boys emigrated. It became a dead place, inhabited mostly by the old, the middle-aged and the very young.

'But I didn't go. I wasn't leavin' this.' He indicated the land before him with a wave of the hand. 'At nights I would go and try to find what excitement there was left in Carewstown. If there was none, I made some. Gamblin' with cards, a wrestlin' match with any man that fancied himself. And there was always a girl or two who was willin' to be cuddled under a hedge, Father Devlin or no Father Devlin.

'Now and then I would go into the village for a few drinks. A few times I got involved in brawls after I had a drink too many. Father Devlin got to hear about it. One Sunday at Mass, he denounced me by name from the altar. Called me a ruffian and a blackguard. I walked out and never went to church again. From then on I set out to oppose Father Devlin in every way I could. Someone had to stand up to him.

'I began to gather a few of the local lads and girls in my cottage at the week-ends for a few jigs and reels. I brought along Johnny Boyle to supply the music.

'Soon the young people of the district – well, what was left of them – started to flock to this place every Saturday and Sunday night. It was the only place left where they could enjoy themselves. I had to turn away most of them, we were that cramped for space. Of course Devlin got to hear about what was goin' on. He ranted and raved from the pulpit. Called my place a den of iniquity. One day he stopped me in the village street and started to threaten me at the top of his voice. Told me if I didn't stop holdin' dances I'd have him to reckon with.

'A crowd gathered round. I waited till he had finished, then told him to go to hell and walked away.

'That did it. I had openly defied him in front of everyone. He knew if he didn't do somethin' about it, his power was gone. I was the serpent in this little Eden he had made.

'We held the dance as usual in my house on the Saturday night. About twenty of us were packed in the kitchen. Two couples had the floor to themselves while Johnny sat by the door sawin' away at the fiddle for all he was worth. We were all havin' great fun when the door was kicked open and Father Devlin and his curate walked in. He had his tall silk hat on his head and he carried his blackthorn stick in his hand.

'Johnny stopped playin' and the two couples that were dancin' came to a standstill. The rest of us just sat there, too stunned to move.

'Devlin walked to the centre of the floor and stood glarin' about him. He raised his stick and let a bellow out of him like a bull. "Get out, ye whelps!" he roared. "Get out before ye feel the weight of me stick!" With that, he lays about him with his blackthorn.

'There was a mad dash for the door. As the young people scampered past him, he struck at their legs with the stick. Then he twisted round to where Johnny was sittin' by the door. He cuffed him across the head and sent him flyin' off the chair. Johnny fell on his back, his fiddle beside him. Devlin raised his foot and brought it down on the fiddle, smashing it to matchwood.

'I went for Devlin. I struck him on the chest with my fist and sent him staggerin' back. I bent to pick Johnny up when Devlin brought his blackthorn down across my back. "Take that, ye red cur!" he roared.

'I collapsed to my knees from the force of the blow. I was stunned for a few seconds. Then I lost my head.

'I jumped to my feet and swung round. Devlin was in front of me, hatless, his stick raised for another blow. I struck him in the face once or twice with my clenched fist and he fell into the arms of his curate. I snatched the stick from his hand and raised it to strike him with it, when Johnny grabbed my arm. "For God's sake, Con, are ye mad?" he shouted. "It's the priest!" He twisted the stick out of my hand and flung it away from him. He got between me and Devlin.

'Devlin lay against the wall, his hand coverin' his eye where I had hit him. Father Nolan held him by the arm.

' "In heaven's name, Father," Johnny shouted, "get out of here if ye value yer life!"

'But Devlin just stood there with his hand over his eye and a bewildered look on his face, all the fight knocked out of him. Father Nolan picked up his stick and hat and led him out by the arm.

'The next day Johnny came to see me. He was worried-lookin'. He had been to Carewstown that mornin' and had met the people comin' from Mass. They told him Father Devlin had been standin' on the steps in front of the church so that the entire congregation could see his bruised face as they passed in.

'Later he told them from the pulpit that I had brutally assaulted him while he was performin' his duties as parish priest. I was leadin' the youth of the parish down the slippery slope to hell, and it was up to the people not to let this happen. For if they did, he warned, then they would pay a terrible price for their indifference. He told them that when the news of what had happened reached the rest of the country, people would ask what class of people were they in Carewstown that they could stand idly by as their priest was physically assaulted tryin' to save their sons and daughters from bein' corrupted.

'That night, it was long after midnight, I was sittin' by the fire readin' a newspaper with only the oul mongrel for company. Suddenly the dog lifted its head and ran to the door, barkin'. I knew there was someone outside. I first thought it was a few of the lads comin' for a game of cards, but as I reached the door I wondered at the lateness of the hour.

'I opened the door. It was a bright moonlit night – mid-June it was. Five men stood facin' me a few yards away. The dog was still barkin' furiously and makin' little dashes at them. As I stood there, one of them called my name. His voice sounded strange, like it was muffled. I took one step forward, and then I saw why. All were wearin' hoods over their heads; pieces of material with slits cut for eyes. One of them carried a cudgel.

'Even then I didn't sense the danger. I thought they were some of the local lads playin' some sort of joke. The little mongrel made one of his barkin' dashes towards them when the one with the cudgel brought it down with all his might on its head, killin' it outright.

'They swarmed all over me before I could do a thing. It was as if they had all been waitin' for one of them to make a move. One stood each side of me holdin' my arms, while another was behind with his right arm hooked round my throat and his left hand grippin' my hair. The remain' two stood in front of me. One of them pushed his masked face into mine. I could see the shine of his eyes. "We'll teach ye a lesson, ye bastard," he snarled, "one ye'll never forget! We won't have any priest beaters in this parish." He drove his fist into my stomach three times while the others held me fast.

'Then they let go of me. I slumped to my knees. They gathered round and started to kick me. Somehow I managed to roll free. I tumbled down the slope there and on to the track. I lay there, winded and bruised from the beatin'. I could hear them smashin' up the furniture. And I could hear the cow moanin' in terror. They had dragged her from the outhouse, and were chasing her towards the fields. She came stumblin' down the slope only a few yards away from where I lay. There were two of them after her, yellin' at the tops of their voices. One of them was the bastard with the cudgel. He kept hittin' her with it.

'Then I heard someone shout: "Now let's burn this kip to the ground!" The thought of what they were about to do made me stagger to my feet. I could hardly stand. I was still winded and the pain in my side was so bad I was sure one of my ribs was broken. Somehow, I managed to crawl up the slope.

'There was a dull roar and the whole house went up in flames! They had saturated the inside with paraffin before puttin' the torch to it. I found a few empty tins of the stuff lyin' around the followin' mornin'. The three of them were leapin' and whoopin' in front of the house. I staggered forward and my foot struck somethin'. I had difficulty bendin' down and pickin' it up. It was the *sleán* I used for cuttin' turf. The blade of it was as sharp as a razor.

'I held it firmly with both hands and made for the man nearest me. He was wearin' a light-coloured shirt. He had been leapin' about like the others, but now he was standin' still and clappin' his hands and cheerin' like he was at a play as the flames shot up through the thatch.

'I aimed at the space between his shoulder-blades and drove the blade of the *sleán* in and down, cuttin' away shirt and flesh from his back with one quick stroke!

'He leapt, screamin' like a madman and then pitched forward on his face. The other two came rushin' towards me. I made a wild swipe with the *sleán* at one who came at me from the left. I missed him. The effort threw me off balance and I fell to my knees. Someone came chargin' directly at me.

'I struggled to get to my feet – then his boot swung up into my face! I can remember a blindin' white flash and a crackin' sound as the point of his boot struck the bridge of my nose. I could feel the pain shootin' through my skull. I went over on my back. The blood was runnin' down my face and into my mouth. I started to choke. I rolled over, coughin' and retchin', and tried to get to my feet.

'One of the bastards must have been standin' over me, waitin' for me to do just that. As I was about to straighten up, he brought his fist down. He caught me behind the ear and I went out like a light!

'I don't remember much after that. I think I came round a few times, before falling unconscious again.

'It was the rain that revived me. It was one of those heavy summer showers. I woke up drenched to the skin. It was daybreak. At first I didn't know where I was or what had happened. Then it all came back to me. I struggled to my feet and stood swayin', feelin' more dead than alive. My face was swollen and numb and my chin and neck and even my chest was crusted with dried blood.

'The cottage and outhouse were blackened ruins. Just a few feet from the doorway the body of the dog lay with its skull crushed in. I stood there lookin' on in the pourin' rain. I kept tellin' myself that this was a nightmare I was havin' and that soon I would wake up.

'I don't know for how long I stood there. Probably only a few minutes. I went into what was left of the cottage. Nothin' remained, but among the ashes I found a fire-blackened tin box where I kept my money. There was about four or five sovereigns and some silver – all I had left in the world. I put them in my trouser-pocket and then went out searchin' for the cow.

'I could follow her tracks easily enough. She had trampled the potato beds flat in tryin' to get away from the men who had been chasin' her. I found her half-in and half-out of a bog-hole. Her hind legs were broken. She was moanin' from the pain, but there was nothin' I could do to put her out of her misery. I had no weapon except the *sleán*, but even if I had, I hadn't the strength to do it.

'I made my way to Johnny Boyle's house. Johnny nearly died of shock when he saw the state I was in. I told him what had happened while he stripped and bathed me. My body was black and blue from the kickin' I had received. Johnny ran his fingers gently down my sides. There were no ribs broken, he assured me. Afterwards he applied a cold compress to my face to take down the swellin'.

'I told Johnny about the cow lyin' in agony out there in the bog. He fetched his knife, sharpened it and went out. He was gone for nearly two hours. When he came back, his boots and trousers were covered in blood.

'I stayed in Johnny's house all that day. Johnny advised me to get away from Carewstown. Sooner or later, he said, Father Devlin and myself were bound to clash again, and if that happened . . .

'He didn't say anythin' more, but I knew what he meant. Those five buckoes whoever they were, would come lookin' for me again. I was too vulnerable, livin' as I was out there alone on the edge of the bog. And I was frightened. I tried to put on a brave face in front of Johnny, but I was nineteen and frightened.

'That night Johnny gave me an old jacket and put a small parcel of food in the pocket. Then I left. I sneaked out of Carewstown like a thief and headed north. Two weeks later I was in Derry and almost penniless. One day I went along the wharf lookin' for work.

'There was a crowd of young people, boys and girls, waitin' to go on board a rotten oul tub of a boat. They were all goin' to Scotland for the potato-diggin'. The boss of the squad had the same surname as my own, but everyone called him Micky Jim. He was from Donegal like the others.

'Micky Jim had been expectin' twenty people but only sixteen had arrived, so he hired me on the spot. We sailed a few hours later. The next mornin' we landed at Greenock. The potato merchant met us on the quay and hurried us off to Buteshire. There we worked like slaves in the pourin' rain.

'The men dug the potatoes from the ground with short three-pronged graips. The women followed behind, crawlin' on their knees and draggin' two baskets apiece along with them. Into the baskets they lifted the potatoes thrown out by the men. When the baskets were filled they were emptied into barrels. These barrels were in turn sent off to the markets and the big towns.

'That's how we worked, from seven o'clock in the mornin' to six o'clock in the evenin', and all for sixteen shillin's a week. We had to sleep in byres at night – aye, and sometimes even in pig-styes. But when November came I didn't go back to Ireland with the others. I moved on to Glasgow and got a job there.

'I stayed there for nearly two years and moved on again. I was a navvy – an itinerant one, movin' from place to place. I worked with thousands of other navvies at the dam-construction works in Kinlochleven. We gutted whole mountains there, destroyed the beauty of that part of the Highlands for ever.

'When that job was finished I moved south into England. Newcastle, Leeds, south-west to Manchester. After that, Birmingham, Northampton, Bedford and finally London. I was in London for two years.

'Three days ago I was sittin' by myself in a crowded pub in Whitechapel, surrounded by dockers and seamen, fishwives and whores, all either laughin' or quarrellin'. The noise was deafenin'.

'A man began to sing. I couldn't see him for the crowd, but I knew from his voice he was a fellow-countryman. Everyone quietened and listened.

'The song was an old one: *The Green Hills of Erin*. He wasn't a good singer, but he put his whole heart into the song. Once he faltered and nearly broke down. I knew how he was feelin', for I felt the same way myself.

'Suddenly I was sick of it all – sick of wanderin' from one town to another, sick of filthy lodgin' houses and of livin' among strangers. Sick of the dirt and the smell of cities. I wanted to see the Partry Mountains risin' up out of the mornin' mist and to feel the pure sweet wind sweepin' in from the Atlantic. I wanted to go back to Carewstown, to my roots.'

Gallagher took off his cap and mopped his sweat-covered face. He had thick fiery-red hair. The sun had revolved a little more to the west and once again they were exposed to its glare.

Gerry put on his straw hat and tilted it down over his eyes. Now I know what to expect, he told himself grimly. It was going to be a contest

71

of wills between himself and Father Devlin. If I allow him to run me out of Carewstown as he did all the others, then I will have failed not only myself but Fintan Butler as well.

He reached for his shoes and began to put them on. He tied the shoelaces with determination. I won't let him break me, he told himself fiercely. I won't!

Gerry stood up and put on his jacket. He placed the overcoat over his arm. Stooping, he took a firm grip on the handle of the suit-case and lifted it. He stood looking down at Gallagher.

'No doubt we will be seeing each other often from now on,' he said.

Gallagher merely nodded, but as Gerry walked up the track he called after him. 'Schoolmaster.'

Gerry turned around.

Gallagher's red hair gleamed in the sun. His voice was hard. 'When ye see Father Devlin, tell him Con Gallagher is back, this time for good.'


## III


The heavy boot swung into Gallagher's side.

Gallagher woke with a start. A big man, red-faced with aggression, stood over him with an ashplant in his hand.

'Get up, ye dog!' he ordered harshly. 'Up!' He raised the stick menacingly.

Two men stood behind him, just inside the doorway of the ruin. Gallagher raised himself slowly and cautiously to one knee. The man took one step back and raised the stick higher.

'Filthy, thievin' tinkers!' he snarled. 'Ye won't steal from me and get away with it. I may have lost the rest of yer tribe, but by Christ I'll make an example of ye!' He lifted the stick above his head.

'Hit me with that stick, O'Malley,' Gallagher snapped, 'and it will be the last thing ye'll ever do!'

At the mention of his name the man's jaw dropped. Gallagher came slowly to his feet, fists at the ready. 'The last man who raised a stick to me inside these walls,' he growled, 'had his face punched in for doin' it!'

There was a tense silence. Then one of the men near the doorway gave a little cry of recognition. 'It's Con Gallagher!'

O'Malley let his stick fall to the ground. His eyes widened with astonishment.

'Well, I'll be damned!' he exclaimed.

Gallagher lowered his fists. He was aware of a dull pain under his ribs. 'And I don't like to be kicked awake!'

O'Malley gave a shrug. 'We thought ye were a tinker. When we saw the remains of a fire and the billy-can outside, we thought ye were a tinker.'

Gallagher felt dwarfed by Bull O'Malley. Although six foot tall himself, O'Malley topped him by two inches. And he was broad – very broad. Years ago someone had nick-named him 'Bull' and the name had stuck. He wore leggings; a billycock hat was set squarely on his head. He had a deep, coarse voice.

'The tinkers have been passin' through here in droves over the past few days, and layin' their red thievin' hands on poultry and everythin' else not nailed or battened down! Some of them have been campin' this side of Carewstown and allowin' their bloody horses to roam all over the place. A whole field of mangolds was destroyed on me two nights ago.'

The two men walked forward from the doorway and placed themselves each side of Bull O'Malley. They stared sulkily at Gallagher.

Gallagher recognised them immediately. O'Malley's two sons, Luke and Sonny. Sonny, the younger, was the image of his father. The likeness was remarkable. He had the same blunt features, the same dark hair and thick eyebrows that almost met over the nose. He was similar in height and build – a giant of a man, but he lacked the aggression of Bull O'Malley. Nevertheless, he tried to copy his father's manner – tried to imitate his brusqueness by declaring loudly, 'Ye've a bloody nerve, Gallagher, comin' back here to Carewstown!'

'Now, now,' Bull O'Malley intervened hastily. 'He's not stayin'. He's just passin' through.' He looked questioningly at Gallagher. 'Aren't ye?' he inquired.

'No,' Gallagher responded firmly, 'I'm stayin' here for good.'

Bull O'Malley stared at him with consternation written all over his face. Neither he nor his sons said anything for several seconds. Sonny O'Malley broke the silence first.

'Well begob, Father Devlin won't like that!' he cried.

'I don't care a shit for Father Devlin!' Gallagher snapped.

'Aisy now, Gallagher, aisy,' Bull O'Malley cautioned, 'the lad didn't mean it like that. But he's right,' he added. 'There *will* be trouble if ye stay. So why don't ye do the sensible thing and move on to some other place.'

'That's good advice Da is givin' ye, Gallagher,' Luke said. 'It would be best for ye and everybody if ye went on yer way.'

Gallagher turned to face him. Luke O'Malley was about a year younger than himself. He was shorter than his father and brother, but tall and muscular nevertheless. He had the black hair and heavy eyebrows of the O'Malleys, but there the resemblance ended. His face was narrow, the eyes deep-set. Gallagher could not recall ever having seen Luke O'Malley smile. The face was rigid, any emotion showed only in his eyes. Gallagher could see undisguised dislike in them now.

'*I* know what's best for me,' Gallagher rejoined. 'But as for everybody . . .' He stared intently at Luke O'Malley. 'Who do you mean by everybody, Luke?'

Luke stared stonily back without replying. The lash of a whip was wrapped round his right hand and wrist and he tapped the palm of his left hand with the short thick handle.

'Unless you mean,' Gallagher went on, 'those . . .' The thought came to him. '. . . those *ten* curs who burnt me out that night ten years ago.' He had baited the hook, now he waited for someone to bite.

Sonny O'Malley gave a derisive guffaw. 'Ten, me arse! Sure, wasn't there only five!'

'How do you know that, Sonny?' Gallagher demanded.

Too late Sonny realised his mistake. Under the fierce glare of his father, his face turned a deep red, and he mumbled, 'I . . . I just heard, that's all.'

Oh, no, Sonny, Gallagher thought, you don't get off the hook that easy. 'Well now, Sonny, if you know how many there were, you must know *who* they were.'

Bull O'Malley cut in before his son could answer. 'Now aisy does it, bucko. How would Sonny be knowin' who they were? Sure, wasn't he just a lad of thirteen at the time.'

'Why don't you let him answer for himself,' Gallagher retorted.

The O'Malleys did not utter a word. They were wary now and on the defensive. Gallagher's suspicions deepened. They were the ones who had reaped the benefits after he had been driven away. The land his father had made fruitful became theirs. Even this ruin of his former home was now their property. He decided to break their silence. He would try one more bluff. Perhaps he could goad one of them into saying something rash.

'The reason why I've come back . . .' He chose his words carefully, speaking slowly, watching their faces for any reaction. '. . .is to seek redress for havin' been assaulted and havin' my house burnt down.' He paused. 'Naturally, I'll have a solicitor actin' for me.'

Bull O'Malley gaped at him. 'Solicitor?'

Gallagher nodded. 'Yes. First, I'm goin' to prosecute Father Devlin for assault and battery. True, I hit him, but that was in self-defence.'

He took pleasure in watching the shocked, incredulous expression on Bull O'Malley's face.

'Good God,' Bull gasped, 'ye don't mean to tell me that ye would take a priest to court?'

'Why not? A priest is not above the law.' Gallagher was beginning to enjoy himself.

'I never heard of such a thing! How could anyone callin' himself a Catholic bring a priest to court, to charge him . . .' Bull's voice tailed off at the audacity of it.

'Bloody renegade!' Sonny spat.

He was amazed at their gullibility, but Luke was not so easily fooled.

'To hell with that for a story, Gallagher!' he rasped in his hard, gritty voice. 'Look at ye – livin' like a tramp. Sleepin' in the open, brewin' tea in a billy-can. Where would ye get the money for legal costs and the like?'

Hesitation would convince all three of them he was lying.

'Walter Carew of the Big House is payin' all costs,' he answered promptly, and as he spoke thought he had gone too far.

The O'Malleys were stunned. The lie was so outrageous they obviously believed it. There was a long silence before any of them could say anything.

Eventually Bull O'Malley managed to croak, 'Walter Carew?'

Gallagher nodded. The brief respite had given him time to think. Not one of them, particularly Bull O'Malley, would dare question the authenticity of his statement by asking Walter Carew. There was an inbred peasant awe and fear there for lord and master.

'I've been correspondin' with Walter Carew,' he said, pausing just long enough to let the information sink in. 'He wrote to me, explainin' that he's not interested in any action against Father Devlin. But he is interested in hearing what Father Devlin has to say when he's cross-examined in court.'

'What do ye mean?' Bull O'Malley demanded.

'The five who attacked me and burnt my house down were never caught, were they? Never identified?'

They stared at him in silence.

75

'Walter Carew thinks Father Devlin knows who they are. Remember how Devlin always boasted that he knew everythin' that was goin' on in the parish of Carewstown? His vigilance committee were always runnin' to him with every titbit of information. He couldn't help but know who they were.' He could see something like fear in Sonny's eyes. It spurred him on relentlessly. 'Bein' a priest, Father Devlin will have to answer truthfully every question put to him. And when he does . . .' he paused dramatically, staring at Sonny, '. . . then God help those five, for Walter Carew is a dangerous man to have as an enemy. Don't forget it was his property that was burnt down. I only rented it. And ye all know what happens to anyone who destroys property belongin' to Walter Carew. Remember the men who maimed his cattle?'

Everyone in Carewstown knew that story. It had happened during the Land War of the early 'eighties. Walter Carew had evicted some tenants and they had taken revenge by maiming a few of his cattle.

They were caught and Walter Carew, who was a close friend of the resident magistrate, saw to it that the jury was packed with wealthy landowners. The culprits had each received seven years' hard labour.

'I won't envy those five buckoes,' Gallagher said, 'if Father Devlin is forced to blow the gaff on them. It'll be at least five years' hard for each of them for arson and attempted murder.'

Sonny gave a startled yelp. 'Attempted murder! Sure it was nothin' only – '

Bull O'Malley gave him a swift dig in the ribs with his elbow, and glared from one son to the other.

'Have ye two nothin' else to do but stand here gosterin' all day?' he snarled. 'Aren't we short-handed enough without the pair of ye wastin' precious time! Clear off, both of ye, outta this!'

Luke tossed his head in the direction of the doorway. 'Come on, Sonny,' he ordered gruffly, 'there's work to be done.'

Gallagher called after them. 'Luke! Sonny!' They turned around. 'Spread the word. Tell all ye meet that I'm goin' to make those five bastards pay for what they did to me.'

Luke's face flamed. 'Deliver yer own threats, Gallagher! We're not yer bloody messenger boys!'

Bull O'Malley spun around towards him. 'Shut yer gob, ye pup, and get out!' he bellowed. 'If both of ye haven't that sowin' finished before nightfall, ye'll answer to me!'

They went without saying another word.

Bull O'Malley turned a red truculent face to Gallagher. 'Stop pickin' on my lads, bucko. Stop tryin' to get them entangled in yer squabble!' He raised the stick slightly. It was an instinctive act, but it made Gallagher flare up with anger.

'I warned ye before about that stick!' he snapped.

Bull O'Malley blinked at him in surprise. He became aware of his raised arm and lowered it, giving an apologetic grin. 'Sure, it's gettin' carried away, we are.'

Gallagher stared at O'Malley with distrust as his manner became conciliatory.

'Now why should we be at loggerheads, eh?' Bull said softly, affecting a heartiness that did not fit the expression in his eyes. 'Come on, now, let's cool down. I never had a row with the Gallaghers in me life. Yer father and meself always respected each other. Come on, now.' He stepped across to Gallagher and laid a heavy hand on his shoulder. 'Amn't I right now, eh?'

Give the devil his due, Gallagher thought grudgingly, but he has a way with him. He gave a nod of assent and Bull O'Malley raised his hand from his shoulder and brought it down again with a resounding whack.

'That's the spirit!' he declared heartily. He turned and stumped towards the doorway. 'Come on now outta this,' he boomed, 'and let's breathe God's fresh air!'

He walked to the edge of the slope above the track and halted. He put the ashplant under his arm, reached into his pocket and took out a silver cigar-case. He nodded towards the distant mountains.

'Notice how clear they are this mornin',' he said to Gallagher. 'Bad sign, that. Rain on the way.' He selected a cigar and snapped the case shut without offering one to Gallagher, who smiled wryly to himself. Bull O'Malley hadn't changed; he was still tight-fisted. He put his hand in his pocket and pulled out a crumpled cigarette packet. One cigarette remained, crushed almost flat. He put it between his lips and threw the packet away.

It landed at Bull O'Malley's feet. O'Malley glanced down at it and gave a grunt. The cheapest brand on the market, he thought. He raised his eyes to the distant mountains and inhaled deeply on the cigar. He blew out the smoke in a long steady stream, and asked casually, 'How are ye goin' to live, now that ye intend stayin' here?'

'I'll get work,' Gallagher replied.

'Here in Carewstown?'

Gallagher detected a note of amusement in his voice.

O'Malley gave a deep chuckle. 'I wish ye luck.'

'There was always work to be had here, especially on the estates,' Gallagher said sharply.

'The estates are bein' broken up!' Bull O'Malley announced triumphantly. He turned his head and grinned at the astonished look on Gallagher's face. 'Ireland is a different country now, bucko, than it was when ye went away. Ever hear of the Wyndham Act?'

Gallagher shook his head.

'The government lent the tenant farmers millions to buy the land from the landlords. And now the landlords are goin' one by one. Two in the district have sold out durin' the past year. And it won't be long before the rest follow. The Hacketts, the Townshends, the Merricks. All goin' back across the water – back to the land of their ancestors. And bloody good riddance!' he added with venom. He stared out over the flat expanse of bogland, puffing contentedly on the cigar, a smug expression on his face.

Gallagher sucked at the cigarette and stared moodily at the ground. 'And Walter Carew?' he asked.

'Sold all but the village and demesne. The demesne has gone to pot! Oul Walter had to let the workmen go, includin' the gardener. Kept only the cook and Tim Skerritt.'

Gallagher gave a gasp of astonishment. 'Tim Skerritt! Why, he must be over ninety years of age!'

'Ah, young Tim, young Tim!' O'Malley explained testily. 'Oul Tim is dead these eight years or more.'

Gallagher dropped the butt of the cigarette and ground it underfoot.

'Oul Walter never comes out now,' O'Malley went on. 'A recluse! Just stays inside that big oul fort of a house with that scatter-brained sister of his.'

'Who bought Carew's land?' Gallagher asked.

'I bought most of it,' O'Malley answered. 'Phil Costello and Malachi Drennan bought what was left.'

So that's it, Gallagher thought. The gombeen man and the two biggest farmers in the district had grabbed every acre of land up for sale, not giving the small-holders a chance.

And they had bought it cheap, he knew. Since the end of the South African war land prices had fallen. Gallagher had seen the consequences of that depression while travelling through the English countryside. The poverty – the apathy. Many of the smaller, poorer villages had become rural slums.

'So ye see, bucko,' Bull O'Malley said, and he did not try to disguise the glee in his voice, 'there's nothin' here for ye.'

And you'll see to it that there won't be, Gallagher thought grimly. Bull O'Malley would not delay in contacting Phil Costello and Malachi Drennan, advising them not to give him work should he ask for it. Where veiled threats had failed, denying him the means of earning a livelihood would succeed. Gallagher groaned inwardly. He had no choice now but to move on. But first he wanted to see Johnny Boyle. 'Is Johnny Boyle still alive?' he asked hopefully. Johnny, he told himself, must be at least sixty now.

O'Malley nodded. 'Aye, but he won't be for long if he continues drinkin' the way he does. He works for me now, ye know. If ye can call it that.'

O'Malley turned to see Gallagher staring questioningly at him. He realised an explanation was expected. 'Johnny was doin' nothin' but mopin' about the house all day. He was drinkin' like a fish, runnin' to seed. I hate to see a man endin' his days like that, so I offered him a job and he took it. Nothin' strenuous, mind. Johnny is not capable of hard work anymore. Only light work. Anythin', as long as it keeps his mind occupied.'

Gallagher did not believe him. He knew Bull O'Malley well enough to know that he never had a compassionate thought for anyone in his life. His suspicions were aroused. He felt concern for his old friend, suspecting O'Malley's motives. He stared out over the bog, lost in thought. The river in the distance sparkled in the glare of the noon sun. A thought struck him.

'Who bought the land Johnny lives on?' he asked. 'Was it yourself or Malachi Drennan? Or was it Phil Costello?'

Bull O'Malley had the countryman's simplicity of manner. He had never learned to disguise his feelings. He flung the cigar away with an angry gesture.

'Johnny bought the land himself from Walter Carew,' he answered with bitterness in his voice. 'Bein' a tenant of his, Carew gave him first preference.' He gave a deep sigh and shook his head slowly. 'I never knew,' he said in tones of bewilderment, 'he had that much money. Johnny was never a thrifty man.'

Lucky for Johnny his wife was, thought Gallagher. When she died, she left one hundred and fifty pounds in the bank in Castlebar. Johnny had never touched a penny of it, despite his remarkable thirst for whiskey. He had left it there gathering interest, anticipating a time when it would be needed for some specific purpose.

Gallagher now knew the real reason for O'Malley's superficial concern for Johnny. Naturally it had to do with the land. The bog before them stretched northward for another half a mile, before giving way to lush pasture land – Johnny Boyle's land. It was a long rectangular strip squeezed between track and river, cut abruptly off at its northern end by the road that ran west towards Westport. Gallagher could understand Bull O'Malley's anger at not getting it. On those five grassy acres, cattle could graze and drink their fill from the clean running waters of the shallow river. O'Malley was not the only one who had his greedy eyes on Johnny's five acres. There was also Malachi Drennan. He too was possessed by the terrible hunger of the Connachtman for land.

Gallagher could remember when Malachi proclaimed to one and all that those five acres should by right of geography be his. The road that was the northern border of Johnny's holding was also the dividing line between his and Malachi's rich and fertile acres.

He could imagine how it was now, with O'Malley and Malachi keeping a careful watch on Johnny and on each other, each wondering which would be the first to persuade Johnny to sell his land. Neither would be above making overtures to Johnny. Like two suitors, Gallagher thought, scheming for the hand of an unsuspecting spinster.

Gallagher made his mind up there and then. I *have* to stay now, he told himself with a feeling of happiness. I have to stay and protect Johnny. He loved Johnny as a son loves his father and he knew Johnny felt the same way about him. He also knew that Johnny would be more than happy to provide him with board and lodging until he got a job.

'I'm stayin'!'

Bull O'Malley stared at him with open-mouthed dismay. '*What?*'

'I'm stayin' here in Carewstown. I'm goin' to stay with Johnny Boyle. And I'll get work, even if I have to go as far as Castlebar to get it.'

Bull O'Malley turned away slowly and stood contemplating the distant mountains, fingers thoughtfully stroking his chin. Gallagher watched white fleecy clouds moving in from the Atlantic, watched their shadows racing down the green and purple slopes of the Partrys. He waited.

At last O'Malley broke the silence. 'Listen, bucko, listen.'

Gallagher turned to face him.

Bull O'Malley stood before him with legs apart. He held the ashplant with both hands across his mid-riff. His face was expressionless. He said, 'Ye want a job? I'll give ye one.'

Gallagher hid his surprise.

'I'll give ye eighteen shillin's a week,' O'Malley continued, 'and ye can have yer meals with the family. Agreed?'

Gallagher hesitated for a few seconds, before agreeing. 'But Luke and Sonny won't like it,' he added.

'Ye leave Luke and Sonny to me,' O'Malley responded grimly. 'They dance to my tune. There's just one thing. . . If yer goin' to work for me, I want ye to drop all this nonsense about bringin' Father Devlin to court. Don't try to rake up old troubles.'

Ah, so that's it, Gallagher thought. It wasn't greed but fear that had prompted him to make his offer.

'Now I know,' Bull O'Malley went on, raising his hand a little, 'I know ye have good cause for wantin' revenge. I know that. But what will the consequences be if yer action against Father Devlin is successful? What will the consequences be if those men who attacked ye and burnt yer house down are identified and sent to prison?'

Gallagher gave a quizzical smile. 'Suppose you tell me,' he answered.

'Faith then, I will!' Bull O'Malley declared boldly. He pointed a long thick forefinger at him. 'Ye do this thing,' he warned solemnly, 'and it never will be forgotten or forgiven! Ye put yer neighbours behind bars, and their kin will bear a grudge against ye till doomsday!'

He glowered at the smirk on Gallagher's face. 'Smile away all ye want,' he growled, 'but there are quite a few long-tailed families in this parish, and I wouldn't like to be in yer boots if ye try to shorten the tail of any one of them!'

'What then,' Gallagher asked placidly, 'would you suggest I do?'

'Don't do a thing! Let sleepin' dogs lie! That way ye will save yerself an awful lot of trouble and grief. And that's good advice I'm givin' ye,' he added.

Gallagher stared silently at the ground, pondering. He had never intended bringing *anyone* to court. But he *did* intend to discover the identities of those five men. And when I do, he told himself grimly, I will deal with them one by one in my own way. He was convinced beyond doubt that the O'Malleys had been involved. Sonny was an oaf and a blabber-mouth. Sooner or later he would let something slip.

'Well then?' Bull O'Malley waited for him to say something.

Gallagher heaved a sigh, and nodded. 'Maybe you're right,' he said. 'Maybe it would be best to leave things as they are.'

O'Malley beamed. 'Good man, good man,' he boomed cheerfully. 'I knew ye would see reason. And ye will be happy workin' for me. I'll see to it that Luke and Sonny will work in harmony with ye. There's me hand on it.'

Gallagher turned away quickly and walked back into the ruins to collect his belongings, pretending he had not seen O'Malley's proffered hand. A handshake signified a truce, but for him hostilities were just about to begin.

81

# Chapter Two

I

Regan, the Deputy Inspector General, was a tall, broad-shouldered, handsome man of slim build. He had neatly trimmed iron-grey hair swept back from his forehead in tightly bunched waves. Despite the warm June sun shining through the windows and the stuffiness of the room, despite the tight-fitting, high-collared dark uniform, he managed to look cool and composed, in marked contrast to Major Calder's sweaty, flustered appearance.

The Major finished reading the monthly report and tossed it contemptuously on to Regan's desk. 'All but worthless!' he commented bitterly.

Regan stared steadily at him from the other side of the desk. He sat upright on the chair with his elbows on the arm-rests. He had formed a pyramid with his hands, resting his chin on the apex.

'It seems fairly comprehensive to me,' he said quietly.

'It's crammed with too much irrelevant material,' the Major complained peevishly. 'There's nothing of value left after you separate the wheat from the chaff!'

Alec Carew sat on the chair next to him with one long leg crossed over the other. He stared down at a spot where the carpet had frayed. Apart from the customary initial greeting, he had said nothing since entering the office with Major Calder a half-hour before. He smoked a long Turkish cigarette. The strong aroma helped alleviate the smell of whiskey and nervous perspiration emanating from the Major.

Regan twiddled the waxed, pointed end of his moustache. He took his time in answering.

'I can only repeat, the returns for last month are the most comprehensive to date. Surveillance of German tourists and businessmen has been stepped up as you requested. And the same goes for any returned emigrants from America. We've given you names and addresses . . . It's up to your people in London to evaluate the importance of the information supplied. I'm satisfied we've done our job thoroughly and efficiently.'

The Major unbuttoned a side-pocket, took out a handkerchief and dabbed his forehead with it.

'I'm not questioning the competence of the Royal Irish Constabulary,' he said. What worried him was that their reports would be similar. Once again he would be accused of laziness and incompetence. The wording of that despatch of more than a month ago came back to haunt him.

*Lamentable paucity of information . . . more initiative and less reliance on . . .*

Suddenly he gave vent to his anger and frustration. 'The only chance I had of getting some real information,' he snarled, 'was ruined by that blockhead of a detective! Jesus Christ Almighty! How did he manage to let Burke slip away from him? A sixty-seven-year old man! How?'

An expression of exasperation crossed Regan's otherwise calm features. Every Friday since it happened, both he and the Chief Commissioner had had to undergo the same questions.

'As I told you last week and the week before,' he explained with ill-concealed annoyance, 'a brawl broke out in the pub and he had to intervene. In the confusion, Burke slipped away unnoticed.'

'That was not his assignment! Any bobby on the beat could have done that!'

Regan raised a hand in protest. 'You should be making your complaints to the Chief Commissioner, not to me. The Dublin Metropolitan Police are responsible for G division. We are responsible for intelligence outside the metropolitan area.'

'The sooner the two police forces are amalgamated the better,' the Major growled. 'That's one of the recommendations I'll be making to the DMI when I meet him in London on Monday.'

Regan gave a slight shrug. 'As you wish,' he said offhandedly, 'but in my opinion there's nothing wrong with the present system.'

The Major lapsed into sullen silence. He was all too aware that he was becoming more cantankerous each day. Everything had gone wrong, and he was dreading this meeting with the DMI on Monday. If only he had something to offer.

'Any news about the whereabouts of Burke?' he asked hopefully.

Regan shook his head. 'Nothing. The Chief Commissioner's men have made inquiries at every common lodging-house in the city.'

'Workhouse? Burke had very little money.'

'That too. They showed his photograph just in case he had entered under an assumed name, but no one like him has been admitted. However, if he should seek admittance, they will notify us immediately.'

'Damn!' the Major muttered.

'To be perfectly candid, Major,' Regan said, 'I think you are overestimating the importance of this man.'

'Burke was a national hero,' the Major declared firmly. 'A legend. And legends die hard in Ireland. If the IRB knew he was back in this country they would seek him out – use him for propaganda purposes. That's why it's imperative we find him and keep him under surveillance until we see who are the people that contact him.'

'Since nothing about Burke's release appeared in the newspapers,' Regan said, 'I think that's highly unlikely, don't you?'

Major Calder shifted uneasily in his chair.

'That acquaintance of yours,' Regan went on, 'that newspaper editor. Did you – ?'

The Major shook his head before he could finish. 'I decided not to use the direct approach. Too many awkward questions would have been asked. You know what newspapermen are like. I thought it best to be circumspect. I contacted my people in London and they suggested letting a news agency handle it.'

'But nothing about Burke appeared in any of the newspapers.'

'No,' the Major grudgingly admitted.

'So he was not worthy of even a few lines.'

The Major said nothing.

'Which proves my point,' Regan said. 'Burke is a nonentity, a nobody. I'll wager that the few people who remember him think he died in prison.'

The Major heaved a weary sigh. He was aware of a dull lethargy creeping over mind and body. He felt sick and tired of it all. This time tomorrow he would be in London. On Monday there would be the conference in Whitehall. And after that . . . He sighed again, but this time with contentment, picturing himself fishing at a mountain stream in some remote Highland glen. Far, far away, he thought, from stuffy offices and musty-smelling files and shabby intrigues.

He rose clumsily to his feet, feeling bloated and short of breath. Too much desk work and too many after-dinner whiskies, he thought, picking up his attaché case from the desk.

'I've a few things to settle before I go,' he said, stretching out his hand across the desk to Regan.

Regan stood up and grasped it. 'Have a good leave, Major,' he said, giving him a warm smile.

'That suggestion of yours about employing Durkin,' the Major said. 'It might be worth a try. Explain it all to Alec here and see what he thinks.'

Regan nodded. The Major withdrew his hand and turned to Carew.

'See you later, Alec. There are a few things I want to go over with you before I leave.'

As he closed the door behind him, both men sat down. Regan took out a cigar-box, and offered it to Carew. Carew shook his head. Regan selected a cigar, lit it and relaxed in his chair. Now that Major Calder had gone, he abandoned his former rigid pose.

'I'm glad to see the Major going on leave,' he drawled, holding the cigar elegantly aloft between two long thin fingers. 'He badly needs a rest. Have you noticed how irascible he has become of late? Of course it has all to do with this Burke business. His own fault, really. It was a crack-brained scheme, I thought. Now if the Major had asked my advice at the very beginning, before . . .'

Carew lit another Turkish cigarette, letting Regan's affected pose and drawling voice flow over him. The voice reminded him of Sinclair. He could feel the old sense of distrust. The Major had warned him about these Dublin Castle people.

'Ruthless opportunists. Untrustworthy, from the DIG down to the most insignificant junior clerk. A treacherous, slanderous lot.'

He waited until Regan had finished, then asked, 'Who is Durkin?'

Regan's eyes squeezed up into humorous slits. 'Billy Boy Durkin?' He gave a deep-throated chuckle. 'A character! Likes to act the buffoon at times. Meeting him will be an experience. Major Calder loathes him!'

'Yes, but what does he do?'

Regan pulled open a desk-drawer and began to root around inside. He fished out a magazine and slid it across the desk to Carew.

'Durkin is a publisher,' he said. 'This is one of his.'

It was a glossy publication, entitled *Society Life*. A dowager wearing a tiara stared out haughtily from the front cover. Carew turned over the pages uninterestedly. It was the usual publication of its kind: society events, society weddings, social announcements. *The marriage arranged between William Purefoy Irwin Hassard, MA, Barrister-at-law, only son of Arthur Warren Hassard, KC, Merrion Square, Dublin, and Pamela Blackiston Houston, only daughter of . . .* He turned the page. *Fashions for Autumn.* There were four fashion drawings, two on each page. Carew studied them for a moment, then looked at the signature. 'There are some drawings here by Miriam Durkin,' he said without lifting his head. 'Is she his daughter?'

'Durkin hasn't any children,' Regan replied. 'Miriam Durkin is his wife.' He flicked cigar ash from the sleeve of his immaculate tunic.

'What do you think of it?' he asked as Carew pushed the magazine to one side.

Carew shrugged. 'A social climber?'

'Exactly. But he also moves with equal aplomb among the lesser breeds. Here, let me show you.'

Regan got up and walked across the room. He paused before a shelf full of dark-blue files. He selected one and gave it to Carew.

Carew opened it, expecting to find a collection of confidential papers and documents, but all it contained was tabloid-sized newspapers, about fifteen or twenty copies clipped together.

'The *Eye-Witness*,' he read.

'Another of Durkin's,' Regan said. 'As you can see, as different from *Society Life* as chalk and cheese.'

Carew turned the pages, glancing at some of the captions. *Don Juan and the Grass Widow. Sid Ayres – his wealth and how he got it. A Dublin pork butcher and his double life.* He paused out of curiosity at one article and began to read aloud. 'Observed a well-known gentleman driving down Harcourt Street on a hackney car on Friday night last at 12.55 am. He pulled up alongside a woman who was walking alone on the footpath.

'After a brief conversation, the pair of them drove off, to where I do not know.

'But I know this much – the lady was not his wife.

'I know the gentleman in question has a wife. She will know when she reads these few lines, the reason why her husband was late home.

'I am sending her by post a marked copy of this paper. This may act as a warning to other husbands who are in the habit of acting as this one has done.'

Carew remarked cynically, 'Something of a moral crusader, I see.' He thumbed through the rest of the issues with a growing feeling of distaste. The opening lines of an editorial caught his eye. *The* Eye-Witness *was started for the purpose of cleansing our city of some of the pests and evils that infect it* . . . The hypocrisy of it irritated him. Under the veneer of self-righteousness he could detect the leer of the sensualist and muck-raker. He closed the cover on the little tales of petty crimes and clandestine love affairs and placed the file on top of *Society Life*.

Regan stared at him through a thin blue veil of cigar smoke, slightly amused by the stern expression on his face.

'Surely most of the stuff in that rag is libellous?' Carew asked.

Regan nodded. 'Durkin has been threatened with actions for slander a few times, but he ignores them – he even laughs at them. The people he writes about in the *Eye-Witness* are all on the bottom rung of the social ladder. Small shop-keepers, clerks, petty criminals . . . The people who cannot afford a lengthy court case or who are afraid to see it through. Dublin is a small city: everybody knows everybody else's business. The whole damn place thrives on gossip! No wonder the *Eye-Witness* sells like hot cakes.' Regan squashed the remains of the cigar in the ashtray, and leaned forward, hands clasped before him on the desk. His face was cold and impassive. 'Let me be frank with you, Captain. I'm not interested in what your opinion of Durkin may be, or for that matter, Major Calder's. Our intelligence branch are only interested in the information he supplies. Turpitude does not concern them.'

'The end justifies the means, is that it?'

'Something like that. Anyhow, that was what Major Calder failed to understand. He does not employ Durkin for intelligence work simply because he does not like him. Apart from his personal dislike for the man, he thinks the very nature of his profession makes him untrustworthy.'

'There may be something in that, you know.'

'Perhaps, but I doubt it. It would have been better to have used Durkin at the start than to waste valuable time having Burke followed in the vain hope that some members of the IRB would contact him. Now that plan has come to nought, the Major has no alternative but Durkin. That is, of course,' Regan added, 'if he consents.'

Carew paused. 'But might Durkin not balk at being asked to work for military intelligence? It could be dangerous.'

'No less dangerous than seeking information in the criminal underworld. If he does refuse, it will not be for that reason.'

'And if he consents, what do I offer in return for his services? Money?'

Regan shook his head. 'Oh no, not money. Durkin is fairly well-off. No, it will have to be something else.' He pondered for a while, twiddling his moustache. Then he smiled. 'Offer him something that will satisfy that grubby little ego of his.'

'What?'

'A knighthood,' Regan answered. 'He will do *anything* to gain that. But to be conferred,' he emphasised, '*only* when Major Calder and yourself consider him to be no longer useful. Understood?'

Carew nodded.

'Which means that both of you will have to dangle that particular carrot before his eyes for quite some time.'

Again Carew nodded. 'But on whose authority?'

Regan made a sweeping gesture with his hand. 'Don't worry about that. Sir William Durkin,' he said, giving another of his deep chuckles. 'God, he's bumptious enough as it is, but when that happens . . .' He shook his head. 'Put a beggar on horseback and he'll ride to hell.'

Carew rose slowly to his feet. 'If there's nothing further to discuss . . .'

His legs felt cramped. He wanted to get out into the fresh air and sunshine, away from this stuffy, drab office. He walked to the window and looked out. A uniformed messenger was striding across the quadrangle with some files under his arm. Under the stone archway just inside the main entrance, an armed sentry stood outside his box. His predecessors must have stood at that same spot over the centuries, Carew thought, armed with crossbow, hackbut and musket.

Very little remained of the once massive-walled medieval fortress. Dublin Castle had been entirely rebuilt during the eighteenth century. This seat of British power and administration was now, as a nationalist newspaper had recently described it, 'an overcrowded and overworked warren of haphazard bureaucracy'.

The rooms beneath were occupied by the Under-Secretary and the Assistant Under-Secretary. Adjoining were the Council Chamber and the law officers' departments, where the Attorney-General, the Solicitor-General and the Lord Chancellor were to be found. In the Lower Castle Yard, two hundred yards away, were the offices of the Chief and Assistant Commissioners of the Dublin Metropolitan Police, the only body of Irish police under any form of local control. Just across the Upper Yard was the Lord Lieutenant himself.

Regan joined him at the window.

'So this is the heart of the web,' Carew commented.

Regan nodded. 'I must show you around some time. Some of the towers from medieval times still stand. The Birmingham Tower, the Record Tower. Red Hugh O'Donnell, the young chieftain from Donegal, was imprisoned there for four years. He escaped during a night of heavy snow and eventually made his way back to Donegal, but he never forgave his former captors. He joined forces with Hugh O'Neill, Earl of Tyrone. Together they waged war on the forces of Elizabeth for nine years, all the time seeking help from Philip of Spain. If the Spaniards had landed up north in Donegal instead of Kinsale in the extreme south, the whole history of Europe would have been changed.'

It could happen again, Carew thought. If war should break out between Britain and Germany, there was a very real possibility of a German expeditionary force landing in Ireland. Whitehall had every reason to be concerned.

'Was this place ever besieged?' he asked.

'Oh yes. It was part of the defences of the old walled city. Dublin at that time was an outpost of English colonialism, and often harassed by raids of the Irish tribes, the O'Byrnes and O'Tooles, who swept down from the hills.'

'The wild and barbarous Irish, eh,' Carew remarked.

Regan stiffened slightly. Carew's words offended his pride.

'Matched, of course,' he said, 'by the barbarism of the English garrison. Irish warriors were decapitated when caught and their heads impaled on top of the Castle walls.

'Once on a foray into the Wicklow Hills, they captured the wife of the chieftain, Fiach MacHugh O'Byrne, and brought her back here. She was caged naked over the portcullis until she died. Over there,' he said, pointing, 'where the archway now stands.'

'There's a different lady there now,' Carew said, nodding towards the statue of Justice which stood with scales upraised on top of the archway.

'Ah yes.' Regan gave a crooked smile. 'But haven't you noticed? She stands with her back to the city.'


II


Durkin moved his fat rump about on the high bar-stool and called for another drink. He sat at the top of the bar with his back to the front door. He was ideally placed to observe the entire bar and anyone who entered or left, even through the side door further down.

It was the usual quay-side pub: shabby and dirty, ill-lit by flickering gas-jets. Down at the lower end, figures were huddled together around tables. There was a furtive atmosphere about the place. He had been told of its reputation, so he had disguised himself as a navvy.

The peak of his crumpled stained cap was pulled down low over his eyes and he had tied a red kerchief around his neck. The jacket was worn and ragged and the wrinkled trousers had a large patch at one knee. On his feet were heavy workman's boots. He had left nothing to chance. He had smeared his hands with dirt and had removed his gold teeth. Before leaving home he had practised his gap-toothed smile in front of the mirror; he had been as careful as any actor about to go on the stage. He had not shaved for several days. He ran the back of his hand over the rough bristles on his cheek and chin and gave a grunt of satisfaction. The disguise was complete.

The publican pulled down the handle of the bar-pump a few times, so that the porter overflowed from the glass and streamed over his hands in a dark-brown flood. He did not trouble to wipe them. He placed the pint glass before Durkin and swept up the copper coins from the counter. He turned away without uttering a word and stumped back towards the till. He had a pronounced limp.

Durkin looked down with misgiving at the minute bubbles forming on the thin coating of froth. As he watched, the froth disappeared completely. He hesitated for a moment, before raising the glass to his mouth and taking a sip. He made a wry face at the sour, bitter taste and plumped the glass down on the counter. Slop! he thought furiously. Bloody bilge water! The realisation that he had been taken advantage of aroused his ire, but his anger quickly subsided. He smiled to himself. It didn't matter – it would make his revenge all the sweeter. He stared at the publican, who was hunched over a newspaper spread out on the counter. I'd love to see his face when he reads my article about him and his pub in the next issue of the *Eye-Witness*. He would post him a copy just to make sure. To Flurry Lynch Esq publican, brothel-keeper, receiver of stolen goods.

The card game was still going on. He had seen the stakes they were playing for on his way to the lavatory: a gold snuff-box, a cameo brooch, some terracotta figurines. Obviously the house of an antique collector had been burgled.

He turned his head a little as the door behind him was pushed open. A whore sauntered past swaying her hips provocatively, leading her latest victim by the hand. Durkin craned his neck as he tried to catch a glimpse of the man's face, but he had his straw boater tilted down over his eyes and his jacket collar turned up hiding the lower half of his face. They passed through the open door beyond the counter; he could hear their feet on the bare stairs as they climbed them to the rooms overhead. The publican placed a bottle of whiskey and two glasses on a tray, and limped up after them.

Durkin shook his head in wonder and eased himself of the stool. Business was brisk tonight. There had been a regular procession up and down the stairs during the hour and a half he had been there. The hot weather has everyone randy, he told himself with a chuckle and pushed open the door. It had rained while he had been inside. It had cleared the mugginess from the air. He stood on the footpath, enjoying the mild cool breeze flowing along the quays. It was a beautiful night. Stars twinkled in the dark velvety blue of the sky and a full moon hung low over the glistening rooftops. I'll go home now, he told himself, home. He decided to walk a little of the way. The exercise would do him good and he would sleep all the better for it.

The pub stood at the corner of a lane, and he set off, heading south. There was a gas-lamp half-way down, and a figure emerged from the shadows and stepped into the pool of light. ''Night, love.'

Durkin swerved on the alert. Sometimes they had a bully or two with them.

She tittered at his nervousness. 'We're all alone, sweetheart. Just you and me, you and me.' She opened her coat; she wore only a short chemise underneath.

Durkin's eyes travelled down the length of her half-naked body. He threw back his head and gave a roar of laughter.

'Clear off, yeh worn-out oul hag,' he jeered, 'yer fit only for the knacker's yard!'

He experienced a swift surge of savage delight as the heavily painted lips started to quiver; as the tears of humiliation sprang to the eyes.

She choked on a sob. 'You bastard!' she uttered hoarsely.

He gave a snort of contempt and turned away. As he did so, she made a grab at him. Her hand clutched his arm; he could feel the nails biting into his flesh. Something snapped inside his head. To be mauled at by one of *them*! He whirled round, his face twisted with hate. He snarled and raised a fist, ready to strike.

She backed away in terror, her hand up before her face. Durkin stood glaring at her, breathing heavily. Suddenly he spun around and strode off down the lane, his heavy boots rapping loudly against the cobbles. As he neared the top, she began to scream and swear.

He turned into the next street, temples throbbing. Christ, how I loathe them! he thought. The rabble, the whores, the beggars, the scum from the reeking tenements. He hated the close proximity of their unwashed bodies; their fetid breaths and foul-smelling rags. Their very presence brought back memories he wished to forget.

He continued uphill through narrow and dirty streets. Groups of loafers stood about at street corners and under streetlamps. They did not give him a second glance as he passed by, dressed as he was in workman's clothes. He wondered what his fate would have been if he had been dressed like a gentleman.

He emerged from a dark squalid alley into well-lit, busy Thomas Street. Trams whined up and down the wide roadway. He crossed to the other side and walked down the footpath, before turning the corner into Meath Street, crowded with Friday night shoppers. He had to push his way through. Now that everything was fresh in his mind, he began to compose the front-page article for the next issue in his head. *There is a public-house on Usher's Quay which is a hot-bed of vice and . . .* But he was unable to concentrate with all the tumult going on around him.

The sounds of flat Dublin voices beat against his ears: the shrill twitterings of haggling housewives; the high falsetto cries of shop-boys standing guard over barrels of pigs' cheeks. People were coming out of the church. A little old priest with a shock of white hair was standing at the foot of the steps, nodding and smiling and shaking hands. As Durkin passed, a woman exclaimed with concern in her voice, 'For God's sake, Father, will yeh go inside outta that before yeh catch yer death standin' there in just yer soutane.'

Further down, a ragged ballad-seller was bawling out a song.

'. . . the day will come when vengeance loud will call,
And we will rise with Erin's boys and rally one and all.
I'll be the man to lead the van beneath our flag of green,
And loud and high we'll raise the cry: "Revenge for Skibbereen!"'

He held a bunch of broadsheets aloft.

'Here yez are, here yez are,' he roared 'Songs for everyone and for all occasions. Songs about courtship and marriage. Songs about the beauties of Mother Ireland. Songs about our patriot dead.' As he saw Durkin approaching, he thrust the broadsheets towards him. 'Here ye are now, sir. A penny each. How about this one? *A Lament for Myles Burke.* One of the forgotten felons of our land. Died in prison . . .'

Durkin had to step into the gutter to avoid him. He swerved round a corner into a dark alley. 'Bloody pest!' he growled under his breath. His heavy boots slithered over wet greasy cobbles. The hubbub began to recede. He was able to think clearly again. *There is a public-house on Usher's Quay which is a hot-bed of vice and crime. One night last week, while sitting at the counter, I observed . . .* He moved down through a maze of narrow and dim-lit back streets, lost in thought, heedless of where he was going. Yet his feet never faltered. He knew without being aware of it which lanes to avoid, which were blind and which were not. He turned a corner, and then another.

Perhaps it was the unnatural silence that made him slacken his pace.

He came to a halt in the middle of a wasteland, suddenly aware of his surroundings. He looked about him in bewilderment.

Whole streets lay in ruin all around him. Here and there, the remains of a tall tenement reared its jagged outline to the night sky. There were no street-lights, but in the bright moonlight everything was as clear as day. Realisation came slowly, and it left him numb with shock. He had avoided this place for nearly forty years. Twenty minutes ago he had walked out from that pub on the quays and had told himself; I'll go home now. It was as if his unspoken thoughts had reached the subconscious, which had guided him unerringly to this spot: the mouth of a muddy laneway in which stood the cottage which had been his home for the first ten years of his life.

He looked about him in a daze, the silence pressing against his ears, finding it hard to believe that this place had once teemed with uproarious life. Then it had been an overcrowded fetid slum, a by-word for squalor and depravity. Brutish toil, poverty and hunger had reduced its inhabitants to the level of beasts. Drunken brawls had been an everyday occurrence. His earliest memory was of two women stripped to the waist, fighting like animals in the filth of the gutter.

A mixture of sounds came drifting back. The raucous bellowings of drunken men, the tolling of a Souper's bell; the shrill pipings of street-urchins.

> Souper, Souper, ring yer bell,
> Souper, Souper, go to hell!

These streets had been the favourite hunting-grounds of the proselytisers. They had come here with Bibles in their hands and gold in their pockets, intent on seducing the impoverished Catholic Irish from their faith. A Mission Hall and school had been established nearby and a soup kitchen installed. There one could fill one's hungry belly and don new clothes. All one had to do in exchange was to recant.

'*Do you repudiate the Scarlet Whore of Rome now, brother? Dost thou renounce its idolatry and pomp? Recant now, I say. Recant, recant, recant!*' The high fanatical voice echoed and re-echoed in his head. It was the voice of his nightmares. He could feel his insides shrivelling up with fear. Once again he was a child of ten, trembling as he stood between his father and mother in the candle-lit semi-darkness, in that bleak cold place that resembled a vault.

The Reverend Frederick Pound, a tall terrifying figure dressed in black, towered over a massive Bible which lay open on its stand in front of him. On either side stood two tall smoking candles. His gigantic shadow covered most of the wall behind. They cowered in terror as his high-pitched voice reverberated throughout the chamber.

'Take the oath now, brother. Cast aside all those popish superstitions and beliefs. Recant, recant, recant. . . !'

Even after all these years he could still feel a pang of shame, remembering his father's whine of protest.

'For pity's sake, sir, enough. Have done with it.'

His mother wept uncontrollably. Why did he do it? he asked himself, tears pricking his eyes. Why? There had been others worse off than ourselves. He had thought the scars had long since healed; now he could feel them beginning to crack open and bleed. Part of him wanted to get away from this place and its painful memories, but the other part forced him to stay, forced him to take the first tentative step down the laneway.

He kept to the centre of the narrow muddy road, side-stepping the pot-holes. There was only waste ground on his right and he could see the gleam of rainwater where it had gathered in hollow depressions. Here and there, fragments of broken wall stood up among the weeds like tombstones. The silence was unnerving. He would have welcomed any sound, even the plaintive miaowing of a marauding cat. He stepped on a piece of glass and it exploded under his heavy boot with the report of a rifle-shot. He stood with thumping heart, nerves on edge.

A long row of cottages on the left stretched away to the lighted street in the distance. They were mere shells now. Most of them were roofless. The small square windows and doorways were boarded up. The public fountain still stood on the narrow, broken footpath. He paused before it, remembering times when he had stood in line with the other children of the neighbourhood, waiting to draw the meagre supply. Sometimes the water became contaminated. Cholera had broken out. The disease had swept through the overcrowded slums like wildfire, wiping out whole families. It had killed his infant brothers and sisters: he was the only survivor of six children. He moved on.

He came to a stop a few yards further down. The cottage facing him was no different from the other hovels. Half the roof was gone and some of the planking covering the doorway had been torn away, probably for firewood. It had left a gap just wide enough for a man to squeeze through. He thought it strange that all the cottages were boarded up except this one – this place where he had been born. It was as if the house itself was offering him admittance. He could not resist the urge to investigate. Curiosity after all was part of his profession.

He squeezed himself through the narrow opening, deliberately

94

creating noise. He felt like a frightened boy trying to maintain his courage by whistling in the dark. Perhaps the ghosts would be scared away.

The ghosts were still here; he could sense their presence as he stood in the dark, the smell of damp and decay in his nostrils. This wretched place had witnessed too much suffering and heartbreak for it to be at peace. Hunger, pestilence, sickness. He could feel the tears welling up in his eyes. He was sorry now he had entered. This ruin was as oppressive as the inside of a tomb. It gnawed at his nerves, played tricks with his imagination. He fancied he could hear someone's laboured breathing. It was only a trick of the mind of course, a remembrance of the time when his father's tortured bronchial gasps had filled this room.

Suddenly the wheezing was punctured by a dry phlegmy cough, and a hand closed around his ankle.

Durkin went rigid with shock, feeling a rush of blood to the heart. He whined like an animal and pulled his leg free. Panic-stricken, he kicked out and kicked again. A moan of pain drifted up from the floor.

He stood trembling, his breath coming in quick short gasps. The urge to dash out into the street was strong, but his curiosity was stronger. He fumbled in his pocket and took out a box of matches. Striking one, he extended a wavering hand.

A hand stretched out towards the flickering match-flame, palm upward, as though to ward off further kicks. An old man's voice pleaded, 'Please, oh, please.'

He moved a step closer. Two terrified eyes stared up at him. High, wide cheek-bones jutted out from a gaunt white-bearded face. The man wore a filthy mud-stained overcoat fastened under the throat by a safety pin. A length of frayed rope was tied around his waist. The match went out and the voice croaked appealingly, 'Don't! Please don't.'

Durkin's fear was swamped by a wave of fury. Christ, to be frightened out of one's wits by a filthy old tramp! He had to get out before he lost control.

He half-ran down the lane, not stopping until he reached the lighted street beyond. Then he leaned against a lamp-standard, holding on to it, gasping for breath. He felt weak with shock, and it was several minutes before he felt strong enough to move on again.

He avoided the short-cuts now, the alleys, the ill-lit back streets, and kept to the main routes. He walked with heavy tread, weighed down and dejected. Only half an hour ago he had felt as pleased as Punch with himself. Now his elation was gone; he had lost it back there in that ruin of a cottage where he had been born. In that laneway outside he had witnessed the abasement of the only two people he had ever cared about; in that laneway he had learned to hate.

In the weeks after they had conformed, the proselytisers called several times with gifts of food and money. They always came in daytime, bearing their gifts openly and with all the fanfare they could muster: tolling their bell, singing their hymns of triumph. They had gained a victory – one of their few victories – and they wanted everyone to see the rewards for conforming.

Beware of Greeks bearing gifts, Durkin thought cynically, crossing the wide entrance to Patrick Street. Further down, the massive bulk of the cathedral towered over the mean tenements surrounding it.

They sent him to a new school, Dr Crawley's school for young Protestant gentlemen, far from his own neighbourhood. There he sat with the sons of merchants and stockbrokers, painfully conscious of their nudges and giggles at his ill-fitting clothes and flat Dublin accent. The teacher, Estridge, humiliated him from the very beginning.

'We have a new boy amongst us this morning, gentlemen. Young master Durkin. One of the new converts. A scrubby little street arab from the slums of the Liberties!

'Come up here, Durkin, and let us all have a look at you. Walk correctly, boy – you will have to get accustomed to wearing boots. Now then, did you wash yourself this morning? Let me have a look behind your ears. Hmmm, just as I thought – black as a pot! And now your hair.'

The cuff across the ear sent him staggering back. 'You verminous little scut! How dare you come here in that state! Go home at once and do not come back until you are scrubbed clean from head to foot!'

Durkin winced, reliving that moment of shame. He walked down Bishop Street. A strong aroma of roasting chocolate came from the biscuit factory. Shrieking, laughing girls came trooping out, their night-shift over. Durkin was barely aware of them. Once again he was in that schoolyard, walking towards the shed.

He had never seen a water-closet before. In the cottage, one used the cess pit at the bottom of the garden. He stood looking at the water in the bottom of the bowl.

'What's this for?'

They stood there, grinning. 'Don't you know?'

He shook his head.

'This is for washing in. You kneel down, see, and when you've finished, you pull the chain. Like this.'

He watched fascinated as water gushed out from the sides. He was obsessed with cleanliness since Estridge's rebuke.

Word spread from classroom to classroom. Every day at lunchtime, the whole school would gather inside the shed to watch him washing his face and hands in the lavatory bowl. Nearly two weeks passed before he discovered what the water-closet was really used for.

He crossed the intersection and continued down Digges Street. Tall, stepped-gabled houses lined one side of the street, the decayed relics of the Dutch and French immigrants who once lived here. Shawled, gossiping women clustered about the open doorways.

Every day after school the ragged barefooted tribe from the cottages waited for him at the mouth of his laneway. Some were former friends. He would walk past them with downcast eyes, his satchel under his arm, acutely conscious of his high hard collar, his new clothes and polished boots.

They would fall in behind him and the chanting would begin.

> Proddy, Proddy on the wall,
> Half a loaf will do ye all,
> And a penny candle to give ye light
> To read the Bible on Sunday night.

He would run then, as fast as his legs could carry him. They would follow in hot pursuit. Stones and foul horse dung grabbed from the roadway would be flung after him.

He boarded a tram in Harcourt Street and climbed to the open upper deck. He was relieved to find it deserted. He sat down on the hard wooden seat as it moved off. It moaned its way southwards between the tall, stately Georgian houses.

The parish priest of nearby St Catherine's had launched a crusade against the proselytisers. In the surrounding streets hate smouldered against those who had conformed. One Saturday night it erupted.

They were sitting in front of the fire when the brick smashed through the window. His father sprang to his feet while William had cowered in terror in the corner. His mother ran to him and held him tight to her breast. He could feel the frantic beating of her heart. Outside, the shouts and screams of abuse began.

'Come out, ye bloody turncoats! Come out or we'll go in and drag ye out! Swaddlers! Bible-thumpers!'

His father pulled the kitchen dresser across the earthen floor in an attempt to barricade the door, but it was kicked open and they stormed in, men and women, howling and cursing. The men grabbed his father and carried his squirming body outside.

The women fell on his mother like a pack of she-wolves, tearing at her hair and face. William screamed, clinging to her skirt, and was dragged out with her into the lane.

Three men stood over his father, kicking him as he lay on the ground. Some of the crowd rushed into the cottage and staggered out again, carrying pieces of furniture. Everything his parents possessed was piled in a heap in the middle of the narrow road. Paraffin oil was sprinkled over it and a torch applied. There was a roar of triumph as the flames shot up. They stripped his father naked and poured tar all over him. A drunken crone came tottering forward with a sackful of feathers.

The tap on his shoulder made him start. He looked up to see the conductor holding his hand out for the fare. He fumbled in his pocket. The tram swerved into the Rathgar road. It swept along between the mid-Victorian houses with their imposing lawns. He alighted half-way up, and walked a little way before turning into a quiet, tree-lined avenue.

Someone was playing a violin in one of the houses. Schubert, he thought. The sweet gentle tones soothed his frayed nerves. This was his world. The Liberties, with its impoverished sinuous streets and bitter memories, was far behind him now.

He was relieved to find the avenue deserted. He dreaded meeting a neighbour who might recognise him in these clothes. He ran down the footpath, not stopping until he reached his house. He pushed in the gate and hurried up the steps. His feeling of panic did not abate until he had closed the door behind him.

He stood with his back against the wall in the narrow dim-lit hallway, a little winded. His reflection stared back from the hall-stand mirror. Good grief, he thought, I look a proper tough. He had crept out of the house dressed like this without Miriam seeing him.

An idea occurred to him. I'll give her the fright of her life, he thought, giggling to himself. The old impish humour was returning; he was himself again; it was as if the traumatic events of the last half-hour had never been. He moved stealthily down the passage. Standing before the door, he turned the knob as gently and as noiselessly as he could. He pushed in the door, shouting at the top of his voice.

'Surrender your virtue or else!'

Miriam half-rose from the chair, her hand to her throat, a startled look on her face. The man sitting opposite her jumped up and whirled round. He was a young man, tall and dark, with a thin moustache. He strode aggressively forward. 'What the devil!'

Durkin gave a yelp of dismay and slammed the door in his face. He stumbled frantically upstairs, into the bathroom and bolted the door. He tore off his clothes, swearing. He turned on the water and with frenzied haste scrubbed the dirt from his face and hands. The man's aristocratic bearing, his well-cut clothes and English accent, told him he was from Dublin Castle. Probably some important official.

'Oh, Christ,' he whimpered, 'what an entrance that was.'

He was about to shave when there was a faint tapping on the door. He pulled the bolt back and opened it. Miriam stood outside. He beckoned quickly. 'Close the door,' he whispered. She obeyed. 'Who is he?' he inquired hoarsely. He was in his underwear, his face lathered, a cut-throat razor held menacingly in his hand.

'A Captain Carew, from the Castle.'

He turned to the mirror and scraped at his face with quick savage strokes. He spoke with difficulty out of the corner of his mouth. 'What does he want?'

She stood behind him, staring over his shoulder into the mirror. 'He didn't say. Only that he had to see you about something important.' She seemed to have difficulty in speaking. Durkin glanced at her reflection and saw her lower lip tremble as though she was about to cry – or laugh. He turned around and glared at her. She wouldn't dare!

Her face was composed. He turned his head back to the mirror and resumed shaving.

'If it's any consolation,' she said, 'he is as embarrassed as you are. He thought you were an intruder.'

Durkin's hand shook a little and the razor nicked his chin. 'Shit!'

'What?'

'Never mind,' he rasped. He washed the soap from his face and dried it. The cut on his chin was bleeding a little and he dabbed at it with the towel. Her expressionless face and calmness irritated him.

'For Christ's sake, just don't stand there like a tailor's dummy!' he snapped. 'Do something!'

'Do what?'

'Get my suit, and a clean shirt. Quickly!'

He searched for and found the small square of alum. He moistened it and held it against the cut on his chin. He waddled into the bedroom and dressed hurriedly. He paused in the act of tying a shoelace and darted an angry look at her.

'Have I got everything I need?' he asked with heavy sarcasm.

'I think so, yes.'

'Then what the hell are you standing gawking at me for? We have a guest – attend to him. Give him another drink.' He noticed the sudden flush spreading over her pale face. Her eyes evaded his.

'You *did* offer him a drink, didn't you?'

'I forgot. I – '

'You stupid bitch!'

'I'm sorry, William. I . . . We started to talk and I forgot. I was showing him my water-colours.'

Durkin lowered his voice to a furious whisper. 'How many times have I told you not to bore our guests by showing them all that rubbish! Never do it again, d'ye hear? Now get downstairs.'

She closed the door before he could say any more. He bent over the shoe and pulled at the lace. It snapped in two and he swore viciously under his breath. He took off the shoe and tied the two parts together.

Ten minutes later he was ready. He stood before the full-length mirror, turning this way and that. He noticed the little speck of dried blood on his chin. He moistened the tip of his forefinger and, pushing his face close up to the glass, rubbed it gently away. He tested his smile. His reinserted gold teeth gleamed back at him. Everything ship-shape, he told himself, giving a little grunt of satisfaction.

He hurried down the carpeted stairs, pausing before the closed door. He was like an actor standing in the wings, rehearsing his opening lines before walking on stage. He cleared his throat, put on a broad smile, opened the door and strode in with hand outstretched.

'My dear fellow.'

Carew stood up as Durkin walked towards him with all the bonhomie he could muster. He brushed aside Carew's expression of apology with a magnanimous wave of the hand.

'I'm afraid I've called at rather an awkward time. I should have made an appointment.'

'Oh bosh! No need, I assure you, Captain . . . Captain. . . ?'

'Carew. Alec Carew.'

'Please, sit down, Captain. Now, what will you have to drink? I'm afraid my wife has been neglecting her duties as hostess.'

'Whiskey, please . . . with a dash of soda.'

Durkin poured two liberal measures from a decanter. 'I hope you were not bored whilst waiting?'

'Indeed, no. I was admiring your wife's sketches and water-colours.'

Durkin handed a glass of whiskey to Carew. 'Oh, Miriam dabbles with the paint brush quite often. Keeps her amused. Her work is rather amateurish, I'm afraid. Lacks the professional touch.'

'I wouldn't say that,' Carew protested mildly, smiling at the dark-haired woman sitting opposite him. She smiled back, lowering her eyes in shy confusion.

Durkin sat between them. 'Miriam tells me you're from the Castle. I know most of the people there. You must be new.'

'I arrived from England six weeks ago. Major Calder is my commanding officer.'

'Ah yes, the Major. How is he?'

'I had a postcard from him a few days ago. He's enjoying his leave in Scotland.'

'Glad to hear it. Well now, and what do you want to see me about, Captain?' He turned his head. 'Miriam, leave us.'

Carew looked away. Durkin's crude manner embarrassed him. He rose as Miriam stood up and bowed gracefully to her quiet goodnight. He did not sit down until she had closed the door behind her. Durkin remained seated, sipping his drink.

'I must apologise for my wife, Captain,' he said. 'Too introverted and shy, I'm afraid.'

Carew pursed his lips thoughtfully, unsure whether to come directly to the point. 'I've been reading some back numbers of your newspaper, Mr Durkin – '

'Oh please.' Durkin raised a hand in protest. 'Do we have to be so formal? I'm Billy to my friends.'

Carew smiled slightly. 'Very well . . . Billy. As I was saying, I've been reading your newspaper. A remarkable publication. Those stories about the criminal underworld for instance. I was most impressed. Tell me, how do you – ?'

'I'm so glad you asked me that,' Durkin interrupted. 'I disguise myself. Sometimes as a beggar or a tramp. Sometimes as a common labourer.' He grinned broadly. 'Like tonight, for instance. I fooled you – admit it now.'

Carew was reminded of a little boy coaxing admiration from an elder. 'You gave me quite a start,' he answered with a smile. 'You looked a veritable roughneck.'

'It's necessary to masquerade as one of the lower classes when I go into the most lawless parts of the town looking for a story.'

'A man like you could be very useful to us,' Carew said.

Durkin's garrulity ceased abruptly. 'Useful in what way?'

'You are a man who keeps his eyes and ears open. You have a way of

101

obtaining information that intrigues me. We need information of a certain kind. I trust you follow my meaning?'

'Politics?'

'In a sense.' Carew hesitated for a few seconds. 'Before I begin,' he continued, 'I must have your assurance that what I'm about to tell you will not be divulged.'

'My dear fellow,' Durkin protested, 'my dear fellow, you are talking to a professional journalist. Why, I have informants whose very lives depend on my discretion.'

'Don't misunderstand me. I'm not suggesting that you are in any way unreliable or indiscreet. But I am about to impart some highly confidential information, and I must have your promise that you will keep it to yourself.'

Durkin put a stubby forefinger to his mouth and winked. 'My lips are sealed, Captain.'

Carew felt a twinge of unease. He's not taking this seriously, he thought.

'Understand there are certain things I cannot divulge. I can only supply you with a few details. Nothing more.'

Durkin nodded.

'Whitehall has informed us,' Carew began after a short pause, 'that the German Secret Service may be in contact with a subversive organisation in this country. Their aim is to use this organisation as a disruptive force should a European war break out.'

Durkin gave a low whistle. 'This organisation, has it a name?'

'The Irish Republican Brotherhood. Have you heard of it?'

'Many years ago. Are you telling me it's still in existence?'

'Yes. We believe it is being supplied with money from a sister organisation in America. That's all the information we have about it. Despite our efforts, we have been unsuccessful in establishing the identity of even one member. The Under-Secretary is very concerned.'

'The Under-Secretary?'

'There was a conference in the Castle a few days ago. Regan and myself discussed the situation with him. It was Regan who recommended you. Rated you very highly, in fact. The Under-Secretary seemed most impressed.'

'Was he really?' Durkin exclaimed with sudden interest.

Carew gave a nod of affirmation. He leaned back in the chair and took a long drink from the glass. The preliminaries are over, he told himself, now's the time to get down to brass tacks.

'We want you to work for us, Mr Durkin. By we, I mean Major

Calder and myself – Military Intelligence. We want you to discover, if you can, the identities of the people who are members of the IRB.'

He paused, giving Durkin time to digest what he had said. He waited for him to say something, but Durkin remained silent, his face impassive.

'If you should consent,' Carew continued, 'and if your investigations should prove successful, then your efforts will not go unrewarded. I have the Under-Secretary's word on that.'

Durkin stared steadily at him. He said in a quiet voice, 'Has the Under-Secretary anything specific in mind?'

'A knighthood.'

Durkin sank slowly back in his chair. He seemed lost in thought, his eyes blank.

'Mr Durkin?'

Durkin blinked, and struggled into a sitting position. He tried to gather his scattered thoughts.

'Well,' he cleared his throat. 'Well, I've always been a loyal man. If you and Major Calder, and the Under-Secretary, think my humble services will be of use, then all I can say is that I shall endeavour to do my utmost for King and country.'

After Carew had gone, Durkin poured himself a full glass of whiskey. He swallowed it in two gulps. He filled the glass again. A knighthood! His wildest dream had come true. I'm going to pinch myself in a minute, he told himself, just to convince myself I'm not dreaming. He sat hunched forward holding the glass between his hands, staring at the empty fireplace. Now and then he raised the glass to his lips and took a tiny sip.

He was slowly becoming drunk. He was unaware of the door opening and closing behind him. It was only when he heard the rustle of her skirt beside him that he lifted his head.

'Oh, Miriam. Nice chap that, eh? Bit stuffy, though.' He chuckled to himself. 'Ye know, they need old Billy Durkin. By Christ, they do! They look down their noses at me and think me a bloody upstart, but when there's dirty work to be done . . .'

'What did Captain Carew want?' she asked.

'Nothing for you to worry your little head about.' He gave a deep long belch and took another sip of whiskey. 'How would yeh like to be called Lady Durkin, eh?' He raised his head and grinned at the bewildered expression on her face. 'How would yeh like to go to the Castle Balls an' have all of them bowin' an' curtsyin' to yeh? All of them – the Regans, the Harrisons, that fat bastard, Calder. Won't that be somethin'?'

His speech was slurred, the flat nasal Dublin accent more pronounced. His face was flushed with excitement and whiskey. She dreaded this drunken, exultant mood of his; it always led to a frenzied sexual assault. She stiffened as his hand wandered over her buttock and hip. He did it absently, staring moodily at the fireplace, sipping his whiskey. He was breathing heavily. She looked down at him. Beads of sweat stood out on his forehead and upper lip. Like an animal, she thought with a feeling of revulsion, a ruttish animal.

His hand slid down her thigh. 'Go on up to bed and wait for me.'

She dug her nails into the palms of her hands and shivered. Mistaking the tremor that swept over her body for desire, he squeezed gently with his hand and whispered, 'I won't be long.'

She walked out of the room without a word.

What a night it had been – the most extraordinary night he had ever experienced. The Fates had always been kind to him, but tonight they had indulged in a little mischief-making. He shuddered, remembering.

He tossed off the remainder of the whiskey. They called him Lucky Durkin. He had risen from obscurity; he had established his own publishing company and had made lots of money, but all that paled into insignificance compared to a knighthood.

'Begob, Billy Boy,' he murmured to himself, 'you've come a long way from that filthy muddy laneway in the Liberties.'

### III

Carew typed slowly and carefully with one finger. He was unused to a typewriter and would have preferred to write his report, but Major Calder complained that his handwriting was almost illegible. With some justification, Carew had to admit; he possessed a peculiar backhanded style.

Durkin has agreed to work for us. Already he has given me the name of a man who, he assures me, is an extremist. The man is Fintan Butler.

Butler has a small business in Thomas Street called Kincora School Supplies (chalk, pens, pencils – that sort of thing). Judging from the decrepit state of the building in which his office and storeroom are located, I imagine it is not a very lucrative one. Although Durkin dismisses Butler as a harmless crank, I have my doubts. The nature of his business compels him to travel all over the country. What an excellent cover if he is an IRB organiser.

Durkin told me that Butler was in the USA in late 1907 and returned to Ireland in December of that year. That was when the Pinkerton Detective Agency sent word that an IRB courier was on his way back to Ireland with a large amount of money for the organisation. Was Butler the courier? We can find out.

I'm going to the Castle this afternoon to see Harrison. I want him to put Butler under surveillance. Discreetly of course. Butler must never have the slightest suspicion that he is being watched. I also want him to find out the name and location of Butler's bank. It will be up to his people to use whatever powers they have to inspect Butler's account. If Butler lodged a large amount of money shortly after his return from America, then I think that that is all the proof we need.

Keep your fingers crossed, Ian. This could be the chance we have long been waiting for!

Alec Carew lit a cigarette. He could feel the heat of the sun against his back. This time tomorrow, he thought, I will be in Carewscourt. Major Calder's leave was coming to an end and his was just beginning. The conference with Harrison should be over by six o'clock. That would give him enough time to pack and catch the late evening train for Mayo. Since his arrival in Ireland, he had neither had the time nor the opportunity to visit Carewscourt. Uncle Walter's weekly letters always ended with a few words of reproach.

*When are you coming? When, when?*

He heaved a sigh, stubbed out the cigarette, and bent over the typewriter again. There was one more thing to report before he could lock up and leave.

The man you have been searching for, Myles Burke, is dead. Nine days ago, the body of an elderly man was taken from the Liffey. The head and face had been horribly mutilated by the propellers of one of the brewery steam-barges that ply the river. The contents of the pockets were: two penny pieces, a roll of string and a razor (brand-new). There was nothing else to identify the man.

The police were of the opinion that the shirt and socks, which were of very coarse material, were prison issue. There was a label inside the collar of the shirt with serial numbers and the word 'London' on it. The shirt was sent to the authorities in England. Harrison's people received word a few days later.

The shirt, together with a complete set of new clothing, was issued to Myles Burke on his release from Pentonville Prison in April of this year.

He plucked the sheet from the typewriter, attached it to the other pages of the report, and put them in a large envelope. He sealed it and put it in the safe. Since Major Calder had put him in sole charge of the filing system, he had had the safe installed for better security. The old wooden filing cabinets were empty. The files they had contained had been too out of date to be of further use and had been packed and dispatched to the military archives in Whitehall. He closed the door of the safe.

Ten minutes later, attaché case in hand, Carew was striding down the steep winding hill towards the city. It was uncomfortably hot and he welcomed the light cool breeze wafting up from the river-mouth as he strode down along the north bank of the Liffey. The brewery buildings dominated the south bank. On the other side of the river, men were rolling barrels of porter on to the wharf and lowering them by winch into a steam-barge. He continued down the quays, past the barracks, past the shabby faded buildings, past the imposing edifice of the Four Courts with its green copper dome. He wheeled to the right, on to Winetavern Street bridge.

A man was hunched over the parapet mid-way across, gazing down at the water. He turned his head. When he saw Carew approaching, he jumped to attention and saluted smartly. He wore a torn, overbig jacket and ragged trousers. The left side of his face was hideously disfigured from eyebrow to chin.

'Good day to yeh, Captain,' he cried. Then the voice suddenly dropped to a wheedling tone. 'If yeh could spare a copper or two for a poor disabled soldier lad.' He pointed to his wound as an old campaigner might point to his medals. 'Shrapnel did that to me, Captain. The Tugela River.' The left eye was missing. The eyelid was sewn to the flesh of the cheek, giving his face a lop-sided look.

Carew rooted among the loose change in his trouser pocket and took out a half-crown. He dropped it into the outstretched palm, and walked on. The man howled his thanks after him.

'God bless yeh, Captain. Yer an officer and a gentleman!'

He walked up the long steep hill towards the cathedral on the crest. God, he thought, what a place to get it. The encounter had disturbed him. It brought back memories of Williamson. On the hospital ship bringing them back to England, Williamson had slashed his throat rather than have his fiancée see his bullet-smashed face.

He passed under the archway that connected the cathedral with the Synod Hall and turned left into Christchurch Place. It was a bedlam of noise. Horse-drawn drays clattered over square-set cobbles; whips cracked; trams whined past, heading east and west. The Castle was only about five minutes' walk away. He looked at his watch. Three-thirty. He was too early. His appointment with Harrison was not till four-fifteen. The thought of having to sit in this heat in a stuffy room waiting for Harrison appalled him. He peered through the railings, down at the enclosed space between the cathedral and the street. A stretch of lawn, shrubbery, trees. An old man sat with his back to the railings and opposite a woman sat sketching him. He gave a little start of surprise, then walked the few yards towards the entrance.

He came up behind her silently, not wishing to distract her from her task. She was completely unaware of his presence as he stood looking over her shoulder. He looked across at her subject.

He was just an old tramp. He sat hunched forward a little, staring vacantly at the ground. His arms rested on his knees, the palms of his hands upturned. He wore a filthy mud-stained overcoat which was fastened under the throat by a safety pin. A rope was tied around his waist.

He watched as she deftly moved the pencil over the surface of her sketch-pad, adding final touches to the face, the white straggling hair and beard, the high, wide cheek-bones.

'A remarkable likeness, Mrs Durkin.'

She looked up, startled. A slow flush spread over her face.

'Oh, Captain Carew. I'm sorry, I didn't recognise you. The uniform.' He had been in mufti when he had called at Durkin's house.

He sat down beside her. 'May I?' he asked, stretching out his hand for the sketch.

She gave it to him. He studied it carefully. It was the expression of the eyes which he found fascinating. He looked across at the old man and back again to the sketch. Yes, she had gauged the mood correctly. The eyes were blank with hopelessness and despair.

'It's a little masterpiece, Mrs Durkin,' he said.

'Oh, please.' She gave an embarrassed laugh. 'Not as good as all that, surely?'

He stared intently at her. 'But it is. I would like to buy it if it is for sale.'

The wide-brimmed summer hat shadowed the upper part of her face. 'You really like it?'

Her lack of confidence amazed him, until he remembered a remark of Regan's. 'The poor woman has all the spirit bullied out of her.'

107

He said, 'I like it. Truly.'

'Then it's yours, as a gift.'

'Oh, no,' he protested. 'Every artist is entitled to his or her reward.'

'Your appreciation is reward enough. But first . . .' She held out her hand. 'I must spray it with fixative, else it will smudge.'

She opened a wooden box which contained her materials and took out a small bottle of amber-coloured liquid. She unscrewed the top. He looked on, watching her movements, studying her profile. Miriam, he thought. There was nothing Semitic about the delicate curved features or the straight nose. Only the jet-black hair and the soft brown eyes revealed her ancestry.

She put the stem of the spray between her lips and blew gently on the sketch resting on her knees. Then she straightened up. 'There, I'll let that dry for a minute or two.' She heaved a sigh. 'Strongbow will have to wait.'

'Who?'

She smiled. 'My reason for coming here was to do a drawing of Strongbow's tomb. I've been commissioned to do a series of line drawings for a guidebook on Dublin. But,' she gave a little gesture of despair, 'this was as far as I got. There was something so terribly tragic about that poor creature sitting over there. Poor soul, he looks as though all the trouble in the world is resting on his shoulders.'

Carew looked about him. 'You know,' he said, 'I pass by this place several times a week, and not once did it occur to me to go inside.' He smiled at her. 'Will you be my guide? I would like to see Strongbow's tomb.'

Once again a slow flush spread over her face. Her eyes evaded his. 'If you wish,' she said.

He thought it strange that a mature woman should blush like a girl just because he had forced a little roguishness into his manner. She handed him the sketch and he placed it carefully in the attaché case. They set off up the footpath. Then Carew halted. 'Wait just a moment,' he said and walked back.

The old man had not moved. He still sat hunched forward, his arms resting on his knees, the palms of his hands turned upwards. Carew took out all the loose change he had in his trouser pocket. This is my day for almsgiving, he thought, and dropped the lot into the hollow of the man's hand. He turned away. The stench from the old tramp's body was sickening.

She was waiting outside the small side door at the western end, a questioning look in her eyes.

108

'Model's fee,' he explained with a grin. Taking her by the elbow, he led her inside.

It was cool and dim inside. The tall, stained-glass windows changed the light to the colour of claret. They walked between the highly polished pews, their feet clicking loudly against the flags, towards the black polished limestone tomb of a Norman knight.

'So that's Strongbow,' Carew said. 'Who was he?'

'Richard de Clare, Earl of Pembroke. He was one of several Norman knights on the Welsh marches who had been impoverished after the Welsh had rebelled and taken back their lands.'

'Wales? How then did he come to be buried in a cathedral in Dublin?'

'Oh dear.' She gave him a look of dismay. 'It is rather a long story.'

'Oh, well.' He shrugged and smiled. 'Someday when you have time, maybe you'll tell me.'

She nodded. 'Someday.'

An awkward silence fell between them. He said, 'Are you going to make a sketch of the tomb? I'll just wander around.'

'Oh no, not now. It's far too late. Some other day. The morning would be better, when the light is stronger.'

They walked away. He shook his head. 'You amaze me. You're not only a talented artist, but you seem to be an historian as well.' He spoke in a low voice, conscious of how the interior of the cathedral echoed to the slightest sound.

She gave a gentle laugh. 'The Anglo-Norman period was my thesis for a degree. I was a merely quoting from memory. Besides, my father was a professor of history.'

How could she have married a boor like Durkin? he wondered. Not only was she years younger, she was also, culturally and intellectually, his superior. They paused at the top of one flight of steps which led to the crypt.

'Shall we?' he asked, his hand touching her elbow.

She hesitated, her hand to her throat. 'Forgive me, it's just that I have a claustrophobic fear of going below ground.'

'Oh well, in that case . . .'

She shook her head. 'No, no, let's go on. Silly really, to give in to these irrational fears.'

They descended the steps slowly. At the bottom she grabbed his arm. In the semi-dark he could hear her sharp intake of breath.

'Would you rather we – ?'

'No,' she said firmly, 'let's go on.'

They walked forward under low curved arches. Lanterns affixed to the walls lit up the passageway. Somewhere, someone was talking. It was a man's voice, hollow-sounding. They turned towards it. The way was dark, and her hand frantically searched for his. He gripped it, squeezing it reassuringly. Hand in hand they picked their steps with care, under an arch and then left into another passageway.

Several yards away a small group of people stood in a semi-circle before a tall, gaunt, middle-aged man, who stood with his back to the wall holding a lantern. He spoke in a monotone.

'. . . originally founded by King Sitric, the Danish King of Dublin, in 1038, and rebuilt by Strongbow more than one hundred and thirty years later. The crypt is pre-Norman . . .'

They walked up and stood on the fringe of the group, listening. Miriam made no attempt to release her hand.

'There are several underground passageways radiating from here,' the guide went on. 'One leads to the Castle and another to Saint Patrick's Cathedral. This one to my right leads to Saint Audoen's.'

'And behind you?' someone asked. 'It looks as though an entrance has been blocked up.'

'Ah yes . . .' The guide half-turned and placed his hand against the wall. 'That tunnel was sealed after the tragic demise of a young English officer.' He turned and faced his audience again. 'It happened in the year 1822. A Lieutenant Blacker of the 78th Regiment of Foot came down here with fellow mourners to attend the funeral of their colonel. It was a fully uniformed ceremony for which a sword had to be worn. That night, Lieutenant Blacker and his fellow officers were due to embark for England, having completed a stay of duty in Ireland.

'During or after the service, Blacker began to wander about the crypt. He came to the entrance of this tunnel behind me, and decided to explore it. In those days the crypt was illuminated by torches. Taking one, the Lieutenant entered. The passage leads down from the cathedral in deeply hewn ramps underneath the Liffey and up again to Saint Mary's Abbey on the north side.

'Somewhere along the passage, Blacker's torch blew out. In the darkness, with all sense of direction lost, he evidently decided the only thing to do was to press onwards. A horrible fate awaited him! He was attacked by a horde of large river rats that populated the tunnels. He drew his sword to defend himself, but in the darkness, the sword struck the narrow roughcast walls and broke. Two days later, a search party found him – or rather what was left of him. He had been picked clean to the bone!'

110

Carew winced as her fingernails dug into the palm of his hand. 'Please,' she whispered, 'please, take me away from here.'

Thinking she was about to faint, he took the wooden case containing her art materials and placed it under his arm, at the same time taking a firmer grip on the handle of his attaché case. He put his free arm around her waist and brought her back up the passageway.

They mounted the steps slowly. 'Can I get you something?' he asked. 'A glass of water?'

She shook her head. 'No, thank you.'

They blinked against the light as they emerged from the wine-coloured gloom of the cathedral. With his arm still round her waist, he guided her to the nearest seat. They were alone now. The old tramp had gone and they were screened from the street by a tree and some shrubbery. She sat with her head lowered, her hand covering her face.

'How do you feel?' he asked.

She took her hand away from her face. 'A little better now. Thank you.'

They lapsed into silence. The sun had gone and the light had changed to a metallic grey. A little wind was stirring; it rustled the leaves of the tree above their heads.

Suddenly she was aware of his arm around her waist and of how close they were.

'Could we sit a little further apart?' she whispered, darting a nervous glance towards the street. 'Someone might see.'

Her agitation amused him. 'What of it? Whoever saw us would assume we were lovers.'

'Don't joke about it, please. In this town gossip travels like wildfire.'

He remembered Regan making a similar remark. He withdrew his arm and moved away a little. 'There, now your reputation is safe.'

She stared at the ground. 'You must think I'm being very silly.'

'I think nothing of the kind.'

Silence fell between them. After a while he said, 'I'm going on leave this evening. When I come back, may I see you?'

She shot a startled look at him, then turned her head quickly away, the colour mounting her cheeks again. 'Why, you are always welcome to call to our house anytime you wish.'

He knew she was pretending to misunderstand. He said, 'That's not what I meant.'

She kept her head averted, deliberately avoiding his eyes. 'I do not think that would be proper.'

'We've known each other for such a short time,' he said, 'and yet . . .'

'No, no!' She shook her head. 'You're mistaken.' She covered her face with her hand and began to weep. 'Please go.'

'I didn't mean to upset you.'

'Please!'

He gripped the handle of his attaché case and stood up. He looked down at her bowed head. 'May I see you again?'

Her voice was muffled by the hand over her face. 'I don't know . . . I'm so confused. Please go.'

He walked away. He stopped near the entrance and looked back. She was sitting with her hands in her lap, staring vacantly at the ground. It was the same way the old tramp had sat and he remembered her comment, 'As though all the trouble in the world is resting on his shoulders.'

# Chapter Three

## I

Father Poole donned his vestments with old shaky hands. Outside, the storm raged unabated. He toddled over to the window and peered out at the deepening darkness. The wind lashed the rain against the glass; he could hear it whining over the roof-tops. He shook his head. Nine days now – nine days of high winds and heavy rain. It was the worst summer in living memory. And cold – as cold as early March. He shivered and turned back towards the fire.

'If I should speak with the tongues of men and of angels, but do not have charity,' he addressed the empty room, 'I have become as sounding brass or a tinkling cymbal.' He had decided to revise his sermon after the meeting with the local grocer's wife which had taken place just after lunch. He stood before the fire, hands outstretched towards the heat, seeing again the stern outraged face.

Was he aware of the number of low lodging-houses in the district which catered for – the thin bitter lips had compressed with distaste – streetgirls? There was one such house only a block away from the church. It was absolutely disgraceful to see the women dawdling in the doorways, conversing with the young men of the neighbourhood. It was an affront to the feelings of decent people! He had listened with his usual forbearance, thinking, Heaven preserve me from zealots and lay clerics. When she had finished, he had given a helpless shrug of the shoulders.

'Well, what do you want me to do? Have the house closed down, is that it? Surely the poor creatures have a terrible enough existence without any one of us trying to deprive them of a little shelter.'

'But they are corrupting – '

'Oh come now!' he interrupted. 'Have you witnessed any of these women soliciting? Well, have you? If so, it's a matter for the police rather than for me.'

'Well no, not actually.'

He had put on his sweetest smile and patted her hand. 'The best thing to do is to let things be, and try to have a little compassion for those poor unfortunates. After all, nowhere does it say that Christ ever rebuked Mary Magdalene for her way of life.'

He could still hear her waspish retort. 'Ach, Father Poole, sure you never try to see the evil in anyone.'

Ah, but I have tried, he thought, every day of every year since I was ordained. All down his priestly years he had searched for him – the unrepentant sinner. He had never encountered him personally. Only once had he seen him, and that had been from the gallery of a court-house. The man was on trial for the rape and murder of a twelve-year-old girl. There had been no remorse, not even after sentence of death had been passed. Instead, he had scoffed and blasphemed.

Father Poole heard the rest of the story from his old friend Martin Fenlan, Catholic Chaplain of Newgate Prison. The prisoner sat alone in his cell, awaiting execution. Martin would enter and close the door while two warders waited outside. The man was a Catholic and Martin would make his appeal: confess and repent, accept the Sacrament. The man's response was always violent. The night before his execution, the prisoner sat in his cell playing cards with two warders. Martin walked in, ordered the warders to leave and to lock the door behind them.

Father Poole never tired of telling the tale and his congregation were never tired of listening to it.

'They unlocked the door of the cell at daybreak. They found the priest sitting beside the prisoner with his arm around him, consoling him. The man was weeping. This was the man, my dear brethren, who had violated and murdered a child of twelve. This was the man who had cursed God and his priest. This was the man who had committed sacrilege by pulverising the Sacred Host – the body and blood of Jesus Christ – into the filth of the cell floor with his boot! Now here he was, weeping like a child, contrite, at peace. He had confessed the sins of a lifetime and had been absolved. A few hours later he walked calmly to the gallows, repeating the prayers of the priest walking beside him.'

The priest straightened up slowly in his chair, wincing as his ancient, sapless body protested at the movement. He sat forward a little with his hands clasped between his knees, gazing at the fire.

'It was a tremendous victory, Martin,' he whispered, ''twas so.' He wagged his head slowly from side to side. 'Ah, but Marty, Marty,' he groaned, 'yeh left a tiny spark of envy in me heart.'

Father Poole had never been ambitious like some; he had never desired the bishop's crozier or the red hat of a cardinal. He had been

114

content to remain a humble parish priest in one of the poorest parts of the city. I did my best, he told himself, but he was not really content. His one and only desire had not been fulfilled. Unlike Martin Fenlan he had never found the one person who would have made his vocation as a priest worthwhile. He had never found the godless, unrepentant sinner, though he had searched for him down all the years.

He thought that at this very moment, somewhere in this city, someone is in danger of losing his immortal soul. Somewhere, someone is plotting revenge with murder in his heart. Somewhere, someone has reached the depths of despair and is but one step away from suicide – the unforgivable sin . . .

He raised his hands in a gesture of helplessness. 'What's the use, what's the use?' he groaned. He was too old and feeble now to be of help to anyone. He would be eighty years of age before the end of the year. Then they would send him away to a home for retired priests where he would while away his time till death claimed him.

'Father Poole, are you there?'

The voice of his sacristan startled him. He was standing in the doorway, the light behind casting his shadow over the polished linoleum.

'Over here, Peter.'

'Why are you sitting in the dark, Father?' the sacristan asked, walking forward slowly so as not to bump into anything. He struck a match and applied it to the gas-jet. He looked down. 'Are you ill, Father?'

Father Poole looked up, blinking against the light. 'Of course not!' he snapped. 'What makes you think that?' He stood up – a little too suddenly – and swayed.

The sacristan made a grab for him, but Father Poole pushed his hand away.

'Leave me be, leave me be,' he ordered gruffly.

Fear made him irritable, but it was not the fear of approaching death. He was afraid they might suddenly decide to send him into retirement, thinking him too old and perhaps senile to do his job. He darted a suspicious look at the sacristan. How long had he been standing in the doorway? Had he heard him talking to himself?

The sacristan looked concerned. 'It's ten minutes to eight, Father.'

'And what if it is?'

'But . . .' The look of concern changed to bewilderment. 'Tonight's the night for the Sacred Heart Sodality. Had you forgotten?'

With a shock Father Poole realised that he had. But he was afraid to

115

admit it. 'Of course I didn't forget! Why do you think I put on me vestments?' He paused, and inquired, 'This is the night for the men, isn't it?'

The sacristan shook his head. 'No, Father, the women.' He clicked his tongue. 'Ach, Father Poole – sure you're covered in snuff!' He produced a handkerchief and flicked it away.

Father Poole waved his hands outwards. 'Shoo, shoo, shoo!' He shuffled past him towards the door. 'Any of the women arrive yet?' he asked over his shoulder.

'Not yet, Father.'

'Then I'll go out to the porch to welcome them.'

'In heaven's name, Father!' The sacristan strode swiftly past him, and stood in front of the door, blocking his way.

'Do you know what it's like out there? The rain, the wind, the cold! You'll catch your death!'

Father Poole glared at him. 'You worry too much, Peter. Stand aside.'

'I'll do no such thing!' the sacristan declared defiantly. 'You're a stubborn old man, so you are!'

'I know I am. Now stand aside.'

The sacristan gave a groan of resignation. 'Oh very well. But you're not going out to that porch without putting something on.'

'Yer an oul fusspot, Peter,' he complained as the sacristan helped him on with his overcoat. As the younger man started to fiddle with the buttons, Father Poole slapped his hands. 'I can do that meself,' he rasped. 'I'm not an invalid, yeh know.'

The sacristan stepped aside. 'It's all very well, but it's I who will have to answer to Father Kinsella and Father Murphy if anything happens to you.'

'Ah, give over yer blether,' Father Poole growled, opening the door.

The man's voice stopped him. 'Father Poole . . .'

Father Poole turned slowly, his hand on the door-knob. 'Now what?' he asked testily.

'I thought you'd like to know. That man is here again.'

'What man?'

'The old man I was telling you about. He's been coming here every day for the past nine or ten days now.'

'Ahhh, *that* man. Every day, you say?'

'Aye, he comes in during the afternoons and doesn't leave until the chapel closes.'

Father Poole heaved a sigh. 'A saint,' he whispered, 'a saint,' and closed the door.

He walked up the narrow side aisle. The church was empty except for the solitary figure sitting in front of the shrine of St Joseph. Candles burned before the shrine and cast a soft glow across the white-bearded face. The man stared vacantly in front of him. The overcoat was fastened under the throat by a safety pin. Father Poole shook his head. Poor creature, he thought; one of life's outcasts.

He opened the side door to the porch. Rain whipped past the entrance. He pulled the collar of the overcoat up about his neck and throat and waited.

The first to arrive was a shawled, stout, middle-aged woman. She mounted the steps slowly.

'Kate Gaffney!' Father Poole exclaimed. 'How dare yeh come out on a night like this. And you a martyr to arthritis. God doesn't expect . . .'

She ignored him, pushed in the unyielding front door with difficulty. The wind rushed in past her. It swept through the church; the flames of the candles before the shrine wavered wildly.

Myles Burke hunched his shoulders as the wind swept against his back. The half-open door let in the sound of the pelting rain and he could feel his insides shrivelling with fear. Death waited outside. He felt like a condemned prisoner listening to the gallows being erected outside his cell window. The church would close in an hour and he would have to go out into the merciless rain and wind. He wouldn't survive the night; in the morning he would be found curled up dead in some alley.

He coughed and clutched his chest, wincing with pain. He coughed again and his mouth filled with phlegm. He pulled out a filthy rag of a handkerchief and spat into it. The phlegm was rust-coloured, stained with blood. He let his head fall back a little and closed his eyes. He found it difficult to breathe.

It was ironic. He had survived the famine, the coffin ships, Bull Run, Antietam, the slaughter of Fredericksburg. It's this bitch of a city that succeeded in killing me, he told himself bitterly. The church was filling rapidly. He could hear the sound of many feet and the creaking of seats. He opened his eyes. Already the pews in front of him were full. Strange, there seemed to be only women. A strong smell of damp arose from rain-drenched coats, shawls, umbrellas.

Suddenly everyone stood up, and as suddenly sat down again. An old man's voice broke the silence.

117

'In the name of the Father, the Son, and the Holy Ghost . . .'
Everyone began to recite the rosary.

Throughout the first two months of summer he had tramped the streets of the city day after day, trying to preserve what little money he had. He had discovered what it was like to be old and penniless and without friends in Dublin. One simply died of starvation or exposure. The only alternative was the Workhouse.

He shifted uneasily in his seat. The Workhouse. It brought back memories of childhood, memories he wished to forget. He shook his head. Never, he thought, never. I would rather have it end like this. His eyes would not stay open. They were heavy from exhaustion and hot with fever. He closed them. Around him the voices droned on and on.

'. . . to thee do we cry, poor banished children of Eve . . .'

He lapsed into a fretful dream. He was struggling through dense undergrowth, fleeing from someone, but who it was he did not know. He was conscious of a terrible sense of danger and the need to get away. Now and then he would pause to catch his breath and listen. In the distance he could hear whoever it was pursuing him crashing through the jungly thickness with the ferocity of a wild animal. He would struggle frantically on, panic-stricken, but it was difficult. The jungle was impenetrable and little light filtered through the lushness overhead. There was hardly any air and he could not breathe.

He awoke with a start, burning with fever and gasping for breath. The congregation was silent now and an old priest with a shock of white hair was speaking from the pulpit.

'We must beware, my dear women, of blindness of the heart and of the spirit . . .'

Myles was painfully aware of the overpowering stench of his body – as if it were decomposing prematurely. His feet wallowed in liquid filth: the boots were worn and broken and let in the rain. They were not his boots. One morning he had woken up in a cheap lodging-house to find his own had gone, together with his overcoat and the parcel containing his spare socks, shirt and razor. Fortunately the thief had left him his own broken boots and overcoat – a mud-stained rag of a thing without buttons. He had tried to keep it closed by tying a piece of rope around the waist and fastening it under the throat with a safety pin.

'. . . Then Jesus said to them: "Amen, I say to you, the publicans and harlots are entering the Kingdom of God before you . . ." '

I would have been dead by now, he told himself, but for the generosity of that British officer. He had been sitting where he always sat in daytime, in that little park in front of Christ Church Cathedral. Without money, he had not eaten for two days. Suddenly a shadow fell across his vision and money was dropped into his hand. He had looked up in astonishment to see a tall khaki-clad figure striding away to a woman who stood waiting outside the side door of the cathedral.

Five shillings and ninepence, he remembered. He had lived on that for more than a week. It had been the only act of kindness shown him since his arrival in Ireland. And as for my own damned countrymen . . . He had been mocked, robbed, kicked. He still carried the bruises from that swine's heavy boot. He had kicked him twice in the side as he had woken half-dazed in the ruins of that cottage.

'. . . for John came to you in the way of justice, and you did not believe him. But the publicans and the harlots believed him; whereas you, seeing him, did not even repent afterwards . . .'

He had been coming to the church every day since the weather turned bad nine days ago. It was the only place where he could sit out of the rain undisturbed. Recently he had discovered that one could obtain a free breakfast of soup and bread at the Mendicity Institution. Every morning for a week now he had been standing in line with two hundred other destitutes in the pouring rain, waiting for the gates to open. He was soaked to the skin.

'. . . Who is weak, and I am not weak? Who is made to stumble, and I am not inflamed. . . ?'

He coughed; this time the pain in his chest was more severe. His breathing was becoming more rapid and shallow, the fever was mounting.

An organ sounded a note and everyone stood up to sing.

> *Tantum ergo sacramentum,*
> *veneremur cernui;*
> *Et antiquum documentum*
> *Novo cedat ritui . . .*

His body was on fire, he was being consumed. He began to rave a little, pleading for someone to give him water to ease the agony of his burning throat, but his feeble croaking was drowned by the loud enraptured hymn-singing voices.

> *Genitori, Genitoque,*
> *Laus et jubilatio;*
> *Salus, honor, virtus quoque*
> *Sit et benedictio . . .*

Benediction was coming to an end. The church would be closing soon. He gripped the back of the seat in front of him and raised himself with difficulty to his feet. The storm outside held no terrors for him now. He welcomed it. He wanted to feel the heavy cold rain beating against his fever-hot face, wanted to raise his head and open his mouth wide and let it trickle down his parched throat.

He moved sideways on weakening legs along the knee-rest, mumbling to himself, delirious, brushing past the hymn-singing women, who drew back in alarm. He forced himself up the aisle, his breath coming in loud painful gasps.

He wobbled from side to side like a drunken man. Terrified faces stared at him from both sides. He could hardly see them: everything was becoming dark. Suddenly his legs buckled. A woman screamed. The sound seemed to come from a great distance away. He did not feel his body hitting the ground.

## II

'Myles, Myles,' his father called. 'Come on, son, come on.'

He whimpered from fatigue and the gnawing pangs of hunger in the pit of his stomach. He shuffled along in his bare feet to where his father and elder brother waited on top of the rise. He tried to hurry, but the steep incline was too much for his weak spindly legs. When he eventually topped the rise, he leaned wearily against his father's side, sobbing.

His father's heavy gnarled hand rested lightly on his thick, tousled hair.

'I know, son, I know. But we'll reach Galway tomorrow or the day after, God willin'. There'll be ships there. You never saw a ship before, did you? Oh, they're big things with sails on them which reach to the sky. Sails? Well, never mind, son. You'll see, you'll see. The ship will take us across the ocean. You and meself and Colm. To Canada or America. Now whist, child, stop your cryin' and let's go on our way in God's name.'

They trudged along the narrow rutted road between fields thicks with the stench of putrefaction: the smell of blighted, rotting potatoes and the sickly sweet smell of decaying flesh. There was not a living man, woman or child to be seen. There were no cattle, sheep, horses, or fowl. The cabins they passed were derelict and whole villages lay abandoned. A light mist had fallen, covering the land like a shroud. The autumn sun, a dull red ball, burned through the haze. Nothing broke the silence. They were travellers in the Land of the Dead.

He was continually falling behind. His father and brother would come to a standstill and wait patiently for him.

'Come on, son, come on.'

It was towards evening when he sat down at the side of the road, unable to go any further. In the distance he could see his father and brother looking back at him. His father beckoned, but he ignored him. The pain in his stomach was a dull ache now; he was too exhausted even to cry. He sat on a grassy mound, his back to a ditch. He closed his eyes. Sleep stole over him. He swayed and fell backwards, clutching the tall grass each side of him in alarm. His right hand touched something – something cold and wet.

An old woman lay in the ditch. Her sightless dead eyes glared up at him from her waxen, emaciated face. Her mouth was smeared green from the nettles she had devoured.

At first his dulled senses could not comprehend – then he screamed in terror.

'Hush, hush.' A cool hand was placed on his fever-hot forehead. He opened his eyes. A nurse looked down at him with concern on her face. He turned his head a little. He could see a cream-coloured ceiling, green walls. He tried to move his arms, but he was covered up to the chin by bedclothes.

The nurse whispered something to him, but his confused brain could not grasp what she was saying. He closed his eyes. He was drifting back, back . . .

Under the starry night sky, the Workhouse looked like a fortress under siege. An army of silent, ragged skeletons surrounded it. Some lay huddled asleep on the ground; others sat around the fires, staring vacantly into the flames. Now and then a child would give a fretful little cry which would dwindle to whimpering sounds of hunger.

They sat near a group crouched over a small fire. He cuddled against his father for warmth. His brother lay asleep at his father's feet. A man with a wild unkempt beard and fierce deep-set eyes sat on a rock facing them.

'D'ye know, 'tis a curious thing,' the man said. 'The people have been waitin' here for days to get inside that Workhouse, and yet 'tis a pesthouse inside. 'Tis so. The place is swarmin' with famine fever.'

121

'Are ye tryin' to get in yourself, friend?' the man asked after a while.

'It's for the New World we're bound,' his father answered. 'We'll reach Galway tomorrow with God's help.'

'Then may the Blessed Virgin wrap her cloak about you and the childer,' the man declared fervently, 'for they're dyin' like flies in the streets of Galway. And those that survive and have the passage money are bein' crammed into the holds of the coffin ships. Stinkin' rotten wrecks the likes of which ye wouldn't cross Lough Corrib in!'

They sat in silence for a while. Somewhere a woman was sobbing and in the far-off distance a dog howled. The man leaned forward a little.

'By yer accent I'd say you're a Mayo man. Have I got ye, now?'

'I am, God help me,' his father answered. 'And I've left my woman and three of my children there – buried in a common grave with a hundred other poor souls.' He wept quietly, to himself.

The man shook his head in sympathy. 'A wirra, wirra.' He heaved a sigh. ''Tis the end of us, the whole godforsaken, downtrodden, degraded Irish race.' His voice turned bitter. 'The Sassenach have won at long last, friend. They have so. They conquered and ground us into the dust, but we survived. When we rebelled, they ground us back into the dust again, and still we survived. They made slaves of us while they grew rich and arrogant on our sweat. We bowed to their insults, but we survived. We worked the land that was once ours; we watched them gorge themselves on what we produced while we tried to exist on potatoes and milk. Now the potato is gone, blighted, and we're finished.'

At daybreak they heard the rumble of heavy wheels coming from the north. The army of wasted, withered wretches came slowly awake, shivering in their rage in the cold morning air. The movement of his father's body beside him caused him to wake. He whimpered from the cold and the dull ache of hunger in his belly.

The rumbling grew louder. Everyone was looking towards the north. A horseman emerged from the morning mist; more horsemen followed. Dragoons. Behind them came a long line of wagons. As the leading horseman, an officer, saw the crowd, he barked an order to his men. Carbines were drawn. They held them upright, the butts resting on the pommels. The crowd watched in silence as they came on.

The officer held himself tall and proud in the saddle. He looked down at the watching silent multitude, his lip curled with contempt. Some of his men looked apprehensive when they saw the size of the crowd; several fingered the triggers of their carbines. The wagoners showed their fear.

They trundled slowly past, the heavy broad-rimmed wagon wheels crushing the small stones of the narrow dusty road into powder. They were piled high. Whatever they contained was covered by tarpaulins held fast by thick ropes.

"'Tis munitions,' someone said.

The man with the wild straggly beard spat sideways. 'Munitions be damned,' he growled. "'Tis food. They're headin' for Galway.' He raised his voice. 'They're headin' for the Galway docks! They're shippin' out food to England and the people starvin' to death!'

A low, angry hum arose from the crowd. A few moved towards the wagons. The officer drew rein and shouted an order to halt, unsheathing his sabre at the same time. His men sat tensely in the saddles confronting the crowd, carbines at the ready.

The crowd drew back slowly, subdued. No one moved, no one spoke. A trooper's horse snorted and tossed its head, pawing the ground with its hoof. Suddenly, the bearded man leaped on to the road and turned to the crowd.

'What's the matter with all of ye?' he roared in Gaelic. 'There's food in those wagons. Let's take it!'

No one moved. The man glared at them. Some stared down at the ground, afraid to meet the challenge in his eyes. Others turned their backs to him and walked away. Then, with a cry of anger and despair, the man spun around and made for the wagon nearest him.

The wagoner raised his whip as the man scrambled up towards him. He drove his fist into the wagoner's face and sent him flying backwards into a ditch on the far side of the road. Then he plucked a knife from his belt and began to slash wildly at the tarpaulin.

The officer spurred his horse savagely and galloped up the road, sabre held straight and rigid before him in the charge position. Someone shouted a warning. The man whirled about, crouching, knife raised. The officer made no attempt to draw rein. As he galloped past the wagon, he gave a backhanded swipe with the sabre . . .

He awoke screaming, seeing blood spurting up like a fountain, seeing the head rolling in the dust. He struggled to sit upright and a pair of hands gripped his shoulders and forced him down again.

'There, now. It's all right, it's all right.' Her voice calmed him. He could barely see her face in the grey dawn light.

Nearby a bed creaked and a voice croaked peevishly, 'For God's sake, nurse, shift me to another ward, will yeh? I can't stand this bloody commotion any longer!' He slipped back into sleep again.

He next awoke to find himself naked on an oil-sheet, being sponged down by two nurses. There was a screen around the bed. They dried and dressed him and removed the oil-sheet. A nurse spoon-fed him some broth. He closed his eyes and drifted off to sleep again. His body felt wonderfully cool. The fever had gone and his sleep was untroubled.

When he awoke once more a doctor, a grave-faced young man, was standing by his bed. 'How do you feel?' he asked, but without waiting for a reply, he produced a thermometer and bent down and placed it in his mouth. He waited for a moment before taking it out. The doctor looked at it and nodded. He examined the patient with a stethoscope.

'Inhale, exhale. Again.' The young man straightened up and smiled. 'You know,' he said, 'there was a time when we gave up all hope of saving you.'

'What happened to me?' Myles whispered.

'Pneumonia. You're over the crisis, although there's still a fair amount of fluid on the lungs. But don't worry,' he assured him, 'we'll get rid of that in time. Then plenty of rest for a few weeks, lots of care and attention, and you'll be as right as rain.'

He turned away to the patient in the next bed. Myles stared up at the ceiling with unblinking eyes. When I'm cured and released, he thought, it will be back to the streets again. He told himself that with luck he might survive the autumn, but when winter came . . . He shuddered.

'O God,' he whispered, 'why did you allow me to live? Why? Why let me go through all that agony again when you know it will end in the same way?'

He closed his eyes and prayed for a miracle. It was a useless act, he knew; he was too much of a realist to believe in miracles.


III


He sat up in the bed as the nurse washed his face. She dipped the sponge in the basin of warm water, squeezed it, then washed the soap away. She dried his face slowly and carefully. Her plump red-cheeked face was level with his. Nurse Keogh, he thought. Of all the nurses, she was his favourite. She was young and soft-natured. She dipped the comb in the water and began to tidy his sparse grey hair. After she had finished she drew back a little and smiled approvingly.

124

'There now, fresh and neat as a new pin.' She picked up a hand-mirror and gave it to him. 'Have a look.'

Myles winced at the death's-head that stared back at him. Fever had burned away the flesh from his face and his eyes looked out from deep hollows. Beneath the jutting cheek-bones, the cheeks had a sucked-in appearance. His face looked unnaturally pale now that they had shaved off his beard: he had an impression of a bleached skull recently unearthed. He shook his head and handed back the mirror.

Nurse Keogh leaned forward and buttoned the collar of his shirt. 'We must have you looking your best when your visitor arrives.'

He stared at her in astonishment. 'Visitor? But I don't know a soul in the world! There must be some mistake.'

She stood up, laughing. 'Oh, no mistake.'

He sighed. It had to be a mistake. On the stroke of three the visitors streamed in, bearing their gifts of flowers, chocolates and bottles of lemonade. He watched them.

Nurse Keogh came in, leading an old man by the arm. He wore a tall silk hat and dark clerical clothes. He shuffled along with the aid of a stick. Nurse Keogh smiled as she brought the old priest to the side of the bed.

'Here's Father Poole to see you, Myles.'

Father Poole lowered himself into a chair and extended a shaky hand. 'My poor man,' he said. 'How are yeh?'

'Father Poole called several times inquiring about you,' Nurse Keogh said as she walked away.

Father Poole took off the tall silk hat and placed it at the foot of the bed. He had thick white hair and a round wrinkled yellow face the colour of cheese. It was then Myles recognised him. He remembered collapsing in the chapel. 'I feel much better, thank you, Father,' he answered.

Father Poole smiled and patted his head. 'Ah, that's grand – excellent. You gave all of us quite a start. Such a commotion, man dear . . . And the women of the Sodality, clucking around like frightened hens . . .'

'I'm sorry, Father, if I – '

Father Poole cut short his apology with a wave of the hand. 'Ah, sorry for what. Sure a thing like that could happen to anyone.' He leaned forward. 'We searched your clothing, trying to find something that would identify you. But there was nothing . . .' He lapsed into silence. He sat hunched forward with both hands resting on the walking stick, his eyes on Myles's face.

Myles knew the priest was waiting for him to talk about himself. When he had regained consciousness, the hospital authorities had asked for his name and he had given it, too weak to think clearly. If he had been a little stronger and his mind more alert, he would have given a false name. Dublin Castle could still have detectives searching for him. He had been apprehensive for a while, telling himself that the Castle could have notified all hospitals and charitable institutions to report the admittance of anyone bearing the name of Myles Burke. But nothing had happened. There had been no official inquiries about him; no one even faintly resembling a detective had entered the ward. Perhaps they are no longer interested in me, he thought. Besides, there must be hundreds of men with the same name in this city.

He said, 'My name is Burke, Father. Myles Burke.'

'Do you have anyone belonging to you, Myles? A wife, children, brother, sister. . . ?'

Myles shook his head. 'No one, Father.'

Father Poole had probed and touched a tender spot. He could feel emotion surging up. Suddenly he gave a tiny gasp and his eyes filled with tears.

Father Poole turned away, embarrassed. There was an awkward silence.

The ward hummed with conversation. Chattering groups were clustered around nearly every bed. Minutes passed, before Father Poole cleared his throat and leaned towards Myles in a conspiratorial manner.

'Tell me, Myles,' he inquired softly, 'where do you go to when you are discharged from this hospital?'

Myles stared at him coldly. 'Go to? There's only one place I can go to.' He could not keep the bitterness out of his voice. 'Back to the streets. Sleeping in the hallways of tenements, trying to exist on what little charity there is in this damned town!'

Father Poole laid a small hand on his arm. 'Would you not go to the Workhouse?'

'Never!'

Father Poole drew back in alarm, startled by the violent reaction. The angry half-shout stilled all conversation in the ward. Father Poole could see heads turning towards them. He plucked at Myles's sleeve.

'Please,' he appealed, 'don't agitate yourself so.'

Myles trembled with anger. 'Never!' he repeated harshly. 'I'm not going to exchange one prison for another!'

They were silent for a while. Then Father Poole cleared his throat a few times and said: 'It's hard at times for one to find the right things to say to a man in your situation, Myles. Undoubtedly you must find the daily existence of life hard, very hard.' He pondered deeply for a moment with lowered head. 'Frankly, I would be concerned if I didn't know you to be a man of indomitable faith.'

'Faith?' Myles echoed in astonishment.

Father Poole nodded. 'Peter, the sacristan, saw you in church every day, despite the fierceness of the weather.' He shook his head in admiration. 'Such devotion! Such piety! You possess a great reserve of spiritual strength, Myles.'

Myles stared at him, dumbfounded. How could the man be so mistaken? The church had been just a place to shelter from the rain.

'So you see,' Father Poole went on, 'I've no need to worry that you will ever allow yourself to be caught in the grip of despair.'

The urge to laugh was replaced by a feeling of irritation. The pious platitudes irked him. 'So you think that, do you, Father? Well, let me tell you something . . . One night, without money, feeling cold and sick and hungry, I found myself in the middle of Butt Bridge staring down at the dark swirling water. The thought came into my mind, why not end it now. A few minutes of agony, and then no more suffering. I asked myself, why carry this pain-racked, decaying carcase of a body around any longer? Why?'

'Stop it!' Father Poole brought the point of his stick down sharply on the linoed floor. 'I won't listen to such talk! You haven't the right . . .' He stopped abruptly and passed a shaking hand over his eyes. Again, a hush descended over the ward.

Father Poole sat with his hand covering his eyes. 'Myles, Myles,' he whispered. 'You have to promise me, no matter how much you are tempted, that you must never even *think* of committing such a deed.'

Myles gave a derisive grunt. 'It's easy for you to talk, Father. You have a fully belly and a roof over your head. But when I leave here it's back to the streets and a lingering death. Why prolong the agony?'

Father Poole shook his head in despair. 'Jesus and Mary help us,' he moaned. He sat hunched over his stick with his chin resting on his hands, his eyes half-closed.

'There is a man of my acquaintance,' he murmured after a while, 'a member of the Sodality, who is looking for a caretaker.' He raised his head, then gave a little start when he saw the look of hope in Myles's eyes. 'Oh, don't build up your hopes, Myles,' he croaked with panic in his voice, 'nothing may come of it.' He gave a little sigh and rose slowly to his feet. 'However, I'll see what I can do.' He picked up his hat from

127

the bed, placed it squarely on his head and stretched out a trembling hand.

'Good-bye now for the present, Myles, and may God look after you. I'll be seein' you soon . . .' He took a few steps, then halted and turned around. 'Remember now – don't despair.'

Myles watched him shuffling down between the beds towards the door, feeling hope beginning to flicker for the first time.

# Chapter Four

## I

They worked feverishly at the hay, making the most of the good weather. After more than ten days of heavy rain and high winds, the weather had changed for the better. There was now only a gentle breeze wafting in from the Atlantic and the sun burned fiercely in a clear blue sky. They worked in three teams of two. Con Gallagher and Johnny Boyle worked the eastern half of the meadow: down past the bottom of the long gentle slope and beyond the dry shallow ditch, Luke and Sonny O'Malley toiled away in the western half. Bull O'Malley and a man he had hired from the village had the north meadow.

Con Gallagher was pitching – gathering a great load of hay on to his fork, raising it above his head and hurling it up to Johnny, who stood on top of the haycock. Johnny would take the load and spread it evenly, pressing with his arms or tramping with his feet. It was hard and exhausting work in the intense heat and both of them were drenched in sweat. Gallagher gathered another load, feeling his tired arm muscles protesting at the strain. He raised the loaded fork. Johnny was still spreading, but doing it slowly and sluggishly. He appeared to be on the verge of collapse. Under the sheen of sweat, his face was white and drawn. He's becoming too old for this kind of work, Gallagher thought. He lowered the fork.

'All right, Johnny,' he said, 'I'll finish it off. Come on down.'

Johnny was too exhausted to argue. He sat down awkwardly, legs dangling over the edge of the cock, then slid down into Gallagher's outstretched arms. Gallagher lowered him to the ground.

'Are you all right?' he asked.

Johnny raised a hand feebly in reply, then let it drop to his side. He lay flat on his back with his eyes closed and his mouth open. The grey stubble on his cheeks and jaws glistened in the sunlight. Gallagher stood looking down at him for a moment, then picked up the hayfork. The cock was nearly completed. He pitched up several more forkfuls, then threw the fork to the ground and unrolled the hay-rope Johnny and himself had twisted. He threw the rope over the haycock, then stuffed one end of it into the cock near the butt. He went round to the far side, pulled hard, and stuffed in the other end. He threw another rope over from the western side, quartering the cock with ropes so that it was held down firmly against the wind. It was the fourth haycock they had built since early morning.

He then stood looking down the long slope, enjoying the gentle breeze flowing against his sweat-covered face. The two O'Malley brothers were completing their third haycock. Three to our four, Gallagher thought contemptuously. And they have a smaller meadow and a level one at that. The sight gave him a feeling of satisfaction.

There was a constant rivalry between himself and Luke and Sonny. Since he had started working for their father, they had adopted an overbearing attitude towards him, treating him like a serf rather than an employee. He had paid back in kind, acting like an overseer, mocking their slowness and physical strength. Nothing delighted him more than to abuse them in front of their father.

Gallagher watched them now, chuckling to himself. Luke was on his knees, trimming the butt of the haycock, while Sonny was standing on top, raking with slow wearisome movements. Gallagher raised his voice.

'Luke, Sonny!'

They looked towards him.

'Get a move on, for God's sake,' Gallagher shouted, 'or both of you will be there till Christmas!' He laughed as Sonny shook a furious fist at him.

He lay down alongside Johnny in the shadows of the haycock, feeling the sweat drying on his body. They had worked non-stop since daybreak.

He thought Johnny had fallen asleep, until he touched his arm and croaked wearily, 'Why the hell do ye have to keep on needlin' those two?'

'I like to see Sonny losin' his rag,' Gallagher answered sleepily.

'You'll go too far one of these days, then there'll be trouble.'

Gallagher yawned. 'With Sonny? I can handle Sonny.'

'Luke's the one you'd want to be wary of.'

Gallagher did not reply; he was feeling relaxed and drowsy. He was just drifting off into sleep when Johnny began to snore loudly. He grimaced, then smiled to himself. Enjoy your rest, Johnny, he thought, you've earned it.

Johnny had welcomed him with open arms when he had walked into his cottage after an absence of ten years. There had been no need to ask for lodgings; Johnny had insisted that he stay with him before he had a chance to bring the matter up. He knew that loneliness had been slowly killing Johnny. It had been the cause of his heavy drinking. But now with him living in the same house, Johnny no longer sought solace in the whiskey bottle. Con had come back just in time.

The sound of voices drifted up from the lower field. Gallagher slowly raised himself and looked down the slope. Two women with baskets hanging from their arms were coming up towards them. The two O'Malley women: mother and daughter. Gallagher nudged Johnny awake, then rose to his feet and walked down the slope towards them. The daughter, seeing him, lowered her head and dawdled, allowing her mother to go on ahead.

Peg O'Malley smiled as Gallagher took the basket from her. He rarely saw her smile. Any woman having a man like Bull O'Malley for a husband would have no cause to, he told himself, as he helped her up the slope.

Johnny made a little bow to her. 'Good day to ye, ma'am. Isn't it glorious weather we're havin' for the hay. Sure, if this keeps up.'

Gallagher knelt and opened the basket, taking out the bottles of tea wrapped in cloth and the thick meat sandwiches. He concentrated on spreading the cloth over the grass and pouring the hot sugary tea into the big delft mugs. He deliberately kept his back to the daughter, Una, as she came up the slope. He could hear the swish of her skirt against the stubble of the field; the faint panting of her breath after the climb. He could see her shadow moving over the grass and he turned his head away. She walked past. He was aware of a quickening heart-beat and a racing of the blood. He was angry; angry that this woman could make him feel like this.

He could hear her talking to Johnny. Johnny said something and she laughed. The laugh irritated him. During all the weeks he had known her, never once had she laughed like that with him. She had spurned all his feeble attempts to be friendly; instead she stood aloof, keeping him at a distance.

To hell with her! he thought savagely. She behaves like her father and her bloody half-brothers. He thrust his voice through their low-voiced conversation.

'Come on, Johnny,' he said gruffly, 'the tea is gettin' cold!' He put his finger through the handle of the mug, and began to sip his tea.

He realised he had been rude. Una O'Malley stared coldly at him. He avoided her eyes and focused his attention on her mother. He smiled at her, trying to make amends for his rudeness. He said without thinking, 'You make a grand cup of tea, ma'am.'

The trite remark made him wince. Peg O'Malley nodded and smiled back at him. She had a strong handsome face and greying brown hair. Her shrewd grey eyes noted the flush on Gallagher's face and she could sense his suppressed excitement. She knew what was wrong with him.

'Well, most of the hay's saved, thanks be to God. Ye've broken the back of it,' Peg O'Malley said as she shielded her eyes against the sun. She looked westward towards the distant mountains, quivering in the heat-haze. 'And just in time, I'm thinkin'. I don't like the look of that sky.'

Johnny raised his head, his mouth busily chewing on a meat sandwich. He washed it down with a mouthful of tea and nodded. 'Aye, I think yer right, ma'am. This weather is goin' to break. We'll have rain before mornin'.'

Gallagher did not say anything. He stood in the shadow of the haycock sipping his tea. Cup to mouth, he glanced at the girl standing beside her mother. She too was shading her eyes and looking towards the west. Una was Bull O'Malley's only child by his second wife. She had inherited the black hair of the O'Malley clan but nothing else. Except that damned superior manner, Gallagher thought resentfully.

She lowered her hand and turned her head a little. High cheek-bones curved to a small pointed chin. For an instant their eyes met; before she turned away with an air of indifference.

Gallagher tossed the dregs of tea away with an abrupt gesture and squatted down beside Johnny. He poured out a fresh cup and reached for a sandwich.

Peg picked up the empty basket. 'Come on, girla. Let's leave the men and let them have their meal in peace.'

'Ah sure don't be rushin' away on our account,' Johnny protested. 'We enjoy the company of yerself and yer lovely daughter. The presence of both of ye makes the meal more enjoyable.'

Peg laughed. 'Indeed now, Johnny, but it's the silver tongue ye have. But we must be goin'. With all the men at the hay, there's double the amount of work for Una and meself, with the milkin' and all.'

The men watched as they moved down the slope. Johnny swallowed his tea, belched appreciatively, and lay flat on his back. He gave a long sigh of contentment.

'Ahhh . . . when the belly is full, the bones like to stretch.'

Gallagher sat down beside him and lit a cigarette. 'You know,' he said, 'I have a great regard for that Mrs O'Malley. A friendly, warm-hearted woman.'

'Well,' Johnny commented dryly, 'if ye love the mother, ye love her brood.'

Gallagher glanced sharply at him, but Johnny's eyes were closed and his face impassive; he seemed to be drifting off to sleep again. Gallagher turned and stared down the slope. Una O'Malley's red blouse was like a flame against the emerald green of the fields.

'She who fills the eye, fills the heart, aye, Con?' Gallagher swivelled round to see Johnny sitting up and smirking at him.

'What the hell do you mean?' he demanded.

'Una O'Malley, that's who I mean. Do ye think I haven't eyes in me head, that I can't see how ye behave when she's around. Aye, and I'm not the only one who's noticed that, I fancy.'

Gallagher threw away his cigarette and ground it savagely underfoot. 'Ah, you're cracked!' he snorted, as a tell-tale flush spread all over his face. 'You're imaginin' things!'

He was aghast to think that the real reason for his odd behaviour had been so obvious.

'Well, ogle her all ye want,' Johnny went on, 'for that's as far as ye'll ever get. She'll marry money – Bull O'Malley will see to that. So ye better come to yer senses and realise what ye are, and what she is. Do ye think her father would ever allow a common farm labourer to court his daughter?'

His words cut Gallagher to the quick. 'By Christ, I'm a better man than Bull O'Malley and those two pups of his!'

'Now none of that!' Johnny snapped. 'We are what we are, both of us. I can accept my lot and ye had better do the same. And if ye want to marry and settle down, then pick a girl from yer own class – there's plenty of them about.'

'Let them stay there!'

Johnny raised his eyebrows. 'Oho . . . so yeh have it as bad as that, eh?'

Gallagher brought the flat of his hand down hard against his knee. 'Who the hell does Bull O'Malley think he is? Does he think he owns the bloody county and everyone in it?'

'Mebbe he will in time,' Johnny said.

'It's that bloody superior way of goin' on that needles me,' Gallagher fumed. 'He acts as though he's God almighty!'

Johnny gave a bitter laugh. 'He has money and land. He can afford to act like God almighty.'

'I suppose if you went back far enough,' Gallagher said with a sneer in his voice, 'you'd find that he came from a long line of pauperised bog-farmers.'

Johnny chuckled. 'Begob, ye wouldn't need to go back as far as that.' He leaned sideways and placed a hand on Gallagher's arm. 'Bull O'Malley's parents were pitchforked out of their cabin by the Carews for fallin' behind in their rent.' He gave a nod and a wink. 'Now there's one for ye.'

Gallagher stared at him in silence.

'Ask anyone around here who's old enough to remember,' Johnny went on, 'and they'll tell ye the whole story. The O'Malleys had to take shelter in a ditch with only a piece of canvas over their heads to keep off the rain. Aye, and they'll tell ye how they had to go from one farmhouse to another beggin' for food. Bull O'Malley was a mere gossoon then, but ye can be sure the memory never left him. He remembers the cold and the wet and the hunger, but most of all he remembers the humiliation. That's what made him the man he is. That's what goads him on.'

'That sort of thing happened to thousands of others in those days,' Gallagher growled. 'They didn't all turn out like Bull O'Malley.'

'I'll grant ye that,' Johnny said. 'There was only the Workhouse, or America if ye had the passage money. But no Workhouse or America for the Bull. Oh no! He worked and scraped from dawn to dusk, hoardin' every penny. He survived the bad times, and when the good times came, he was able to buy a patcheen of land and marry and settle down.

'It was hard goin', tryin' to support a wife and two small boys on a few acres of sour bottom land. But the Bull survived, schemin' and hoardin' his gold, workin' like a man possessed. They say the hardship killed his first wife. When a man has the land hunger, he doesn't let a small thing like an ailin' wife stop him. Rumour had it that he ignored her complaints because he didn't want to spend the money on a doctor.

'Well, anyway, Bull O'Malley clawed his way up, enlargin' his holdin' all the time. A few poor acres one year, a patch of cutaway bog the next. Whenever he heard of a family breakin' up and goin' off to America, or an old couple ailin' and nearin' death, he'd be hoverin' about their place like a vulture waitin' to pounce. And at auctions, he'd outbid everyone else.

'And that's how he did it. In twenty years' time, all this part of Mayo will belong to Bull O'Malley and his sons and grandsons.'

Johnny leaned heavily on Gallagher's knee and raised himself slowly. He walked out from the shade of the haycock and stood looking to the north.

134

'Come here for a moment,' he said.

Gallagher joined him. Johnny pointed to where the Big House stood on a hill a mile and a half away.

'The Carews won all of this land with the sword and drove our people to the mountains and the bog. The Carews have been our lords and masters for more than two hundred and fifty years. But now Walter Carew is nearly finished. Debt and bad management have brought him to the edge of ruin. He had to sell all the land outside the demesne at a time when land prices had fallen to rock-bottom. Bull O'Malley bought it for a song.'

Johnny gave a deep laugh. 'That must've given Bull an awful lot of satisfaction. Buyin' the land of the man who had thrown his father and mother out on the roadside.' He stood with his hands in his trouser pockets, staring at the house in the distance. 'That house, and the demesne, that's what Bull O'Malley wants. And by God he'll get it, or me name is not Johnny Boyle!'

He turned round to face Gallagher. 'And ye are the one,' he said with sarcasm in his voice, 'who has notions about his daughter. Begob, ye fly high, I'll say that for ye. But 'twill be all the harder when ye hit the ground!'

Gallagher was silent. He stood staring at Carewscourt, a brooding look on his face. Then he gave a twist of the shoulders and bent down to pick up the hay-fork.

'Come on,' he rasped, 'we've wasted enough time gosterin'. There's work to be done!'

II

Gerry Troy swung the hurley. There was the smack of leather against ash and the ball soared towards Con Gallagher. It hit the turf three feet in front of him and bounced as he raced forward. He could hear the pounding feet of the Castlebar men behind him and the cries of the Carewstown team supporters. He swung wildly with the hurley as the ball fell and hit it, all his strength behind the swing. The ball shot forward with the speed of a bullet – direct for the goalkeeper's head. The goalkeeper dived for the ground just in time. The Carewstown team and their supporters went wild. The match was nearing its end and it was their first goal; they had not even scored a point.

Gallagher trotted back down the field and was surrounded by his own team. They cheered and clapped him on the back. Gerry Troy, the captain, embraced him.

'A bloody marvellous shot that, Con,' he cried. 'We might be victorious yet.'

Gallagher grunted. With only ten minutes to go and the Castlebar team leading by one goal and two points, it was highly unlikely.

They waited tensely, gripping their hurleys with both hands. The Castlebar goalie, furious with himself for having lost his nerve, gave the ball a vicious swipe and sent it soaring. It started to fall about five yards in front of the Carewstown goal and there was a frantic attempt by the team to intercept it.

There was a mêlée in the goalmouth; bodies bunched together; hurley sticks clashed. Someone gave a scream of pain, a whistle blew and everyone came to a confused standstill. The referee came running up as Sonny O'Malley staggered about holding his hand to his head, blood running down the side of his face.

Luke ran to his aid. He grabbed him by the arm and steadied him. Then he turned a furious face to the referee.

'I saw it all,' he fumed. 'It was deliberate. That bastard . . .' He pointed a finger towards a member of the Castlebar team. An argument developed and the spectators rushed over from the sidelines to see what was wrong.

Gallagher knelt on one knee and placed the hurley stick in an upright position in front of him, resting his weight on it. It had been a good match, he thought; it was a pity it had to end in a squabble. He felt sorry for Gerry Troy as he watched him intervene, trying to make peace. The schoolmaster had attempted to do an awful lot during the few months he had been in Carewstown. He had told Gallagher how he had tried to revive Gaelic culture and sport in the district only to be constantly opposed by Father Devlin.

When he tried to start an evening class for the teaching of Irish, Father Devlin had raised objections. The educational authorities, he declared, frowned upon any attempts made by schoolteachers to revivify the Irish language. Even if classes were held after normal school hours and instruction given free, he felt as school manager that he must uphold the wishes of the authorities, therefore he could not allow such a class to be started. Not to be daunted, Gerry next proposed that he be allowed to teach Irish dancing to the schoolchildren.

Dancing led to immorality! Father Devlin thundered. He had

enough trouble in the past trying to stamp it out. There would be no teaching of dancing, Irish or otherwise, in his parish!

Gerry had been prepared for him when he broached the subject of starting a hurling club. Surely the good Father could not object to that. The young men of the parish had nowhere to go to in the evenings and week-ends. There was only the pub, and did not drinking lead to immorality? Father Devlin had been hoist with his own petard. He had no choice but to give his consent, reluctantly. He had even considered accepting Gerry's offer of being club treasurer. It had amused Gallagher greatly when Gerry told him that Father Devlin had declined when he learned that he, Con Gallagher, was a member of the club.

Gallagher rose to his feet. Things had simmered down. The spectators and teams were now intermingled and there was a great deal of talking and laughing. This had been Carewstown's first game and Gerry had invited the Castlebar team for a friendly match. They had come down by train with about fifty of their supporters, men and women. The whole of Carewstown seemed to be here.

The Castlebar goalie approached Gallagher with a rueful smile on his face.

'Man, dear,' he said with a shake of the head, 'ye nearly killed me with that shot.' He said it without malice.

Gallagher smiled back at him. 'It wasn't intentional. I'm very raw like the rest of my team. But thanks for takin' it like a sportsman. I wish there were more like you.'

He nodded towards where Sonny O'Malley sat at the edge of the playing field, while Luke tended his cut head. Standing beside them, with her hand on Sonny's shoulder, was a tall plain-looking girl. Honor Costello, Phil Costello's daughter. She and Sonny were keeping company.

The goalie shrugged. 'Hurlin' is a rough game. If he can't accept a knock on the head, he'd better take up golf instead.'

Now that the match was over, there was a carnival atmosphere. Some of the Castlebar boys were taking a keen interest in the girls from Carewstown.

The goalie laughed. 'There will be a few marriages made here today, I'm thinkin',' and gave a low whistle of admiration. 'My God,' he exclaimed, 'what a beauty!' He pointed. 'Who is she?' he asked Gallagher.

Gallagher glowered. 'Una O'Malley.'

She stood a little distance away, surrounded by three admirers. One of them was a member of the Castlebar team. He stood very close to Una, his head inclined towards hers, talking and laughing. Now and then she would lift her head and smile into his face. He was a tall handsome lad with dark curly hair.

The goalie grinned. 'That's Stevie Jordan, one of our full-backs. Man, dear, but those other two are wastin' their time tryin' to compete with Stevie. A terror with the women, that lad is.'

Gallagher looked on with murder in his heart, but he held himself in check, swallowing his rage and when he heard Una O'Malley laugh at some remark, he turned on his heel and walked away. The goalie stared after him, surprised at his abrupt departure.

Both teams used the adjoining field for changing: a high hawthorn hedge provided privacy. Gallagher took off his jersey, togs and boots and began to put on his clothes. He stood apart from the others. He wanted to be alone. There was a sickly feeling in his stomach. More members of both teams came through the gap in the hedge. Gallagher tied his bootlaces. He stuffed his jersey, togs and boots into his old haversack, buckled it and thrust the hurley stick through the straps. When he stood up, Luke and Sonny O'Malley were only a few feet away from him. Sonny had a makeshift bandage tied around his head; he was still a little groggy on his feet.

'You look quite the wounded hero, Sonny,' Gallagher laughed. He wanted to vent his pent-up feelings of jealousy and frustration on someone. Sonny O'Malley was the perfect victim.

Sonny scowled at him. 'Go to hell, Gallagher!' he rasped. 'I'm in no mood for yer smart remarks.'

'Leave Sonny alone!' Luke snapped. Luke stood facing him, holding his shirt in his hands. He was naked to the waist. His taut muscular body was tanned deep brown by the sun.

'Still mollycoddlin' him, Luke?' Gallagher taunted. He was in the mood for a fight, but Luke just stood there, glaring.

Then he began to put on his shirt slowly. He put his head through the neckband and pushed his arms into the sleeves. The shirt was bunched up about his chest when someone shouted, 'Where are the O'Malley brothers?'

Luke turned around, pulling down the shirt as he did so.

Gerry Troy and three members of the Castlebar team came striding up towards them. Gallagher stiffened. One of them was Stevie Jordan. The four men formed a rough semi-circle in front of Luke and Sonny. Luke stared at them suspiciously.

'What do ye lot want?' he asked with hostility in his voice.

Gerry's laugh sounded forced. 'We're a delegation – a delegation of goodwill.'

One of the men stepped forward and extended a hand towards Sonny. 'No hard feelin's, I hope? I wouldn't like to go back to Castlebar and leave ye here thinkin' what I did was deliberate.'

By now a small crowd had gathered. Sonny seemed confused. He looked appealingly to Luke. Luke gave a curt nod.

'I suppose I'll have to take yer word for that,' Sonny grumbled and shook hands.

Gerry Troy gave a hearty laugh and slapped Sonny on the shoulder. 'That's the attitude to take, Sonny. Sure, what's a game of hurling without a smack on the head. It's all part of the game, so it is.' He turned round to the crowd. 'Well, what do you Castlebar boys think of the Carewstown team?' he shouted. 'Do you think we will be county champions some day?'

There were good-humoured cries of derision.

'Ah now lads,' Stevie Jordan shouted, 'let's be fair, let's be fair. We thought we would walk away with the game, but we won only by one goal and two points. And that's nothin' to boast about, considerin' we're the best team in the county and we were playin' against a bunch of inexperienced lads. A little more trainin' on their part, and they could trounce us the next time.'

Gerry took a step towards him. 'Then there will be a next time?' he asked eagerly. 'I'll put my lads through their paces and we could be ready for you on the first Sunday in September.'

'I'm willin' for one,' Stevie Jordan declared readily and turned round to the others. 'How about the rest of ye?' he cried.

There were roars of approval and someone shouted, 'Ye can be sure he's willin', Mr Troy, for when he comes down again it won't be just for the hurlin', aye, Stevie?'

Stevie Jordan grinned and wagged a finger. 'Now, now, Paddy, no tales out of school.'

Someone laughed, and said, 'It'll be for Una O'Malley.'

Stevie Jordan's face turned red. Everyone laughed at his embarrassment, but the laughter faded away as Luke O'Malley thrust his way through the crowd and confronted Stevie. His face was white with anger and one powerful fist was clenched.

'Is what he says true?' he demanded harshly.

Stevie was completely taken aback. His mouth fell open and his eyes went blank with confusion. He was speechless for several seconds, finally stammering, 'What . . . what do ye mean?'

'My sister's name has just been mentioned,' Luke said in a low, dangerous voice, 'and I get the impression that ye are interested. Am I right?'

Stevie Jordan looked as if he suspected his friends of having arranged all this as a practical joke, but the expression in Luke's eyes told him he was wrong. Sonny O'Malley went and stood beside Luke, scowling darkly at Stevie.

Stevie looked apprehensively from one brother to the other. He tried to affect an nonchalant manner. 'Well, what of it?' he asked lightly. 'She's not engaged to be married, is she? If not – '

'No, she's not engaged to be married,' Luke interrupted, 'and if ever she does, it won't be to someone like ye – an underpaid counter-jumper with the arse outa his britches!'

Angry blood rushed to Stevie Jordan's face; he began to choke and stutter with outrage. 'Who the bloody hell. . . ?'

Gerry Troy pushed his way in between them. He laid a hand on Luke's shoulder. 'Now, Luke, there's no need for this.'

Luke flung his hand away. 'Keep yer nose outa this, Troy!' he snapped. 'It's got nothin' to do with ye!'

Now that someone had come to his aid, Stevie Jordan became bolder. 'No one's goin' to tell me what I can and can't do!' he declared aggressively. 'The girl's of age. She knows her own mind. And if she likes me and I like her – '

Luke grabbed him by the collar of his jersey. He drew Stevie towards him until their faces almost touched.

'Now ye listen to me, townie,' he growled, 'ye're a stranger down here and ye may not be aware of a few things, so let me enlighten ye. It doesn't do to cross the O'Malleys – '

'And those that do,' Sonny butted in, 'live to regret it.'

Luke's grip tightened on the collar. 'So I'm warnin' ye,' he went on, 'stay away from Una. Because if ye don't, I'll cut that yellow hide of yours to ribbons with my whip! And this,' he added in a voice full of menace, 'is the first and last warnin' ye're ever goin' to get. Understand?'

No one spoke. If he cares about her, Gallagher told himself, he'll tell Luke to go to hell even if it means being battered into the ground by both of them. But Stevie Jordan did not say anything. His face was pale and his underlip quivered. Fear showed in his eyes.

'I'm waitin' for yer answer,' Luke said. 'Are ye goin' to stay away from Una?'

Stevie's eyes swivelled towards his team-mates as though expecting to see someone coming to his assistance. But no one moved; no one said anything. Gallagher sensed that quite a few of them envied his reputation as a Lothario; perhaps some of them had lost their girls to him. If that was the case, he could understand their satisfaction in witnessing his humiliation.

Luke did not relax his grip on Stevie's collar. He held it with his left hand and raised his clenched right fist threateningly.

'Answer me, yeh bastard!' he grated. 'Are ye goin' to stay away from Una?'

Stevie Jordan lowered his head and nodded dumbly. Luke released his hold and placing his fingertips against Stevie's chest, he pushed him away contemptuously.

Everyone watched Stevie Jordan as he walked slowly away, his head lowered. Then Sonny O'Malley gave a loud derisive guffaw and Stevie Jordan's shoulders twitched as though someone had laid a lash across them.

Gallagher shook his head. A little while ago he had been jealous of Stevie Jordan, now he felt sorry for him. News of what had happened would spread through Castlebar like wildfire. Stevie Jordan was finished, both as a man and as a lover; the vicious tittle-tattle of an Irish provincial town would see to that. Gallagher picked up his haversack. Walking away, he raised his hand in salute to Gerry Troy. Gerry was grim-faced.

Striding down the road towards Carewstown, Gallagher told himself that not only had the O'Malleys destroyed Stevie Jordan, they had destroyed the Carewstown hurling club as well. Word of what had happened would soon reach Father Devlin and he would make capital out of the incident to forbid all future matches, using the excuse that they were the cause of rowdiness.

'Damn the O'Malleys!' Gallagher snarled. 'Damn them to bloody hell! They've ruined everything!' He strode on, the haversack swinging from his shoulder. He had been the first to leave and he had the road to himself.

Nearing the village of Carewstown, he heard the sound of wheels. He looked behind him. A horse and trap were approaching. He knew it was the O'Malleys: everyone else from Carewstown had gone to the hurling match on foot.

Luke was holding the reins and Sonny was sitting beside him. Behind them, Una O'Malley and Honor Costello were sitting opposite to each other. Luke was keeping the horse at a gentle trot.

Gallagher stood at the side of the road and waited for them to pass.

This section of the road was dangerously narrow, only just wide enough for a horse-drawn vehicle. He waited patiently. When they were about six or seven yards away from him, he saw Luke reaching down beside him with his free hand. He brought up a hurley stick and, with full force, struck the horse's hindquarters with the flat of it. The horse broke into a wild gallop.

Gallagher dived sideways into the ditch behind him. His weight fell on the haversack hanging from his right shoulder and his hurley stick snapped in two. The ditch was shallow and his long legs stuck up over the edge; he felt the hub of the swiftly moving wheel scraping the sole of his boot. Above the clatter of wheels and hoofs he could hear Honor Costello screeching with laughter.

He scrambled furiously out of the ditch, one side of his face and jacket smeared with mud.

'You murderous bastard!' he roared as the trap disappeared in a cloud of dust down the road.

After Johnny had gone to bed, Gallagher sat staring moodily at the glowing embers of the turf fire, smoking cigarette after cigarette. Something disturbed him. He knew it had nothing to do with Luke trying to run him down; nor had it anything to do with Stevie Jordan's brief flirtation with Una O'Malley. It was something else – something he had seen or heard that had made an impression on his subconscious. It lay festering in some dark corner of his brain, giving him no peace. He knew he would not sleep feeling like this, so he started to go back over the events of the day, trying to jog his memory. Something was telling him that this disquietude of mind had originated when both teams had been changing.

Luke had been facing him while putting on his shirt. It was bunched up about his chest when Gerry Troy called out and Luke had turned around. . . .

Then Gallagher remembered and jumped to his feet knocking his chair backwards. He stood, trembling a little, seeing again the broad muscular back, the deeply tanned skin, the broad white scar running down between the shoulder-blades.

He walked into Johnny's room. It was dark, save for the small red-globed lamp burning beneath the picture of the Sacred Heart. Johnny was asleep, snoring contentedly. Gallagher sat down on the side of the bed and shook him awake.

'Wha. . . ?' Johnny mumbled sleepily. 'Is it time to get up already?' A little light filtered in from the other room. Gallagher could make out the outline of his head.

142

'No. Listen, Johnny.' Then he told him.

When he had finished, he waited for Johnny to say something, but Johnny did not utter a word. His long silence made Gallagher suspicious. He sensed that Johnny had known all along.

'Luke was one of the five who attacked me and burnt my house down that night ten years ago, wasn't he?' he asked harshly. 'He was the one I went for with the *sleán*.'

He remembered the pain of his bruised and battered body, the flames shooting up into the night sky and the masked men leaping and whooping in front of the burning house. His hands closed instinctively as though he was gripping a *sleán*. In his mind's eye he could see himself staggering towards the broad back of the man who was standing and cheering and clapping his hands as the flames shot up through the thatch. He raised the *sleán* and aimed at the space between the shoulder-blades.

Johnny's voice broke his reverie. 'Why are ye askin' me these things?'

'Because I need proof,' Gallagher answered. 'I want to know if Luke O'Malley was missin' for a long while after. I cut away the flesh from the back of a man that night, and it would have taken weeks for him to recover from an injury like that.'

'How the hell do I know if Luke was missin' or not!' Johnny replied exasperatingly. 'It's been ten years. I can't remember that far back.'

Something in his voice told Gallagher he was lying. 'Very well, Johnny,' he said quietly, 'I'll go to every pub in the village if I have to, till I find someone who can remember.'

Johnny was silent for a while. Then he said in a low voice, 'Luke was missin' for five or six weeks. I can't remember exactly for how long.'

'Where was he?'

'The county infirmary. The O'Malleys tried to keep it a secret. Said Luke had gone to England for a holiday. But one day a few years ago, big mouth Sonny let it slip out accidentally while we were workin' in the fields together. Then he got down on his knees and begged me to keep my mouth shut. Said his father and Luke would have his life if they ever found out he told. What are ye goin' to do?'

Gallagher's voice was hard. 'First I'm goin' to beat Luke to a pulp! Then I'm going to make him tell me who the other four were. And then I'm goin' to do the same to them, one by one!'

'Don't do it.'

'*Whaat?*'

'Don't do it. Forget Luke or the others ever did anythin' to ye. Just . . . just let sleepin' dogs lie.'

'For Christ's sake!' Gallagher exploded. 'Have you gone soft in the head? They put the torch to my house and half-killed me! I was forced to roam the roads of Scotland and England for ten years. And you're askin' me to forget!'

'Someone is goin' to get killed,' Johnny said. 'If ye must have yer revenge, then take Luke to court if ye have enough proof.'

'I don't want to have no truck with the law,' Gallagher growled. 'I'll settle this my own way. I just want to lay my hands on Luke.'

'Ye may try to beat up Luke, but as sure as God, he'll try to *kill* ye. He's that type. Ye found that out for yerself today when he tried to run ye down.'

Gallagher gave a disdainful snort. 'Luke is all piss and wind like his father and brother.'

'Don't fool yerself!' Johnny rapped. He gripped Gallagher's arms. 'Now ye listen to me,' and Gallagher could feel his sour breath against his face. 'A few years ago, tinkers who were passin' through here stole some of Bull O'Malley's poultry. Luke set out after them in the trap with Sonny and two labourers who were workin' for their father. They found the tinkers about three miles beyond the village. There were four of them. A young man and an old man and two women. They had a pot of water on the boil and the women were cleanin' out the birds when Luke and the others found them. Luke was carryin' that bull-whip of his. He ordered Sonny and the other two to take the old man and the women aside. Then he went for the young tinker man. He flogged him – flogged him to within an inch of his life. He would have killed him if Sonny and one of the labourers hadn't dragged him away. The tinker lost an eye.' He released his grip on Gallagher's arms and lay back.

'Are you tryin' to frighten me?' Gallagher asked with a trace of amusement in his voice. 'For if you are, you're wastin' your time. I can take Luke, whip and all.'

'I'm tryin' to tell ye what Luke is like,' Johnny answered peevishly. 'He's dangerous. There's somethin' wrong with that fella. There's somethin' in him that's eatin' him up with hate. Did ye ever look into those goat's eyes of his? Jesus!'

He was silent for a moment; then he said in a low deliberate voice, 'Con, forget what Luke and the others did and forget Una O'Malley, and on the day ye ask any other girl to marry ye, I'll transfer this house and this land to ye, legally. Bull O'Malley and Malachi Drennan have had their eyes on these five acres for years. But they'll never get them. They'll be yours if ye do what I'm askin'. And I'll never be in the way if

144

ye bring a woman here. Just build a small extension to this house and that'll be my home. I'll be happy and content as long as I'm not alone. What d'ye say?'

Gallagher released his breath in a long sigh. 'You're askin' an awful lot of me, Johnny,' he said.

'I know I am.'

Gallagher was silent for a while. He rose slowly from the side of the bed.

'I'll think about it,' he said.

He closed the door of Johnny's room and went into his own and undressed. But he could not sleep. He could feel hate flooding through him. He wanted to destroy the O'Malleys – to destroy them as they had destroyed him.

## III

'Dammit and double dammit!' Johnny Boyle exclaimed testily. 'If I have to stay in this bed any longer I'll be fit for the madhouse, so I will.' He sat propped up against the pillows; the plaster cast on his injured foot made a huge bulge in the bedclothes.

Gallagher was shaving in front of a small mirror affixed to the white-washed wall. He had placed the oil-lamp on a small table beside him to give himself light.

'I'll be here till Christmas,' Johnny moaned, 'stuck in this bloody bed.'

Gallagher finished shaving. He washed away the soap from his face, and cleaned the razor.

'It's your own pigheadedness that has you there,' he said. 'Why the hell didn't you wait and let me fix that gutter? Or why didn't you ask Luke or Sonny to do it?'

'Sure wasn't it Luke who told me to fix it,' Johnny retorted. 'Ye know how bossy he can be.'

'More fool you for obeyin' him,' Gallagher said. 'And the mornin' that was in it – cold with the frost an inch thick on the ground. No wonder the ladder slipped.'

He put the razor away, picked up the basin of sudsy water and walked to the back door. He pushed it open with his foot and tossed the

145

contents of the basin into the clump of bushes outside. He walked back and placed the empty basin on the washstand. He opened the small door lower down and took out a tin box and put it on the floor. Then he sat down on a stool and took off his boots. From the tin box he produced a tin of polish and a brush.

Johnny stared at him in mystification as he began to apply polish to the boots. 'Goin' out?' he asked.

'No.'

Gallagher took a rag from the box and started to rub his boots vigorously. His uncommunicativeness irritated Johnny.

'When ye've finished,' he said waspishly, 'ye can bring that lamp over beside me so I can read me book.'

Gallagher nodded. He put his boots and tied the laces, then stood up and picked up the lamp. He placed it on the chair beside the bed, alongside Johnny's book. Johnny reached for it. It was the only book in the house besides an old battered dictionary. Gallagher had found it in the bottom of his haversack. It was a dog-eared, musty-smelling western entitled *Wild Bill on the Vengeance Trail*. Johnny had read it twice and was now reading it again. There was a scarcity of books in Carewstown nowadays. The habit of reading had nearly died out in the district. The only ones who did read were the older people, and they had to be content with the weekly *Mayo Examiner*.

Johnny opened the book, found the place he had marked, and commenced to read in a voice a little above a whisper, 'It was approachin' sundown when the trail-weary stranger rode into Abilene. . .'

Gallagher walked into his own room and closed the door. The only thing that annoyed him about Johnny was his inability to read silently. He lit the oil-lamp and took from the shelf a bottle of hair-oil. He soaked his hair with it, wrinkling his nose at the heavy scent. He stood before the dressing table mirror, brushing his unruly red hair severely down across his skull. His own reflection repelled him. The coarse surly features, the heavy peasant jaw, the broken nose that twisted a little to one side. He turned away. He dried his hands and wound a red kerchief around his neck.

When he walked back into Johnny's room, Johnny raised his head a little, nose twitching. 'What's that peculiar bloody smell?' he asked. He looked questioningly at Gallagher, but Gallagher's eyes avoided him. Then Johnny noticed his glistening hair.

'Jesus, Mary and Joseph,' he gasped, 'what's that ye have in yer hair?'

'Hair-oil,' Gallagher replied, his face burning.

'Hair-oil!' Johnny echoed. 'Well, I'll be . . . And is the oul dropeen of water not good enough to keep that red thatch of yours plastered down over yer skull? Hair-oil no less!' He spat in disgust. 'Foulin' the air! Ye have the place smellin' like a kip-house!'

Gallagher turned away, annoyed. Taking the broom lying against the wall, he began to sweep the earthen floor. Little clouds of dust flew up under his vigorous strokes.

Johnny stared at him open-mouthed. 'What in the name of God are ye doin'?' he asked in amazement.

'What does it look like I'm doin'?' Gallagher answered shortly. 'The place needs tidyin'.'

'Begob it does not, then,' Johnny shouted. 'It suits me well enough as it is. Agh!' He swept a protective arm up across his face. 'Will ye give over yer bloody sweepin',' he spluttered. 'Ye have me nearly suffocated with the hurin' dust!'

Gallagher swept the dust into a corner, then turned and faced him. Johnny glared. 'Are ye gone mad or what?' he shouted. 'Dollin' yerself up like a Fancy Dan at this hour of the night. Sweepin' the floor – '

'You're goin' to have company,' Gallagher interrupted.

Johnny ceased his tirade, and raised his eyebrows inquiringly. 'Am I, faith. And who's callin'?'

Gallagher hesitated for several seconds, before answering. 'Una O'Malley said she would call to see how you are.'

Johnny's malicious grin revealed his few remaining teeth. 'Oho,' he crowed, 'so that's the reason for yer funny behaviour. No wonder yer done up to the nines. I was wonderin' – '

There was a gentle tap on the window-pane.

'Come in, girla,' Johnny called, 'come in and welcome!'

Gallagher put the broom hastily aside. 'I'll leave you and Lady Muck alone together,' he whispered 'I'm goin' to my own room.'

'Don't be so ill-mannered!' Johnny exclaimed reproachfully.

'It's you she wants to see, not me,' Gallagher retorted, striding out. He closed the door of his own room, sat down on a chair and lit a cigarette.

He was smoking his fourth three-quarters of an hour later when he heard Johnny calling him. He rose reluctantly from his chair, stubbing out his cigarette.

He entered Johnny's room just as Una O'Malley was rising from Johnny's beside chair. The oil-lamp had been put back to its original position on the sideboard. She did not turn her head as he entered the room, but kept her gaze fixed on Johnny's face. Johnny had some parcels in his lap; his face was a little flushed.

'What do ye think of this, Con?' he cried. 'Here's this girl sayin' she's goin' to walk all the way home by herself and insistin' that she will be perfectly safe. Did ye ever hear the like! And a tribe of drunken tinkers camped in that boreen near Kinsella's field.' He looked up at Una O'Malley with an expression of indignation. 'Is it barbarians ye think we are, girl, that we would let ye go home unescorted. And ye after comin' all this way just to see how I was keepin' and bringin' me books to read and a freshly baked apple tart. Boys oh boys.' He smacked his lips. 'There's nothin' I like better than Mrs O'Malley's apple tarts.'

Una laughed. She put a blue woollen scarf on her head, crossed it under her chin and draped an end over each shoulder. Johnny reached for her hand and grasped it.

'Thank ye for comin' to see me, Una,' he said earnestly. 'Yer presence is like a ray of sunshine.'

She smiled at him. 'It won't be long until you are on your feet again, Johnny,' she said. 'Then the two of us will do the two-handed reel at Sonny's engagement party.'

Johnny put on a mournful face. 'Ah girla,' he sighed, shaking his head, 'me dancin' days are over for a good long time to come. Ye'll have to find someone else to dance with.'

She withdrew her hand from his, and laid it lightly on his shoulder.

'Never mind, Johnny. There will be other times.'

Johnny's face brightened. 'Indeed there will be, girla. Sure, I'll dance at yer weddin'.'

Gallagher turned away and walked out of the room. He went into his own room and put on his jacket. He had left the door open and he could hear Una saying good-bye to Johnny. He lit a cigarette and then put the packet and the matches in his pocket. He loitered deliberately for several minutes before walking out.

Una was waiting patiently for him outside the house. They walked in silence up the narrow rutted track towards the Westport road. When they reached it, they turned right and walked eastwards towards the crossroads. It had been a cloudy, rain-troubled day, but now the night sky was clear and a new moon had risen. It was bright enough to read by.

The village began at the northern side of the crossroads. A row of whitewashed cottages gave way to solid two-storey houses, shops and pubs. The tall spire of the Protestant church on the northern outskirts dominated the village. The more humble Catholic one lay hidden in a sunken cul-de-sac west of the village street.

148

They turned their backs on the village and walked southwards down the road towards the O'Malley farm, a mile and a half away. They kept to the left of the road, in the shadow of the long, high stone wall of the Carewscourt demesne. Neither of them had said anything since leaving Johnny's house.

Gallagher could feel sweat breaking out on his forehead. This was the first time he had ever been alone with Una O'Malley and he could think of nothing to say. For God's sake, he told himself, say something – anything.

'So . . . Sonny is gettin' engaged.'

'Yes.'

'Honor Costello?'

'Of course.'

Now that he had broken the silence, he hoped she would talk, but she did not. She continued to walk along quietly by his side. He lit a cigarette, feeling that she was enjoying his discomfort.

'When will the weddin' be?' he asked.

'A year's time – maybe longer. The house will have to be built first.'

'Oh, and where will that be?'

'Where the ruins of the old Workhouse now stand. Sonny has some men clearing away the rubble.'

'But . . .' he turned his head to her in surprise, 'that's Phil Costello's land.'

'It will be Sonny's when he marries. It's Honor Costello's dowry.'

Gallagher emitted a low whistle. Phil Costello had only two children to leave his one hundred rich acres to: his daughters, Honor and Stacia.

He gave a bitter laugh. 'Faith then, I think I'll use me charms on Stacia Costello. It would be worth me while.'

'Then you'll have to move fast,' Una O'Malley said, and he could detect a note of amusement in her voice, 'for Luke has his eye on her.'

So that's it, Gallagher thought. What Johnny had said was true. Bull O'Malley was forcing his two sons into marriage with the two Costello sisters in order to gain the Costello acres. In years to come, all this part of east Mayo would belong to Bull O'Malley and his sons. There was certainly no love involved. If Honor Costello was plain, her sister was downright ugly.

They walked past the entrance of a boreen, the left side of which was the boundary wall of the demesne. The road stretched away before them between high, wild hedges. Gallagher could feel the hate he had for the O'Malleys stirring inside him like a sickness.

'I suppose,' he said sneeringly, 'Luke was captivated by Stacia

149

Costello's good looks.' He tossed away the cigarette with an angry gesture. 'Jesus Christ!' he exclaimed contemptuously, 'you O'Malleys would sell your souls for a few acres of cutaway bog!'

Una O'Malley came to an abrupt halt. She turned towards him as he came to a standstill: her face was a white blur in the shadow of the hedge.

Her voice trembled. 'How dare you! How dare you say such a thing about my family? You . . . you . . . foul-mouthed lout! You insolent, arrogant nobody!'

Her words inflamed him. 'An arrogant nobody, am I?' he snarled, taking a step towards her.

She stood defiantly, arms by her side, small hands clenched. He towered over her, fuming with rage.

'And what are the O'Malleys?' he spat. 'What are they, aye? By Christ, I'll tell you! Scum! The scruff of the ditches! Landgrabbers! Your father is pushin' your step-brothers into marriage with the two ugliest women in Mayo just for the land that goes with them. Aye, by God – and it won't be long before he sells *you* to the highest bidder!'

She slapped his face. Before she could withdraw her hand he grabbed her wrist and held it, lowering his face to hers. His voice was low and harsh.

'There's a local wealthy farmer who goes to a certain pub in the village at week-ends and drinks into the early hours. When he's in his cups, he likes to boast to anyone who will listen about how he's goin' to have Una O'Malley for a wife in exchange for seventy acres of his best.'

'Liar!'

'A widower who wants a young woman for a wife so that she can give him the children he never had. A man who wants heirs of his own blood to inherit his land and wealth.'

'You slanderous, filthy-minded cur!'

'A man old enough to be your father!'

'Enough! Let go of me!'

'I'll put a name to him – Malachi Drennan.'

She began to struggle then, trying to release herself from his grip, panting from her exertions. But he held her firmly by the wrist with no difficulty. When she started to pound his chest with her free hand, he grabbed that wrist too. Powerless, she suddenly burst into tears.

'Luke and Sonny will kill you for this,' she sobbed.

He pulled her roughly towards him and crushed his mouth down on hers. Taken completely by surprise, she offered no resistance. When he drew back his head he released his hold on her wrists at the same time.

150

She staggered back a few steps, and stood, shocked, breathless, her hand covering her bruised lips. She remained like that for a moment, then took her hand away.

'You animal,' she whispered hoarsely, 'you loathsome animal.'

'Now you can run home and tell them I molested you and tried to make love to you. Tell them if they want to do somethin' about it, to come tonight. Tell them to bring tins of paraffin as they did the last time. Your father and your step-brothers have had their eyes on Johnny's land for years, now this is the only way they are goin' to get it – by burnin' the house down and drivin' the two of us out of the district. And they'll have Father Devlin's support when he hears what I did to you. He too will be glad to see me gone. So tell them to come – and tell Luke and Sonny they won't have to wear hoods over their heads this time!'

Una O'Malley stod motionless and silent. After a while she spoke, her voice weak and bewildered. 'What are you talking about? I don't understand a word. What has Johnny got to do with it?'

'He holds land your family wants. They know he will never sell. They also know that he intends to give it to me. So the only thing they can do is wait for an opportunity to get rid of us both. *Now* they have the opportunity – they'll never have a better one. Go home and tell them how I nearly violated you. But when they come this time, they won't catch me unprepared!'

Her voice was incredulous. 'You're mad! My family would never do anything like that. Not to you, not to Johnny, anyone . . .'

Of course, he told himself, they would have hidden everything from her – the baby of the family. They would have drawn a veil between her and all that was mean and sordid about themselves. Now he began to rip that veil ruthlessly away, telling her all that had happened that night ten years ago without omitting a single brutal detail. When he had finished, she was stunned with horror.

'You've no proof it was Luke or Sonny!' Her voice was shrill.

'No proof!' Gallagher gave a sarcastic bark of a laugh. 'Luke has a wide scar runnin' down his back from the wound I gave him. He spent nearly six weeks in the county infirmary while your father told everyone he was away in England. Why did he lie?'

'I don't believe you.'

'Ask Johnny. Sonny let that piece of information slip out accidentally.'

He could sense her dismay; nevertheless her voice was bold and challenging.

'If you are so sure Luke and Sonny are guilty, why have you not accused them to their faces? You're vociferous enough with your accusations in my presence, yet you work alongside them every day without opening your mouth. Why? Is it because you're not absolutely sure that they are the guilty ones? Or is it because. . . ?'

She did not finish the sentence, but the implication was clear enough: her voice was tinged with contempt.

'You think I'm afraid, don't you?' he retorted angrily. 'Well, maybe I am. I'm afraid of what I might do if either of them says anything that might provoke me! In the past I used to jeer at them; now I keep silent and try to avoid them.'

'Why not avoid them altogether by not working for my father?' she responded tartly.

'Because I need the money, that's why!' he answered hotly. He twisted his mouth into a sneer. 'That's somethin' a spoiled brat like you would never understand!'

He expected her to say something, but she was silent. 'I will be leavin' your father,' he went on, 'when I have enough money saved. Then I will be gettin' my own place. Johnny made a bargain with me. "If you want to live in peace in Carewstown for the remainder of your life," he told me, "then forget what the O'Malleys did to you." '

'Johnny has a head of sense on his shoulders.'

' "Pick a girl of your own class," he said, "and on the day you ask her to marry you, I'll transfer this house and this land to you." '

'Johnny was always the generous man.'

' "And forget Una O'Malley," was his advice, "she's not for you. When she marries, it will be for land and wealth and not for love!" '

He could hear her sudden sharp intake of breath; it sounded like a stifled cry of pain. 'Oh no, no!' She shook her head. 'Johnny would never say a thing like that about me. He would never say such a cruel thing. Never!'

Her voice broke and she clapped her hands to her face.

Gallagher could feel the venom draining out of him as he looked down at her, watching the slender shoulders heaving, listening to the muffled sobs. He felt pity then. Her step-brothers, particularly Luke, stood in the way of any man coming near her. She was being isolated and preserved, but for whom? She was paddocked like a prize mare until the highest bidder in the shape of Malachi Drennan came along.

Instinctively he reached out and grasped her shoulders with both hands.

'Stop it, now, stop it,' he ordered gruffly. 'I'm sorry.' He paused,

152

then said, lying to stop her crying, 'You're right, Johnny never said that.'

Her sobs slowly ceased. He took his hands away from her shoulders, and she lowered her hands from her face. He stood shame-faced before her, watching her dabbing at her eyes with the tiny handkerchief she had taken from her pocket.

She sniffled a little. 'Why do you invent and say such horrible things? Why?' she whispered hoarsely.

He shrugged his shoulders. 'I don't know.' His voice was low; all the anger had gone out of him. 'I suppose it's because I've bottled up all my hate, all my jealousy and frustration. Then something happens and I lose my head and it all comes out and I hurt someone.'

'Jealousy. Frustration,' she said in a puzzled voice. 'I don't understand.'

He gave a weary sigh. What was the use of hiding anything any longer? Let her mock if she wanted to after he told her. 'I think it was *you* I wanted to hurt more than Luke and Sonny. I wanted to hurt you and degrade you because. . . .' He hesitated. 'Because I love you and I know I can never have you.'

He could not go on. He had always envied the man who could talk with ease to a woman about his intimate feelings for her; he could never do it. He was glad he could not see her face clearly in the moonlit darkness. He waited now for her sardonic laugh.

She stood still for a moment with her head bowed, then turned and walked away without saying a word. He followed her and they walked side by side down the road in silence. Nearing the O'Malley farm, she turned and faced him.

'Don't come any further with me,' she said. 'I don't want my father or my step-brothers to see us together.'

Any other time he would have been angry; now he accepted what she said with an indifferent shrug. 'All right. I understand.'

'It's necessary that you do understand,' she said. She took a step towards him and placed her hand on his arm. The familiar gesture surprised and amazed him.

She looked up into his astonished face and said in a low matter-of-fact voice, 'If we are to become lovers, we shall have to keep it a secret. No one must know – especially my father and Luke and Sonny. If they should ever find out . . .' She dug her nails into the flesh of his arm. He was stunned and speechless.

She gave a little groan of exasperation. 'Oh God – I'm trying to tell you I love you and all you can do is stand there like a statue.'

153

But when he tried to take her in his arms she pushed him away gently.

'Is it just teasin' me you are, Una O'Malley?' he growled.

'You told me you would be getting your own place when you had enough money saved. You told me that Johnny would give you his house and land on the day you asked a girl to marry you. Have you a girl?'

He shook his head. 'No,' he said, and added bitterly, 'What girl would have me with a face like this?'

'I would.'

She raised herself standing on her toes, and kissed him. Then she was gone into the darkness, swiftly and silently like a phantom, leaving him flabbergasted in the centre of the road.

# Chapter Five

## I

Carew lay on the bed in his pyjamas reading the newspaper. His eyes roamed over the small type indifferently. The paper was four days' old. It took that length of time for *The Times* to reach Carewscourt from London, where it was posted every morning. His Uncle Walter declared that *The Times* was his only link with civilisation. In spite of the fact that the Carews had been in Ireland since the middle of the seventeenth century, he still regarded himself as an expatriate living among a semi-barbarous people in a semi-barbarous land.

Carew folded the paper and put it down on the cluttered tray beside him. Every morning at eight-thirty, a servant girl woke him and gave him breakfast on a tray. Breakfast in bed, he mused; Uncle Walter and Aunt Emily are spoiling me.

He lit a cigarette. He drew long and hard on it, before exhaling slowly, watching the faint blue tobacco smoke coiling lazily up towards the damp-stained ceiling. It was going to be another long, hot, tedious day with nothing to do. He was bored – utterly and completely.

He gave a slight sardonic grunt, remembering how excited he had been in that railway carriage on his way to Carewscourt. It had been raining heavily – and it was to go on raining heavily for another nine days. At first it had not mattered that the rain prevented him from going outdoors; there was so much to talk about between himself and Uncle Walter; they had not seen each other for twelve years. But after a few days, with no sign of the weather clearing, he began to feel like a prisoner. There was nothing to do but read, but it was impossible to read for long with Aunt Emily prowling about. She was always seeking him out for one of her little chats. She had been very lonely before he arrived, with no one to talk to but her brother, Walter, and he was the most taciturn of men. The only other occupants of Carewscourt were the cook, Mrs Joyce, and two maid-servants, and they kept strictly to themselves below stairs.

After those first few chats with his Aunt Emily, Alec soon realised that she was slightly senile. During the course of a conversation, her voice would slowly fade away, and she would lapse into silence, staring away from him with blank eyes, a wistful smile on her face. She would remain like that for a while, lost in her own little world, completely unaware of his presence. She was apt to confuse the past with the present, talking of events that had happened forty or fifty years ago as though they had happened only the day before. Even though his father had been dead for twenty years, she talked about him as if he were still alive. She was a small, frail old lady in her late seventies with remarkably clear, unwrinkled skin and wide blue eyes. She had lost all sense of time; she still dressed in the fashions of the late 1880s.

As for Uncle Walter . . . Alec heaved a sigh. After the excitement caused by his arrival had died down, Walter Carew had retired to the library. There behind locked doors, surrounded by old crinkly documents, title deeds and maps of the estate, he had resumed his writing of the history of the Carew family from the time of Richard Carew's arrival in Ireland with Cromwell's army. He had been working on it for more than ten years. The work occupied every waking hour of his day. It had become an obsession; he was terrified he might die before he could complete it.

The ancient grandfather clock in the corner chimed ten times. Carew yawned and stretched. The cigarette had burned away between his fingers and he dropped it hastily into a cup on the tray beside him. It hissed out in the dregs of tea. Carew felt a sudden spurt of irritation. Christ! he thought, I'm becoming more like an Irish peasant every day. Lazy – slovenly in my habits.

He swung himself off the bed and took off his pyjamas. Naked, he walked across to the washstand. He poured water from the china jug into the basin. He had become used to washing and shaving in cold water. There was no piped water in Carewscourt. Barrels of drinking water were delivered from the village once a week. A few dilapidated rainwater tanks at the back of the house supplied other needs. On his arrival, he had asked for hot water to be brought up to his room at nine sharp the next morning, but the sight of one of the young servant girls struggling up the stairs from the kitchen with the huge kettle of boiling water had made him feel so guilty and ashamed he had not asked again.

He dried himself, opened the door of the large mahogany wardrobe and took out his clothes. He examined them carefully for signs of mildew before putting them on. The whole place reeked of damp. The top floor directly overhead had been abandoned for years. The roof was in an appalling state and the supporting beams were rotten. He had overheard his uncle warning the two maid-servants not to go up there because it was too dangerous. The warning was unnecessary. Neither the cook or the two girls would go anywhere near the top floor; that part of the house was reputed to be haunted.

Alec descended the broad staircase slowly. His ancestors stared at him from their portraits on the wall. Soldiers, churchmen, squires. The soldiers predominated. Carews in lace collars and bucket boots; in Ramillies wigs and steel breastplates. The uniforms were different but the faces were the same: narrow and stern with a hint of cruelty in the eyes. The exceptions were his father and his Uncle Julian.

He paused before the portrait of his father. The face smiled benignly at him. No sign of the Carew hardness there, he thought, only the softness of the Hammonds. The face was round and smooth, almost effeminate. As the eldest he had inherited the estate on the death of his father, but he had relinquished it to his brother Julian, the second elder. Henry Carew had chosen the Church as some of his forebears had done. Not for him the life of a squire; not for him rain-swept, windswept Mayo with its barren mountains and bogs. For him the small, ancient Saxon church of Clayton, nestling at the foot of the Sussex Downs. There he had been content.

Alec moved down two steps and stood. He was always impressed by the striking resemblance between his Uncle Julian and his father. There was a difference of course; he could see it in the eyes. The lips were full and sensual; the face flabby with a look of self-indulgence about it. He too had abandoned Mayo, leaving an agent to manage the estate and collect the rents. He had lived the life of a roué in the fleshpots of London and Paris, squandering the Carew fortune in gaming saloons and on an army of mistresses. He died, burnt out by his excesses, at the early age of forty-four. His younger brother, Walter, inherited a bankrupt estate.

There was a noticeable gap between that and the next portrait. Walter Carew had placed the painting of himself further down, dissociating himself from his weaker, lecherous, spendthrift brother. A taciturn man, he had no other way of expressing his hatred and contempt for the man who had brought disgrace to the family and ruin to his beloved Carewscourt. He stared out at the world, arrogant and proud, helmet under his arm, resplendently handsome in his Dragoon officers' uniform. He had posed for that portrait at the age of twenty-two; a year later he was in the Crimea. Carew felt a twinge of envy. His uncle had participated in one of the most epic cavalry actions in modern

157

history – Scarlett's Charge of the Heavy Brigade at Balaclava. Three hundred, he thought with pride, against four thousand. Hopelessly outnumbered, they had charged up that slope, cutting and slashing their way through the serried ranks of Russian cavalry, forcing them back, back . . .

He shook his head in wonder, and walked down the stairs to the hall, and out into the bright morning sunlight.

He stood at the top of a long flight of wide stone steps. His Uncle Walter was seated at a table at the foot of them, writing away. He wore a heavy buff-coloured cardigan and on his head was a wide-brimmed straw hat. Carew gave a little groan of exasperation. He marched down the steps.

His uncle turned stiffly round in the chair. 'Good morning, my boy.'

'Good morning, sir.'

Walter turned back to the ledger, writing slowly and carefully in his beautiful copperplate script.

Alec sat down on a step and lit a cigarette. Carewscourt stood on the only elevated ground for miles around. The ground fell gently away before him. He could see over the tops of the trees of the demense; over bog and river and plain to the distant Partry mountains.

'Wisps of smoke out there on the bog.'

'Breakfast fires,' his uncle explained without lifting his head. 'They've been cutting turf since daybreak, making the most of the good weather.'

'Must be like a swamp after all the heavy rain we've had. Treacherous, barren place, a bog.'

Walter Carew raised his head and stared at the grey tendrils of smoke climbing up from the brown barren waste. 'Yes,' he murmured, lowering his head and continuing to write. 'And yet,' he said, 'I had a tenant who reclaimed a good part of it. Made it fertile. Best tenant I ever had. Not one of the yahoos from around here. Donegal man. Gallagher by name.'

'What happened to him?' Carew asked without interest.

'Oh, he died. Son took over. Then some hooligans burnt the house down and ran him out of the district. Never did find out what they had against him.'

Carew stared at the view, trying to imagine what it had looked like in Richard Carew's time. The river in the distance had been the western boundary of the Cromwellian plantation. The defeated Irish had been banished to the territory beyond it, then a vast tract of wild forest, bog and poor infertile soil. The hill on which Carewscourt stood was the frontier, the edge of the wilderness.

158

He remembered the old map in the library, said to have been drawn by Richard Carew himself. Beyond the river had been a forest, one of the great primeval oak forests of ancient Ireland. In there had lurked the defeated and the dispossessed, with hatred in their hearts, their gaze uplifted towards the distant hill where the walls of Carewscourt rose higher and higher with each passing day. Forays had been made at night; scaffolding had been torn down and a few workers employed in building Carewscourt had been killed. Richard Carew had to keep sentries armed with matchlocks on watch day and night.

Years later, long after Carewscourt had been built and with an uneasy peace prevailing, Richard's two sons, beardless lads in their mid-teens, crossed the bog and river and entered the forest. When they did not return that night, Richard led a search party for them at first light the following morning. At dusk they found them. Their throats had been slashed open and their bodies stripped naked.

Alec knew the story well. It had been told to him many years ago when he was a boy, shortly after he had arrived in Carewscourt. The man who told it, an old groom on the estate, was a traditional story-teller. He had used words and gestures to their best effect, creating a vivid picture of what had happened more than two hundred years before.

He told of how Richard Carew and a band of twenty armed men had ridden into Irish territory, searching for the murderers. They found them a few days later, taking refuge in a small village of thatched mud-walled cabins at the foot of the Partry mountains. There were four of them; they had shared the dead youths' clothing between them. One of them was an old man. He was an O'Conor and a direct descendant of the last High King of Ireland. Once he had been chieftain over the lands which had been rewarded to Richard Carew for his services to Oliver Cromwell.

A racing mountain stream ran through the centre of the village. The four men were forced to kneel at the edge of it with their hands bound tightly behind them. Then, as the whole village looked on, Richard Carew drew his sword and decapitated them one by one. The old chieftain was the last. He died cursing the Carews, seed, breed and generation.

As punishment for having harboured the killers of his sons, Richard had the village crops destroyed and the livestock slaughtered. Then his men put a torch to the thatch roof of every cabin before they rode away. That was in early November. By spring of the following year, two-thirds of the village had died from exposure and hunger.

From that time, they called Richard Carew 'The Exterminator'. He had the great oak forest beyond the river cut down, ensuring that never again would it provide shelter for outlaw or wolf. The clearance made Richard a very rich man. Timber was urgently needed in England for ship building, house construction, charcoal . . . Richard's fellow colonists, well aware of the enormous profits to be made from timber, did as he had done. By the beginning of the eighteenth century they had stripped Ireland bare of her forests.

A piece of verse he had heard long ago came drifting back to Carew; the lament of some long dead, long forgotten Irish poet surveying his ravaged country.

> But now the woods are falling,
> Other lands are calling
> And John O'Dwyer of the Glen!
> You're worsted in the game.
>
> Now I'm lonely, roofless,
> Since all the hills are woodless;
> The north wind stings me bloodless
> And death spreads in the sky . . .

Charlotte, Richard Carew's wife, became a recluse after her two sons had been murdered. She confined herself to the upper part of the house, severing all contact with her husband and the other members of the household. By day she remained behind locked doors in the room near the north wing which her two sons had shared. Food was left outside the door. At night she emerged, wandering the corridors of the upper floor, a lighted candle in her hand, wailing her grief.

Carew glanced at the open ledger on the table. 'In that history you are writing,' he said offhandedly, 'do you mention the old legend about Charlotte? The servants used to say that she only cries when a Carew is about to die. You know, like the banshee.'

Walter Carew slowly raised himself upright in the chair and stared stonily at him for a full ten seconds without uttering a word. Then he turned away and reached for his pen.

'You'll forgive me if I terminate this conversation,' he said in a vexed voice. 'Time is precious, and I don't intend to waste any more of it by listening to your nonsense!'

Carew sat forward and rested his elbows on his knees. Let him be, he told himself; irascibility is a symptom of old age. The sun was high in the sky now and he could feel the heat of it on his head and shoulders. It

160

was going to be another long, hot, boring day. Away below, a tall figure moved slowly through the trees of the demesne. Tim Skerritt. The Skerritts had been stewards of Carewscourt for generations.

Tim Skerritt emerged from the trees on to the gravel drive. Carew watched him as he walked towards the gate-lodge. Why, he wondered, am I always ill at ease when I'm with Skerritt? Perhaps it was the evasive eyes; perhaps it was the permanent sly grin on the long narrow face which gave the impression that Skerritt was always secretly laughing at him. There was even a hint of mockery in the way he tugged deferentially at his forelock whenever he encountered him.

'A soft day, Master Carew.'

Carew grunted. *Master* Carew. Even after all those years, he thought, it's still Master Carew.

Tim Skerritt had been his playmate. When he had first arrived at the then strange, adult world of Carewscourt, he had been delighted to find another boy of his own age living on the estate. They had played together among the trees of the demesne. *The Last of the Mohicans* had been his favourite book at the time; he had insisted on being Hawkeye and Tim Skerritt on being the treacherous Indian, Magua. And he had looked and behaved like a wild Indian, Carew thought with a feeling of wonder. Tall and skinny in his ragged clothes, his skin tanned a deep brown by the sun, stealing from tree to tree in his bare feet. Tim Skerritt had taught him how to catch a trout with his bare hands; had taught him how to light a fire in the open without the aid of matches or flint. He had also taught him songs which, Carew discovered afterwards, were seditious.

> They come, they come, see myriads come
> Of Frenchmen to relieve us.
> Seize, seize the pike, beat, beat the drum
> They come, my friends, to save us.

Only a week ago, a drunk in the village had been arrested for singing that song. Carew smiled wryly to himself. Obviously the spirit of rebellion was still alive in Mayo – and the fear of it, considering the over-reaction of the police constable. But then, as he remembered the constant requests for information from London, the same fear was shared by the chiefs of Intelligence in Whitehall. Whichever foreign power captured Ireland held a pistol aimed at Britain's heart. It would be a mad gamble of course, to launch an invasion from a European port and hope to evade the British fleet. But the French had done it. In the autumn of 1798, three frigates carrying more than a thousand soldiers had sailed into Killala Bay. The French quickly took the town of Killala and made it their headquarters. Irish peasants from all over Connacht rushed to join them. A few days later, the French general, Humbert, marched south and smashed and scattered the vastly superior British force under General Lake at Castlebar. It was said that the British cavalry, in their mad haste to get away, rode over their own infantry in the narrow streets of the town.

Alec turned his head. Walter Carew was hunched over the ledger, writing away. It was all there, faithfully recorded in his uncle's stiff and formal style. He had borrowed the ledger one night and read how a member of the Longford militia came galloping up on a foam-flecked horse to the doors of Carewscourt, yelling that the French and Irish had scattered Lake's army to the four winds and that they were coming south and for everyone to flee, flee, flee if they valued their lives. . . .

Panic then. The entire household running hither and thither, gathering belongings; women screaming . . .

His great-grandfather, Nigel Carew, a widower with one child, a lad of sixteen, had remained cool and calm. He was in command of the local corps of yeomanry and quickly gathered about ten of them for the defence of Carewscourt. The rest of his men fled with the servants and the local gentry.

Then they waited. Day after day, they watched the north road with muskets at the ready, expecting to see columns of blue-uniformed men marching towards them, but they never came. Word eventually reached Nigel Carew and his men that the French and their Irish allies had marched eastwards towards the midlands. Two weeks later, at a place called Ballinamuck, the small French army surrendered after a short battle against a numerically superior British force and were taken prisoner.

The Irish rebels were butchered without mercy. Some escaped the massacre and tried to make their way back to their own districts. Among them were four of Nigel Carew's tenants. When Nigel learned of their whereabouts, he began to hunt them down with the aid of his yeomen. Some of the local gentry and squireens, who had returned now that the danger was over, joined in the fun.

'This is better than fox-hunting!' one of them laughed as he mounted his horse.

One by one, the rebels were captured. Three of them were hung. The fourth managed to elude his pursuers by escaping into a bog where no horse could follow. Nigel Carew and his men followed on foot. With them was Nigel's sixteen-year-old son, Roderick. A local man had been bullied into guiding them through the treacherous, quaking waste.

After two days they found him, an exhausted scarecrow of a figure hardly able to stand. They stopped a short distance away from him and stood, undecided as to what to do: there was no tree in the desolate barren bog from which to hang him. Then Nigel Carew drew his sabre and thrust it into the hand of his youthful son and pushed him forward.

That night in the huge draughty dining room of Carewscourt, with the flickering candlelight and a roaring log fire throwing dancing shadows on the walls and ceiling, Nigel Carew and his friends celebrated drunkenly and uproariously. At the head of the table sat Roderick Carew, pale-faced and quiet. Outside a storm raged; rain lashed against the windows. Nigel Carew staggered to his feet, face flushed from too much claret, and raised his glass in a toast to his son.

'I have blooded my son!' he cried. 'I have fleshed my bloodhound!'

Uncle Walter heaved a sigh and slumped back in the chair, his hand covering his eyes.

Alec looked at him with concern. 'Is anything the matter?'

'Just a touch of dizziness. I'll be fine in a few minutes.'

'You're overdoing it, you know.'

'I know,' Walter admitted in a weary voice. 'I've been working here since early morning.'

'Leave it be for today,' Alec advised.

'I could be dead before tomorrow,' Uncle Walter answered abruptly, taking his hand away from his eyes. 'No, I'll keep on at it. You see, I've nearly completed it. Another page or two, and it's finished.'

'Really?' Alec gave a delighted laugh. 'Why, that's wonderful!' Uncle Walter gave an ironical grunt. 'Is it? I'm not so sure. Writing this damn history has kept me alive for more than ten years. Now that it's finished . . .' He gave a helpless gesture with his hand and lapsed into silence.

Alec leaned back and tilted his head. A dark speck marred the faultless blue of the sky. He screwed up his eyes against the glare. A hawk hovered. Suddenly it swooped down towards something in the bog and vanished from sight.

After a little while, Walter said, 'Tell me, have you ever thought of marrying again?'

The question took Alec by surprise. 'I must confess I haven't given it much thought.'

'You should, you know. You're not getting any younger. How old are you now?'

'Thirty-two.' His uncle had mentioned every Anglo-Irish family in the district, hoping, he suspected, that he would meet some girl and take a fancy to her. He had met a few he had liked, but they all had lacked something, he thought; some mysterious quality which Miriam Durkin alone possessed. Although he had only met her briefly, he did not want to meet any more girls. He was tired of making comparisons. Miriam was a part of him now; he was unable to put her out of his mind. He asked himself, I wonder what this old warrior's reaction would be if I told him I had fallen in love with a married woman? Undoubtedly it would be one of shock and horror.

'Look here, my boy . . .' Uncle Walter turned stiffly towards him. 'Don't think I'm trying to interfere in your personal life but . . .' He paused, chewing on his underlip, embarrassed. 'The fact is,' he went on, 'there are only a few years remaining for your Aunt Emily and myself. And when we are gone, all this . . .' he waved his hand 'all this will be yours.' He sat back in his chair. 'You are the last, Alec,' he said, 'the last of the Carews. I want you to marry; I want you to have sons; I want them to inherit Carewscourt. 'Sometimes,' he went on in a low voice, 'I lie awake at night thinking of what would happen to this place if you should die without issue.' He wagged his head slowly from side to side. 'You have no idea, no conception of what it's like here in Mayo. They're land hungry – they fight like hungry dogs over a few miserable acres. Things have changed. It's not like the old days.'

He stirred slightly in his chair, agitated. 'Damn Gladstone! Damn the Liberals!' His voice shook with anger. 'I knew what was going to happen more than twenty years ago. I could see all this coming. And now this damned Wyndham Act . . . God! That I should live to see the day when a British government would do this to us. Don't they know – don't they realise? Allowing the Irish peasants to buy land – did the government think they would be satisfied with just that? Now look at what is happening. Now they are demanding Home Rule! *Demanding!* God above! In my father's day they would not have dared even to think like that! When his coach drove the roads, they scuttled out of his way into the ditches like rats!'

He pointed. 'Out there, beyond those gates, during the great famine, they gathered in hundreds, howling for food. When it was refused, some of them tried to climb over the wall. It was then my father ordered the gates to be opened and the dogs turned loose on the crowd outside. That was the way.'

He said no more; his brief tirade had exhausted him. Alec made no comment. He knew better than to contradict anything his uncle said.

He always tried to be reasonable and logical in his arguments, but he knew reason and logic would be wasted on Walter Carew. He was too narrow-minded and prejudiced – and bigoted. When Henry inherited the estate and gave permission for a Catholic church to be built in the village, Walter had violently opposed the decision, but Henry had stood firm. His brother Julian had sided with him. Nevertheless, Walter's objections had been strong enough for them to yield a little. Certain stipulations were made. The church had to be located out of sight in a sunken cul-de-sac west of the village street. Furthermore, its spire could not exceed thirty feet – it could not be allowed to dominate the Protestant church at the northern entrance to Carewstown.

Alec sighed. His uncle seemed to be unaware that time had passed him by. There were times when he spoke as though he was living in the days of his ancestor, Richard; regarding himself as a feudal overlord with the power of life and death over his vassals. Poor, pathetic old man, he thought, watching as his Uncle Walter picked up his pen again and consulted some notes, preparing to conclude his long chronicle of the family. As if we were royalty, Alec thought with an amused smile; as if we were Tudors or Plantagenets. He felt sorry for the old man.

The demesne plantation was now very much smaller than it had been when Alec was a boy. Then it had covered about two hundred and fifty acres, but it was now reduced to less than twenty. There was a saying in Ireland that the 'selling of the trees' presaged the decline of the family. Certainly the fortunes of the Carews had declined over the years. When Uncle Walter inherited the estate, he had to sell the land around to pay for Julian's outstanding gambling debts, at a time when land values were constantly falling. All that remained was the demesne and the village.

The other great Anglo-Irish landowning families had suffered as well. A succession of ruinous harvests, coupled with falling land prices, had gravely reduced income from land. Most had been forced to sell their private woodlands, which had been reverently preserved since the eighteenth century. Travelling mills came over in force from England and Scotland and commenced the wholesale felling of demesne timber.

The wood was sold in bulk, mature and immature, for a lump sum and the land was left to become profitless rabbit-infested scrub.

There was very little replanting. A series of Land Acts shook the confidence of the landlords as they recognised in them a forewarning of the change in the ownership of Irish land. The Wyndham Act of 1903 gave the deathblow to the old landlord system which had existed for centuries. A hundred million pounds was advanced by the British government for tenants to buy out the farms they rented from the landlords. The landlords were given a bonus of twelve per cent to induce them to sell. Only a few – men like my uncle, Alec thought with pride – resisted the offer.

He could understand his uncle's concern. Word had reached Carewscourt that several of the big landowning families in the county had sold out and had gone to England. How long would it be, Carew wondered, before the Hacketts and the Merricks and the Townshends did the same?

We Anglo-Irish are a dying breed, Alec thought with despair. The Big Houses in the district were now mostly inhabited by people of his uncle's generation. The younger people had abandoned rain-swept, wind-swept Mayo for the bright lights of London and Dublin. Confined to their own class and religion, the marriage prospects for the young women who remained dwindled with each passing year. Conversing politely over the tea-cups in the huge drawing-rooms, he sensed their quiet desperation. Once, as a guest of the Hacketts, he had taken a stroll through the rose garden with Jessica Hackett. She had confronted him and, blushing furiously, had offered to be his mistress if he would promise to marry her eventually. He had declined, trying to be as tactful as he knew how.

'Thank God, thank God!' Walter sighed and lay back in the chair.

Alec turned towards him. 'Sir?'

Walter gestured with his hand. 'I've finished it.' He shook his head. 'I thought I would never live to see the day.'

Alec forced enthusiasm into his voice. 'Marvellous! Congratulations, sir.'

Walter closed his eyes. 'Ten years,' he murmured wearily, 'ten years of writing and careful research. God, but I'm exhausted.'

What a terrible waste of time, Alec thought. He has neglected his duties writing that damned family history and leaving Tim Skerritt to manage the estate. God knows what way we are financially.

Uncle Walter remained seated with thumb and forefinger pressed against his closed eyes. Alec was beginning to think he had fallen asleep, when he took his hand away from his face and turned towards him.

'I've been thinking. Could we have it published? Know anything about the publishing business?'

Carew suppressed a groan. 'I'm afraid I don't,' he replied. He detected a note of excitement in his uncle's voice and thought that it would be something for the old man to look forward to, seeing his work in print. It might add a few more years on to his life. Nevertheless he tried to dissuade him.

166

'We have to be realistic. Naturally, *we* find the history of the Carews fascinating. But would a publisher – or the reading public for that matter? I think not.'

'As it is now, I agree,' Walter Carew said, the excitement still in his voice. The idea had taken firm root in his brain and Carew knew that he was not going to be easily discouraged. 'It needs the professional touch. It needs to be rewritten by one of those writer chaps. Know any of them in Dublin?'

How odd, Alec thought, I've been thinking about her all the time since I came here, trying to think of some way of seeing her again. And now, just as I was giving up all hope . . .

'Yes,' he replied, 'as a matter of fact, I do. A man called Durkin. Journalist.'

'Good?'

'Very.'

'Do you think . . . If you asked him?'

'Let's invite him to stay with us for a few days, then you can ask him yourself.'

'That's a splendid suggestion! But do you think he will come?'

'He might, if he's not too busy.' In fact I'm *sure* he'll come, Alec told himself. He could imagine Durkin boasting about it to everyone. 'I'll take a little walk before lunch. I'll go to the post office in the village and telegraph the invitation.'

'Do that, do that!' Uncle Walter's voice was full of enthusiasm.

'And his wife. We must invite her too, of course.'

'Of course.'

'She's an artist. I'm sure she would be delighted to do a few pen and ink drawings of Carewscourt and its surroundings. We could use them to illustrate your history if ever it is accepted for publication.' Without his realising it, Alec's voice had become as enthusiastic as his uncle's.

Uncle Walter looked at him with gratitude. His nephew had suddenly alive. There were two spots of colour in his cheeks and his eyes were bright and lively. He looked so animated compared to his usual dour self that Walter was compelled to remark, 'You know, Alec, I've never seen you looking so happy and excited.'

Durkin's arrival at Carewscourt was dramatic. A series of small explosions one morning brought Alec running out to the top of the steps. There he had stared in amazement as Durkin came chugging up the drive in a cloud of black smoke, driving that wonder of the age, an automobile. It was a two-seater, painted a vivid yellow, with bright red mudguards. Carew's immediate response was that it was garish and vulgar, like Durkin himself.

Durkin was dressed for motoring in a long white dust coat and cap. He wore leather gauntlets and goggles covered his eyes. His wife wore a similar coat and a veil covered her face to protect against the dust of the road.

Durkin had struggled out of the car helpless with laughter, delighted with all the excitement he was causing. Mrs Joyce, the cook, came panting up from the kitchen with the two maid-servants behind her, her hands and wrists covered in flour, while Uncle Walter and his sister peeped wide-eyed from behind the curtains. It was the first motor car they had ever seen. Indeed, it was the first motor car seen west of the Shannon. Alec learned later that Durkin had created panic and excitement driving through the towns and villages of Roscommon and east Mayo.

Durkin quickly made himself at home in Carewscourt. He lost no time in becoming familiar with each member of the household, treating each one differently. With Walter Carew he was courteous and knowledgeable and enthusiastic. Any doubts Walter may have had about having the book published, were quickly dispelled by Durkin's gushy optimism.

'There are no doubts in *my* mind, sir,' he boomed, flashing his gold-toothed smile. 'This is a work of major historical importance. Of course – if you will forgive me for saying so – it is a bit stilted in its present form. But rest assured, when I have finished with it . . .'

In Emily Carew's presence he was kind and polite and remarkably subdued, listening with infinite patience when she lapsed into wistful nostalgia as she recalled the days when Carewscourt was the centre of social activity in this part of Mayo.

'Oh, the balls we had! All the officers from the garrison at Castlebar would come down. I remember this very handsome young subaltern I was dancing with . . .'

Durkin would nod and smile gently as the tiny bird-like voice meandered on.

From the moment of his arrival at Carewscourt, Durkin adopted an over-familiar attitude towards Carew, calling him Alec, trying to give the impression that they had known each other for years. One evening Walter invited the Hacketts and the Townshends over. Durkin soon made himself the principal object of attraction. He dominated the conversation, holding the Hackett and Townshend women spellbound as he told of how he had broken up a white-slave ring in Dublin, and how he had rescued an innocent young girl from a fate worse than death. As the evening wore on, Durkin became very drunk. He alluded to certain activities 'in which the gallant Captain and myself are involved. Cloak-and-dagger stuff, ye know. Very hush-hush. Not many people know about it.'

Alec glared warningly at him, but Durkin replied with a broad conspiratorial wink, and slurred, 'We know the score, don't we, Alec?'

Alec was appalled; he swore under his breath. No one, not even his uncle, knew that he was attached to Military Intelligence.

Miriam Durkin was so markedly different from her husband. She was unobtrusive and shy. She was clearly embarrassed at times by Durkin's bumptious behaviour. Not once since she and Durkin arrived had Alec had a chance to talk to her alone. Somehow she always happened to be in the company of someone, Walter, Emily or Durkin. She had even formed friendships with the cook and the two maid-servants. He had a feeling that she was deliberately avoiding him – that she feared to be alone with him.

But she was alone now. He stood at the window of his room, watching her. She sat on a chair at the edge of the trees, an easel in front of her, painting. Durkin had retired to the library with the ledger and a notebook. He had locked himself in as he did not want to be disturbed by Emily.

He walked out of the room and down the broad staircase. The door of the dining room was open. Alec paused in the hall and looked in. Thick golden bars of sunlight slanted down from the tall narrow windows. Between the windows, in the cool shade, his uncle sat upright in a chair, asleep. His head was thrown back and his mouth hung open. Alec stared at him for a few seconds, then walked out into the heat and glare of the mid-day sun.

He strolled along by the front of the house until he reached the north wing, where he turned down the grassy slope towards the trees. Miriam Durkin raised her head. When she saw him approaching, she lowered her gaze to the canvas before her and began to dab at it with the brush. He could sense her nervousness and paused deliberately to light a cigarette, as he ambled casually towards her. She continued with her painting, not raising her head as he leaned against the tree trunk behind her. 'Do you mind if I watch?' he asked. 'If I make you nervous by standing here, please say so.'

'You are not making me nervous,' she said, but he could hear the tremor in her voice. She was working on a water-colour painting of Carewscourt. It was a three-quarter view. The house stood out on the canvas, stark and majestic on its hilltop, against a light-blue background of sky.

'You've succeeded in making an ugly house look beautiful,' Alec said.

'Imposing rather than beautiful,' Miriam replied. 'When I first saw it in the distance, dominating the surrounding countryside, looking so magnificent, it reminded me of the Acropolis.'

'The Acropolis,' Alec repeated and smiled. 'My uncle would be delighted to hear you say that. He loves this place.'

'This painting is for him,' she said. 'But first I want to do a line drawing from it, which can be used as a frontispiece for the book when it is published.'

*If* it is published, Alec thought, watching the delicate movements of her paintbrush.

He said, 'You have been avoiding me, you know.'

'Oh, come now . . .' She gave a laugh, as though she found his assertion absurd, but her laugh sounded a little forced.

'Must you pretend – '

'You have a wife!' she cut in harshly, staring at him coldly.

'*Have!* Who told you that?'

'Your aunt.'

He sighed. 'My aunt, it grieves me to say, gets things confused. She's no longer worthy of credence.' He tossed away the cigarette. 'My wife died some years ago,' he said. 'She killed herself.'

He had forgotten how sensitive she was. His bluntness shocked her. 'How terrible,' she whispered.

As he started to speak, she forestalled him. 'Please! Don't talk about it.'

'But I want to talk about it!' he insisted. 'I *have* to talk about it. Please, try to understand. I've kept it bottled up inside me for so long.'

Nevertheless he hesitated. He thought, I want her, but I'll lose her if I tell her everything. If I tell her it was I who was responsible for my wife's death, she'll turn away from me in horror and disgust.

'Very well, then,' she said, 'talk about it if you think you must.'

He was reluctant to begin and his hesitancy made her look questioningly at him. He sighed. He had to tell her, no matter what the consequences.

'Valerie and I married on impulse. The South African war had just broken out and I had received my embarkation orders. It was a mad time. Everyone seemed to be infected with patriotic fever. No one was thinking rationally. I suppose Valerie and I were no exception.'

At long last he was able to talk to someone about it. He talked on, feeling a great relief, thinking, it's not surprising Catholics are able to preserve their sanity; they can unburden themselves in the confessional. Miriam sat sideways on the chair, her head bowed, listening silently and sympathetically.

'I'm just trying to explain how things were at the time. The war was over and it was a small peacetime army again. Officers who wanted to stay on were discouraged from doing so. And certainly the army people did not want incapacitated ones. That's why I studied so hard at the Staff College. When I left I went straight to Whitehall. The department I was attached to was fighting an uphill battle against prejudice from the old school clique and the niggardly allowances from the Treasury. We had to work hard to justify our existence. And we did; from nine o'clock in the morning to eight at night, six days a week.

'Our marriage suffered. There were bitter quarrels between Valerie and me. She was alone all day and bored to distraction. She had no women friends. I should have known that eventually some man would come along and take advantage of the situation. Ironic – it was I who first introduced him to her. His name was Dennis Sanquest, a politician, a Liberal. Handsome chap, and charming, very charming. They became lovers, but Valerie didn't know that Sanquest regarded her as a mere plaything – someone he could have a little fun with; someone he could display before his friends as his latest conquest.

'When she arrived at his flat one night and told him that she had left me after admitting everything, he was furious. The scandal would ruin him and mean the end of his political career if he should be named as corespondent in a divorce case. He discarded her without a thought. Abandoned by everyone, she rented rooms in Bloomsbury. She had a small private income which was sufficient for her needs. She was completely alone.

'I did not know what had happened to her after she left me. Nor did I care I felt, when she walked out of our home that night, she had walked out of my life forever. I was dazed at first – numb with shock. The anger came later. I destroyed everything that reminded me of her:

171

photographs, mementoes. One morning a letter arrived. It was from Valerie. She begged for my forgiveness. I tore the letter in two and threw the pieces into the fire. I did not reply. Instead, now that I knew where she was living, I contacted my solicitors and instructed them to start divorce proceedings.

'A week later I received a frantic letter from Valerie imploring me not to go through with it. She admitted she had made a dreadful mistake and appealed for a reconciliation. Again I tore up the letter and did not reply.

'More letters followed, each one more urgent than the last. I did not answer any of them. She made appointments to meet me at different places: restaurants, art galleries. I did not keep any of them. It was not that I did not love her. I did, despite the fact that she had been unfaithful. But the more intense the love, the more intense the hate. I wanted to make her suffer. I knew that I would take her back eventually, but I wanted to torment her with indifference. I wanted to drive her to the very edge of despair.

'Finally, a letter came which was different from the others. She was making one last appeal. She wanted me to take her back. She wanted both of us to start all over again. She wanted me to go to her rooms in Bloomsbury that night, to talk things over. She would be attired for the street, ready to go. Her things were already packed. "Please come and take me away with you," she wrote. "I'll be waiting. I'll wait all night if necessary so long as I know you'll be coming. But don't fail me this time, Alec. Please! Because if you do . . ." ' He paused, then went on. 'She threatened to take her life if I did not arrive.

'At first I thought it was a ploy – a ruse designed to panic me into running to her, but then something told me it was not. Perhaps it was the handwriting. It was wild and erratic, as though she had been writing under severe emotional strain.

'And yet when the time came for me to go to her, I hesitated. I decided not to go until the following morning.'

He ceased talking. Miriam raised her head and looked at him. He was leaning against the trunk of the tree, staring with blank unseeing eyes at the ground. She did not say anything, waiting for him to speak.

'The next morning,' he went on in a flat emotionless voice, 'I rose late. I washed and shaved and had breakfast, then sat down by the window and read the morning newspaper. It was a Sunday – a grey spring morning and raining a little. The window was open at the top and I could hear the church bells ringing in the distance. I felt relaxed and, for the first time since Valerie had told me of her unfaithfulness, happy.

'I knew what I was going to do. I would leave at about noon and walk to Bloomsbury. On the way I would stop at a restaurant and have lunch and then continue, taking my time. I wanted to see the look on Valerie's face when she opened the door. I wanted to catch her unprepared.

'As noon approached, I put on a raincoat and hat. I stood before the mirror in the hallway, fixing my tie, whistling. It was one of those moments one remembers forever: the moment of supreme happiness just before disaster strikes. I opened the halldoor. A fat policeman came puffing up the steps towards me. Was my name Carew? he asked. I told him yes it was and brought him into the hall. He began to talk. All the time his eyes deliberately avoided mine; he kept them fixed on a picture on the wall behind me.

'A woman had thrown herself from Waterloo Bridge, he told me. It had happened in the early hours of the morning. There had been a witness who had raised the alarm. The body had been retrieved from the river after a lengthy search. Three keys attached to a metal disc had been found in the pocket of the woman's coat. The address of a house in Bloomsbury was engraved on the disc. The police had gone to the house and had entered the flat rented to the dead woman. On a table in the living room they found a letter addressed to me.

'He talked on, but I was no longer listening. I stood there, my senses numb. I was in a state of shock. I kept telling myself that it was all a mistake, some kind of ghastly mistake.

'We travelled through the streets in a cab. Then something suddenly occurred to me and I nearly cried with relief. Valerie was not dead! This was nothing but an elaborate hoax perpetrated by her in revenge for all the suffering I had caused her. And this man sitting beside me was not a policeman. Why, he didn't even look like a policeman. He was probably an actor she had hired to impersonate one. I nearly laughed out loud. My nerves were so strained I was probably on the point of hysteria.

'We alighted at the morgue. As we climbed the steps I kept hoping to see Valerie standing there, a mischievous smile on her face, the whole episode a cruel joke. But it was a man who was standing inside, a policeman. He led the way. I tried to keep despair at bay, telling myself that some sort of mistake had been made. The detective pulled the sheet away from the face.'

He was silent then. Miriam raised her head and looked at him.

'Was it your wife?' she whispered.

He nodded. 'Yes, it was Valerie.' His hands were covered in sweat and he thrust them into his his trouser pockets. He turned towards the house and stared at it with brooding eyes.

'There was an inquest. The letter she had left for me remained in the possession of the police as evidence. It was read aloud in court. It contained nothing censorious. She blamed herself for everything that had happened. I sat there listening, feeling sick with guilt and remorse. I kept telling myself that I had killed her – had killed her as surely as if my own hands had sent her plunging down into the muddy waters of the Thames. I told myself, if there is any justice in the world I should be punished for it. I wanted to pay for my crime. I would have welcomed even a reproachful speech from the coroner but all I got from him was an expression of sympathy.

'It was the same with my fellow officers. I received nothing but sympathy and understanding from them. They tried to lift me out of my depression. They approached me one by one with invitations: some drinks over a game of cards; a night out at the theatre . . . But I said no to all their offers. I simply wanted to be left alone. I asked for more work – anything to keep my mind occupied.

'It was the nights I feared. I began to have strange dreams. Not nightmares, but unusual and disturbing dreams. They were nearly all about Valerie. They never varied. I would find myself searching for her. When I did find her, she always managed to evade me like a will-o'-the-wisp, and then I would lose her again. Sometimes I would wake up weeping with frustration and despair.'

Alec lapsed into silence.

'Do you still have those dreams?' Miriam Durkin asked after a minute or two had passed.

'No, not now,' he answered, 'not since I arrived in Ireland. Perhaps London had something to do with it. There were too many unhappy memories there.'

He said no more. Now that he had told her everything, he expected her to condemn him for what he had done, but she said nothing. He searched her eyes for signs of contempt and loathing, but all he could see was sympathy.

He gave her a long intent look. 'I can't imagine a future without you, Miriam.'

She blushed and turned away to face the easel. 'You will have to put me out of your mind,' she said quietly.

'I can't.'

'You must.'

'You know I love you. And you feel the same way about me. I know you do. Don't deny it. We have a right to be happy.'

'But I'm married – '

174

'To a man you loathe! Do you think I haven't noticed.'

'That's not true!' she protested in a shrill voice.

He could see she was agitated. He placed a hand on her shoulder. 'Miriam . . .'

A twig snapped.

They both turned, staring apprehensively into the cool green dimness. He caught a glimpse of a tall thin figure moving away through the trees.

'Who is it?' she whispered with fear in her voice.

'Tim Skerritt. My uncle's steward.'

'Do you think he heard?'

'I don't know.'

Instinctively she reached up and gripped his hand resting on her shoulder.


### III


At breakfast, Walter Carew expressed a wish to see the family solicitors in Castlebar and Durkin readily offered to drive him.

Shortly after lunch, Durkin, attired in his motoring outfit, climbed into the car and gripped the steering wheel. Walter climbed in beside him, trying hard not to show the fear he felt for the mechanical monster.

'You will drive carefully, won't you, Mr Durkin?'

'Never fear, sir, never fear,' Durkin laughed. 'I'll get you there safely and back. We'll be home before dusk.'

Alec had to twist the starting-handle six or seven times before the engine exploded into life and the car began to shudder and shake. Walter gripped the side with one hand and his hat with the other, as they drove up the road in a cloud of black smoke. Alec and Miriam tried to comfort Emily as she stared after them, wide-eyed and trembling.

It was a glorious day, warm and sunny with hardly a cloud in the sky, but by late afternoon a fresh breeze was beginning to blow in from the west. It increased steadily in force. As evening approached, Alec stood at the top of the steps, hair blowing wildly in the wind, watching the heavy black storm clouds moving in from the Atlantic. I hope to God, he thought, Durkin does not try to get back before the storm breaks. Durkin's car had no roof. A severe drenching would kill his uncle.

175

A half-hour later the storm broke. Carewscourt, standing on its hill high above the surrounding countryside, took the full brunt of it. The rushing wind and rain dashed against the thick stone walls. By nightfall, Alec felt as though he were inside a fort under attack. The wind repeatedly struck the house with the force of a battering-ram. He could hear it scaling the walls in fury, screaming over the roof.

He sat to the left of the huge fireplace. Miriam was facing him, with Emily between them, her tiny body upright on the chair, staring at the crackling log fire.

'I do hope Walter and Mr Durkin are safe,' she wailed as another violent burst struck the house.

Alec stretched out his arm and laid a comforting hand over hers. 'Of course they are. At this very moment, Walter and Mr Durkin are snug in their beds in a hotel in Castlebar.'

'But suppose they left before the storm broke?'

'Then they would have been here hours ago. Castlebar is only about twenty miles from here and Mr Durkin's automobile can do twenty-five miles an hour.'

Emily's eyes widened in horror. 'Twenty-five miles an hour!' Again the wail of distress. 'Oh poor Walter!'

Alec patted her hand. 'There, there. You must not upset yourself.'

There was a lull in the storm. They could hear the rain drumming against the windows. It was as if the attacking force had drawn back their battering-ram and steadied it for one final assault. Alec braced himself; he found himself counting. One, two, three. There was a rushing sound as though a speeding train were charging towards them. It hit in an explosion of noise. He could feel the house shudder. The window frames rattled violently and glass cracked with the sound of a pistol shot. Miriam cowered in terror, her hand up to her throat. Emily sat with her hands in her lap, quite unperturbed.

Alec grinned reassuringly at Miriam. 'This house was built to last. The walls are of solid stone and eight feet thick. There's no need to be afraid. Carewscourt has stood successfully against the elements for more than two hundred years.'

Emily nodded in agreement. 'You must not let the strong winds frighten you, my dear. Here in Mayo we get them quite often. Although,' she added, 'not usually quite as bad as this. But Alec is right. This house could withstand a hurricane. I remember the night of the Big Wind. I was only a little girl at the time. Heavens, what a night. Anyone who experienced it will never forget it. It was like the end of the

176

world! They said whole fields were ripped up into the air! Imagine! And yet this house, standing on a hill, survived.'

'I do hope your husband will succeed in getting the book published when the manuscript is completed,' Emily said to Miriam, changing the subject. 'Walter is so looking forward to seeing his work in print. Poor Walter, he worked so hard writing the family history. He allowed me to read it. It's most comprehensive. Such a pity he does not mention Charlotte's ghost.'

Miriam Durkin stared at her, wide-eyed. 'Charlotte's ghost?'

Alec groaned, but before he could interrupt, Emily started to explain.

'A poor tragic creature. She became insane after her two young sons were murdered. She haunts this house, you know. Oh yes, indeed. I have often heard her crying at night. And yet Walter never mentions that.'

Miriam glanced fearfully over her shoulder. The flickering flames of the fire and an oil-lamp standing on the dining room table provided the only light. Most of the room lay in deep shadow. Outside, the storm howled about the house as though a pack of wild wolves were trying to get in. Rain lashed the window-panes.

'Now, Aunt,' Alec said, 'you promised Uncle Walter you would never talk about that again. There are no ghosts.'

Above the noise of the wind and rain there came a long tearing sound followed by a heavy thud. Miriam started. Alec smiled to allay her fears.

'A tree falling,' he explained. 'I'm afraid this storm is going to cause an awful amount of damage to the plantation below.'

'I am not the only one to have seen Charlotte,' Emily went on as though nothing had happened. 'A guest, Colonel Merrick's wife, was in one of the rooms upstairs brushing her hair by candlelight in front of the mirror, when she saw this face peering over her shoulder. Poor woman, she was dreadfully upset.'

Alec swore under his breath. If I don't stop her, he thought, she'll leave Miriam a nervous wreck. 'Aunt Emily . . .'

Emily smiled. 'Yes, Alec?'

'Forgive me for saying so, but all this talk about Charlotte is making Mrs Durkin rather nervous. That, and the storm.'

Emily looked dismayed. She turned to Miriam, her hand fluttering towards her throat. 'Oh my dear, do forgive me. I had no idea.'

Miriam smiled nervously. 'You must allow for us city dwellers, Miss Carew. Some of us find it hard to adapt to country life. We never experience the full impact of storms such as this, and Carewscourt is so

177

huge. Our house in Dublin would fit in one corner of it.' She gave a weak smile. 'And now to know that it is haunted makes me a little apprehensive.'

'Oh, but you should not be frightened of Charlotte,' Emily protested. 'She would never harm anyone. She just cries. It's so sad to hear her. At times, listening to her, I cry myself.'

Alec sighed and stood up. 'I think it would be a good idea if we all had some sleep,' he said. He walked across the dimly lit room to the sideboard on which a number of candlesticks stood. He lit one of the candles.

Emily rose slowly to her feet. 'I do hope Walter and Mr Durkin are safe,' she said again.

Alec stood beside her holding the candlestick. The candle-flame wavered slightly in the draughty room.

'They are asleep in their beds, Aunt,' he said. 'They have better sense than we have.' He offered his arm to her. She placed a small delicate hand on it and bade Miriam good-night. Out in the dark cold hall she stopped him at the foot of the stairs.

'No need to see me to my room, Alec,' she said, reaching for the candlestick. She held up her hand against his protest. 'Please. We have a guest who is sitting all alone.'

Nevertheless he stood watching the frail figure mount the broad staircase, her shadow moving past the portraits of her ancestors on the wall. He could hear the wind moaning through the house. On such a night as this, he told himself, one could believe in ghosts and phantoms, and yet this small, fragile old lady climbs up into the whistling darkness unafraid.

He waited until he could no longer see the reflection of her candle, before going back to the dining room.

He found Miriam crouched against the fire, her arms crossed over her breasts, each hand gripping a shoulder. He could see the relief on her face as he entered. He immediately went to the sideboard and poured two glasses of brandy. He walked over to her and held out a glass.

'What is it?' she whispered.

'Brandy.'

'I never – '

'Take it. It will settle your nerves.'

He sat down opposite her sipping the brandy. She did likewise, then coughed and made a face.

'Keep on sipping,' he said. 'It will do you good – make you sleep.'

'Sleep,' she echoed and shuddered. 'I don't think I'll be able to sleep tonight.'

'You must not believe anything my aunt tells you. All this nonsense about ghosts is just a figment of her imagination.' He decided to divert her thoughts to other things. 'How did you meet your husband?' he asked.

The question took her by surprise. She stared confusedly at him for several seconds, then lowered her head, gazing into the glass she was holding. After a moment she spoke.

'William lodged at our house. My mother was dead and my father, due to ill health, had to retire from the university on a small pension. It was far too small for the three of us to live on. We were forced to take a lodger . . .'

'I don't understand. You said the three of you.'

'I have a younger sister, Rhoda. She's married now and living in England.'

'Miriam and Rhoda,' he said. 'They're Jewish names, are they not?'

'My mother was a Jew. Her family disowned her for marrying a Gentile. The same thing happened to my father. His people were strict Presbyterians. They cut him off without a penny.'

She said no more. She stared at the fire, lost in thought. The crashing wind had dropped to a vicious whine, but the rain had intensified and its thunderous noise filled the room.

'You're neglecting your drink,' Alec said.

'Oh.' She raised the glass slowly to her lips.

'What made you decide to marry . . . William?' He hesitated over the name. Durkin, he thought, is one of those men destined to go through life known only by their surname.

'My father died. Rhoda and I had to fend for ourselves. Both of us had a very sheltered upbringing, you understand. On our own, we couldn't cope with life, with things in general. Then William took over – began to take care of us. He was such a tower of strength.'

She hesitated and he could sense her reluctance to continue. 'He became another father to you both,' he spoke for her.

'Yes.'

'And when he asked you to marry him, you accepted, because you did not want to lose your new-found security.'

She stared at him coldly. 'You're very perceptive.'

'Do you love him?'

'I married him.'

'That's not what I asked you.'

She looked away and stared at the fire again. 'No,' she murmured.

An awkward silence grew between them. He glanced at his watch.

'It's getting late,' he said. 'I think we should retire.' He lit a candle and handed it to her. She grasped the candlestick firmly. She had forgotten about the storm and the terrors the house held for her, but when Alec closed the dining room door and the cold whispering darkness enveloped them, her fear returned.

They walked slowly up the broad staircase, Alec holding the oil-lamp a little above his head. They could hear the wild rush of the wind and the pattering of rain against floorboards from the deserted upper floor. God, Alec thought, half the slates must have been blown away.

The paused at the entrance to the long corridor. It stretched away into the darkness towards the empty north wing. The noise of the storm was muffled now. They were hemmed in on all sides by thick heavy stone, but still the wind managed to snake in through innumerable cracks and crannies. It came moaning towards them out of the blackness. Miriam had to shield the candle-flame with her hand as it fluttered wildly. They moved up the corridor, their footfalls against the bare boards sending out hollow echoes. Miriam could feel her courage ebbing with each forward step. It vanished completely as Alec opened the door for her and she stood on the threshold, looking into the dark, listening to the wind whining away outside the house.

'Come in with me,' she pleaded.

He walked in before her and she followed reluctantly, closing the door behind her. He placed the lamp and the guttering candle in its holder on a low table in the centre of the floor. They formed a small aura of light, leaving both ends of the room in total darkness.

He said, 'I'll leave the lamp and candle with you. There's a candle in my room.'

As he turned to go, she cried out in a panicky voice, 'Alec, don't leave me alone tonight!'

He turned and faced her. She stared back at him, her cheeks flaming.

He said gently, 'I won't leave you, Miriam.'

She walked slowly to the bed and sat down. She took off her shoes, and lay down fully clothed, covering herself with a heavy quilt.

He stood watching her, then stooped and removed his shoes. He snuffed out the candle and, putting his face over the glass chimney of the lamp, blew out the flame. He moved slowly and cautiously across the pitch-dark room until his knees touched the edge of the bed. He got under the quilt and lay sideways on the bed, facing her. He could feel her breath against his face. They lay like that for a while, not saying a word. Then he reached out and placed his hand on her hip.

'Please,' she whispered, 'don't make love to me. Not now, not tonight. When we get back to Dublin there will be time for that, but you'll have to be patient with me. You'll have to give me time.' She began to weep. 'You've destroyed the belief I had in myself,' she sobbed. 'I never thought I would surrender . . . myself . . . the principles I've always cherished. I never thought I would be involved in an adulterous affair. I never thought I would become one of those people William is so fond of writing about in that filthy newspaper of his.'

She cried herself to sleep. Alec turned on his back and stared into the darkness. He lay for a long time, listening to the storm as it blew itself out.

# Chapter Six

## I

Myles Burke gave a final wipe to the brass knocker, the letter-box and door-knob with the polishing cloth and then closed the heavy door on the cold winter night. In the feeble light his hand searched for the bolt, found it and shot it home. The sound echoed hollowly throughout the tall empty house.

He moved to the table in the hall and put the cloth and tin of Brasso in the wicker basket alongside the dusters, the tin of polish and a bunch of keys. He put his arm through the handle of the basket, picked up the oil-lamp and moved down the hall on slippered feet. He stopped outside a glass-panelled door on the left. One hand, hampered by the basket, tested the handle. The light from the oil-lamp shone on the brass plate.

**EDWARD H CORCORAN**
Commissioner for Oaths

Satisfied, he shuffled down into the back passage and opened the door of the closet under the stairs. A scuttling noise startled him. He thrust the lamp in among the mops and brooms, but he could see nothing. He waited for a few seconds, but the noise did not repeat itself. He placed the basket on one of the shelves and closed the door. He would go down into the cellar tomorrow and put down some rat poison.

He paused as he always did at the foot of the stairs, his left hand holding the lamp, his right hand resting on the banisters. The thought of the long climb to the top of the house always daunted him. Father Poole's plaintive voice came back.

'Begob, Myles, I'd be a more frequent visitor if it wasn't for these stairs. Man, dear, it's like climbin' the Matterhorn.'

He began to climb the stairs slowly. His giant shadow mounted the wall at the top of the stairs. He paused for breath as he reached the landing, then continued. He was used to seeing people with swollen jaws and pale nervous faces walking up these two flights to the rooms on the first floor.

# THOMAS DUNLEAVY
## Dentist

He twisted the door handles, ensuring the doors were locked. Once he had forgotten to lock Mr Corcoran's office and had been harshly reprimanded. For one terrible moment he thought he was going to be dismissed. He was determined never to let that mistake happen again.

Genteel respectability ended at Mr Dunleavy's landing. There was no lino covering on the stairs leading to the second floor. His feet thumped loudly on bare boards. Shamefaced, shabbily dressed people mounted these stairs to the offices of Mr Samuel Gold (Personal Loans Arranged). His mouth twisted with distaste.

He reached the third floor. The rooms of the Hibernian Literary and Debating Society. Voices drifted up through the floorboards every Thursday night.

Home Rule. The dawn of a new era?
Is the Irish Literary Revival coming to an end?

He climbed the last two flights with effort. His own rooms were squeezed under the roof. He opened the door of the front room and closed it behind him. He could feel the heat as he entered. The coal fire burned steadily away in the grate. The gas-jet projecting from the wall above the fireplace filled the room with a greenish glow. The room was sparsely furnished with an ancient sideboard, a small kitchen-dresser, a table and two chairs. In one corner stood a gas-stove on which a black kettle simmered gently. A few books occupied the space between the two small windows.

Myles blew out the lamp and placed it on the sideboard. He moved to one of the windows to draw the curtains, but before doing so he peered out. The quays were deserted. A wind was rising, blowing from the west. He could see it skimming over the surface of the black waters of the Liffey far below. He shivered and drew the curtains. He put two spoonfuls of tea into the teapot, then poured in the scalding water from the kettle. He cut two thick slices of bread and spread yellow, salty butter over each one. He poured the tea into a mug, added milk and sugar, then sat down at the table and began to eat and drink. The clock ticked away on the mantelpiece.

I've Father Poole to thank for all this, he thought. He raised the mug to his lips and sipped the hot sugary tea, remembering the day when he had sat for the first time in Mr Corcoran's office.

Mr Corcoran had stared stonily at him through the pince-nez

183

fastened on to his thin beak of a nose. He had a bony wizened face and an unhealthy pallor. He cleared his throat several times before speaking.

'Frankly, Mr—er—Burke, we prefer a married couple fulfilling the duties of caretaker.'

Myles had sat on the edge of the chair with his hands clasped between his knees, listening to the legal measured tones, telling himself, I'm not going to get it, I'm not going to get it.

'This house is rather big and your duties would be many. Too many, I'm afraid, for a man of your years.'

He had groomed himself as best as he could for the interview. Father Poole had sent a large parcel containing clothes and shoes to the hospital just before he was released. All were second-hand, but they were far better than the stinking rags he had been wearing.

Mr Corcoran lowered his head and examined his finger-nails. 'However,' he said, 'Father Poole has been persistent – very persistent,' he added with a trace of exasperation in his voice. He paused for a while, before saying, 'We are prepared to give you a month's trial.'

Three months had passed since then. He washed down the last of the bread with a mouthful of tea and stood up. He picked up the mug and small plate, walked to the door and opened it. There was a small sink on the landing. He turned on the tap and washed them, then brought them back into the room and dried them with the tea-cloth. He placed them on the kitchen-dresser, then put away the milk, sugar and butter. From the top of the kitchen-dresser he took down a jar. It was an old brown-coloured stone ink jar he had rescued from Mr Corcoran's waste-paper basket. He poured what was left of the hot water from the kettle into it, then pressed the cork firmly down into the opening with the palm of his hand. He then wrapped a piece of red flannel around it and placed it under his arm.

He walked into the bedroom. He had left the gas low so that the room was poorly lit, but he could see well enough. He pulled back the bed-clothes and put the jar underneath them. The bed would be well warmed by the time he got into it in about an hour from now. It was a double bed. The middle-aged married couple who had been caretakers before him had been dismissed on the spot for gross drunkenness.

He walked back into the front room and placed the keys on the sideboard and then hung his jacket on the inside of the door. He brought a chair over to the fire and raised the flame of the gas-jet. He walked over to the shelf between the windows.

His library. Every Saturday afternoon, with the offices closed for the weekend, he would stroll along the quays and browse among the second-hand book barrows. It was amazing the bargains one could find. *Paradise Lost* had cost him a mere twopence. *A Tale of Two Cities*: threepence. He took down a book and walked back to the fire. This one had cost him sixpence, a lot out of his ten shillings a week wages, but it was worth it. It was an old favourite, *Les Misérables*.

He sat in front of the fire and found his place. Jean Valjean's long and tragic life was coming to an end. Myles had more understanding and sympathy for this character than for all the others he had ever read about. The years of imprisonment; the relentless pursuit by the police official, Javert.

Books had prevented him from going mad in prison. The nights when he could not sleep had been the worst, when the dark thoughts of despair and depression came creeping into the mind. On those nights, he would sit up and light a candle. He had hoarded the butt-ends of candles as another prisoner would hoard pieces of food. With the candle-flame held close to the page, listening for the measured tread of the warder on the stone-flagged corridor outside, he would allow his thoughts to escape to the sun-drenched wilderness of *Coral Island*; to the wind-swept moors of *Wuthering Heights*. One night he had found himself chuckling at the merry escapades of Mr Pickwick; another night he had wept uncontrollably at the death of Little Nell. The prisoners who went insane were those who were illiterate and without imagination. As he began to read, he was faintly aware of the rising wind and of the rain beating against the windows.

II

Myles sat before the fire, waiting for Father Poole to arrive. It was Sunday evening. He could hear the bells of St Patrick's in the distance. It was the hour of evensong.

From the time Myles had been made caretaker, Father Poole had been a regular visitor every Sunday evening. He liked listening to Father Poole; he had a fund of stories about his boyhood and youth in the Dublin Liberties; stories about the colourful characters who once lived there. Zozimus, the famed blind balladeer from Faddle Alley; his old friend, Stony Pockets; the poet, James Clarence Mangan.

185

'Poor Mangan,' Father Poole would sigh, 'the street-arabs gave him an awful time – and I was one of them, God forgive me.'

It was hard to believe that Father Poole was eighty years of age. He had been born in 1829, the year of Catholic Emancipation.

The heavy sound of the door-knocker came beating up from the bottom of the house. Myles rose from his chair. The oil-lamp on the sideboard was already lit. He picked it up and opened the door of his room. Half-way down the stairs he could hear Father Poole's feeble voice moaning through the letter-box.

'Hellooo . . . anyone at hooome?'

He opened the hall-door. Father Poole stood outside leaning on his stick, shoulders hunched a little.

'A cold night, Father.'

'But bracing, Myles, bracing,' Father Poole said and stepped in.

At the foot of the stairs, Father Poole paused and transferred his stick from his right hand to his left. Myles stood beside him holding the oil-lamp aloft, his right hand under Father Poole's left elbow.

It took them nearly ten minutes to reach the top of the house. When they entered the front room, Father Poole sat down wearily on the nearest chair. Myles took the tall silk hat from his head and the stick from his hand, but when he offered to take off his overcoat, Father Poole waved him away.

'In a minute or two. I'm out of puff.'

Myles stood over him, waiting patiently. After a while Father Poole began to unbutton his overcoat. Myles helped him to take it off and hung it up. He picked up the two chairs and placed one on each side of the fireplace. But Father Poole did not sit down. He stood in the centre of the room, hands joined, looking around him, nodding in approval.

'Ah yes, yes, very cosy. You're as snug as a bug in a rug here, Myles. You are so.'

He put on his glasses, walked over to the windows, and peered closely at the titles of the books. 'Any new acquisitions, Myles?'

'Not since the last time you were here, Father.'

Father Poole looked over his shoulder. 'Tell me, Myles, did you ever read a book called *Handy Andy*?'

'I never did, Father.'

Father Poole heaved a sigh. 'Ah, a pity. A grand book, grand.' After deliberating for a little while, the priest selected one and carried it towards the fire.

'*Paradise Lost*,' he read aloud.

'Ah yes.' Myles smiled. 'Of all the books I've ever read, there are only two which are particular favourites. That's one of them.'

'Really?' Father Poole muttered abstractedly, turning over the pages. 'Of course,' he said, 'certain critics have argued that while Milton appears to be on God's side, his real sympathies seem to be with Satan.' He continued turning the pages. 'Now where,' he growled, 'are those lines I'm looking for?' He stopped and gave a little grunt of triumph. 'Ah, here we are.'

> Here we may reign secure, and in my choice
> To reign is worth ambition, though in Hell:
> Better to reign in Hell, then serve in Heaven.

Father Poole raised his head and stared at Myles over the tops of his glasses. 'Better to reign in Hell, than serve in Heaven,' he repeated. 'There now, Myles, doesn't those few lines tell yeh all yeh need to know about Satan? Can't yeh sense all the insufferable pride behind them? Ah . . .' He shook his head. 'Is it any wonder he was cast out of paradise?'

Myles shrugged. 'Perhaps I never read *Paradise Lost* as carefully as I should have,' he said.

Father Poole paused at a page. Ah, but you did, my friend, he thought, you did. The page, like all the others in the book, was musty and brown with age, but the red ink drawn under four lines of type was fresh. Not more than a week old, Father Poole surmised. He read the words underlined.

> What though the field be lost?
> All is not lost; the unconquerable will,
> And study of revenge, immortal hate,
> And courage never to submit or yield.

Father Poole closed the book. If you want to know a man, he thought, first examine the books he prefers. He rose slowly from the chair.

'I'll put this back where it belongs.'

'Oh, just leave it on the floor beside you, Father,' Myles said.

'I'll do no such thing! It's too valuable a book to be left lyin' around.'

He walked stiffly over to the bookshelf and stood before it, taking down one book after another, turning the pages, pretending to browse. It gave him time to think.

What did he know about this man, Myles Burke? Very little, he had to admit. He remembered Myles in hospital blurting out something about prison. But he was not the criminal type. Political prisoner? Most likely. There were quite a few of these old Fenian diehards around, still bitter after all those years about their humiliating defeat, still hating the Catholic Church for its condemnation of their movement. Is Myles like that? he asked himself.

> . . . study of revenge, immortal hate,
> And courage never to submit or yield.

Those lines had appealed to him; perhaps they matched his own thoughts. Father Poole put a book back on the shelf and took down another. What concerned him more was the fact that Myles had once contemplated suicide. True, extreme poverty and hardship had driven him to the point when suicide must have seemed preferable to the life he was leading. But this Myles Burke was different. He was a cultured, educated man, yet he lacked the simple faith of the poorest of the poor. And his disregard for the consequences of such a terrible sin was horrifying, horrifying.

Father Poole gave a weary sigh. This should be an occasion for rejoicing. At long last his prayers had been answered. He had found the one he had been searching for all those years – the one wavering on the brink of eternal damnation. All I can do, Father Poole thought despairingly, is to try and give him the spiritual strength to resist such a temptation. He would have to probe this man first and get to understand him. But probe with caution, he told himself, with the utmost caution.

He put the book back on the shelf and returned to the fire.

'Yeh have a most interestin' collection there, Myles. Indeed yes. Yeh have a cultivated taste in literature.'

'I'm glad you think so, Father.'

Father Poole reached into the pocket of his jacket and took out his snuff-box. He sprinkled some snuff on the back of his hand and sniffed it. He smiled apologetically at Myles.

'The only little luxury I allow myself, Myles, apart from a nip of brandy during the cold winter nights.'

'I'm afraid I have none to offer you, Father,' Myles said. 'Rules of the house, you know,' and he uttered a mirthful little bark.

Father Poole stared at him in amazement. He had never seen Myles Burke laugh before.

Silence fell between them. The clock on the mantelpiece ticked away loudly in the stillness. Father Poole sat forward a little on the chair, his hands outstretched towards the fire. Myles sat upright, hands on knees, staring at the leaping flames. After a while Father Poole straightened up

188

with a groan and lay back in the chair. He stared at Myles with his heavy-lidded eyes, a slight smile on his face.

'D'ye know, Myles,' he said softly, 'it states on your hospital record that you are a Catholic, and yet I never see you at Mass. I stand up there in the pulpit every Sunday mornin' looking down at the upturned faces searchin' for yours, but in vain. But then of course,' he added, 'you probably go to St Audoen's. It's much nearer.'

Myles stared back at him, stone-faced. 'I never go to Mass,' he answered curtly.

'And the Sacraments?'

'Never.'

'And yet Peter, the sacristan, used to see you sittin' in St Catherine's every day. Sittin' there from early afternoon till the church closed at night.'

'It was just someplace to sit. Someplace to shelter from the cold and the rain.'

'I see.' Father Poole bit his underlip. Myles eyed him warily. He was tense now – on the defensive. Father Poole noticed his hands gripping his knees, the whites of the knuckles showing.

'We are old men, Myles,' Father Poole sighed. 'We've tramped the long hard road of life, sweated and toiled along it. We stumbled and fell many times, and yet always managed to struggle up again and continue. But we are nearin' the end of that road, my friend. And when we do come to the end of it, we can take our rest – our eternal rest.'

He paused, waiting for Myles to say something, but Myles stared fixedly at him, saying nothing.

'But some have difficulty reachin' the end of that road, Myles,' he went on. 'They wander off the highway and into the bush and get lost. Then they roam aimlessly about, frightened and confused, trying to get back. Sometimes, with luck, a guide appears. Then they follow him obediently, relyin' on his knowledge and experience to get them back to safety.'

Again he paused. 'Let me be *your* guide, Myles,' he said, quietly.

'I'm not lost!'

'I regret to say I think you are. When a man reaches the winter of his life, there's nothin' he can look forward to but death. Then he turns to God, not away from Him. And He is waitin' for you, Myles. He wants you to destroy willingly the barrier you've erected between Him and you. Go to Him – go to Him absolved and with a contrite heart. Receive the Blessed Sacrament at the Holy Sacrifice of the Mass.'

Myles began to twist about on his chair, agitated. 'Leave me be, Father, leave me be.'

189

Father Poole went relentlessly on. 'You told me once that going to a Workhouse was simply exchanging one prison for another. Were you in prison, Myles? You can confide in me. You can trust me.'

Myles hesitated before answering. 'Yes, I was in prison.'

'Perhaps you think the crime they sent you to prison for makes you unworthy of God's mercy. If you think that, then you're wrong. Very wrong. God loves all sinners.'

'The crime they sent me to prison for!'

Father Poole was taken aback by the harsh voice and the sudden change in behaviour. Myles' body was trembling with anger and outrage.

'Are you implying that I was a common criminal? A thief perhaps?'

Father Poole gave a hasty wave of denial with his hand. 'No, no, of course not.'

'They sent me to prison for trying to free my country. And if that's a crime then I plead guilty. Gladly! Proudly!'

Father Poole nodded. 'Ah, I see. A political prisoner. A Fenian.'

'Yes, a Fenian. One of the men who fought and lost. We paid a terrible price for our defeat. Imprisonment – condemned by the Catholic hierarchy from the pulpit. Remember the words, "Eternity is not long enough nor Hell hot enough to punish the Fenians!" Even in prison we were denied spiritual comfort. The prison chaplain came to me in my cell and tried to make a bargain with me. If I renounced my Fenian oath he would hear my confession and give me communion. I told him to go to hell! And you tell me there is a barrier between God and me. It was not *I* who erected it!'

'Oh, Myles, Myles.' Father Poole shook his head. 'All of that was so long ago. Times have changed and so has the attitude of the Church. The Church will gladly welcome you back into the fold. There's nothing to prevent you from unburdening yourself to me right here and now if you wish to do so.'

'Ah, I see. The Church can break her own rules when it suits her, is that it?' Myles asked with heavy sarcasm.

Father Poole sighed. 'Try to understand. There was a time when a priest had to sneak like a thief through the back streets and alleyways of this city in order to say Mass in some garret or other. Perhaps he would say it in some lonely place in the hills with someone on the lookout for the searching redcoats. Freedom to worship our religion in our own country has been bought dearly with blood and tears – and you do not surrender that sort of freedom easily. If anything should jeopardise that freedom – an insurrection for instance – the Church, without hesita-

190

tion, will condemn it. And it does not matter in the slightest if that insurrection is justified or not.'

'And as the poor rebel goes to the gallows,' Myles commented bitterly, 'the Church looks idly on.'

'Rebellions have never succeeded in Ireland,' Father Poole said, 'and yet they are always attempted. Ours is a bloody history, Myles. A horrible series of futile uprisings against impossible odds and always ending in butchery and defeat for the rebels. And the sad aftermath – the executions, the transportations, the wailings of the widows and orphans. Good God,' he said in an angry voice, 'do we ever learn!' He shook his head. 'But no more, no more. The Fenian rebellion was the last.'

'I wouldn't be so sure about that if I were you!' Myles exclaimed harshly.

Father Poole glanced sharply at him. 'What do you mean?'

'Ireland is still not free. There will be more rebellions until she is!'

'Ahhh!' Father Poole made a gesture of annoyance with his hand. 'You're out of date. Time has passed you by. This is the twentieth century, the age of progress, the age of miracles. A man climbs into a machine and takes to the air and crosses the English Channel. Think of it – a machine that flies. The eighth wonder of the world! We're livin' in the dawn of a new enlightenment. Men no longer take to the barricades to redress wrongs. They sit at conference tables and discuss them in a civilised manner. And you sit there like a dog chained to a stake fixed in the past, mouthin' your worn-out shibboleths, still full of hate for England and your Church, too arrogant to make your peace with God. You're a rebel without a cause, Myles. A museum piece! A poor, pathetic old man.'

Father Poole drew back as Myles stood before him, trembling, his glaring face twitching.

'How dare you!' he grated. 'How dare you use your condescending ways on me! So I'm an object of pity, am I? Why you snuff-sniffing, yellow-faced, craw-thumping pious old hypocrite! What do you know!'

Father Poole blinked in dismay. I've antagonised him, he thought. He had allowed himself to be carried away. He had gone too far. He had been rash when he should have been circumspect. O God, I've lost him, he groaned to himself, lost him.

Myles stooped and brought his face close to Father Poole's. 'Do you know how I spend my week-ends?' he hissed.

Father Poole shook his head.

'I roam the streets, searching, hoping to meet an old comrade from the past. Sometimes I go into a public-house and sit there with a glass of lemonade in my hand, eavesdropping, hoping to hear some treasonable conversation. But I'll find the men I'm looking for sooner or later. Then I'll offer my services. We'll plot and plan together for the day when it's opportune to strike!' He gave a long shuddering sigh and gulped, tears in his eyes. 'My God,' he choked, 'how I long for that day!'

'You long for that day,' Father Poole repeated. 'And yet when you were sick and hungry, wanderin' through the streets, you had reached the point when you thought life was not worth livin'. You thought of committin' suicide. Remember?'

Myles shrugged. 'When you're ill and have sunk to the depths of despair, black thoughts enter your mind. I toyed with the idea of committing suicide, but I knew in my heart and soul I would never take my own life. That's the coward's way out!'

Father Poole sighed. 'I spent many a sleepless night worryin' about you; prayin' for you. I wanted with the help of God to coax you away from such terrible thoughts. I wanted to save you from being damned for all eternity.'

'So that's why you've been clinging to me like a leech all these months. Ever watchful – my guardian angel. Well, you need not concern yourself any longer. When I die it will not be by my own hand, but fighting for my country.'

Father Poole's mouth compressed into a thin hard line. 'I see,' he said, feeling anger stir within him. 'And how many young minds will you poison with your wild dreams of glory before that happens? How many immature lads will you lead against trained troops, to be slaughtered like sheep? You want to sacrifice yourself in a bloody revolution that will have no hope of success, and you want to sacrifice hundreds, perhaps thousands of young lives with you! And for what? So that your name may someday appear in the footnotes of history books!'

'There is no such thing as a bloodless insurrection.'

Father Poole glared up at him from beneath white shaggy eyebrows. 'I hope to God,' he quavered, 'somethin' happens that will divert you from the path you have chosen. When I think of all those young lives already in jeopardy . . .'

'Why don't you pray for a miracle, Father,' Myles said sardonically. 'Perhaps it will occur. Perhaps I'll die from natural causes before I can do any mischief. Or perhaps I'll fall under the wheels of one of those damned automobiles.'

'Or perhaps some distraught parent will kill you!' Father Poole snapped. 'Socrates, yeh know, was forced to drink hemlock for corrupting the youth of Athens!'

Myles gave a sharp intake of breath. His mouth worked soundlessly for several seconds before he found his voice.

'Get out!' he choked, spittle forming on his underlip. 'I've listened to you and your sanctimonious blabberings for the last time! Now get your things and clear out of here! I never want to see you again, do you understand, never!'

Father Poole sighed and rose slowly from his chair. He had difficulty putting on his coat. Myles stood glaring at him, not offering to help. Father Poole placed his tall silk hat on his head and picked up his stick.

He turned towards Myles, his hand on the knob of the door. 'I'll pray for you, Myles,' he said in a low voice.

'Get out!'

Ten minutes later Father Poole walked painfully, with the aid of his stick, up the steep deserted street that led to his church. It was a bright moonlit night and frost glistened on the rooftops. I won't let go of this man, he vowed. I'll storm Heaven with my prayers!

He began to pray silently to himself. He was a firm believer in the power of prayer.


III


He stumbled through the snow, half-frozen, half-insane with grief and despair. The blizzard had swept on and now a full moon hung low in the dark-blue cloudless sky. He struggled from one field to another, making for the safety of the hills.

Once he heard rifle shots far behind him. The sounds made him go a little faster, but progress was slow and difficult and he was near the point of exhaustion. He would have to rest. A snow-covered hedge loomed up ahead of him and he made for the shelter of it. As he reached it, the ground fell away from under him and he rolled down into a deep ditch. There was water at the bottom covered by a thin skin of ice and he splashed into it face first. He scrambled frantically out, coughing and spluttering. He tried to climb the other side, but the snow was too deep and soft and he kept sinking into it. Finally his strength gave out. He had pushed himself to the limit. Semiconscious, he slid slowly down, his feet and legs sinking into the freezing slush at the bottom.

He lay there unable to move, his body half-buried in the snow. Soon he was aware of the paralysing numbness creeping up his body. He knew he was freezing to death, yet he made no effort to stir. The desire to live had died three hours before in that village street amid the swirling snow, the volley of rifle-fire and the screams of wounded and dying men.

Defeat! He gave a low moan of despair. Inept leadership and disastrous hesitations had brought them to this. And treachery. They had been waiting for them, forewarned, rifles at the ready. And they had blundered into them, half-blinded by the wind-driven snow. A few volleys and it was all over. Now the men were scattered and being hunted down like wild animals. A hoarse shout followed by a flurry of shots cut through his benumbed senses. Two more shots rang out. He raised his head, listening. The sounds had come far away to the right. The military had placed picquets along the base of the foothills to prevent anyone escaping into them. If he stayed he would be captured. He knew what capture meant. Rotting in prison for the best part of his life, or a dishonourable death at the end of a rope. Far better to die fighting it out.

He groaned in agony as he pushed himself up into a kneeling position. He sank further into the water. He had no overcoat. He had covered a dying comrade with it on the outskirts of the village. He fumbled in the pocket of his jacket with stiff frozen fingers. He carried a flask of brandy for emergencies. He unscrewed the top with difficulty and drank the entire contents in quick gulps. He threw the flask away and began to rub his hands vigorously together until circulation was restored. He could feel his strength returning; could feel the brandy coursing through his veins, filling him with a warm glow.

Suddenly he crouched as a cry broke the stillness and another cry answered it. The sounds came from the left this time and were much nearer. They were closing in! There was a belt around his waist with holster attached. He drew out the heavy Colt revolver. The ice-cold butt burned the skin of his palm like a flame. This time he was able to make his way up the side of the ditch without much difficulty. He peered over the top. The full bright moon and the reflection of the snow made a mockery of the night. The long line of hedge bordering the next field was a good fifty yards away. He could see himself floundering across in the moonlight, exposed, a struggling dark blot against the shining whiteness. An easy target. But he could not stay here and wait to be captured. He had to go on.

194

Gripping the butt of the revolver, he scrambled to his feet and pushed himself forward. The snow was almost knee-deep; it took him nearly ten minutes to reach the hedge at the other side of the field. Then he rested for a few minutes and pushed on again. He was half-way across the next field when they caught sight of him. There was a cry to halt, then they opened fire, but he was just outside their range; bullets kicked up the snow about five yards away to his left. He did not pause to rest when he reached the next hedge, but continued on, driving his exhausted body ruthlessly onwards. But there were no more cries to halt; no more shots. He had broken through the picquet lines.

He pushed on; the ground was rising; he was almost into the foothills. He could feel hope returning. How many more had broken through? Enough, he hoped, to form several companies and carry on the fight, using guerrilla tactics. They would wipe out the shame of their ignominious defeat!

He did not see the soldier until he was almost on top of him. He must have been crouched behind a bank of snow watching him all the time as he came struggling and panting up the long slope. He stood up, long rifle and bayonet pointing, and challenged him in a frightened voice. He came to a stumbling halt with the point of the bayonet less than a foot away from his chest. He stood swaying, almost on the point of collapse, his arms hanging limply by his sides, the revolver dangling from his right hand. His breath came out in quick tortured gasps. At first his tired dulled brain could not comprehend what had happened. Then realisation came seeping in. Captured – and he had almost made it to safety. His whole body sagged with despair. A sob escaped him. Perhaps it was that that made the soldier lower his rifle, out of a sense of pity.

As the point of the bayonet moved down from the level of his chest he acted without thinking. He brought up his arm in one swift movement and pulled the trigger. The revolver bucked and flared and the figure before him leaped and fell back with outflung arms.

But he had not killed him. As he struggled past the soldier grabbed his ankle. He snarled with fear and pointed the revolver down at the white blur of the face and fired –

He awoke with a start, the explosion of the revolver ringing in his ears, his heart thumping, beads of perspiration on his forehead, trying to collect his thoughts. His trouser legs were scorching from the fire and he twisted to one side. His foot touched the book he had been reading

195

before he had fallen asleep. The only sounds in the room were his heavy breathing and the loud ticking of the clock on the mantelpiece. Ten minutes to nine. He had been asleep for less than half an hour.

The sound of singing came drifting up from the quays below. He limped over to the window, pulled the curtains across and looked down. Crowds of people were coming down the quays, all heading eastwards. Young people mostly; some were singing and prancing along in the middle of the roadway. He was puzzled for a moment, then he suddenly remembered with a slight feeling of shock. Of course – it was New Year's Eve. They were all going to Christchurch Place. There they would gather about the old cathedral and sing and dance till midnight when the bells would herald in the New Year.

He had never felt so lonely, so isolated. Even in prison he had not felt like this. Alone in one's cell at night, one was always conscious of human life on the other side of the stone wall. Even to hear the slow, measured tread of the warder in the corridor outside brought an odd feeling of comfort. He had never felt so abandoned as here at the top of this tall silent house on Usher's Quay.

Something had happened to him after the severance from Father Poole. The hatred that had motivated him for so long had inexplicably withered and died. There had been a vacuum for a while until remorse came seeping in. A memory came back to haunt him: the cold-blooded murder of a soldier on a bleak snow-covered hillside. The man had lowered his rifle in compassion at his sorry state and he had shot him.

'God forgive me,' he whispered, 'God forgive me.'

There was a pagan belief that the soul of a murdered person never entered Paradise, but wandered the terrestrial regions seeking retribution. Reason told him that was all nonsense; but reason was being steadily eroded by a terrible unnatural fear over which he was losing all control.

He could hear more singing on the quays below: still more revellers on their way to the cathedral. The old year was dying. He thought, I'll be sixty-eight this coming March. One year nearer the grave. He was overcome by a feeling of terror. I'll die unshriven, with the murder of a man on my soul! I'll be damned for all eternity! He gripped his arms in fear, his nerves at snapping point. It was as if his mind was a leaking vessel, his sanity seeping out like water.

I've got to get out of here, he told himself frantically; out, quick, before I go mad! He grabbed his overcoat which hung on the inside of the door. He put it on, together with his hat and wrapped a muffler close about his neck. He descended the stairs slowly in the dark, his hand holding tightly on to the banister rail. He could feel the cold of the house and the walls threw back the echoes of his footfalls on the bare stairs. It was like being inside a tomb.

He pulled the heavy hall-door shut and stood on the steps. The cold made him gasp; it nipped his cheeks. It will snow before morning, he told himself. He could feel it – almost taste it. But the sky was clear; stars twinkled. He walked down the quay and turned into a narrow cobbled street, his head bent, and his hands buried in the pockets of his overcoat.

He paused at Wormwood Gate as a rocket shot up into the night sky and exploded a half-mile away to the east. He could see the outline of the cathedral on the ridge. The noise of the crowd surrounding it could be heard even at this distance. He turned away and headed eastward, keeping to the safety of the deserted side streets. Unruliness frightened him; he felt so vulnerable in his frailty.

As he turned the corner into Bridgefoot Street he stopped, daunted by the steep slope before him. He rested for a few minutes, before pushing himself on. Despite the lateness of the hour, some children were still playing on the footpath. Ragged slum children, singing their absurd street rhymes.

> Lizzie Daly sells fish,
> Three ha'pence a dish.
> Cut the heads off,
> Cut the tails off . . .

When he reached Thomas Street he backed into a deep doorway to allow the boisterous crowd to pass by. All Dublin seemed to be heading for Christchurch Place tonight. The dark bulk of St Catherine's faced him on the other side of the wide road. He waited until the street was clear of people and traffic, then stepped forward. He came to a halt in the middle of the road. It was a hallowed spot. Here Robert Emmet was executed more than a hundred years ago. His portrait hung over the fireplace in every tenement room and whitewashed cabin. The ordinary people kept his memory alive in maudlin ballads.

> Bold Robert Emmet, the darlin' of Erin,
> Bold Robert Emmet, he died with a smile . . .

A cynical grunt escaped him. He died with a smile, did he? Faith then, the man who wrote that never saw Emmet being executed, or any other man for that matter. He continued on across the road and down by the side of the church, heading south towards Pimlico, trying to

197

imagine how it had been on that September day all those years ago. The Dragoons with swords drawn, sitting stiff-backed on their restless mounts; the noisy rebellious crowd; the pale-faced young man standing on the platform, waiting to die. Then the drop and the slim, lithe body jerking violently at the end of the rope. No merciful sudden death for that poor romantic young fool, he thought grimly. No quick snapping of the neck, only slow strangulation. The body was still twitching when it was flung on to a table and the head hacked off, blood spurting like a fountain. It was said that every mangy cur in the neighbourhood gathered in packs after the execution, greedily licking the blood from the cobblestones.

The starry-eyed idealists who start revolutions, he told himself, are incapable of visualising the horrors that lie at the end of them. He thought of Emmet's followers, twenty-one in all, who were hanged from the shafts of upturned carts in the narrow streets of the Liberties. Who remembers them? He shook his head. No one, he told himself. They were the forgotten ones like myself. Father Poole was right. Rebellions have never succeeded in Ireland; always they have ended in butchery and defeat. He was astonished at the change in him. It was as if reason had finally dominated a lifetime of emotion. He groaned with weary anger. I've wasted my entire life!

He found himself walking slowly through narrow and murky slum streets flanked by tall tenement houses. The houses had triangular gables and brought back memories of Rotterdam and Brussels. The old Huguenot silk-weaving quarter, but the trade was dying and the silk looms were now few. Groups of men and youths hung about the street corners. He could sense their apathy and hopelessness as he passed. Dublin was not an industrialised city like Manchester or Birmingham; the city's industries of brewing and distilling could only absorb a fraction of the labour force. Here in these slum streets existed an army of the unskilled, all trying to wrest a living anyway they could. Here was hunger and despair and disease . . .

He continued down a cobbled footpath towards a pump where a woman was drawing water. A solitary street-lamp shed feeble green light, leaving most of the street in shadow. This was Jonathan Swift's Dublin. The Dean of St Patrick's had strolled through these streets with muddied cloak, doffing his beaver hat in salute to the fond greetings of beggar and artisan. He wandered aimlessly on from one squalid street to another. Newmarket, Blackpitts, Long Lane.

He came to a halt and stood staring with nostalgia at the windows of the hospital. Lights burned dimly in the wards. Which ward was I in?

Ah, that one on the second floor. Last window on the right, that's where my bed was. Wonder who's in it now? Whoever he is, I envy him, no matter how sick he may be.

He shuffled past the police barracks – formerly the Archbishop's Palace – and turned the corner into the cathedral close. Silence enveloped him. He could hear the echoes of his footsteps on the pavement. Beyond the tall railings was the churchyard, the tombstones a ghostly grey in the starlit night. Opposite, the Deanery. Only one window showed light behind a lowered red blind. Had that been Swift's study? He could picture him hunched over his desk, busily writing . . . forever writing. Never sentimental; always satirical. *Drapier's Letters*; *A Tale of a Tub*; *Gulliver's Travels* . . . He paused outside the side entrance of the cathedral. He sleeps in there now. His beloved Stella also. Companion? Wife? Mistress? No one will ever know for sure. Swift took that secret with him to the grave.

In Patrick Street the pubs had closed, but the ejected patrons still clustered about outside. Voices were raised in song and there were cries of 'Happy New Year!' He made his way through them and turned into steep Hanover Lane. He mounted the slope with effort, breathing hard. He felt exhausted. I must have been walking for nearly an hour, he thought. With luck I may be able to sleep tonight, without dreaming, without lying awake in sweating fear, listening to the sounds creeping up the house.

When he reached Francis Street he paused to catch his breath. There was a bitter cold wind arising. He looked up. Dark heavy clouds were crawling across the sky, blotting out the stars. As he watched, the first few flakes of snow came swirling down. He pulled the collar of his overcoat up about his ears and crossed the road, entering a maze of narrow, ruined streets. His pace slackened when he reached Meath Street. He was on his way home.

Fear returned and his mouth went dry. Ten minutes from now he would be climbing the stairs in the dark. Who knows what would be waiting there? Perhaps tonight, in these last dying hours of the old year, he would show himself.

'O Christ,' he whimpered, shuddering. He forced himself on. There was nausea in his stomach and sweat was gathering on his forehead. It was an effort to put one foot before the other. The church loomed above him.

Suddenly his legs buckled and he went staggering sideways against the railings. He clutched at a rail and held on, heart thumping, the blood pounding in his ears, his mind wailing for mercy.

A bell tolled above his head. Only then did he realise he was outside a church – Father Poole's church. Acting on impulse he pushed in the gate. Holding on to the railings, he moved down the passage between the church and the presbytery. When he reached the door he pulled on the bell and waited. The snow was smothering everything in whiteness, deadening all sound.

After a minute he heard footsteps, and the door was pulled open. A young priest faced him. He was of medium height and of slim build, with a pale sensitive face.

'Yes, what is it?' he asked.

Myles opened his mouth, but all he could utter was an unintelligible croak. His throat felt parched and raw.

'Yes, what is it?' the priest asked again, a note of impatience in his voice.

'Father Poole,' Myles managed to utter hoarsely. A snowflake landed on his lower lip and immediately dissolved.

The priest shook his head. 'No, I'm sorry. Father Poole is not available. Is it urgent? A sick call? I'll go myself.'

Myles shook his head. 'No, no, no sick call,' he said, regretting now he had rung the bell. 'It's of no consequence. Just tell him Myles Burke called,' he said and moved away. He heard the door close behind him, but just as he reached the gate it was hurriedly opened again and a voice called, 'Just a moment! Please wait!'

He turned, watching the priest coming towards him through the falling snow. He had put on his overcoat and was pulling the collar up about his ears. As he came into the light of the street-lamp Myles could see an exasperated look on his face.

'You did say your name was Myles Burke?'

Myles nodded.

'Father Poole became very excited when I mentioned your name, and very annoyed when I told him I had let you go. Was he expecting you?'

'No.'

'Odd, somehow I got the impression he was. No matter. Come along.'

The priest led him down a passage, knocked and opened the door and entered the room. Seconds later he poked his head through the doorway and beckoned. Myles walked forward reluctantly.

Father Poole sat beside a crackling fire, his breviary on his lap, watching. As Myles came into view, his hat in his hand, all arrogance gone, he thought, All praise to almighty God, he's come at last.

'Come in, Myles, to the fire and don't be standin' out there in the cold. Come in, man.'

Myles edged in, hands twisting the brim of his hat, while the young priest stood at the door looking curiously on.

'Forgive the lateness of the hour, Father,' Myles mumbled apologetically.

Father Poole pointed to the chair opposite him on the other side of the fireplace.

'Sit down there, Myles, and thaw out. Man, dear, yeh must be perished with the cold.'

He hoped the tremor in his voice went unnoticed, for he was appalled at Myles's appearance. The grey skin; the red-rimmed eyes; the sunken cheeks. The eyes had a darting, hunted look.

Father Poole turned his attention to the curate standing by the door.

'Robert, two glasses of brandy, like a good lad.'

'Now, Father,' the young priest protested, 'you know how I disapprove of – '

'For medicinal purposes, Robert,' Father Poole interrupted. 'When you reach our age, you'll know what it feels like to have frost in yer bones.'

The young priest poured brandy from a decanter and handed each man a glass.

'Leave us now, Robert,' Father Poole said.

'Only for a short while, Father,' the young priest rejoined. 'It's very late.'

Father Poole sighed as he closed the door. 'That's Father Kinsella, one of my two curates,' he explained. 'D'yeh know what it is, Myles. I'm Parish Priest and yet the pair of them treat me like a child.' He raised his glass. 'Here's wishin' you a Happy New Year, Myles,' he said and raised the glass to his lips.

Myles did not drink. He held the glass between his hands, staring shamefacedly down at it. 'You're making it very hard for me, Father,' he muttered.

'How so, Myles?' Father Poole inquired, placing the empty glass on a low table beside him.

'Your kindness, your hospitality. When I think of the abuse I gave you . . .'

Father Poole raised a hand. 'Ahhh, will yeh stop. Sure I was just as bad. Forget it now and drink yer brandy. Go on, 'twill do yeh good.'

Myles drank slowly. Father Poole gazed thoughtfully at him, noticing the way his hand shook.

Myles drained the glass. A full two minutes passed before he spoke.

'Father Poole, you can't imagine the hell I've been through these past few weeks.'

'If there is anythin' troublin' you, Myles,' Father Poole said, 'I would suggest you talk about it. It doesn't do, yeh know, to bottle things up.'

Myles raised his head and stared at him with wide terror-filled eyes. 'Oh, God, how I fear him,' he whispered. 'If he would only leave me in peace.' Suddenly his face crumpled and tears sprang to his eyes. He bowed his head. A sob tore free.

'Fear who, Myles?' Father Poole asked with concern.

'The man I killed,' Myles replied brokenly. 'The man I murdered.'

'You murdered a man?' Father Poole gasped, horrified. 'God between us and all harm! When did this happen?'

'When?' Myles passed a hand dazedly across his forehead. 'Oh, a long time ago. After the Tallaght fight.'

'The man was a soldier?'

'Yes.'

'Of course, in battle, one has to defend – '

'It wasn't like that. The man had pity for me and I shot him!' He paused. 'Now, at night, in that big old house, I can sense his presence. Sometimes I think I can see him.'

'Nerves,' Father Poole stated firmly, 'just nerves – and an over-wrought imagination. My advice is to see a doctor, Myles. A good tonic can work wonders.'

'I don't want to die in a state of mortal sin! I don't want to die with a man's death staining my soul! I want God's forgiveness for the crime I committed!'

Father Poole was startled by the expression of terror on the face and the rising hysteria in the voice. He raised his hand.

'Calm yourself, Myles, for heaven's sake!'

'I want to confess! I want your absolution!'

Father Poole nodded. 'Yes, yes, but calm yourself first.' He stood up and took his stole from the shelf where he always kept it. He placed it around his neck and sat down again covering his eyes with his hand. This was the moment he had been waiting for since his ordination. No longer need he envy his long-dead friend, Martin Fenlon, for having saved the soul of an unrepentant sinner. The envy was dead now. Victory was his. He had achieved his life's ambition. He waited patiently. Myles began to talk in a slow calm voice. Father Poole listened, now and then muttering a few words of encouragement whenever the voice faltered.

'God is all merciful, Myles,' Father Poole said when Myles had finished. 'He understands your agony of mind. All He wants is for you to be truly sorry. And you are sorry, aren't you, Myles? For all your sins?'

Myles nodded. 'Yes, Father. Truly sorry.'

'Then that's all God wants. He wants you to come back to Him, contrite, beggin' forgiveness. Like the prodigal son.' He paused. 'Say an Act of Contrition now, and I'll give you absolution.'

Myles looked at him helplessly. 'I'm sorry, Father, I've forgotten. It's been so long.'

'Never mind,' Father Poole assured him. 'Just repeat after me . . .'

Outside the snow beat against the window-panes. Above their heads the clock ticked away the last thirty minutes of the old year. Father Poole closed his eyes and joined his hands, Latin phrases stumbling over his tongue. Myles stared in wonder at the beads of sweat standing out on his forehead.

The mumblings ceased and Father Poole opened his eyes and smiled. 'You are absolved, Myles. Your sins are forgiven.'

'I feel so much relieved, Father.'

'You have made an old man very happy, Myles.'

'Pray for me, Father.'

'I've never stopped prayin' for you, Myles. And I'll pray for him, the man you killed.'

'And for all the other men I killed.'

Father Poole stared at him for a long while. The clock ticked away in the silence. 'All the other men you killed?'

Myles nodded. 'But I never felt remorse about them the same way I did about him. I slew them in the heat of battle. It was kill or be killed.'

'What battle was that?' Father Poole asked dazedly. A feeling of disquiet was beginning to stir in his brain.

'Oh, there were quite a few. Bull Run, Fair Oaks, Antietam. But the bloodiest of all was Fredericksburg. Have you ever heard of the Battle of Fredericksburg, Father?'

Father Poole shook his head.

'Garret Lysaght covered himself with glory in that battle, leading his men in one final suicidal charge. Less than a hundred men took part in that assault. Only two survived – Garret Lysaght and myself. Oh yes,' he nodded in affirmation, taking the stunned look on Father Poole's face for disbelief. 'When night fell, Garret and myself managed to crawl back to our lines carrying the colours with us, even though both of us were wounded. The military histories never mention my name though. I am always referred to as Lysaght's "second-in-command".'

Father Poole raised a trembling hand to his forehead. Oh God, he thought, how could I have been so stupid, so blind. He had been dealing with human nature all his life; he should have been able to

203

recognise the symptoms before now. The moroseness; the sudden upsurges of rage. What was the name of that word mentioned in that handbook on psychology – the one in the chapter on sudden changes of personality? Schiz . . . schiz . . . But he was too upset to remember clearly. He lowered his hand and stared at the man sitting facing him. So relaxed now; yet only a short while ago he had been in the depths of despair.

'. . . we were transferred to a hospital in Washington. Later, we were brought to the White House and personally decorated by Abraham Lincoln himself. You have heard of Abraham Lincoln, Father? Why of course you have. The President of the United States of America.'

Father Poole shook his head and sighed. The poor creature, he thought, the poor creature. The only way he could escape from the harsh realities of life was to lose himself in books, allowing his imagination to take over, seeing himself as the characters he read about.

'. . . I met Garret Lysaght in Paris many years later. He planned to attack Pentonville Prison in London and release the Fenian prisoners there . . .'

No longer is he able to differentiate between fantasy and reality, Father Poole told himself. He could feel tears pricking his eyes. The poor creature, the poor creature.

'. . . but we were betrayed by a British Secret Service agent posing as a Fenian officer. Arrests were made all over London. I was caught like a rat in a trap in my lodgings. I was forced to shoot it out with detectives before being overpowered.'

Father Poole uttered a low groan. Sweet God, he thought, from where did he get that from? Some trashy novel about spies and anarchists?

'. . . Then someone took a grip on my hair and pulled. I was dragged face downward across the floor and on to the landing and then down the stairs . . .'

Father Poole moved restlessly, agitated. I can't listen to any more of this, he thought wildly. He was overcome by a feeling of anger. God had played a cruel joke on him. His eyes filled with tears, tears of rage and frustration.

Myles ceased talking. 'Why are you crying, Father?' he asked in astonishment.

Father Poole tried to smile through his tears. 'Just tired,' he whispered, 'just tired.'

Myles rose to his feet. 'Forgive me, Father. I did not mean to keep you so – '

There was a sharp knock, and the door was pushed open. Father Kinsella strode into the room, rasping with annoyance.

'Really, I must protest!'

Father Poole covered his eyes with his hand, not wanting his curate to see his tears.

Myles began to apologise. 'My fault entirely. I did not realise how late it was.'

Father Kinsella looked at Father Poole, lying slumped in his chair, his hand still covering his eyes.

'There you are, you see,' he exclaimed in a shrill voice, 'he's overtaxed himself! I should not have allowed you to see him!'

'I'll go at once,' Myles said. He bent down towards Father Poole. 'Goodbye, Father. We'll meet again soon.'

Father Poole raised a hand feebly in farewell, and let it drop back into his lap.

Father Kinsella stood in the open doorway, looking up at the sky. 'You're in luck,' he said to Myles, 'it has stopped snowing.' He gave a curt nod to Myles's goodnight and closed the door.

Myles crunched his way homeward. The streets and roofs of the houses were covered with a thick mantle of snow. It gave a curious dignity to the tall crumbling tenements, covering the squalor and ugliness with purifying whiteness.

He too felt cleansed. For the first time in his life he was aware of a blissful inner peace. He was no longer afraid to go home. Father Poole and his prayers had exorcised that particular fear forever. The vision of Father Poole's weeping exhausted figure came back to him. Burdened with the weight of my sins, he told himself grimly.

Just as he reached the bottom of the hill a church bell began to ring out. More bells joined in, this time from the top of the hill behind him. He stopped to listen. There were churches and cathedrals all around this spot which once had been the centre of the old mediaeval town. A ship's siren moaned from down river. Then all the bells joined in with wild abandon, ringing joyfully and merrily, welcoming in the New Year.

# Chapter Seven

## I

'God save all here!' Father Devlin boomed, taking off his tall silk hat as he strode into the wide, big, lamp-lit kitchen of the O'Malley farmhouse. A tall, middle-aged man followed him. He had a narrow mournful face, tapering to a long pointed chin. His iron-grey hair was parted in the middle and he had the mutton-chop whiskers of a bygone age.

Bull O'Malley and his wife rose from their chairs before the fire, Peg holding a basket containing wool and knitting needles.

'Why, Father Devlin!' Bull O'Malley exclaimed. 'And Malachi! Well, well! Come over here to the fire. This is a pleasant surprise. Peg, fetch the whiskey.'

Father Devlin lifted his hands in protest. 'Now, now, now . . . Please, Mr O'Malley, don't go to any trouble on our account.'

'Ah, wisha, Father,' Bull O'Malley said in a grieved voice, 'what trouble. Here now, let me help ye off with yer coat and hat. Come on now, Malachi, don't stand on ceremony here. Make yerself at home.'

Father Devlin, divested of his overcoat, seated his bulk on the chair facing the fire. He was a powerfully built man, over six feet tall with sleek black hair greying at the temples. The outward tips of his bushy eyebrows were tilted upwards slightly, giving him a demonic appearance. There was a striking similarity between himself and Bull O'Malley. Both were tall beefy men with the heavy, strong-boned features of the Irish peasant. A stranger would have taken them for brothers.

''Tis a cold night to be travellin' the roads, Father,' Bull O'Malley said, sitting down beside him. Courtesy forbade him from asking the reason for this unexpected visit. Father Devlin called twice a year to collect the Easter and Christmas dues. Malachi was a more frequent visitor. But the two of them together?

''Tis, 'tis,' Father Devlin agreed. 'But I like to visit my parishioners, cold weather notwithstanding.'

Malachi Drennan sat down beside the wide fireplace.

'Father Devlin's trap broke an axle,' he explained to Bull O'Malley.

'It did, it did,' Father Devlin said, nodding his head. 'And 'tis a great inconvenience.'

Bull O'Malley clicked his tongue in sympathy. 'Will it take long to have it fixed?' he asked.

'I'll have it by the end of the week, I've been told,' Father Devlin replied. 'In the meantime, Malachi here has kindly offered to drive me in his own trap anywhere I wish to go.'

Malachi lowered his head in embarrassment. 'Only doin' my Christian duty, Father,' he murmured humbly.

Father Devlin clapped him on the shoulder with a large heavy hand. 'And it does ye every credit, Malachi me son,' he boomed, 'indeed it does.'

Peg came in carrying a tray with three glasses of whiskey. She went from one man to the other. Father Devlin raised his glass in a toast.

'And here are my best wishes to the O'Malley family. May they remain in good health and continue to prosper.' He turned his head. 'And to you, too, Malachi.'

The two men raised their glasses in salute towards the priest and sipped reverently. Peg sat down, picked up her basket and resumed her knitting.

Father Devlin drained his glass, smacking his lips appreciatively. 'And where,' he asked, 'are the family?'

'Sonny has set the date for next year,' Bull O'Malley said. 'Easter Monday. It's yerself will be marryin' them, I hope, Father.'

'Indeed and I will,' Father Devlin declared, face beaming, 'and with pleasure.'

Malachi Drennan leaned forward with a sly smile on his face. 'Faith, and I'm thinkin',' he sniggered, 'Luke won't be long after him.'

Bull O'Malley chuckled and drained his glass. 'Indeed and I think ye may be right, Malachi,' he said, coughing a little as the whiskey burned his throat. 'It's about time those two lads of mine settled down and started to raise families. The testin' of a man is when he has the responsibility of a wife and children.'

Father Devlin nodded in approval. 'True, true.'

'Ye've two fine lads there, Barney,' Malachi said, addressing himself to Bull O'Malley.

Father Devlin nodded in agreement. 'Two fine upstanding young men,' he said. 'A credit to their parish – and to their parents,' he added.

'They're hardworkin' lads, Father,' Bull O'Malley said, 'both of them.'

'Indeed and I've heard great accounts of them,' Father Devlin said. 'It's a pity the other young men of the parish don't follow their example. Slack-mouthed idlers most of them, I'm sorry to say. I see them in the village day after day, standin' outside the public houses with their hands in their pockets, passin' remarks on the people passing by.' His face darkened with anger. 'D'ye know what it is,' he growled, 'a few years in the army would do some of those boyos a power of good. And a harsh taskmaster of a sergeant over them. Man, then they'd hop to it!'

He twisted round to Bull O'Malley. 'Is that fellow Gallagher still workin' for ye?' he asked sourly.

Bull O'Malley nodded. 'He is, Father,' he said.

Father Devlin faced the fire again, scowling. 'That scoundrel sets a bad example for the other young men of the parish. He's a trouble maker! Always was and always will be. Whenever I meet him in the village,' he said bitterly, 'which is not very often, I'm glad to say, he walks right past me without even raisin' his cap in respect . . .'

'Oh my,' Bull O'Malley murmured in sympathy.

'. . . without even as much as touchin' the peak! Why, once he looked me right in the face and sneered. Actually sneered!'

'What class of a Christian would ye call that!' Malachi exclaimed.

'Of course he was away in England for a good many years,' Bull O'Malley offered by way of explanation.

'Ah well,' Malachi sniffed loftily, 'that explains a lot.'

Peg ceased her knitting and raised her head. 'More whiskey, Father? Mr Drennan?'

Both men looked at her in mild surprise. Her quietness and unobtrusiveness had made them forget her presence. Father Devlin raised his hands in mock horror.

'Heavens no, Mrs O'Malley!' he exclaimed. 'Ye'd have that young curate of mine sniffin' the air like a hound. He'd probably think I was after spendin' the entire night in a shebeen.'

Bull O'Malley and Malachi laughed.

Then Father Devlin looked about him. 'And where is the girl?' he asked.

'Out visitin' friends, Father,' Bull O'Malley answered.

'How old is she now?'

Bull O'Malley scratched his head. 'She'll be twenty-two in . . .' He turned to his wife for confirmation. 'April, isn't it?'

Peg O'Malley nodded.

'And is she keepin' company?' Father Devlin asked.

'She is not, then, Father,' Bull O'Malley stated emphatically.

208

'Has she ever mentioned anyone – men, I mean?'

'She never did, Father.'

'It could be that the girl has a vocation. Tell me, has she ever talked about becomin' a nun?'

Bull O'Malley's mouth dropped open. 'A nun! Una?' Then gasped, and started to laugh as though Father Devlin had made a joke, but ceased abruptly at the stern look on Father Devlin's face.

'Forgive me, Father, but the thought of Una becomin' a nun . . . Not that she doesn't take her religion seriously,' he added hastily, 'she does. But I know me own daughter well enough to know that she doesn't want to lock herself inside a convent for the rest of her life. She's too high-spirited a girl for that.'

'High-spirited. Hmmm.' Father Devlin frowned, shook his head and sighed. 'And she's nearly twenty-two, you say. A full-grown woman.' He shot a reproving glance at Bull O'Malley. 'It doesn't do, ye know,' he said sternly, 'to let the years slip past like this. I don't approve of late marriages, especially for women. A woman should be married young and have all her children before she's forty.'

Bull O'Malley gave a shrug. 'I suppose you're right, Father.'

'There's no supposin' about it!' Father Devlin snapped. 'I am right!'

Bull O'Malley could feel his temper rising. If it had been any priest other than Father Devlin he would have told him to go to hell and mind his own business. But he knew Father Devlin would never tolerate such talk from any of his parishioners. He was a good man to have for a friend but a dangerous one to have for an enemy.

'The fact is, Father,' he said, trying to keep the anger out of his voice, 'there's not a man in this parish I'd allow my daughter to marry!'

Father Devlin opened his mouth to say something, but Bull O'Malley raised his hand in objection. 'Now hear me out, Father. Una has a good home here and she wants for nothin'. She gets anythin' she asks for: clothes, money – anythin'. I spoil her, I admit it.' He thrust his face aggressively towards Father Devlin, who sat looking quietly and steadfastly at him, his hands joined over his paunch.

'Now you tell me, Father, what man in this parish could give her the comforts she's used to? Eh? Could he give her the best of food or pay for a doctor if she fell sick or buy her fine clothes or anythin' she fancies? Answer me that.'

'Not very many, I have to admit, Mr O'Malley,' Father Devlin replied.

'Them and their few miserable acres,' Bull O'Malley went on contemptuously. 'Paupers, that's all they are! Aye, and I daresay there's quite a few would give their right arm to marry Una – and the dowry that goes with her. But by God,' he added grimly, 'let one of them approach me and I'll take the pitchfork to them!'

'Now, now, there's no need – ' Father Devlin began.

'There's that Brady girl that married the Finnegan fella,' Bull O'Malley rasped. 'Now there's an example for ye! I remember that girl when she was the grandest lookin' creature on two feet. Then she married Finnegan. A bog farmer with a few sickly cows. Now look at her! Livin' on the edge of starvation with two small children! Goin' around practically in rags! Workin' on that small farm from mornin' to night! And Finnegan spendin' what little money he has on drink, rollin' home at all hours of the night from the pubs in the village, drunk as a lord. And to think his wife is the same age as Una! My God! The woman is only twenty-two. To look at her now ye would take her for fifty-two. And ye are wonderin' why Una is not married. Well, that's the reason! Who around here could give her the life and comfort she gets here? Who? Answer me that if ye can, Father Devlin.'

There was a brief silence. Then Malachi Drennan cleared his throat and croacked, 'I could, Barney.'

The quick deft hands abruptly ceased their knitting. Peg glanced sharply across at Malachi who was staring intently at her husband, two bright spots of red on his pale cheeks. Bull O'Malley gaped back at him as Father Devlin sat in silence staring at the fire. Eventually Bull O'Malley found his voice.

'*You*, Malachi?' He forced a smile on his face, prepared to accept Malachi's assertion as a joke. He even tried to laugh. 'Why, you're nearly as old as meself.'

Malachi straightened up in his chair, an aggrieved look on his face. 'Well now, Barney, ye may think yerself an old man but I don't think of meself as such!' he exclaimed testily. 'Why, I can reap a field with the best of them. I'm up at the crack of dawn every mornin' milkin' the cows, attendin' to the poultry, sowin', reapin'. Pick any two young men ye fancy and by God I'll work them into the ground, so I will!'

'But Una is not quite twenty-two,' Bull O'Malley protested.

'And I'm fifty-six years of age and I say what of it,' Malachi retorted. 'I have me health, thank God. Aye, and I have all me hair and most of me teeth and that's more than many men ten years younger can boast of!'

Before Bull O'Malley could get a chance to reply, Father Devlin raised a conciliatory hand and waved it like a flag of truce.

'Now men, men,' he said, laying a hand on Bull O'Malley's shoulder,

'I can understand your surprise at Mr Drennan askin' for the hand of your daughter. It's a natural reaction. If I was not a priest and if I was in your position, I imagine I would feel the same. But I don't think Mr Drennan . . .' he shot a quick look in Malachi's direction, before turning a sympathetic face to Bull O'Malley 'I don't think Mr Drennan intended that he should ask for your daughter and expect you to make a decision on the spur of the moment. Isn't that so, Malachi?'

Malachi gave a dumb nod.

'No, no, no,' Father Devlin continued, 'nothing like that at all. He is merely makin' a formal proposal of marriage and is simply askin' you as the girl's father to think about it. Take all the time you want. There's no hurry.'

Bull O'Malley's heavy eyebrows were drawn down in a confused frown. His agitation was plain as he rubbed the palm of one beefy hand against the back of the other, as if he were suffering from a skin irritation.

'Well, as you say, Father,' he mumbled, avoiding Father Devlin's penetrating stare, 'I'll have to think about it.'

'Of course you'll have to,' Father Devlin boomed cheerfully, 'it's only to be expected.'

''Tis only the difference in the ages,' Bull O'Malley persisted.

Father Devlin heaved a sigh. 'Do ye know what it is, Mr O'Malley,' he said, 'I seriously think we attach too much importance to this question of ages between man and wife. I really do. Take for instance a young couple just married. For a short while it's all sunshine and roses. Then the children start to arrive and the husband has to stay at home at nights with the wife and help look after them. Gradually, all kinds of little problems begin to crop up. Responsibility after responsibility is laid on the husband's shoulders. Then the burden becomes too much for him and he becomes restless. He begins to long for the happy carefree days when he was single. And that, by the Lord Harry . . .' he slammed a fist into the open palm of his left hand, 'is how all the trouble starts!'

Then he spread his arms wide. 'Now a mature man would not do any of these things,' he said. 'He would not, faith. He would be steady and sensible and considerate and would not have that rovin' gleam in his eye. His wife and family would come first. And that's what every household needs – a steady, sensible hardworkin' man. Someone like Malachi here.'

'Aye, I know what ye mean, Father,' Bull O'Malley said. 'But Una is of age and it's *she* who will decide who she wants to marry. With my blessin' of course,' he added hastily. 'She may be of age, but I won't allow her to marry someone who can't provide for her!'

'Yes, yes,' Father Devlin nodded, 'so ye told me.' He rubbed his chin reflectively. 'But do ye really think,' he said after a short pause, 'it's wise to allow a young person to make a decision of that sort? Marriage is a very important step to take. It requires prudence and foresight, qualities, alas, sadly lackin' in so many young people.' He laid a hand on Bull O'Malley's sleeve. 'The best marriages of all were the made marriages,' he said authoritatively. 'And yet people scoff nowadays at the old traditional ways, sayin' that the day of the match-maker is gone. Tommy rot!' he snorted. 'Drivel! Tell me, Mr O'Malley, did ye ever hear of any of those marriages turnin' out bad? Did ye now? Answer me truthfully.' He glared as if an answer to the contrary would be taken as heresy. He gave a triumphant bellow as Bull O'Malley shook his head. 'Of course ye didn't! And I never did either. And the reason why the made marriages were happy ones is because the people who arranged them were mature level-headed people.'

Bull O'Malley suppressed a sigh, and stared gloomily at the fire. There was no point in arguing any longer. Father Devlin had an answer for everything.

Peg sat rigid her basket on her lap, knitting forgotten, keeping in check the smoulderings anger inside her. She knew that Father Devlin and Malachi Drennan had rehearsed carefully before coming here. Her sidelong glance had caught a quick exchange of looks between them as if Father Devlin were silently saying, 'I've done my share; now it's your turn.' She waited.

Malachi cleared his throat. 'I have a great regard for the girl, Barney,' he said. 'I want ye to know that.'

Bull O'Malley merely nodded.

'She would never lack anythin' she desires,' Malachi went on. 'Money, clothes . . .'

Bull O'Malley grunted.

'She would never have to lift a hand to do an ounce of work – not as much as wash a cup. There would be servants to do all that.'

'Why, the girl would have the life of a lady,' Father Devlin said.

'She would, Father, she would,' Malachi responded eagerly. He took a deep breath. 'D'ye know,' he ventured cautiously, 'if the marriage ever did take place, all this part of Mayo would belong to the O'Malleys and the Drennans. If I should have children, all my land would go to them – your grandchildren, Barney.' He looked towards Peg, who was staring at him with undisguised loathing. He turned his head hastily away.

There was a long, awkward silence. Father Devlin decided this was the time to be mute and neutral. He sat looking at the fire with lowered eyelids, a contented expression on his face, looking like a big over-fed cat.

Malachi could feel beads of sweat on his forehead. He had played all his cards but one – his last and best.

'If your daughter should ever consent to be my wife, Barney,' he said, 'I would be willin' to sell seventy acres of my land to you – but only to you.'

He knew the power Bull O'Malley had over his children. He knew he was forcing his two sons into loveless marriages with the Costello sisters so that they could gain the Costello acres. He knew Una O'Malley would never marry him unless she was forced to do so by her father. Therefore he had to bribe Bull O'Malley, but the bribe had to be big enough and tempting enough for him to be unable to resist it.

Peg O'Malley watched her husband apprehensively. She cherished a forlorn hope that he would curse Malachi Drennan for a damned lecher and order him and Father Devlin from the house. She gave a low moan of despair as Bull O'Malley spoke.

'Which seventy acres are ye talkin' about, Malachi?'

Malachi licked his lips. 'The southern part of me farm borderin' the Westport road. Between the village and the river.'

Bull O'Malley stared at him in astonishment.

Father Devlin took out his watch and looked at it. 'Good heavens!' he exclaimed. 'Is that the hour it's at?' He put the watch back in his waistcoat pocket and rose to his feet. 'I greatly fear, Malachi,' he boomed, 'we've worn out our welcome. We're keepin' Mr O'Malley and his good lady from their beds.'

'No indeed,' Bull O'Malley protested, 'yerself and Malachi are welcome to stay as long as ye like.' He followed them out.

Malachi climbed into the trap and took the reins. Father Devlin got in alongside him. Then Father Devlin placed a hand on Bull O'Malley's shoulder and lowered his head towards him. 'I'm glad we've had this little talk, Mr O'Malley,' he said in a low voice. 'I hope ye'll give it plenty of thought.'

Bull O'Malley nodded.

'And I'm doin' this just as much for the girl as for Malachi,' Father Devlin continued. 'I want ye to know that. It's important that ye understand.'

Bull O'Malley nodded again. 'I do, Father, I do.'

Malachi clucked his tongue, shook the reins and the mare, happy to be moving again after standing in the cold for so long, trotted briskly away. Bull O'Malley closed the door and walked back into the kitchen where Peg still sat on the chair, holding the basket on her lap.

'Not a word about any of this to the lads or Una,' Bull O'Malley said. '*Especially* Una.'

'She will hear about it sooner or later,' Peg replied.

'Well, when she does hear about it,' Bull O'Malley snapped, ''twill be from me and only me! So ye keep yer bloody mouth shut!'

She glared up at him. 'Your not going to encourage her to marry that old goat?'

'Of course not!' he answered hotly, but she could detect the lack of conviction in his voice. She said no more.

A little later she lay in bed beside her snoring husband, staring into the darkness. She was unable to sleep. She could hear voices and movements in the kitchen below. Una had arrived home first, followed by Luke and Sonny. She knew Una had been with Con Gallagher, not with friends as her father and half-brothers thought. Una confided all her secrets to her. She would tell Una about the visit of Father Devlin and Malachi Drennan.

Malachi Drennan could not sleep either. He lay awake in the big double bed where for sixteen years he had striven desperately to create the heirs to inherit his many rich acres, but there had been no children. He did not worry too much in those early years of his married life, telling himself that some women were slow to conceive, but after twelve years and his wife still childless, he had to accept the painful fact that she never would have any. The thought drove him to despair and drink. He was the last of his line. There would be no one to carry on the Drennan name, no one to inherit his land. When he died the O'Malleys and the scruff from the hills would fight like tinkers for possession, dividing up the land generations of Drennans had fought and died for – had even apostatised for. He shifted restlessly on the bed, thinking of what would happen if he should die without issue.

When his wife died he began to look around for another; someone who would give him the children he needed. But there were few marriageable girls left. Carewstown had suffered like every other parish in Mayo from emigration. Each year saw the exodus of the young to the El Dorado they called America. The few that were left he had rejected after investigating them and their backgrounds. One belonged to a family with a long history of ill-health; another was a slattern with a fondness for the bottle; yet another had a family who had a habit of making other people's homes their own. He had crossed them off one by one until there was no one left but Una O'Malley.

But she was unobtainable. Bull O'Malley and his sons doted upon her, treating her like a queen and letting no man near her.

This made him desire her all the more. Whenever he visited the O'Malleys he found himself secretly staring at her, letting his eyes roam over her full breasts and wide hips, gauging her breeding possibilities as he would a heifer at a fair. At nights he imagined she was beside him in bed, naked and wanton, submitting eagerly to his advances. He had had to confess his carnal thoughts to Father Devlin and had been severely censured. Perhaps that was why Father Devlin had volunteered to act as match-maker, preferring to have him married rather than have him fornicate, as he had in the past, with the tinker women passing through the district.

'Remember Saint Paul's advice to the unmarried, Malachi. "But if ye do not have self-control, let ye marry, for it is better to marry than to burn." '

But seventy acres! He winced. That was nearly one-third of his holding, but if he wanted Una O'Malley that was the price he would have to pay. And she would marry him – Bull O'Malley would see to that. He had seen the look of greed on Bull O'Malley's face and he smiled to himself in the dark.


II


They sat at the kitchen table sipping tea, waiting. Luke and Sonny had taken off their jackets and high hard collars and now sat with their shirt sleeves rolled up, the noon sun shining through the windows warming their backs. They could hear Doctor McCann moving about in Una's bedroom overhead.

'Maybe it was somethin' she had for breakfast,' Sonny said.

Peg, sitting at the head of the table holding a cup between her hands, nodded. 'Maybe.'

They had been about to leave for Mass when Una had suddenly taken ill. Sonny, alarmed at the deathly pallor of his half-sister's face, had jumped into the trap and had driven furiously to the village for the doctor. Luke lit a cigarette.

215

'She hasn't been lookin' too well lately,' he murmured.

Peg closed her eyes. Oh God, she thought, that this should happen now and himself away. Why didn't Una tell me? Was it because she was ashamed? Did she think I wouldn't understand? She sighed, and wondered if all she had done to help the young couple could possibly have been worth it. But then she remembered how they would look at each other, the tenderness in Con's face as he gently held Una in his arms mirrored by the shining happiness in Una. Oh yes, it had all been worth it.

They heard the door close and the heavy clump of feet on the stairs and rose to their feet as Doctor McCann stepped into the kitchen. He was a tall heavy-set man of about sixty, bald, with a brick-red face and a walrus moustache. He stood looking at them in silence, his leather bag in his hand, tweed suit smelling strongly of pipe tobacco.

'Well?' Luke asked.

Doctor McCann shrugged his shoulders. 'Nothing to be unduly alarmed about,' he said in his clipped Northern accent.

'What's wrong with her?' Luke asked impatiently.

The Doctor ignored him and turned his attention to Peg. 'Your daughter is pregnant, ma'am,' he said quietly. He waited for her reaction, anticipating the floor of tears and the hysterics. Her calmness surprised him. He pursed his lips thoughtfully. You knew all along, he thought.

'What's that ye said?' Luke hissed.

The Doctor turned to face him. Luke's face was ashen. Sonny stood behind him, his mouth open.

'I said the girl is pregnant,' he replied. 'Two months, I would say.'

'Yer wrong!' Sonny cried wildly. 'Ye've made a mistake!'

Doctor McCann turned an exasperated face away and addressed himself to Peg. 'And where's himself?' he inquired.

'In Dublin,' she replied in a low voice. 'He won't be back till Friday.'

Luke suddenly strode forward, brushing past the doctor, making for the stairs. Doctor McCann grabbed him by the arm and held him.

'Where are you going?'

Luke turned a venomous face to him. 'Upstairs. I want to have a word with that . . . that . . .'

'You will not go near her!' Doctor McCann released his grip and blocked the way to the stairs. He knew how to deal with Luke. Thrusting his big red face forward he jabbed Luke in the chest with a thick forefinger.

'Now you listen to me, laddiebuck,' he growled. 'That girl up there is

216

my patient, and if you harm her or the child she is carrying, then you'll answer to me – and the law,' he added grimly. He turned to Peg. 'I'm leaving her in your care, ma'am,' he said. 'I'll drop in tomorrow to see how she is.'

Peg O'Malley nodded. 'Thank you, doctor.' She shifted her gaze to Sonny. 'Sonny, drive the doctor home.'

Doctor McCann waved a hand. 'Thank you, but no. A walk before lunch sharpens the appetite.' He hesitated for a few seconds, then gave a curt nod. 'Well, good-day to you all,' he said, and walked out.

When the door closed, Luke turned to his step-mother. The look in his eyes frightened her: there was the look of murder in them.

'I want ye to go upstairs to yer daughter,' he said in a low, hard voice, 'and ask her to answer one question. I want her to give you the name of the man responsible.'

She stood erect with her arms by her sides, hands clenched, nails biting into the flesh of her palms. She could not let Luke see how frightened she was. She took a deep breath and then spoke, keeping her voice low and steady.

'There's no need to ask Una. I know who the father is.'

Luke's eyes narrowed. 'You know. *How* do ye know?'

Sonny took a step forward. 'Tell us who he is,' he cried, 'and by Christ we'll – !'

'Stop that!' Peg O'Malley commanded sharply, looking from one to the other. 'I'll tell you,' she said, 'but first both of you will listen to what I have to say.'

They stood side by side, glaring, waiting impatiently for her to speak.

'One night a few months ago – early spring it was . . .' She told them about the visit of Father Devlin and Malachi Drennan; of how Malachi had asked for Una's hand in marriage; of how he had offered to sell seventy acres of his best land to their father if the marriage took place.

They stared at her in silence, too stunned to speak. It was Sonny who managed to find his voice first.

'*Malachi Drennan*! Are ye tellin' us that he's the one responsible?'

'Of course not!' Peg O'Malley snapped. 'My God, Una wouldn't allow him to touch her!'

'I hope Da booted that oul goat outta the house!' Sonny exclaimed.

Peg O'Malley's lips curled. 'He did not, faith,' she answered bitterly, 'he was ever so polite. He told Drennan and Father Devlin he would think about it. He told me not to open my mouth to either of you and Una until such time when he would tell all three of you himself. But I told Una the next morning when all of you left the house. I warned her

217

that Drennan was trying to bribe your father with land and that I thought your father would accept the bribe!'

Luke took a step forward, his face white with anger. 'Ye can't talk about Da like that!' he rasped.

She stood her ground, her chin thrust out defiantly.

'I can,' she answered boldly, 'and I will. Ever since, your father has been a constant visitor to Drennan's house. No doubt they sit at the table, plotting and planning, making arrangements. Your father has been at Una to marry Drennan, cajoling her, pleading with her, aye, and threatening her! Forcing her into a loveless marriage the same way he's forcing you pair into marrying the Costello sisters. And all to satisfy his lust for land!' Tears sprang to her eyes. 'You can't imagine,' she choked, 'the hell that girl has been goin' through these last few months. You can't . . .' She plucked a handkerchief from her sleeve and dabbed her eyes with it. She raised her tear-streaked face to her step-sons. 'Can't you see?' she wailed appealingly. 'Can't you understand? All the harassment she's been receiving from your father made her desperate. Getting pregnant was her only way of escape!'

Luke was unmoved and spoke harshly. 'I want the name of the man who made her pregnant. I want it now!'

She gave a sigh of resignation and turned away, avoiding his eyes. Either she told him or he would force it from Una. 'Con Gallagher and Una have been lovers for about a year now.'

He gave a sharp intake of breath. 'Jesus! Gallagher! Gallagher of all people!' He turned to Sonny. 'Get into the trap and wait for me. I'll be with ye in a minute.' Then he made for the stairs, taking them two at a time. He went to his room and took down a whip which hung from a peg on the wall.

It was a South African *sjambok*, a heavy whip nine feet long, the lash not of leather but of rhinoceros hide. A war veteran had sold it to him; part of the booty plundered from some Boer farmhouse. The lash was wound tightly around the heavy handle; it resembled a police baton. His step-mother was waiting for him, her back to the door.

'Where are you going?' Her voice was shrill with fear. Then she saw the whip and her hand flew to her throat. 'Oh God no!'

'Stand aside,' Luke ordered.

She shook her head. 'No! Please, Luke, don't do anything until your father comes back.'

'Da can have what's left of Gallagher after I'm through with him!'

'If you attack Con Gallagher with that whip you'll go to prison. You nearly killed that tinker lad with it. You were lucky to get away with that. You won't be so lucky next time.'

Luke gripped her shoulder, digging his fingers in so hard she winced with pain.

'Ye connivin' bitch!' he gritted. 'Ye knew all along. Ye knew she was seein' Gallagher and ye kept yer mouth shut. Well ye'll pay – ye and that little 'hure upstairs! Now out of my way!'

She moved aside. Luke pulled open the door and strode down the drive to Sonny who was waiting in the trap. Luke took the reins from him and struck the horse's hindquarters with the handle of the whip. The horse broke into a furious gallop.

Luke stood with legs wide apart, hitting the horse with the whip-handle everytime it showed signs of slowing down. They passed the tall figure of Doctor McCann walking home. He stopped and stared after them. Twenty minutes later Luke pulled back on the reins as they reached the crossroads. The main street of the village faced them on the other side of the Westport road.

Luke jumped down from the trap. 'Leave it here and follow me,' he ordered.

He turned left at the crossroads, Sonny at his heels. A hundred yards further on he turned left again, striding down the rutted track that led to Johnny Boyle's house.

Johnny was sitting with his back to the window reading when the door was kicked open. Luke marched in, Sonny behind him. Luke stood in the middle of the floor, looking about him, tapping the palm of his left hand with the handle of the whip.

'Where is he?' His strong white teeth were bared. 'Where's Gallagher?'

Johnny stared at him open-mouthed.

'Are ye deaf!' Luke almost spat the words. 'I asked ye where's Gallagher?'

Johnny struggled to his feet. 'He's not here. In the village, I suppose.'

Luke took two long-legged strides to the nearest bedroom door and kicked it open, the whip raised menacingly. When he saw the room was empty he turned and walked through the open doorway of Johnny's room, searching. Johnny watched him in a daze.

'What are ye doin'?' he asked as Luke came out of the room. 'What's wrong?'

'Don't act the innocent with me, Boyle!' Luke snapped. 'They've been meetin' here a few nights a week for the past year, haven't they?'

'Who?'

'Who the hell do ye think! Una and Gallagher.'

'Why of course they meet each other here,' Johnny declared,

pretending he did not know what Luke was getting at. 'This is his home, isn't it. And the girl comes to see me – has been comin' ever since I met with the accident last year. She brings me books, cakes . . .'

'Then they go out.'

'Con escorts her home, as is only right and proper.'

'They make love . . . in the dark.'

'Ahh, yer cracked!'

'She rolls about the ditch with him like a bitch in heat!'

'Why ye filthy-minded cur!' Johnny roared, his face flaming. 'Don't ye dare malign the girl in my presence and under my roof!'

'She's carryin' Gallagher's baby!' Luke blurted, his voice breaking. Tears appeared in his eyes. Johnny was stunned.

Luke had exposed himself. In one brief moment of weakness he had allowed the mask to slip.

Then Johnny saw and understood the reason for Luke's attitude towards Una O'Malley, the reason for his murderous hate for any man that desired her. These were not the angry tears of an outraged brother, but those of a betrayed lover! Johnny was stunned with the shock of it. Luke O'Malley was in love with his own half-sister! He glared into Luke's moist, agonised eyes, loathing on his face.

'So that's how it is, is it?' he said grimly.

For a second or two Luke did not comprehend. Then, with horror, he realised that Johnny knew – had discovered the secret he had managed to keep hidden from everyone for years. He turned his burning face away from the old man's contemptuous stare, a sick feeling in his stomach.

'What class of a twisted, unnatural bastard are ye?' Johnny growled disgustedly.

Luke gave a shuddering sigh that was almost a sob and a tear rolled down his cheek. Sonny stared wide-eyed at him, dumbfounded.

Johnny took one step back. His eyes on Luke, he hawked up a mouthful of phlegm and spat it towards Luke's feet. It landed on the toe-cap of his shoe.

'Get out!' Johnny snarled. 'Get out of me house, ye degenerate!'

Luke stared at him, face twitching. He opened his mouth as though he was about to speak, then spun about and strode out of the house, leaving Sonny in a daze. Sonny turned in bewilderment to Johnny, then lumbered out after his brother.

Luke strode furiously up the track towards the Westport road. Sonny had to run to catch up with him.

'What's the matter with ye, Lukey?' he cried, coming alongside him. 'Why did ye let that oul bastard treat ye that way?'

Luke did not answer him. His face was grim; beads of sweat glistened on his forehead. They mounted the slight slope and, turning right on to the Westport road, walked towards the village. There were five public-houses in Carewstown. Four were on the main street; the fifth was on the western edge of the village. This was the one known to be frequented by Con Gallagher. A narrow lane branching off the village street led to it.

Luke and Sonny headed towards the wide square of open ground which lay at the end of the lane. To the left was a long low building with a blank, grimy whitewashed wall and a broken, galvanised roof. It was used as a piggery and the stench hovered about it. A low stone wall ran across the far side of the square. This was the eastern boundary of Malachi Drennan's farm. There was a row of whitewashed thatched cottages on the right. A ragged child in bare feet stood outside an open door, finger in mouth, staring shyly at them. Beyond the cottages stood the public-house, a ramshackle two-storied building, its whitewashed walls now a dirty grey. There was a long wooden seat outside. Two old men were sitting with glasses in their hands, enjoying the mid-day sun.

'Lukey,' Sonny whispered nervously, 'mebbe we'd better wait and let Da deal with this.'

Luke turned a white vicious face to him. 'If ye've lost yer nerve, then don't come!' he snapped. 'I'll handle this by meself!' Heaving a sigh Sonny followed him.

The two stood just inside the door, blocking the sunlight. The interior was gloomy; tobacco smoke hung motionless in the thin air. In a corner a drunk was singing quietly to himself. A group of men were leaning against the bar, their backs to the doorway. There was a low hum of conversation. Luke recognised Gallagher.

'Gallagher!' Luke's voice was high and harsh. All conversation ceased and everyone turned around. Surprise showed on Gallagher's face.

'What are you two doin' here?' he asked.

'I want a word with ye, Gallagher.' The menacing tone of Luke's voice caused a few of the men at the bar to stiffen expectantly: they could sense trouble coming. One or two noticed the whip in Luke's hand. This was not going to be another dull Sunday afternoon.

'What about?' Gallagher asked, leaning nonchalantly against the bar.

'Outside!' Luke snapped. 'This is personal.'

Gallagher could not resist the old urge to tease. He reached behind him, lifted the pint of porter he had been drinking and began to sip it, making no effort to move.

221

'You can talk freely here, Luke,' he drawled. 'These are all my friends.' He gave a grin. 'What's it all about, eh? Is it that ye can't manage the farm with yer Da away, and ye want me to take charge. Is that it?'

There were a few partially smothered sniggers. The sounds enraged Sonny; his face turned red with temper.

'Don't ye dare mock us, Gallagher!' he shouted. 'Not after what ye've done!'

'What have I done?' Gallagher asked, smiling.

Before Luke could stop him, Sonny bawled, 'Ye've made Una pregnant!'

There was a sudden hush. The smile vanished from Gallagher's face. Luke turned to Sonny, the whip raised as if he were about to strike him. 'Ye and yer big stupid mouth!' he snarled. 'Shamin' us before everyone!'

Just that once, Gallagher thought, stunned. Just that one brief moment of madness . . . Then the bitter tears of self-reproach. He had tried to comfort her, putting all the blame on himself . . .

'Step outside, Gallagher,' Luke ordered.

Gallagher sighed. They have a right, he told himself. If it was my sister, I too would come looking for the man responsible. He walked forward. Luke and Sonny stepped aside to let him pass.

He blinked against the strong sunlight, taking off his jacket, heading for the centre of the square. There was a vicious crack like a pistol-shot and the lash struck him across the back, splitting open the shirt, tearing the skin. He screamed with pain, dropping the jacket, twisting around to see Luke swinging his arm back and over.

This time Luke aimed for his face. Gallagher flung up his arms, protecting his eyes. When he heard the crack he ducked and the lash cut the air above his head. He fell back.

Luke took a few steps forward, then flicking his wrist, sent the lash out at waist-level. He had shortened the distance between himself and Gallagher. The lash struck Gallagher under the ribs and encircled his waist. He grabbed it and tugged, pulling the handle from Luke's hand. He threw it away, gritting his teeth against the searing pain of his back, but the pain of his injured pride was worse. To be flogged like a dog! He walked towards Luke, fists up. Luke advanced to meet him. Gallagher stopped and waited, shoulders hunched.

Luke displayed his lack of skill. He drew back his arm, aiming for Gallagher's eyes, making his intention obvious and leaving himself wide open for a counterpunch. As Luke's arm curved in towards his head, Gallagher flung up his left arm and blocked it, driving his fist into Luke's midriff.

Luke's breath exploded against his face. Eyes bulging, he collapsed, hands feebly clawing at his mouth. Gallagher hammered him again and again. Luke went down on one knee. Gallagher grabbed his hair with his left hand and swung with his right. His hard knuckles ripped open the soft flesh over Luke's eye. Luke screamed, blood running into his eyes and down his face. Then Gallagher let go of his hair and Luke flopped face downward into the dust. He lay moaning, his hand against his injured side.

Gallagher stepped back, breathing heavily. The crowd from the pub and the cottages stood watching twenty feet away. All the children had been rushed indoors the moment the trouble started. Someone shouted a warning and Gallagher whirled around to see Sonny charging towards him. He had forgotten about Sonny.

He waited until Sonny was almost on him, then swiftly side-stepped and struck out. Sonny took the blow on the temple and staggered sideways. He fell on his knees, momentarily stunned, his back to Gallagher. Gallagher waited, tense, fists at the ready. Sonny was tall and broad and as strong as an ox. He was capable of killing a man with his bare hands.

Sonny shook his head a few times, trying to clear his fuddled senses. He gave a roar of rage, scrambled to his feet and turned round, his right arm raised. Gallagher drove his right fist into his stomach and followed it up with a left to the mouth. Sonny went staggering back, arms flailing, spitting blood and fragments of teeth. Gallagher walked after him, halting only to hit, weaving and ducking the wild swings of the powerful fist. He broke Sonny's nose and closed his left eye. He began to work on the body, aiming for the solar plexus all the time.

Sonny began to cry from pain and fear. He was on his own now. All his life he had relied on Luke and his father to support him in his bullying and to bolster his courage. Now there was no one. Gallagher drove his fist into his face and sent him sprawling on his back.

Sonny lost his nerve, knowing that if he stood up again Gallagher would hammer him. He scrambled away on all fours, not stopping until he reached the dirty blank wall of the piggery twenty feet away. There he sat, cowering against the wall, blubbering like a child, the blood from his broken nose streaming down his face.

Gallagher gave a contemptuous snort. Sonny was finished as a man in Carewstown. His exhibition of cowardice would never be forgotten. Gallagher felt a warm glow of satisfaction. You've paid, you bastard, he thought, for what you did that night ten years ago.

It came back to him then: the shooting flames, the moaning of a cow in terror, the booted foot swinging into his face. He faced the crowd, and he raised his voice so that all could hear.

'There's not a man or woman here who doesn't know what happened to me one night ten years ago! Five men came to my place and beat me up and put the torch to my place. All wore hoods over their heads. But I know who two of them were. One was that cowardly bastard behind me . . .' He jerked his thumb over his shoulder towards Sonny cowering against the wall. 'Another was Luke O'Malley. And by God I'll prove it!'

He strode towards Luke, who lay moaning on the ground. He had forgotten about Una; the only thought in his mind was revenge. He bent over Luke, gripped his shirt with both hands and tore it apart, exposing Luke's back from neck to waist. The broad white scar against the deeply tanned skin was visible for all to see, running down the full length of the back from between the shoulder-blades.

'See that scar?' Gallagher cried, pointing down. 'I gave that to him with a *sleán*!'

Luke lay on his belly, the dusty ground soaking up the blood from the gash above his eye. He still held his hand against his battered side; it was black and swollen. Gallagher picked up the whip. He flicked his wrist and sent it cracking high over Luke's prostrate body. Luke flinched.

'I want the names of the other three, O'Malley,' he grated. 'I want them now and you're goin' to tell me. If you don't, I'll give you a few more scars to remember me by!'

Luke managed to shake his head.

Gallagher brought his arm back and over and laid the lash across Luke's bare back. Luke screamed, writhing in agony.

'Their names!' Gallagher roared.

Luke shook his head and again Gallagher brought the lash down across his back. Luke's refusal to tell enraged him. Then something snapped inside him; all the choked up hatred he had for Luke suddenly spewed out. He began to flog Luke unmercifully, bringing the lash down across back, buttocks and legs again and again. Luke began to scream then – screaming out names; screaming for him to stop, but Gallagher did not hear. He had lost all control. He saw everything through a red mist.

A woman's hysterical wail rose above the crackings of the whip. 'For God's sake stop him! Stop him before he kills him!'

Her cry galvanised some of the men into action. Three of them

224

charged towards Gallagher. One of them came up behind him and hooked an arm around his throat while another snatched the whip from his hand. Then both of his arms were grabbed and held firmly. Gallagher struggled; a man cuffed him across the mouth as one would a bucking horse. He quietened down then, shaking his head like a man coming out of a deep sleep. His eyes were glazed. They held him firmly until the madness drained out of him.

Luke lay on his belly squirming in agony, whimpering like a puppy, his hands clutching at sparse tufts of grass. His back was a bloody torn mess. Twenty feet away, Sonny sat against the wall of the piggery, paralysed with fear, staring at the writhing body of his brother with open-mouthed horror.

Johnny Boyle pushed his way through the crowd gathering about Gallagher, cursing himself for not having arrived sooner. I could have prevented all this, he told himself despairingly. He came to a halt before Gallagher, trying to control his temper.

'Ye wouldn't listen to me, would ye!' he rasped. 'Ye wouldn't listen to good advice. I told ye not to have anythin' to do with Una O'Malley. Now ye'll do five years' hard for what ye've done to Luke!'

He thrust his hand into the pocket of his jacket. Somehow he had known what the outcome of all this was going to be. He gathered what money he had just in case Gallagher was forced to flee. It was all wrapped up in a knotted kerchief. He pushed it into Gallagher's hand.

'Here,' he said roughly, 'there's nearly seven pounds in that. Enough to get ye far away from here.'

Gallagher pushed it back at him. 'I'm not takin' that!' he exclaimed harshly. 'I'm not goin' to run away!'

Johnny slapped back his hand. 'Don't be a bloody fool!' he cried. 'D'ye want to rot behind bars for five years!'

'He's right, Con,' one man said. 'And that bastard,' he added, nodding towards Luke, 'is not worth doin' time for.'

Someone picked up Gallagher's jacket from the ground and handed it to him.

'Make yer way down to the station,' he said. 'The train from Castlebar is due there in about an hour. If ye leave now ye'll catch it.'

'The O'Malleys left their horse and trap at the crossroads,' Johnny said. 'Take that.'

Gallagher shook his head. 'I'm not runnin' away like I did the last time.'

Johnny grabbed him by the shirt collar. 'If ye won't think of yerself,' he said in a low voice, 'then think of the girl. Don't leave her to face Bull

O'Malley alone.' He paused. 'Take her with ye. Peg will help. She's an understandin' woman. Catch that train and the pair of ye will be in Dublin before nightfall.'

'And if the peelers come lookin' for ye,' someone said, 'we'll say we saw ye headin' north towards Castlebar.'

Still Gallagher stood undecided, holding the jacket in one hand and the money in the other.

'For Christ's sake!' Johnny half-shouted in exasperation, 'yer wastin' valuable time! Go! Now!'

Gallagher put on his jacket slowly, reluctantly, then he put the bundle of money into his pocket. He stared into Johnny's face for several seconds, turned abruptly on his heel and strode away without looking back.

A man raised his voice. 'Good luck to ye, Gallagher,' adding in an undertone, 'ye'll need it, God help ye.'

There were tears in Johnny's eyes as he watched him turn into the laneway and out of sight; he had a feeling he would never see him again.

There was an unnatural silence, like the uncanny hush immediately following an explosion. Everyone stood in shocked, silent groups. Suddenly the stillness was broken by a distressful wail that came from the other side of the square. All turned to stare at Sonny. He still sat crouched against the wall, hugging his sore and battered body, the lower part of his face caked with blood.

'Help him,' he cried appealingly, 'someone help me brother.'

A woman turned and ran into a cottage. She came out bearing a basin of water in which a cloth and a bar of soap floated. She moved towards Luke.

Her husband stepped out from the crowd and stopped her. 'Where are ye goin' with that?' he demanded sternly.

She nodded past his shoulder. 'That poor lad's back is in a cruel state. It needs to be bathed and – '

He punched the basin out of her hands. 'Not for that hoor!' he snarled. 'Not for that Judas! He can lie there and bleed to death!'

He turned a livid, stubbled face to the crowd. 'Dick Brogan, Stevie Kerrigan and Peter Mullen were never particular friends of mine,' he asserted harshly. 'They were always too chummy with the O'Malleys for my likin'.' His eyes roamed over the faces in front of him. 'We all know,' he said in a lowered voice, 'that it was the O'Malleys who burnt out Con Gallagher that night, for they were the only ones who had somethin' to gain. But we never knew who the other three were.' He nodded his head slowly, his face a rigid mask. 'But now we know – and so will everyone else from here to Castlebar, includin' the peelers. And all because of . . .' he half-turned and spat at Luke, 'that fuckin' informer there!'

He went and stood over the crumpled heap that was Luke. 'By Christ, O'Malley,' he hissed, 'there'll be hell to pay when Brogan, Kerrigan and Mullen hear how ye betrayed them. From now on yer life won't be worth tuppence!' He turned and walked towards his cottage, his wife following him.

Then the crowd began to disperse slowly; silently. Luke O'Malley had committed the unforgivable sin – he had informed on his friends. They shared with the rest of their race an almost paranoiac fear and hatred for the informer. Life in Carewstown was dull and easy-going, but beneath the surface there was fear and distrust. They were conscious of being constantly under surveillance. They knew that the village police sergeant and constable were there not only to deal with ordinary crime but to report on any political activity in their district. A drunken utterance against the Crown or the singing of a rebel song in the presence of a policeman would result in one's name being forwarded to Dublin Castle as being politically suspect. One learned to be circumspect when a member of the Royal Irish Constabulary was around.

But the informer was far more dangerous. He was one of the community, he knew everyone, their backgrounds and where their sympathies lay. He was dangerous because he was unknown. He could be the next-door neighbour, a friend, a blood relation. His treachery was motivated by a variety of reasons. Greed was paramount. English gold had always been readily available for information of a political nature.

That night they sat around the turf fires discussing the events of the day. It did not matter to them if Luke's betrayal of his friends was the culmination of a long-standing feud between himself and Gallagher concerning land. An informer was an informer. In time to come Luke O'Malley could betray local patriots fighting to free their country. There was trouble coming; there were rumours that the Irish Republican Brotherhood were organising. If trouble did come, survival would depend on knowing who could be trusted and who could not.

They talked of many things. Of how Luke and Sonny were brought by cart to the infirmary in Castlebar; of the 'roasting' they would get from Father Devlin for not coming to their aid; of what Bull O'Malley would do when he arrived home from Dublin. They speculated on Luke's future standing in the community after he was discharged from hospital. But Luke's future was already being decided in a little room attached to the school-house on the outskirts of the village.

Gerry Troy, the schoolmaster, sat at a table with three other men. The three were the nucleus of a newly formed Irish Republican Brotherhood circle. After thoroughly investigating their backgrounds and their political beliefs, he had approached them one by one. All were now sworn-in members of the organisation.

One was Tim Skerritt, the steward of the Carewscourt estate; another was the youngest son of a small farmer; the third man was going to reside permanently in Castlebar where he had obtained a position in a draper's shop. In time he too would recruit and form an IRB circle there, but he would have to be careful; Castlebar was a garrison town.

Tim Skerritt was doing all the talking. He had been Gerry Troy's first recruit. Gerry was impressed by his practical approach to things and his determination to get things done. He had the qualities of a born leader.

'I propose that we banish the two O'Malley brothers from this part of the country for good,' Tim Skerritt said. 'Make it so hot for them here they'll have to leave!'

'That's a bit extreme, isn't it, Tim?' Gerry protested.

'An informer is an informer,' Tim Skerritt said, repeating what he had heard so many times in the village that day. He leaned forward across the table, staring intently at Gerry. 'I'm thinkin' ahead, Gerry,' he said. 'I'm tryin' to work out in my mind what we could do in this district if a general rebellion should break out.' He paused deliberately, before continuing. 'I think a small guerrilla unit of not more than twelve men would be most effective. We could raid police barracks for arms; quarries for explosives. Then we could destroy lines of communication: wreck telegraph wires, blow up bridges and railway lines. They would have to send troops down from Castlebar to seek out and destroy us. Then we would have to go on the run, move from place to place, rely on the people to feed and shelter us. It would mean havin' to place our lives in their hands. A guerrilla unit can only operate in a district where the people are staunch and know how to keep their mouths shut.'

Gerry nodded. 'Of course.'

'That's why it's necessary we weed out the undesirables *now*.' Tim Skerritt insisted. 'We have to make this whole area safe and secure for a guerrilla unit to operate.'

'But if you make trouble for the O'Malleys,' Gerry said, 'the police will blame Brogan, Kerrigan and Mullen. They will harass them even if they don't arrest them.'

'That's what I'm hopin' they will do,' Tim Skerritt said with a grim smile. 'I want them out of the district as well. Brogan in particular. He would sell out his own father if the price was high enough.'

There was a brief silence. Then Gerry inquired in a quiet voice, 'What are you going to do to the O'Malleys?'

Tim Skerritt shrugged. 'I don't know yet. But we'll think of somethin'.'


## III


Bull O'Malley walked steadily under the hot mid-day sun. Sweat trickled from under his billycock hat, down his hot perspiring face, down inside his high stiff collar. His suit-case was heavy, and because of the heat he was forced to carry his overcoat. He stopped to rest, cursing under his breath.

'Just wait till I get home,' he muttered furiously, 'I'll give those two lazy hounds of mine a piece of me mind!'

Luke and Sonny knew he was coming on the afternoon train; they should have been waiting at the railway station with the horse and trap. He picked up the suit-case and carried on. His breathing was laboured. That's what a week in Dublin does for you, he thought. All that idleness; eating too much; drinking too much; going to bed in the early hours of the morning. Nevertheless he had enjoyed himself. A man needed a holiday after working hard all the year round.

It did not occur to him to bring his wife with him. When Una had asked him why not, he was astonished. 'Bring yer mother? In the name of God, girla, is it mad ye are! Who the hell would do the cookin' for the lads?'

He quickened his pace, longing to be home. He wanted to throw off his jacket, kick off his boots, sit under the tree at the back of the house and drink a jug of cool buttermilk.

He turned the slight bend in the road. He could see the dog stretched out in front of the gate about a hundred yards away. It lifted its head, then, catching his scent, came charging towards him, barking with delight.

'Get out of me way, ye mangy hoor!' O'Malley snarled, giving it a kick. He opened the gate, walked up the drive, and stopped, staring at the bicycle leaning against the wall. There were only about three bicycles in Carewstown and he recognised this one. It belonged to the police sergeant. The uneasiness he felt when he got off the train returned. Mickeen Gavan, the porter, had been unusually quiet, his eyes evasive. Normally, Mickeen would detain you as long as he could, jabbering away about this, that and the other. O'Malley pushed in the door and walked into the kitchen.

Sergeant Hanafin was sitting at the table with Peg O'Malley. His note-book was open in front of him and his helmet was on the table. He was a tall, burly man of about fifty with greying hair. His moustache was wax-tipped, military fashion. Peg sat at the head of the table. Her face was white and drawn. She stared apprehensively at her husband.

Bull O'Malley lowered the suit-case to the floor, a fluttering feeling in his stomach. 'What's wrong?' he asked hoarsely.

The sergeant was not one to be hurried or flustered. 'Sit down, Mr O'Malley,' he said in a slow ponderous voice, as though he were inviting a weary traveller to take his ease.

'For God's sake!' Bull O'Malley snapped. 'Has there been an accident or what?'

There was a movement to his left and he turned. Sonny ambled reluctantly towards him. His father's jaw dropped at the sight of his son's face. A plaster lay across his nose and his face was bruised and swollen.

'Jesus, Mary and Joseph!' Bull O'Malley managed to gasp. 'What the hell happened to ye?'

'All in due time, Mr O'Malley,' the sergeant intervened. 'I'll explain it all to you.'

Bull O'Malley threw his overcoat on to a nearby couch and sat down heavily. 'Holy God above!' he exclaimed angrily. 'I can't leave this place for one bloody week!'

The sergeant sighed sympathetically. ''Tis not a happy homecomin', right enough.'

'I'm waitin', sergeant.'

'Well, there was a bit of a fracas between your two lads and Con Gallagher. It happened in the village at the bottom of Donovan's Lane. There was a good deal of fisticuffs. But I'm afraid that's not the worst of it. Gallagher used a whip on your boy, Luke.'

Bull O'Malley stared at him dumbfounded.

'Luke had to be sent to the infirmary in Castlebar,' the sergeant went on. 'The lad took a savage beatin'. That Gallagher is an out and out blackguard!'

230

Bull O'Malley swallowed. 'Lukey, is he . . . serious?'

Sergeant Hanafin fingered his waxed moustache. 'Sixteen stitches above the eye, several fractured ribs, but his back was the worst. Gallagher cut the flesh to ribbons, nearly killed him.' He shook his head, sucking at his teeth. 'Barbarous, barbarous.'

'How long . . . how long will he be in. . . ?' Bull O'Malley could not speak further; he could feel his throat constricting.

The sergeant shook his head. 'Hard to say. The lad was left lyin' in the dirt. The doctors are afraid of infection, you see.' He shot a curious glance at Bull O'Malley. 'D'ye know, you'll hardly credit this, but not one of that crowd from the pub or the cottages lifted a finger to help. Not one.' He heaved a sigh. 'God bless and save us, what class of people are inhabitin' the earth nowadays.'

Bull O'Malley glared at Sonny. 'And what the hell were ye doin' when all this was goin' on?' he demanded harshly.

'Now, now, now,' the sergeant said soothingly, 'sure the poor lad was in a bad state himself. Just look at him.'

'Where's Gallagher now?'

'I wish I knew.' The sergeant scowled. 'When I made inquiries, I was told he was last seen headin' for Castlebar. They deliberately sent me on a wild goose chase. I should have known better than to take the word of any of that crowd from Donovan's Square.'

'Johnny Boyle will know,' Bull O'Malley growled.

'He says he does not. However, I think he's lyin'.'

'I'll get the truth out of him.'

'Now, Mr O'Malley,' the sergeant said sternly, 'I strongly advise you not to; you'll only get yourself into serious trouble. Leave this to the law. We'll get Gallagher, never fear.'

O'Malley snorted. 'Aye, and when the sky falls we'll all catch larks. What was the row about anyway?'

Sergeant Hanafin closed his note-book, put it in his breast-pocket and buttoned the flap. Then he stood up and put on his helmet.

'Your wife and son can tell you all about that, Mr O'Malley,' he said. He did not want to be around when they told him; he had enough to do without becoming involved in a domestic squabble. He inclined his head to Peg. 'Good-day now to ye, ma'am.' He shifted his gaze to Sonny. 'A cold compress might take down that swellin' . . .' He walked to the door, Bull O'Malley behind him.

He paused at the threshold, squinting at the sky. 'That's a powerful bit of sun,' he commented, 'but I wouldn't say no to a wee drop of rain. Me poor oul garden is in a sorry state for the want of it.' He wheeled his

231

bicycle down the gravel drive, Bull O'Malley walking beside him. At the gate the sergeant paused again, one foot on the pedal.

'I think you should know,' he said, 'that Gallagher forced Luke to admit that he was one of the party that burnt down Gallagher's house.' He stared up the road. 'Luke also named Sonny, Dick Brogan, Stevie Kerrigan and Peter Mullen.' He paused just long enough for Bull O'Malley to understand the implication of his words. 'Gallagher made Luke confess in front of about twenty witnesses – that bloody rabble from the pub and the cottages.' He ran the tip of his finger along the handlebars, waiting for Bull O'Malley to speak.

There was a lengthy silence. Then Bull O'Malley asked with anxiety in his voice: 'What do ye think will happen?'

'Nothin', unless Gallagher is found. If he is and if he can prove that Luke and Sonny and the other three were the guilty ones, then he won't be goin' to prison alone. If I were you, Barney, I wouldn't be too keen on wantin' to have Gallagher caught.'

Bull O'Malley sighed and nodded. 'I suppose yer right,' he said. He looked at the sergeant, searching his face. 'Everythin' is all right, then?'

The sergeant stroked his chin thoughtfully. 'It didn't take long,' he said slowly, 'for word to reach Brogan, Kerrigan and Mullen about Luke informin' on them.'

'Ach!' Bull O'Malley waved his hand contemptuously. 'Those three! Sure what can they do?'

Sergeant Hanafin looked at the ground and said softly: 'That house Sonny is havin' built for himself and his future wife . . .'

'What about it?' Bull O'Malley asked testily.

'It was burnt to the ground the night before last.'

'Jesus Christ!'

'That's not all,' Hanafin continued. 'Threatenin' letters – unsigned of course – have been sent to your house addressed to Luke and Sonny. Slogans have been painted on walls in the village. Brogan, Kerrigan and Mullen are tryin' to stir up trouble against your two lads.'

Bull O'Malley's red face turned a deeper shade. 'Arrest the bastards!' he spluttered. 'Arrest them!'

'How can I, without proof?' the sergeant replied.

'But ye know it's them! Who else could it be?'

Sergeant Hanafin nodded. 'Aye, I know it's them. I can't arrest them without proof, but I can make it damn hard for them to live here.' He threw a leg over the saddle of his bicycle, and stared solemnly at Bull O'Malley. 'You know what the Brogans are like, Barney. A vicious tribe – injure one and you injure them all. So you'd better see to it that

232

Luke and Sonny don't go often to the village. If they do go, let them leave before nightfall. It's a long lonely road between here and Carewstown.' With that warning Sergeant Hanafin cycled up the narrow dusty road leaving Bull O'Malley staring after him.

Sonny was sitting at the table with his mother. Bull O'Malley marched across the kitchen floor and glared down at the battered, apprehensive face.

'What caused all this trouble?' he growled.

Sonny gulped. 'Well,' he began hesitantly, 'it all began when Una took sick and we had to get the doctor . . .'

'Una!' Bull O'Malley exclaimed in astonishment. 'What has Una got to do with what happened?'

'Never mind, Sonny,' Peg said, rising to her feet, 'I'll explain.'

She walked up to her husband and faced him. She did not hesitate. 'The doctor found that Una was pregnant,' she said calmly.

For the first time in her married life she saw pain in her husband's eyes, as though she had plunged a knife into his body. It gave her a feeling of vindictive pleasure. 'Con Gallagher is the father,' she went on blandly, brutally, turning the knife in the wound, watching the pain intensify. 'When Luke was told, he went to the village looking for Gallagher, taking Sonny with him. He used the whip on Gallagher, but Gallagher managed to take it away from him and then used it on him.' She waited, watching as the pain and bewilderment slowly dissolved into murderous fury.

'Where is she?' Bull O'Malley hissed between clenched teeth. 'Where is that little . . . little. . . ?' He was apoplectic with anger.

'She's gone away with Con Gallagher,' Peg answered coolly. 'They're probably married by now,' she added, not bothering to disguise the satisfaction in her voice.

'Where to?' Bull O'Malley choked. 'Where to?'

'I don't know. Dublin, England maybe.'

He wanted to smash everything about him into smithereens, but he managed with iron self-will to control himself.

'By Christ, that little bitch will regret this to her dyin' day!' His voice shook with anger. 'She'll regret it – and so will that penniless bastard she ran away with. Before the month is out, the pair of them will be starvin' to death in some filthy slum!'

'I doubt it,' Peg O'Malley said.

'What the hell do ye mean?'

'I gave Una seventy pounds before she left. That should keep the two of them in reasonable comfort for a while – at least until Una has her baby.'

233

'You did what!' He took a step towards her. 'Where would ye get seventy pounds?' he asked suspiciously.

'I broke open the tin box you keep your money in. After all,' she said with mockery in her voice, 'you did say you'd give Una her dowry when she got married.'

He struck her then, across her face, sending her head swinging to one side. As she turned to face him, the mark of his huge hand was already apparent.

'You'll never do that again,' she said in a low voice.

'I'll do it,' he bellowed, 'anytime I feel like doin' it!'

'No you won't, because I won't be here. I'm leaving you, leaving you for good.'

Both men stared at her in shocked silence. Bull O'Malley gave a derisive snort. 'Leavin' me, are ye? And where would ye go to, tell me that?'

'Back where I came from. Galway.'

He guffawed contemptuously. 'What, back to that slum in the Claddagh? Back to that poky little shop, livin' off the takin's of penny bags of bullseyes and a few pence worth of paraffin oil!'

'That's it,' she replied, 'that's exactly where I'm going. My sister is a widow now without kith or kin. The two of us will live at the back of the shop. And we'll be happy.'

'Ye'll bloody well starve!' he shouted. He could not believe it, but she was in earnest.

'Near enough to it,' she said. 'But I'll be living with my own people. In the Claddagh we're all poor and no one is ashamed of it. There are no Bull O'Malleys there, no beggars on horseback. They judge a man for what he is, not for how much money he has or the amount of land he possesses.'

He towered over her, breathing hard, trying to curb his temper. 'So I'm a beggar on horseback, am I?' he mouthed hoarsely. 'That's the thanks I get for takin' ye out of a bloody hovel and givin' ye a proper place to live. Ye never knew what it was to have a dacent meal in yer belly until ye married me!'

'I can't deny that,' she whispered.

'Yer damn right ye can't! Anythin' I ever did was for me family. I clawed me way up from nothin'!' There was pride in his voice.

'But you became greedy, Barney,' she said, 'you became so greedy you were willing to sell your own daughter like a beast at the fair, forcing her to marry a lecherous oul wretch that's old enough to be her father. And all because you wanted to lay your hands on seventy acres of his land.' She saw a flicker of shame in his eyes.

234

'I made no promise to Malachi,' he blustered.

'You're a liar!'

His face flamed. 'Don't ye dare call me that, ye bloody cow!' he roared, half-raising his fist.

She did not move, but stood facing him defiantly. 'Yes, that's it,' she said calmly, 'that's your answer for everything. Go on then, hit me! For all the good it will do you. For all the good it ever did for your sons. What happened to Luke and Sonny had to happen sooner or later. If it had not been Con Gallagher it would have been someone else.' She gave a weary sigh. 'I'm not blaming them. I blame myself for looking on and allowing you to poison their minds. If I hadn't been such a coward maybe they might have turned out better.'

'So it's my fault, is it?' His voice was bitter. 'I make men out of them and for that I'm at fault. I teach them never to let anyone outsmart them; I teach them to better themselves. I gave them a sense of pride. Ach!' He waved a hand in contempt. 'What am I explainin' all this to ye for? Ye don't understand.'

'I understand better than you think!' she snapped. 'Oh yes, you taught them well,' she said in a sarcastic voice, 'and they were good pupils. You taught them so well,' she went on, 'you've made the name O'Malley hated and feared for miles around. Men spit when your name is mentioned. They have a saying: If Bull O'Malley was dividing Ireland, you can be certain he wouldn't leave himself last.'

'Ye've said just about enough,' Bull O'Malley snarled dangerously, his face twitching.

'I haven't said nearly half-enough,' she retorted recklessly. She paused, composing herself, and added quietly, 'I'm glad Una is gone from this house. She's safe from you, from Luke.'

'Luke!' he echoed, a puzzled look coming over his face. 'What the bloody hell are ye talkin' about? If the lad was a bit stern with her at times, it was only for her own good.'

'That's not what I meant.'

'Then what in Christ's name do ye mean? I can't make head or tail –'

'All you can think about,' she cried, 'is how to make more money; how to lay your hands on someone's holding; how to get more cattle, more sheep, more of this, that and the other. You can find out before anyone else who it is that's in trouble over rates or who's in debt or who's emigrating, so that you can get in first and grab their paltry few acres. You can tell at a glance what it is that ails a cow or a sick calf better than any vet. And yet when it comes to what is happening under your own nose and under your own roof, you're blind! Blind and stupid!'

235

Sonny darted forward and grabbed his father's upraised arm. 'Don't, Da,' he pleaded, 'don't . . .'

Bull O'Malley glared down at her, his mouth working soundlessly. If it had been a man who had called him that to his face, he would have smashed him to a pulp.

'Get out of me sight,' he managed to croak, 'get out of me sight or I'll . . .'

'I'll get out of your sight,' she said. 'Soon I'll be out of your sight for ever.' She looked at Sonny. 'Get the trap ready. I want you to drive me down to the railway station in about half an hour.' She turned and walked towards the foot of the stairs. She climbed them slowly, without hurry.

The two men stood silently in the huge kitchen. They could hear her moving about in the room over their heads. The sounds of her packing stirred Bull O'Malley's smouldering rage. Suddenly it burst into flame.

'Very well then, go!' he shouted, shaking his fist towards the ceiling. 'Go and be damned to ye! Who needs ye! Barney O'Malley needs no one! D'ye hear me – no one!'

# Chapter Eight

## I

Three men ruled Ireland: the Lord Lieutenant, his Chief Secretary and his Under-Secretary. Both the Lord Lieutenant and the Chief Secretary were politicians and had to spend a good deal of time in London attending Cabinet and Parliament; therefore the Under-Secretary, who was a Civil Servant, was the effective head of British Administration in Ireland for most of every year. An Irish politician once described the Administration in nautical terms.

'The Lord Lieutenant wears the insignia of command and signs the log, the Chief Secretary is Captain of the ship, while the Under-Secretary is the man at the wheel.'

The Under-Secretary was a tall thin man of about sixty-eight. He had a neatly trimmed white beard and used a pince-nez for reading. He had the appearance of a scholar and the reserved manner of a clergyman: he had indeed been a professor of logic and before that a Presbyterian minister. He sat at the head of the table carefully scrutinising the document in front of him as if it were a religious text which he had to examine for scriptural errors. When he came to the end he sighed and straightened up, removing the pince-nez.

'This then,' he said, staring with mild reproof at the impassive faces of Regan and Harrison, 'is all the information we have on the Irish Republican Brotherhood?'

Regan, the Deputy Inspector General, nodded.

The Under-Secretary looked at the document again and shook his head. 'Not much,' he murmured reproachfully, 'for nearly three years' work, to say nothing of the expenditure.' He raised his head and spoke directly to Harrison, the Assistant Commissioner. 'I see here,' he said, tapping the paper lightly with the pince-nez, 'G division poached the ordinary detective branch for recruits.'

Harrison flushed slightly. 'That was at the insistence of Military Intelligence,' he answered curtly.

'Oh really?' The Under-Secretary stared questioningly at Major Calder and Captain Carew.

'The War Office,' Major Calder explained, 'were pressing Captain Carew and myself for more and more information about the IRB. When I asked Special Branch for extra men for surveillance work, I was told there were no extra men available. Therefore, I suggested they get some from the ordinary detective branch.'

The Under-Secretary nodded slowly. 'I see,' he said, carefully replacing the pince-nez. He studied the document again. They stared at him in silence, waiting. Carew thought, we're like a bunch of schoolboys nervously watching the master studying the exam papers.

'Er, this fellow, Butler,' the Under-Secretary said softly without raising his head. 'It states here that he is under constant surveillance. How many men have been assigned to watch him?'

Harrison cleared his throat. 'Four.'

The Under-Secretary lifted his head in surprise. 'Four? That many?'

'It's a round-the-clock surveillance.'

The Under-Secretary turned to Major Calder. 'Is Butler that important?'

The Major nodded. 'We have every reason to believe he's a member of the IRB Supreme Council, therefore it's vital we know who are the people he contacts. If we could arrest the Supreme Council we could demoralise the entire organisation.'

The Under-Secretary stroked his beard thoughtfully.

'We know for a fact that Fintan Butler is an IRB courier,' the Major continued. 'He's been to the United States three times during the past two years and returned with large sums of money, which he carries in a money belt. The money is lodged in a bank under the name of Andrew Kinsella. Kinsella is the IRB treasurer. We have a complete dossier on him.'

The Under-Secretary shook his head ponderously. 'I would dearly love to know,' he murmured, 'how much money they've accumulated.'

'The bank allows us to inspect their account,' Harrison said. 'The last lodgement, that is the money Butler brought back from the States, brought the amount up to five thousand pounds. But there have been a series of large withdrawals since then. There's less than a thousand pounds left.'

'Which means Butler will have to go back soon to the States for more funds,' Regan said.

'What is the money being used for?' the Under-Secretary asked.

Major Calder shrugged. 'Obviously to revivify the IRB. We know the Germans are contributing most of the money.'

'Arms?'

The Major gave a brief shake of the head. 'The amount of money is too small. Perhaps the odd purchase of a revolver or two, but that's all.'

'I see.' The Under-Secretary gave another of his slow nods. 'A revolutionary organisation without teeth. Not much of a threat, wouldn't you agree?'

The Major gave him a long hard look, but said nothing.

The Under-Secretary placed both hands on the table and lowered his head. This was the first of the new weekly meetings he had initiated. Until now monthly meetings with the heads of military and police intelligence had been sufficient, but not any longer. Events were moving too fast. The forthcoming introduction of the third Home Rule Bill had aroused wild reactions in the North of Ireland.

Two Home Rule Bills had been introduced by the Liberals during the past twenty-five years. Both had been defeated. The second Bill had passed through the House of Commons only to be thrown out by the House of Lords which could reject all legislation except money bills. But now the power of the Lords had been cut down by an Act of Parliament, and they could only postpone the enactment of the Home Rule Bill for two years. Most of Ireland was jubilant. Home Rule was just around the corner. Ireland would have her own Parliament once again.

But there was no jubilation in the North. The Ulster Protestant Unionists, the descendants of the English and Scottish settlers who had been planted there in the seventeenth century, reacted with fury and dismay to the news. Violence had broken out, and there had been anti-Catholic riots in Belfast. There was talk of preparing an Ulster provisional government and creating an Ulster Volunteer Force. What really disturbed the Under-Secretary was the report he had received two days ago about the smuggling in of arms for this new Volunteer army. He gave a long weary sigh and removed the pince-nez.

'You know,' he said, raising his head, 'I've been reading these reports concerning the IRB for the past two years, and have occasionally succeeded in extracting useful information from them.' He paused deliberately, slowly switching his gaze from one side of the table to the other. 'But I think the time has come,' he went on, 'when the same microscope should be employed in another part of Ireland, namely the North.

'Information should be collected as to the goings-on in parts of Ulster of organisations which lately have been supplied with arms and are being detailed for eventualities.'

Major Calder stared coldly at him. 'Are you saying,' he asked in his rough Scots burr, 'that you now consider the IRB to be no longer of any importance?'

The Under-Secretary shook his head slowly. 'No,' he answered softly, 'I'm saying that I now consider the IRB to be of only *secondary* importance.'

Our of the corner of his eye the Major could see Harrison smirking, and he felt his temper rising. Carew, sensing the other man's agitation and fearing he was going to say something rash, gave a warning glance.

'I dread to think of what will happen,' the Under-Secretary said, 'when the Home Rule Bill is passed. If trouble does come, the police are going to be put under enormous pressure.' He turned solemnly to Major Calder. 'I would therefore suggest that you military chaps use your own sources for gathering information.'

'We haven't any.' The Major's tone was brusque. 'We're totally dependent on the police for information. We merely give directives.'

'Then that will have to cease, at least until this emergency passes.'

'The War Office will have something to say about this.' The Major declared threateningly.

The Under-Secretary remained completely unruffled. 'I put my views to the Chief Secretary,' he said calmly, 'before he left for London. He agrees with me whole-heartedly. So much so, he intends to call to the War Office to explain the situation himself. So you see,' putting on a sweet smile, 'there is really nothing for you to worry about, Major Calder.'

He addressed himself to Regan and Harrison. 'If you gentlemen have any questions. . . ?'

They shook their heads.

The Under-Secretary rose stiffly to his feet. 'In that case, until Monday next, gentlemen.'

Regan gave a sigh and unbuttoned the side pocket of his tight-fitting uniform for his cigar-case. The Under-Secretary strongly disapproved of tobacco and alcohol. Harrison sat in smug satisfaction at the look of surliness on Major Calder's face. Carew was studying the file in front of him intently.

'That fellow,' the Major growled, referring to the Under-Secretary, 'should be retired. He's completely out of touch with the situation.'

'Oh, I don't know,' Harrison drawled, 'what he said made a lot of sense to me.'

Carew turned over a page in the file, pretending he had not heard. Harrison had never tried to conceal his dislike for the Major and

Carew. According to Castle gossip, he had behaved in the same way towards the Major's predecessor. Perhaps, Carew thought, some overbearing staff officer had once ruffled his feathers. Harrison was a man who loved to harbour a grudge.

Carew spoke to Regan, deliberately ignoring Harrison. 'How long, do you think, could the IRB exist without funds?'

Regan removed the cigar from his mouth and shrugged. 'Hard to say,' he answered. 'Judging from the large amounts withdrawn from their account over the last six months, not very long, I would imagine. Why do you ask?'

'If Major Calder and I are about to be deprived of your services,' Carew answered evenly, 'then we'll have to use another and faster method of disrupting the IRB organisation.'

'Oh,' Harrison's voice was tinged with sarcasm, 'and how do you propose to do that?'

Carew eyed him coldly. 'By discrediting them with the Irish-Americans and the German Embassy in Washington.'

They waited for him to elaborate as he unbuttoned the side pocket of his tunic and took out his cigarettes. The Major had scotched his suggestion when he mentioned it to him over lunch, but the Under-Secretary's unexpected decision had now left them with no alternative. He lit the long Turkish cigarette, taking his time. Harrison drummed his fingers impatiently against the surface of the table.

Carew drew long and hard on the cigarette. 'I take it both of you have read the dossier on this man, Kinsella?' he said, giving a brief nod towards the folder in front of him. Regan nodded.

'Get to the point, will you!' Harrison exclaimed testily.

'Rather foolish of the IRB, wouldn't you say,' Carew went on calmly, addressing himself to Regan and plainly ignoring Harrison, 'entrusting their funds to a man who was imprisoned for embezzlement.'

Regan gave an indifferent shrug. To him the question was irrelevant. 'They may not know what he's done. It was a long time ago.'

'It would be something though, wouldn't it,' Carew persisted, 'if Kinsella started to dip into the funds for his own personal use. If he did, and the news reached the States, the money would be cut off immediately. And with no funds, the IRB would find it hard to exist.'

Harrison snorted irritably. 'You're wasting our time with mere suppositions.'

Carew flushed with sudden anger. 'I don't believe in wasting anyone's time,' he snapped, 'least of all our own. Thanks to the Under-Secretary, he's left us with precious little of it to waste!' There was a

241

cut-glass ashtray near his elbow and he savagely ground out the cigarette in it. He took a deep breath. Careful, careful, he told himself, don't let him get you rattled.

'Now, now, gentlemen,' Regan said gently, 'no acrimony, if you please.'

Carew glared at him.

Regan smiled back. 'But I would be obliged if you would come straight to the point, Captain Carew.'

Carew gave a curt nod. 'Very well.' He leaned across the table, hands clasped, and stared steadily at Harrison. 'I want Kinsella forced into a situation where he will have no option but to steal from IRB funds.'

Harrison looked puzzled. 'What do you mean, "forced into a situation"?'

'Kinsella,' Carew explained 'is a weak little mouse of a man. An underpaid scrivener in a solicitor's office. He's a widower and the father of a large family. The eldest is a priest in St Catherine's. The second eldest, a girl, looks after the house and the rest of the children. All, with the exception of the priest of course, have to exist on Kinsella's meagre salary.' He paused. 'What do you think would happen if Kinsella should lose his job? Remember he's fifty-seven. At his age he would find it hard to get another.'

Harrison gave a gesture of indifference. 'That's a hypothetical question. However, I think it would make him rather desperate.'

'Desperate enough to steal?'

'Possibly. But you seem to forget Kinsella regards himself as a patriot. To him, stealing from the IRB would be tantamount to treason.'

'I've had someone investigate Kinsella's past,' Carew said. 'Do you know what made him steal from his employer all those years ago?'

Harrison shook his head.

'Drink. Kinsella is a dipsomaniac. He spent most of his time in the prison hospital, being dried out. Although he has not taken alcohol in twenty-five years, the craving for it is still there. If anything disastrous should happen to him, such as being dismissed from his job, the urge to seek solace in the whiskey bottle might be far stronger than his strength of will. If Kinsella were to go on a binge, he would drink his way down to the last penny of whatever money is available, irrespective of who it belongs to.'

Harrison turned in bewilderment to Major Calder. 'I don't understand. What is all this leading up to?'

'Captain Carew will explain,' Major Calder said.

'We want you,' Carew said, 'to arrange to have Kinsella dismissed from his job.'

Harrison stared at him in stoney silence.

'Counsel your men to be discreet,' Carew continued, 'we don't want Kinsella to suspect that the police were involved.' He relaxed back in the chair. 'Shouldn't be too difficult,' he said. 'I'm sure Kinsella's boss, being a member of the legal profession, will be shocked when he learns that an employee of his was once convicted for embezzlement.'

Carew said nothing more. Both he and the Major waited for Harrison to say something. Regan gazed abstractedly up at the ceiling, puffing away at his cigar. He was not responsible for G division or the metropolitan area, so this had nothing to do with him.

Harrison cleared his throat nervously. 'As both of you know,' he said, glancing from Carew to Major Calder, 'the Chief Commissioner is about to undergo an operation. However, as soon as he is released from hospital, I will submit your request to him.'

'Oh, that won't do at all!' Major Calder protested. 'That could be months away. No, no, Harrison, this will have to be done within the next two weeks. You alone will have to decide and take the responsibility.'

It was the Major's turn to smirk.

Harrison glowered. If he refused, he knew Calder would immediately send a report to the War Office that he was deliberately being uncooperative, and the War Office would use its influence to have him demoted or transferred. He gave a curt nod. 'Very well. I'll see what I can do.'

Carew was about to reach down for the attaché case resting against the leg of the chair when Harrison leaned forward towards him, his face contorted with bitterness and dislike. 'But let me tell you – both of you,' darting a venomous look at Major Calder, 'that this is without doubt the most degrading and distasteful thing I've ever been asked to do!'

Carew lifted his shoulders in a gesture of resignation. 'Yes, well, there are many things we have to do in this business that are distasteful. Nevertheless we have to do them.'

Major Calder was chuckling as they walked across the Upper Castle Yard.

'By God, I've never seen Harrison so nettled.' His voice suddenly turned serious. 'But be careful, Alec; he'll do you harm if he can.' They passed under the stone archway and went out into Castle Street. The cold night air had a bite in it.

The Major said, 'You mentioned to Harrison you had someone investigate into Kinsella's past. Who?'

'Billy Durkin. I put him on to Kinsella. Durkin struck up an acquaintance with him – told him he was a traveller in ladies' underwear. They're great chums now, Durkin has even been invited out to the house several times.'

The Major gave a disdainful snort. 'Leave it to Durkin,' he growled.

'Oh, Durkin is not such a bad chap,' Carew said and immediately thought, Why do I always jump to Durkin's defence whenever he's criticised? Conscience? Because I made a cuckold of him?

They walked down Cork Hill past the City Hall. The late evening rush was over and Dame Street was almost deserted.

The Major caught Carew by the arm. 'They serve a damn good steak over in the Ormond,' he said. 'Care to come along? Later we can have a chat about this business over a few drinks.'

The look of appeal on the Major's face made Carew feel sorry for him. The Major was a lonely man. He shook his head.

'I'm sorry. It will have to be some other time, Ian. I have a lot of things to do.'

The Major smiled and nodded. 'Of course,' he said. 'I understand.'

Something in his tone made Carew glance at him sharply. He thought, does he suspect?

The Major still retained the grip on his arm as though reluctant to let him go. 'One thing I don't understand,' he said. 'If Kinsella steals from the IRB fund, how do you propose to blazon the news abroad?'

'Simple. Give Durkin all the facts and let him publish them in the *Eye-Witness*.'

'Good God, yes!' The Major uttered a crow of delight. 'That sort of thing would be meat and drink to Durkin. I can imagine the headlines. "Secret society funds stolen by treasurer" or "IRB funds blown on booze"!'

Carew nodded. 'About a thousand copies will be forwarded to our Embassy in the States. They will send some to the German Embassy in Washington and distribute the rest among Irish-American organisations throughout the country. So you see,' he added with a smile, 'Durkin can be useful.'

'I suppose he is,' the Major conceded grudgingly. 'Nevertheless I can't stomach the fellow. He's an ill-mannered brute.'

Carew sighed, wanting to leave. Miriam will be there now, he thought, waiting. He was only half-listening; the Major's constant tirades against Durkin bored and irritated him.

244

'Neither do I trust him. No one knows anything about the fellow's past, but I'll wager it was an unsavoury one . . . I wonder why he's always so bloody vindictive?'

Carew lost his patience. 'You too would be vindictive,' he blurted, 'if you were driven out of your home by a howling mob just because your father had apostatised!'

The Major's eyes widened. 'You don't say!' He shook his head. 'Well I'll be jiggered.'

Carew cursed himself for being so rash. 'That's in confidence, Ian.'

'Oh, don't concern yourself, old boy,' the Major assured him breezily. 'My lips are sealed.'

Are they, wondered Carew. All he has to do is to tell one person and then everyone in the Castle will know, from the Chief Secretary down. He told himself: I'll have to be more careful; have to keep to myself the things Miriam divulges about her husband's past. Pillow talk; lying together on the tossed bed, all passion spent. She always chose that moment to talk about Durkin, and always in a disparaging way. Perhaps, he thought, it helps to salve her own conscience.

He said: 'I really must go, Ian . . .'

Alec strode down Dame Street, impatient to be home. Durkin had gone to London to make final arrangements for the forthcoming publication of *The Carews of Carewscourt*. He would not be back until Friday evening. His absence meant that Miriam could stay with him in his flat until Durkin returned. Four days, Carew thought joyfully, four whole days! They had not been alone together since Durkin had gone to Belfast six months ago.

At Foster Place, one of the new taxicabs stood alone among the horse-drawn vehicles for hire. He walked towards it, past the sullen stares of the lounging jarvies.

'Wilton Place,' he said and climbed in. He lay back on the seat in the dark interior with the attaché case resting on his knees as the driver cranked up the engine.

I did the right thing, he told himself, renting that flat. Obtaining the Major's permission had not been difficult. It was necessary, he had told him, for an Intelligence officer to have private quarters. There he could entertain certain people who might be useful – people with information to give but who were afraid to be seen entering a barracks or Dublin Castle. . . . The taxicab moved off slowly, making a wide turn in front of Trinity College. He gazed idly out; the lighted shop windows in Grafton Street went sliding past before his tired indifferent eyes. At the top of the street the cab turned left and headed eastwards along

245

Stephen's Green. Already the prostitutes were out, patrolling the pavement in front of the park railings. He closed his eyes.

I wonder whether Uncle Walter will be well enough to attend the reception when *The Carews of Carewscourt* is published? He shook his head sadly. Highly unlikely, he told himself. His uncle had not been the same since Emily died. Her death had come as a great shock to him. Somehow Walter always believed he would die first. All alone now, Alec thought, all alone in that big rambling house . . .

They were approaching the canal bridge. He leaned forward and tapped the driver on the shoulder.

'Stop here.' He wanted to walk the rest of the way. He alighted, paid the driver, then turned right, heading west, the tree-lined canal on his left. The thought struck him suddenly. Maybe she didn't come – maybe she changed her mind. He was filled with dismay. He swerved right into Wilton Place. A short row of tall elegant Georgian houses overlooked the grounds of a lawn tennis club. Only a few of them were residential. The house he lived in was at the end. His flat was on the top floor. Underneath was a dentist and on the ground floor an estate agent. They had arranged between themselves that if by chance Miriam was seen entering the house by day, she could always pretend she was visiting the dentist. He paused before mounting the steps. The house was in darkness: the dentist left at six o'clock. He looked up. Faint light showed through the blinds on the windows of the top floor flat. She had come! He climbed the steps. His hand shook a little as he inserted the key in the lock.


II


He opened his eyes slowly and yawned, stretching his satiated body between the warm sheets with the lazy sensuousness of a cat. He moved his leg and was immediately aware of the cold empty space beside him. He struggled into a sitting position, rubbing the sleep from his eyes, and lay back against the headboard.

Miriam was seated in front of the dressing table with her back to him, brushing her hair. She was fully dressed.

He glanced at the clock. It was ten-thirty. 'Why are you dressed so early?' he asked in surprise. 'Are you going somewhere?'

'Yes,' she answered in a low flat voice. 'Home.'

He could see her face in the mirror. She stared stonily into it as she brushed and brushed away.

'But Durkin doesn't arrive home until tomorrow night,' he protested, trying to keep the disappointment out of his voice.

'I forgot to mention,' she said, 'we have a maid now. I gave her a few days off when William went away. She'll be back this afternoon. If she doesn't see me there, she'll wonder where I am. She could mention it to William. He likes to know where I've been when he's away. Not that he's suspicious. He's just naturally curious.'

He sighed. 'I see. You're right, of course. We have to be careful.'

'Careful! I'm tired of being careful!' she snapped. 'I'm sick to death of looking over my shoulder everytime I come here, wondering and dreading if someone who knows me has seen me and can guess what I'm coming here for!'

There was a touch of hysteria in her voice and picking up her hairbrush again, she began to attack her hair with swift savage strokes.

'What I want to know,' she said in a voice as cold as ice, 'is when do I cease to be your mistress and become your wife? When does this clandestine affair come to an end? You'll have to tell William sometime, so why not now?'

He stifled a groan. 'Miriam, Miriam, be reasonable. I can't tell him now – not the way things are at present.'

'Why not?' she demanded. 'Tell me – why not?'

'Think of the scandal it would cause. You couldn't keep a thing like that hidden for very long, not in this damn town. I would have to resign my commission.'

'There's Carewscourt. You told me your Uncle Walter is willing to hand over the entire estate to you anytime you wish.'

'That's true. But . . .' He hesitated.

'Yes? But?' She sat stiff and motionless, waiting.

'It's not that simple. You see, my uncle has certain fixed views, certain principles which he adheres to rigidly. Marriage in his eyes is sacred; adultery the unforgivable sin. While I was in South Africa, Valerie came to Carewscourt for a holiday. By all accounts, she and Uncle Walter got on famously. Later, when he learned of her infidelity, he destroyed every photograph and memento of her he could find. She had given him some gift, something which he cherished very dearly. He smashed it to pieces. So you see, if he should find out about us, he's quite capable of disinheriting me.'

'I see,' she said after a while. 'So we have to go on meeting like this,

247

ever watchful, always circumspect in our behaviour when in company so no one will suspect – '

'Don't talk like that!' he interrupted harshly.

'It means of course,' she went on in the same level tone, 'that you will not be free to make a decision until your uncle dies. Am I right?'

'I'm afraid so,' he answered in a weary voice. He flung the bedclothes away from him. Sitting on the side of the bed, he put on his slippers. He stood up and reached for his dressing gown. 'Try to have a little patience, Miriam,' he said.

She turned to face him, her face flushed with anger. 'Patience!' she cried. 'I'm almost thirty years of age! I want a child! And if we have to wait until your uncle dies, I'll be too old to have one!' Tears sprang to her eyes – tears of despair and frustration. She began to weep quietly.

He knew the sensible thing to do was to remain silent and let her cry away. He sat down on a chair with his back to the window and lit a cigarette. 'How is it you never had a child for Durkin? He looks virile enough.' He asked when she had stopped crying.

'Oh yes, he's virile,' she murmured, dabbing at her eyes with a handkerchief. 'But he refused to have a child in spite of all my pleadings. Why, I don't know. Perhaps he was afraid of the responsibility, or perhaps it was pure selfishness. It would be just like him to regard a child as a competitor for my affections.'

There was a brief silence. Then she spoke to the mirror, 'There were times when he was drunk, when I tried to take advantage of him, thinking he might forget to use one of those . . . *things*!' She paused, embarrassed and ashamed. 'But drunk or sober, he was always careful.' Her voice turned bitter. 'You are like him in that respect!'

'That's not fair!' he protested. 'I'm cautious for a different reason. I have to be careful for both our sakes!'

He walked over to her and placed his hands on her shoulders. 'I want children too, Miriam,' he said. 'Heirs to inherit Carewscourt.' They stared into the mirror, studying each other's face. 'There's something I have to tell you.'

'What?'

He hesitated, wondering if he was doing the right thing by telling her. 'I'm in Military Intelligence. Do you know what that means?'

She shook her head slowly. 'I'm not sure. Has it anything to do with spying?'

He gave an amused little laugh. 'In a way.' His voice turned serious. 'Your husband works for us. He tries to gather information about a certain underground political organisation.' He felt a spasm of cold foreboding as he spoke.

'Is it dangerous,' she asked, 'this work William is doing?'

'It could be. He's indispensable, Miriam. At the moment he and I are working on a scheme which could wreck this political organisation for good. It will mean a knighthood for him if we succeed.'

'A knighthood.' He stared at her, watching an expression of contempt steal over her face.

'When the time comes for you to tell him about us,' she said, 'perhaps the pain will not be all that great. After all, he may consider a knighthood a fair exchange for a wife.'

'Oh come now.' He felt he had to make some kind of protest, no matter how feeble. 'He's your husband. He loves you, in his fashion.'

'I hate him!' she exclaimed venomously. 'Loathe him!'

He sighed. Am I the only one, he asked himself, who cares anything for Durkin? Durkin thinks so, he thought, remembering his drunken, maudlin behaviour one night. 'Alec,' he had blubbered, pawing at his sleeve, 'yer the only true friend I have in the whole wide world. The only one I can trust . . .'

Alec appealed to her. 'Can't you appreciate the predicament I'm in? If I do as you suggest and tell Billy about us, he will do his damnedest to destroy me in revenge. He will deliberately wreck this scheme of ours. The outcome – a court-martial and a dishonourable discharge. Uncle Walter would not only disinherit me, he would disown me!' He pressed his fingers gently into her shoulders. 'Try to have a little patience and understanding,' he said softly. 'Things will work out. You'll see, you'll see.'


III


'. . . the author has set out to do something extremely difficult,' the Chief Secretary went on, holding a copy of *The Carews of Carewscourt* in his hands, 'and has abundantly succeeded in doing it. What is remarkable about the book is the vigour and originality of style. Books on family history, I venture to say, tend to be rather ponderous and dull. This one is the happy exception.'

There were about sixty people in the large hotel dining-room; they

249

stood in respectful silence, listening to the mild cultured voice with its Northumbrian accent.

'This is not just another history of an Anglo-Irish family. It is much more. As historiographer to the Carew family, Mr Durkin graphically describes the lives and customs of . . .'

Carew stood on the edge of the crowd gathered in front of the Chief Secretary. He could see Durkin's flushed, simpering face as he listened to this praise from the second most important person in the land. Beside him stood Walter Carew, *The Carews of Carewscourt* clutched tightly to his breast. He still looked as if he could not believe that the book had at last been published. He had risen from a sick bed despite his doctor's objections and had travelled all the way from Mayo just to be here. A nurse had accompanied him; she stood beside him now, a little overawed by her surroundings. They were all here – the cream of Castle society.

Carew smiled to himself. By God, he thought, one has to admire Billy Durkin.

Durkin had invited the Castle crowd to the reception for the launching of his book. All had politely refused; it was their way of expressing the dislike and contempt they had for him. Undismayed, Durkin invited the Chief Secretary, knowing him to be a literary man. He had dedicated the book to him and had delivered a copy of it to him in person. Naturally the Chief Secretary was flattered and accepted Durkin's invitation with pleasure. The news of his acceptance circulated rapidly round the Castle. Immediately all the rejections were revoked.

You had the last laugh, Billy, Carew thought, remembering his apt comment as the Chief Secretary entered followed by the people who had spurned the invitations.

'Here comes the Pied Piper,' Durkin chuckled, 'and the rats behind him.'

He dragged his mind back to the Chief Secretary's speech, but he could not concentrate. His mind wandered away again. He looked uninterestedly over the crowd. It was composed of the usual sort one saw at Castle functions; the well-dressed, well-bred men and women who hovered about the Lord Lieutenant and his Chief Secretary, looking for favours, hoping for titles. Sprinkled among them were a few gentlemen of the press, book reviewers from the loyalist newspapers. The representatives of the nationalist press were conspicuous by their absence.

'. . . some student of history yet unborn will count himself fortunate

250

in having a book such as this. May I express a wish that he will regard it not merely as Anglo-Irish history or as a partisan account of what happened, but as an essential part of the whole . . .'

The Chief Secretary nodded appreciatively to the sustained clapping and stepped down from the low dais. He moved among the dress suits and the long flowing gowns; a few polite words here, an introduction there. How many of those who applauded and were now shaking his hand, Carew wondered, hated him and the party he represented? The Liberals had steadily eroded the power of the Anglo-Irish, especially landowners like his uncle, by a series of Land and Reform Acts. It was ironic that the Chief Secretary was now helping to push through the Home Rule Bill, the Bill which would abolish his office for ever, although it was rumoured he was more than pleased to have his name go down in history as being the last Chief Secretary of Ireland.

'Drink, sir?'

Carew turned gratefully to the waiter standing behind him. More waiters and waitresses were weaving through the crowd bearing trays of drinks and delicacies. Carew swallowed a mouthful of whiskey, and made his way towards his uncle.

'How are you, sir?'

Walter Carew stared at him with moist eyes; the book was still clutched tightly to his breast.

'My boy, my boy,' Walter Carew croaked in a trembling voice, 'if only your Aunt Emily were alive to see this day.'

Will I be like this one day? Carew asked himself. Decayed and old, my last remaining years devoted to a three-hundred-page genealogy which nobody will be interested in buying, let alone reading. He could see Durkin making his way towards them, his face beaming. His uncle had spent years on research and had contributed two-thirds towards the cost of publication, yet Durkin was getting all the credit. Lucky Durkin, he thought sourly.

Durkin's eyes were feverish with excitement. He laid a hand on Walter Carew's arm. 'The Chief Secretary wishes to have a word with you,' and he led the old man away towards the waiting, smiling aristocratic figure.

Carew groaned to himself. His uncle was becoming increasingly inarticulate of late, and he no longer made much sense. He did not want to witness the embarrassing and one-sided conversation that was about to take place. He moved through the gossiping groups, his glass in his hand, acknowledging with a smile or a nod some face he recognised. He was relieved that no one tried to engage him in conversation. The one

251

person he wanted to see was not here. Durkin had apologised for his wife's absence; a very bad headache had left her indisposed. Alec had been looking forward to meeting her; they had not seen each other for nearly two months. He felt dismayed and wondered if she were deliberately avoiding him, if it was all over between them.

Alec stopped suddenly at the sight of the figure standing near the open door. He was so obviously out of place he was attracting suspicious glances from one or two of the waiters. He stood there holding a bowler hat in his hands, a small, middle-aged man in a shabby grey overcoat. Grey seemed to be his natural colour: greying hair, grey, straggly moustache, grey mournful face. The only relieving colours were the white stiff collar and the black tie. He's wandered in here by mistake, Carew thought. Maybe The Sick and Indigent Roomkeepers' Society are holding a conference elsewhere in this building.

A hand touched his elbow. 'I say, you're Captain Carew, aren't you?' Carew turned around.

A tall, slim, fair-haired young man stood before him. 'I didn't wecognise you out of uniform,' he said. He had a beaky nose and smooth polished features. 'I'm Courtney,' he announced in a high-pitched effeminate voice. 'We were introduced once, but then,' he said with an accusing glare, 'you pwobably don't wemember.'

Carew recalled having seen him at a few Castle functions; he had an idea he was attached to the Chief Secretary's office. 'Of course I remember,' he replied. Silence followed; Alec could not think of anything else to say. In desperation he blurted out, 'How are things?'

'Tiptop, thanks.' Courtney edged a little closer. 'Mind if I ask you a question?'

Carew eyed him with distrust. 'That rather depends on the question,' he answered guardedly. It was difficult trying to understand what he was talking about, the lisp was so pronounced.

'I'm curious as to why your uncle commissioned a tyke like Durkin to wite the book. Surely there must have been plenty of chaps who could have done the job equally well. Billy Durkin, after all, is no gentleman.'

'My uncle was interested in his writing ability,' Carew answered curtly, 'and that only.'

'But Durkin's a bounder,' Courtney protested, 'an absolute bounder!' He glanced swiftly over his shoulder, then leaned forward towards Carew, hand up to the side of his mouth. 'I say,' he giggled, 'have you heard the latest about Durkin?'

Carew shook his head. He wrinkled up his nose as Courtney's face almost touched his. The odour of Eau de Cologne was overpowering.

'They say Durkin's father exchanged his weligion for a bowl of soup!'

A nerve leaped in Carew's head. God damn and blast Calder! Why couldn't he keep his big mouth shut!

'I never pay any attention to malicious gossip,' he said coldly.

'Oh, this isn't gossip!' Courtney exclaimed. 'This is stwaight from the horse's mouth, I swear!' He gave a tiny squeak of dismay. 'Oh, Holy Moses, there's that old bore Henwick with Agnes. I'll have to dash over and wescue her. Old Henwick, you know,' he sniggered, his mouth against Carew's ear, 'is absolutely furious he was not proposed for this year's Honours List.' He squeezed Carew's arm. 'That'th what you get, I told him, for openly pwaising the Conservatives.'

He was gone, leaving his sweet heavy scent lingering in the air. Carew gulped down the remainder of the whiskey. God, he thought, what a town for wagging tongues. He remembered something Swift had written about the Dublin of his day. 'I ever feared the tattle of this nasty town. It is not a place for any freedom, but where everything is known in a week, and magnified a hundred degrees . . .'

Durkin came towards him a little unsteadily, a full glass of whiskey in his hand. There was a scowl on his flushed face.

'What was that blabbermouth Courtney whispering to you about?' he growled. 'Something about me, I bet. Slimy, scandal-mongering scut of a nancy boy!' Durkin snarled under his breath.

Carew sighed wearily. 'That type is not worth getting upset about, Billy.'

'He's a bloody mischief-maker!' he rasped. 'He spreads stories about you, me and everyone.'

'About me?'

'He says you keep a mistress.'

It was as if someone had unexpectedly dashed cold water in his face. He stared at Durkin in shock and dismay.

Durkin laughed; here and there a gold tooth gleamed.

'Ha, ha, who's upset about Courtney now?' He came a little closer and gave a broad suggestive wink. 'Who is she, eh?' he whispered, grinning. 'Who is the little bit of fluff?'

Carew composed himself with an effort and forced a smile. 'You're not thinking of exposing my little secret in the *Eye-Witness* are you, Billy?' He expected Durkin to throw back his head and roar with laugher and he was taken aback as Durkin looked at him with genuine hurt. He laid a hand on Carew's sleeve.

'You think I would do a thing like that to you?' Tears showed in his eyes. 'Never say anything like that to me, Alec, not even in jest.

253

You're my friend, my only friend. You're true-blue. I'd trust you with my life.'

Carew winced. His earnest declaration of friendship and trust made him feel guilty and ashamed. He needed another drink badly. Durkin followed him.

He picked up a glass of whiskey from the table and swallowed half the contents in one gulp. He turned his head a little. The man in grey was still standing near the open door, holding his bowler hat in his hands. Carew's curiosity was aroused.

'I say,' he said to Durkin, 'who the deuce is he, do you know?'

Durkin looked over his shoulder, and swore softly. 'Good Christ! I didn't think he'd come.'

'Do you know him?'

Durkin grinned foolishly. He was more than half-drunk. 'Our mutual friend,' he giggled, 'Andy Kinsella.'

'Who?' At first Carew did not comprehend and then it dawned on him. He stared incredulously at Durkin. 'You can't possibly mean . . .'

'I was drunk when I invited him,' Durkin protested. 'I didn't think he'd take me seriously.'

'God dammit!' Carew's voice rose a fraction and several people stopped talking to stare at him. He lowered his voice.

'How the hell,' he hissed in Durkin's ear, 'could you be so stupid as to invite an IRB man here!'

Durkin shrugged helplessly. 'He's been tagging along at my heels like a bloody mongrel all morning. To get rid of him, I told him I had to go home and change my clothes as there was a reception for the launching of my book at the Hibernian at two o'clock. I told him he could come if he wished, but emphasised it was a formal dress affair, thinking that would discourage him. Christ!' He shook his head in amazement. 'I didn't think he'd have the nerve to show up.'

'Well, get rid of him!' Carew hissed again. Horrified, he could see Kinsella coming towards them. Durkin brushed past to intercept him. He put his arm around Kinsella's shoulders and brought him forward. 'This is Mr Kinsella, Alec. Mr Kinsella, poor fellow,' he said, 'lost his job a few weeks ago and is rather upset about it.' He lowered his head. 'After how many years, Andy?' he asked softly.

'Fifteen years, Mr Durkin,' Mr Kinsella answered in a breaking voice. 'Fifteen years, and then to be dismissed, discarded like an . . . an oul shoe.' A tear rolled down his cheek. 'If it was something I did wrong, a spelling error or a misplaced comma in a will or contract . . . But to be sacked without even the hint of an explanation . . .'

Mr Kinsella's voice tailed off into silence. He stared at the drinks arrayed on the linen covered table in front of him. He was mesmerised. Both men watched the peculiar expression on his face. It was an odd mixture of fear and desire.

Kinsella knew all he had to do was to reach out and take one, but he did not. With an effort, beads of perspiration standing out on his forehead, he turned away.

Durkin grinned. 'Have a drink, Andy.'

Kinsella licked his lips. 'I'll have a lemonade.'

Durkin snorted. 'Lemonade! Sure that's a drink for women and kids. 'Here . . .' he picked up a glass of whiskey and placed it in Mr Kinsella's hand.

Kinsella stared at the glass in terror and apprehension as if Durkin had just handed him a live bomb.

'Drink it,' Durkin urged, 'it'll do yeh the world of good. Man dear, yer nerves are in tatters.'

Kinsella shook his head, his eyes still riveted on the glass. 'No, no,' he whispered. 'I couldn't. Ye've no idea what this stuff does to me.'

But his resistance was beginning to dissolve. Carew could see it in his eyes. He watched with a feeling of guilt and remorse. Up to now, Kinsella had been a name in a file. Carew had planned his destruction with coolness and detachment, working it out on a sheet of note-paper as he would a mathematical problem. He never expected to meet Kinsella in the flesh, never expected to witness the result of his action. He felt a sudden urge to dash the glass from Kinsella's hand, but he did nothing – said nothing. He stood motionless as a grinning Durkin slowly pushed the glass towards the weakening mouth. Kinsella gave a low moan of surrender, closed his eyes and raised the glass to his lips. He had the look of a man about to commit suicide.

Carew walked away, cursing Durkin in his heart. Someone stepped in front of him and he stopped abruptly. The man looked vaguely familiar. He was tall and stout with a florid complexion. He held a glass of brandy in one hand and a large cigar in the other. He immediately began to talk about the current political situation in a rich fruity voice.

Carew tried to concentrate, but his thoughts were on the ugly little scene taking place a few yards behind him.

'I think the Liberals are committing political suicide with this Home Rule Bill. Don't you agree?'

Carew sighed and nodded. 'Yes.' The tension was draining out of him. He felt as if he had just witnessed some savage rite in a distant jungle but he was back in civilisation again, back among his own class, back among the cultured accents, the refined manners and the vicious little tittle-tattles. Durkin would never be at home here, no matter how hard he tried. He was forever tainted by a background of brutishness and squalor.

The man took a swig from the brandy glass and leaned forward in a confidential manner. 'Tell me,' he said in a low voice, 'have you heard the latest concerning. . . ?'

# Book Two

Book Two

# Chapter Nine

## I

They unloaded grain from the *Robert Ellis* in the intense heat of the July afternoon. The ship had to clear the Port of Dublin before ebb tide, which was less than two hours away, and the men who were unloading her were being hurried and harassed unmercifully. Bonuses had been promised to the stevedores and windlass men to speed up the unloading by hustling the workers. The casual labourers of the docks were being driven by threats and curses to the point of collapse.

Down in the hold, half-naked men were feverishly shovelling the grain into tubs. An hour before they had been working knee-deep in it; now it barely covered their ankles. They shovelled without uttering a word, breathing strenuously through their nostrils. Some had covered their mouths with scarfs and handkerchiefs against the choking dust and flying wisps of chaff. From the deck, their sweating bodies could hardly be seen through the thick golden haze.

Men drew up the grain-filled tubs from the hold, guiding the ropes with their hands. Canters emptied the tubs into sacks; weightmen pushed the sacks on to scales. The railer carried each sack on his back to the top of the gangplank where the Tally Clerk numbered the sacks off as they were transferred from ship to dock. Along the cobbled dockside, horse-drawn drays waited in a long queue. As each dray was fully loaded with the bulging sacks it moved off, the horse straining under the weight. The air was full of flying fragments of straw and husk, caught and swirled around in a wild dance by the breeze blowing up from the river mouth.

Con Gallagher was railer. It was a job which could only be given to the strongest man. At the weighing scales, a few feet away from the hatch, he stood with legs apart, his back to the scales, aching arms over his shoulders. Two men lifted the heavy sack and he grasped it, staggering up the deck bent double with the terrible load on his back, feeling the crushing weight forcing him down, down.

The top of the gangplank comes into view . . . booted feet. He comes to a shuffling halt and tries to straighten up. The heavy sack slides down to the left, almost knocking him off balance. Two men pick it up and stagger down the gangplank with it. The Tally Clerk makes another tick. Gallagher turns slowly about, gasping for breath, his heart pounding against the wall of his chest. There is a red mist before his eyes and he grasps the rail, waiting for his vision to clear.

'Get movin', damn yeh!' a voice roars, and he stumbles forward, dazed from exhaustion. The deck sways before him. Both arms dangle helplessly, his eyes have a glazed look and his mouth hangs open. The Tally Clerk stares at the retreating figure with awe. Nearly one hundred and seventy tons have been hauled up from below since early morning and all carried on Con Gallagher's back!

He stands with his back to the scales once again, aching arms over shoulders, waiting for the two weighmen to lift the sack so that he can grasp it. His hair and sweat-drenched shirt and trousers are covered in dust and grain; a gritty slime, a mixture of sweat and dirt, runs down his steaming face. He has the appearance of some primeval creature that has just shrugged itself up out of the earth.

Down in the hold they shovel as fast as their sweating tortured bodies will allow. Two men have collapsed; they crawl away from their furiously shovelling comrades and lie in a dark corner of the hold, chests heaving, trying to protect with their hands their eyes and mouths from the swirling clouds of dust and chaff. No one heeds them – three more tubs after this and they're finished. The thought of climbing out of this hell-hole into the clean river-swept air gives them extra strength. They shovel more furiously than ever before.

From the bridge, the Captain watches another grain-filled tub being hauled to the surface. He consults his watch and then inspects the sky. With luck his ship could clear the port within the hour and reach the mouth of the Mersey before nightfall. In the distance the roofs and spires of the city are etched sharply against the cloudless blue of the sky. Up river near the Custom House, the furled masts of a sailing vessel stand tall and proud. The Captain raises his binoculars. For a full five minutes he lets his eyes rove over her admiringly as if she were a beautiful woman. He is moved by memories and nostalgia. Fewer and fewer, he tells himself, with each passing year. Twenty years from now they'll be just a memory. But once . . . once they rode the oceans of the globe majestically like the queens they were . . . Coming over the rim of the world in the red burst of morning, silent as a ghost, canvas full-bellied before the trade winds. And now – obsolete;

260

victims of the ruthless laws of commerce. Progress, he thinks bitterly.

Down below a whistle blows and the last tub is hauled to the surface. Then, one by one, the men laboriously climb the ladder out of the hold. One by one, they stagger over to the rail and rest, staring down at the dark waters of the river. Dust and sweat dries into a filthy crust on the naked upper parts of their bodies.

The Captain stares down at them sympathetically for a minute, then moves to the open window and raps out an order to one of the crew resting against the ship's rail. The man, a Lascar in a dirty yellow jersey, silently obeys. A moment later he steps out from the galley with a bucket of water dangling from one hand. The long bony fingers of his other hand tightly grip the handles of four chipped enamel mugs. He places the bucket down beside the men, then hands them the mugs as they gather round.

They dip the mugs into the clear cold water and drink greedily. There are eight men and four mugs; a man drinks then hands the mug to a waiting comrade. Con Gallagher staggers over to them, his face blank and stupid with fatigue. A man hands him a mug. He tries to grip the handle, but his fingers are stiff and rigid. Somehow he manages it. He bends down slowly, stiffly, like an old man and fills the mug and drinks the contents in one gulp. He remains half-crouched over the bucket and digs the mug into the water again and drinks, but slowly this time. Then he straightens up in easy stages, groaning with pain.

The Lascar stands silently and looks on. They do not notice his nose crinkling up in disgust at the overpowering stench of their bodies. They themselves are unaware of it. In the overcrowded tenements of the Dublin slums, the odours of the human animal are as natural as the scent of hawthorn to a countryman.

Then they cross the deck in a straggling line. From a bundle at the ship's rail they select their garments: soiled shirts; shabby ragged jackets. . . . They stumble down the gangplank.

There are crates covered by a tarpaulin on the dockside. They clamber up, then stretch themselves flat. They are oblivious to everything but the sensuous relief, the ecstasy, as their tortured bodies at long last find rest. Some fall into sleep immediately; the rest are content just to lie there, staring up into the blue of the sky, feeling the breeze sweeping across their bodies like a caress.

They walked up the quays in the gathering dusk, heavy boots resounding against the flagstones. A train rumbled across the loop-line bridge in the distance, heading south. Their steps were unhurried; fatigue dragged at the muscles of their legs, at every sinew in their bodies.

Kit Byrne gathered what moisture there was in his mouth and spat sideways. 'How many tons do yeh think we shifted today?' he asked.

Con Gallagher groaned wearily. 'Jesus Christ . . . it feels like it was a thousand.' He came to a halt and stared curiously at his companion. 'Why do you ask?'

Kit Byrne leaned against a wall. He took off his cap and passed the palm of his hand over his bald head. He was a tall, tough, wiry man with a narrow, gnarled bitter face. He was thirty-seven years of age, but premature baldness and a life of brutish toil made him look older.

'I know how many tons we were paid for,' he said. 'I'm askin' yeh how many tons do yeh think we shifted?'

Gallagher gave a helpless shrug. 'For God's sake, Kit, I'm the railer, not the bloody tally-man. It was bad enough carryin' the sacks without havin' to count them.'

Kit's face was lined with exhaustion, but the deep-set eyes burned with anger. 'Well, I've been countin',' he growled. 'There were eight of us shovellin' the grain into those tubs and I counted every tub that was hauled up. It's all in here,' he said, tapping his hollow temple with his finger. 'I know. I know how many sacks were filled from each tub and I know how much each sack weighs. It's a simple matter of arithmetic. And this I tell yeh – we shifted nearly one hundred and seventy tons since this mornin' and McEvoy paid us for a hundred and forty-five.'

Gallagher looked at him in disbelief. 'You'd better be sure of yer facts, Kit,' he said.

Kit nodded solemnly. 'I'm sure. And this is not the first time – it's been happenin' all along. I've been watchin' and calculatin'. We're bein' paid less than what we're entitled to and the remainder is goin' into McEvoy's pocket.'

Gallagher clenched his fist. 'If what you say is true – '

'It's true, Con. Take my word for it.'

'Then by Christ, the two of us will go over McEvoy's head and ask to see – '

Kit Byrne's scornful laugh interrupted him. 'For God's sake have sense! They'll tell yeh to go to hell and get out. They'll also see to it that ye'll never get a job on the docks again. The employers,' he added bitterly, 'are cheatin' us as well as the bloody stevedores. The whole damn system is rotten – rotten and corrupt!'

The docks were quiet in the growing darkness. Along the drab line of warehouses and sheds the lamplighter moved with his long pole tipped with flame. One by one the gas-lamps flared into life. Kit Byrne put his hand into the pocket of his ragged jacket and took out a handful of silver and copper coins. He looked at the money he was holding as though estimating the weight.

'And this,' he said with weary anger in his voice, 'is all I have after slavin' in that bloody hold since day-break. I go home to the missis now and drop this into her lap and tell her to feed both of us and the four kids and pay rent for that stinkin' dogbox of a room in that bloody kip of a tenement. Jesus!'

He turned his head and looked back along the broken pavement. 'He's still there,' he muttered with hatred in his voice, 'sittin' at the top of the bar like Lord-bloody-Muck, swillin' beer that's been paid for by every poor divil he employs. If yeh don't buy beer for the stevedore on pay day, yeh won't be hired when the next boat comes in. Most of them will stagger home stocious to their wives and kids with not even two copper pennies to rub together and the bloody publican rakin' all in and maybe givin' a backhander to McEvoy for payin' his men in a pub.'

'Put a cork in it, Kit.' There was weary irritation in Gallagher's voice. 'Talkin' and lettin' off steam is not goin' to change the system.'

'No, it won't!' Kit retorted. 'Somethin' a hell of a lot more is needed!' He slapped the cap back on his head and straightened up. Gallagher took a crumpled pack of cigarettes from his pocket and offered one to him. 'Here, have a smoke and calm yerself.'

They walked on, keeping in step, cigarettes hanging from their mouths. It was dark now and warm, very warm. Heavily perfumed women with garish doll faces strolled past them, heading for the moored ships. A different trade took place on the docks at night.

'There's trouble on the docks in Liverpool and up in Belfast,' Kit said. 'The Trade Unions have moved in, organisin' the unskilled labour and the employers are fightin' back. They're threatenin' to bring in scabs if there's a strike. There'll be blood shed, mark my words.'

Gallagher did not say anything. His face was tired and expressionless. Kit's constant talk of rebellion was tiresome and irritating, especially since it was so ineffectual.

'It's about time somethin' like that happened here,' Kit went on.

'That's what we need – organisation. If we had that we could change things on the docks – change them for the better. Do yeh know what would happen if all the unskilled and casual labour on the docks were organised into a Trade Union?'

Gallagher gave a brief shake of the head. 'No.'

'They could destroy the whole rotten system overnight,' Kit said. 'And if their demands were not met they could close down the docks by goin' on strike. Dublin, more than any other sea-port city in these islands, depends on imports. We'd have the employers in a stranglehold! And that would only be the beginnin'. Man, we could bring everythin' in this city to a halt!'

There was sarcasm in Gallagher's voice. 'You seem to have given a great deal of thought to the matter, Kit.'

'Aye, I have,' Kit replied. 'And I'm not the only one,' he added.

'Blather and pipe dreams won't get you anywhere,' Gallagher said. 'Yer just wastin' yer time.'

Kit grabbed him by the arm, bringing him to a halt. They stood underneath the loop-line bridge. A train rumbled by overhead. 'This isn't blather, Con,' Kit said seriously. 'I've been meetin' certain people over the past few weeks. They want to know what conditions are like on the docks and I've been givin' them the facts. I'll tell yeh this – we're goin' to be organisin' pretty soon.'

Gallagher heaved a weary sigh. 'I'll believe it when I see it happenin'.'

'You'll see, you'll see!' Kit uttered vehemently. 'We're on our knees now but soon we'll be standin' on our feet and then all hell will break loose! The workin' man will come into his own. We'll get rid of the bloody slave-drivers and those fat, easy-livin' bastards of capitalists! We'll destroy the slums and the bloody slum landlords with them! Are yeh aware,' he asked, jabbing a finger at Gallagher's chest, 'that we have the worst livin' conditions in Europe? Do yeh know that? Thousands livin' in rotten overcrowded slums, dyin' of starvation and consumption and every other kind of disease yeh can think of! And the children – thousands dyin' – '

He checked himself. But it was too late; by the feeble light of the streetlamp he could see the spasm of pain shooting across Gallagher's face.

'Oh Christ, I'm sorry, Con,' he blurted, 'I didn't mean . . .' His words stumbled over each other in awkward apology.

Gallagher gave a curt nod. 'Goodnight, Kit,' he said and strode off into the darkness, leaving Kit Byrne mute and miserable. Another train rumbled heavily overhead, drowning out the sounds of Gallagher's retreating footsteps.

Kit cursed himself for his stupidity. When Gallagher's two children died within two weeks of each other, Gallagher had isolated himself from everyone in the working gang, wanting to be alone with his grief. They let him be, covertly watching him as he worked away with a silent ferocity that was disturbing. At lunch-time he would sit apart from the rest, devouring his sandwiches with wolfish clamps of the jaws. Other times he would just sit and stare into space, lunch untouched. No man dared to approach him. The brooding face, the red-rimmed staring eyes, the hands that constantly clenched and unclenched, were enough to daunt anyone. They let him be, telling themselves that in time the fury and the sorrow would pass. It took a long time.

Kit walked on, lost in thought, remembering the day during lunch-break when they had been sitting down eating and drinking and talking among themselves. Gallagher as usual sat a little distance away, munching and drinking in moody silence. When he finished, he stood up and walked over, sat down beside them and lit a cigarette.

Kit recalled the sudden silence that had descended on the group. All conversation withered and died, they felt uneasy and embarrassed. Now and then a man's eyes would slide sideways, guardedly and furtively, at the tall red-headed man sitting quietly with a smoking cigarette between his fingers, gazing abstractly across the river.

Clearing his throat he said to no one in particular: 'I hope the weather holds till we finish. Those clouds far off look threatenin' . . .'

No one replied. Kit sighed. He could still experience the relief, a relief shared by the others, when Gallagher spoke for the first time after weeks of silence. They resumed work with lighter hearts. One or two of the men began to whistle, a thing no one had done in a long time. Things were almost the same as they had been, but not quite. Each man found himself weighing his words carefully when talking to Gallagher. Certain words and topics, such as children or children's ailments, were taboo. There was a living nerve in their presence and the wrong word dropped accidentally could so easily touch it. The pain would be terrible to witness.

But there had been no slip of the tongue, Kit thought bitterly, till I opened my big stupid mouth! He continued up the quays, a tall, thin exhausted figure, racked by guilt and remorse.

# III

Gallagher picked his way along the broken, uneven footpath of the narrow, ill-lit slum street. The heat had brought the denizens of the tall crumbling houses out to seek some fresh air. Women clustered about the open halldoors, gossiping. Men and youths lolled against the area railings or sat on the wide steps playing cards and pitch-and-toss. Ragged bare-footed children frolicked in the gutters. High Georgian houses flanked the street. Once the homes of the nobility in the eighteenth century, they now housed the sweated poor of the city. Light glowed dully from oil-lamp and candle behind ragged torn curtains; washing hung from jutting poles resting on windowsills. Gallagher moved through the hubbub. Dublin voices, flat and nasal, bawled, drawled and bickered.

The lower end of the street was silent and deserted; most of it lay in ruins. The tall tenement house he lived in stood at the corner of a laneway; timber supports propped up its sagging side-wall. As he prepared to mount the steps, a movement near the mouth of the laneway made him pause. At the edge of light from the flickering gas-lamp, a woman stood smoothing down her skirt. Beside her, unconcerned and unashamed, a man urinated noisily against the wall.

Gallagher's mouth tightened with disgust. He mounted the steps and walked through the open doorway. In the unlit hall he groped for the banister rail, found it and climbed the stairs slowly. The stench clogged his nostrils. It was the stench of the tenements: the sweat of unwashed bodies, sewage, stale cabbage water, rotting timbers.

When they first moved in it hadn't been like that – or perhaps they hadn't noticed. Despite the stench, the rats, the stultifying dirt all round them, Una made a haven of their rooms. They were always clean and tidy, but that was in the days when she was proud of herself, of her love for Con, and of her growing pregnancy. He smiled to himself as he remembered her wide-eyed astonishment on reaching Dublin. There were no fields, she could not see the sky, but she was happy because she was with him. He remembered her surprise that you had to pay for food – at home they had been self-sufficient and he remembered how they had laughed at her naievety when she spent his week's wages on one piece of beef. She had always taken good food for granted, but as the realisation of what they had done, and the difficulties they must face, dawned on Una it seemed to Con that a small piece of her died.

In the beginning they had been swept along by their love for each other. Nothing could shake that sure foundation, not even the disapproving priest who married them only to save their child from being born out of wedlock. Una was not afraid of him and his moralising. What did he, a mere priest, know of the love between a man and a woman – nothing, or he would not have said the things he did. It was not a sin to love as they loved.

And when the baby came, oh, how happy his Una had been. They worshipped the child, a baby girl named Margaret. The birth was easy, and Una was strong. She had not really needed the help of the slattern from downstairs. The baby was healthy, and it touched Con to see Una look after her with such a fierce protective pride. He knew his child could come to no harm with such a mother. But Farley had come along too quickly, and this time Una was ill while carrying him. The stench of the tenements penetrated her very soul, and she was sick nearly every time she went out. She was no longer able to go shopping for the food that Margaret needed to keep her strong, and as her time drew near Una grew steadily weaker.

Farley's birth was hard, and this time they had needed help. Una was left drained by it, and Farley did not thrive as his sister had, but he was beautiful in his fragility. Although Una did her best, she had not the strength to fight against the encroaching dirt and disease. Once the epidemic hit the tenements Con knew his children were doomed for there was no cure for diptheria, and his babies could not fight it. They spent their last precious pennies on the doctor, but he was as despairing as his patients. He could not help. Con thought they would have been better off buying some decent food.

Strangely, it was Margaret who died first. He had come home to find Una sitting with Farley pressed close to her bosom and Margaret in their bed. He knew at once she was dead, but Una would not let him near the small body. The three of them sat together all night, clutching each other in their mutual grief, unable to offer any comfort for they had not the words to say what they felt. In the morning Con had taken his Margaret to the undertaker. He carried her himself, wrapped in the sheet in which she had died. He felt ashamed carrying his pathetic bundle through the streets, but there was nothing else he could do.

Two days later when he got home from work he found Una still holding Farley, for she had not let go of him since Margaret died. But now their son was dead, and when Una looked up on his return the light had gone from her eyes. He knew that Dublin had taken her soul just as surely as it had taken the souls of their babies.

He arranged the pauper's funeral. He thought his heart would break at the sight of those small coffins. Each seemed no bigger than a shoe box. He had made the wooden cross himself, and carved their names on it. He knew it would not last, but it helped a little to ease the bitterness in his heart. He had failed his children and he had killed the strong, healthy country girl he had brought to this hell-hole they called the capital city.

Something squirmed under his boot in the dark. He kicked out and the rat squealed in fright; he could hear it scuttling down the stairs below him. He stood for a few seconds listening, then moved on up. At night they had to keep the oil-lamp burning, with the rats tearing at the skirting, fearful for the children. But not now, he thought with a stab of pain, they had no children to protect.

He came to the top landing. There were two doors. One led to the front living-room, the other to the back bedroom which also served as a kitchen. He stood before the bedroom door, hesitating, wondering what kind of mood she would be in tonight. He took a deep breath and twisted the handle.

'I'm home,' he announced, trying to force a little gaiety into his voice.

The wick of the oil-lamp standing on the rough deal table had been lowered so most of the room lay in shadow. Her head and shoulders were silhouetted against the window. There was no response to his entry. He stood in the middle of the room with his hands in his pockets staring at her, feeling like an intruder. He waited patiently until she rose silently. Her movements were heavy and weary, like those of an old woman. He gave a silent groan of despair.

He took off his jacket and cap and threw both down on a nearby sofa. He sat down at the table. The table was bare except for the oil-lamp and a folded newspaper. He spread the newspaper out before him and turned the tiny wheel on the oil-lamp. A tongue of flame shivered upwards and he could see his shadow quivering into life on the damp-stained wall opposite. He bent his head over the newspaper, trying to concentrate on the small print, but his thoughts were distracted by the sounds and movements behind him. The clink of delft, a knife sawing through bread; milk being poured into a jug. He could hear her moving towards the fireplace. There was no gas in any of the houses on the street; cooking had to be done over an open fire.

He folded the newspaper and put it to one side as he heard her slow footsteps coming towards him. She came up to the table with a loaded tray. A plate of potatoes, cabbage and meat was placed before him. She put down a knife and fork, a cup and saucer, a jug of milk and a bowl of sugar. She walked away and came back with a steaming teapot and began to pour into the cup. She was silent. He thought they were like two strangers alone in a strange room, trying to find words to start a conversation.

'Are you goin' to have somethin'?' he asked.

'I'm not hungry,' she answered listlessly.

He caught her by the wrist. It felt so thin and fragile in his huge calloused hand. 'Please . . .' he appealed. 'Take somethin'. You know how I hate to eat alone.'

He let go of her and she moved behind him to the kitchen dresser. He picked up the knife and fork. Suddenly he felt ravenous and began to wolf the food. She sat down at the head of the table with a cup of tea and began to sip at it, holding the cup between her hands, elbows resting on the table. She stared silently past him at the window with blank eyes. Now and then he stopped eating to steal a sidelong glance at her. She did not notice; it was as if he were not there.

He stabbed at the last morsel of food on the plate with the fork and swallowed it, then washed it down with his tea, draining the cup in one gulp. He made an attempt to break the awkward silence, feigning pleasure.

'Ahh, man alive, I needed that.'

She did not speak, did not move, but continued sipping the tea, staring unblinkingly at the window. The cheap alarm clock on the sideboard ticked loudly in the silence.

She had aged considerably over the last few months. She had lost weight and the plumpness was gone from her face. Her skin was taut and dry and her eyes stared out from hollows. God, he thought, if she were to go back to Carewstown now no one would recognise her.

'Did you do anythin' today?' he asked.

'I went to the cemetery,' she murmured, speaking for the first time.

He felt a swift surge of irritation. 'Una, not again!'

She looked down into the cup she was holding between her hands. 'There was nothing else to do,' she said quietly. 'You were gone since early morning. I just couldn't sit here doing nothing. Thinking, remembering.'

He stretched out his hand and placed his fingertips lightly against her arm. 'Now listen to me, Una. You can't go on like this. You'll have to snap out of it.' He paused, and said in a low voice, 'What happened, happened. Life must go on.'

There was a sharp intake of breath. She began to tremble, gripping the cup between her hands until the whites of the knuckles showed. She

269

jerked her head up, lifting her face to the ceiling, staring upwards in agony.

'Life!' She choked. 'In this . . . this . . .' Tears began to stream down her face. 'Oh God,' she wailed, 'how I hate this place! How I hate this filthy, stinking house . . . this street . . . this city!'

Once again he reached out, taking the cup away from between her hands. She was gripping it so tightly he was afraid it would break. She lowered her head and let her hands flop to the table. He covered one of them with his, squeezing it tightly.

'Shhh, there now, girla,' he whispered, trying to comfort her.

'If only we could go away,' she sobbed. 'Anywhere.'

'Please, Una,' he begged, 'don't upset yerself. Please.' He felt so helpless.

'Anywhere where there's no hunger or disease, where there's no consumption or malnutrition or, or . . .' she almost spat the word '*diphtheria.*' Her voice rose to a near-screech. 'Oh merciful God, my babies!'

It will be all right in a while, he told himself, when the crying and the hysteria stop. It's when she doesn't cry, when she just sits there staring at nothing, those are the times I fear most.

He sat still and silent, watching her as she cried, her head buried in her folded arms resting on the table. He remained like that until she fell asleep, exhausted, drained of emotion. Then he stood up and took two steps to the head of the table. He lifted her up in his arms. He was shocked at the lightness of her body. She moaned a little as he lifted her, but made no resistance.

He carried her across to the bed. Bending slightly and freeing one hand, he drew the bedclothes back and lowered her gently. He took off her shoes and began to undress her. It was like putting a tired, sleepy child to bed.

He drew the bedclothes up to her chin and walked back to the table. He lowered the flame of the oil-lamp until the room was in semi-darkness. Then he picked up a kitchen chair and brought it back with him to the bed. As he sat down on it she gave a shuddering sigh and stirred a little. He put out his hand and gently began to brush back stray strands of hair from her forehead. He moved his hand down a little. He thought she was asleep until his fingers touched her open eyes.

'There now,' he whispered, 'there now. Go to sleep.' He smoothed the eyelids down with his fingertips, feeling the moistness of tears on the long eyelashes.

'Don't go away,' she breathed, 'don't leave me.'

270

'I won't leave yeh, pet. I'll stay here. Just go to sleep.'

He had lost count of the times their evenings had ended like this since the children died. It had been much worse before, he thought, much worse. Nothing ever lasts, he told himself, not even grief. There has to come a time when she will cry herself dry, when she will begin to live a normal life again. Then, in time, perhaps another child . . . Her breathing was even and regular now and he slowly withdrew his hand, knowing that she was asleep. In the room underneath an argument was starting; loud voices filtered up through the floorboards. Joe Mooney, he thought.

Every pay night it was the same. Joe coming home after spending most of his money on drink; the inevitable quarrel with the wife; the children cowering under the bedclothes waiting in fear for their father's temper to explode from the constant nagging. He tensed a little as the bickering, shrewish voice rose to a screech. 'Yeh bloody drunken waster. . . !'

There was a shouted curse, the sound of a blow and a woman's scream of pain. A plate broke against a wall . . .

Una stirred uneasily as a child screamed in terror from the room below. She uttered a little whimper and Gallagher stretched out his hand and began to stroke her hair gently. 'Shhh . . . there now, there now.'

His action brought back a vivid memory of last winter when his infant daughter had woken, crying from some frightening dream. He had sat like this, beside the crib he had made himself, soothing away the fears of the night with gentle strokes of the hand, crooning comfort into her ear . . .

A faint scratching began in the far corner of the room. He lifted his head, senses suddenly alert. He moved his foot, scraping the sole of his boot across the bare floorboards. The action of tiny claws ceased abruptly at the sound.

Like the other tenants of the house, he fought this never-ending battle against the rats. You tried to repair the rotten skirtings of the rooms which they gnawed away with their sharp teeth; you stuffed broken glass into the holes and boarded them up and they simply avoided these places and gnawed their way through someplace else. Like any war, you had your victories and defeats. You hunted them in the cellars and backyards and on the stairs, killing them with boot and shovel or with whatever other weapon that came to hand. And still they came, breeding and multiplying in the squalor.

They had their casualties and you had yours: infants attacked in their

271

cribs; the old and infirm in their beds. There were children on the street who bore rat-inflicted disfigurements – a half-chewed ear; a gnawed nose-tip. One night, Joe Mooney's wife, eight months pregnant, had woken to find a rat nibbling at her milk-swollen breast.

He raised his hand and wiped the sweat from his forehead. The room was warm and stuffy. He unlaced his boots, walked silently in his stockinged feet towards his cap and jacket. He fumbled in the pocket of his jacket for cigarettes and matches, then moved towards the chair at the half-open window. It was a little cooler here, but not much. A sour stench rose up from the outdoor privy below. He could hear voices in the lane to his left. There was the sound of a bottle breaking followed by a man's hoarse oath and a woman's bawdy laugh. The lane, dark and flanked by ruins, was used by the prostitutes.

He smoked away. A sickle moon hung low in a star-lit sky. A memory came drifting back: sitting outside Johnny Boyle's cottage on a warm summer's night such as this, smoking a cigarette, watching the reflection of moonlight on the river in the distance, feeling the cool, clean, heather-scented breeze against his face . . . He was engulfed by a feeling of homesickness; his throat felt thick and tears pricked at his eyes. He had a feeling he would never see Carewstown again.

Six months ago he had written to Johnny Boyle, wanting to know how things were in Carewstown – wanting to know if the police were still looking for him for the injuries he had inflicted on Luke and Sonny O'Malley. He had instructed Johnny not to post his reply in Carewstown but to give it to a mutual friend, a train driver, and have him post it on his arrival in Dublin. As a double precaution he had not given his address, but that of the local post office.

Johnny's letter arrived two weeks later. It was all about the O'Malleys. Bull O'Malley's wife, Peg, had long since left him and had gone back to her sister in Galway. And Luke and Sonny O'Malley were also gone – to where no one knew.

Luke's betrayal of his friends had resulted in a savage retribution. The house Sonny O'Malley was having built for himself and his future wife was burnt to the ground. The two brothers found themselves boycotted. No one would speak to them. They would not be served in any of the shops or pubs in the village. Walking home one night, they had been attacked by a body of men wearing masks. As they ran for their lives, a shotgun was fired after them.

The following day they were gone from the district. Nobody knew for definite where they had gone; some said America; others said they had bought a farm in Kerry and Bull O'Malley would not tell. He would not divulge their whereabouts, even to the two abandoned Costello sisters, who were threatening breach of promise.

Gallagher flicked the tip of his cigarette out of the window: it curved high over the ruins at the back like a shooting star. He thought, well, I had my revenge, but I never thought it would be so complete. Bull O'Malley, according to Johnny, was drinking heavily in the pubs of the village almost every night – drinking himself to death.

A sharp little cry of pain cut off his thoughts abruptly. He picked up the oil-lamp, and walked over to the bed. He stood looking at her, holding the lamp aloft. She lay on her back, asleep and breathing fiercely, both hands clutching the bedclothes. He knew it was a bad dream she was having. She had not had one night's untroubled sleep since the tragedy. He stood, unmoving, waiting for the features to relax, waiting for the hands to let go of the bedclothes. Her face was glossy with sweat; damp strings of hair lay across her forehead.

He put the lamp back on the table and blew out the flame. He undressed in the dark, and naked slid gently in beside her. She stirred a little, then turned away to face the wall.

She did not know about Johnny Boyle's letter; she did not know that her mother had gone back to Galway, that her two step-brothers had been forced to flee Carewstown. Nor did she know that her father, lonely and embittered, staggered home drunk nearly every night to an empty house. Why should I tell her? he thought, she's suffered enough.

He feared for her sanity. There was nothing left to remind her of the children. He had made a bonfire of the cribs and the infected clothing. Nothing remained, except that tiny grave in the corner of the cemetery which she haunted. He had made the cross himself and painted it black; a neighbour had painted their names in white.

Margaret Ann Gallagher
Age 16 months
Farley Gallagher
Age 5 months

Oh God, he thought, I'm not sure if you exist, but if you do, if you can hear me, help her. Don't mind me. I'm of no account. All I can offer is my strength, and that won't last forever. But it's all I have. All I ask is, don't let her suffer, give her peace of mind.

He groaned in despair and stretched his aching body. 'What's the use,' he whispered, 'there's no one there to listen. There never was.'

Faint moonlight shone through the uncurtained window. He could hear the faint chimes of a distant church bell. Midnight. There were no sounds from the rooms below: everyone in the house was asleep. In the silence, the marauding rats were beginning their nightly assault. He could hear the persistent gnawing starting again in the far corner of the room.

They are the only ones that thrive in this dunghill, Con thought. It's ourselves that sicken and die.

# Chapter Ten

## I

Durkin stood at the edge of the platform, surveying the crowd in front of him. They stood in small groups talking, huddled against the cold of the raw November morning. A few carried floral wreaths. Durkin began to count, his eyes roving over them. Be accurate, he told himself, always be accurate. There was enough material here to fill four pages of the *Eye-Witness*.

His lips moved soundlessly. Thirty-eight, thirty-nine . . . Fifty-two in all, he estimated, including the piper. The piper stood alone and apart, cradling his bag-pipes in his arms. He was dressed in green. Green tam-o'-shanter, green tunic, green kilt, green woollen stockings. The only relieving colour was the black of his gleaming buckled shoes. He was shivering. His face and bare hands and legs were mauve from the cold.

Durkin chuckled at the sight. He walked slowly forward, his hands deep in his overcoat pockets, sauntering in and out through the crowd, eyes roaming over faces, ears alert, hoping to catch some snippets of information.

Quite a few were speaking in Gaelic. It irritated Durkin not being able to understand what they were talking about. Bloody nationalists, he thought sourly; Gaelic-speaking fanatics. He had no real hatred for these people, just a good-humoured contempt. Constantly he mocked them in his newspaper. He had coined a name for them, 'Rainbow Chasers', and the name had stuck. He stopped and lit a cigar. He looked leisurely about him. He recognised one or two faces: a popular poet of patriotic verse; a retired professor of history. Intellectuals mostly. All looked as though they were living on the edge of poverty. Shabby-genteel, he thought with a sneer. His eyes roamed over them with ill-concealed contempt. And these are the people who want a free and independent Ireland. He knew some of them wanted to free their country by peaceful means; he also knew there were others who wanted to use physical force.

275

*Physical force.* He shook with silent laughter at the thought of this bunch of scholastic dreamers leading a rebellion against the greatest Empire on earth. Most of them were middle-aged. The youngest was about thirty-five. And the oldest? Ahh . . . undoubtedly Methuselah over there.

The man was about five yards away. He stood with his back against the wall, in front of a huge poster advertising Bovril. He clutched a wreath to his chest, a tall, seared, ancient figure in a shabby grey overcoat that hung loosely on his gaunt frame. He was staring solemnly at the ground, his eyes obscured by the brim of the soft, weather-stained hat. He looked so frail and pale. It's not worth his while coming back from the cemetery, Durkin thought, sniggering at his own cruel wit.

He consulted his watch. The train should be here soon, then the lamentations will begin. It was a sad occasion for the people around him. The return of the mortal remains of Garret Lysaght to his native land for burial. He had expected to find the station overflowing with people, but he had found only this pathetic few.

The faithful few, he thought, like Methuselah over there. Once again his eyes rested on the old man facing him. One of Lysaght's contemporaries, he surmised, possibly an old comrade-in-arms. The man had remarkably high, wide cheek-bones that gave him an alien appearance.

His gaze shifted to the two men talking earnestly beside him. One was short and stocky, the other tall and thin with black hair and a falcon nose. He was holding a few papers in his hand. Durkin gave a grin as he recognised the tall man: he always took pleasure in baiting Fintan Butler. He threw the cigar away and sauntered over.

'Hello, Butler,' he said, giving a wide gold-toothed grin and glancing at the papers in Fintan Butler's hand. 'Is that the transcript of the graveside oration you're holding?'

Butler was wary. He gave a curt nod. 'Hello, Durkin,' he said.

His companion uttered a few words in Gaelic. *'Conas atá tú.'*

Durkin looked at him and then at Butler. 'What did he say?' he asked.

'He said "How are you?" ' Butler replied.

'Well why didn't he say it in English? Doesn't he know the language?'

'Of course he does. But he prefers to speak in Irish.'

*'Bhfuil Gaeilge aige?'* the man said, turning his head to Fintan Butler.

'What did he say?' Durkin asked again.

'He wants to know if you speak Irish,' Butler answered with a trace of irritation in his voice.

'*Me?*' Durkin threw back his head and guffawed. 'Taw shay mahogany gaspipe,' he spluttered. 'How about that, eh?'

The man scowled at him. He had a face like a bulldog.

'What is it you want, Durkin?' Butler asked wearily.

Durkin widened his eyes and spread his arms as though his reason for being here should be obvious. 'Why, to report on this most moving event of course. What else?'

'The funeral of an old rebel would hardly be of interest to the sort of people who read that rag of yours, Durkin.'

'True,' Durkin admitted with a mischievous grin. 'They'd be more interested reading about the people *attending* the funeral. Holy God! What a collection of eccentrics and misfits.'

'*Snáthháin!*' Butler's companion growled, baring yellow teeth.

Durkin turned to him, flashing his gold-toothed smile. 'I don't know what you said, friend,' he bantered, 'but it didn't sound very nice.'

'Is that why you came here, Durkin?' Fintan Butler inquired in a cold voice. 'To observe us and then poke fun at us in that scandal sheet you call a newspaper?'

'Partly,' Durkin replied, still grinning, 'and partly to learn more about Lysaght's past exploits.'

'Read the history books, Durkin.'

'His exploits in the bedroom I mean, not those on the battlefield. Tell me, wasn't he found in bed with someone's wife?'

His voice was a little loud. He heard a movement behind him, and turned to see Methuselah glaring at him; the hands holding the wreath were trembling with rage. Durkin turned his back to him. That's the trouble with these nationalists, he thought, they're too damned touchy.

'Why don't you go away, Durkin,' Fintan Butler said in a bored, slightly exasperated voice, 'and circulate among your cronies in Dublin Castle. I'm sure you'll be able to dig up someone's murky past in that place. Or will you?' he added, as if struck by an afterthought. 'Your Castle friends behave so damn righteously, perhaps they really do lead unblemished lives.'

'I doubt it.' Durkin was enjoying himself. He was always trying to pierce Butler's armour of reserve, and never quite succeeding. Perhaps, he thought, this time. 'Each one of us has something in his past he wants to keep hidden. We all have our guilty secrets.'

'Have you a guilty secret, Durkin?' Fintan Butler asked.

'*Me?*' Durkin exclaimed in mock outrage. 'Why, I'm as pure as a vestal virgin!'

'Then there's no truth in the rumour that's going round?'

'What rumour is that?'

'That your father was tarred and feathered for apostatising.'

Durkin's jaw dropped and his face was aflame. Jesus, he wailed to himself, how the hell did he find that out? This bloody town!

He tried to laugh, but it sounded weak and false in his ears. He tried to think of something witty to say, but all he could produce was a feeble, 'Well, I must be off, Butler.'

A smile hovered about Fintan Butler's mouth. 'Must you?' he asked, raising an eyebrow. 'What a pity – and just when the conversation was becoming *so* interesting.'

Durkin swallowed hard. 'Good-bye, Butler,' he said, and turned to the other man. He tried to put a little joviality into his voice. 'And *adieu* to you too, my Erse-speaking friend.'

The man displayed his yellow teeth again, this time in a vicious grin. '*Póg mo thóin!*' he uttered coarsely.

Durkin turned a puzzled face to Fintan Butler. 'What did he say?'

'Kiss my arse!' Butler translated with a sweet smile.

There was a distant prolonged wail and Fintan Butler turned swiftly away, his companion pushing Durkin rudely aside as he followed. A deflated Durkin stood watching them as they marched up the platform, followed by the crowd, to meet the incoming train.

'Move aside – you're standing in my way.'

Durkin turned around. Methuselah stood glowering at him, holding his wreath in one hand.

Durkin flushed with anger. 'I'm damned if I will!' he snapped. 'Walk round behind me!'

'I'll walk *through* you, you fat pig, if you don't get out of my way!'

Startled, Durkin took two hasty steps back and Myles Burke walked slowly past his amazed, open-mouthed face. The hand holding the wreath trembled a little. That corpulent, loud-mouthed swine!

The train came rumbling in, filling the station with a loud, grinding, ear-aching, screeching noise as it slowly came to a halt. Steam hissed in clouds over the engine and platform.

A silent crowd gathered before the van. The doors were slid open and men appeared, carrying a high, long packing-case. They lowered it gently to the platform. The lid was removed and the sides prised away. The men stooped and lifted with strain a brown oak coffin. Somewhere in the crowd a woman began to weep loudly as Fintan Butler and three other men lifted the coffin to their shoulders. They walked slowly down the platform towards the entrance.

Myles Burke joined the crowd who were picking up pieces of the broken packing-case. Some were holding the fragments reverently as though they were pieces of The True Cross. Myles stooped stiffly to pick up a chip and he placed it carefully in his pocket, then shuffled along with the crowd following the bearers, trying to protect the fragile wreath from the crush. By the time he reached the street, the coffin had already been placed in the hearse and the procession was about to move off. Myles attached himself to the tail of the cortège. The green-clad piper marched with slow measured steps ten yards in front of the hearse. As they crossed the bridge and turned right on to the north quays, he began to play.

The slow, poignant, grief-laden air wailed over huddled roofs and across the dark sluggish waters of the river. It was a *caoine*; a poet's lament for the High King of Ireland.

Leading the cortège, Fintan Butler choked back the tears as he recognised the piece. MacLiag's lament for King Brian Boru and the kings and princes who fell at Clontarf. He had composed the music for it when still a student in the seminary.

> Oh, where, Kincora! are thy valorous lords?
> Oh, whither, thou Hospitable! are they gone?
> Oh, where are the Dalcassians of the Golden Swords?
> And where are the warriors Brian led on?

They slow-marched four abreast, keeping in step to the long drawn-out dirge, past the military barracks, past the church. . . . Now and then a few people stopped and stared; here and there men raised their hats and caps in silent tribute. Myles turned towards the long line of shabby buildings on the other side of the river. He picked out the house where he lived. The two small windows of his room were the only ones covered by blinds as a mark of respect. He marched slowly on, keeping in step to the mournful wailing of the pipes.

> And where is Donogh, King Brian's worthy son?
> And where is Conaing, the Beautiful Chief?
> And Kian and Corc? Alas! they are gone –
> They have left me this night alone with my grief!

As they came to O'Connell Bridge the noise of the pipes died away. They stopped to allow the hearse to make the wide turn into Sackville Street, before moving on again. A policeman near the O'Connell Monument stood rigidly to attention, his hand touching his helmet in salute. He did not lower his hand until the tail of the cortège turned the corner. They moved slowly up the principal street of Ireland's capital city. The hustle and bustle went on all about them. Trams whined up and down on both sides of the street; automobiles hooted their horns. The street was crowded; people seemed to be scurrying in all directions. No one paid them much attention; a few curious glances here and there, that was all. The long-haired poet walking beside Myles cast a disdainful look about him. 'Boors!' he exclaimed scornfully.

The piper, in defiance of the general indifference, started to play *Let Erin Remember*. But Erin no longer remembered, thought Myles bitterly; she no longer cared. There were no flags at half-mast, no shutters covering shop windows as a mark of respect. Dublin turned away its cold commercial eye as the small weary column marched slowly up the long slope into North Frederick Street.

'Oh, God,' a man behind Myles uttered hoarsely, 'we're bringin' the mortal remains of Garret Lysaght through the heart of the city so that all can pay homage. A man who devoted his whole life to free his country and his people . . .' His voice broke on a sob of anger. 'And no one gives a damn, not a bloody damn!'

'He was the noblest of warriors,' the long-haired poet declared. 'He should be buried with the kings and illustrious dead at Clonmacnois. A man any country would be proud of . . .' As they crossed the intersection into Blessington Street, he glared at a group of loafers outside a public house.

God in heaven, Myles thought despairingly, what was it all for? All the agony, all the years spent in prison. Tears welled up in his eyes. He started to weep – not only for himself, but for Garret Lysaght and all his old comrades. The Fenians were fading away; each passing year saw fewer and fewer of them. Soon it will be my turn, he thought, and then there will be none of us left. . . .

They turned the corner into Phibsborough Road. Despite the cold, Myles was sweating. There was a nagging pain above his left breast-bone and his breath was coming in tortured gasps. He turned to the poet walking beside him.

'How far away are we now?'

'Not far, not far.'

They crossed over the canal bridge. Now that they were on the last mile to the cemetery, the piper began to play a final tune. The slow, sweet, sad air drifted down the shuffling column, stirring the emotions, touching the heart-strings. It told of a battle fought and lost; of patriots dying on the gallows; of prisoners in chains waiting to be transported to Van Diemen's Land . . .

It brought back a memory to Myles. He was sitting with others inside a horse-drawn prison van on their way to the docks.

'Where are dey takin' us to, aw?' the little lad from Watergrasshill had asked nervously. 'Is it Van Diemen's Land, mebbe, aw?'

Everyone had been silent and morose, except Joe Furlong. Joe laughing, Joe making quips at the two guards sitting in sullen silence with carbines across their knees.

He shook his head. Even after all these years he still experienced a feeling of awe, remembering. We on the way to prison for fifteen years, he thought, and Joe laughing and joking as if we were going on a picnic. Nothing could break his spirit, nothing. He sighed. Dead, I suppose. Dead and forgotten like Garret and all the others.

The cortège came slowly to a halt. Myles, lost in thought, walked on – straight into the man in front. He drew back dazed and bewildered.

'Where are we?' he asked.

'Cemetery,' someone replied.

II

'. . . now here he lies, at rest in his own native soil, embraced by the earth of the country he loved so well. His life, his courage, his unswerving devotion to the cause of Irish freedom, should be an inspiration to us all. Ireland's loss is our loss. Ah, Jesu, but we'll miss him.'

Now and then a gust of wind snatched away the sound of Fintan Butler's voice as he stood over the open mouth of the grave. Myles Burke, standing at the back of the crowd, was finding it difficult to hear all that was being said. He stood alone and apart, holding the wreath in his right hand, his eyes on the tall thin austere figure dressed in black, standing at the graveside. Fintan Butler paused, then unfolded a long sheet of paper and began to read from it. Myles leaned forward a little, left hand behind his ear, trying to hear. Butler's high stilted voice came drifting towards him, punctuated by gusts of wind.

> Fear no more the heat o' the sun,
> Nor the furious winter's rages;
> Thou thy worldly task hast done,
> Home art gone, and ta'en thy wages:

Golden lads and girls all must,
As chimney-sweepers, come to dust.
Fear no more the frown o' the great,
Thou art past the tyrant's stroke . . .

Myles gave up the effort of trying to listen. Besides, he knew those lines from *Cymbeline*. Appropriate, he thought, most appropriate.

Fear no more the lightning-flash,
Nor the all-dreaded thunder-stone,
Fear not slander, censure rash . . .

The wind was getting stronger, blowing steadily from the west, driving low dark-grey clouds before it. It whined across the cemetery, forcing Fintan Butler to raise his voice.

No exorciser harm thee!
Nor no witchcraft charm thee!
Ghost unlaid forbear thee!
Nothing ill come near thee!
Quiet consummation have;
And renowned be thy grave!

The last word spoken, Fintan Butler folded the paper carefully and put it in his overcoat pocket. He stooped and picked up a small ball of clay from the mound of freshly dug-up earth and tossed it into the open grave.

'*Ar dheis Dé atá sé,*' he announced in a high emotional voice and turned away.

The grave-diggers clustered round with their long shovels began to fill in the grave. They worked quickly: fifteen minutes later, task completed, they put their shovels in a cart and moved away.

People began to place wreaths on the grave; some stood to mutter a prayer or two before walking away. Myles remained where he was, waiting for them all to go. It started to rain. The long-haired poet was the last to leave. He lifted a woebegone face to the falling rain and exclaimed dramatically:

'You see . . . even the heavens weep!' then spun about and strode off down the narrow path.

Myles was alone. The only sounds were the moaning wind and the hissing rain. He stepped forward, moving slowly and carefully between the gravestones and monuments of weeping angels. Garret's grave was the first in an untouched plot of ground. It looked so abandoned and forlorn despite the small mound of wreaths and flowers. Myles placed his wreath with the rest. Attached was a card on which he had written, *From an old comrade*, but the rain had almost obliterated it. There was a strong smell of damp arising from the upturned earth. He was breathing heavily, and his heart was thumping. Easy, easy, he cautioned himself. He stood motionless, waiting for the rapid beating of his heart to slow down.

Since that morning, he had been conscious of his own impending death. I'm seventy years of age, he thought, looking at the grave.

'Soon I'll be with you in the clay, old friend,' he whispered. 'I'm the last now – the last survivor of that last charge at Fredericksburg.' Tears blurred his vision.

He started to murmur a little prayer, then stopped. Prayer seemed a somewhat conventional tribute for so unconventional a man. He could remember when both of them had shared a mutual contempt for the pious demeanour of others. No, there was only one tribute – one gesture – Garret Lysaght would have appreciated.

He came to attention and brought his arm up in a rigid salute, his fingertips touching the brim of his hat. He would not have done such a thing if there had been anyone present, but he had the whole windswept, rain-swept cemetery to himself.

'We'll never see the likes of him again,' the voice croaked behind him. He hunched up his shoulders in fear, startled, but his fear was only momentary. It was quickly swamped by anger. To be spied on like this! He twisted around, a hot word of rebuke on the tip of his tongue.

His anger evaporated at the sight of the small pathetic figure crouched against a tombstone. He must have been there all the time, Myles thought, shielding his back against the wind. The ancient wizened face under the bowler hat was blue with the cold. The hat was the only thing he was wearing that seemed to fit. The overcoat was far too big for his small frame and the trouser legs fell in folds over the big boots. He was obviously the recipient of cast-offs. He detached himself from the tombstone and came towards Myles. He was weighed down by the overbig overcoat. The rain had turned the clay into mud and he nearly slipped. Myles caught him by the arm.

'Steady now.'

'I'm all right, I'm all right,' the man mumbled, freeing his arm, but not in an offensive way. He looked at the grave with weak watery eyes. He had a white drooping moustache.

'I knew him well, yeh know,' he said nodding towards the grave. 'I did, bedad.'

His flat, Dublin accent was cracked with age. It startled Myles a little to hear it; it could have been Father Poole talking.

The man sighed. ''Tis the end of an era, so it is.' He seemed content to stand there for the remainder of the day, lost in his memories, oblivious to the rain and wind.

Myles was impatient to be gone. 'Well, I must go now,' he said.

The man did not say anything – did not move. He stood staring at the grave with blank eyes. Myles shook his head and moved away. He picked his steps with care, afraid of slipping in the heavy mud. He gave a sigh of relief when he reached the gravel path.

He was a good distance down it when he heard the cry. He stopped, listening. Perhaps, he thought, it was the wind. The cry came again, a faint wail of distress. Oh, God, Myles thought, he's fallen – maybe broken a leg. He hurried back as fast as he could, but when he reached the grave there was no one there. He searched over a jungle of gravestones and monuments. He thought he heard a cry above the sound of the wind and falling rain, but he was not quite sure. It seemed to come from the left, beyond some shrubbery, about ten yards away. He moved towards it.

He found the man standing in the middle of a narrow path, blubbering. When he caught sight of Myles his voice rose to a wail.

'I'm lost,' he howled, 'lost. I can't find me way out!'

Myles tried to soothe him. 'There now, there now . . .' he said softly as though he were speaking to a child. And like a child he guided him out of the maze, leading him by the hand. The man fell silent, but when they reached the gravel path leading to the entrance, he began to whine away in his cracked voice.

'I should've stayed in the cab like I was told. Fintan will never forgive me. Now how will I get home?'

Myles groaned. Compassion had forced him to go back, now he was saddled with a responsibility he did not want. But he could not abandon the poor creature.

'But yeh see, I had to get out of the cab and follow after,' the man continued, 'I had to pay me last respects to an oul friend . . .'

Myles nodded, not paying any attention. 'Yes, yes, but if you could try and hurry, just a little . . .'

But the man could not, even if he had wanted to. 'I remember when they were takin' us to Kingstown in a prison van. It was after the 'sixty-seven risin', yeh understand. Well . . .'

The rain was growing heavier. Myles's overcoat and trouser legs were sodden. Oh God, he thought, I'm going to catch pneumonia again. The thought filled him with dread. He felt hatred for this man he was helping. Only for him, he thought savagely, I would be in a tram now heading for home. The man's incessant prattle was gnawing at his nerves.

'There we were, eight of us and two guards with carbines, cooped up in a little dog-box of a prison van. There was meself and a little Cork lad from Watergrasshill. Then there was Costigan and a Donegal man named MacGrory . . .'

Jesus, Myles thought despairingly, will he ever stop. Jabber, jabber, jabber . . . He was only half-listening. His thoughts were on a warm cosy room, on a plate of thick Irish stew. He could see the lumps of meat and potato. His stomach rumbled. He had not eaten since early morning.

'. . . Then there was a fella with a French name. A silk weaver from the Liberties . . . Huguenot descent. What's this his name was? Fouchard? No, that wasn't it. Feeney? No, that's an Irish name. Ah, dammit to hell!' he exclaimed exasperatedly. 'I've bloody well forgotten!'

'Fouvargue,' Myles said indifferently.

'Who?'

'Fouvargue – he killed himself afterwards in Pentonville.'

The man halted and Myles with him. He thrust his face upwards, his eyes searching Myles's face. Myles recoiled a little.

'Who are you?' the man whispered.

'I don't understan – '

'Your name!' the man demanded fiercely, his hand clutching Myles's sleeve.

'Burke, Myles Burke.'

The man's mouth dropped open, revealing rotten black stumps of teeth.

'Jesus, Mary and Holy Saint Joseph!' he whispered. 'Myles Burke! I thought you were dead years ago.' Tears started to roll down his cheeks. 'Myles, me oul comrade.'

Myles stared uncomprehending. 'Who. . . ?'

'It's me,' the man explained in a choking voice, 'Joe.'

'Joe?'

'Joe Furlong.'

Myles echoed, 'Joe Furlong.' Then realisation came. Shock hit him like a blow to the body. He was stunned.

*This is Joe Furlong?* The Joe Furlong of the prison van, laughing and joking? He shook his head in disbelief. It couldn't be. Joe, the troublemaker of Pentonville, constantly defying the authorities, emerging after ten days of solitary confinement, thin and wan, but still laughing

285

and joking. Joe, handsome, quick of mind and body, devil-may-care. *This is Joe Furlong?* He was so dazed he was not aware of the sound of approaching footsteps.

'*Mr Furlong!*'

They turned to see the tall dripping figure of Fintan Butler striding towards them in obvious annoyance. His black hair was plastered over his head with rain. His voice was shrill with anger.

'What possessed you to leave that cab! Do you realise I've been looking everywhere for you!'

Joe ignored him. With one hand still clutching Myles's sleeve, he made a quick grab at Fintan.

'Fintan, Fintan,' he shouted, 'do yeh know who this is? Do yeh know who's standin' in the livin' flesh right before yer eyes?'

'Mr Furlong!' Fintan Butler's voice rose to a shout. 'Will you come along this instant before you catch your death!'

'But Fintan – '

'Come along!' He tugged firmly at Joe's arm, but Joe resisted, stamping his foot like an angry child.

'No, I won't!' he shouted. 'Not until yeh hear what I have to say!' He pointed a finger at Myles. 'This is none other than Myles Burke himself,' he declared in a voice choking with emotion. '*Lieutenant* Myles Burke, the last survivor of that final charge at Fredericksburg. Garrett Lysaght's second-in-command. The man who shot his way through the picquet lines after the Tallaght fight . . .'

Myles winced.

'. . . the man involved with Garret in the Pentonville affair . . .'

Joe stopped talking. The excitement was too much for him. He stood holding on to Myles, gasping for breath.

Fintan Butler put an arm round his shoulders.

'Please, Mr Furlong,' he said, all anger gone from his voice, 'calm down.' He turned an astonished face to Myles. 'Is what he said true? Are you really Myles Burke?'

Myles nodded.

'My God,' Fintan Butler gasped, 'I thought you died years ago in prison.'

Myles shivered. He could feel the rain seeping through his clothes. 'For God's sake,' he exclaimed testily, 'could we talk about this in the comfort of a cab? If we stay here any longer we'll all die of pneumonia!'

# Chapter Eleven

## I

Alec Carew walked towards the entrance of the Lower Castle Yard, the cold January air nipping his cheeks. The bells of the nearby cathedral were ringing the hour. Eleven o'clock. Never before had he known the officials and civil servants to work this late. Every department seemed to be having an emergency meeting. The House of Commons had approved the third reading of the Home Rule Bill and the Ulster Protestant Unionists had formed a Volunteer Force to resist it. The dreadful prospect of a civil war was looming on the horizon.

He returned the sentry's salute at the gate as he marched out and turned into Dame Street. He decided to walk home for the bitter cold air was like a tonic to his tired senses. He had been cooped up for too long in that long narrow room with the Under-Secretary, Ian Calder, Regan and the rest.

The Under-Secretary had tried to allay the fears of those who had been alarmed at the news from the north of Ireland. A private army of one hundred thousand men had been created, almost overnight.

'But lacking arms.' The Under-Secretary had permitted himself a slight smile. 'Four hundred rifles have been seized by the Customs in Belfast.'

The smugness in his tone had irked Carew. 'Yes,' he said, opening a folder, 'but several hundred arrived safely, packed in crates marked as zinc plates. Moreover, we have just received information from a most reliable source that six Maxim machine-guns and two hundred and fifty thousand rounds of ammunition have been landed safely at Portrush.'

The Under-Secretary's face showed a mixture of annoyance and scepticism. 'Reliable source? How reliable?'

He had hesitated before answering. 'Billy Durkin of the *Eye-Witness*.'

Assistant Commissioner Harrison gave a contemptuous bark of a laugh which Carew ignored. Besides, he had another bit of information

287

which was to wipe the smiles off both their faces. 'We reported direct to Whitehall. They checked immediately. The Vickers Company produced a copy of a receipt for six machine-guns and ammunition. One of the names on the receipt was an F H Crawford. Crawford is the arms purchaser for the newly created Ulster Volunteer Force.'

Carew smiled to himself. Lucky Durkin, he thought, always at the right place at the right time. Durkin, acting on a tip-off, had been in Portrush for a different reason. He had scooped the other papers by discovering the whereabouts of Ireland's greatest bigamist who was living in that northern seaside town with his sixth wife.

He turned into Grafton Street. How dare they sneer at Durkin? He had accomplished more than the lot of them combined. Even now he was risking his life sending reports from the north about the activities of the Ulster Volunteer Force. Carew strode on, swinging his attaché case in his gloved hand. He was taking a risk walking alone through the streets at night with a case full of confidential documents. In fact he was disobeying orders. All Castle personnel taking confidential papers home were now required to hire a cab or taxicab, or use one of the chauffeur-driven cars at their disposal in the Lower Castle Yard. Security was being tightened up as a result of the northern crisis.

He crossed the road and headed east along Nassau Street. A light fog was descending. The tops of the bare trees beyond the railings of the college opposite were swathed in a thickening grey veil. He seemed to have the long narrow street to himself. The offices and shops were long since closed and the only light came from the street-lamps. A thought came into his mind. What if he had been followed from the Castle? This would be an ideal place for an attack. A swift blow from behind and the attaché case with its precious contents snatched from his lifeless fingers . . .

He gave an abrupt rasp of annoyance. For God's sake, get a grip on yourself. Nevertheless he stopped and turned, looking and listening. The long stretch of damp deserted pavement vanished into fog. There were no sounds except the faint moaning of a tram in the distance. He pressed on. Nerves, he told himself; this damn northern business has us all rattled.

But never again would he take such a risk. Among the papers in the attaché case was a notebook containing names and addresses of informants, men he and Major Calder had recruited to work for Military Intelligence. He was not only putting his own life in danger but other lives as well by walking home alone. But there's no danger, he tried to assure himself, the Irish Republican Brotherhood is now a demoralised and discredited organisation.

288

From the elegance of Merrion Square Alec walked into the shabbiness of Mount Street, remembering the meeting a little over a month ago. The Under-Secretary had sat at the head of the table looking through his pince-nez at the copy of the *Eye-Witness* resting on the blotting-pad.

'Crudely written,' he commented, 'but effective. Our Embassy in the States arranged to have copies sent to every Irish-American organisation in the country. Copies were also sent to the German Embassy in Washington. So we can safely assume,' giving one of his rare smiles, 'no more money will be coming in to swell the IRB coffers. And without money the organisation will cease to exist.'

'Let us hope so,' Harrison said.

Regan, the Deputy Inspector General, picked up his copy and chuckled. 'I like the headline. "IRB funds blown on booze." ' He raised his head. 'It says here Kinsella used up nearly a thousand pounds. That true?'

'No, no,' Major Calder replied. 'Durkin wildly exaggerates. He drew out four hundred pounds over a period of seven or eight months. Some of it was used to support his family, but most of it was spent on drink. Poor devil, he couldn't help himself. Durkin says he was swilling a bottle of whiskey a day.'

'Poor devil is right,' Harrison said, and Carew remembered his look of contempt. His gaze never wavered as he said with undisguised malice in his voice, 'I'm sure you'll be interested to hear that Kinsella died in hospital early this morning. Cirrhosis of the liver.'

The canal bridge came into view. Carew turned right and headed west towards home. The fog lay thick and heavy along the canal: visibility was suddenly reduced to about ten feet. A man leading a plodding horse emerged from the murk, the horse laboriously pulling a canal barge. The barge moved silently through the fog, ghost-like, piled high with turf. The greenish glow of a street-lamp appeared in the distance. As he drew nearer, he could see the dim outline of a figure standing beneath it. Prostitutes roamed the streets of this district after nightfall.

She stood waiting, hand on hip. She was fashionably dressed in tight-fitting dress, wide-brimmed hat, fur stole. She took a step forward to meet him, but stopped, daunted at the sight of his officers' greatcoat and cap. He acknowledged with a curt nod her enticing smile and walked on, a little surprised. He had expected to see one of those ravaged veterans of the streets, but she was young and quite beautiful. He carried her image with him through the foggy darkness: the painted sensual mouth; the wide curved hips. Lust stirred in his blood like a fever. I've been celibate for too long, he told himself. He found his steps faltering, wanting to go back to her, but he crushed the thought before it could take root. He tried to think of something else.

But he could not collect his thoughts – could not think clearly. It was as if the fever in his blood was infecting his brain. He had a sudden and erotic vision of Miriam. A groan escaped him, a groan of anger and frustration. Durkin was up north for nearly two weeks now. In the old days, Miriam and himself would have spent every night together during his absence, but the affair was over now; over for good.

Nevertheless, he paused before mounting the steps and looked up, hoping to see light in his windows of his rooms on the top floor. She had never returned the key. The tall Georgian building reared up into the fog, dark and abandoned. The estate agent and the dentist left for home each evening at six o'clock. He stood before the door, fumbling in his pocket for the key.

He climbed the unlit stairs: there was a strong smell of beeswax. He unlocked the door of his room and walked in, moving slowly and carefully in the dark towards the fireplace. He put the attaché case down on the floor beside him and groped for the matches on the mantleshelf. He struck one and applied it to the gas-jet. There was a pop and it flared into life, filling the room with a greenish glow. He took off his cap and greatcoat, and shivered. The room was as cold as an icebox. The fireplace was set for lighting. He struck a few more matches: tiny flames began to dance upwards and there were crackling sounds as the kindling caught alight. He took off his tunic and put on a cardigan. He knew there was a cold meal prepared for him in the kitchen, but he was not hungry.

A woman came every afternoon to clean to flat. She raked out the fireplace, made the bed and generally tidied. She also collected the mail and left it for him on the silver tray on the sideboard. He poured a large whiskey, placed an easychair in front of the fire and sat down. He took a sip and lay back, the fire warming his legs.

Silence pressed against his ears. This is like the old days, he thought; that black period following Valerie's suicide, sitting alone brooding, trying to drown my memories in alcohol.

Their affair came to an end in that little out-of-the-way tea-room off Leeson Street which they used as a rendezvous. There had been a bitter quarrel between them three nights before when Durkin had been away on business. It had started in the usual way: she demanding that he tell Durkin everything so that she could obtain a divorce; he trying to explain that that would result in him being disinherited and losing Carewscourt . . .

She sat at the table, hands in lap, tea untouched, listening to the same arguments. '. . . To tell Durkin about us now, at a time when he's risking his life supplying us with vital information, would be an act of treachery . . .' She remained silent for a long while after he had finished talking. Then, face composed, said quietly: 'I've decided to end this affair of ours, Alec . . .'

He stared contemplatively at the fire. She had made him promise never to try and see her again. He had kept to his promise, often declining Durkin's repeated invitations to visit. He did not want to go to that house, did not want to witness their happiness.

'I don't know what's come over Miriam lately,' Durkin told him, face flushed from drink, as they sat in the hotel bar. 'She's changed – for the better. All love and affection. Of course she was always a dutiful wife, but never so . . . so responsive.' He gave a suggestive wink and leered. 'Know what I mean?'

She's atoning for her sins, he thought bitterly, standing up and walking over to where the whiskey bottle stood. He brought it back with him to the fire and placed it down on the floor beside the chair. Then he sat down and filled the glass. He took a deep swallow and lay back in the chair with a sigh. This was the only thing that eased the pain – that helped him to forget . . .

He sat like that for a long time, drinking and brooding. Eventually he fell asleep. When he awoke the fire had burnt itself out and he felt chilled to the bone. He rose dazedly to his feet and stood, swaying a little, senses reeling. Slowly the room came into focus. His gaze rested on the silver tray on the sideboard. A light-blue envelope lay on it. He took a few unsteady steps across the room and picked it up. It was a telegram.

He clumsily tore open the envelope. He read it, then read it again, slowly, trying to concentrate, trying to fight off the effects of the whiskey clouding his brain. It was from his uncle's solicitor in Castlebar. *Regret to inform you, your uncle, Walter Carew, died in his sleep yesterday evening. Deepest sympathy.*


II


Alec stood outside the churchyard, solemnly shaking hands with everyone as they came up to him, accepting their condolences with a slight sad smile and a 'Thank you . . . you are so kind . . . so very kind . . .' There were about thirty mourners in all: the Hacketts, the Merricks, the Townshends, the Bricketts, the Henshaws . . . Elizabethan and Cromwellian names. Our ancestors, he thought, have held Ireland for the Crown for centuries, and now they're fading away.

> The tumult and the shouting dies;
> The Captains and the Kings depart . . .

He watched as they moved slowly down the village street in the pale winter sunshine towards the line of waiting carriages. The vast majority belonged to his uncle's generation. A dying breed, he thought sadly and with despair; we Anglo-Irish are a dying breed . . .

The family solicitor, Bob Egan, sat waiting in his car. Carew opened the door and moved in beside him. 'Wait a while, will you, Bob, till they all go.'

'No hurry,' Egan answered. He sat behind the wheel smoking a pipe; squat, middle-aged, bowler-hatted; a heavy brown moustache adorned his upper lip.

'D'ye know,' Carew said reflectively, 'sitting in that church and looking about me, I couldn't help thinking back to when I was a boy. Then there must have been a congregation of at least four hundred. Now . . .' He shrugged and heaved a sigh. 'There are so few of us left . . .'

Egan grunted. 'There'll be fewer by the time summer comes,' he said, the pipe between his teeth. 'The Hacketts and Henshaws are selling out and going to England.'

Carew winced. He stared bleakly through the windscreen. The carriages were moving off one by one.

> Lo, all our pomp of yesterday
> Is one with Nineveh and Tyre . . .

'Have you decided what you're going to do about Carewscourt?' Egan asked.

Carew shook his head. 'No . . . but I'm not going to sell out like the Hacketts and Henshaws, if that's what you mean.' The last carriage was moving away. Carew said: 'Could we wait a little longer? I don't want to pass any of them on the road. Somehow it wouldn't seem proper.'

'I'm in no hurry,' Egan said and leaned back in the seat, puffing away at his pipe. After a short silence, he said: 'That steward . . . Skerritt, isn't that his name?'

'Tim Skerritt. What about him?'

'Do you trust him?'

Carew looked sideways at him. 'What exactly do you mean?'

Egan took the pipe from his mouth. 'I'll come straight to the point,' he said. 'Carewscourt is on the verge of bankruptcy. The estate has been badly mismanaged for years. Your uncle gave over the complete running of the estate to Skerritt. The older your uncle became the less inclined he was to bother about how things were going. I heard rumours – but only rumours, mind – that Skerritt let the land for grazing without your uncle knowing. It's also rumoured that he sold timber from the estate, allowing the men to come in after nightfall to cut down the trees. The estate is losing money, and I've a strong suspicion a lot of it is going into Skerritt's pocket.'

'Can you obtain any definite proof?' Carew asked.

'I'll take the estate books back with me to Castlebar and hand them over to the auditors. If there are any discrepancies they'll find them. Of course Skerritt can always claim that he was carrying out your uncle's instructions and with your uncle dead, who is there to say that wasn't so? I was rather hoping you would remain longer. There's much to discuss. Is it necessary for you to leave for Dublin tonight?'

Carew sighed wearily. 'I'm afraid so. I was given compassionate leave rather reluctantly. This northern business . . .'

'I see.' Egan put the pipe back in his mouth and started to suck on it, holding the bowl between forefinger and thumb. 'Well,' he said after a while, 'if you are not going to sell Carewscourt, you'll have to reside there and take charge. And you can't do that if you're in the army.'

'You mean resign my commission?'

'You'll have to. If you remain in the army and leave Skerritt in charge, he'll run the place into the ground, ruining you in the process. Then you'll have no choice but to sell.'

Carew shook his head slowly. 'I can't . . . I just can't resign now, not with all this trouble brewing.'

Egan shrugged his shoulders. 'Well . . . you'll have to make a decision, one way or the other.'


III


The train moved slowly northwards between the flat green fields of east

293

Mayo. Carew had the first-class compartment to himself. He sat beside the window reading the letter from Egan.

I strongly suggest you personally discharge Skerritt for incompetence. Perhaps a gratuity of £200 will salve his injured pride. Considering his dishonesty, this may seem outrageous to you, but you must take into account his years of service, and the fact that the Skerritts have been stewards of Carewscourt for generations.

I have communicated with a man in Tyrone who would be willing to take on the job of steward of Carewscourt. I know him personally and can vouch for his integrity. He is of good Ulster Presbyterian stock; sober, industrious . . .

Egan came to Dublin one weekend to discuss matters in detail. He had brought with him a briefcase full of documents, including a report from an agricultural expert who had inspected the estate. The chief recommendations were that the rich grassy lands of the estate be used for cattle rearing. Yearlings could be sold for fattening to farms in Westmeath and Cavan. Existing timber should be felled and sold and the ground replanted with fast-growing commercial timber . . .

Carew sighed and put down the clipped pages beside him on the seat. Nothing but suggestions and recommendations. Where the hell is all the money to come from? he asked himself.

He had put the same question to Egan. 'Your uncle's legacy, of course,' had been the answer.

'There will be precious little of that left if I do as you suggest.'

'Then sell Carewscourt.'

'No!'

'Very well, then . . .'

Carewscourt had marvellous potential, Egan assured him, but it would require large injections of capital not only for restocking and replanting, but for byres and haysheds and the like. Then there was the house itself. It was too big and the top floor and north wing were in a ruinous stage. They would have to be demolished and the house made smaller and more compact.

'It will mean spending every penny of what your uncle left you,' Egan told him. 'But after a year or two under proper management, the estate should start to pay for itself. Besides, the rents from the village will provide a steady income.'

It was then he produced a single sheet of flimsy paper from his briefcase and handed it to him. 'Several copies of that have been circulated around Carewstown . . .'

Carew lit another cigarette and looked out of the carriage window. The countryside looked so fresh and green in the spring sunshine. He put his left hand inside his tunic; he had placed the folded paper carefully between the flaps of his wallet. He pulled out the piece of paper. It was a typewritten carbon copy.

No more rents for the new Lord of Carewscourt! The Carews have grown fat and rich on the blood and sweat of the people of this district over the past two hundred and fifty years. The present Lord's ancestor won these lands with the sword and drove the owners – your forbears – into the wilderness of bog and mountain. These lands are rightfully yours! Why pay rents to the descendant of the man who stole them.

The day of the landlord is over! No more evictions! No more throwing helpless families out on the side of the road and demolishing their humble cabins into dust! The Ascendancy are crumbling away like their mansions and demesnes. Next will be their army and the lickspittles who support it!

Listen to the wind, friends. The might of England is about to be challenged by the might of Germany. A great war is coming – and coming sooner than most people think. Keep in mind this watchword: England's difficulty is Ireland's opportunity!

He folded the paper and put it back inside the wallet. Rabble-rousing stuff, he thought, remembering Egan's words.

'Who wrote it?' he had asked.

Egan shrugged. 'Nobody knows. The police sergeant gave it to me to give to you.'

Carew stretched out his legs and relaxed. He watched the flat, green, monotonous landscape go sliding past. He could feel the accumulated tension of the past few weeks slowly draining away. He had been granted leave only because things up north had quietened down. He smiled wryly to himself, remembering the morning headlines, and wondered how Regan and Harrison and the other police officials had reacted to the news.

Six masked men armed with cudgels had surprised and overpowered five policemen in their barracks at Partry in west Mayo. After tying up their victims, they stripped the barracks of its arms: five carbines, one revolver and seven hundred rounds of ammunition. It was obviously the work of some extreme republican group, the papers said, possibly the IRB. Partry, he reflected; that was about fifteen miles south-west of Carewstown. His lips formed into a thin grim line. Gun-running up north, he thought, and now raiding for arms down here . . .

295

A prolonged wail drifted from the engine as the train slowed down. Carewstown. He assembled the papers strewn over the seat beside him and stuffed them hurriedly into the attaché case. Leave had been given so unexpectedly there had been no time to make arrangements. He had dashed off a telegram to Carewscourt telling Tim Skerritt to meet him at the station with the gig. I hope to hell he received it in time, he thought, or he would have to walk the two miles to the demesne.

But Skerritt was there, waiting. He took Carew's suitcase from him while Carew kept his attaché case on his lap as he settled himself in the seat. Skerritt climbed up beside him and took the reins.

As they moved off, Carew said: 'Sorry for such short notice.'

'I only received your telegram an hour ago,' Skerritt said. 'It sent cook into a tizzy.'

'Tell her not to bother preparing anything for me. I'm going to the village first to attend to some business. A light cold supper when I return would be welcome, though.'

The horse trotted along the narrow dusty road between high blooming hedges. Carew breathed in the clean, sweet, country air. It was invigorating. He raised his voice above the noise of wheels and hoofs.

'By the way, ask Mrs Joyce to prepare a room for a guest who's coming tomorrow. He'll be staying for the weekend.'

'A guest?'

'Yes, an architect from Dublin. He's going to inspect the entire house. The top floor and the north wing will have to be demolished.'

Skerritt shook the reins. 'Giddyup outa that!' he rasped and the horse broke into a canter.

Carew held his attaché case tightly, swaying with the motion of the gig. Was there something the matter with Skerritt? he wondered. He seemed on edge. Has it anything to do with my unexpected arrival? Was he involved in some skulduggery when my telegram arrived? He hoped so; it would make the task of dismissing him that much easier.

A dog barked furiously at them from behind the closed gate of a drive leading up to a farm-house and up ahead they could see two figures standing in the middle of the road. The two policemen stood motionless, their boots and trouser legs caked with mud. The sergeant raised his hand in a tired salute to Carew.

'What's wrong, sergeant?'

'Just searchin', sir.'

'Searching? For what?'

'I suppose ye read about those arms that were stolen from the police barracks in Partry, sir?'

'Of course. But Partry is more than fifteen miles from here.'

'Sixteen to be exact, sir. But I don't think they hid them in that district, knowin' that the whole area would be combed.'

'What makes you think the arms are hidden in *this* district?'

'Ah, we had a stroke of luck there, sir. Two nights ago, about three miles from here, a tinker and his woman were sleepin' in the ruins of a cottage. The cottage stands at the side of a boreen. Durin' the night they heard noises outside and got up and peeped out. There in the moonlight they saw several men and a horse and cart passin' by. There was a load on the cart covered by tarpaulin . . .' The sergeant paused.

Carew stared at him in bewilderment. 'What's so unusual about that, sergeant?'

The sergeant smirked a little, pleased with his own cleverness. 'The boreen is very narrow and full of potholes. Why use it when there's a perfectly good road runnin' parallel with it only thirty yards away?'

Carew nodded slowly, comprehending. 'Why indeed, sergeant.'

'They didn't want to take a chance meetin' anyone on the road, ye see, sir.'

'Of course.'

'And they were headin' north-east, in this direction.' The sergeant took a step closer and lowered his voice a little. 'I trust Mr Egan gave you that paper? That inflammatory piece of – '

Carew nodded. 'Yes, yes, thank you, sergeant.'

'Somehow I think it's all connected,' the sergeant went on, 'the raid on the barracks and this stirrin' up of trouble against the gentry.'

'You may be right, sergeant.'

'There's trouble brewin', sir,' the sergeant pronounced gravely. 'South of here, near Lough Mask, Colonel Peacock's home was raided and his collection of sportin' rifles stolen together with five hundred rounds of ammunition. A box of gelignite was taken from a quarry on the Roscommon border.'

'I see.' Carew stroked his chin thoughtfully. 'This indeed is serious, sergeant. Any idea who's involved?'

'No, sir. But we'll get 'em, never fear.'

Carew returned his salute. 'Good hunting, sergeant.'

Skerritt clucked his tongue and urged the horse forward. Carew waited for him to make some comment, but Skerritt maintained a stony silence. He sat upright, holding the reins loosely in his hands, his eyes on the road in front.

He betrays himself by his silence, Carew thought.

The ground sloped gently away from the road. In the distance he could see the brown of bog and sheen of river. He shifted his gaze again to the road ahead. Carewscourt came into view: the long, high, crumbling wall of the demesne with the plantation of tall trees beyond. The sight of them made him think of the rumours Egan had heard about Skerritt selling timber from the estate and pocketing the proceeds. As they drove past he could not help saying, 'Have you been thinning out? Seems to me there are fewer trees now than before.'

'Windfalls,' Skerritt replied tersely, staring straight ahead. 'We had quite a few heavy storms last winter.'

As they reached the crossroads, Carew said: 'Stop here. I'll walk the rest of the way.' Somehow he did not want Skerritt to know where he was going. He strode up the village street. On the other side of the road, two shop-keepers chatted in adjoining doorways. An old man led a donkey and cart down the middle of the road. There was a lazy, sleepy atmosphere about the place.

Half-way up the street he turned into a sunken cul-de-sac. There the Catholic church was located. Walter Carew's bigotry had been legendary so he was not surprised at the look of astonishment on the housekeeper's face when he asked to see the parish priest.

She ushered him into the study and went in search of Father Devlin. He took off his cap and placed it with the attaché case on a nearby chair. He waited, with his back to the fire. There was a crucifixion scene on the wall facing him. The room was sparsely furnished. A well polished mahogany table, a bookcase, a sideboard. There were two leather armchairs on each side of the fireplace. Despite the bookcase, he did not think Father Devlin was one of those scholarly types of clergymen. The room was stamped with a rugged masculinity: the sporting prints on the walls; the aroma of cigar smoke; the decanter of whiskey on the sideboard. There was a heavy step in the passage outside. The door opened and Father Devlin walked in.

Carew was surprised: he did not expect to see such a huge man. He walked towards him, hand outstretched in greeting. 'Good afternoon, Padre. I'm Alec Carew.'

A big ploughman's hand gripped his.

Carew said, 'I'm the new master of Carewscourt. As such, I felt I should call and pay my respects.'

Father Devlin beamed. 'Delighted, delighted. Please, remove your coat and make yourself at home.' He walked heavily to the sideboard and picked up the decanter. 'I know you army chaps prefer whiskey to tea and scones,' he said, giving a booming laugh.

Carew, divested of his greatcoat, accepted the full glass Father

298

Devlin thrust towards him. Father Devlin raised his glass in a toast. 'Your very good health, sir.' They both took a sip. Father Devlin waved towards the chair. 'Sit down, sit down.'

He has the rough manners of a peasant, Carew thought, though he felt completely at ease in his presence. I wish I was always so relaxed, he thought ruefully, remembering the tension he always experienced at the Under-Secretary's weekly meetings. There, manners were impeccable; tempers always under tight rein. Yet one could always sense the hostility building up all round . . .

He took another sip from the glass. 'This is an excellent whiskey, Padre,' he said.

'Yes it is, isn't it,' Father Devlin agreed, raising the glass to his mouth. 'A publican here in the village gave it to me for a Christmas gift.' He chuckled. 'But gift or no gift, I told him, if it's inferior stuff, I'll denounce ye from the altar.'

Carew smiled as Father Devlin gave another of his booming laughs, comparing his joviality with the Reverend Slater's depressive manner. If he had told the pastor of his own church that he intended spending more than twenty thousand pounds on reviving Carewscourt to its former glory, he would have been rewarded with a simple: 'Oh, really . . . that's nice.' Father Devlin's bubbling enthusiasm on the other hand, inspired him with courage and confidence.

'Splendid, splendid!' Father Devlin crowed. 'My dear sir, you are exactly what this poor country of ours needs. One becomes disheartened, ye know, hearing that old dirge about Mayo being unworthy of investment.'

'Apart from the estate,' Carew said, 'a great deal of work will have to be done to the house itself. It will have to be altered considerably. I intend to use as much local labour as possible. Unskilled, unfortunately. I've been informed that there are no tradesmen in the district.'

'Alas, no.' Father Devlin shook his head regretfully. 'Hewers of wood and drawers of water, I'm afraid.'

Carew swallowed a mouthful of whiskey. 'I'm extremely optimistic, Padre. I have a report from an agricultural expert who inspected the estate. His opinion is that Carewscourt has marvellous potential. And when that potential is realised, quite a few local people will be employed on the estate. Think of what that will mean to the traders and shopkeepers in the village.'

'A blessing,' Father Devlin said. 'And who can tell, the other big land-owners may follow your example. So much of their land is lying idle.'

299

'We Anglo-Irish, Padre, may pledge our allegiance to England, but we owe a debt to Ireland, our adopted country. We have an obligation, not only to our country, but to the community as a whole. It was Drummond, was it not, who said: "Property has its duties as well as its rights." '

'Property has its duties as well as its rights,' Father Devlin repeated slowly. He smiled. 'You have just provided me with the text of next Sunday's sermon, Captain Carew. Ye have indeed. Ye know,' he went on, 'I'm always telling my flock to respect the law and the rights of property owners. I don't tolerate poachers and suchlike in my parish. I do not, faith. I tell my people from the pulpit, the law must be respected. And they obey, Captain. They listen to their priest.'

'Not all of them, I'm afraid, Padre.'

'What's that!' For a second he forgot to whom he was speaking; all he was aware of was that someone had contradicted him. Then he forced a smile; his way of apologising for the harshness of his voice. 'I'm sorry, but I don't understand.'

Carew produced the sheet of paper Egan had given him and, leaning forward, thrust it into Father Devlin's outstretched hand. 'It should not be too difficult to discover who the author is. There can't be that many typewriters in the district, surely.'

Father Devlin pondered for a minute. 'Three, as far as I know,' he said gazing thoughtfully at the fire. The Reverend Slater had one and so had Troy, the school-teacher. The third belonged to Shelia Tighe, the publican's daughter, who was doing some sort of secretarial course . . .

He scrutinised the paper again. Then he noticed something. 'Excuse me a moment, Captain,' he said and went over to his small writing-desk in the corner. He pulled open a drawer, and took out a manila folder in which he kept his correspondence. He turned over hand-written letters until he came to a type-written one. This he picked up and examined closely. 'Captain . . .' There was a note of excitement in his voice.

Carew put down his glass on the hearth and took the note from Father Devlin.

The contents puzzled Carew. They dealt solely with educational matters.

'The machine on which this letter was typed,' Father Devlin said, standing over him, 'has a defective key. The letter "m". Observe how it drops below the level of the rest of the type.'

Carew nodded. There were dropped 'm's on every second or third line.

300

Then Father Devlin handed him the other sheet of paper. 'This is the one you gave me. Notice the "m's" again – the same defective key.'

Carew nodded. 'My God, yes I see . . . both letters were typed on the same machine.' He noticed something else: the capital 'T's' on both sheets of paper had half a serif missing at the base. He gave a low grunt of satisfaction.

'Who does the typewriter belong to?' he asked.

'Gerry Troy, the school-teacher.'

Carew looked up at him in surprise. 'The school-teacher?'

Father Devlin nodded, his face grim. 'But he won't remain a school-teacher for very long. I'm the school manager and I'm going to run him out of the school and out of the district. I'll also see to it he never gets another job teaching again.' He reached out for the papers. 'I'll keep the evidence if ye don't mind.' Father Devlin gave a smile of satisfaction. Troy had been a thorn in his side since he came to Carewstown four years ago. He had become too popular with the people, and that was dangerous. He regarded himself as their champion, demanding this and that on their behalf. His recent request for starting a lending library had been but one of many over the last few years.

Well, your days in Carewstown are numbered, bucko, thought Father Devlin, placing the papers in the folder and putting it back in the drawer.

Carew sat a little forward, the glass between his hands. 'Tell me what you know about this fellow Troy, Padre.'

Father Devlin took a sip from his glass. 'Well, I know he's a native of Limerick city. He spent a few years in Dublin at the Teachers' Training College before coming here.'

'I see,' Carew pondered a moment. 'Strange, don't you think, for a city man to settle in a quiet out-of-the-way place like this. Usually they prefer a city post.'

Father Devlin gave a slight shrug. 'I suppose . . .'

'Unless of course,' Carew said, 'he was sent here deliberately.'

Father Devlin stared at him, puzzled. 'I don't understand.'

'Padre, did you ever hear of a secret organisation called the Irish Republican Brotherhood?'

'Yes, of course. Many years ago. It died out after the Fenian rebellion, didn't it?'

Carew shook his head. 'Not really. In fact, it has become very active over the last few years. I've an idea Troy was sent here as an IRB organiser.'

Father Devlin stared at him open-mouthed.

'Furthermore,' he continued, 'I think he might have been involved in the raid on the police barracks in Partry. I don't think he actually participated, but I'll wager he and some others planned it.'

Father Devlin was genuinely shocked. 'Great heavens,' he gasped, 'I had no idea . . .' His face was grim. 'All the more reason why he should be ejected from his position and from the district immediately.'

Carew shook his head. 'I think it would be a mistake,' he said, 'to act rashly.'

Father Devlin spread both arms wide. 'What then do you propose I do?' he asked.

'Do nothing,' Carew replied. 'Let Troy go on thinking no one suspects him, but keep him under close surveillance. Find out who are the people he associates with in the district. Pay particular attention to outsiders who may visit him, especially if they are from Dublin. It's vitally important we find out who Troy's superiors are.' He paused, his eyes on Father Devlin's face. 'I was told you are a firm believer in law and order, Padre.'

Father Devlin nodded. 'You were told correctly, Captain.'

'Therefore a loyal man?'

Father Devlin hesitated before answering, wondering what all this was leading up to. 'Of course.'

'Good. I want you to cooperate with Sergeant Hanafin.'

'I will,' Father Devlin answered quietly. An inner voice whispered caution. He had waded into the surf, willing to let his feet get wet, but now he felt he was being dragged out beyond his depth.

'Supply Sergeant Hanafin with all the information that comes your way. I'll have a chat with him after I leave here and will explain all . . .'

Later that night, after he had finished supper, Carew wrote a letter to the District Inspector, explaining everything that had happened and making a few suggestions. He suggested that Troy's mail should be intercepted and opened, the contents copied, then the envelope resealed and delivered to its destination. He signed the letter in his usual backhand style and put it in an envelope. He laid it on top of a large pile of papers relating to the estate. He sighed wearily. He would have to go through all those before retiring. He reached for the cup near his elbow and took a sip. He made a face: the tea was cold. Nevertheless he drank it. The thin quivering flame of the oil-lamp on the table feebly kept the encroaching shadows of the huge dining room at bay.

There was a knock, and Mrs Joyce, the cook, came in with a tray in her hand. She was a stout middle-aged woman with a broad red-cheeked genial face.

302

'I came to collect the things, sir,' she said, 'that is if yer finished.'

Carew straightened up in the chair. 'Yes, yes, of course, come in.'

She was panting a little after her climb from the kitchen. Carew sat watching her, as she placed the supper things on the tray.

'Why didn't you send one of the maid-servants up, Mrs Joyce?' he asked. 'This isn't your job.'

The upper part of her face was in shadow. 'The fact is, sir, Brigid and Mary are afraid to come up the stairs after dark.'

He gave a little snort of irritation. 'Nonsense! The girls are being silly, that's all.'

She lowered her head, avoiding his eyes. 'No, sir,' she said in a low voice, 'they're not bein' silly.' She paused, then said: 'They're terrified. And to tell ye the truth, so am I.'

'Terrified? Of what?'

She raised her head a little and looked at him; he could see fear in her eyes. 'It happened just a few nights ago, sir.' There was a slight tremor in her voice. 'Noises, footsteps. Overhead and on the stairs. Brigid and Mary had to sleep with me. They were frightened out of their wits!'

Carew smiled, to ease her fears. 'Come now, Mrs Joyce. You're a sensible level-headed woman. It's a very old house and badly in need of repair. It's only natural that you would hear noises in the stillness of the night. The wind, a loose floorboard.'

'No, sir!' Her voice was emphatic. 'None of those things. I came out and stood at the foot of the stairs, listenin'. I could hear the sounds plainly. They came from the top of the house. Footsteps, and the sound of somethin' bein' *dragged*.'

And the sound of chains too, I shouldn't wonder, Carew thought cynically, but said nothing.

'Ye don't know what it's been like,' Mrs Joyce whimpered, 'for three helpless women livin' alone in this great big barracks of a house.'

My God, Carew, thought, she really is frightened. 'What about Skerritt?' he asked.

'Oh, him!' Mrs Joyce exclaimed contemptuously. 'It's all right for him. He's safe and snug in his lodge down at the gate. When I told him about the, the disturbances, he laughed and called us three silly biddies.'

Carew tossed the remains of the cigarette into the empty fireplace and picked up the oil-lamp from the table. 'Come along, Mrs Joyce,' he said. 'I'll escort you downstairs.'

'Will ye be stayin' with us for long, sir?' Mrs Joyce asked, gasping a little as they descended the stairs.

'About ten days or so,' Carew answered.

'Thank God for that at least,' Mrs Joyce breathed thankfully.

They moved up the stone-flagged passage. Carew opened the door leading to the kitchen and stood to one side, holding it open as she struggled past with the loaded tray. She put down the tray with a sigh of relief. The kitchen was ablaze with light. There were oil-lamps everywhere.

He was amused. 'All right now, Mrs Joyce?' he asked, smiling.

She gave him a grateful look. 'Thank you, sir. We'll all sleep aisy in our beds tonight now that you're here.'

He chuckled quietly to himself all the way back to the dining room. 'Ghosts and hobgoblins and things that go bump in the night,' he murmured, closing the door behind him. He put the oil-lamp in the centre of the table and reached for the papers in his attaché case. He selected Egan's letter from the pile and read it again. He decided to reply to it.

Dear Bob.

I intend to do as you suggest and dismiss Tim Skerritt for incompetence. Perhaps, as you say, the £200 gratuity will do the trick.

Can you arrange a meeting between myself and this man from Tyrone? Your office, I think, would be the most suitable place. If he is competent and industrious as you say, then I am willing to allow him to run the estate any way he likes. With someone dependable in charge, I can stay on in the army. When the northern crisis is over, perhaps then I can resign my commission . . .

It was after midnight when he finished the letter. His eyes were heavy with fatigue. There was more work to do, but he told himself that enough was enough. He put his papers away and went out into the hall. As he closed the door, he stood, listening to the uncanny silence. Each time he came back to Carewscourt he found it hard to adjust. He walked slowly up the broad staircase, his footfalls echoing and re-echoing throughout the vastness of the house. Disturbing the ghosts, he thought with a smile.

But the smile was forced. He was aware of a cold feeling creeping over him. He held the oil-lamp over his head as he walked along the corridor tense, the darkness skulking away from the quivering flame of the lamp. When he reached his room and closed the door behind him, he gave a long sigh of relief. The palms of his hands were clammy with sweat. He had been absent from Carewscourt for so long he had forgotten how unnerving it could be at dead of night.

He undressed and put on his pyjamas, and climbed into bed, but the weariness he had felt only a short time before had left him. He lay on his back, staring up into the darkness. For once there was no wind blowing, just a light breeze which sighed through the half-open window, unloosing a thousand whispers throughout the room.

Suddenly the years fell away and he was a boy of twelve again, new to Carewscourt, listening to the wind moaning through the house, unable to put from his mind the servants' stories of Charlotte's lamenting ghost roaming the upper floors. He lay awake for a long while, remembering, till sleep claimed him.

Several times during the night, he awoke, restless, disturbed by dreams, finding it difficult to adjust to a strange bed. Eventually, from sheer exhaustion, he fell into a deep sleep.

He dreamt he was a boy, climbing the stairs to the deserted upper floor in the dark, a lighted candle in his hand. Below, he could hear his uncle urging him on.

'You must not run away from the thing you fear. Confront it and conquer it!' To show cowardice was to incur his uncle's wrath. He was more afraid of that than whatever it was that lay waiting for him at the top of the house. Up and up he went into the moaning dark. He found himself standing at the entrance to the long corridor which stretched away towards the empty north wing. The wind came moaning towards him; he could feel it flowing up against his face. The candle-flame flattened, wavered violently, and went out. He was blind and helpless in the pitch-dark.

Then he heard it: a thumping sound. It came again, a slow heavy tread. His blood turned to ice. Something was coming towards him in the dark. . . . He struggled up into a sitting position, breathing harshly, his body oily with sweat. A sliver of moonlight lay across the carpeted floor. He raised a shaking hand to his face. The nightmare had been so vivid, so real. . . . Even now he could still hear the thumping sounds. . . .

He jerked his head upwards, ears straining. Something was moving along the corridor overhead. There was the slow heavy sound of a footfall – he could actually hear a floorboard creak.

The blood rushed to his heard, and he went rigid with shock and fear. This can't be, he told himself incredulously, this can't be. There was no one else in the house but himself, the cook and the two maidservants. The floor above had been deserted for sixty years. The sounds of footsteps were moving away, towards the right, in the direction of the stairs. He remained in the same position, nerves taut, listening. Gradually the sounds faded away.

He did not move, ears alert for the slightest sound, but there was only silence. A faint breeze whispered across the room from the half-open window. He lowered his head gently to the pillow and pulled the bedclothes up to his chin. He felt cold – ice-cold. Within him there was fear; a deep, primitive, paralysing fear which prevented him from leaving the safety of the room to investigate. It was only with the coming of light did he feel shame for his lack of courage.

Somewhere outside a cock greeted the false dawn. He got out of bed, walked to the windows and pulled the curtains wide. The first grey light of day entered the room. Again the cock crowed. The terrors of the night had gone and a new day was dawning. He took off his pyjamas, washed and shaved in cold water, and dressed. A whiskey bottle and glass stood on a small low table in a corner near the window. He filled the glass, and sat down on the side of the bed, sipping the whiskey and smoking a cigarette, castigating himself for his cowardice. I'm no better than Mrs Joyce and the two maidservants, he told himself bitterly, cowering in my room. He had discovered something shameful about himself, and now he had to redeem himself. Now – before the sun rose; while the house was still dark and silent, the three women below still asleep.

He stood up and walked to the table and lit the oil-lamp. It was almost pitch-dark in the windowless corridor. He walked slowly down it towards the landing, holding the lamp aloft. An oval window high above the landing gave some light. He paused at the foot of the stairs leading to the top floor. This was the nightmare all over again. He took a deep breath and started to climb.

He paused on the landing and looked down. Already his shoes were covered in dirt. The strong smell of damp and decay filled his nostrils. The whole damn upper floor is disintegrating, he thought. He halted at the entrance of the long corridor leading to the north wing, holding the smoking lamp high. It stretched away into the malevolent darkness. The stench of damp and decay was overpowering. The territory of my nightmare, he thought. Along this corridor according to legend, the ghost of Charlotte Carew roamed at night, wailing her grief for her two murdered sons.

He braced himself. He intended to walk to the north wing, inspecting every room along the way. It would be a test of courage – and an act of penance, he told himself grimly, for the sin of cowardice.

He put one foot forward cautiously. He would have to watch each step he took; the floor was rotten with age and neglect. He tilted the lamp downward a little – then froze. He stood staring down in disbelief

306

for several seconds, then gently lowered himself until he was squatting on his haunches holding the lamp at knee-level.

There were footprints all over the dirt encrusted floor.

He examined them intently. There were no boot marks, but he could clearly see ribbed patterns. Whoever had been up here had been in their stockinged feet.

The footprints led out from the corridor and up into it. He straightened up and then, with the lamp tilted downward, began to follow the trail up the corridor. It came to an end outside the second door on the right. He paused before it, then turned the handle. The door yielded stiffly, rusted hinges groaning. The dust of generations lay thick on the panes of the window facing him, blocking all light.

It was wide and high like all the rooms in Carewscourt. A pile of rubbish lay in the corner to the left of the window. He halted in the centre of the room and looked about him. The room was bare. The rusted iron bars across the window mystified him. Then he saw the remains of an old rocking horse sticking up from the pile of rubbish. Of course, this was the old nursery. His father and uncles and aunt had played here when they were children. How long ago? he wondered. Eighty years? Seventy at least . . . He lowered the lamp. The dust was inches thick on the floor. Footprints everywhere. On the floor beside the crumbling skirting-board was a deep rectangular impression as though a heavy box had been placed there. He took a step towards it then lowered himself to his haunches. He saw the object immediately and picked it up. He rose slowly to his feet and stood looking down at what lay in the palm of his hand.

There was no need to go any further, no need to walk to the north wing inspecting every room, testing his courage. He cursed himself for a damn fool, and went back to his own room. He walked to the window and examined the clip of ammunition. Army ·303. He put the clip in his trouser pocket and lit a cigarette, then sat down on the side of the bed.

The sheer audacity of it stunned him.

Sergeant Hanafin was right. The arms stolen from the police barracks in Partry had been taken to this district. And Tim Skerritt was one of the party involved. Perhaps he was the leader. Certainly it had been his idea to use Carewscourt as an ammunition dump, knowing it would be the last place on earth the police would think of searching.

'But my unexpected arrival upset everything, didn't it, my friend?' Carew muttered, remembering Skerritt's agitation on his arrival. All the time he was with Father Devlin, Skerritt must have been running around all over the place contacting his friends, making arrangements

307

to have the arms and ammunition removed that night. He could imagine them gathered about the front steps in the early hours of the morning, removing their boots so as not to make any noise.

The proper thing to do of course was to go to the sergeant with the evidence and have Skerritt arrested. But would Skerritt talk? Would he tell the whereabouts of the arms and divulge the names of his friends? Treachery was the unforgivable sin to men like Skerritt. Skerritt would rather go to gaol than inform. He would regard imprisonment as some kind of martyrdom, willingly endured for love of country. Besides, he told himself, if Skerritt were to be arrested and put on trial, the resultant publicity would be harmful to himself and to Major Calder.

God, yes, Alec thought, Harrison would do his utmost to embarrass him, especially in the presence of the Under-Secretary. He could imagine him at the weekly conference sitting at the table with a smirk on his face.

'Do you not think it ironic, Captain, you and Major Calder spending so much time and energy tracking down the IRB, and all the while an active group of them were operating under your very nose in Carewstown, using your own house to store stolen arms?'

He shook his head. No, my friend, I'll never give you the opportunity to make fun of me. Whatever happened, he told himself, the news about the stolen arms being stored in Carewscourt must never leak out. He would have to get rid of Tim Skerritt immediately. Frighten him so he would leave the district. With Skerritt gone, the people involved with him might take fright and leave also. If that happened, the IRB circle would be smashed. Troy would have to start recruiting all over again.

As for the stolen arms and ammunition, he would simply tell the sergeant he had found the clip on the road. That would make the sergeant intensify his efforts; possibly he would call for reinforcements to help him with the search. And if they were not found, it did not matter all that much. He had an idea they had hidden them somewhere in the bog or possibly in a ditch. If they were left for any length of time in places like that, damp would rust the weapons and render the ammunition ineffective. He threw the cigarette into the fireplace, opened the door and walked out of the room. He knew what he had to do.

He strode down the steep gravel drive towards the gate-lodge. The morning air had a bite in it but he was oblivious of the cold. Light showed in the windows of the lodge. Skerritt, he thought, must be having his breakfast. He pounded on the door.

'Who's there?' a voice called from inside.

'Captain Carew. Open up!'

A bolt was drawn and the door opened. Skerritt stood in the doorway, blinking in the early morning light. He was unshaven and unkempt. Carew pushed past him to the room beyond. A mug full of tea and a plate of eggs and bacon were waiting on the table. I've interrupted his meal, Carew thought grimly, now I'm going to ruin his appetite.

'What's wrong, Captain?' Skerritt asked.

Carew took out the clip of ammunition from his trouser pocket and placed it in the centre of the table.

'One of you dropped that on the floor of the old nursery last night as you were sneaking out with the arms and ammunition.'

Skerritt looked at the clip, then raised his eyes to meet Carew's accusing stare. 'I don't know what yer talkin' about, Captain.'

'The arms and ammunition stolen from the police barracks in Partry,' Carew snapped, 'that's what I'm talking about! I want to know where they are now. I also want the names of the people involved.'

Skerritt stared back at him, poker-faced. He knew it was no use pretending.

'Ye'll get no information from me,' he answered in a low determined voice.

Carew nodded slowly: it was an admission of guilt. 'This is a political offence, Skerritt. They'll make an example of you. I wouldn't be surprised if you get ten years.'

Skerritt swallowed. 'I won't be the first or last to suffer for my country.'

Carew sighed. As I suspected, he thought. A waste of time trying to make him give any information. 'Skerritt,' he said, 'your people have served my family well and faithfully for almost a hundred years. For that reason – and for that reason only – I'm going to give you a chance . . .'

He leaned forward, hands resting on table. 'Pack your things and get out! Catch the noon train for Dublin. And when you get there, hide yourself – under an assumed name if you want to stay out of gaol.' He picked up the clip of ammunition and held it in front of Skerritt's face. 'At ten o'clock tonight, I'm going to Sergeant Hanafin with this. And from that moment on, you will be a wanted man!' He straightened up. 'And if ever you get caught and you tell them I gave you this chance, I'll deny it. Remember, they'll believe me more than they will believe you.'

Carew turned and walked out of the room and out of the house, slamming the door behind him. He was half-way up the drive when he

309

heard a shout. He turned. Skerritt was standing in the middle of the drive outside the lodge.

'Sons of whores!' he screamed, raising a threatening fist. 'Ye've rode roughshod over us for centuries! But ye won't for much longer! Yer finished – ye and the Hacketts and the Henshaws and all the bloody rest of ye. . . !'

Carew turned contemptuously on his heel and strode up the drive towards the house.

# Chapter Twelve

## I

Dusk was gathering as Gallagher reached the suburbs of the city. He strode south-east between rows of neat red-brick houses. Lights were beginning to appear in the windows. He pulled the collar of his shabby jacket up about his neck and throat. The raw autumn evening had a foretaste of winter in it. A speck of rain touched his cheek; immediately he quickened his steps. He was acutely aware of his worn jacket and broken boots. Another soaking like the last, he told himself, and I'll be laid up in bed again. It would be disastrous if he should fall sick; incapacity meant starvation.

He strode on, fighting fatigue. I must have covered nearly twenty miles since morning, he thought, looking for work. He tried not to think of the coming winter with no money for food or rent.

'Christ help us,' he groaned, 'Christ help us all.'

It was the second month of the lock-out. Some years before, in a room in a Dublin slum tenement, with a candle stuck in a bottle for light, a new Union had been founded; a Transport and General Workers' Union, representing the unskilled as well as the skilled. The Union grew rapidly. It was militant from the start, using the tactic of the sympathetic strike. For the first time the exploited unskilled workers and labourers had a voice. Trouble began to flare up in the cities and docks of Dublin and Cork.

The employers watched the growth of the Union with alarm. They formed a federation and came together to discuss what action they could take against it. They decided to bring in strike-breakers whenever a strike organised by the Union occurred. Violence erupted. The tactics of the employers became so crude and dangerous, the Lord Lieutenant was forced to intervene. Nevertheless the Administration supported the employers as did the police. Fierce clashes took place on the streets of Dublin between the constabulary and the strikers. One sunny Sunday morning, baton wielding police savagely attacked a huge crowd attending a proclaimed meeting and left hundreds injured and bleeding. 'Bloody Sunday' passed into legend.

Shortly after, four hundred Dublin employers pledged themselves not to employ any person belonging to the Transport and General Workers' Union. A document was handed to tens of thousands of Dublin workers demanding they sign an agreement forswearing the Union. Failure to sign meant instant dismissal. Thousands refused and were thrown out of work.

The great lock-out had begun.

A tram whined past him, heading for the city. Gallagher was tempted to run after it and jump on board. But he killed the urge. The two pennies in his pocket would be better spent on a loaf of bread. He pulled the peak of the cap down lower, shielding his eyes against the light slanting rain. He marched doggedly on, footsore, the muscles of his legs aching, senses numb from exhaustion. It was eight o'clock by the time he reached the city centre.

Sackville Street was strangely deserted for the time of evening; it was usually full of life. There were no lingering, laughing, chatting groups. To linger these days was to attract the attention of the police. They seemed to be everywhere; standing about or sauntering up and down in pairs, stern and imposing in their tall helmets and glistening waterproof capes. Sturdy hands, he knew, were resting on batons under the capes.

He could feel their eyes on him as he strode past. The shabby rough clothes and unkempt appearance marked him as an object of suspicion: he was one of *them*. He might have been wearing a uniform. Most of the shops were closed. The shops selling foodstuffs were not only closed but shuttered as well. To display food when a quarter of the city's population were starving was to invite plunder.

He turned a corner and walked down a passageway between a hotel and an office building. It was dark except for a light above a side-door leading into the hotel. The hotel kitchen had several small windows almost at pavement level. One was half-open. There were clattering sounds of delft being handled and a strong kitchen smell drifted out. An assortment of aromas assailed his nostrils. Saliva gathered in his mouth. He had not eaten since morning; breakfast had been a thick slice of unbuttered bread and a mug of tea. He increased his pace towards the street beyond.

Soon he was in his own area; the narrow ill-lit cobbled streets; the tall crumbling tenements. This was the battlefield. For weeks past, the police and the starving locked-out workers had clashed here, attacking and counter-attacking up and down the streets. Baton-wielding police had stormed the tenements, kicking in the doors, clubbing the people old and young alike, smashing the miserable sticks of furniture. Then the counter-attack; the ragged multitude of the slums fought with every weapon they could lay their hands on. He side-stepped holes in the footpath. Splinters of paving and cobbles had been ripped up with pick and crowbar and used as ammunition. No one had bothered to clean up the débris littering the road and path. It could be used again in another battle. The small dingy shops were all closed. For weeks they had provided the people of the district with food on credit in the hope that the lock-out would be short-lived. But the lock-out continued and now they were closed from lack of custom or else had gone out of business.

It was the silence and the almost deserted streets he could not get used to. Before the lock-out these streets teemed with life after nightfall: noisy gossiping groups on the steps and about the open halldoors; ragged barefoot children crowding the gutters. Now the children lay shivering with cold in the fireless rooms, whimpering from the gnawing pains of hunger. At lease I haven't that to face when I arrive home, he told himself. If my children were alive now . . . He winced, picturing himself standing empty-handed before them, their pinched hungry faces staring up into his . . .

He climbed the stairs slowly in the dark. As he came to the top landing he hesitated, fearing the look that would come over her face when he told her he had come home with no money. He took a deep breath and turned the handle. She was sitting hunched forward at the black, empty fireplace, a black shawl over her head and shoulders. As he shut the door she turned her head towards him. Her face was in shadow under the cowl of the shawl. He thought, Say it now . . . now when I can't see her face.

He stood with his back to the door, arms spread wide in a gesture of defeat. 'There's nothin'! Not a thing! I tried everywhere. All day. Out in the country beyant Finglas. I tried every farm-house for miles around.'

He did not intend to raise his voice, did not intend to make it sound so harsh. It echoed in the almost bare room. Most of the furniture was gone. What little they had, had been sold or pawned to buy food. All that remained was the table, the kitchen dresser, three chairs and a bed. He waited for her to say something. But she was silent, and turned her head away. He hung his jacket and cap on the back of the door, walked to the table and sat down.

He groaned wearily. 'I thought, since there was no work in the city, I'd find some in the country. At a farm mebbe, milkin' or diggin' a drain

313

or choppin' firewood – anythin'.' He gave a bitter laugh. 'What I didn't know was that every other man had the same idea. Christ! I've had more doors slammed in me face!' He turned towards her. 'D'ye know what,' he said, 'one bastard even threatened me with a pitchfork!'

She remained still and silent. Her silence was worse than any harsh words of reproach. He let his head collapse into his hands, pressing his thumbs against his eyelids, feeling weariness and despair creeping over him. Oh God, he groaned to himself, what's the use, what's the bloody use? The chair creaked as she rose slowly to her feet. He could hear her footsteps on the bare floorboards as she moved towards the kitchen dresser behind him. He remained in the same position, head resting in his cupped hands, eyes closed. A drawer was pulled open and he wondered: what she was rooting there for? There was no food.

Her arm brushed against his and he opened his eyes. She put down a plate in front of him. 'Eat,' she murmured and she sat down, her back to the window.

He looked down at the plate. There were three sausages and a slice of dry bread on it. The sausages looked as though they had been cooked the day before. The grease on them had congealed into thick blobs of grey, but it was food. Saliva gathered in his mouth. He did not bother with a knife and fork. He put a sausage in his mouth and bit it in half. It was stale and hard, but he did not care. He had not eaten since early morning. He was about to put the other half in his mouth when he noticed she was staring at him. He felt his face burning with shame and guilt and he lowered his hand from his mouth.

'Where's yours?' he asked.

She shook her head slowly. 'I had mine.' Her voice was flat and lifeless. The shawl no longer covered her head and in the lamplight her face looked gaunt and worn.

He ate the sausage self-consciously, staring at the plate. The sausage was hard and gristly. A thought struck him and he raised his head and looked at her sharply. 'Where did you get this food? You had no money this mornin'.'

She did not meet his suspicious stare. 'What does it matter where or how I got it?' she answered wearily. 'It's food. Eat it and be thankful.'

'What the hell kind of an answer is that?' he snapped.

She was silent, and a bright red spot appeared on her cheek. Shame? Guilt? A sickening, terrible thought grew in his mind. 'I asked you a question, woman!' There was anger and fear in his voice.

She stared steadily at him. 'Do you really want to know?'

He nodded dumbly, dreading her reply. Some of the wives of the locked-out workers had sold themselves for the price of food.

'I went out after you left this morning. I couldn't bear just to sit here all day, moping. I walked the streets. I thought, maybe there's someone who wants a woman to clean, to wash dishes, scrub floors. Anything, so long as it pays.' He could see her trying to maintain control. Her small hands were clenched so tightly the whites of the knuckles showed. 'I must have walked every street in the city, looking for work, but there was nothing, nothing. There were hundreds like me, men and women, walking the streets looking for work and not getting it. Everywhere you saw them. You could see the hunger and despair in their faces. I saw a woman with a babe in her arms and she begging. She just stood there on the footpath with one hand held out and she crying with the shame of it . . .' Tears trickled slowly down her face. She made no attempt to wipe them away. 'There was this small eating-house opposite Ship Street Barracks. I stood outside it, trying to gather courage to go in and ask for some work. I had been refused so many times. There were some soldiers standing outside the barrack gate and they were staring at me in a way I didn't like. I became nervous. I suppose that's why I walked into the eating-house without thinking.

'I was a dingy, cheap-looking place. It was only half-full. I walked through to the kitchen. There was a woman there in charge. I asked for some work; cooking or washing dishes . . . She shook her head and said she was sorry. I started to leave. I remember feeling weak, light-headed. I stumbled and she caught me. She led me to a chair and told me to sit with my head down. Then she filled a glass with water and made me sip it. She was very kind.'

He stared at her with narrow eyes, his face a rigid mask. The food at his elbow was now forgotten. He was no longer hungry.

'I sat there for a little while. I watched the woman putting some food in a paper bag. When I was leaving she gave it to me . . .' She gave a quick frightened look at him. 'When . . . when the customers go,' she went on in a faltering voice, 'they sometimes leave a little of the meal on the plate – '

'Christ!'

His cry of rage silenced her. She cowered in fright as he jumped up sending the chair toppling backwards. His face was twitching. 'So that's where you got it!' she shouted. 'The leavin's of the table! Fuckin' pig food! Swill!'

A nerve beat wildly in his head. He grabbed the plate of food from the table and flung it in fury against the wall. It shattered into fragments. She backed away as he took a step towards her, hand raised threateningly. 'How the hell could you do it!' he shouted, eyes wild.

315

'How could you lower yerself to . . . to . . .' His face was twisted with rage and there was foam on his lower lip. 'Have you no pride?' he bellowed.

'No!' she screamed. 'No! I've no pride! I'm hungry!'

The fury of her outburst checked him. He was shocked and confused by the sudden transformation. She was crouching like a cornered animal, prepared to scratch and claw if touched. They faced each other, breathing heavily, like two battle-weary combatants, watching and waiting to see who would make the next move. He could feel the anger draining from him. Suddenly he gave a deep sigh and let his raised arm flop to his side. It was a sign of surrender and defeat.

'It's a pity you have so much pride,' she sneered. 'Maybe if you had a little less you could have brought home some money for food.'

He looked away from her contemptuous glare. 'I did me best,' he mumbled.

'Your best wasn't good enough!' she snapped. 'All you have to do is to put your name on a piece of paper and you won't have any trouble getting work.'

He glared at her in anger and amazement. 'Ye want me to scab? What kind of a man do you think I am?'

'Other men have done it!'

'Well, I'm not one of them!'

'Pride again.'

'Yes! Pride!'

Her lips curled. 'Do you know what pride is? The jump of a cock on his own dunghill. Well, jump and shout all you want to, Gallagher. It's the only thing you can do!'

He struck her on the side of the face with his open hand. She staggered sideways with a yelp of pain. He had never struck her before. He towered over her, stunned, unable to believe he had done such a thing. His mouth worked soundlessly. He wanted to say he was sorry, but somehow the words would not come. He could feel emotion swelling up inside him, choking him. Suddenly he turned about and strode to the door, grabbing his cap and jacket.

She listened with fear in her heart as his booted feet thundered down the stairs.

Durkin put down the cup on the saucer and dabbed at his mouth with the napkin.

'More coffee, Mr Durkin?' ffrench-O'Carroll smiled at him from across the table.

Durkin shook his head and smiled back. 'Thank you, no.'

Doherty, the heavy-set man sitting beside Durkin, burped gently and tapped his chest with stubby fingers. 'A wonderful meal, Maurice,' he said, addressing ffrench-O'Carroll, 'but I know I'll suffer for it in the middle of the night. Smoked salmon and myself . . .' He burped again and smiled apologetically.

ffrench-O'Carroll rose slowly to his feet. 'Let's adjourn to the study, shall we.' He led the way.

The study was warm and cosy. The leaping log-fire in the huge fireplace filled the room with heat. 'Please, gentlemen . . . be seated,' ffrench-O'Carroll said and walked towards the sideboard. As both men sat down, he half-turned to them, decanter in hand. 'Brandy? Mr Durkin . . . Mr Doherty?'

Durkin nodded and Doherty said: 'I shouldn't really, but . . .' He was one of those corpulent men who perspire freely after every meal. The wide fleshy face with its thick blunt features was oily with sweat. His breathing was laboured; tiny red veins dappled his cheeks. A man who never stinted himself of the good things in life, Durkin thought, and was now paying for his excesses.

ffrench-O'Carroll approached them with a brandy glass in each hand. Durkin accepted one with a word of thanks. He took a sip, savouring the brandy on his tongue before swallowing it. He smacked his lips. He was no connoisseur, but he knew enough about brandy to know that this was first-rate stuff.

ffrench-O'Carroll's note requesting that he dine with him had arrived by post three days ago. He had been astounded, for he had met O'Carroll only a few times before, mostly at Castle functions. He had always found him stand-offish and aloof. Not a man, Durkin told himself, to lavish hospitality on a mere acquaintance. He still did not know why O'Carroll had invited him. During dinner he had been evasive, speaking only of trivial things, exchanging pleasantries . . .

Thick wine-red curtains covered the windows; they could hear the fierce rain beating against the window-panes.

'By jingo!' Doherty exclaimed, 'winter's coming in with a vengeance, and no mistake.'

Durkin glanced at him. 'Tricky Dicky' Doherty. He was an employer of sweated labour and one of the biggest slum landlords in Dublin. Durkin disliked him intensely. Doherty, in his opinion, was a fat, coarse pig.

'I'm reading your book, *The Carews of Carewscourt*, Mr Durkin,' ffrench-O'Carroll said. 'Excellent. I find the historical background really fascinating.' He raised his glass in tribute. 'I congratulate you.'

Durkin simpered. 'Thank you.'

'Is it selling well?'

'Er, moderately. It received some good reviews in the English papers.'

'And here at home?'

Durkin grinned ruefully. 'Not so good. The nationalist newspapers were particularly hostile.'

ffrench-O'Carroll gave a languid wave of the hand. 'Oh, ignore *them*. There's no true literary criticism in Ireland. If the critic doesn't like your politics or your religion, he'll slate your work even if it is a masterpiece. Provincialism at its very worst.'

'Such attitudes destroy one's desire to write another book,' Durkin said, aggrieved.

ffrench-O'Carroll nodded sympathetically. 'Nevertheless you should not allow yourself to become disheartened, Mr Durkin,' he said.

Doherty shifted impatiently about on the chair. 'Don't you think it's about time we got down to business?' he grumbled, his eyes on ffrench-O'Carroll.

Annoyance showed on O'Carroll's face. 'Very well,' he answered curtly.

Durkin waited patiently, holding the brandy glass between his hands. His chair faced the fire and he was beginning to feel hot and uncomfortable.

He had arrived dressed for the occasion, resplendent in gleaming white dickey front and dinner jacket, expecting O'Carroll and guests – if there were any – to be dressed the same. When one was invited to dine with one of the most powerful and wealthiest men in Ireland, one could not dress otherwise.

But O'Carroll and Doherty had been dressed informally in plain dark suits. He had stood before them in the hallway, mouth open in dismay, feeling foppish and foolish. Doherty had sniggered openly at his appearance. O'Carroll had been impassive, but there had been a glint of amusement in his eyes.

'This unfortunate situation which is disrupting everyday life in Dublin . . .' ffrench-O'Carroll began, running the tip of his tongue over his thin lips. He turned towards Durkin. 'What's your view, Mr Durkin? To be more precise, do you approve of the action the employers took, locking out thousands of workers because they refused to sign a document forswearing the Transport and General Workers' Union?'

Durkin stared at him, wondering what all this was leading up to. He hesitated. O'Carroll, he knew, was vice-chairman of the Employers' Federation and had been one of the leading instigators in forcing the workers to sign. If he were to say he disapproved, O'Carroll would take it as an adverse criticism of himself and his methods. He gave a non-committal shrug. 'I neither approve nor disapprove. I'm . . . neutral.'

O'Carroll took another sip of wine, and nodded approvingly. Durkin was not quite sure if the nod meant he was satisfied with the taste or the answer.

'I'm glad to hear it, Mr Durkin. You must be the only journalist in Dublin who is. Every other member of your profession seems to have embarked on a crusade on behalf of the locked-out workers. We, the employers, have been vilified in print. We have been described as arrogant swine, rapacious rogues, barbarians . . .' He drained his glass in one gulp and placed it on a low coffee table beside him, a sour expression on his face. There was a folded newspaper on the table. He picked it up. 'Allow me to read for you an excerpt from an article in this morning's paper, Mr Durkin. It's described as "An open letter to the Masters of Dublin," and begins . . .' He brought the paper up close to his face. 'I address this warning to you, the aristocracy of industry in this city, because, like all aristocracies, you tend to grow blind in long authority . . .' He paused, eyes moving down the page, then said: 'Ah yes, here we are . . . Listen to this . . . "You may succeed in your policy and ensure your own damnation by your victory. The men whose manhood you have broken will loathe you, and will always be brooding and scheming to strike a fresh blow. The children will be taught to curse you. The infant being moulded in the womb will have breathed into its starved body the vitality of hate . . ." ' He folded the paper and put it back on the table. 'And that,' he said bitterly, his face dark with anger, 'from the pen of one of the most distinguished writers in the land.'

'That sort of thing,' Doherty growled, 'incites the ragtag and bobtail to create further trouble. It's bad enough when that scurrilous Union

319

rag publishes stuff like that, but when a highly respectable newspaper like the *Irish Times* . . .'

'Precisely.' ffrench-O'Carroll nodded his head in agreement. 'I think the newspapers should act in a responsible way and not publish such emotional, high-flown drivel.' He shot a glance at Durkin. 'What do you think, Mr Durkin?'

Again Durkin gave a non-committal shrug. 'The newspaper letter columns are open to all. There's nothing to stop the Employers' Federation from replying to denunciatory comments such as that.'

'And engage in a slanging match with every Tom, Dick and Harry who thinks he was born with ink in his veins?' ffrench-O'Carroll shook his head. 'No thank you.'

'You could issue a statement,' Durkin suggested.

O'Carroll nodded slowly. 'True, but with a hostile press, we would run the risk of being misinterpreted. The fact is, Mr Durkin, we have decided to publish a book, a book which will explain our side of the situation. We feel it's necessary to inform the public of the damage being done to the economy of the country by ruthless socialist agitators. We also feel it's our duty to warn the people of what godless socialism can do to our Christian way of life.' He paused, his eyes on Durkin's face. 'That is why I invited you here. We would like *you* to write the book. We hope you will accept.'

Durkin was taken completely by surprise. He never suspected this. He tossed off the brandy in one gulp, then stared at the fire, the empty glass between his hands, pondering.

ffrench-O'Carroll said: 'We will pay you five hundred pounds. A most generous offer, you will agree.'

Durkin tried to think, but the brandy and the wine he had consumed during dinner had fuddled his brain. He found himself mumbling, 'Very kind of you . . . I'm honoured. If you think I'm capable of such an undertaking . . .'

'Then you accept?'

Durkin raised a flushed bewildered face. 'Oh . . . er . . . yes. Yes, of course.' He blinked a few times, like a man awakening from sleep. Then he thought, Why the hell didn't he ask me earlier? All through dinner I could have thought the whole thing over. He was conscious of a growing feeling of resentment. He had been taken unawares and had committed himself rashly without a thought for the consequences. He did not want to take sides in this damned lock-out. Not once had he mentioned it in the *Eye-Witness*. Politics and intrigue were his interests, not labour disputes. But once this book bearing his name was

320

published, he would be known far and wide as the official propagandist of the Employers' Federation.

Doherty gave a deep contented sigh. 'Well, that's that,' he said, and stretching himself out in the armchair, closed his eyes, his hands folded over his ample stomach.

ffrench-O'Carroll smiled. 'I'm so glad you've consented. And do forgive me for not coming to the point before now. You see, I had to sound you out first. I thought perhaps your sympathies might lie in the other camp. I'm afraid I will have to give you a time limit, Mr Durkin. It's important that the book be published as quickly as possible, to combat this vicious propaganda campaign being waged against us. But then of course,' he added with a smile, 'you newspaper chaps are accustomed to meeting deadlines.'


III


The rain had dwindled to a light drizzle. Gallagher marched on; marching the fury out of him; marching to the point of exhaustion. Eventually he was forced to halt. He leaned against a street-lamp and held on to it, chest heaving. He was soaked to the skin.

The anger he felt was directed against himself. He could still see her cowering against the window, the red mark where he had struck her vivid against the pallor of her cheeks. Is that what I've become, he asked himself bitterly, a wife-beater? Wife-beating was a way of life in the slums. Perhaps it was the grinding poverty and the look of hunger and want on the faces of the children that did something to a man; it gnawed away at his pride until there was nothing left but a savage snarling brute.

He sighed – from weariness, from hunger, from despair. He looked about him. He was not quite sure where he was; somewhere in the southern suburbs, he suspected. He had marched on and on in the heavy rain, unheedful of the direction he was taking. He was standing on a wide tree-lined avenue, flanked on both sides by two-storey mid-Victorian red-brick houses with huge front gardens.

The homes of the well-to-do, he thought. Someone was playing slowly on a piano. There was an air of smug respectability about this avenue. No hunger or despair lurked behind these doors; no

321

whimpering cries of starving children disturbed the night. He sighed again and thought, I'll rest here for a few more minutes, then I'll go . . . I'll go back humble and contrite and beg for her forgiveness.

He leaned against the street-lamp, one arm wrapped around it. The avenue was deserted . . . almost. He could hear the sound of approaching footsteps. Ahead, a figure emerged from the haze of fine rain, the thickset figure of a man wearing a fawn overcoat, with a homburg set squarely on his head. He walked swiftly, his head down against the slanting rain. Gallagher watched him coming towards him. Then the thought suddenly came to him. If she could swallow her pride, he told himself, so can I. He stepped into the middle of the footpath. Durkin almost bumped into him. He came to an abrupt halt and looked up, startled.

Gallagher said, 'I'm tired and hungry, friend. Any money you can spare will be welcome.'

Durkin's plump face retained its look of startled surprise for a few seconds. His mouth hung open. Gallagher caught the whiff of brandy and the spicy aroma of rich food. The face was vaguely familiar.

The look of surprise on Durkin's face swiftly changed to one of anger. 'I've nothing to spare,' he snapped, 'nothing!' and swerved to pass by. Gallagher instinctively grabbed him by the shoulder.

Durkin twisted round, face flaming. 'Take yer paw off me, yeh scruffy bastard!' he snarled.

Gallagher released his grip and Durkin spun on his heel and strode off, leaving Gallagher rooted to the spot, stunned. He stared at the retreating back open-mouthed. It was not the violent reaction or the harsh words that shocked and amazed him, but the accent – the flat nasal accent of the Dublin slums. It was inconsistent with the expensive clothes and the elegant surroundings.

Suddenly fury surged up, almost choking him. Tears of rage and humiliation sprang to his eyes. Fists clenched, he strode forward.

Durkin heard the footsteps behind him and stopped and turned. Gallagher grabbed him by the lapels of the overcoat and rammed him against the railings in front of a house. He shoved his face up close and Durkin recoiled from the sour smell of his breath.

'Right, you fat pig!' Gallagher rasped. 'I asked you civil enough, now I'm goin' to take all of it. Hand it over!'

Durkin began to struggle, trying to free himself. Gallagher took a firmer grip on the coat and lifted him a little, forcing him back until the spiked tops of the railings dug into his shoulder blades. Durkin bellowed with fear and pain and jerked his head back. His hat fell from his head into the garden. He roared again and slammed a meaty fist into the side of Gallagher's face. Gallagher let go of him and cuffed him several times across the mouth with the back of his hand, splitting open a plump lower lip and breaking a tooth. Durkin could feel the salt taste of blood in his mouth.

Suddenly his resistance collapsed. He sagged against the railings and throwing back his head, he started to howl like a dog. His high-pitched cries echoed and re-echoed along the length of the avenue.

Gallagher frantically tore open the overcoat with both hands; a button flicked his cheek. He plunged a hand inside Durkin's dinner jacket. His fingers closed on a wallet – a wallet thick with banknotes. He felt a rush of elation; there was enough here for Una and himself to get out of the country – to America even. He pulled the wallet out. Durkin gave a roar of outrage and tried to grab it. Gallagher slapped his hand away and took to his heels. He sprinted down the wet pavement holding the wallet tightly in his hand. Behind him he could hear the man he had just robbed screaming for help. He had covered about thirty yards when he saw the figure charging towards him. He saw the spiked helmet and lamp-light glistening on a waterproof cape and swerved violently to the left, almost leaping on to the road. The policeman came to a skidding halt and threw his baton. It bounced off Gallagher's shoulder as he raced past.

Further down, the second policeman was waiting for him, standing wide-legged in the middle of the road with baton at the ready.

Gallagher shouted a curse and tried to stop his mad headlong rush. He dug the heel of his boot into the wet surface of the road and slipped. Both legs shot up from under him and he came down on his side, sliding for several feet and ending in a puddle. He was winded and stunned. He had lost his cap but he was still clutching the wallet.

The sound of heavy boots pounding against the road pierced his dazed senses. He scrambled hastily to his feet. Both policemen were running towards him, one coming from the front and one from behind. He rammed the wallet into the inside pocket of his jacket and stood, fists rolled into tight balls. He stood sideways, twisting his head from left to right, keeping his eyes on both of them.

The policemen slowed down now that he was on his feet and prepared to fight; they came towards him slowly and cautiously: the cornered animal was also the most dangerous. One of them unbuttoned his cape with one hand and let it fall to the ground to give his baton-arm more freedom.

Gallagher looked wildly about, trying to fight down a rising panic. He

323

was trapped and there was no way out. This was not the slums; there were no gaping hallways or dark laneways to escape into. The solid houses of the avenue with their dark curtained windows and locked doors were like hostile onlookers, refusing sanctuary.

The policemen crept towards him weaving their batons in front of them, sure of their victim. He could feel the sweat of fear breaking out on his skin. A stage of savagery had been reached in this conflict between locked-out worker and police. They could bludgeon him to death and no one in this neighbourhood would lift a finger to help. He was an intruder – a barbarian from the slums who had assaulted and robbed; his death would be a warning to others. He spun about in desperation like a rat trapped in a cage.

Then he saw it; it lay beyond the dripping gardens in the half-light – a short stretch of blank wall between two houses. Panic-stricken, he had missed it before. It was about ten feet high. Beyond lay back gardens and freedom. He spurted towards it.

One of the policeman gave a startled shout as he saw where Gallagher was making for. Gallagher could hear the rapid beat of their boots as they came after him. There were high railings and a closed gate in front of him. He banged down the latch and pushed with his shoulder and the gate flew open. He raced up twenty feet of narrow path then leaped high at the end of it, bringing both hands forcefully down on the top of the wall.

He screamed then – screamed in agony as the pain shot through him. In the dim light he had not seen the double row of sharp jagged glass embedded in the top of the wall as a safeguard against intruders. He hung, the palms of both hands impaled on two bayonet-like pieces of glass, toe-caps scraping against the wall, breath coming in sobs, blood streaming down wrists and under the sleeve of his jacket. Then a pair of strong hands grabbed his hips and pulled.

He screamed again as his body went backwards, as the glass ripped open the palms of his hands. The policeman staggered back under his weight and toppled off the footpath. Suddenly his feet slipped on the wet grass. He fell clumsily on his back, Gallagher on top of him. Gallagher could feel his breath exploding against the back of his neck.

Gallagher rolled off him and staggered to his feet. He stumbled down towards the gate, kicking aside the policeman's hand as he tried to grab his ankle. The other policeman was waiting for him with baton raised. Gallagher shuffled to a halt, his torn and bleeding hands hanging down by his sides, half-dazed by shock and pain. He stood helpless and defenceless as the policeman walked towards him, bulky under the waterproof cape, swinging the baton in his hand.

He halted two feet in front of Gallagher and swung the baton back, aiming for the side of Gallagher's head. As the arm swept down, Gallagher suddenly blocked it with his left arm and kicked with all his might.

There was a strangled curse and the policeman went reeling back, dropping his baton and going down on one knee, hands gripping his injured leg. Gallagher was about to take a step towards him when the baton struck him behind the ear. There was a vivid flash, then darkness.

The policeman stood over him, breathing hard, baton in hand. Then he glanced at his companion. 'Are ye all right, Matt?'

Still resting his weight on one knee, the other policeman nodded, fingers gingerly pressing his shin. 'Nothin' broken as far as I can tell,' he answered, biting his lip. He stretched out a hand. 'Help me up.' When he had been assisted to his feet, he began to move slowly about in tiny circles, testing his injured leg and swearing softly under his breath.

'He stole my wallet,' a voice said behind them.

They turned their heads. Durkin was standing in the open gateway, dabbing at his bleeding mouth with a handkerchief. His thin hair lay in disordered strands across his forehead.

The policeman standing over Gallagher bent down and turned him over on to his back. Gallagher was unconscious. His mouth hung open and he was breathing harshly through his nose. They were inside the light from the street-lamp and the policeman caught sight of Gallagher's upturned palms.

'Jesus,' he breathed. He ran his hands down both sides of Gallagher's jacket. Feeling the bulge, he reached inside and pulled the wallet from the inside pocket. He held it up. 'This it?'

Durkin nodded.

The policeman unbuttoned the flap of his breast pocket and placed it carefully inside. 'Ye can open it down in the station to see if it's all there. How much is in it?'

'Nearly fifty pounds,' Durkin answered thickly. His cut lip was stinging like mad and every time he spoke the jagged remains of the broken tooth cut his tongue.

The policeman shook his head. 'Foolish to be carryin' that amount around these times.'

Durkin began to shiver a little. 'You see,' he began in a quavering voice, 'it happened like this . . .'

'Yes, sir,' the policeman interrupted gently, 'ye can tell us all about it later.' He could see that the man was suffering from shock. Best give him something to do, he thought. 'If ye wouldn't mind, sir . . . I dropped me cape a little way down the road. I would be obliged if ye would fetch it. As ye can see,' nodding down towards Gallagher, 'we've got our hands full here.'

Durkin ambled off without a word.

The policeman looked down at Gallagher. 'Come on,' he said to his companion, 'let's get this fella down to the station and let the doctor have a look at him . . .'

They half-carried, half-dragged Gallagher between them down the avenue, holding him under the arm-pits. His head hung limply down. When they came under the light of a street-lamp, the policeman with the injured leg said: 'Wait a minute.'

They halted. The policeman bent down and examined the back of Gallagher's head. The hair was matted and soaked with blood. The policeman looked behind. There was a trail of blood leading away up the footpath. 'Holy Christ,' he breathed, 'the hoor's bleedin' like a stuck pig!'

'Serves him right,' his companion said. 'Come on. It's twelve calendar months for this boyo at the very least. Assault and battery. Robbery. Resistin' arrest . . .' He winced as pain again attacked his injured leg. 'As far as I'm concerned,' he gasped, 'they can lock him up and throw away the bloody key!'

# Chapter Thirteen

## I

*Furlong (Dublin) – 23rd November, 1913, at the South Dublin Union. Joseph, late of 26 Emorville Ave, SCR Deeply regretted by his loving son, James, daughter-in-law, Alice . . .*

Myles Burke heaved a sigh and let the newspaper drop to the floor. He sat with his hands on his knees staring into the fire. He was touched by a feeling of guilt. I should have kept in touch with Joe, he told himself. I should have kept in touch, at least made inquiries about him . . .

He could hear the sound of voices coming from the room underneath. He rose slowly from the chair and reached for his jacket. It was Thursday and the Hibernian Literary and Debating Society were having their weekly meeting. And an important one, according to Mr Dineen; a most distinguished visitor was expected. He lit the oil-lamp and walked slowly down the stairs to the landing below.

The door of the room was wide open and light poured out on to the landing. Holding the oil-lamp, Myles peeked in. There were about twenty people there already, seated before the low platform. Myles noticed a clerical collar here and there. Usually about twenty-five people attended these meetings – thirty at the very most. But tonight was going to be an exception; he could hear more people coming up the stairs. He stood waiting, holding the lamp high to give more light.

A party of eight people came up towards him; there seemed to be more women than men. Perhaps, he thought, tonight's meeting is about the suffragette movement. They passed before him into the room. He wrinkled up his nose at the smell of perfume. Then he descended the stairs, taking his time.

Mr Rochford was standing at the half-open halldoor, looking up and down the quays. Mr Dineen and Mr Fogarty were seated at a small table in the hall. On the table between them stood a bottle with a lighted candle stuck in it. Two people, a man and a woman, were standing before them. Mr Fogarty was inspecting their membership cards and Mr Dineen was writing their names in a book.

'I'm really looking forward to hearing Mr Sanquest speak,' the man said. 'How on earth did you manage to get an MP?'

Mr Dineen laughed gently. 'It wasn't easy, I can assure you, Mr Powers.'

'I saw Mr Sanquest once,' the woman said in a breathless voice. 'He was addressing a meeting. He was so forceful, so handsome, so . . . virile.'

Mr Dineen smiled politely.

Mr Fogarty turned his head to see Myles standing a few feet away with the lighted oil-lamp in his hand. 'Burke,' he said sharply, 'provide some light to the foot of the stairs for Mr and Mrs Powers.'

Myles meekly obeyed. He led the way up the hall holding the lamp high, the couple following behind. Then he stood aside and raised the lamp higher as they mounted the stairs.

He did not like Fogarty. Fogarty was bossy and rude. Once, in a fit of temper, Fogarty had called him a doddery old fool. No, he did not like Fogarty; he did not like his overbearing manner; he did not like his pimply skin or his supercilious parrot nose. He shuffled back to the table on slippered feet.

Fogarty looked up as Myles gave a polite cough. 'Well?'

'Miss Price told me you wanted to have a word with me.'

'Ah yes,' Fogarty said, turning sideways on the chair towards him. 'We are expecting a very important person tonight. Mr Dennis Sanquest, a Member of Parliament. Now, Burke . . .' Fogarty raised a finger as though he were making an important point in one of his lectures, 'after Mr Sanquest arrives, this halldoor will be closed. I want it to remain closed. Under no circumstances open it for any latecomers. I don't want anyone walking in while Mr Sanquest is speaking. Now, is that understood?'

'Perfectly, Mr Fogarty.'

'Good. Now wait there. We'll need the light from that lamp when Mr Sanquest arrives.' Then Fogarty turned to Mr Dineen and began to converse with him in a low voice.

Myles moved up the hall a little, then halted and stood with his back to the wall. His arm was tired from holding the lamp. He waited as he had been told, not daring to move or complain. Standing in the cold with the draught from the half-open halldoor sweeping up against him, he saw himself through their eyes: a fawning, servile lickspittle.

He knew Mr Corcoran had given him the job of caretaker only as a

328

favour to Father Poole. He also knew Mr Corcoran would be glad to be rid of him as he was too old. The knowledge that Corcoran had it in his mind to dismiss him given the slightest pretext, filled him with terror. He had forced himself to submit to every indignity uncomplainingly, maintaining a passive silence when under verbal attack from even the most junior of Corcoran's clerks. He had deliberately murdered his pride in order to survive.

'It's quite a feather in our cap,' Fogarty said, 'having Mr Sanquest addressing our Society. It puts us on the map, so to speak.' Fogarty was vice-chairman of the Hibernian Literary and Debating Society.

'Don't I know it,' Mr Dineen said. 'It's a great honour, a great honour indeed.'

Dineen was chairman. He was tall and loose-limbed and had a narrow sensitive face. He was a poet and tried to look like one: he wore his hair long and sported a huge bow tie. He was also a literary critic and two of his plays had been produced at the Abbey Theatre. He called to the man at the door. 'Any sign of him, Dick?'

Mr Rochford, the treasurer, poked his head in, shook it and withdrew it. He maintained his vigil at the halldoor, slapping his arms to keep warm. He had on only his jacket and his college scarf was wound about his neck. He was twenty-three years of age and a devotee of Dineen. He even wore his hair long like him.

'I will tell you this,' Fogarty said, leaning forward, his acne showing starkly in the candle-light, 'our friend has moved remarkably fast through the ranks of the Irish Parliamentary Party. Only a few years ago he was a nobody on the backbenches. Now look at him.'

Dineen chuckled. 'Johnny Redmond will have to be careful if he wants to remain leader of the Party with our friend around.'

Rochford opened the door wider to allow more people to pass through. There were five in all. One by one they handed their membership cards to Fogarty while Dineen wrote their names in the book. Myles moved over to the foot of the stairs and stood waiting with the lamp. Four of them came towards him. The fifth remained standing looking down at Fogarty and Dineen. Fogarty stretched out his hand. 'Membership card, please.'

The man produced a small pasteboard card. 'Press,' he said. He was of medium height, thickset, wearing a fawn overcoat and with a homburg set squarely on his head.

'Oh, really?' Mr Dineen showed sudden interest. '*Times*? *Freeman's Journal*?'

The man grinned: gold teeth gleamed.

329

'Neither. The *Eye-Witness*.'

'Oh . . .'

There was a brief awkward silence. Then Mr Dineen said: 'Third floor, Mr . . . er. . . ?'

'Durkin's the name,' the man answered breezily and walked away. As he started to climb the stairs he glanced at Myles standing at the banister rail with the lamp.

Myles walked back to his place at the wall. He had encountered that man before, but when or where he could not remember. All he knew was that it had been something unpleasant.

Rochford pushed open the door wide and ran into the hall. 'There's a taxi approaching. I think it's him!' and ran out again leaving the hall-door wide open. The candle-flame wavered wildly in the breeze and went out. Fogarty and Dineen stumbled to their feet, Fogarty swearing. 'Matches, matches!' he cried.

'I haven't any!' Dineen responded despairingly. They made their way to the door and ran down the steps.

Myles stood in the middle of the hallway, waiting. He could see the beam of headlights across the entrance and could hear the sound of a running motor. Then a group of men appeared, climbing the steps. Fogarty preceded them. He came rushing up to Myles. 'Lead the way with that lamp,' he hissed. Myles climbed the stairs slowly, his aching arm holding the lamp high above his head. He could hear them coming up behind. Dineen said something and a deep voice answered: 'No, no . . . the honour is all mine, I assure you . . .'

When Myles reached the second floor landing he became aware of a commotion above. He raised the lamp as high as he could and looked up. Faces were peering over the banister rail. Someone shouted: 'He's arrived! He's coming up the stairs!'

Myles sighed wearily. When they reached the third floor landing they were immediately surrounded by a cheering, clapping crowd.

Myles tried to force his way through towards the stairs leading to his own rooms, but he was trapped. Above the noise he could hear Dineen's high-pitched voice. 'Please, ladies and gentlemen! Allow Mr Sanquest to enter. If you would all go inside and take your seats, *please!*'

Myles felt himself being pushed into the room. He tried to turn about and struggle back, but it was like fighting against a strong current. He was swept along by the excited crowd which an exasperated Mr Dineen with waving arms drove before him as if he were herding unruly sheep into a pen. The room was long and narrow and lit by two gas-jets. Rows of wooden chairs, six to a row, stretched from one wall to half-way

330

across the floor, leaving a narrow passage from the door to the window at the rear.

Myles selected a chair. The rows in front of him were quickly filled. He found himself sitting alone at the very back, the lighted oil-lamp in his hand.

Then a sudden hush fell as Dineen rose to his feet and stood facing them on the low platform. Seated at a table behind him were Fogarty, Rochford and Sanquest.

'Ladies and gentlemen,' Dineen began and cleared his throat. 'Tonight, the Hibernian Literary and Debating Society is graced with the presence of one of the most distinguished members of the Irish Parliamentary Party . . .'

Myles felt like an intruder sitting there. Perhaps, he thought, I could walk to the door quietly without being noticed . . . He half-rose and the chair scraped noisily against the bare floorboards. Several people in front turned their heads and glared at him. 'Shhh!' whispered one and raised a finger to his lips. Myles sat down abruptly.

'. . . a man whose maiden speech in the House of Parliament a few years ago made such an impression on us all. A man who, before a crowded House, castigated no less a personage than Bonar Law for his treasonable activities with the Ulster Unionists . . .'

Sanquest sat with a slight smile on his face, his eyes wandering over the faces before him. They came to rest on a woman in the front row. She was a handsome lady of about thirty-six with a wide sensual mouth. Nice plump figure, he thought, staring intently. Their eyes met. She lowered her head when she saw him staring at her, a slow flush spreading over her face. Sanquest felt the old excitement beginning to stir. The pursuit was on. He would insist on Dineen introducing him when the lecture was over. He was near enough to see the wedding ring on her finger. He shifted his gaze to the man sitting beside her.

Fat and grey with a drooping walrus moustache. A good twenty to twenty-five years older, Sanquest thought. All I need is just a few minutes alone with her when all this is over. He shifted about on the chair. The married ones were always the most reluctant; always feigning outrage. That made it all the more exciting.

'. . . In the crucial years ahead,' Dineen went on, 'it's a comforting thought to know that the destiny of this country rests in the capable hands of men of the calibre of Mr Sanquest . . .'

There were several cries of 'hear! hear!' followed by a burst of clapping. An elderly gentleman two rows in front of Myles staggered to his feet and cried in a choking voice: 'You're a credit to you country, sir. A credit, I say . . .' Someone else shouted: 'Stout fellow!'

Dineen held up his hand for silence, 'And now,' he cried in his high-pitched voice, 'without further ado,' turning sideways and stretching out his hand towards the man sitting at the table 'I give you the Honorable Dennis Sanquest, MP!'

The room exploded into a furious burst of clapping as the tall burly figure stood up and moved round the table to the front of the platform. Dineen sat down at the table beside his colleagues. The applause continued for a full minute until Sanquest smilingly raised his hand in good-humoured protest. As the clapping died away he nodded his head in appreciation. He cleared his throat. 'Mister chairman, ladies and gentlemen . . .' then, catching sight of one or two clerical collars, bowed in deference. 'Reverend Fathers . . .'

He paused then and lowered his head, pondering. It was a theatrical gesture. A moment passed: there was dead silence. Then he raised his head, his eyes roaming over the upturned faces.

'My friends,' he began in a deep melodious voice, with the slightest trace of a Cork accent, 'Ireland is fast approaching the most significant period in her troubled history. She is no longer content to remain the Cinderella of the United Kingdom; she no longer intends to beg with outstretched his arms for the rights that justly belong to her. She asks – nay, she demands – that the Parliament taken from her more than a century ago be returned!' There was another outburst of clapping and Sanquest raised his hand for silence. 'Self-government is on the way!' he announced. 'The Home Rule Bill will become law in September of next year when it receives the Royal assent. . . .'

Again another outburst of clapping; again the raised hand for silence. 'Of course there are those who violently oppose the Bill,' he said, smiling. 'The Conservatives and their friends, the Ulster Unionists. But . . .' he paused dramatically, 'but, my friends, no matter how strongly they object, once the Bill becomes law, they will have to abide by it!

'England has given her word that the Irish nation will have Home Rule by 1914, and England's word is good enough for me!'

Where and what would I be now, Myles asked himself, if the Fenian rebellion had succeeded all those years ago? Perhaps standing on a platform like this windbag, addressing a cultured audience, an honoured citizen of the Republic.

Then he shook his head in exasperation, annoyed with himself. What the hell is the matter with me? What's the use of dreaming like this? I know what I am – a nobody. I'm old and almost helpless and living in constant fear of being thrown out on the street, ending my days in the Workhouse like Joe Furlong. . . .

'Where are they now,' Sanquest cried, flinging an arm out dramatically, 'those who preached the gospel of violence? Where are they now – those who said that Ireland could not gain control of her destiny through constitutional means? Where are they now – the hillsiders, the Fenians, the secret societies. . . ?

'How silent now are the voices of the fanatics,' Sanquest went on. 'No more appeals to the youth of Ireland to rally round the banner; no more goading them to go forth with pitchfork and pike into the mouths of cannon and rifle . . .'

Sanquest savoured his words as though they were choice morsels of food. He experienced a thrill seeing the effect they were having on the audience. '. . . Yes, my friends, the voices of the fanatics are silent now. Reality has caught up with them. One stroke of the pen and Ireland will be a nation once again. And without one shot having to be fired – without one life lost. Those madmen who wanted to match the raw untrained youth of this country against the experienced soldiers of the greatest Empire on earth, are doomed. Yes, my friends, they are finished . . .'

Myles squirmed restlessly about on the chair. Why do I submit to all the insults and indignities? Why? So I can keep this aging, decaying body alive for a little while longer? What if they throw me out – I've enough money saved to keep me alive for six months. And after that. . . ? He shrugged. If I die from starvation and exposure in the corner of some filthy alley, what of it? At least I'll die a free man.

Then he thought of Joe Furlong ending his days in the Workhouse and tears welled up in his eyes. He began to weep quietly for all his dead comrades, the men who had fought and lost . . .

'Away with them!' Sanquest thundered, 'away with all of them, I say. The rebels, the firebrands, those few remaining Fenians . . .'

Myles jerked his head up and glared at the tall burly figure facing him thirty feet away.

'Let them slink away from the bright light of reality into the darkness of despair. There let them cringe and gnash their teeth in frustrated rage. Let them perish there in ignominy. Let them – '

Myles kicked the leg of the chair in front of him as he struggled to his feet. 'Shut your filthy mouth!'

There was a stunned silence. Heads twisted around to the tall seared figure standing with the lighted oil-lamp in his hand, his face twisted with fury. 'How dare you stand there and insult the men who fought and suffered for this country!' Myles shouted hoarsely, shaking with rage. 'Why you dandified, loud-mouthed bastard, you're not fit to wipe their boots!'

Sanquest recovered quickly; he was used to hecklers. Mockery usually silenced them. He gave a booming laugh. 'Send that man back to the lunatic asylum where he escaped from!'

Someone in the audience tittered, but the words cut Myles like a whip. His lips peeled back, revealing the few remaining rotting teeth. 'Why you syphilitic sonofabitch!' he roared, the veins of his neck bulging, 'I'll tear your rotten tongue out!'

He began to stalk down the passage towards a white-faced Sanquest, one hand clawing the air. Suddenly he realised he was still holding the lamp. He halted and glared at it as a slave would at his chains. He gave a roar of rage and drew back his arm and threw it full force at the figure standing on the platform.

Sanquest darted to one side, threw his arms wide as one foot shot into space over the edge of the platform, then swallow-dived with a terrified yell towards the people seated in the front row.

The room shook with the impact and the lighted oil-lamp flew over the heads of the men seated at the table and struck the wall behind them. The glass chimney exploded and the paraffin-drenched wallpaper caught alight. A sheet of flame raced upwards towards the ceiling.

Instantly there was pandemonium. Women screamed and men shouted and chairs were overturned as everyone dashed madly for the door. Myles was flung against the wall as people scrambled past. He struck back with his fist, still consumed with rage. Through a red mist he saw Fogarty pushing his way towards him, his face conforted with fury. He came to a halt and started yelling, jabbing at Myles' chest with his forefinger.

Myles could not hear what he was yelling about with the uproar, nor did he care. He had a score to settle with Fogarty.

Fogarty raised his voice to a scream and pushed his head forward, thrusting his parrot nose towards Myles like a weapon. Myles drove his clenched fist at it. 'So I'm a doddery old fool, am I!' he roared, and experienced a savage pleasure as Fogarty went reeling back with his hand covering his nose, blood spurting between his fingers.

Then Myles sagged, suddenly exhausted. His body was covered in sweat and he could feel his legs shaking. He reached out and grabbed a chair and pulled it towards him, then sat down. Everything looked out of focus. He closed his eyes.

Gradually he recovered. He became aware of the silence and of a faint burning smell. There was a droning sound as if someone was speaking in a low voice some distance away. He raised his head and opened his eyes. The room looked as though it had been shaken by an earthquake.

334

Chairs were scattered and overturned all over the floor. Some were broken; a few in the front row were completely smashed. Fogarty was sitting on a chair beside the door with his head thrown back and holding a blood-soaked handkerchief to his nose. Rochford was standing over him and talking to him in a soothing voice.

Dineen was still sitting at the table on the platform. His hair was tossed and his bow tie undone. He was staring steadily at the room before him, a dazed expression on his face. Thin veils of smoke from the doused fire hung about his head like gunpowder fumes. He looked like an exhausted general surveying the carnage of a battlefield.

Behind him, a large patch of cracked wall showed where the wallpaper had been burnt away. The paper surrounding the patch was blackened and singed. 'I can't believe this has happened,' Dineen wailed. 'I just can't believe it!' He turned his head to the two men at the door. 'How is Mr Fogarty?' he asked.

Rochford turned to him. 'The bleeding seems to be stopping. He'll be all right in a little while.'

'And Mr Sanquest?'

'Just winded. But he injured Father Kane when he fell on him. I think the Father's arm is broken.'

'Oh, God,' Dineen wailed again.

'I'm more worried about that fellow, Durkin,' Rochford said, 'and of how he's going to report what happened here tonight in that scurrilous rag of his. He can make us the laughing-stock of Dublin.'

Dineen looked despairingly about the room. 'This is a nightmare,' he whimpered.

Rochford walked slowly up the room towards Myles, who was sitting calmly on the chair with folded arms. Rochford came to a halt and stood looking down at him, breathing heavily through his nostrils. His face was white. 'You damned old . . . old . . .' He paused, lips trembling, trying to think of the strongest noun to use. '. . . scoundrel.' Tears of rage began to appear in his eyes. 'Wait till Mr Corcoran hears about this,' he choked. 'If I were you I'd start packing my things now before . . .'

Myles gave an indifferent wave of the hand.

Fintan Butler gave a tired sigh and closed the ledger and placed it on top of the other. Then he stood up and carried both to the small safe in the corner. It was the end of the financial year. He had made a fair profit which surprised him, considering he had largely neglected his business for other things – things of national importance.

The teapot on the gas-ring was boiling. He opened the small cupboard near the window; inside on a shelf was a mug, a spoon, a tin of condensed milk and a packet of tea. He put a spoonful of tea into the boiling water, stirred with the spoon, then turned off the gas. There were two cheese sandwiches wrapped in paper in the pocket of his overcoat hanging on the door.

The office was small and sparsely furnished; it was illuminated by a hissing gas-jet located over the door leading to the storeroom. It was bitterly cold: although there was a fireplace, he had decided against lighting a fire, telling himself it was almost April and the weather should be turning milder. Besides, it helped to keep down costs. The rent for the office and storeroom was thirty-five shillings a week, a sum he could ill afford.

He munched a sandwich and washed it down with a mouthful of tea and thought about the meeting last night which had been held in this very room. There had been himself and four others – all members of the Supreme Council of the Irish Republican Brotherhood.

'No more trips to America for me!' He had been emphatic about that. Someone else would have to go as courier. 'I'm well-known to the police,' he had argued. It was not arrest he was worried about, but the confiscation of precious funds. The British Embassy in the United States had done the organisation grave harm by distributing copies of the *Eye-Witness* containing Durkin's article on Kinsella's embezzlement of IRB funds. The money from America had suddenly dried up as a consequence.

But now a trickle was starting to flow again. Most of it was German money. The action of the Ulster Unionists in arming themselves to resist Home Rule had prompted the German Embassy in Washington to recommence its financial support of the IRB. If the British government allowed itself to be intimidated by the Ulster Unionists and reneged on its promise in granting Home Rule to the southern Irish, then civil war might result. And with her hands full with civil war in Ireland, Britain would be unable to come to the aid of France should a European war break out.

He poured for himself another cup of tea, then lit a cigarette. Tobacco was his only vice: he smoked sixty cigarettes a day. He lay back in the chair and lazily blew smoke-rings towards the grimy ceiling.

How the hell did Durkin find out about Andy Kinsella? he asked himself. Of course Durkin had got it all wrong, describing Kinsella as the IRB treasurer. It had been decided to deposit all money coming from America in a private bank account in the name of someone whom the police would never suspect of being a member of the IRB: a meek, well-behaved individual above suspicion. Poor Kinsella had been the ideal choice.

The money thus deposited established a central fund, used in the early years to revivify the ailing organisation and later for the purchase of arms. The seizure by the Castle authorities of what remained of the fund had not resulted in the disintegration of the IRB as British Intelligence had hoped. Every IRB circle throughout Ireland was independent of each other, financial and otherwise. Each circle had its own governing body consisting of Centre, sub-Centre, Secretary, Treasurer and Section Officers. . . .

He dropped the butt into the dregs of tea in the bottom of the cup and glanced at his watch. Ten minutes to seven. He had a journey to make; he hoped it would not be a fruitless one. He put on his overcoat and turned off the gas-jet.

He made his way slowly down the stairs in the dark. When he closed the halldoor behind him he stood, breathing in the cold fresh air. He had been cooped up in the small stuffy office all day and he felt a little dizzy. Thomas Street was quiet now and almost deserted. This was the time of evening he liked most, when everyone was at home taking their ease after supper. He had the streets almost to himself. He crossed the road and began to saunter along the footpath, heading east.

Standing outside the halldoor, he had seen the detective lurking in the doorway opposite. Now he could hear his footsteps following a good distance behind. He was being watched day and night. One simply had to learn to live with it.

A slight breeze was blowing from the south, driving tatters of cloud before it. Suddenly the moon was exposed, full and low, bathing everything in a harsh blue light. He sauntered on. Wide Thomas Street ended at the entrance to what had been the old walled town. He followed the curve of path into Cornmarket, then came to a standstill at the top of the wide steps leading down into Cook Street. The tower of St Audoen's rose up into the night sky, moonlight glinting on rough uncut stone. He gazed at the lights of the city across the river.

Here where he was standing had once been the heart of the old Norse town. He tried to imagine what the view from this height had been like then. He closed his eyes and conjured up a vision of narrow streets of post and wattlework houses below at the foot of the slope; of flat green meadows on the far side of the river. In his mind's eye he could see the Norse citizens of the town crowding this ridge, staring with bated breath towards the north-east where the fleet of their allies lay off shore; the allies they had summoned from the Hebrides and the Orkneys and the Isle of Man to do battle with the High King, Brian Boru, and his Irish army. . . .

He descended the steps slowly in the dark, hearing as the multitude on the ridge had heard, the clash of arms and the screams of triumph and agony. He saw as craven Sitric Silkenbeard had seen from the safety of his watchtower within the town walls, the defeated Norse racing into the surf as they attempted to reach their ships. . . .

He passed under St Audoen's Arch into Cook Street. The street was deserted, except for an old woman in a shawl shuffling along the narrow footpath. He walked slowly up between crumbling tenements and the old city wall. In his eyes, brick tenements were transformed into post and wattle cabins; gas-lamps became rushlights and above him on the walls, flaxen-haired Dublin Norse gazed across the river at the camp-fires of the victorious Irish and wailed for their warriors who had gone to Valhalla.

He turned left into Winetavern Street. A tram rumbled past the mouth of the street and a man was playing a rollicking tune on a barrel-organ outside a public-house. He was back in the twentieth century again. When he turned the corner, he increased his pace, conscious once again of the detective on his tail. Perhaps, he thought, I can shake him off somewhere along here. He strode on down the quays, a tall thin figure dressed in black. He had become accustomed to wearing clothes of that colour since his student days at the seminary.

When he came to a quiet section of the quays he halted abruptly and stood in the shadows, listening. He could hear the quick beat of footsteps coming towards him. The detective following was matching his long-legged stride. I'll have to give him the slip somehow, he thought, I can't let him follow me all the way. His mind was clear and alert now; the fantasies of ten minutes ago where gone.

He knew he was held in high esteem by the members of the Supreme Council. They knew he was dedicated and hard-working; they respected his intellect and sound judgement. But they did not know of his secret moments, the times when his mind was swamped by wild fantasies more bizarre than any weaved by an ancient Norse saga writer. He saw himself as another Brian Boru – his hero and inspiration. He too would one day lead an Irish army against the English and break their power over his country for good as Brian had done with the Norse. And perhaps, like Brian, he too would die a glorious death at the moment of victory. . . .

He crossed O'Connell Bridge. Sackville Street, the principal street of the capital, was coming to life. People were coming from other parts of the city and from the suburbs, to the theatres, the restaurants. It was spring, and groups of youths and girls flirted under the electric street-lamps. Trams whined to and fro and automobiles hooted their way through the crowded roadway.

Despite the crowds and the hubbub, there was an air of relaxation. He could sense it. No more groups of police standing at corners, hands resting on batons. No more fear of being caught up in a baton-charge. The great lock-out had ended and the locked-out workers and strikers had gone back to work after having been starved into submission. The lock-out had lasted for an incredible six months. What police there were seemed to be more tolerant than usual, and the prostitutes loitering under the portico of the General Post Office flaunted themselves brazenly without fear of harassment. He crossed the road at Nelson Pillar and continued on up on the east side of the street. He knew without looking around that the detective was still following him.

He turned a corner into a side street. At the lower end a large crowd was going in by the side entrance of the pro-Cathedral. It was Lent and a mission was being held. He strode down towards them. He was in luck: it was a mission for men and he mingled with the crowd climbing the steps. Once inside, he moved swiftly towards the main entrance and pushed his way down through the crowd coming up the steps between the pillars. He crossed the road into the shadows and walked quickly towards a street-lamp standing on the corner. He swerved round the corner and made for a laneway a few yards down.

The laneway was narrow and dark and lined on one side with stables. He stood in the recess of one, his back to the door, watching the mouth of the laneway. Behind him, on the other side of the door, he could hear a horse snorting and moving about. There was a smell of hay and horse dung. He waited in the dark and watched. He had only caught a brief glimpse of the detective, but he had seen enough to be able to recognise him: he was tall and wore a light-coloured mackintosh.

A minute passed. There was the sound of footsteps and a man and woman came into view. Two minutes later an old man hobbled past with the aid of a stick. He waited for another five minutes, then moved cautiously up the lane. At the entrance he looked left and then right. The only living thing he could see was a cat sniffing at something in the gutter.

He walked swiftly down the narrow slum street, between tall Georgian tenement houses. Further down, a group of ragged urchins were kicking a tin can about the cobbled roadway. He crossed the intersection of Gardiner Street, then came to a slow halt at the entrance to a long narrow street which stretched away before him into the gas-lit darkness. He hesitated before entering the brothel quarter, then stepped forward, stomach nerves fluttering. He had memorised the address; it was among the high numbers and he had to cross to the north side of the street. The numbers went backwards: one hundred and twelve, one hundred and eleven . . .

In the areas of shadow between the flickering gas-lamps, the whores waited in ambush along the narrow uneven footpath. They lounged against the railings and before the open doors. He walked past – past the leering painted faces and the whistles and the crude invitations. He winced, shocked to hear such filth coming from the mouths of women. He was uncommonly innocent for a man of thirty-seven. His youth and early manhood had been spent in the seminary where vice was simply a subject for discussion in lectures on moral theology.

Eighty-eight, eighty-seven, eighty-six. A girl came into view, standing under a street-lamp. She lolled against it, smoking a cigarette. As he approached, she grasped the light rainproof coat she was wearing and pulled it wide open. He started at the sight of naked flesh, and hurried past. Her mocking laugh followed him down the footpath. My God, he thought furiously, when this country gains its freedom, we'll wipe out this . . . this . . . He was prepared to go to any lengths to free his country; he was willing to condone massacres without a qualm, yet sexual immorality profoundly shocked him. Sixty-eight, sixty-seven . . . Sixty-six was a Stone and Marble Works. He halted at the house adjoining it. Two women stood in the open doorway. Both were wearing shawls and one was cuddling an infant to her breast. He climbed the steps under their curious stares. 'I'm looking for a Mr Burke,' he said. 'Myles Burke. Perhaps you can tell me – '

'Top floor back,' one of the women said.

He nodded his thanks and walked into the dark hallway. A voice followed him.

'Watch out for Saucy Sal, mister. She's a man-eater.' He could hear their giggles as his hand searched for the banister rail in the dark.

He began to climb the stairs slowly. The stench made him almost retch. Behind a door a child was crying fretfully. God above, he thought, what chance has a child, growing up in a place like this. Hunger, disease, moral corruption . . . Yet these excursions into the stews strengthened his resolve; he wanted to destroy everything he saw and create a whole new world. Whenever doubts crept into his mind about what himself and his comrades were trying to achieve, he would visit these streets of shame and squalor to convince himself of the righteousness of their cause.

He reached the third-floor landing, a little breathless after his climb. Suddenly light pierced the darkness from above and he looked up. Someone was holding a lamp over the banisters; he could make out the outline of a head. He continued his climb, the light aiding him.

The woman stood waiting at the top of the stairs, holding the lamp above her head. As he climbed the last flight of stairs towards her, a strong smell of cheap perfume suddenly clogged his nostrils.

'Comin' in for a short time, love?' She brought the lamp close to herself, displaying her wares, and he recoiled at the sight of the heavily painted mouth and cheeks, the eyelids darkened with kohl, the strawberry-coloured dyed hair. He shook his head. 'I'm looking for Mr Burke.'

She indicated with her head the room behind her. 'In there. But he's not in.' She smiled. 'Would you like to wait in my room?'

'No, no,' and winced at his hasty, high-pitched reply. 'No, thank you,' he added in a gentler tone.

She shrugged. 'Suit yourself,' she said, turning the knob of the door of her room. 'You can go in if you want,' she added. 'He never locks his door.' Then she entered her own room and closed the door, leaving him standing in the dark.

He stood, undecided. Then he took a few steps forward. His hand closed around the door-knob and twisted and pushed. He stood in the doorway, nose twitching at the stale smell. He put his hand in his pocket and took out a box of matches and struck one. A small table stood in the centre of the room with an oil-lamp on it. He removed the glass chimney and applied the dying flame of the match of the wick. The room seemed to shudder into life around him.

He stood beside the table and looked about. The room was small and almost bare. A table, a single narrow bed in the corner, two wooden chairs and an upturned tea-chest on which some books were stacked. He walked on bare floorboards to the window and looked out, but he could see nothing in the dark. The window was uncurtained and two missing panes had been replaced by cardboard.

He could hear the woman in the adjoining room singing in a low voice; the sound was so clear he felt as if he were in the same room. He reached out and touched the wall with its damp peeling wallpaper. It was just a partition made of deal. Some enterprising landlord had divided a single room into two. The sound of singing stopped and he could bear her moving about. Then water began to trickle into something and he squirmed on the chair with embarrassment. There was no privacy, even when one was performing one's most intimate functions. He tried not to listen; tried to focus his thoughts on something else.

He looked around, then raised his eyes to the ceiling. It was crusted with dirt, but he could see what appeared to be the remains of decorative plasterwork. Of course these houses had once been the homes of the aristocracy back in the eighteenth century. In the huge drawing-rooms — now partitioned and crammed eight or ten to a room — periwigged ladies and gentlemen had conversed over glasses of claret, or had danced the slow stately minuet to the tunes of a harpsichord.

The woman in the next room had resumed her singing. A thought came to him: I could be sitting in the home of a complete stranger. What if it is a different Myles Burke? There could be hundreds of men of that name in this city. He tried to calm himself. I'll just have to wait and see, he thought.

It had been a long search. He had gone to that old tall house on the quays looking for the caretaker, to be met by a wrathful little man named Corcoran.

'No, Burke is no longer caretaker here. He's gone, and good riddance! He went berserk one night and caused a panic. Nearly burnt the place down! No, I don't know where he is now. Try the prison! Try the lunatic asylum!' Later, after he had calmed down, he had referred him to Father Poole.

But Father Poole shook his old white-haired head. 'I can't help yeh, Mr Butler. I don't know where Myles is now. Perhaps he's dead. If he's not . . . then do as Mr Corcoran suggests and try the asylum.'

Then he had raised his head, showing sad troubled eyes. 'It does not surprise me to hear that Myles Burke became violent. It does not, faith. I could see when I saw him last that he was on the verge of a mental breakdown. He looked so agitated. And as for what he had to say . . .' He shrugged, giving a sigh. 'Pure fantasy. Said he had murdered a man . . . said he had participated in battles long ago. He even told me he had been decorated by President Abraham Lincoln.'

342

Fintan smiled, remembering the look of astonishment on Father Poole's face when he said, 'But he really *was* decorated by Abraham Lincoln, Father.'

There was the sound of a footstep outside the door and a hand fumbled with the door-knob.

The door opened slowly and Myles stood in the doorway, a parcel of groceries under his arm. Under the brim of the old weather-stained hat, the eyes were wide and curious – and a little fearful.

Fintan said: 'I hope you will forgive this intrusion, Mr Burke. My name is Fintan Butler. We met before.'

Myles closed the door behind him. 'I don't recall . . .'

'It was at the funeral of Garret Lysaght. We came back in a cab with poor Joe Furlong, God rest his soul.'

Myles nodded slowly. 'Ah yes. . . .' He placed the parcel of groceries on the table. Then he took off his hat and overcoat and hung them from a nail on the inside of the door. 'How did you find out where I lived?'

Fintan sat down. 'Purely by accident,' he said as Myles moved back from the door to the only other chair and sat down facing him. 'In my spare time, I sit on the committee of a charitable organisation. Enquiries are often made – neighbours are most helpful – about people who may be in need of our help. A list is made of names and particulars. Your name was on the list. I checked with two of our members. The description they gave convinced me that you were the man I had been searching for.'

Myles held up a hand in protest. 'I won't accept charity. I told that to the two who came here – '

'Please, Mr Burke . . .' Fintan interrupted, 'you misunderstand. The reason why I came here has nothing to do with charity.'

Myles sat with his hands on his knees and waited for him to explain. Fintan rose and brought his chair a little closer, conscious of the thinness of the partition behind him. 'Mr Burke,' he said in a low voice, 'I'm a member of the Irish Republican Brotherhood.'

He expected some kind of reaction, but there was none. Myles did not move or say anything, just continued to stare impassively at him. It was as if he had said, 'I'm a member of the local football team.'

'When I told my friends in the organisation that you were still alive, they couldn't believe it. They thought you had died in prison years ago.' He leaned forward a little. 'You may not be aware of the fact, Mr Burke, but your exploits in the past, your unswerving loyalty to the cause of Irish freedom, has been an inspiration to us all.'

Myles gave a slight grunt.

'When the time comes – when we have achieved our freedom – rest assured, the Fenians will not be forgotten. They will be remembered and honoured.'

He was disconcerted to see the old man smile sardonically. Myles wagged his head slowly from side to side. 'My friend – my poor misguided young friend . . .' He sighed deeply. 'Don't waste your life on impossible dreams. Just devote all your energies to your profession or trade and do the best you can. And if you're not married, then search around for some nice girl and settle down. Have plenty of children. Forget everything else. Just grow old in peace and comfort and become fat and dandle your grandchildren on your knees. Don't end up like me. Don't grow into an embittered old wreck living in a garret of a stinking slum tenement, existing on the edge of starvation.' He twisted about on the chair in agitation. 'For God's sake grow up, boy!' he rasped. 'Let my life serve as a warning rather than an example!'

Fintan stared at him in dismay. He had not expected this, he had not expected this at all. In the silence he could hear movements outside on the landing. There was a knock and a door was opened and then banged shut. On the other side of the partition he could hear a man's voice. There was silence for a few seconds; then the man spoke and the woman laughed.

'I'm sorry to find you like this, Burke. So . . . so disgruntled.'

Myles looked at him from under shaggy eyebrows. 'Disgruntled? Is that what you think?' He gave a dry chuckle and shook his head. 'No . . . not disgruntled. In fact, I'm now happier and more content than I've ever been in my whole life.'

Fintan stared at him in disbelief. 'Happy! In this place?'

'Oh yes. I'm seventy-two years of age now. I have a little money saved and I have enough to pay for rent and food. And I'm free! I can go where I please and do as I please. No longer am I at everyone's beck and call. And I have my little pleasures. A good book by the fire at night . . . If you knew what my life had been like, you would call this happiness.'

Movements on the other side of the partition could be plainly heard. A bed creaked and the woman began to laugh, a deep throaty laugh that gave an impression of skittishness, lewdness, expectation. . . .

Fintan was shocked and outraged. Suddenly he leaned forward towards Myles and hissed: 'In heaven's name, how do you stand it?'

Myles looked at him in amazement. Then, comprehending, simply shrugged. 'Oh, *that* . . . she has to live.'

Fintan stared at him open-mouthed. 'It doesn't shock or upset you?'

Myles smiled and shook his head. 'Listen, when I was caretaker I

344

would lie in bed at night listening to the wind moaning through the empty house below. I would have welcomed any human sound, even that of a child crying from the adjoining house. But the houses on both sides were empty too. Sometimes I heard the wind calling my name . . .' He paused, staring with blank eyes at the floor. 'It was only my imagination of course – and nerves. But it's a terrible thing, a terrible thing to live like that. Isolated . . . in complete silence. All human sound is desirable. Even that,' he added, nodding towards the partition.

The rhythmical sounds of love-making went on. The woman gave a cry and Fintan twitched. 'My God,' he whispered furiously, 'has she no respect for people's feelings!'

'Don't be so hasty to condemn her,' Myles admonished gently. 'She only sells her body to survive.' His voice turned bitter. 'I sold my pride, my self-respect. . . .'

Fintan had an overwhelming desire to clap his hands to his ears to prevent himself from having to listen to what was going on on the other side of the partition. Instead he had to sit on the edge of the chair, praying silently for the sounds to cease.

'You haven't told me why you wanted to see me,' Myles said.

Fintan raised a hand to his forehead; he was confused and over-wrought. Everything seemed to be going wrong. 'There was a meeting last night,' he said, keeping his voice low, 'between myself and several members of the Supreme Council of the Irish Republican Brotherhood. There was a unanimous vote of agreement at the conclusion of the meeting concerning yourself.' He paused, then said: 'We would like you to become a co-opted member of the Council.'

Myles remained sitting in the same position, his hands resting on his knees. He stared at the floor for a while, pondering. Then he lifted his shoulders slightly and let them fall again. 'Frankly,' he said in a weary voice, 'I don't see why I should attach myself to the council of a revolutionary organisation when there's not going to be a revolution.'

'But there will be,' Fintan cried, then lowered his voice, aware that he could be heard in the next room. 'Some day,' he added lamely.

'Ah yes . . . some day,' Myles repeated, giving a sigh. Then he raised his head and glared. 'The Irish Republican Brotherhood is obsolete. Obsolete! In a few months from now the Home Rule Bill will become law and your organisation will be just a historical curiosity. So forget your dreams of an armed insurrection and of an independent Irish Republic. A year from now, Johnny Redmond and his Party will be comfortably installed in the new Parliament here in Dublin; they will swear their allegiance to King and Empire and that, my friend, will be that.'

Fintan shook his head, despair showing on his face. 'How I misjudged you. On the way here, I thought I would find the Myles Burke I had read about.'

'What you found,' Myles interposed, 'was a tired cynical old man who simply wants to be left alone.' He felt sorry for this idealistic young man facing him; he reminded him of himself when he was young and full of romantic ideas. 'Come down to earth, my friend, and face reality. The people of Ireland no longer want rebels advocating violence. They want Home Rule and parliamentary debate. And that's what they are going to get.'

'You're forgetting the north and the Ulster Volunteer Force. They intend to fight if Home Rule is imposed.'

'And you're forgetting our own new Irish Volunteers.'

Fintan gave a snort. 'Formed with the aim of ensuring the passage of the Home Rule Bill throuugh Parliament. A volunteer army without arms! With a university professor as Commander-in-Chief and Johnny Redmond in control!'

Myles spread his hands. 'If the Ulster Loyalists continue to resist after the Home Rule Bill becomes law, let the government send the British Army against them. All we will have to do is to sit back and watch.'

Fintan looked at him intently before speaking. 'Listen,' he said in a low excited voice, 'one of our men has stumbled across some vital information, information which will cause an uproar if the public gets to hear of it. A little over a week ago, a Cabinet order was sent to the Commander-in-Chief of the Army at the Curragh ordering him to send troops to protect arms depots in Ulster which are in danger of being raided by the Ulster Volunteers. Nearly every officer refused to obey that order; moreover, they threatened to resign their commissions rather than undertake military operations against the Ulster Volunteers.' He paused. 'This is a mutiny, no matter what others may call it.'

For the first time he saw a glint of interest in Myles's eyes, but there was scepticism in his voice. 'How did your man come across this information?'

'He's a medical student here in the city. He has a friend who's a Lieutenant stationed at the Curragh. This officer was ordered to go on leave. Not granted leave, mind you, but ordered. He was one of the very few who objected to what he considered to be treasonable activities on the part of his fellow officers. As a consequence he found himself blackballed in the officers' mess and sent packing. He was very bitter about the whole affair and told everything to our man when he was in his cups.'

Myles grunted. 'Interesting.'

'Don't you see what this means? The Cabinet cannot risk large-scale defections from the Army. Not now – not when a European war could break out at any moment. They will have to give an assurance to the mutineers that they will not be used in any operation against the Ulster Loyalists. And when that assurance is given, the Ulster Volunteers can act with impunity, knowing that the British Army will not march against them. They will threaten the government with civil war if Home Rule is imposed, and rather than have that happen the government will abandon Home Rule.'

Fintan smiled. 'We have quite a few active IRB men in the towns and villages close to the Curragh Camp. Two nights ago, in a hotel in Naas, some high-ranking British officers were celebrating. One of our men is a waiter in the hotel and was able to pick up some useful information. The officers had good reason to celebrate. They had received "good news" from London, as one of them put it. I'm sure you can surmise what the good news was.'

'The officers had been given the assurance they had asked for.'

Fintan nodded. 'Exactly.'

'What do you think will happen now?'

'The government will renege on the Home Rule Bill, that's what will happen. All they have to fear is Johnny Redmond's wrath, and what is that compared to the Ulster Loyalists threatening civil war and the army officers threatening mutiny? And they have nothing to fear from the Volunteers under Redmond's control. They are unarmed and therefore ineffective. As for the Irish people . . .' He shrugged. 'They will be betrayed and cheated once more. But this will be the last betrayal. This time the people will react in fury. They will discard Redmond and his Party and turn to the men who want a free and independent Irish Republic. With Redmond out of the way we can gain control of the Volunteers and arm them. We'll smuggle in the arms somehow. Money to purchase them will come from America.' Fintan's face flushed with excitement. 'But we must be ready. We must be thoroughly organised.'

He rested a hand on Myles's knee. 'Over the past few years we have been busily recruiting all over Ireland, except parts of the western seaboard – Connemara, south Mayo . . . It's essential we have men in the fishing villages along that stretch of the coast. There are scores of little inlets where a fishing boat carrying arms could sneak in unseen.'

'Why haven't you recruited there before now?'

'We sent an organiser, but he was arrested. That part of the country is so sparsely populated. Villages few and far between. The police are on the alert since our man was arrested. A stranger wandering about for any length of time is bound to be stopped and questioned.' He stared intently into Myles's face. 'What we need is someone who would not arouse suspicion. An elderly man on legitimate business, for instance.' He paused. 'Someone like yourself.'

'Me?' Myles jerked upright, startled.

'I have a small business,' Fintan explained. 'School supplies. I employ two men on a commission basis. They go to schools and retailers around the country, showing samples, taking orders. We pride ourselves in that we only stock items of Irish manufacture. It sometimes helps. *You* could be our salesman for Connemara and south Mayo.

Myles was dismayed. 'But I know nothing about that sort of thing!'

'There's nothing to it,' Fintan said, waving his objection aside. 'I can teach you everything in a matter of days. You simply go from town to town and village to village with a few samples. You'll be supplied with a price list. Write down any orders you get and post them to our office in Dublin and we will despatch the goods.'

Myles shook his head doubtfully. 'I don't know, I don't know.' Yet there was a feeling of pride and hope. He was needed. 'What would I have to do?'

'The important thing,' Fintan said, 'is to settle in a particular place long enough to get to know the people. There's good material in every town and village. You were an officer once and therefore a good judge of character. But do not approach a man until you have thoroughly investigated his background or until you have reported to me first. Send me a written report, giving all the details. Send all reports in our business envelopes addressed to me personally. One must be suspicious, even of the Post Office. I will supply you with the name and address of a man in east Mayo who will be of help to you.' The woman next door laughed, a loud bawdy satisfied laugh that filled the room. Fintan lit a cigarette, her laughter in his ears. Suddenly Blake came to mind and he thought:

> The Harlot's cry from street to street
> Shall weave old Ireland's winding sheet . . .

Myles Burke sat dozing in the heat of the midday sun. He was protected from the glare by the sloping roof over the small recess on the platform of the railway station. The porter, a small man with a wizened face, stepped from his tiny office and mopped his face with a handkerchief. He was hot and uncomfortable in his uniform. Steel rails reflected the glare of the sun and wavered in the heat-haze. The fields had lost their green freshness, and looked brown and scorched after nearly two weeks of unbroken weather. The porter walked slowly towards the man dozing in the shade, his heavy boots sending out slow loud claps against the stone flags.

Myles slept peacefully. The porter looked down at him with pursed lips, his hands in his trouser pockets. Everything the man was wearing was new, even the hat resting on the small suit-case on the seat beside him.

'Is it that yer waitin' for somewan?'

Myles opened his eyes and blinked. 'Did you say something?'

'I was wantin' to know if ye were waitin' for someone.'

'Oh, yes. Mr Troy. Perhaps you know him.'

'The schoolmaster is it? Sure I know him well. A friend of yours?'

'A friend of a friend.'

The curious little eyes stared steadily down under the visor of the cap.

'I'd say now,' he said slowly, stroking his chin, 'ye're a Dublin man. Am I right?'

'That's correct.'

'A Commercial, mebbe?'

'In a way,' Myles answered, irritated by the man's inquisitiveness. He was exhausted and drowsy and wanted to go back to sleep.

'Ye'll not find,' the porter said, 'much money floatin' around here. 'Tis scarce as hobbyhorse manure. Not with this drought an' all. The crops are in a cruel state for want of a drop of rain. 'Now if it's medicine for cattle and sheep yer sellin' – stuff for the warble fly or the fluke worm, my advice . . .'

Myles decided to satisfy the man's curiosity once and for all or he would get no peace. 'It's nothing like that. I travel in school supplies – pencils, pens, copy-books. Things like that.'

'Begob, is that a fact now? When I was a gosoon goin' to school divil a bit of pencils or copy-books we had. No, faith, just a slate and a bit of chalk, that's all.'

'Indeed?'

A gate opened on squeaky hinges and a low-sized powerfully built man clad in tweed trousers and white shirt strode purposefully towards them. The porter turned his head at the sound of footsteps, then bawled, 'Ah, the boul Gerry, here's a man stewin' in the heat for the past hour waitin' for ye.'

Myles rose slowly to his feet. Fintan described him well, he thought, but he didn't mention the beard.

Gerry Troy wore a wide-brimmed straw hat and his face was tanned a deep brown by the sun.

'Mr Burke?'

Myles nodded, and caught a brief flicker of dismay in his eyes. He had obviously expected a much younger man.

'I'm sorry for keeping you waiting. Any luggage?'

'Just the suit-case.'

Gerry picked it up and led the way, Myles following, hat in hand. The porter came after them.

'D'ye know if Bull O'Malley received any news about his two lads at all, at all, Gerry? No? Ah, that's children for ye. A trial from the moment they step out of the cradle. I was just sayin' to the wife the other day . . .'

There was a horse and trap on the road outside the station. Gerry opened the little door at the rear and Myles climbed in and sat down. He put his hat on, then took the suit-case from Gerry. Gerry climbed in and picked up the reins.

The porter banged the door shut and raised a pair of aggrieved eyes. 'Sure yer always in some rush or other, Gerry,' he whined. 'Never the time for an oul chat.'

Gerry shook the reins and turned a grinning face over his shoulder. 'Ah, you and your oul chats, Mickeen Gavan,' he laughed. 'Aren't you the lucky man that has nothing to do all day.'

'Aye, begob,' the porter shouted as the horse broke into a trot, 'and all day to do it in!'

Gerry gave another laugh and smacked the horse's hindquarters. 'Poor Mickeen,' he shouted above the noise of the wheels, 'was born with a double dose of misfortune. A curiosity any woman would envy and an acute case of verbal diarrhoea.'

The horse trotted on between high hedges, kicking up the dust of the road. Myles coughed a little, shielding his mouth with his hand.

'And how is Fintan?' Gerry shouted.

'Active,' Myles shouted back.

'Stay at my house for a few days. I'll acquaint you with the situation here. Then move on to Castlebar. There's a man I know there who will be of help to you.'

Myles nodded and watched the road in front, screwing up his eyes against the flying dust. He could see a speck in the distance. It was a man on a bicycle coming rapidly towards them. Gerry pulled on the reins and the horse slowed to a halt. The sun glinted on a uniform button and Gerry gripped Myles's knee.

'Say nothing. Let me do all the talking.'

The policeman stopped alongside them and rested a hand on the shaft. His dark uniform was powdered with dust.

'A glorious day, sergeant..'

The sergeant nodded. ''Tis that, Mr Troy.' He produced a handkerchief from his hip pocket and started to mop his face with it. 'Ah, but we'll pay for it later on in the year,' he said heavily. 'The crops, ye know.' He shook his head and sighed. 'I pity the farmers. Barney O'Malley's fields are in a cruel state for want of rain.'

'How is Bull O'Malley these days?' Gerry asked.

'Despondent, Mr Troy, very despondent. His wife gone, his daughter gone. And now he's just received a letter from Sonny sayin' he's followin' Luke to America.'

Gerry gave a whistle of surprise. 'I didn't know Luke was in America.'

The sergeant sighed again. 'Ah sure the poor lads tried their hand at farmin' down in Kerry, but things didn't work out right.' His eyes shifted to Myles. 'Is that yer father ye have there, Mr Troy?'

Gerry gave a laugh. 'Sure me poor father is dead and buried these twelve years or more. No, no, this gentleman is a salesman. School supplies. Pencils, pens, copy-books. And all made in Ireland, so I've been told. That's what we should all do, sergeant; support our native industries. Keep the money in the country. Import the raw materials and make the goods ourselves. The only cure for emigration.'

The sergeant nodded absently and gazed with vacant eyes down the road. 'Aye, ye may be right.'

Myles sat mute and tense. Experience had taught him to say as little as possible in the presence of a policeman. He sat, hot and uncomfortable under the blazing sun, wishing the schoolmaster would go.

'That youngster of yours,' Gerry declared, 'is a born scholar. He's my prize pupil.'

'D'ye say so, now?'

351

'Aye, I do. I hope you've picked a good profession for him. One that will give him plenty of scope for his talents.'

'I was thinkin' of the Civil Service,' the sergeant said, fingering the strap under his chin. 'Oh, a secure job and a pension at the tail-end of it, that's the ticket.' Then he straightened up in the saddle. 'Well, I must be off. Duty calls. Good-day to ye now, Mr Troy.' He turned towards Myles. 'And good luck to you, sir.'

Gerry clucked his tongue and urged the horse forward. This time he allowed it to saunter.

'Was it necessary,' Myles asked peevishly, 'for you to tell him about me?'

Gerry nodded, his face grim. 'Yes, it was.' He jerked a thumb back over his shoulder. 'He's on his way down to the railway station right now to have a chat with Mickeen Gavan. First, he'll talk about the weather and the crops, then he'll drop a casual remark about the stranger in Gerry Troy's trap and chatterbox Mickeen will tell everything he knows. Better to tell him myself first. If I had been secretive and tight-lipped about you he would have become suspicious. Ger on, ye bitch!' he rasped and the horse broke into a trot. It was a while before Gerry Troy spoke again. 'I made a mistake calling you Mr Burke in the hearing of Mickeen Gavan. When Sergeant Hanafin writes his report to Dublin Castle, he'll mention you. You can be sure of that. A stranger in the district is always reported. So from here on, be on your guard.'

Myles felt the familiar icy finger of fear touching his heart. He gripped the edge of the suit-case and forced himself to concentrate on the dusty road ahead. It ran straight for about fifty yards, before curving gently round a bend. As they turned the bend he saw it: a massive structure standing on a hill in the distance. He jerked upright in shock.

'That place!'

Gerry lifted his head. 'Ah yes, Carewscourt. Where our lord and master lives.' Myles swayed with the motions of the trap, his eyes fixed on the massive building, so stark and bleak against the blue of the sky. He could not believe it existed. He had thought it was a picture created by the subconscious – part of the landscape of his nightmares, but in the nightmares he was always approaching it from the opposite direction.

Slowly the house fell out of sight, hidden by the tall hedges flanking the road. He stared straight ahead, knowing what he was going to see. It was like experiencing another nightmare, this time in reverse. He thought aloud.

'There's the long high wall, and the plantation of tall trees beyond . . .'

Gerry turned his head. 'What did you say?'

There was no reply. The deep-set eyes stared trance-like past his shoulder towards the long crumbling wall of the demesne. Gerry shrugged. The horse had slowed down and hoofbeats plodded on and on. Gerry yawned and closed his eyes, the reins held loosely in his hand, feeling the heat of the sun on his back. Myles sat upright on the seat, hands gripping the suit-case, the long high wall of rough uncut stone moving slowly past his vision. Then the gates of the demesne came into view: old and rusting: one hung down loosely from broken hinges.

A murmuring grew inside his head; slowly it swelled into a roar and before his eyes a ragged starving multitude swarmed before the gates howling for food. The gates remained closed. In desperation, two men began to climb the wall. It was then they opened the gates and turned the snarling dogs loose . . . He turned his head away from the scene, but more agony was to be seen on the road ahead. All along on both sides, in the ditches and fields, they lay in their hundreds. Ragged, hollow-eyed, emaciated. The dead, the dying. . . . They passed the crossroads, the horse laboriously pulling its load up the village street. A wheel rolled over a stone and Gerry awoke with the jolt.

He yawned and rubbed his eyes and turned his head towards Myles, smiling apologetically. 'This damned heat makes one . . .' and stopped, startled by the expression on Myles's face. He pulled on the reins, bringing the horse to a halt. 'Are you feeling ill, Mr Burke?'

Myles shook his head. They had reached the northern outskirts of the village opposite the Protestant church. Myles rose stiffly to his feet and opened the little door at the rear and stepped down, leaving the suit-case on the seat.

Gerry watched, puzzled, as Myles walked slowly on cramped legs up the road. He came to a stop at a gate leading into a field and stood, gazing. Then Gerry understood. 'Ah, don't be so modest, man,' he called. 'There's no one in sight. Piss into the ditch!'

But Myles just stood there as if he had not heard. Then after a while he opened the gate and walked into the field.

Gerry waited. After ten minutes had passed, he gave a hiss of impatience and jumped down from the trap and strode up towards the gate.

Myles was standing in the middle of the field, his hat in his hand, staring into the distance.

'What in the name of. . . !' Gerry swore under his breath and walked

353

towards him. 'Is anything the matter, Mr Burke?' he asked as he reached him. Myles turned to look at him. His eyes were glazed. Then he turned his head away and pointed towards the west. 'There was a Workhouse, way over there.' Gerry followed the direction of his finger and nodded. 'The ruins were there up to a few years ago. It was destroyed by fire back in the 'eighties, so I've been told.' He turned his head, staring at the profile. 'Were you here before?'

Myles nodded slowly, still looking towards the west. 'A long, long time ago . . . The Black Forty-seven. I was only a child.'

Gerry stared at him in awe.

'We had travelled from the village of Turlough, more than thirty miles away. There were seven of us. My father and my mother, my three sisters and my brother, Colm, and myself. We were walking to Galway. From there, we hoped to sail on a ship for America.'

He turned stiffly around and stretched an arm out towards the road. 'Out there, on the road, in the village, in the fields and boreens, was a vast army of starving wretches trying to get into the Workhouse. Many were dying from hunger and fever . . .'

He paused, eyes narrowed against the sun, seeing it all . . . 'We settled down for the night outside that church over there, intending to move on to Galway the following morning. It was bitterly cold and some of the people had built a bonfire not far from where we were lying. A large crowd gathered around it. A few were sick with fever. In those days they called it the famine fever. Typhus . . .' He lowered his head, his eyes wandering over the greenish-brown parched grass. 'And here,' he whispered, 'where we're standing, they dug a huge common grave.' He took a deep breath, trying to keep his voice from shaking. 'They threw them into it, men, women, children . . .' He was unable to go on.

Gerry looked slowly all about him. 'The local people,' he said in a muted voice, 'call this place *Páirc na Marbh* – the Field of the Dead.'

Myles squeezed his eyes shut like a man in pain, letting the hat fall from his hand. Tears began to creep out from beneath the eyelids. 'They're down there,' he gasped, 'under our feet, all those poor souls, my mother, my sisters . . .' He gave a moan and slowly slid to his knees, shoulders shaking, sobs tearing at his throat.

# Chapter Fourteen

## I

Major Calder was a frequent visitor to the Officers' Mess of his old regiment, the King's Own Scottish Borderers, and had been from almost the first day of their arrival in Dublin. There were still a few old chums serving with the 'Kokky-Olly Birds' including Major Craig, a burly bluff Scot with cropped coppery hair and a broken nose: he had once been the boxing champion of the regiment.

Alec Carew always tried to find some excuse for not going whenever Major Calder invited him along. He felt uncomfortable and out of place in the company of these Scots. He found them uncouth compared to their English counterparts. And he disliked Jock Calder's friend, Major Craig. He was too aggressive and outspoken, particularly when he was in his cups, which was quite often. He too had risen from the ranks like Major Calder, and never missed an opportunity to make caustic remarks about the 'Pedigree Pups' whenever Carew happened to be present. He was fond of baiting people, especially the young subalterns, who were afraid of him. But he was not in a baiting mood tonight as Carew could see, sitting only a few feet away from him. He lay sprawled in a leather armchair, a glass of whiskey in his hand, his face flushed and scowling. There was an air of tension in the Mess. A rumour had gone round that the battalion – indeed the whole Brigade – were being sent north to confront the Ulster Volunteers. The Ulster Volunteers were now a force to be reckoned with. Nearly twenty-five thousand rifles and three million rounds of ammunition had been landed at Larne on the east coast of Ulster three months before. Most of the money for the arms had been donated by rich supporters and members of the British Conservative Party. With the Home Rule Bill about to become law in eight weeks' time, Protestant Ulster was on a war footing. According to barrack-room gossip, certain Scottish and Welsh battalions were to be sent north, as English regiments with anti-Home Rule officers in command could no longer be relied upon to carry out orders.

'I've been told,' someone said, 'that the Ulster Volunteers have light artillery.'

'Oh, they're well armed,' Major Calder conceded, 'but not to that extent.' There were about fifteen officers gathered in the long high-ceilinged room. It was near midnight and the whiskey had flowed freely: tobacco smoke hung motionless like mist. Most of the senior officers were wearing their 'Number Ones'; dark-blue tunics and tartan trews. All the subalterns were dressed in khaki tunics and kilts. The CO, Colonel Lamont, stood in front of the empty fireplace, a glass of whiskey in his hand. There was a grave expression on his face as he listened to the conversation.

'What are they like, these Ulster Volunteers?' Craig asked, looking sideways at Major Calder. 'Well trained?'

'Alec can answer that better than I,' Calder replied. 'He was up north for a few weeks acting as an observer.'

All heads turned towards Carew who was sitting in a deep leather armchair sipping his whiskey. He lowered his glass and looked over at Craig, meeting his bleary, baleful stare. He gave a slight shrug. 'A little sloppy with their foot-drill,' he said, 'and rather clumsy performing manoeuvres, but otherwise good. For a volunteer army, that is,' he added.

'Musketry?' another officer inquired.

'Fair. But then lack of arms was the trouble. All that is changed now, of course. In another few months they will be as good as any professional army.'

Then the Colonel spoke. 'All the more reason why they should be forcibly disarmed before they reach that stage. The government cannot allow a private army to exist outside the law.'

A deep uneasy silence followed the statement. Some of the officers stared fixedly into their glasses. The silence became so unbearable, Carew felt compelled to say something. 'Yes, sir, I agree. It would be disastrous to delay.' He could hear a faint hiss of annoyance coming from Calder and he turned his head towards him. Calder deliberately avoided his eyes, but Craig, sitting next to him, glared venomously.

Carew looked away, feeling a flush spreading over his face. He had made a mistake voicing his opinion. After all he was here only as a guest. From the moment he arrived he had been aware of a feeling of hostility directed towards Colonel Lamont. The Colonel was openly anti-Conservative in his politics. He blamed them for urging on the Ulster Loyalists into committing what he considered to be an act of treason.

The Colonel raised his head and stared abstractedly up at the ceiling.

'There is a very real possibility,' he declared in his clear, Eton accent, 'of war breaking out between Britain and Germany. It could happen at any moment. And yet the Ulster Loyalists have been in collusion with the Germans, if my information is correct. They were allowed to sail their ship carrying the arms through the Kiel Canal unhindered. Naturally the Germans want a civil war to break out in Ireland. With a civil war in her own back garden, Britain would be unable to go to the aid of France should she be attacked.' He gulped down a mouthful of whiskey. Then his eyes roamed over their faces. 'In my view,' he said with a touch of harshness in his voice, 'the Ulster Loyalists are traitors, and the sooner we render them powerless the better.'

There was silence for a while. Then Craig drawled thickly, 'There are many officers in this room who would not agree with you, sir.' He stared moodily at the glass of whiskey in his hand.

The Colonel lazily raised an eyebrow. 'Oh . . .' His tone was soft. 'Of course, every man is entitled to his opinion.' He paused, then looked searchingly about him, his eyes finally coming to rest on a few subalterns standing together. 'But the first duty of a soldier is to obey orders, no matter what his private opinions may be.' Then he smiled, bleakly. 'Ours not to reason why, you know.'

The subalterns smiled wanly back at him, sipping nervously at their drinks. Craig gave a gusty sigh. 'Aye, Colonel, that's where the conflict lies. Duty or what you believe in.'

The Colonel looked down at him again, his face expressionless. 'Perhaps,' he said softly, 'you would care to define the distinction?'

Major Craig lifted the hand holding the glass and brought it slowly to his mouth. His arm was the only part of his body that moved. He still lay sprawled in the chair, his attitude one of studied insolence. He took a sip, then raised his head and gazed thoughtfully at the ceiling. 'Well, Colonel,' he said in a slow deliberate voice, 'if I am ordered north, I will go. If I am ordered to confront an Ulster Volunteer, I will do so. If I am ordered to shoot him, I will raise my revolver and I will take careful aim . . .' then he lowered his gaze and stared with half-closed eyes at his superior officer '. . . but I'll be damned if I will pull the trigger.'

One of the subalterns gave a sharp intake of breath and Carew stiffened a little. Calder began to clean his pipe, glad of something to do, dissociating himself from everything that was happening around him. Colonel Lamont's face was a frozen mask. He lifted his glass to his mouth and drained it. Then he lowered his head and stared at the floor, not wanting to look at anyone while he addressed them; what he was about to say was intended for everyone.

'This battalion,' he declared in a cold precise voice, 'may have to go up north. We may have to fight the Ulster Volunteers. If I give a certain order,' he paused deliberately, 'will it be obeyed?'

The silence which followed was answer enough. A muscle twitched in the Colonel Lamont's cheek.

It was Craig who broke the silence. 'If it's the order we think it is, I doubt it.'

The look of shocked disbelief on the Colonel's face changed to one of anger. He held himself rigid, trying to keep his wrath under control. Suddenly he gave a gesture of dismissal. 'Ach, this is insane – insane. We've all had far too much to drink. We'll be our normal selves in the morning.'

Major Craig lifted his glass. 'I admit I'm fu' . . . but I bloody well mean what I say.'

The Colonel placed his empty glass on the mantleshelf and nodded curtly. 'Goodnight, gentlemen,' he said and strode stiffly out of the room.

No one moved; no one said anything. Then a tall wiry officer exclaimed in a shocked voice: 'Malcolm, for Christ's sake!'

Craig shrugged. 'Well, what of it? It had to be said. It's how we all feel, isn't it?'

## II

Durkin sat morosely at a table in the hotel bar, brooding over his whiskey. Two elderly gentlemen, residents of the hotel, were conversing quietly in a corner. It was very warm and the windows were wide open. The street outside was strangely silent for a sunny Sunday afternoon. Everyone's at the seaside enjoying themselves, Durkin thought sourly and swallowed his whiskey. It was his fifth glass since he had walked in more than an hour ago.

He glanced at the clock behind the bar and swore softly under his breath. Those bastards, he thought savagely. They had promised faithfully to be here at the appointed time, and they had failed him, his so-called friends. They had all agreed to go to a race-meeting at Fairyhouse and then back to Monto for drinks and, as Freddy Mulligan the tick-tack man had put it, 'a romp with the jolly girls'.

358

Not one of them had turned up. He swore again. Damn them, he thought, thinking of the long boring day ahead of him. He had been looking forward all week to having some fun with 'the lads'. He had even bought a new hat for the occasion, a straw boater. He tilted it up from his perspiring forehead and rose from the chair and walked across to the bar and ordered another whiskey. The barmaid accepted his money without a word of thanks. Dressed in black satin, she looked uncomfortably hot and irritable.

I bet she's wishing she was out on the Hill of Howth on a day like this, Durkin thought with malice, rolling in the heather with a man. He experienced a stab of pleasure knowing that someone besides himself was miserable and frustrated.

There was a folded newspaper near his elbow and he picked it up and spread it flat on the counter. He began to sip the whiskey, his eyes wandering over the page. Not a thing, he thought, not a cursed thing worth getting excited about. A man had died of sunstroke in Greystones; there had been a drowning tragedy in Arklow; a mother of six had been sentenced to six months' imprisonment for stealing a loaf of bread and a pound of sugar.

The silly season, he thought, turning a page. Even the foreign news was dull. They were still kicking up a fuss about the assassination of that Archduke in Sarajevo. Where the hell is Sarajevo? he asked himself and shrugged. Somewhere in the Balkans, I suppose. Always trouble there. But exciting nevertheless. Not like Ireland – not like Dublin. You'd die of boredom in this miserable kip of a city. He sighed and swallowed what remained of the whiskey in one gulp.

The barmaid was wearily adding up some figures on a list. She had her back turned to him and he contemplated her voluptuous satin-encased body with melancholy lust. Desire stirred in his loins and he closed his eyes with a silent groan. Jesus, he moaned to himself, this bloody heat would make even a saint feel randy.

Behind the closed eyelids he could feel tears of self-pity beginning to form. Shouldn't feel like this – shouldn't have to. No married man should. If only that bitch would respond. But she just lies there like a bloody corpse. What the hell is wrong with her anyway? Never used to be like that. For a brief while a few years ago she behaved in bed like a bloody nymphomaniac. But now! A wail arose in his brain. It's not fair! I'm only human! Why can't she. . . ?

He opened his eyes, seeing everything through a blur of tears. He swept a hand across his eyes, feeling a savage rage swelling up inside him. To hell with her! I'll be damned if I'm going to humiliate myself by asking for my conjugal rights. I shouldn't have to ask . . .

Engrossed with his thoughts, he had not been aware of a growing clamour in the distance. The barmaid ceased her calculations and turned her head. Then she looked questioningly at Durkin. 'What's that?'

Durkin shrugged and waddled over to the windows. Roars and shouts shattered the tranquil peace of the street outside. Above the uproar he could distinguish the tread of marching feet. He leaned out and looked down.

They came marching into view from the left, a long column of Scots soldiers, three abreast, kilts swinging, rifles on their shoulders, bayonets glinting in the sun. And running alongside on the footpaths on both sides of the column, shouting and taunting, a large crowd of civilians, mostly youths with a few girls among them. Durkin watched a ragged urchin picking up a stone from the gutter and throwing it.

'What's happening?' The barmaid was close behind him, trying to peer down into the street over his shoulder. The two elderly gentlemen were standing at the other window, staring silent down. Durkin could feel the softness of her breast against his shoulder blade and her excited breath against his ear. Once again he experienced a twinge of lust and tried to concentrate on what was happening in the street below. He saw a soldier wiping blood from his smashed mouth with the back of his hand and replied: 'Trouble,' and hurried out of the bar and down the carpeted stairs.

He stood beside the hall-porter in the doorway, blinking against the strong sunlight, watching the troops marching past and the yelling jeering mob running alongside them. He grabbed the arm of a passer-by, a perky little man in a cloth cap and serge suit. 'What the hell is happening?'

The man was as excited as a puppy. 'Great news!' he yelped. 'A yacht sailed into Howth Harbour with hundreds of rifles and ammunition for the National Volunteers. About a thousand of our lads were waiting to unload her. Then those bastards,' jerking a thumb over his shoulder, 'were sent out to stop them.' He threw back his head and gave a shrill laugh of delight. 'But all they got for their trouble were a few broken heads and about a dozen rifles! Bejay! If the Loyalists up north can bring in rifles, so can we!'

Then he broke away to join the crowd, to join in the taunting and the cat-calling. Durkin stood watching as the head of the column wheeled right into Talbot Street. Then he joined the throng. Something was going to happen – he could sense it. Boredom and frustration fell away from him. One became tired of writing about shabby little love affairs and assignations; a little blood and thunder would be a welcome relief. Suddenly he chuckled to himself. Lucky Durkin, he thought, always in the right place at the right time.

Major Craig marched at the head of the column, leading it up the long narrow shop-lined street, swagger-cane in hand, teeth clenched, face dark with fury, his eyes firmly fixed on the tall column of Nelson Pillar in the distance. He tried to ignore the prancing figures on either side, tried to ignore their taunts and shouts.

'Hey, Jock, does yer mother know yer oot!'

'G'wan yeh hoors! Go up north and seize the rifles of yer pals, the Ulster Volunteers!'

'Hoot, mon, yer drawers are slippin'!'

The long street was the boundary line of the vast area of slumland to the north. Attracted by the commotion, the ragged youths and barefooted street arabs came swarming out from the side streets and laneways. They mingled with the crowd on the footpaths, adding their own particular style of invective to the jeers and insults being hurled at the troops.

The quiet Sabbath serenity of Sackville Street was ruptured as the column swung left into it, accompanied by the howling mob. The rag-tag and bobtail from the festering slums of Monto, brutalised by poverty and baton wielding police during the recent lock-out, darted close to the sweating, furious soldiery and began to pelt them with anything they could pick from the roadway and gutter: stones, tin cans, horse droppings. The younger ones danced along, taunting them with song.

> Sew, sew yer petticoat, yer petticoat, yer petticoat,
> Sew, sew yer petticoat, yeh dirty Scottish Borderer . . .

Durkin waddled along the footpath at the rear of the crowd, sweat running down his face from under his new straw boater. 'Holy God, boy,' he panted to himself, 'you'll have to cut down on those bloody whiskeys.'

The soldiers at the tail of the column were suffering the most. Not only had they to endure the abusive crowd on both sides, but those behind as well, who were snapping at their heels like a pack of ferocious mongrels. Now and then restraint broke and they turned about, making savage feints with their fixed bayonets at their tormentors.

The column wheeled right in front of the O'Connell Monument and continued up the north quays towards their barracks, which was a mile upriver.

361

Major Craig shot a backward glance over his shoulder. 'Captain Haig,' he barked, 'take command!'

He swerved smartly left; three quick strides took him to the pavement. There he stood with his back to the waist-high river-wall, legs apart, holding his swagger-cane level across his stomach.

He watched his men marching past. Exhausted, goaded beyond endurance, they were almost at breaking point. He glared at the yelling, jeering mob coming up behind them. His mouth tightened. He was not going to allow that damned noisy rabble to follow his men all the way back to their barracks. As the last section came marching towards him, he stepped into the centre of the road and ordered it to halt.

Durkin pushed his way through the crowd on the footpath, his hip brushing against the river-wall, wondering why the people up in front had suddenly come to a standstill. He could see two women struggling back through the crowd, their faces white with fear. He was cautious by nature, but the six whiskeys he had consumed made him feel reckless. He pushed his way through to the front of the standing, suddenly silent crowd, then halted abruptly, startled, giving a sudden involuntary hiccup of fright.

Thirty soldiers were lined across the full width of the quay ten yards away, their rifles aimed at the crowd. Six in front were kneeling on one knee. The silence was suddenly shattered by a girl's scream of terror. 'Jesus, they're goin' to shoot!' A youth gave a guffaw. 'Ah, sure they're only coddin'.'

But Durkin was not so sure. He was near enough to see the murderous looks on the faces of the soldiers. Suddenly he was seized by panic. He was about to turn around and fight his way back when everything exploded in a flash of red flame. A bullet struck his shoulder and sent him spinning around like a top. His face struck the pavement and he could feel the pain as his teeth cut into his tongue. His mouth filled with blood. He lay face downward, stunned, the echoes of the volley and the terrified cries of the seagulls from the river in his ears. Then there was silence.

He lay still, feeling the blood from his mouth pouring down over his chin in a warm sticky stream and forming into a red puddle on the dusty pavement inches from his face. There was no pain where the bullet had struck, just a numbness as though he had just been kicked by a horse. He could feel the blood running down his arm and over his hand and in between his fingers and there was the strong acrid smell of cordite which caught at his breath and made him cough. Long strands of hair hung down over his eyes and he could feel the warmth of the sun on his

362

uncovered head. I've lost my hat, he thought stupidly, my new hat. . . .

Resting his weight on his good arm, he slowly heaved himself up and flopped awkwardly back against the river-wall. He sat on the footpath with his legs spread wide apart. He felt dazed and light-headed and gazed at the heaped bodies before him with a curious air of detachment. His left foot touched that of another man. The man lay sprawled face downwards on the road, his feet resting on the footpath. On the narrow roadway the bodies lay in untidy heaps. Under one mound he could see the thin, bare, grimy leg of an urchin twitching spasmodically. He was reminded of a freshly caught fish flopping its life away on a river-bank.

He raised his eyes and met the blank stare of a matronly-looking woman sitting on the pavement directly opposite, the upper part of her body wedged in the narrow closed doorway of a shop. She wore a wide-brimmed hat which lay drunkenly askew and under a short open jacket an immaculate white blouse, in the centre of which a bright-red stain was beginning to spread in all directions.

Durkin and herself stared solemnly at each other over the heaped, sprawled bodies. They were like two tired guests silently congratulating each other on their sobriety, at a party where everyone had disgraced themselves by falling down drunk.

As Durkin watched, the woman, slowly and gracefully, began to slide sideways. She came to rest against the side of the doorway and lay, eyes popping, mouth hanging open, a look of complete surprise on her face.

Durkin turned his head lazily away, the sun warming his face. He felt weak and drowsy and had a desire to sleep. Faint whimperings of pain came from the roadway and here and there a body began to stir. His half-closed eyes wandered over the carnage. Then his journalistic mind took over. He found himself starting to count, recording and filing away in his brain facts for future reference. He had counted up to twenty-seven when something kicked against his left foot.

He turned his head to see the man who had been lying at his feet starting to crawl away on his hands and knees. But the movement must have caused an artery to burst; blood began to spurt out from under the man's trouser leg and over the heel of his boot. Durkin watched fascinated as the figure moved reptile-like over the tram-lines, leaving a trail of blood behind it.

He could feel his stomach heaving. He turned his head sideways and poured the contents of his stomach on to the pavement. Then he lay back against the river-wall and closed his eyes, vomit and blood from his injured mouth rolling down over his chin. He was too weak to wipe it away. In the distance he could hear the frantic jangling of an ambulance bell. . . .


## III


Carew told the driver to stop when they came to Merrion Square. 'I'll walk the rest of the way.'

It was after midnight and he had the streets to himself. Far off, a ship's siren sent out a long moan of warning. Troop-ship, he thought, heading for Liverpool under cover of darkness to avoid submarines. He continued on along Mount Street, the echoes of his footsteps in his ears. It was hard to believe that at this very moment the flower of Europe were slaughtering each other on the blood-drenched fields of France and Belgium. The war was only eight days old, and already the combined casualties were five times greater than those suffered during the whole South African War. What was the killing and wounding of forty-two Dubliners compared to that? he asked himself.

Nevertheless the Bachelor's Walk massacre had happened at the worst possible time – ten days before war had been declared. The military, about to embark on a massive recruiting campaign, had started to look frantically about for a scapegoat. They found one – Harrison, the Assistant Commissioner of the Dublin Metropolitan Police. In order to placate Irish opinion, Harrison had been dismissed from office for 'provocatively' calling out the military to deal with the landing of arms at Howth.

The Under-Secretary was also going: his successor was due to arrive in early October. And as for the King's Own Scottish Borderers . . . His grip on the attaché case tightened.

They had been sent to England en route to France, the day after war had been declared. Their presence in Dublin had been an embarrassment to the authorities, especially with a recruiting campaign about to be launched. It would have been disastrous if any of the battalion had been forced to stand trial for murder, as the nationalist newspapers had demanded. But the sudden outbreak of war had overshadowed everything else. In the excitement and euphoria, the King's Own had been quietly shipped out.

Where are you this night, you Scottish Borderers? he wondered, turning into Herbert Place, ignoring the prostitutes standing in the shadows. Probably trudging along some road, heading for the Belgium frontier, about to be thrown in front of the advancing German steamroller. Sacrificial lambs, he thought, remembering the two Staff Officers congratulating each other on having got rid of 'that troublesome lot'.

He turned into Wilton Place; the short row of tall elegant Georgian houses were all in darkness. He mounted the steps then stood, fumbling in his tunic pocket for the key. Now with the war on he would have to give up this flat. The old easy ways had gone; his presence in barracks was now required. He closed the heavy halldoor behind him and started to climb the stairs slowly in the dark. Just as well, he told himself, this place holds too many memories.

As he walked up the last flight he could see light coming from under the door. He silently cursed the cleaning woman for her carelessness. Sure enough, the door opened when he tested the knob. Then he halted, stunned, not believing his eyes, staring open-mouthed at the figure sitting by the fire. She stared back at him, white-faced.

'I have a key,' she said in a low voice. 'Had you forgotten?'

'Miriam,' he managed to whisper, closing the door slowly. He removed his cap and placed it with the attaché case on a chair. He was still in a daze.

She turned her head away and stared at the fire, waiting apprehensively for his reaction. She began to twiddle with the wedding ring on her finger as though she were trying to take it off.

Seeing how nervous she was, he sat down on the chair beside her and placed a firm hand over hers. 'Stop that. There's no need to feel nervous or upset. I'm glad you're here. Very glad.'

She released a long deep sigh as though she had been holding her breath for a long time. 'I've been sitting here for the past four hours,' she said. 'Several times I got up to go, then changed my mind.'

'I'm glad you didn't go.'

'I was at the hospital, visiting William.'

'How is he?'

'The wound is healing nicely. It became infected, you see. He'll be in hospital for another week.'

A week, he thought. We'll have a whole week together. He said, 'I simply couldn't spare the time to visit him. Just as well, I suppose. This uniform would not be a welcome sight in the hospital. I believe the wards are still full with the Bachelor's Walk victims.'

'Yes,' she said in a low voice, staring at the fire. She was silent for a few seconds, then she said in the same flat, low tone, 'In the bed beside William, there's a boy of fifteen who will be crippled for life. And directly opposite, with a screen round the bed, there's a young man who had half of his jaw shot away. He was to be married in a few weeks, a nurse told me.' She shuddered a little. 'Terrible,' she whispered, 'terrible . . .' Then her voice turned bitter. 'And William Durkin lies there with his arm in a sling, laughing and joking. Lucky Durkin, he calls himself. Always manages to get out of the tightest of corners. Even when the British Army shoots at him, they can't even aim straight. And the crippled and the mutilated lie there quietly and listen to him.'

'Please, Miriam, don't upset yourself.'

'No, Alec. Let me talk about it. I want to. I sit beside his bed and listen to all his boastful talk, and I can feel the silence from the other beds. I can feel the hate and resentment building up around us. Sometimes I feel like screaming at him to shut up. But I don't. I just sit there and say nothing. I just sit there and ask myself how he can be so insensitive with all that suffering around him. You would imagine he would keep quiet, content to just lie there thanking God for having escaped so lightly. And he *has* escaped lightly compared to those other poor victims in the ward. The child crippled for life, the young man with half his face missing.' She began to weep. 'God forgive me, but when I first visited him in hospital after the Bachelor's Walk shooting, when I saw it was just a shoulder wound, I thought, if only that soldier had aimed a little more to the right. I never knew I could think things like that. Never.'

He put his arm around her shoulders. 'Don't talk any more about it,' he murmured gently. 'Let's talk about ourselves instead.'

'Do you remember when I broke off our affair?' she said. 'I deliberately pushed you out of my mind and tried to start all over again with William. I became the ideal wife: caring, loving, passionate even, when I knew that was the way he wanted me to be.' She sighed. 'But it was all pretence – and one can never remain like that for very long. Gradually I lapsed back into the way I had been before. After a while I became despondent. All I could see ahead of me was a long lonely life, shared with a man I detest.'

Silence fell between them. They sat holding hands, staring at the fire. We're like a middle-aged married couple, he thought, content just to be in each other's company.

After a while she said, 'Each evening on my way to the hospital to

366

visit William, I see the troops marching down the quays towards the docks on their way to France. I stand and watch them, searching for your face.'

He laughed gently. 'I'm a desk wallah. The fighting is for the other poor devils.'

'But they could send you to France?'

'Highly unlikely. I'm needed here in Ireland. The nationalists won't let this war pass without trying something.'

'Will you be in danger?' she asked, raising her head to look at him.

He smiled and shook his head. 'We now know who the trouble-makers are. We have them under close watch. If they try to start a rebellion, we can easily nip it in the bud.'

'Have you thought of what you are going to do about us?'

It was his turn to be silent for a while. 'I can't resign my commission until this war is over, Miriam.'

'Oh, God.'

'Don't say that. Don't despair.'

'This war could last for years.'

'It doesn't have to affect us. We don't have to wait until it ends. Just be patient for a little while longer, that's all I ask. Billy Durkin's usefulness is coming to an end. When we no longer need him, I'll tell him about us. I'm sure he'll agree to a divorce. Then we can be married. When this war ends, I'll leave the army and return to Carewscourt. It will be a different Carewscourt from the one you remember, Miriam. It won't be that big, gloomy barracks of a place that terrified you. The top floor and the north wing are going to be demolished, and I intend to electrify the place, using wind-power. It's perfectly feasible . . .'

He stopped when he saw her smiling. Then he grinned. 'I do get carried away, don't I?'

'Like a little boy with his first train set.'

'The last time I was in Carewscourt, I remember thinking: What an empty place it is without Miriam. I thought I had lost you. But everything's different now.'

'I'm so happy it frightens me,' she said, resting her head on his shoulder. 'I feel we'll have to pay a price for this happiness of ours. I don't know why I should feel like this. Perhaps it's because I've been so unhappy all the years I've been married to William. Now when I do find true happiness, it makes me uneasy. I'm filled with foreboding.'

'Perhaps your forebodings are justified. Billy Durkin may agree to a divorce or he may not. He could turn nasty and write about us in the

*Eye-Witness* in his own particular venomous style. He could paint you as the greatest Jezebel in Ireland.'

'I don't think I'd care. But you will have to face censure from your superiors. You will also have to face the cries of outrage from the Castle clique.'

'Perhaps, perhaps not. Maybe the war will change people's attitudes. Infidelity is just another casualty of wartime. The long separations; the boredom of those who stay at home.'

'We could be worrying needlessly,' she said. 'William may consider a knighthood suitable recompense. That is if he ever gets one. He has the impression he's been fobbed off with empty promises.'

Carew sighed. 'His long wait is nearly over. The shooting and wounding by British soldiers of a man working for Military Intelligence created a good deal of embarrassment in certain circles. A knighthood would be one way of compensating him.'

She stared at the fire, grim-faced. 'People are shot and killed,' she said quietly, with bitterness in her voice, 'maimed and mutilated, but William survives and gets a knighthood. Lucky Durkin.'

He squeezed her hand. 'Not so lucky,' he whispered.

# Chapter Fifteen

I

The massive prison gate closed with the sound of muffled thunder. Gallagher walked away down the long drive without looking back. He carried a brown paper parcel containing a spare shirt and socks. He crossed the road and turned the corner into Berkeley Road. Only then did he experience a sense of relief. The prison was out of sight and now he really felt free.

He turned left into Eccles Street. People were coming down the steps of the hospital. Visiting hour was over. He could feel their eyes on him as he marched past. He was suddenly conscious of his shabby worn jacket and cropped hair – the mark of a convict. He increased his pace, his face burning with shame. It was only four-thirty in the afternoon, but already dusk was gathering. The distant spire of a church was lost in a smoke-blue haze. He strode on, feeling the cold January air against his skin. He had been released three days early. What a surprise Una will get, he thought. She was not expecting him until Monday.

Respectable middle-class houses gave way to slums. No longer was he conscious of his appearance; here no one cared what he looked like. A group of men were lounging outside a seedy public-house. As he walked past a voice hailed him. He turned and a man detached himself from the group and came towards him. At first Gallagher did not recognise the thin figure with the cap and shabby clothes. Then the narrow gnarled face came into view.

'Hello, Kit.'

Kit Byrne displayed broken, tobacco-stained teeth in a wide grin. He gripped Gallagher's arms. 'The hard man,' he croaked delightedly. 'Jasus, but I'm glad to see yeh.'

Gallagher smiled. 'It's nice to be back among friends, Kit.'

Kit released his grip. 'Come in and have a pint.'

Gallagher, keenly aware of his empty pockets, shook his head. 'Some other time, Kit. The missis will be waitin'.'

'Ah, come in outa that. She's been waitin' this long, a little longer won't make any difference.' He held up a finger. 'One pint,' he declared solemnly, 'one pint and no more. Then I'll let yeh go home to yer love-nest.'

Gallagher shrugged helplessly and followed him into the pub.

The public-house was nearly full. Gallagher was surprised. When he went to prison during the lock-out, public-houses in the working-class areas had been closed from lack of custom.

'There doesn't seem to be any shortage of money,' he said.

'The war,' Kit shouted above the hubbub and called for two pints. Gallagher sat on a high stool, resting his back against the wooden partition of the snug. Kit placed a pint of stout in his hand and Gallagher took one long swig.

Kit grinned at the look of contentment on Gallagher's face after he had swallowed. He produced a packet of Woodbines and offered one.

'Did the swine give yeh a hard time of it, Con?' he asked gently, striking a match.

Gallagher inhaled deeply, and nodded. 'Hard enough, Kit.'

'Fifteen months,' Kit breathed. 'Jesus, but that was a savage sentence.'

Gallagher felt wonderfully relaxed now with his drink and cigarette. It had been so long since he had either. 'Robbery and assault, resistin' arrest. They made an example of me, Kit.'

'It was all in the newspapers,' Kit said. 'Do yeh know who the fella was yeh robbed and beat up?'

'A fat pig named Durkin. Funny, I'm sure that's the same bastard I had a dust-up with years ago in Westland Row railway station.'

'Durkin publishes that rag the *Eye-Witness*,' Kit said. 'He wrote a book for the Employers' Federation durin' the lock-out. Of course, Durkin whitewashes the employers, describin' them as noble, upright, conscientious men defendin' the Christian way of life against godless socialism. Bullshite!' he growled and gulped down a mouthful of stout. His eyes narrowed dangerously. 'It's a pity yeh didn't finish off the bastard when yeh had the chance, Con. But no matter, I'll get the hoor meself one of these days. I know him to see.'

Gallagher reached for his pint on the counter. It was then Kit noticed the white scar above the ear. 'Christ,' he hissed, 'the bastard must have near opened yer skull with his baton!'

Gallagher, glass to his mouth, shrugged. He took a swallow and showed the scarred palms of his hands. 'I got meself a couple o' weeks in hospital, though.'

370

Kit grinned maliciously. 'But the police are not the cocks of the walk they used to be. No, be Christ! We've a Citizen Army now.' He nodded in affirmation to Gallagher's curious stare.

'Aye, the strikers took enough of their batonin'. We organised ourselves into companies and got an ex-Army man to train us. We've uniforms and rifles now.'

Gallagher shook his head slowly in amazement. 'Holy God, the whole world is gone bloody mad. War; private armies . . . I feel like I've been in prison for fifteen years, not fifteen months!'

'Most of the National Volunteers joined the British Army at John Redmond's request,' Kit went on. 'Only a few thousand left who are willin' to fight for an Irish Republic.'

'So the Citizen Army and the Volunteers are allies, is that it?' Gallagher asked. He was a little confused.

'No, that's not it,' Kit answered sourly. 'The Volunteers want a free Ireland, but the Ireland they want is a hell of a lot different from the Ireland we have in mind. Oh, I grant yeh, there are many Volunteers who are sympathetic to the socialist cause, but there's plenty more who look down on us and call us Marxists and anarchists and rabble-rousin' agitators and the like. Their Commander-in-Chief told us straight to our faces that he didn't want anythin' to do with an organisation that's in conflict with the police. How about that, eh?' he spat. 'There's yer patriotic Irishman for yeh!'

Same old Kit, Gallagher thought with tender amusement, still the same old fire-brand.

'I'm tellin' yeh, Con, if the British left Ireland tomorrow and the people who are in command of the Volunteers took over, there would be no difference in the way of things. We would still be livin' in the stinkin' slums scrapin' for a livin' and fightin' the police. And if we got outa control, they would call out the army, only the soldiers we'd be fightin' would be wearin' green uniforms and not khaki, and that'd be the only difference.' He dropped the butt to the floor and lit another cigarette. Then he leaned forward towards Gallagher. 'Let me tell yeh, Con, there were many in the Volunteers who were rubbin' their hands with glee when the lock-out ended and we had to crawl back to the employers with our tails between our legs. They thought we were finished – broken. They thought the Transport Union was finished and the Citizen Army along with it. And they were nearly right. The Union funds were exhausted and the Citizen Army began to break up as the men went back one by one to work. But things have changed for the better since this war started. The Union is gettin' back on its feet and the Citizen Army is reformin'.'

Kit talked on and on and Gallagher sat there, nodding now and then but not really listening, his mind on other things. When Kit stopped to take a swig from his glass, he took advantage of the pause.

'Listen, Kit, I've got to get work. I've *got* to. I can never go through again what I went through before. I'll take anythin' that's goin'. I don't give a damn what it is!'

Kit said nothing for a while. He sat on the high stool with the pint glass in his hand, the cigarette drooping from his lower lip, his face screwed up in thought. 'Well,' he said slowly, 'things were pretty bad on the docks for a time. After the lock-out was over, many of the lads who had been out found themselves on the blacklist. But things are improvin' – the war's changed everythin'. The factories are workin' full blast with all kinds of contracts. I hear they're even goin' to make munitions out in Parkgate. Money's beginnin' to flow like water. This is goin' to be a long war.' He grinned and winked at Gallagher. 'Don't fret, boy. I got me job back and so will you. I'll see about it first thing on Monday mornin'.'

Gallagher felt a lump in his throat. The past fifteen months had been a nightmare. Now, at last, there was a glimmer of hope; a chance to climb out of the deep bog of despair; a chance to regain his self-respect. He lowered his head, afraid Kit would see the tears forming in his eyes.

Kit snorted, trying to hide his embarrassment. 'Ah, will yeh go on outa that.' He swiftly changed the subject. 'How's the missis?'

Gallagher raised his head and shrugged. 'Oh, she's all right. She's workin' in a factory in Stafford Street. The money's fair.'

They became aware of a band playing in the distance, the brass notes harsh and strident. A hush fell on the bar as everyone paused to listen to the jaunty, rollicking martial air.

Kit Byrne was the first to break the silence. 'There they go,' he declared with pity in his voice, 'another batch movin' out. A few weeks from now, they'll be in the trenches. Poor buggers.'

Conversation slowly started again as the sound of the band faded away. Kit pointed a warning finger at him. 'Whatever yeh do, keep clear of Sackville Street. The place is swarmin' with recruitin' sergeants tryin' to coax every man that passes into takin' the shillin'. If yeh have to join an army, join the Citizen Army and fight for the workin' classes and not for any effin' King or Empire. It's the workin' class of Europe that's fightin' and dyin' in this bloody war, while the capitalists are makin' fortunes from munitions and guns and everythin' else that can kill or maim. Jasus, will we ever learn!'

Here we go again, Gallagher thought. It was time to leave. He drained the glass. 'Thanks for everythin', Kit,' he said, taking the paper parcel from the counter.

Kit waved his thanks aside. 'Ah, for what?' He gave a crude grin. 'There's nothin' like a pint of stout to give a man strength. And yeh'll need it when yeh get home. Man, she'll be sittin' by the fire waitin' and pantin' for the sound of yer footsteps on the stairs. Away with yeh now, outa that.' Kit's shout halted Gallagher at the doorway. 'Hey, Con, don't overdo it. Yeh'll need all yer strength for work on Monday mornin'!'

Gallagher grinned. 'You can't talk,' he retorted, 'you with four at home.'

'Five,' Kit crowed, raising his glass, 'five we have now and another on the way. Sure with me outa work and all that time on me hands, what the hell else was there for me to do!'

The cold air made him shiver as he walked into the street. He pulled the collar of his jacket up about his neck and strode on. He headed east, through narrow slum streets. Kit was right; the war had changed everything. The last time he had walked through these streets, an air of apathy and despair had hung over them. Now it was like the old days before the lock-out. Gossiping women clustered about the open doorways; children played in the gutters; the small dingy shops of the neighbourhood had re-opened and were doing a roaring trade.

There were khaki uniforms everywhere. He had to weave through a crowd of gaping admirers surrounding one returned hero. The soldier stood with his back against the lamp-post, cap pushed back from his forehead.

'Jasus, I'm tellin' yez,' he exclaimed, 'I never saw anythin' like it in all me natural. There we were, rifles at the ready, and chargin' towards us, whole squadrons of Uhlans with lances the length of the bloody street!'

Gallagher turned the corner and down towards the tenement he lived in. Two elderly women standing at the corner of the laneway stared at him with naked curiosity. He ignored them. He mounted the broken steps and walked into the dark hallway.

He was unprepared for the stench after such a long absence; it made him almost retch. Holding his breath, he climbed the stairs slowly. As he neared the top flight, he could feel the banister wobbling under the weight of his hand. He paused and explored cautiously with his foot. Most of the banister-rails were missing. During the long bitter months of the lock-out, the tenements had been cannibalised of anything that would burn. The banister-rails must have been the last when every-

373

thing else had been used up. Safety had been sacrificed for a little comforting warmth. The stupidity of it made him fume. Una staggered up these stairs every day carrying buckets of water from the back yard. If she should stumble and fall . . . He drove the thought from his mind and continued up, the banister trembling under his hand like a frightened animal.

He opened the door, and stood in the doorway. He could hear the clock ticking in the darkness. Una was not home yet. The factory closed at six o'clock and she would not arrive till half-past. He closed the door and groped his way in the dark towards the fireplace. He found the matches on the mantelshelf and struck one, then walked to the table on which the oil-lamp stood. Placing the paper parcel down beside it, he removed the glass chimney and applied the match-flame to the wick. Then he replaced the chimney and straightened up and looked around.

The room, with its few miserable pieces of furniture, was as he remembered it. Most of what little they had possessed had been sold or pawned for money to buy food during the lock-out. But now he could see that a few things had been added. There were new ornaments on the mantelshelf and there was an armchair facing the fireplace. He walked over and examined it. It was second-hand but in good condition. How she must have scrimped and saved out of the little she earns to buy that, he thought with pride. The room was cold. He lowered himself to his hunkers before the fireplace and struck a match. He remained in the same position until the small mound of coal and sticks and tightly rolled newspaper were well alight, then stood up slowly, groaning a little. There was stiffness in his limbs and he could feel weariness creeping over him. He had been unable to sleep the night before; the thought of being released the following day had kept him awake all night. He sat down on the armchair and leaned back with a sigh of contentment. What a surprise she'll get, he thought, when she opens the door and sees me sitting here. He closed his eyes, feeling the heat of the fire against his legs. A minute later he was fast asleep. The dreams that came to him were pleasant ones, full of joyous surprises.

He opened his eyes slowly, blinking. The black fireplace filled his vision. He stared at it dazedly, not knowing where he was. The clock ticked loudly above his head and in the distance he could hear the sounds of a drunken brawl. His awakening senses gradually absorbed it all. Full realisation was like a physical blow.

Time passed slowly. He lay stretched in the armchair, twisted a little to one side like a man in pain, his knuckles pressing his eyelids shut.

374

The clock ticked away remorselessly and from the street below a woman was singing in a drawling drunken voice.

A sigh escaped him and he took his hands away from his eyes. Then he straightened up slowly in the chair. He felt like a recaptured prisoner waking up in his dismal cell after a short spell of precious freedom, with nothing but a sweet memory to sustain him throughout the years ahead. He rose to his feet on stiff cramped legs. The fire was just a heap of smouldering ash in the grate. He experienced a shock when he looked at the clock. My God, he thought, have I been asleep that long?

He could feel anxiety mounting. Where could she be at this hour? He tried to console himself with the thought that she might be working overtime. He sat down and waited. Now and then he stood up to glance at the clock, then sat down again. Each time his anxiety grew. Ten o'clock; ten-thirty. By ten forty-five he was pacing the floor. Where the hell is she?

He came to a halt between the table and the door when he heard the footstep on the landing outside. The door opened. She came to an abrupt halt when she saw him standing there and her hand flew to her throat.

He realised he was standing with his back to the oil-lamp and that his face was in shadow. 'It's all right, Una,' he said quickly, 'it's me, Con. They let me out before my time was up.'

She remained frozen in an attitude of sudden fright. She wore a wide-brimmed hat and a long dark coat. The coat was open and underneath he could see a soiled working-smock.

Then she closed the door slowly and took a few faltering steps towards him. He advanced to meet her. Something about her face made him stop. There was a slackness of the mouth and her eyes were curiously blank. He thought it was fatigue until she came up to him, then he caught the smell of drink on her breath.

He stood still, unable to move with the shock, his arms hanging down by his sides. She placed her hands on his shoulders and pushed her face up to his, her mouth twisted in a loose-lipped foolish grin. When she kissed him he could taste the whiskey on her mouth. He twisted his head away in disgust and took a step back. 'You're drunk!' He heard his own shocked voice repeating: 'You're drunk!'

She stared at him blankly, not quite comprehending the reason for his sudden anger. He glared at her with fury and pain in his eyes as she swayed unsteadily on her feet.

The look of revulsion on his face startled her. Shame and humiliation cleared the fog from her brain. Then a rush of anger followed. She was angry for having allowed herself to fall into this drunken state, and angry with him for catching her unawares by arriving home too soon.

'What of it?' Her voice was shrill. 'What if I am? I . . . I need somethin' . . . somethin' . . . I work hard . . . I need somethin' to . . . to make me forget all of this . . .' She waved her hand about indicating the room and almost lost her balance. She staggered sideways on high-heeled shoes and grabbed the table for support. The oil-lamp wobbled dangerously.

He made no attempt to help her. He stood motionless, watching, not wanting to touch her.

'It's easy for you to talk,' she mumbled, and hiccuped slightly.

'Who were you with?' he demanded, trying to keep his voice steady.

The blank eyes met his, then wavered. 'Friends, just friends . . .' Then she glared angrily at him when she saw the suspicious look on his face. 'It's not what you think!' and her voice rose to that shrill note again. 'You can wash that that filthy thought from yer mind once and for all!' Tears began to form in her eyes. 'How dare you, how dare you think such a thing? I'm not like that.'

'Then tell me – who were you with?' He lost all control. 'Tell me who you were with!' he roared, 'or by Christ I'll . . .' He raised his fist and she cowered back in terror.

Then the words began to tumble out in her haste to explain. 'Some of the girls from the factory, their fellas had joined up and they were being sent out to France and they wanted to see them off and, and the rest of us went with them for company . . . just for company. That's all. And after the ship had sailed, everyone was cryin' and . . . and there was this public-house . . .' Her voice faded to a whisper and he could see the terror in her eyes as she stared at his raised fist.

He lowered it, remembering the last time he had stood in this room, she crouched terrified against the window, the mark of his blow on her face. He turned his back to her and walked over to the fireplace. He stood before it, hands gripping the edge of the mantelshelf. 'How long has this been goin' on for?' he asked in a low voice.

'What do yeh mean?'

He could feel his control snapping again. 'Jesus Christ!' he rasped, darting a savage look over his shoulder. 'This drinkin'!' he snapped. 'What the hell else do you think I mean?'

Her reply came hesitatingly, her voice tremulous with nerves. 'A . . . a while. When we get paid, some of the women I work with and myself . . . Well, why shouldn't I? What else is there for me to do? All the time here on me own. Fifteen months of it, being on me own. Sittin' here night after night, starin' at the fire. I could feel the room closin' in on me. Why shouldn't I have a little drink? What's the harm in that? It makes me sleep an' . . . an' . . .'

Even the soft Connacht accent had gone. She now spoke in that flat nasal Dublin drawl that never failed to grate upon his nerves. He groaned silently, listening to the voice behind him, and thought: Christ above, this isn't happening. This is some bloody nightmare I'm having.

'Go to bed, Una!' he snapped.

There was a brief silence, and then he heard her short unsteady footsteps coming towards him. She placed a gentle hand on his shoulder but he shrugged it away without turning around.

'Go to bed,' he said again, speaking to the clock in front of him. 'Go to bed,' and then between clenched teeth: 'and sleep it off!'

She moved away slowly towards the bed and he could hear her sobbing quietly while she undressed. Then the bed creaked as she climbed into it. He remained standing before the fireplace, hands resting on the mantelshelf. He longed desperately for a cigarette to calm his overwrought nerves. He stood like that for a long time, waiting for her to fall asleep. Then he turned about and started to undress. He put his mouth over the glass chimney of the oil-lamp and blew out the flame, then tiptoed towards the bed on bare feet. He drew back the bedclothes and climbed in, then turned away from her, keeping to the edge of the bed. He closed his eyes and tried unsuccessfully to sleep. In his mind a nagging voice kept repeating: is this the way it's going to be from now on? What will she be like twenty years from now?

A picture began to take shape behind the closed eyelids. He could see a dingy snug at the end of a bar and the gossiping crones within, crouched around a table, glasses of porter in their withered hands. He could see her among them, a black shawl round her shoulders, straggling wisps of grey hair hanging down over her face. Flat nasal accents drawled in his ear with startling clarity: the petty scandals, the lewd jokes and her screeches of wild laughter, bawdy and coarse like the laughter that drifted up from the lane outside at night.

Con moaned aloud and was immediately aware of her stirring at the sound. He tensed as she sidled up against his back and laid a tentative hand on his side. Then the whispered apologies began to slur away against his ear and he could smell the sour fumes of whiskey on her breath.

He lay rigid, trying to ignore the entreaties for forgiveness and the whimpering cries of need.

Suddenly he twisted round with a muttered curse, unable to endure it any longer. He took her brutally, callously ignoring her cries of pain and protest, wanting to hurt and humiliate, wanting to destroy all feelings of love and tenderness she had for him. But when he rolled away, exhausted and satiated, it was with a feeling of horror and self-loathing. He lay on his side, listening to her muffled sobs. Now we've both degraded ourselves, he thought wearily.

He remained awake long after she had fallen asleep, listening to the ticking of the clock, listening to the rats gnawing away in the darkness.

## II

All sailings between Dublin and Liverpool had been cancelled due to the presence of German submarines in the Irish Sea. With everything on the docks at a standstill, all casual dockers had been sent home. Gallagher did not mind; in fact he was glad. The day was warm and sunny and he intended to make the most of it. He slowly drank his tea, then placed the mug down on the table and lit a cigarette.

'I was thinkin' we might go to the Phoenix Park,' he said. 'Then maybe take a stroll through the Zoo. Like the old days. Remember the times the chimpanzee snatched the cap from my head?'

She smiled at him from the other end of the table and nodded. Everything's going to be fine, he thought. They had passed through a long dark tunnel of pain and despair and in the darkness had almost lost each other, but that was all in the past. Happiness made him feel generous.

'Remember that hat you were admirin' in the window of that shop in Sackville Street? I'll buy yeh that, then we can get on the tram at Bachelor's Walk and . . .'

She protested that the hat was too expensive, but he grinned and waved a hand. She laughed at his extravagance and he thought; my God, the years I've been waiting to hear that. She continued to smile, sitting at the table with her needlework. He stared at her, a puzzled look on his face. 'Why do you keep smilin'?' he asked.

She shook her head, concentrating on her work, the enigmatic smile still on her face.

'Don't tease me, woman!'

She raised her head and looked at him. 'Oh,' she said, a mischievous look in her eyes, 'I'll tell you, eventually.'

'For God's sake!' but he relented and folded his arms and grinned at her. 'All right so, I can wait.'

'It might be a long wait,' she bantered.

'I'm a very patient man.'

She looked at him coyly, a blush spreading over her face. 'Well, if you must know . . .' but she was interrupted by the rapid pounding of feet on the stairs. There was a hasty knock, and the door was pushed open. Kit Byrne came into the room, panting. He was bareheaded and his face was a blotchy red and streaming with sweat.

'Con,' he began, then paused, gulping for air. He deliberately ignored Una, keeping his eyes firmly fixed on Gallagher. 'The dispute at the North Wall with the Steam Packet Company . . . About a dozen policemen beat up the picket we placed outside the shed where the office clerks are blackleggin'. They beat them up bad. Hanratty is in hospital . . . But that's not all. The police let it be known that they would be back in the afternoon. They said if they found another picket there, they would baton them into the ground!'

Una felt a swift rush of anger at Kit Byrne's intrusion. He was a firebrand, always urging violent action against the police. Now he had brought his violence with him into her home. She had been grateful when he had got Con's job back for him on the docks, but her gratitude had turned to hate when he had induced her husband to join the Citizen Army.

'Three lads are on picket now,' Kit went on, 'but they want protection. I've two men waitin' for me in the street outside, who are willin' to guard them. Then there's meself. How about you?'

Gallagher heard Una's sharp intake of breath. He said, 'Four men are not goin' to be much protection against twelve policemen with batons.'

Kit's voice was harsh. 'We're goin' to protect the picket with rifles!'

'Oh my God!'

Both men looked at Una. She sat at the table, her hand to her mouth, her face white.

Gallagher glared at Kit, silently cursing him for his big mouth and lack of tact.

'We're wastin' precious time, Con,' Kit snapped. 'There are three lads walkin' up and down on picket duty and we're standin' here jawin'. The police could be on their way this very minute. Are yeh comin' or are yeh not?'

Gallagher reached for his jacket and put it on.

Una rose to her feet as he reached the door. 'Don't go!' she implored. Kit was already half-way down the stairs.

'I have to,' he said helplessly, and ran from the room.

She followed him, hurrying down the stairs. 'Do you want to be sent back to prison again?' she wailed.

He stopped on the landing below and looked up. Her tear-stained face appeared over the banister-rail. 'Don't, Una,' he pleaded.

'They'll put you away for three years this time!' she shrilled. As he prepared to move away, she leaned over the banister-rail, and her weight made it tremble. His startled shout of warning made her move back hastily. He paused for a few seconds looking up, heart thumping, then moved away, running down the stairs. She made one last desperate attempt to hold him. 'There's a baby on the way!'

He halted in the doorway. So that's what she was about to tell me when Kit burst into the room, he thought. Then he ruthlessly drove all thoughts of her from his mind and ran down the steps.

He turned the corner into the laneway. Half-way down, Kit, Charley Norris, the carter, and another man were yoking the horse to the cart. Charley was another Citizen Army man whose cart on more than one occasion had been used for transporting smuggled arms and ammunition from the docks.

Kit walked into the stable and Gallagher followed. It was used as an arms dump by the local company: it was gloomy and smelled of hay, oats and horse-dung. They walked to a dark corner and shifted a bale of hay out of the way. Kit knelt and prised up a floorboard with the aid of a penknife. He reached into the opening and hauled up a bundle wrapped in oilskin. Gallagher took it from him, and carried it out and placed it on the cart, Charley Norris throwing two sacks over it. Then Kit walked out and bolted the stable door. He had a carton of ammunition stuffed into the pocket of his jacket. They climbed on to the cart, Charley taking the reins. The flick of a whip, the horse broke into a canter.

The cart rattled noisily over the cobbles. As it turned into the street, Gallagher saw the accusatory figure of his wife standing in the doorway, staring coldly at them. He turned guiltily away as Charley urged on the horse. 'Hupp, hupp!' They swayed to and fro with the wild motions of the cart. Charley flogged the horse unmercifully, keeping it at full gallop. The streets were bathed in sunlight. The loveliness of the day was like a reproach to Gallagher. He felt bitter resentment towards Kit Byrne. It seemed to him that the little happiness Una and he were trying to build was constantly under threat from outsiders.

From Custom House quay they turned left, heading east. The docks were quiet: it was lunchtime. In the distance they could see three men on picket duty, pacing up and down. Charley pulled hard on the reins when they reached them. Gallagher and Kit and the other man jumped down from the cart. One of the men on picket gave a sigh of relief.

'We thought ye were never comin',' he said. 'There was a polisman here about twenty minutes ago to see if another picket had been placed. When he saw us, he went hotfoot back to the station to tell his mates.'

Gallagher and Kit placed the bundle on the ground and unwrapped it. 'Charley,' Kit said, lifting his head, 'take the horse and cart out of sight. Down the side street there . . .'

The rifles were long and cumbersome. They were old Italian thumb-lock rifles, part of a consignment that had been smuggled in between slabs of marble. There were four. Kit Byrne gave one each to Gallagher and the other man and to Charley Norris when he rejoined them. Gallagher, Kit and Charley were Citizen Army men and well used to handling arms. The fourth man, a young docker by the name of Tommy Ward, held his rifle across his chest with both hands, staring at it in amazement. 'Holy God!' he exclaimed. 'When were these last used? The battle of Waterloo?'

'They'll do well enough!' Kit Byrne snapped.

'About six or seven of the office clerks who are blackleggin',' one of the men on the picket said, 'are havin' their lunch in that shed over there.'

Kit nodded grimly. 'Right – we'll fix those bastards!' He turned to the man who had spoken. 'You and yer mates parade up and down. Give us a shout if yeh see the police comin'.' He grinned and jerked a thumb towards the shed. 'We'll flush these hoors out. It's about time the scabs were taught a lesson.' He tugged the carton out of his pocket and began to distribute the ammunition. They loaded the rifles.

'Let's go,' Kit said. They walked across the road, into the shed. It was cool and gloomy inside. Six men were sitting round an upturned box, playing cards. A seventh looked on, smoking a pipe.

'Stay here,' Kit murmured. He strolled casually towards the card players, his rifle by his side. The man standing smoking the pipe saw him first. Shock and fright rooted him speechless to the spot.

'Who's winnin'?' Kit inquired genially.

They looked up and then they saw the rifle. One of them twisted around. When he saw three men with rifles standing in the entrance, he cringed, giving a low moan of despair. He was in shirt-sleeves like his companions. To show they were not ordinary working-men, they had retained their waistcoats and high stiff collars.

Kit's affability quickly vanished. 'Office clerks,' Kit growled contemptuously. 'Pen-pushers tryin' to do men's work.'

He kicked out savagely and sent the box flying. The clerks jumped to their feet and backed away against the wall as Kit walked slowly forward, the muzzle of his rifle pointing at them. Cards and money were scattered all over the floor.

'Listen, yeh scum. From now on, if we find any scabs workin' on these docks, we're not goin' to waste time warnin' them. Instead we're goin' to let bloody daylight through them!' He raised the rifle for emphasis.

They stared at him in silence.

'Now grab yer belongin's,' Kit ordered, 'and walk out ahead of me.'

There was an immediate scramble for jackets and hats. Relief showed on their faces; all of them had thought they were going to be shot. They hastened towards the entrance, Kit walking slowly behind. Gallagher and the two men moved aside to let them pass. But as they reached the road outside, Kit's shout brought them to a standstill.

They stood in the middle of the road, bunched together like frightened sheep, blinking in the strong sunlight. Kit ambled towards them, the rifle cradled in his arms. He knew they were going back to the firm that employed them to report what had happened. He came to a halt before them; then he smiled, revealing broken, tobacco-stained teeth.

'You lot look pale and flabby,' he said, eyes glinting mischievously. 'No exercise, that's what it is. Must be all that sittin' behind desks, tottin' up figures.' He indicated with a nod of the head. 'See the entrance to that street up there? The one with the pillarbox at the corner?'

All turned as one man and stared. A red pillarbox gleamed in the sun more than a hundred yards away.

'Right,' Kit said. 'Now yer all goin' to run towards it and I'm goin' to aim this rifle at yer backs. I'm goin' to count to thirty, and then I'm goin' to pull the trigger. If yer all not around that corner before I finish countin' . . .' He shook his head sorrowfully.

One of the clerks, a corpulent, pimply-faced man with glasses, protested in a squeaky voice. 'I can't run fast,' he whined, 'I've got flat feet.'

'You better run fast,' Kit said grimly, 'or yeh'll get a bullet up the arse!' Now that lunchtime was over, a crowd of dock workers were beginning to congregate. They stood about in groups, looking on with open amusement. The scabs were hated more than the police.

Kit raised his rifle and took aim. 'Start runnin'!' He began to count. 'One, two . . .'

The clerks backed away; then they turned about and ran. They started off at full pelt with the flatfooted man panting behind, mocked by the laughs and jeers of the onlookers. They had covered about thirty yards when they began to slow down from exhaustion. By the time they reached the pillarbox, they were almost on the point of collapse. Then Kit pointed the rifle towards the sky and fired.

Everyone looking on laughed uproariously as the exhausted clerks suddenly jerked into life and started to scramble frantically round the corner. Kit gave a howl of triumph. 'That's the way to settle strikes,' he yelled, 'a rifle in yer hand and not a bloody scab on the horizon!'

Gallagher was the only one who did not laugh. Kit's behaviour disturbed him. Kit had always been reckless; he was more so now with a rifle in his hands. He was like a fractious child with a dangerous toy. Gallagher thought of the coming encounter with the police. He was not going to allow murder to be committed.

Charley Norris wiped tears of laughter from his eyes. Then he remembered the cards and money the clerks had left behind. 'Hey, are we goin' to leave all that money lyin' about for someone else to pick up. There must be a few quid in there.'

They stood their rifles against the wall and hurried in. Gallagher remained outside. He had been wondering what to do about Kit; wondering how to render him ineffective. Now an opportunity had unexpectedly presented itself. He walked forward to where the rifles lay against the wall . . .

They picked up the money that lay scattered over the floor: there was a little over two pounds in copper and silver. Kit pocketed his share. 'We'll celebrate our victory over the scabs with a few pints later on,' he chuckled.

Charley Norris had gathered the cards together. 'How about a game of pontoon while we're waitin' for the police to show up?' Kit shrugged and Tommy Ward nodded. They were about to sit down when Gallagher gave a warning shout. They ran towards the entrance.

'They're a good distance away yet,' Gallagher said, looking west, shielding his eyes with his hand. 'They're marchin' in columns of three. Twelve men in all. Grab yer rifles,' he ordered, 'and then stay in here out of sight. We want to surprise them.' He raised his voice, shouting across to the three men on picket who were standing still, nervously watching the approaching police. 'Keep walkin' up and down. And don't keep lookin' in this direction. We don't want them to see us till the last minute.' He had taken command and they were obeying his orders without question, even Kit. Though he had been promoted to sergeant in the Citizen Army over Kit, he had never been resentful, he had to

383

concede that. 'Kit,' he said, 'when Tommy and myself walk out, you and Charley remain hidden. When the peelers march past, come out then and cover them from the rear. With ourselves facin' them and you two behind, they might think twice before startin' anythin'.'

He stood in the entrance, watching. The police were much nearer now, near enough for him to see the stripes on the sleeve of the man on the outside. As he watched, the sergeant rapped out an order. Batons suddenly appeared. Gallagher shot a glance at the picket. They had come to a standstill and were staring apprehensively at the oncoming police.

Gallagher gave a low whistle. They turned their heads towards him. He grinned and gave a nod of assurance. Then he turned to Tommy Ward standing behind him. 'When we walk out, keep a distance of about six feet between us.' Tommy nodded, licking his lips. He was tense and nervous and held the rifle awkwardly as though he was afraid of it.

'For God's sake,' Gallagher snapped, 'hold that rifle as though you know how to use it!' He turned away and watched the approaching police. When they were about thirty feet away from the picket, he said curtly, 'Come on,' and stepped out into the sunlight.

The police did not notice them; their attention was concentrated on the three men on picket who were standing helplessly like sheep about to be slaughtered. They marched towards them, batons swinging. One, a red-faced moustachioed giant striding alongside the sergeant, was grinning maliciously.

Gallagher's long legs took him across the road in three seconds. He halted at the edge of the footpath in front of the picket, facing the oncoming police, rifle held loosely in his hands, the butt resting against his hip-bone. Tommy Ward took a position a few feet away and a little behind him. The police came to a stumbling halt. The three in front halted so suddenly, those behind marched right into them, pitching them forward. The portly sergeant was almost thrown on his face. Within seconds, the confident aggression and smart marching discipline was gone. A bunch of surprised, confused figures stood before him.

'That's as far as you go!' Gallagher shouted.

They stared at him dumbly from a distance of fifteen feet. The sergeant was the first to recover. 'You men are under arrest,' he announced authoritatively. 'For illegal possession of arms and obstructing officers of the law in the course of their duty.'

Gallagher grinned. 'Sergeant, tell your men to go back the way they came. Because if you don't . . .' He raised the rifle and took aim. Tommy Ward did likewise.

The sergeant gnawed at his chin-strap, undecided. The constable beside him took a step forward, his face twitching.

Gallagher rapped out a warning. 'If that red-faced hoor on your left takes one more step, I'll blow his bloody head away!'

The sergeant shot out a restraining arm. He glared at Gallagher. 'I'm giving the pair of you one more chance. Hand up those rifles!'

Gallagher could feel his heart beginning to beat faster. This was the moment of truth. For years, the police had bullied and harassed the Dublin workers without fear of reprimand. For the first time they were being openly challenged. The docks were coming alive. Word of what was happening had spread like wildfire and the dockers had stopped working. A huge crowd of them were watching a distance away.

Gallagher decided to help the sergeant make up his mind. He could see Kit and Charley outside the shed, rifles at the ready. 'Don't shoot till I give the word, Kit,' he shouted.

The police whirled around. Gallagher could see the naked looks of dismay when they saw that they were covered front and rear.

'Give the order to charge, sergeant,' Gallagher warned grimly, 'and we'll wipe out half of you with two volleys before you even get half-way!'

A sudden hush fell. No one moved. The crowd of dockers looked on with bated breath.

Then the sergeant heaved a sigh and placed his baton back in its leather case. He barked an order for his men to do likewise. He glared at Gallagher. 'We'll be back – and we'll have the military with us.'

'Do that,' Gallagher said, 'and we'll have the entire Citizen Army waitin' for you. And when the shootin' starts, every Irish soldier servin' at the front will be notified. Take that message back with you and make sure it's understood.'

The sergeant gave an order and they reformed into columns of three and marched away. Gallagher lowered his rifle, watching their retreating backs. He could hear Tommy Ward's huge sigh of relief and turned his head. Tommy was wiping the sweat from his forehead. 'Jesus,' he breahed, 'that was close. I thought any minute they were goin' to charge.' He shot a worried look at Gallagher. 'If they had – would you have fired?'

Gallagher shrugged. 'How the hell could I? I emptied the rifles when you three were in the shed.' Tommy Ward's mouth dropped open and Gallagher laughed at the look of consternation on his face.

Gallagher lay on his back on the tarpaulin-covered crate and watched the seagull hovering almost motionless against the cloudy autumn sky. It was lunchtime and he felt full and drowsy after his meal. The taste of bread and cheese and hot sugary tea was still in his mouth. A cigarette now and his contentment would be complete, but the effort of rising and searching the pockets of his jacket for the crumpled packet of Woodbines seemed too great. He preferred to lie still, feeling the September breeze cooling his sweat-covered body, listening to the voices of the other men resting nearby. They were talking about some big battle that was going on at a place called Loos . . .

People, he thought, talk of nothing else these days. It was the thirteenth month of the war and already the combined casualties exceeded five million. The death of friends brought it all sharply home. Tim Murphy, Jim Gannon, Billy Myers, lads from neighbouring streets. 'Snowball' Brannigan had come home minus both legs and Mick O'Toole was blind for life.

He shifted his thoughts to pleasanter things. Una was big with child now and feeling a little helpless. Soon it would be all over. Next summer, he thought, or maybe the summer of the following year, we'll take the child out to the clean fresh air of the Dublin hills, or maybe to Sandymount. I'll build a sandcastle, take him by the hand, paddle our feet in the little streams left by the outgoing tide.

'What's up, Willie?'

The half-shout from one of the men broke his reverie. He raised himself a little, resting his weight on an elbow, and turned his head.

A youth, face flushed and perspiring from hard running, stood panting several yards away. Gallagher recognised him; he came from the same street as himself. The man shouted the same question again and the youth's eyes swept over the faces of the men, some of whom were climbing to their feet, sensing trouble. Then he caught sight of Gallagher and tensed.

Gallagher could feel fear twisting inside him like a knife. He scrambled to his feet and grabbed his jacket and cap.

The youth began to stutter, unnerved by the terrible look on Gallagher's face. Gallagher caught the words 'accident' and 'banisters' and grabbed him by the lapels of his shabby jacket.

'Where is she?' he demanded fiercely.

'Hospital.'

He broke into a run, seeing in his mind the banister-rail bursting apart and the swollen body of his wife hurtling down the stairwell. By the time he reached Butt Bridge he was completely out of breath. He leaned over, chest heaving, seeing the water below through a red mist. When his breathing returned to normal he ran on, pushing people out of the way, unaware of the curious stares as he raced along the footpath. Charging across the road towards the hospital, he narrowly missed being run down by a tram.

The hall-porter tried to calm him. He gripped him, holding him steady. When he had pacified him, he led him by the arm towards the waiting-room.

'Aisy now, aisy, she's in good hands. Now, will yeh like a good man sit here and wait and try and get a grip on yerself, because yer not doin' yerself any good behavin' like this.'

The man's soothing voice and easy manner calmed Gallagher. He sat on the bench in the small waiting-room, oblivious to the stares of other people there, twisting his cap in his hands, feeling the turbulent emotions slowly draining from him. After a while, he reached into his pocket and pulled out the packet of Woodbines and lit one. He sat leaning forward, elbows resting on knees, smoking and brooding.

He castigated himself for not having made the banister-rail more firm. Then reason intervened and he told himself he had done everything possible. The whole damn house was crumbling from dry rot. Time and again he had inserted pieces of wood as substitutes for the missing rails, but when he tried to drive in the nails, parts of the banister came away in this hands. It's a miracle, he told himself, the house has not collapsed into the street, like the tenements in Church Street.

Kit is right, he admitted, the whole system is rotten and corrupt. Huge profits were made by the slum landlords. Cram as many as possible into the tenements and make them pay, seemed to be the motto. Many of the houses were owned by high officials in the Corporation who neglected to carry out necessary repairs. By God, he thought, the only way to change things is with a rifle in your hands.

The clock above his head ticked away the time. Outside, the light was fading from the sky. A porter came in and switched on the lights and drew the curtains. Con sat twisting the cap between his hands and waited.

He was falling into a doze when a hand touched his shoulder. He looked up to see a nurse standing over him. He followed her down a long corridor, conscious of the loud sounds his heavy boots were making.

A doctor was outside the closed doors leading to a ward. He was tall and thin with a young solemn face and serious brown eyes that regarded Gallagher dolefully through horn-rimmed glasses. They seemed to be too big for him, for he continually kept pushing them up his long thin nose. He did not speak until the nurse had gone.

'Your wife, Mr Gallagher,' he began, and paused. Gallagher stared at him and waited, a sick feeling in his stomach. 'Is going to be fine.' He smiled and pushed the glasses up the long bony ridge of his nose. 'Yes,' he said and nodded, 'she's a very lucky young woman.'

Gallagher's mouth was dry. She could not survive a fall like that, he thought, without some kind of injury.

'And the baby?' he managed to croak. He waited for the answer, knowing he was going to hear the worst. Just be thankful, he told himself, Una has been spared.

The doctor smiled again and placed a hand on his shoulder. 'Don't worry. She's going to have a fine healthy baby. When she fell, she hit the wall sideways. Somehow she managed to retain her balance and didn't fall down the stairs. A badly bruised shoulder, though. And she suffered a nasty bump on the side of the head. Otherwise, apart from shock, she's fine.'

Gallagher gulped painfully; for one horrible moment he thought he was going to burst into tears. He took a deep breath. 'Is it all right if I . . . if I . . .'

The doctor nodded. 'Yes, certainly. But don't stay too long. We've given her something, so she may be a little drowsy.' He opened the door. 'Down at the end,' he said in a low voice. 'The bed with the screen round it.'

Gallagher crept between the beds in his heavy boots, trying to avoid making any noise, the curious stares of the women patients on him. He was thankful for the screen they had placed round the bed; it gave them a little privacy.

She lay still with her eyes closed, the bedclothes drawn up to her chin. One side of her forehead was swollen, the skin a purplish-black. He lowered himself slowly on to the chair, not wanting to wake her. The chair gave a slight creak and her eyes flickered. He leaned forward and whispered: 'Una.'

She looked at him with blank drugged eyes.

'Everything's goin' to be all right,' he said softly. She continued to stare mutely as he went on, assuring her that the baby was fine, telling her that things were going to change for the better. 'And when you come home – '

She interrupted him, her voice harsh. 'I'm not going back.'

He looked down at her with a puzzled frown. 'What do you mean?'

She said slowly and deliberately: 'I'm not going back to that house ever again.' She turned her head. 'It killed my two babies. It nearly killed me and the baby I'm carrying.'

'But where will you go?' he asked after a short pause.

She faced him. 'I'm going back to Carewstown – back to my mother and father.'

His mouth fell open in dismay. 'You don't mean it,' was all he could say.

'Oh yes,' she said firmly, 'I do mean it. I'm going back. If I have to go down on my knees to my father and beg for his forgiveness, I'll do so. This baby is not going to be born in a stinking slum tenement. It's not going to be reared where there's diphtheria or consumption, all that filth and disease. I'm not going to lie awake all night fighting sleep, listening to the rats scraping away at the skirting, dreading that I might fall into a doze and then wake up to find one gnawing at my baby's face.' She spoke without emotion. Gallagher could find nothing to say.

'I'm going to bring up my child where there's plenty of clean fresh air and green fields to play in. Where there's plenty of simple, wholesome, nourishing food.'

He thought, Now I will have to tell her.

He waited until she had finished, then he told her, keeping his voice low and soothing, gently brushing back the hair from her forehead with the palm of his hand. There were tears in her eyes as he finished. 'I see,' she whispered.

Silence fell between them. She lay still, her eyes fixed on the ceiling. Eventually she said in a low voice, 'My father must be a very lonely man.'

Gallagher sighed. 'A changed man,' he said. 'The old bullyin' ways are gone. He was drinkin' heavily, the last I heard.'

'Loneliness,' she said after a while, 'is a terrible thing. Perhaps I will not have to go down on my knees and beg him to take me back. Perhaps he will receive me with open arms. We need each other now.'

He said in a low voice, 'I can't go back with you, Una. You realise that, don't you? If I went back to Carewstown they'd make me pay for what I did to Luke.'

'I don't expect you to go back with me,' she said wearily. 'I know right well what they would do to you.' She gave him a tender look. 'I'm not leaving you,' she said earnestly, 'don't think that. It will only be for a short while. Until the baby is a year old. That will give you enough

time to scrape some money together, then you can send for me. We'll
find some place. Galway, Clare . . . Kerry, even. I don't care where it
is. We could buy or rent a cottage with a patch of ground where we
could grow vegetables. And you could get work on one of the big farms.
You wouldn't have much trouble finding work on a farm with this war
on. But no more cities!' she uttered harshly. 'I don't want to live in a city
ever again!' He was aware of the silence in the ward. Beyond the screen,
he knew that every patient was listening to what they were saying.

'This baby is more important than both of us,' she murmured,
speaking away from him. 'I don't know what kind of reception I'll get
when I go back to Carewstown. If it's a hostile one, then I'll swallow my
pride and be repentant. I'll do anything to give our child a chance to
survive.' She sighed. 'We don't count any more, neither of us.' She
faced him once more. 'It wasn't this accident that made me decide what
I had to do. I was determined to do this a long time ago. Since the day
Kit Byrne called and dragged you into trouble on the docks. When I
heard about the rifles, I made up my mind there and then that I would
not allow you or Kit or any of those trouble-makers to bring distress
down on me or the child I'm carrying.' She stared steadily at him for a
full minute, then said quietly, 'Do you think I don't know where you go
to those nights when you arrive home late? Or those past few weekends
when you've been missing?' She paused, still staring intently at him.
'You've been in the hills with the others, haven't you, drilling with
rifles? And all this talk, all this talk about bombs being made and
ammunition being hoarded.' She glared at him. 'For what?' she hissed.
'What's it all for?'

He avoided her accusing stare.

She gave a little moan and closed her eyes. 'I have this terrible fear
that won't go away,' she whispered. 'I can see the same fear on the faces
of the people; a look of apprehension, as though they are expecting
something to happen.' She heaved a sigh. 'When I was a girl in the
convent,' she said in a faint faraway voice, 'there was a nun who told us
about this island somewhere where there was a volcano which rumbled
day and night. All the people who lived on the island were afraid, but
they went on living there. And still the volcano rumbled and rumbled
and sometimes belched smoke and flame. But the people on the island
did not leave. They just went on doing the same things day after day as
though everything was normal, ignoring the volcano, hoping it would
not explode, telling themselves that if they ignored it, it would
somehow stop its rumbling and die.

'When she told that story, I thought that was a terrible way to live. I

390

tried to imagine what it was like living like that, but I just couldn't.' She paused, and opened her eyes. 'But now I know what it's like,' she uttered softly in a trembling voice. 'We're sitting on a volcano in this city. We can hear the rumbling under our feet, and all we can do is wait and pray that it won't explode.'

# Chapter Sixteen

I

Myles Burke sat on a high stool at the end of the bar, his back against the wall, listening to the fierce argument going on in the dingy smoke-filled tavern. For the past hour he had sipped his port, observing and listening. Rough voices, mouthing loudly in Gaelic and English, had discussed politics, the fishing, the crops, the weather. Then someone had declared in a loud voice that the war would be over this coming summer. 'Summer, how are ye!' another voice had shouted derisively. 'Will ye have sense, man. Sure they haven't even started. Faith then, it won't be this summer or next summer or the summer after that again. This war is goin' to last for years!' An argument had developed.

Myles picked up his glass, his eyes wandering over the weather-beaten faces of the men before him. Big brawny men, dressed in high-necked woollen jerseys and rough homespuns: small farmers and fishermen. He felt conspicuous in his dark overcoat and hat, his high stiff collar and tie. A man near him tossed back his drink with an angry gesture, then plonked the pint glass down on the counter.

'And who the hell cares,' he shouted, 'if the Germans and the French and the English and the Russians bate the livin' daylights out of each other! What of our own country, aye? What about the men, women and children shot down in the streets of Dublin by British soldiers? What about them, aye?'

There was a sudden hush. It was the moment Myles had been waiting for. Say something, he told himself, before they start arguing about something else. His dry cracked voice broke the silence.

'The man is right. The English taught us a lesson. Now let us profit by it.'

All heads turned towards him. In the six weeks since his arrival at this isolated spot at the edge of the Atlantic, they had spread rumours about him. The latest one was that he was a professor from a Dublin university holidaying here in Connemara. Once he had overheard two

392

fishermen talking about him. 'Oh a very knowledgeable man. But nothin' stuck-up about him. Faith, no. Comes into the pub nearly every night for his glass of port and sits with the men and has a chat. Aye, begob, and several times stood a round of drinks for us all. Oh, a proper gentleman . . .' He had said nothing to discourage the gossip; his silence simply strengthened the belief they had in their own rumours.

He stared solemnly at them like a priest about to give a sermon. He spoke, slowly and deliberately, raising his voice so that everyone could hear.

'For years they've been promising us Home Rule. Then, when it's almost in our grasp, they allow the Ulster Unionists to bring in thousands of rifles and millions of rounds of ammunition to wreck it. And when the British Army is ordered north to wrest the arms away from them, every high-ranking officer from the Commander-in-Chief down refuses. So the Ulster Unionists drill openly with their illegal arms and the police look on and do nothing. Yet let any man here,' he declared, raising his voice higher and pointing a finger, 'let any man here walk through the village with an unlicensed, rusting fowling-piece in his hand and he will be clapped in gaol. When we are successful in bringing in arms like the Unionists, the British Army shoots down innocent civilians in revenge.' His mouth twisted in a sneer. 'And as for John Redmond and his Irish Parliamentary Party. Remember when he boasted he had Home Rule in the palm of his hand? Now he's going around the country enticing the young men to join the British Army and fight in this war – John Bull's favourite recruiting-officer.'

They stared in reverent silence, listening to every word. They were simple men, ignorant of the world beyond the boundaries of their own county. They accepted without question every word he uttered; he was after all a professor, a 'very knowledgeable man'.

'We should be grateful to the Ulster Unionists for leading the way. They challenged the British government with rifles in their fists and forced them to renege on their promise of Home Rule. Now that we have rifles, we can demand an independent Irish Republic.'

Someone at the back and out of sight raised his voice. 'Faith then, if it was only a yacht that brought them in, we mustn't have all that many.'

There's always a detractor in every crowd, Myles thought with a twitch of irritation. 'There was another landing off the Wicklow coast,' he answered sharply. 'But what if we have only less than two thousand rifles? We have enough to make a stand. We have enough to train men to be soldiers.' He paused, his eyes drifting from face to face. 'Remember this . . . if we intend to strike, let us do it before this war ends. If we wait until the war is over to demand independence, then England – if she wins – will smother this country with men and munitions and crush us. We are so weak; they are so strong.'

He lowered himself from the high stool buttoning his overcoat, still staring intently at them. 'What Ireland needs now is men of action – men who are not afraid to fight and die for her. If we let this golden opportunity pass, we will be condemned by future generations.'

He walked out into the moonlit darkness. He was only a few yards away from the tavern when he heard the voices rising in argument once again. He walked slowly up the village street, his boots crunching against the loose pebbles of the road. The statements he had just made were treasonable in wartime. What if they were repeated within earshot of a policeman? Every village had its blabbermouth. His mission as an IRB organiser was a secretive one; he had been cautious up to now, taking no risks. It was stupid exposing myself like that, he thought. Fintan would be furious if he knew.

'I'm too old for this job,' he muttered, 'too old.'

The village was behind him now and the track wound before him into the darkness. For the past twenty months he had been travelling these western counties of Mayo and Galway, going from town to town, village to village, acting as a salesman for school supplies, organising and recruiting for the Irish Republican Brotherhood. It had been necessary now and then to go back to Dublin to collect more samples and to confer with Fintan Butler. Then back again. First north to Castlebar, then west to Westport and Louisburgh, then south into Connemara. Clifden, Ballyconneely, Roundstone. Finally he had come here to Carna where he had been staying for the past six weeks, the longest he had ever stayed in one place. He would remain one more week with the Fahys, then move on to the city of Galway where he would try to recruit more men for the Brotherhood. After Galway, it would be back to Dublin for good, his mission completed.

How many men had he recruited and sworn in? He tried to remember: everything in the nature of written lists of names was tabu. The last had been the postmaster in Clifden; he went back from there. 'Nine,' he murmured after a while, 'only nine.' Not many for twenty months of painstaking work. Fintan should have sent a younger man, he told himself with a feeling of despair. He tried to console himself with the thought that those nine recruits would form IRB circles in their own districts. The moon was full and low and his lengthened shadow moved before him up the track. A harsh land, this Connemara; harsh, rugged and astonishingly beautiful. The sea was a mere fifty yards away

394

to his left and he could hear the waves breaking against the rocky shore. It was the only sound that broke the uncanny silence – that and his own plodding footfalls on the rough track. He was a city man and the silence of the countryside unnerved him. Stories he had heard sitting at the Fahys' fireside at night came back to haunt him. Tales of the Banshee and the Pooka and the *cóiste bodhar*, the death coach with its headless horses . . .

He shivered and increased his pace a little. Here, on the very edge of Europe, legends and superstitions were part of everyday life; here, reality and unreality were intertwined. In this wilderness he felt as if he were in another world. Dublin, with its bright lights and bustling activity, seemed a million miles away. He forced himself to think of other things. Think of the welcome you'll get from Dan Fahy when you walk into his kitchen, Myles told himself.

Dan: big, genial and easy-going. His wife, the opposite in temperament and physique: a tall gaunt woman from the Glenties, silent and shrewd. Myles could not remember ever having seen her smile. He had a feeling she resented his presence in the house.

Then there was Donal Ruadh, their son, a lad of seventeen. Tall and thin like his mother, with a thatch of fiery red hair and a face covered in freckles. He was a highly impressionable lad, easily excited.

His hand closed round the naggin of whiskey in his overcoat pocket. His present for Cait, Dan's mother, a woman of great age. Suddenly he realised he did not want to go back to Dublin. He wanted to stay here in Carna with the Fahys. He wanted to sit at their fireside on winter nights listening to their stories of ghosts and Banshees; he wanted to rest his back against the white-washed wall of their cottage on a summer evening, watching the sun slowly sinking below the rim of the ocean. He was almost seventy-four. I want to die here, he told himself.

He picked his way with care along the rough track in the moonlight, arguing silently with himself. Remaining here would be an act of desertion. Fintan Butler's last letter had contained a suggestion that something important was about to happen in Dublin. An insurrection? It was possible. He knew something was afoot. But the thought of ending his days here in peace and quiet and among friends had taken root. He could feel his sense of duty being eroded by an inner voice. *Don't go. Stay. You're too old . . . too old . . . too old . . .*

What more does Fintan expect of me? he whined to himself. I've done everything he asked of me. I've suffered enough for the cause – the best years of my life were spent in prison for it. What more can be expected of a tired old man?

He came slowly to a standstill in the centre of the track. In the distance he could see the lights of the Fahys' cottage winking in the darkness. He sighed wearily. I'll ask Dan to let me stay with them for good. I'll ask him first thing tomorrow morning. Fintan will understand, he thought. The night was mild. January was coming to an end and there was the scent of spring in the air.

He paused as he reached the door. He could hear voices inside. They were saying the Rosary. He could hear Dan voicing the Litany, his voice rising and falling.

> Morning Star . . .
> Help of . . .
> Refuge of Sinners . . .
> Comforter of the afflicted.

There was silence then, but he still waited a little while before entering and giving the traditional greeting, 'God save all here.'

'And forever treat ye kindly for yer prayer,' Dan responded, rising from his chair facing the fire. 'Come in and sit down, Myles,' indicating a low three-legged stool left of the fireplace. Donah Ruadh, sitting on his father's right, stood up in greeting. Dan's wife was busy at the kitchen-dresser: it was time for supper. An oil-lamp burned low on a kitchen table in the centre of the floor.

Myles reached into his overcoat pocket and took out the naggin of whiskey. He walked over to the old woman. A black shawl covered her head and face and most of her body. From under a long black skirt, two bare heavily veined feet peeped out. She went barefoot, winter and summer. Myles offered her the naggin of whiskey.

Dan started to protest. 'Ah shure, what are ye doin' things like that for? Ye have the old woman spoiled rotten . . .'

A thin, age-withered arm reached out and greedily grabbed the bottle and withdrew it into the folds of the shawl. The toothless mouth mumbled its thanks in Gaelic.

Dan sighed. 'I met a man on the road today,' he said, 'and him after drivin' down from Clifden. Well, the things he was after tellin' me . . .'

Dan's wife, grim-faced and silent, squeezed between her husband and son and lifted the simmering kettle from the hook over the turf fire. Dan moved his chair nearer to Myles to allow her free passage as she made her way back towards the table with the kettle. He had a broad good-natured face and a bald head: thick grey stubble covered his jaws and cheeks.

' "Dan," sis he, "the town was alive with police and sojers. Faith, I niver saw so many uniforms in one place. Well, didn't five Peelers stop me just outside Clifden and search the cart. And do ye know who was in charge? Oul Sergeant Broy who used to be stationed over in Maam . . ." '

Dan's wife gave mugs of tea to the old woman and to Myles.

'Well, this man,' Dan continued, 'sis he to the sergeant: "What's up, sergeant, at all, at all? Is it a German invasion ye are expectin' or what?"

' "Begob," sis the sergeant, "there are a few people in this town who would welcome the Germans with open arms if they landed. Stand up now and let me see if there's anythin' under the seat."

' "Look all ye want," sis the man, "for if it's stolen goods yer after, ye should know me better than that."

' "Stolen goods, is it?" sis the sergeant. "Faith then, it's guns we're lookin' for this time."

' "Guns?" sis the man.

' "Aye, rifles," sis the sergeant. And there and then didn't they toss everythin' he had in the cart this way and that. Begob, they even looked under the cart to see if he had anythin' strapped to the bottom. And when they had searched the cart, they searched him to see if he was carryin' any documents of a military nature . . .'

He paused to take a mug of tea from his wife and a slice of buttered soda bread which he bit into, chewed rapidly, then washed down with a mouthful of tea. 'Well, when this man got into Clifden,' he said, belching slightly, 'there were sojers in the streets with rifles in their hands, and the Peelers were goin' into the pubs and hotels and lodgin'-houses makin' enquiries. And when me friend was leavin' Clifden a few hours later, who did he see bein' brought under escort to the barracks but O'Flaherty the post-master.'

He stopped talking and looked at Myles. 'Why, you know him, don't ye, Myles? Didn't ye lodge at his house when ye were in Clifden durin' the summer?'

Myles stared back at him with a look of dismay, the hand holding the mug of tea half-way to his mouth. All eyes were on him. 'No, no,' he replied quickly. 'No, Dan, it's not the same man. It was someone else with the same name, that's all.' He turned his head away from Dan's questioning stare and raised the mug to his mouth, trying to hide his consternation.

O'Flaherty arrested! Fear squeezed his heart. What if he talked? He sipped his tea, remembering the small intense man, his eyes burning with patriotic fervour. Myles realised now he had brought excitement into the humdrum life of the post-master. At the time he had thought he would make an excellent Intelligence agent because he had access to all mail, including military, passing through Clifden. O'Flaherty fancied himself as a guerrilla leader. Given rifles, he could strike down from the mountains with his men and attack patrols, police barracks, outposts . . . He had been full of assurances; there would be no trouble forming a guerrilla band; there was excellent material in Clifden and the surrounding area.

Myles put his empty mug down on the hearth beside him. What had happened? Did O'Flaherty approach the wrong people? Had someone informed? Perhaps O'Flaherty had sent a written request through the post to Dublin asking for rifles and it had been intercepted by the authorities.

'Ah shure,' Dan said, 'there's quare things happin' throughout the country. There's trouble brewin'.'

'Then God keep it away from us if it does come,' Dan's wife said, in her clipped Donegal accent, crossing herself with one hand.

Donal Ruadh thrust his red head forward, face flaming. 'By God,' he cried in a high falsetto voice, 'the police and sojers had better not come down here searchin' and arrestin'! If they do they'll get a different reception than they got in Clifden!'

'Hush, *a mhic*,' his mother appealed, laying a hand on his arm.

The old woman stirred. A narrow face the colour of yellowed parchment and crisscrossed with lines emerged from the cowl of the shawl. 'A Tinker man and his woman,' she croaked, 'stopped at the house today for a drink of milk and a biteen of soda bread. They had come down from the north. Three nights ago they were camped near Nephin Beg. They told me they had seen the Black Pig and he wanderin' over the hills and bogs. As big as a cow he was, and the bristles on his spine standin' up like a hedge. And his eyes – Christ between us and all harm – his eyes a fiery red, like the pit of hell itself!'

Donah Ruadh guffawed. 'Black Pig, how are ye!' he chortled. 'Ye and yer Banshees and Fairies and pishogues. Was it listenin' to a Tinker's tall tale ye were? And I suppose when they had yer attention diverted with their lies and stories, they were robbin' everythin' they could lay their red thievin' hands on!'

The old woman shuddered with rage; one gnarled bare foot stamped against the powdery peat-ash on the hearth. 'Shut yer gob, ye red divil!' she screeched. A long thin arm shot out from the folds of the shawl towards her son. 'Dan Fahy,' she cried, pointing, 'Dan Fahy, are ye listenin' to me? The Black Pig . . .' her screech drowned his feeble protest, 'the Black Pig has always meant trouble, sorrow and war. 'Twas always so, so it was. Didn't Saint Colmcille himself prophesy that the last great battle of the Gael would be fought in the Valley of the Black Pig? Didn't he? And that a woman would walk a day's journey without seein' a man. And didn't the MacDaragh twins see a man wanderin' along the sea-shore and him with two thumbs on his right hand?'

She gazed into the red embers of the fire and began to rock gently on the small stool, moaning to herself. 'And don't I be after hearin' in the stillness of the night when the whole world is asleep, the cry of the Banshee, and she moanin' and wailin' to herself . . . It's the nature of the Fahys to be hearin' the Banshee,' the old woman groaned, rocking herself. 'Six families she cries for. The Fahys and the Hyneses and the O'Briens and the Sionnacs . . .' A wind was rising, coming in from the sea: they could hear it sighing over the house. It flowed down the chimney, stirring the embers of the dying fire. 'It's only for them that's sprung from her own tribe that she'll raise her voice. It was the Banshee who told King Brian Boru that he was goin' to meet his death at Clontarf . . .'

Myles stared at her in awe. He wished he had been born with artistic ability. He would paint her as she was now. He would portray her as Mother Ireland; the once proud and beautiful Queen, now old and withered with sorrow . . .

'There are signs and warnin's to be seen,' the old woman whispered, 'and those that ignore them are fools. Last evenin' there was blood in the sky . . .'

'Ah, will ye cease yer blether, woman,' Dan groaned. 'If trouble comes it comes and there's nothin' we can do to stop it.'

'Aye,' cried Donal Ruadh vehemently, his voice breaking on a high note, 'but them that starts the trouble will have it thrown back in their teeth! The lads of today will not allow themselves to be pushed around like their fathers and grandfathers were!'

'Don't talk to yer father like that!' his mother snapped.

'Ah whist, Nan,' Dan protested, 'shure Donal is just young and hot-headed.'

Myles looked on with a feigned air of detachment. He had been impressed by the youth's rebellious nature. Donal Ruadh also had qualities of leadership. Myles had seen him leading his hurling team with dash and fury, he had watched him urging on his team to greater efforts when they had been on the verge of defeat. Such energy, he had told himself, could be channelled in another direction.

He had begun his tutelage of Donal Ruadh two weeks after his arrival. He had imbued him with a sense of patriotism; had held him spellbound with tales of valour, recounting his own exploits on the fields of Antietam and Fredericksburg. He had used flattery. 'It's lads like you who will free Ireland from her seven centuries of bondage.' He had advised. 'Control your energy, use it to organise the youth of the district into an effective fighting force.' He had urged patience. 'Train with the hurley sticks for the present. The rifles will come later, never fear.'

Myles observed Donal Ruadh's behaviour with satisfaction. He had moulded him into his way. It was a triumphant end to his recruiting mission. This would make up for all the failures.

'Wild talk like that brings trouble, that's what I say. Amn't I right, Myles?' Dan said.

Myles blinked at him. 'I'm sorry, Dan, I wasn't listening. What was that you said?'

'I was just sayin' to this lad of mine here that if he goes around shoutin' his mouth off, some blabbermouth is goin' to repeat what he said and the next thing we'll know we'll have the Peelers bangin' on the door.'

Myles hesitated. He did not want to voice an opinion; he did not want to take sides. To agree with Dan out of courtesy was to contradict himself in front of Donal Ruadh.

'Well now, Dan,' he said, choosing his words carefully, 'if a man has certain opinions which other people regard as seditious, then he should share his opinions only with people he can trust.' He spoke directly to Dan, but his words were intended for Donal Ruadh. 'If the young men of Ireland have decided to control the destiny of their country, there's nothing you or I can do about it. They've been hoodwinked long enough by England and that crowd of renegade Irishmen sitting at Westminster. They have seen their country dragged through the mire by the Conservatives and the Ulster Unionists. They look around and see the best land in the country held by Lord This and Colonel That – the descendants of those who stole the land from their forebears. They see the few pitiful acres they were reared on, boggy, rocky land that wouldn't feed a snipe. They see their brothers and sisters and friends crowding the emigrant ships because there is no living for them in their own country, and yet Lord This and Colonel That grow fat and prosperous on thousands of rich grassy acres that rightfully belong to those same young people.' He shook his head. 'No, Dan, it's not for you or me to say to the young men of Ireland to stop. Sooner or later they

400

will take to the hills with rifles in their hands and take back all that was stolen from them. Ireland was taken from us by force and young men like Donah Ruadh here will win it back the same way.'

'Oh, the boys will be makin' the pikes like they did in the old days,' the old woman cackled, 'and they'll be drillin' in the hills. They will, faith. And the French will come in their big ships to help us and the redcoats will be flyin' for their lives.'

'Stop it, old woman!' Dan's wife said harshly. 'There's been enough talk of war and trouble for one night.'

Dan stretched his arms above his head, yawning. 'Ahhh . . . 'twill be a hard day's work I'll be havin' in front of me tomorrow, so I will . . .'

Dan, Donal Ruadh and the old woman, hugging her naggin of whiskey, shuffled off to bed. Dan's wife was washing the mugs in a basin of water. Soon she too would go to bed, and then Myles would put a few sods of turf on the fire to keep it alive till morning. Finally he would arrange the settle bed in front of the fire, undress and lie down. He was a little surprised when Dan's wife came over to speak to him.

'Two policemen were here this mornin' askin' questions about ye,' she said in a low voice.

His heart skipped a beat.

'The old woman was asleep in her room and himself and Donal Ruadh had gone to the village. They said they had come to take particulars of the year's tillage. They were civil enough, makin' harmless conversation about this and that. One of them asked how many were livin' in the house and I told him there was just himself and me and the young lad and the granny. Then the other asked what interests the young lad had, had he any ambition for a trade or career or what.

'Content enough to scrape a livin' from the few acres we have, I told him, and the odd bit of fishin'. He nodded at that and said, "And what does he do in his spare time, ma'am?"

' "He's precious little of that," I told him, "but he's a divil for the hurlin'."

' "Ah, that's the way to have him, ma'am," he said, "keeps him out of mischief." He sat at the fireplace smokin' his pipe while the other sat at the table fillin' in the forms and askin' how many acres of potatoes we had and how many acres of oats; what was my full name and my husband's full name . . . After a while the one at the fireplace said: "I heard there's a stranger lodgin' with ye, ma'am."

' "A stranger?" I said.

' "Aye, ma'am," he said, "an elderly gentleman from Dublin."

' "Faith, I wouldn't be callin' Mr Burke a stranger," I said, "for he's now almost one of the family."

' "Is that what his name is?" he said. "Tell me now, what class of business is he in?"

' "Well now," I told him, "I wouldn't be knowin' that, for I never asked."

' "Some say he's a retired professor here on holiday," he said.

' "He could be," I said.

' "Well now, ma'am," he said, "ye would want to be very careful who ye let stay under yer roof these days, for there's all classes of quare individuals travellin' around the country bent on divilment. This man that's stayin' with ye, for instance. We've had a report that an elderly gentleman answerin' his description was up in Clifden some time ago and he recruitin' for a proscribed organisation."

' "Proscribed organisation?" I asked him. "And what might that be?"

' "Politics, ma'am," he said, "dangerous politics."

'They stood in the doorway before leavin' and the one who had been askin' all the questions said, "We would like to have a chat with this Mr Burke, ma'am. We'll drop in the day after tomorrow. We'd appreciate it if ye didn't mention that we've been here. And a word of caution: keep him away from the young lad." And with that they left.'

She stared at the fire in silence, her face expressionless. He knew she was waiting for him to speak, but there was nothing he could say.

'I brought seven children into the world in this house,' she said after a while. 'I buried two. Ten years ago, the eldest left for America, and one by one the others followed. I know I'll never see them again. Now all I've left is Donal Ruadh. When he's out at the fishin' and the weather is bad, I'm half out of my mind with worry, and I don't stop worryin' till he's back inside the four walls of the house. When he's sick with a cold and starts to cough, I'm sick with fear. The two children I lost died of consumption. When a letter comes from one of his brothers or sisters in America, I'm afraid he may get the urge to wander and follow after them. I live in constant dread that I'm goin' to lose him one way or the other. I do everythin' to make him happy and content. I spoil him without shame. I give him money for his pocket which I can't afford. The only happiness I know is when I see him sittin' contentedly in the corner readin' a book or playin' in the big field at the hurlin'.'

She looked at him. He was taken aback: her eyes were full of hatred. 'It's to me grief and sorrow the day I let your shadow fall across my door,' she whispered venomously. 'Is it blind or stupid ye think I am that I can't see or know what's happenin'? Haven't I seen the pair of ye together and ye whisperin' the poison into his ear? What did Donal Ruadh ever know of politics or guns or such things till ye told him? Now he talks of nothin' else!'

402

He wilted under the fury of her glare.

'I want ye gone from here first thing tomorrow mornin'. Go back to where ye came from. Ye can make any excuse ye want to himself. But go ye will – for if ye don't, I'll tell the Peelers meself what it is yer up to. I'll make an informer of meself if I have to. I'd do anythin' to save Donal Ruadh. Aye, I'd commit murder to save him!'

Her harsh sharp-featured face was thrust towards him: the lips were peeled back, revealing yellow crooked teeth. He was reminded of a snarling, spitting cat.

'Get away from this place! Away! And take this curse with ye! I hope and pray that the cause ye tried to drag my son into will perish in blood – and ye and yer kind along with it.'

## II

Myles shuffled over to the small window of the ticket office. 'What time is the train from Limerick due in?'

The man looked up, then squinted at a timetable beside him. 'Three thirty-five,' he answered brusquely.

Myles glanced up at the clock on the wall. Three more minutes. He walked slowly back to the seat and sat down. A girl was arranging newspapers and magazines in the kiosk opposite. Myles watched as she came out and placed a newspaper placard outside.

VERDUN:
GERMAN ATTACK REPULSED

He wondered if he would be able to pick out Gerry Troy in the crowd: it was nearly two years since he had seen him last. He had been sent to meet Troy as he was the only one besides Fintan Butler who knew him by sight. Fintan had been emphatic. 'It's imperative Troy be intercepted and not allowed to reach his destination . . .'

He rose hastily to his feet as the crowd came surging down the steps. The last time he had seen Gerry he had been wearing a beard. But he could see no bearded men among the oncoming crowd. Panic surged up and took control. Then his eyes fell on a low-sized powerfully built man wearing a soft hat and tweed overcoat. He was carrying a Gladstone bag. There was something familiar about the short quick step. He stepped out in front of him.

403

'Mr Troy?'

The man came to an abrupt halt. A heavy moustache adorned his upper lip. Myles gave a sigh of relief: there was no mistaking the strong-boned face and the lively brown eyes. 'Hello, Gerry,' he said and stretched out his hand.

Gerry Troy took it hesitantly, a puzzled look on his face.

'It's me, Gerry. Myles Burke.'

Gerry's face cleared and his mouth spread in a wide grin. 'Of course,' he boomed, 'of course.' He tightened his grip and Myles winced. The crowd swept past them.

Myles said: 'I'm here to escort you, Gerry. A few people want to meet you concerning your letter. There's a cab waiting.'

Gerry nodded. They followed the crowd out into the bright spring sunshine.

Myles climbed into the cab after Gerry and slammed the door shut. They sat facing each other. Gerry turned his face to the window, looking out as the cab turned on to the quays and began to move downriver. 'A long time since I was in Dublin,' he murmured.

He has aged noticeably since I saw him last, Myles thought. 'What caused you to leave Carewstown, Gerry?'

Gerry sighed. 'Somehow the police discovered I was involved in the arms raid on the police barracks in Partry. I was involved of course, though in a passive way. Anyhow, I had to get out of Carewstown fast.'

He turned his face to the window again, not wanting to talk any more about what had happened. He had not told the whole story; he had not told how he had unmasked himself as an IRB organiser by writing and distributing a half-dozen typewritten sheets advising against payment of rents to the new master of Carewscourt. He had acted on impulse. There had been a rumour that the new owner of Carewscourt was about to increase the rents. There had been a feeling of smug satisfaction watching Father Devlin ranting and raving from the pulpit, holding up one of the typewritten sheets. 'I'll find out sooner or later who the author of this is, and when I do, heaven help him! I'll have no socialist agitator in my parish.'

Gerry did not know then that Father Devlin already knew. He found out later when he approached him about the formation of an amateur dramatic society. He had expected Father Devlin to reject the idea, and he had been right.

'No, no, no!' Father Devlin had been unyielding and more hostile than usual. 'Ye've been a thorn in my side from the very day ye came here, Troy. First it was the hurling club, then the lending library, now this!'

404

'It's my belief, Father, you want to keep the people of this parish in apathy and ignorance!'

Father Devlin's face turned dark with fury. 'How dare ye talk to me like that! How dare ye, ye . . . ye impudent upstart! I've tolerated your arrogant behaviour for far too long. You're dismissed from your post. Pack your things and get out!'

'Dismissed am I? Why? Because I'm not afraid of you and speak my mind? You'll have to have a better reason than that.'

A triumphant look appeared on Father Devlin's face. 'Well now, bucko, it just so happens I do have a better reason.' He walked to his writing-desk and came back with several sheets of paper in his hand. He placed one down on the table. 'That's one of the sheets that was circulated around Carewstown tellin' the people not to pay any more rents to the new master of Carewscourt. Your handiwork, Troy.'

'You can't prove that.'

Father Devlin placed two sheets on the table. 'Here are two typewritten reports on educational matters you sent me at different intervals. Look closely. All three have something in common. Your typewriter has a defective "m" and "t", Troy. As good as any signature, bucko.' He grinned maliciously, picking up the sheet and holding it aloft between forefinger and thumb. 'Now I'm goin' to write a letter to the Educational Authorities and I'm goin' to send this along with it. Your career as a teacher is finished, Troy. If ye know what's good for ye, ye'll clear out of Carewstown tonight. Sergeant Hanafin has been keepin' tabs on ye for some time past. He suspects ye of bein' an IRB organiser. He thinks ye were involved in the Partry arms raid.'

Gerry had left Carewstown the day after his confrontation with Father Devlin, his career as a teacher at an end. He went back to his native city of Limerick, where he managed to get a job as a clerk in a bacon-curing factory. Soon after he joined the Irish Volunteers and was promoted to Captain. With the split in the Volunteer movement, John Redmond, the leader of the Irish Parliamentary Party, had gained partial control of the Volunteers. On the outbreak of war he urged them to join the British Army, hoping that a grateful Britain would grant self-government after the war was over. The vast majority of the Volunteers responded to Redmond's appeal and joined up. Before the end of 1914, the Irish Volunteers, once one hundred and eighty thousand strong, had been reduced to a mere ten thousand. In Limerick city, the two battalions were so depleted they had to be formed into one. Gerry Troy was made Battalion O/C.

In the New Year of 1915, the Chief-of-Staff of the Irish Volunteers, an eminent historian and Professor of Early Irish History at Dublin's University College, made a brief tour of inspection of the city battalions of Cork and Limerick. In Limerick he had a meeting with the Battalion O/C, Gerry Troy. It was a happy reunion, for Gerry had been a student of his in the old days. A friendship developed: from then on, both corresponded with each other.

The Chief-of-Staff was a prudent man: he was opposed to an insurrection on the grounds that the Volunteers were insufficiently armed. His policy was to build the Volunteers into a well-armed, well-trained force that would be strong enough after the cessation of hostilities to demand implementation of the Home Rule Act which had been placed on the statute book. There were many who supported this course of action, including Gerry Troy. Disquieting rumours began to reach the Military Council – all members of the Irish Republican Brotherhood – about a certain amount of friction going on in the Limerick City Battalion which was destroying its effectiveness as a unit. Gerry Troy, now a devoted advocate of his mentor, the Chief-of-Staff, had taken disciplinary action against several officers and men who were openly in favour of an armed insurrection. The Military Council were seriously perturbed: they had prepared plans for an insurrection in which the Limerick City Battalion were to play an active and vital part.

Gerry Troy had sent a letter by courier to the Chief-of-Staff, expressing his concern about certain matters which had arisen and stating his intention of coming to Dublin for an urgent meeting. The courier had delivered the letter, not to the Chief-of-Staff, but to one of the members of the Military Council. The Council, after each member had read the contents, handed it over to Fintan Butler, giving him permission to take whatever action he considered necessary.

The cab came to a halt and they alighted. Gerry stood on the footpath holding his Gladstone bag, trying to get his bearings. This seemed to be somewhere in the Drumcondra area, but he was not quite sure: it was a long time since he had been in Dublin.

They walked up the footpath, then turned left into a quiet cul-de-sac. There were about twelve houses on either side; small red-brick houses with bay windows and long gardens in front. There was nobody about: at the other end was a high blank wall and beyond a tall building which Gerry judged to be a convent. He followed Myles down the narrow footpath.

Myles came to a stop outside the last house on the right and pushed in the gate. The house adjoining was vacant; an auctioneer's 'For Sale' sign stood inside the railings.

Myles knocked three times. The house had an unlived-in look: the front garden was overgrown with weeds and paint was peeling from the door and window frames. A bolt was drawn and the door was opened a little. A tall thin young man with a pale face and long hair smiled at Myles and glanced at Gerry standing behind. Gerry recognised him at once: he had seen his photograph quite recently on the frontispiece of a slim volume of patriotic verse. The man opened the door wider. Gerry followed Myles down a narrow passage which, presumably, led to the kitchen. He heard the door being closed behind them; then the bolt was shot home. A cautious lot, he thought.

Myles knocked once and opened a door and walked in, followed by Gerry. Three men were sitting at a table. One of them stood up and walked forward, hand stretched out in greeting. 'Nice to see you again, Gearóid,' he said in Gaelic.

Gerry shook his hand; only then did he recognise Fintan Butler. He had grown a moustache and his hair was going grey at the temples. Fintan released his hand and waved it towards a chair. 'Sit down. Earnán,' he said, addressing the long-haired young man who had opened the door, 'take Gearóid's things, will you.' Fintan sat at the head of the long narrow kitchen table. Gerry sat down at the other end, facing him. Myles was already on his left: he still had his hat and overcoat on as though he did not intend to stay for very long.

Fintan lit a cigarette; there was a saucer at his elbow half-full with cigarette butts; wreaths of tobacco smoke hung motionless above the table. There was a brown manila folder in front of him. He opened it and removed a single sheet of foolscap. 'Well now, Gearóid,' he began, 'the letter you sent to the Chief-of-Staff – '

'That letter was strictly confidential,' Gerry interrupted sharply. 'It was meant for the CS and for him only. In fact,' he added, glancing sideways at Myles, 'I was somehow given the impression that he was to be here.' He stared suspiciously at the two men sitting to the right and left of Fintan Butler. One was of slight build. He had a thin sensitive face and wore glasses; two fountain-pens were stuck in the breast pocket of his neat dark suit. He looked like an accountant. The man facing him had the appearance of a countryman. He had hanging jowls and a pug nose; the heavy mastiff features made him look as though he had a permanent scowl. Looking at him, Gerry was struck by the resemblance to a bulldog.

'You state here,' Fintan said, looking down at the sheet of paper in front of him, 'that you're worried about certain matters which have arisen in your battalion.' He raised his head and stared at Gerry. 'Would you care to discuss them?'

407

'Only with the CS. Where is he?'

'He has more important things to attend to. Now, what's troubling you, Gearóid? Perhaps I can help.'

'How can you? This is Volunteer business. You're not in the Volunteers, are you, Fintan?'

'Yes. I'm also in close touch with the Military Council. You could in a way,' giving a slight smile, 'call me an intermediary.'

Gerry had lost faith in people over the past few weeks. He had encountered nothing but treachery and deceit, but you have to trust someone, he told himself. He knew he could trust Fintan – Fintan was his friend. He leaned forward, finger-tips pressing against the table top.

'A few weeks ago,' he said, speaking slowly and deliberately, 'my Vice O/C and Adjutant were missing from parades for more than a week. They told me afterwards they had been summoned to HQ by several high-ranking Volunteer officers. When I asked them why they had been summoned, they told me HQ wanted firsthand information about the arms situation in the Battalion. I accepted what they told me, and I didn't pursue the matter. I was too busy drawing up a new training programme for the summer months.

'Then something odd occurred. One night when we were discussing the training programme, my Vice O/C let slip a remark – something about all this being a waste of time as we would be in action before the summer. When I asked him what he meant, he would not elaborate.

'I became suspicious. I made a few discreet inquiries among the rank and file. Most of them were evasive, but I managed to pick up enough information to convince me that the Battalion was preparing for an insurrection, and I was being deliberately kept in the dark!'

He waited for their reaction – the sudden startled movements; the cries of anger and dismay. But nothing happened. Bulldog-face scowled down at the table. The man facing him had his eyes closed; he was hunched forward over the table, the lower part of his face buried in his cupped hands. He looked as if he were praying silently to himself.

Fintan released a smoke-ring from his mouth, watching its progress as it curled upwards towards the ceiling. 'It was necessary, Gearóid,' he drawled, 'to keep you in the dark. There's going to be an insurrection very soon, and your Battalion will play an active and vital part in it. Therefore we need a Battalion O/C we can trust – whom we can rely upon to carry out orders.'

Gerry stared back at him, stunned.

'Your close association with the Chief-of-Staff is well known, Gearóid. He's been praising you to all who will listen, asserting that you are one of the few officers he can depend on to carry out his orders. And we all know what those orders are, don't we?'

'All this,' Gerry whispered, 'is unbelievable . . . unbelievable.'

'Our people in America,' Fintan continued, 'have been in touch with the German Government through the German Embassy in Washington. On a certain date, a German ship will land thousands of rifles and millions of rounds of ammunition on the south-west coast. All railway and telegraphic communications will be cut to prevent British forces rushing to the scene. The arms will be distributed between the Kerry, Cork and Limerick Brigades, but it's essential that some of the cargo reach the west of Ireland. A train will be commandeered to carry the arms from Limerick across the Shannon into Clare, therefore it will be the task of the Limerick City Battalion to prevent the British garrison from leaving the city. They will have to be kept confined inside their barracks. The streets will be barricaded and manned. When the other Brigades have mopped up all resistance in their areas, they will march on Limerick to reinforce the Battalion. On the day of the arms landing, the Volunteers will strike in Dublin. We are confident we can hold out until the Munster Brigades, having captured Limerick, reach Dublin.'

Gerry gaped in dismay. 'My God,' he uttered hoarsely, 'my God.' He quickly pulled himself together. 'And what does the Chief-of-Staff have to say about all this?'

'He knows nothing about it,' Fintan answered calmly.

The chair scraped noisily against the tiled floor of the kitchen as Gerry half-rose to his feet. He leaned forward over the table towards Fintan, his face turning red with anger. 'Are you telling me,' he grated, 'that the whole Volunteer army is moving towards insurrection and its Chief-of-Staff knows nothing about it?'

Fintan nodded, unperturbed. 'Considering his views on the matter, it was necessary to keep him in the dark.'

'Like I was!' Gerry snapped.

Fintan nodded again. 'We all know how much influenced you are by the CS. That's why your Vice O/C and Adjutant were given different orders regarding your Battalion.'

'And that letter I sent?'

'You should have chosen a more trustworthy courier, Gearóid. He delivered it direct to a member of the Military Council. So, best let the CS remain in happy ignorance.'

Gerry slumped wearily in his chair. 'You've betrayed that man,' he mouthed bitterly, 'the man who launched the whole Volunteer movement.'

Fintan lit another cigarette. 'His was an ideal name under which to launch such a movement. If it had been openly fathered by known separatists, it would have been instantly suppressed.' He paused. 'We've used him for what he was worth, now we don't need him any more.'

'And me?' Gerry asked sarcastically. 'Am I to be discarded too?'

Fintan took a puff of the cigarette. 'I had great hopes for you, Gearóid. But you've changed. You've become too cautious.'

'Realistic is the word. You want me to use my Battalion to prevent the British garrison from leaving the city, do you? With what? I've only enough weapons to arm less than one-third of my force. Howth Mausers and Martini-Henrys – all single-shots. The only modern rifles we have are four Lee-Enfields, and we've only forty rounds for each of those. The only additional arms are shotguns and a few muzzle-loading Queen Annes. How the hell do you expect me to besiege the barracks in the city with what I've got? And do you think the British are going to remain cowering behind the walls of their barracks? They'll break out and storm the barricades, using hand-grenades. They have machine-guns and light artillery. The whole Battalion will be wiped out! You're mad – all of you. But by God,' he said with determination, rising to his feet, 'I'm going to see the CS and inform him of what's going on. He'll soon put a stop to this insanity!' He turned around. The long-haired young man was standing with his back to the door. He was smiling and had a revolver in his hand.

'Sit down, Gearóid,' Fintan said quietly. 'You're not going anywhere.'

Gerry sat down slowly and glared at him.

'What does that mean?' he demanded.

'It means you are under arrest,' Fintan replied. He drew long and hard on the cigarette. 'You'll be released when the rebellion starts. Then you can join us if you wish.'

Gerry sat at the table, breathing harshly; brooding. Minutes crawled by. Then he sighed, and waved a hand in a gesture of resignation.

'Oh well,' he said wearily, 'at least I'll have plenty of time in which to make my mind up.'

'No you won't, Gearóid,' Fintan said. 'Time is running out fast – for all of us.'

Myles was cleaning the revolver. It was a heavy, long-barrelled weapon of antique make. God only knows where this came from, he thought; probably from some dingy warehouse in a back street in Hamburg. It had been smuggled in with a dozen single-shot rifles, all relics of the Franco-Prussian war. He gave it a final wipe with an oily rag and put it back in the holster.

He opened the worn leather pouch and removed the bullets one by one, carefully examining each one as he did so. Only thirty rounds had been supplied with the revolver. Three had been fired during testing. He rejected four which were slightly dented and put the remaining twenty-three back in the pouch.

Dusk was gathering. Outside, the usually busy street with its long line of shops was quiet. He rose to his feet and walked to the mantelshelf and picked up a box of matches. He struck one and applied the tiny flame to the gas-jet. It flared into life with a dull pop and he threw the wasted match into the fireplace. The fireplace was full with ash, all that remained of the many documents and despatches and lists of buildings to be seized. This was the last day of peace: tomorrow the rebellion would start at twelve noon.

He walked slowly to the windows and pulled down the blinds. It was warm and stuffy. He wrinkled up his nose: too many cigarettes had been smoked last night. Something else remained – a sense of fear. It lingered in the room with the stale smell of tobacco-smoke. He had seen it on the faces of the officers of the Battalion as they sat around the table. They tried to disguise it, but he was an old soldier and knew the signs: the jerky pull of a cigarette; the high-pitched laugh; the constant twitching of an eyelid. It happened to the bravest of men. He sat down at the table again and checked the items on it for the umpteenth time; there was nothing to do but wait and he had to occupy his mind somehow. The revolver, ammunition, water bottle, a roll of bandage and a small bottle of iodine. . . .

The clock ticked away in the silence. The furniture shop below had been closed since six o'clock; there were no other occupants in the house. It was for that reason Fintan Butler had rented the rooms. At night, after the furniture shop had closed, the front room was used by the officers of the Battalion as a meeting place. The bedroom had been used to store ammunition. Up to a few days ago, there had been a trunk under the bed containing a thousand rounds of Mauser ammunition, a dozen crude bombs made of lead piping and a few slabs of gun-cotton. During the bitter cold nights of early spring, Myles had been compelled to sleep in a freezing bedroom; lighting a fire would have meant risking being blown to smithereens.

He drew the sword from its scabbard. As a weapon it was useless; the point and edges were blunt with age. An officer in the Battalion, an actor from the Abbey Theatre, had given it to him; he had worn it in several productions of patriotic plays. He held it up to the light with both hands, searching for spots of rust that might still be on the blade. But there were none. He lowered it; it was surprisingly light. The days when officers went into battle with swords had long since gone. Nevertheless Myles intended wearing it as a gesture – a gesture to the past, when battles were fought without the aid of machine-guns or poison gas, when generals and brigadiers personally led their men into battle. At Gettysburg, Brigadier-General Armistead charged at the head of his men, hat on the point of his sword, into the mouths of a thousand rifles. . . .

A church bell tolled the hour. By now, the German ship carrying the arms should be nearing the south-west coast. Under cover of darkness, no lights showing, evading the British destroyers and sloops patrolling the coast. And on shore, clustered about that little harbour in Kerry, hundreds of Volunteers waiting to unload her. If everything went as planned, an Irish Army would be created overnight, an army that would advance on Dublin from the south-west, reducing military and police barracks piecemeal as they marched.

The halldoor slammed and he halted, listening, suddenly tense and alert. Only two people besides himself had a key: the Battalion O/C and Fintan Butler. He knew that all the Dublin Battalion O/C's were at a meeting with the Military Council and Fintan was down in Kerry. He could hear heavy footfalls on the stairs. He opened the flap of the holster and drew out the revolver. The door opened slowly. It took a few seconds for him to recognise the exhausted, bedraggled figure standing in the doorway.

'Fintan!'

Fintan Butler closed the door and dragged himself over to the table and flopped down on the chair. He buried his face in his hands.

'It's all over, Myles,' he moaned, his voice muffled by the hands covering his face. 'We're finished.' A sob broke from him. 'The ship was intercepted by a British sloop. The German crew scuttled her.' Tears were running down his unshaven cheeks. 'All those thousands of rifles and millions of rounds of ammunition gone,' he whispered brokenly, 'and with them our hopes . . . our dreams . . .'

Myles put the revolver down on the table. He was surprised at how calm he felt. That was one advantage of being old; you could accept disaster more readily than the young.

'What happened?'

Fintan shook his head wearily: his eyes were red and raw from lack of sleep. 'The ship was not to arrive before Easter Sunday. We were emphatic about that. A premature arrival would warn the British that an insurrection was impending. But she arrived too soon! She was sighted off Inistooskert island two days ago.' He lapsed into silence, staring down with dull exhausted eyes at the table. Myles sat facing him, waiting patiently for him to continue. The clock on the mantelshelf ticked away the minutes.

Fintan heaved a tired sigh. 'It was heartbreaking, Myles, heartbreaking, to see hundreds of men being ordered to disperse. I saw men crying. Some were smashing their rifles against the stone walls bordering the road.'

'We can still make a stand,' Myles said, trying to lift him up out of his misery, 'with the arms we have.'

Fintan gave a slow shake of the head. 'The Chief-of-Staff has ruined everything,' he said with bitterness in his voice. 'He was not told until the eleventh hour about the coming insurrection. Naturally he was appalled. When he was told that the arms ship was on the way he agreed to go along with us. Then the news reached him . . .' He straightened up slowly and reached with both hands into the pockets of his waterproof, searching. 'He sent couriers hotfoot to every Brigade in the country with countermanding orders . . .' He threw a crumpled ball of paper across the table. Myles picked it up and smoothed it out flat.

*Volunteers completely deceived. All orders for special action are hereby cancelled, and on no account will action be taken.*

'Some of the Limerick men told me,' Fintan went on despairingly, 'that there have been arrests all over the city. All Troy's fault,' he added, trying to keep his voice steady.

Myles stared at him, eyes wide with astonishment. 'Gerry Troy?'

'He's still being held prisoner here in Dublin. When he didn't return home to Limerick, his landlady became worried and informed the police. They searched his rooms.' Fintan's control snapped. 'The damn fool kept a diary,' he cried, banging the table with his fist. '*A diary!* God knows what it contained,' Fintan whimpered, running a trembling hand through his hair. 'Names and addresses. Yours, mine.'

Myles began to chuckle derisively. 'What a collection of amateurs you all are. Professors, school-teachers, poets, dreamers, all playing at

413

soldiers. Just as well the ship did go down. The insurrection would have ended in slaughter with an incompetent crowd like that in command.'

Fintan rose wearily to his feet. 'They'll tear the city apart to get at us now, Myles. I was followed here. Get some clothes together. With luck we might get out of the city before the raids begin.'

'I'm too old to run, Fintan. I'm staying here.'

'They'll put you in prison for the rest of your life!'

'They won't get that chance. I'll meet them at the top of the stairs with the revolver. They won't capture me alive this time.'

'For God's sake, Myles!' Fintan's voice reached a high hysterical note. 'It's madness talking like that. Collect your belongings and come with me now. There's no time to lose.'

'There's plenty of time. They won't come till the early hours. That's when we are at our lowest ebb.' He gave a bitter laugh. 'Believe me, I know what I'm talking about.'

'Please, Myles,' Fintan implored in a breaking voice, 'come with me. I beseech you!'

The intensity of the appeal made Myles suspicious. He stared quizzically at the tall travel-worn figure standing at the door, his hand on the knob. Suddenly he understood. Of course, he does not want to run away alone. In time to come, he can always counter accusations of cowardice by claiming that he wanted to help the legendary Myles Burke reach safety before he could be arrested.

'Best go now, Fintan,' he said quietly. 'Save yourself.' They stared silently at each other for several seconds, then Fintan turned shame-facedly away and opened the door.

Myles sat motionless listening to the rapid beat of his footsteps down the stairs. When the halldoor slammed he sighed. He felt no contempt, just pity. You poor wretch, he thought, you poor romantic wretch.

Where will he go to? Myles wondered, rising to his feet. Suddenly he remembered Fintan telling him that he had an aunt, the only surviving relative, who owned a small hotel in Wicklow somewhere near the coast.

He lit a candle, and opened the door. Certain things had to be done.

He descended the stairs slowly, holding the lighted candle aloft. First he bolted the halldoor: there were two bolts, top and bottom. They'll have trouble breaking that down, he told himself. Then he shuffled down the passage and did the same to the backdoor. By the time they had smashed down either one he would be waiting for them, prepared to sell his life dearly.

He climbed the stairs and entered the bedroom. He struck a match and lit the gas-jet, then blew out the candle. He opened the door of the wardrobe and took out his uniform. He undressed and put it on, taking his time. Lastly he put on the new boots. He did not like wearing leggings or puttees. When he was fully dressed he inspected himself in the mirror. The uniform was ill-fitting and hung loosely on his gaunt frame, but what did that matter. In a few hours from now it would be ripped by bullets and drenched with blood. He closed the wardrobe doors and turned off the gas-jet.

He walked into the front room, leaving the door open behind him. He put on the holster-belt, and strapped the holster to his leg. He loaded the revolver, placed it in the holster and buttoned the flap. The sword he would not need. He lifted a chair and brought it over to the window. He measured the distance from the window to the open doorway. Four quick strides would bring him to the doorway, two more to the head of the stairs. No, they would not take him by surprise this time.

He lowered the gas-jet until it barely illuminated the room. Then he groped his way back to the window and raised the blind. The window was open and he welcomed the cool air against his face. He lowered himself on to the chair; there was nothing to do now but wait.

He stared down, watching a youth and his girl sauntering along the footpath on the opposite side of the street. The city was strangely quiet for a Saturday night. Of course it was Easter and many people were spending the holidays at the sea or in the country. It had been a cold, wet spring, but now the weather had turned warm and sunny. Myles smiled to himself. He felt completely at peace now. No more living in poverty, struggling to keep alive. No more undercover work, ever fearful of arrest.

A church bell tolled at every hour. Nine o'clock; ten o'clock; eleven; twelve . . .

The sleepin city was silent now. He sat and waited. He could hear someone singing. Then a soldier and a woman came strolling into view. The soldier had his arm round her waist and the woman was singing in a drunken voice.

> Boys in Khaki, Boys in Blue,
> Here's the best of Jolly Good Luck
> to you . . .

The place must have been under surveillance for a long time, he thought. The path to it had been too well trodden by men on the run. Will they raid here first? he wondered. He smiled grimly to himself. They'll expect to find a dazed old man in nightcap and nightshirt, hands up to his face in terror. What a shock they'll get when their flashlights focus on me standing at the top of the stairs in uniform, revolver at the ready. For the first two or three it will be the last thing they'll ever see . . .

He yawned, and rubbed his eyes with the tips of his fingers, trying to keep them open. How long have I been sitting here? Two hours? Three? He had to keep awake. Then an inner voice whispered: but you need a little rest. When the time comes, you'll need all your wits . . . He nodded in reply. 'Just a little catnap,' he whispered and closed his eyes.

When he opened them again, the street outside was grey with the first light of day. He jerked upright on the chair, his hand clawing at the flap of the holster, giving a hoarse shout of dismay. But his startled shout was the only sound that broke the silence.

He paused, heart thumping, listening. He could not hear a sound. Then, from under the window, a cat began to mew. The sound reassured him; it was as if a sentry he had posted had just given the 'All's well'. He rose, groaning at the stiffness of his legs, and took a few steps towards the table. He found the matches and struck one and took a few more steps towards the fireplace. He held the tiny flame in front of the clock on the mantelshelf. Ten minutes to four. He had been asleep for nearly four hours. He swore softly and made his way back to the window. He sat down on the chair and unbuttoned the flap of the holster. They will come now. This was the time chosen by security forces for raids and arrests: the hours of the dogwatch just before dawn.

He waited. Even if they didn't come for him first, they would raid the homes of the other members of the Battalion who lived in neighbouring streets. Each man had his weapon with him. If there were raids, some resistance would take place. In this stillness even the single report of a gunshot would travel a long way.

He waited, straining his ears for the slightest sound, watching the light becoming brighter. He could now see the names over the shops on the opposite side. He shook his head. It was unbelievable that Dublin Castle should delay after what had happened. Delay meant giving your enemy valuable time – time to regroup, time to salvage something from the wreckage.

A patch of sky was visible from where he sat. He lay back in the chair and watched it; watched it slowly changing colour from a sombre grey to a delicate pink.

It was Easter Sunday.

Then a church bell began to ring out. Another joined in, then another – all joyously proclaiming the news across the awakening city: Christ has risen.

# Book Three

# Chapter Seventeen

## I

Durkin sat in the hotel dining-room sipping his coffee. Bright morning sunlight shone through the tall narrow windows. Durkin's eyes roamed over the chattering groups at the tables. It was Dublin's most fashionable hotel. Only at Castle functions would one see such an assemblage: lords and ladies; wealthy landowners; bankers; business-men. . . . Durkin felt like a fish out of water.

'Good morning, Mr Durkin.'

Durkin looked up. ffrench-O'Carroll stood smiling down at him. He had on a smart grey overcoat; one hand rested on a walking-stick, the other held his hat and kid gloves. 'May I sit down?'

Durkin half-rose from his chair. 'Please do. Coffee?'

'You are most kind.'

Durkin beckoned and the waiter hurried over. He gave the order, glaring balefully at the retreating black back. He had been kept waiting for a full ten minutes before being served, yet there had been an immediate response to his signal when ffrench-O'Carroll had been observed sitting at his table. The waiter was back inside a minute. 'White or black, sir?' Durkin looked on, scowling. Bloody lackey, he thought sourly; kiss his boots if he asked him to. They're all the same, fawning on titles and wealth. Then he smiled to himself. Wait till this supercilious old swine hears I'm going to be made a knight. He had been told in confidence that ffrench-O'Carroll's name had been proposed for the New Year's Honours List, but had been struck out by the Chief Secretary.

'Do you usually have your morning coffee here in the Shelbourne, Mr Durkin? I've never seen you here before.'

'No, not usually. I've just driven in from Kingstown. My wife had to go away to England.'

'Oh . . . really?'

'Yes. It will be a sad journey for her, I'm afraid. She received word

419

two days ago that her sister's husband had been killed in action in France. Her sister is very upset and Miriam decided to go over and stay with her for a while.'

ffrench-O'Carroll sighed sympathetically. 'Dear me. This terrible war.'

Durkin sipped his coffee and thought: You hypocritical old bastard – you're hoping it will last forever. You with your money invested in munitions and the devil knows what else.

'I can no longer bear to read the casualty-lists in the newspapers,' ffrench-O'Carroll whispered sorrowfully, stirring his coffee. 'All those thousands of young men. Tragic, tragic.' He raised the cup to his mouth and took a sip. 'I hope your wife has a pleasant crossing, Mr Durkin.'

'Well, Miriam has not gone yet. Submarine scare in the Irish Sea. The mail boat won't leave until a destroyer escort is provided. God knows how long the delay will be.'

ffrench-O'Carroll raised an inquiring eyebrow as if to say, Where is your wife now?

Durkin gave a slight shrug. 'No sense coming back into the city with all that luggage and then having to return to Kingstown again. Miriam decided to book into the Royal Marine until the boat sails.'

ffrench-O'Carroll nodded. 'A sensible thing to do.'

'I had intended staying with my wife,' Durkin continued, 'then we encountered a dear friend in the hotel lobby who graciously offered to keep her company until the boat is ready to leave. You may remember him. I introduced you that time the new Under-Secretary arrived. Captain Carew, Captain Alec Carew.'

'Ah yes, now I remember. Tall chap, wore a moustache. I thought him a trifle distant.'

'Oh, you know what some of these English officers are like. Aloof. Although in Alec's case, I think it's shyness.'

ffrench-O'Carroll nodded again. 'I daresay,' he said and raised the cup to his lips. He kept it there, taking tiny sips, trying to keep a serious face. He had a clear remembrance of Durkin's wife and Captain Carew sitting in a corner in Jammett's restaurant: staring into each other's eyes; holding hands under the table . . .

And Durkin, tracking down every little case of infidelity for his scandal-sheet, and he himself the biggest cuckold of them all. He almost choked on his coffee and put down the cup hastily. Dabbing at his mouth with the table-napkin, he saw Durkin looking at him with narrow suspicious eyes.

420

'Forgive me, Mr Durkin, a thought just crossed my mind which I found amusing.'

'Oh?'

ffrench-O'Carroll gave a dismissive wave of the hand. 'It's of no consequence.' He decided to change the subject at once. Durkin had a reputation for being uncannily perceptive at times. 'His Grace the Archbishop wrote to me recently. He was most impressed by your book.'

Durkin looked at him in astonishment. *'The Carews of Carewscourt?'*

ffrench-O'Carroll tittered. 'No, no, the one you wrote for the Employers' Federation. *Crusade in Dublin.'*

'Oh, that one.'

'His Grace was appalled, positively appalled, by some of the revelations. He had no idea socialism was so widespread in this fair city of ours.'

'Dublin is an excellent breeding-ground for socialism,' Durkin said. ffrench-O'Carroll and his friends, he knew, were owners of slum property. 'Grinding poverty . . . the slums . . .'

'Er, yes.' ffrench-O'Carroll nodded solemnly, lips pursed. 'Nevertheless, the book made it clear to many that the employers were not the ogres the socialist press made them out to be. Now most people realise that there are two sides to every story. You explained our side of it admirably, Mr Durkin.'

Durlin blushed a little. 'Thank you.'

'Any more books in the offing?'

Durkin leaned forward over the table. 'The Army people have commissioned me to write one on the exploits of the Irish Regiments at the front,' he said in a low voice. 'Purely a propaganda piece – to aid recruitment, ye know.'

ffrench-O'Carroll beamed. 'Why, that's wonderful news. From one success to another, eh? You're beginning to make your mark in the world of letters, Mr Durkin.'

Durkin chuckled. 'I hope so, I hope so.' Flattery always put him in a good mood. 'May I drive you somewhere? My car is outside.'

'Is that your car? I was admiring it just before I came in.'

'The latest Ford model,' Durkin announced with pride. 'Had her specially painted.' He was touched by a little doubt. 'You don't think the colours are too garish, do you?'

'Not at all. Walking through Dublin nowadays, one sees nothing but mourning black and drab khaki. A little . . . er . . . gaiety is uplifting.' ffrench-O'Carroll rose slowly to his feet and reached for his hat and gloves and walking-stick. 'Thank you for your kind offer, Mr Durkin, but I would really enjoy a stroll through Stephen's Green. It's such a beautiful morning.' He extended a hand. 'So nice meeting you again.'

Durkin stood up and shook his hand. He was about to tell him about his coming knighthood when ffrench-O'Carroll forestalled him. 'Soon I will be calling you Sir William,' he said softly, smiling. 'I heard the good news. Congratulations.'

Durkin sat down a trifle deflated. Still, he had detected a little envy in the voice. He took out his cigar-case. Sir William, he thought. Not bad for a ragged little urchin who had clawed his way up from the slums of Spitalfields. He snapped his fingers at the waiter and ordered another coffee.

He relaxed in his chair. He would stay on in London, himself and Miriam, and settle there permanently. Dublin, he told himself, is too provincial. Here he had too many enemies and very few friends. Then he thought, No, only *one* friend – Alec Carew. Dear Alec . . .

He took a mouthful of coffee. A good offer had been made for the *Eye-Witness* and *Society Life*. Together with the money he would get for the house and furniture, he would be richer by nearly thirty thousand pounds. Not bad – not bad at all. He was already well-heeled financially. They call me a muck-raker, he thought with a smile, but it has paid off handsomely.

The change would do Miriam good; she was looking peaky of late. Listless; feeling sick in the morning. A thought struck him. Jesus! She's not pregnant, is she? He dismissed the thought. Of course not. How could she be? We haven't made love in . . . How long has it been? Seven months? Eight?

He stared moodily down at his coffee, the cigar burning away between his fingers. Always some sort of excuse whenever he approached her. He had now reached a stage when he no longer bothered. One could always find sexual relief elsewhere: the little waitress from the café in Grafton Street; the war-widow who had her own house in Serpentine Avenue.

Nevertheless he loved Miriam; she was the only woman he had ever loved. He had told her that often enough, but her response always lacked warmth and passion. Perhaps, he thought hopefully, things will change when we settle in London.

London. The thought cheered him up. The New Year; Buckingham Palace; the King. 'Arise, Sir William.' He chuckled to himself. *Lucky* Sir William.

422

'Please, Alec, don't say any more. What you suggest is madness – madness.'

'I've five days' leave, Miriam. We could spend them together somewhere.'

'Impossible! I'm leaving for England. They say the destroyer escort will arrive tomorrow morning.'

'Cancel. You can leave at the end of the week. Durkin will never know.'

'Don't speak so loudly,' she said, but the hotel lounge was almost empty.

'I couldn't believe my eyes,' Carew said in a low voice, 'when I saw you and Durkin walking in. It's been three months since I saw you last. I've been to Jammett's several times hoping I'd find you there.'

'How did you happen to be here – here of all places?'

'A friend of mine is a member of the Yacht Club. I was going to spend my leave sailing around Dublin Bay.'

'I've already booked a room,' she protested weakly.

'Tell them you've changed your mind. Tell them you're going back to Dublin, that you're afraid to travel now with all this talk about submarines in the Irish Sea. They'll understand.'

'How about you?'

'I was waiting for my friend to arrive before booking a room.' Then he laughed at the expression on her face. 'Don't look so startled. He's not due till one o'clock, and that's two hours away. I'll leave a note at the reception desk, telling him I had to go back to Dublin on urgent business. I've everything I need here with me,' he added, touching the leather travelling-bag on the ground beside him.

She sat in silence, folded hands in her lap, pondering. Then she heaved a sigh and rose slowly to her feet. 'I'd better go and arrange things.'

He ordered a whiskey and soda. The hotel was on the sea-front. From where he was sitting he could see the yachts sailing out from the harbour, gliding over sun-speckled blue-green water. The whiskey was placed before him on the low table and he paid for it. Then he lit a cigarette and lay back in the chair. It was time to relax . . . time to take things easy after the feverish excitement of the past few days. He reached for the whiskey and took a sip, remembering the tension in the drawing-room of the Vice-Regal Lodge as they watched the Lord

Lieutenant pacing up and down, a worried look on his face, holding the dispatch in his hand, the dispatch informing him that a German ship carrying arms and ammunition had scuttled herself off the south-west coast.

'I'm going to cancel my official visit to Belfast. I'm not leaving Dublin until I've secured the arrest of all the rebel ringleaders.'

'In that case I'd like to consult with some of my staff as well as the Commissioner of the Metropolitan Police,' Colonel Coxton said.

'On what charge?' the Under-Secretary intervened. 'To hold them on a charge of "hostile association" would need the agreement of the Home Secretary.'

'They could be kept on remand,' the Lord Lieutenant replied. 'Anyway, I'll sign the warrants and accept full responsibility.'

'Let us not be too hasty,' the Under-Secretary demurred. 'Prompt, aggressive action on our part might stir up a hornets' nest, and that's the last thing we want. No, delay a little; let them lull themselves into thinking they are not going to be arrested. Besides, if we are going to carry out a joint military-police swoop, it's going to take about five days to make the necessary arrangements.'

'And what,' Major Calder asked with heavy sarcasm, 'if the nationalists decide to start a rebellion in the meantime?'

'Oh come now,' the Under-Secretary said, a smile creasing his dark features, 'all they have are less than two thousand antiquated rifles and a limited amount of ammunition. And with the German ship with its precious cargo at the bottom of the sea, the rebels must now realise that the game is up. No, my dear fellow, no one but a lunatic would start a rebellion knowing that the chances of winning are hopeless.'

A hand touched Alec's shoulder. 'I've arranged to have my luggage sent to the railway station,' Miriam said, sitting down beside him.

'Let's go someplace off the beaten track,' he said, 'somewhere where there's no risk of being recognised.'

She lowered her head, contemplating the carpet. She said, 'There's a place I know in Wicklow, a tiny village by the sea. There's a small hotel . . .'

'Sounds perfect,' he said, grinning.

She shook her head slowly. 'This is all mad – simply insane.'

'Yes,' he laughed, 'but who cares? It's spring – people do mad things in spring.'

The Commandant held himself erect before the sixty-odd armed men standing at attention. He was a small dapper man with a heavy black moustache. His polished leggings and Sam Browne belt gleamed in the bright morning sun. Myles Burke and Tim Skerritt stood a little behind him.

The Commandant cleared his throat nervously. 'Men,' he announced in a loud voice, 'in less than an hour from now, at twelve o'clock precisely, the Irish Republic will be declared. At this very moment, the other battalions are marching to seize the principal buildings in the city. The General Post Office, Dublin Castle, City Hall . . .'

They stood in the centre of what had been a slum court; a narrow lane led out from it into the street beyond. On all sides stood the crumbling remains of two-storey houses. The surrounding area had been a by-word for squalor and overcrowding; now it lay in ruins. A whole wasteland of rotting tenements and ruined courts and alleyways lay about them.

'This is the day we've all been waiting for!' the Commandant cried, trying to force confidence into his voice. 'Now at last our hopes and dreams have been realised.' He paused. The sixty-odd men should have been two hundred and fifty. The countermanding order and the confusion that followed had reduced his battalion to little more than one-fifth of its original strength. 'This battalion has the responsibility of preventing British reinforcements from entering the city from the west. Barricades will be erected. One section will capture the Four Courts and hold it.'

Myles stared stonily back at the curious glances from some of the men in the front row. He could see himself through their eyes – a tall, ancient, ridiculous figure in an ill-fitting uniform, as obsolete as the sword hanging by his side.

'That countermanding order of the Chief-of-Staff's,' the Commandant continued, 'caused a great deal of confusion. The other Dublin battalions are in the same situation as ourselves. All are operating with only a fraction of their normal strength. Nevertheless a stand has to be made. If we can hold out long enough, the rest of the country will rise with us. Failure . . .' he paused deliberately, 'failure means that our children and our children's children will have to carry on the fight. For their sake we must not fail. This time we have to win. We have to! If anybody wants to withdraw now, he is at liberty to do so.'

No one moved; no one said anything. Then a Volunteer directly in front of him raised his voice. 'Well, by God, I don't like this! I don't mind fightin',' he uttered hoarsely, 'if there's a chance of winnin'. But this is madness! We'll be outnumbered and outgunned. Once the barricades go up we'll be sealin' off our means of retreat. We'll be caught like rats in a trap!'

The Commandant did not say anything. His face was expressionless.

The man turned to face his comrades. 'Don't yez understand?' he cried. 'Yez haven't a ghost of a chance. None of yez!' He spun on his heel and strode towards the laneway. A pale-faced lad of about seventeen broke ranks and followed him. The Commandant's voice brought them to a halt.

'Volunteers! Leave your rifles and equipment behind!' As the sounds of their footsteps faded away, he pulled himself erect.

'Right,' he said briskly, 'each officer has his orders. Proceed at once with your men to your posts.'

Each section moved off. Eighteen men remained standing at attention. The Commandant turned round to Tim Skerritt.

'Lieutenant, take your men to North King Street. Erect the barricades at once. If British reinforcements disembark at Broadstone Railway Station, I'll try and send some men to assist you, but don't count on it. Good luck.' He marched away, straight-backed and purposeful.

Tim Skerritt led his men up the laneway and into the street. Myles walked slowly after them. He felt so old, so helpless. I'm a liability rather than an asset, he thought, standing in a doorway watching them erect the barricades. He knew he would be only in the way if he tried to help.

They planned to erect two barricades about thirty yards apart in North King Street, one facing east, the other facing west, with a distance of about thirty yards between. Two streets cutting into this defensive position from the north were also to be barricaded and manned. The entire area now controlled by the Volunteers was shaped like the letter 'T'. The horizontal top section was North King Street, both ends being the barricades facing east and west. The broad stem stretching south contained headquarters and a casualty station and was lightly defended on both sides by small pockets of Volunteers. The base was the Four Courts, a massive building with a green copper dome overlooking the River Liffey.

Myles watched Volunteers rolling empty barrels out from a public-house; they placed them side by side across the width of the narrow street. Then, acting on Tim Skerritt's order, they entered the tenement houses for more material for the barricade. There were cries of protest and outrage as Volunteers staggered out of doorways carrying mattresses, sofas, armchairs. . . . The angry owners followed them out.

'Here, what the hell do ye think yer doin'? Come back with me bloody mattress!'

'But the Republic will repay ye, ma'am,' one Volunteer tried to explain.

'Republic me arse! Give it back, ye bloody daylight robber!'

A crowd gathered outside the barricade being erected: men, women, children. The women were more abusive than the men. 'Bloody bowsies! Why don't yez go to France and fight the Germans!'

Tim Skerritt faced them from the other side of the half-completed barricade. He stood with legs apart, hands on hips.

'Listen, you people,' he shouted. 'There's goin' to be heavy fightin' in this area in a short while. My advice is to get yerselves and yer families out and away from here as quick as possible.'

'Ah, go an' stuff it!'

'It'll take more than a bunch of hooligans playin' at soldiers to move me outa me home!'

Skerritt shook his head and was about to turn away when shots rang out in the distance. A sudden hush fell on the crowd. There was another burst of gunfire: it came from the south – from the direction of the quays.

The sounds galvanised Skerritt into action. He twisted round towards his men, who, like the crowd, were standing motionless, listening. 'Get this bloody barricade up quick!' he roared.

The men responded immediately. Standing their rifles against a wall, they fell to making the barricade higher and firmer. Pieces of furniture were thrown on to it. A Volunteer came running from a stable with a length of stout rope. Several men helped him to bind the flimsy structure together. Skerritt waved to the crowd. 'Clear out of here quick!' he shouted. Most of them hurried to their homes. About a dozen remained, a few children among them.

Suddenly a Volunteer came sprinting round the corner of a side street twenty yards away. He ran towards the barricade waving his rifle in the air. 'Cavalry,' he yelled, 'comin' up behind me!'

There was a frantic clatter of hooves against cobbles. Then they burst into the street: three troopers led by a sergeant. One was slumped over the saddle, wounded. They milled about in confusion, horses snorting and rearing. The sergeant was the first to see the crowd and the barricade: he did not hesitate. Aiming his carbine, he spurred his horse forward into a charge as his men galloped away in the opposite direction.

The crowd scattered in panic as the sergeant fired. The bullet struck a little girl running for the safety of a doorway. The impact flung her tiny pinafored body three feet into the air like a rag-doll. Skerritt and his men scrambled for their rifles lying against the wall.

Myles tugged the heavy revolver from the holster as the sergeant urged his horse over the barricade; raised it as he rode past; aimed at a spot between the shoulder blades as he galloped towards a bend in the road fifty yards away. He pulled the trigger. There was a roar and a flash and the weapon jumped in his hand.

Skerritt saw the man's cap fly into the air, with half his skull inside it. The body toppled out of the saddle and bounced into the gutter. The horse continued on, hooves pounding against the cobbles, empty stirrups swinging. Skerritt stood watching it, holding the rifle loosely by his side. He was dazed with shock; everything had happened so fast. Behind him, he could hear someone whimpering; he could not tell if it was a man or a woman.

He placed his rifle back against the wall. He wouldn't need that single-shot obsolete weapon now, not with a modern carbine lying in the roadway and a bandolier of ammunition on the dead man. He walked slowly forward, hands clammy with sweat, his eyes on the body lying sprawled in the gutter, the shattered head resting in a spreading pool of blood. Nausea stirred in the pit of his stomach. I hope to hell, he thought, I'm not going to disgrace myself by throwing up.

The Angelus began to ring out from the nearby Capuchin Friary. It was twelve noon.

# Chapter Eighteen

I

Durkin motored slowly along St Stephen's Green. The canvas top was down and the noon sun was warm and pleasant against his face. He turned right into Grafton Street. The narrow fashionable street looked more elegant today. The warm Easter weather had brought out women by the score, anxious to display their finery. Durkin was dazzled by the colourful attire and the wide, feathered spring hats. It gave him a warm happy feeling, but suddenly his mood changed. Something sinister had appeared on the scene – an ugly stain on the pretty picture. Coming towards him on the opposite side of the street were about forty or fifty men marching in columns of three; Citizen Army men in dark bottle-green uniforms, long cumbersome rifles on their shoulders. As he drove past, he noticed a few women among them. Where's that mob off to? he wondered. Route march probably. He made a face. Whole bloody lot should be conscripted and sent to France. There they'd get all the fighting they were looking for.

He became immersed in the heavy traffic sweeping round the wide curve in front of the Bank of Ireland. Automobiles, traps, side-cars, charabancs . . . everyone seemed to be heading for Fairyhouse. He was to meet 'the lads' there. Being of the racing fraternity, they always had a few good tips. He expected to win a bundle. And afterwards, down to Monto for a gay romp with the jolly girls. The old brothel quarter seemed to have been given a new lease of life since this war had started.

He drove over O'Connell Bridge, his yellow and red Ford a vivid splash of colour among the drab vehicles. The traffic slowed down again. Something was holding it up in front. He edged into the kerb and cut off the motor, wondering what the hell was going on. He opened the door and got out and strode up the footpath. There was a large crowd in front of the General Post Office. He gave a hiss of exasperation. Another damned recruitment meeting, I suppose.

The crash of breaking glass startled him. He could see it showering out in bright splinters as the windows of the Post Office were smashed from within. He stepped hastily out on to the road and joined the onlookers, weaving in and out towards a little man who was shouting angrily. 'A nice state of affairs, when a body can't go into a post office without being thrown out by a gang of hooligans with guns in their hands!' Durkin tapped him on the shoulder.

'What's happening?'

The little man threw up his hands. 'The whole world has gone stark ravin' mad, that's what's happenin'!' he howled. 'The Volunteers and the Citizen Army crowd have commandeered the Post Office. They've just declared war on the British Empire. Did yeh ever hear the like! And would yeh look up there.'

Durkin raised his head. Two flags waved in the breeze. One was a tricolour of green, white and orange. The other was green-coloured with the words 'Irish Republic' in white and gold. 'They'll bloody well clear outa there when the military arrive,' the little man said venomously.

Durkin pushed his way through the crowd towards the entrance. Better go inside now and see what's going on, he told himself, before the military arrive to arrest the whole lot of them. He chuckled. Good old Durkin – always at the right place at the right time. He could see the headlines: *Exclusive interviews with the Leaders. Once again your roving reporter was on the spot* . . . I hope to hell, he thought, no other reporter got here first.

A pimply youth of about seventeen barred his way with a fowling-piece. 'Yeh can't come in here,' he said sternly.

Durkin grinned and pushed the barrel of the gun aside with a beefy hand. 'Go home and play with your marbles, sonny,' he said and swept past him through the revolving doors.

It was pandemonium inside. The vast hall echoed with the noise of shouted commands, the clattering of equipment, the pounding of booted feet. Uniformed figures scurried about in all directions. Durkin was pushed and jostled. An officer near him was shouting instructions at a group of men fortifying a smashed window with loaded mail-bags. Durkin pushed his way towards him. 'Excuse me, General . . .'

'No civilians allowed in here,' the officer snapped. 'Get out!'

'I'm a newspaper reporter. What's all this about?'

The officer stopped a man rushing past with a bundle of broadsheets in one hand and a pot of paste in the other. He selected a sheet and handed it to Durkin. 'Here – that's what it's all about.'

Durkin glanced at it.

*IRISHMEN AND IRISHWOMEN: In the name of God and of the dead generations from which she receives her old tradition of nationhood, Ireland, through us, summons her children to her flag and strikes for her freedom . . .*

Durkin did not read on. He glanced at the names under the heading: *Signed on behalf of the Provisional Government* and grabbed the officer by the arm.

'The signatories of this proclamation, can I interview them?'

Exasperation showed on the officer's face. 'Certainly not! This is not the time or place for press interviews. Now get out! Sentry!'

The boy who had been guarding the entrance had followed Durkin in. He hurried over.

The officer shouted at him. 'I told you not to admit any civilians. Now escort this man out and don't let it happen again!' He spun about on his heel and strode away.

The boy nudged Durkin with the fowling-piece. 'Get movin'.' When he did it again, Durkin twisted round towards him, face flaming with sudden rage.

'Do that again, you pimple-faced little swine,' he shouted, 'and I'll take that blunderbuss from yeh and break it across yer thick skull!'

Two men standing nearby, supervising the unloading and distribution of ammunition, turned round at the commotion behind them. One walked over and placed his hand on Durkin's shoulder. 'You're Durkin, aren't you?'

'What of it?' Durkin snarled, turning round to face him. The hand was still on his shoulder; it tightened into a grip.

The man was in the uniform of the Citizen Army. He was tall and thin and had a narrow gnarled face. Then he grinned widely, displaying broken tobacco-stained teeth. He turned his head round towards his companion standing a few feet away. 'Hey, Con,' he shouted, 'here's an old friend of yours.'

Durkin watched the tall man coming towards them with a rifle in one hand. He too was in a Citizen Army uniform; there were sergeant's stripes on his sleeves.

Kit chuckled, his hand still clutching Durkin's shoulder. 'We've a prize specimen here. Durkin of the *Eye-Witness*.'

The man's eyes narrowed. He wore a wide-brimmed soft hat pinned up one side, Australian style. The rough-hewn face with its bushy red eyebrows and broken nose looked vaguely familiar to Durkin. The man's hands were scarred.

431

'That was an eloquent speech you made in court,' the man said. 'It helped to put me away for fifteen months.'

Then Durkin remembered. He tried to get away but Kit's firm grip held him fast. Gallagher turned to the youth with the fowling-piece. 'Get back to yer post. We'll take care of this.'

Durkin watched the retreating back with a growling feeling of panic. He tried to wriggle himself free. 'Let me go!' His squeal of terror was drowned by the general uproar.

Kit, his rifle slung across his back, reached out with his other hand and grabbed Durkin by the lapel of his jacket. 'So we're a bunch of godless socialists, are we?' he rasped, pulling Durkin to him so that their noses touched. 'How much did the Employers' Federation pay yeh to write that damned book?'

Durkin tried to turn away – away from the glaring hate-filled eyes and the stench of decayed teeth.

'Thousands of poor families starved into submission and a bastard like you waxin' fat on their misery.'

Durkin struggled, trying to release himself. His straw boater fell from his head. 'My hat,' he gasped.

Kit raised a heavy foot and stamped on it, crushing it flat.

'What the hell is going on here?' It was the officer Durkin had accosted five minutes before.

Kit turned his head without releasing his grip. 'We know this man,' he said. 'He's a Castle spy. He's been seen in the company of a British Intelligence officer. Release him, and he'll go straight to the military and tell them everythin' he's seen here.'

The officer looked at Durkin's sweaty face and desperate, imploring eyes. 'He told me he was a newspaper reporter.'

'He is. The *Eye-Witness*.'

Distaste flickered over the officer's face. 'Very well,' he snapped, 'put him in the basement with the other prisoners,' and stalked away.

Kit released his grip and Durkin staggered back a little. Gallagher caught him by the arm.

'So yeh came in here just for somethin' to write about in that newspaper of yours, did yeh?' Kit said.

Durkin stared apprehensively at him for a few seconds, then gave a reluctant little nod.

Kit Byrne chuckled. 'Right,' he said, grabbing Durkin's other arm, 'we're goin' to show yeh all yeh wanted to see. Maybe yeh'll live to write about it.'

They pushed their way through towards an open doorway, half-

432

carrying, half-dragging Durkin between them. When they began to climb the stairs, Durkin became suspicious and then panicky. 'Where are yeh takin' me?' he yelped.

They did not answer but continued to climb, dragging him up with them, standing aside as some Volunteers came clattering down the stairs. As they passed, Durkin shouted, 'Help!'

The last man halted and looked up from three steps below. Gallagher gave a curt jerk of the head. 'On yer way!' he ordered. The man looked at the sergeant's stripes on his arm and continued on down.

Durkin started to whimper as they hauled him up the stairs. He knew they were going to take him into an empty room and shoot him. When Kit kicked open a door at the top of the stairs he drew back. Gallagher pushed him forward and he stumbled out into the open air.

He was on the roof of the Post Office. He stood, dazzled by the sun in his eyes, feeling the cool breeze drying the sweat on his face, looking over the roofs of the city. Away to the north-east he could see the peninsula of Howth jutting out into the bay. Kit and Gallagher followed him out. He looked around him. There were about ten other men on the roof. His fear suddenly left him. They could hardly shoot him here in front of so many witnesses.

Suddenly there was a crackling sound in the distance. He twisted about, staring towards the south-west from where the sounds were coming. 'What's that?'

Kit chuckled. 'Dublin Castle is under attack. Yer pals are in a right fix now, Durkin. Probably hidin' under their desks, sayin' their prayers.'

There was a fresh outburst of firing and Durkin cringed a little, feeling terribly exposed here on the top of the building. It would not take long for the British to react: soon this roof would be under sniper fire from the surrounding buildings.

Nelson Pillar towered above them – towered above every other building in the city. All an artillery officer had to do, once he got the range right, was to aim just a fraction to the left of the Pillar. . . .

Kit pushed him forward towards the north end of the roof. Above his head the rebel flags fluttered in the breeze and the statues of Hibernia, Mercury and Fidelity stared serenely eastward from above the pediment. He paused to take a quick look down into the street, leaning over the stone balustrade. The crowd was still there, ebbing and flowing. He felt a stab of envy: only a short time ago he had been one of them. Opposite, they were erecting a barricade across the mouth of Earl Street which led eastward towards the railway station. Heavy pieces of furniture taken from nearby shops were being piled up in an untidy heap. Suddenly he gave a yell of dismay. 'My car! They're taking my car!'

Three uniformed men were pushing his yellow and red automobile across the street towards the barricade. Gallagher and Kit joined him. Then Gallagher guffawed and slapped him on the shoulder. 'Just regard it as your contribution to the cause.'

Durkin watched helplessly as they placed his beloved Ford sideways in the centre of the barricade. They had stopped a coal-cart and several Volunteers were unloading it. They staggered over with heavy sacks of coal on their shoulders and dumped them into the car, piling them up on the seats. Then a Volunteer raised his rifle and stove in the windscreen with the butt.

Durkin closed his eyes, unable to watch. Even at this distance he could hear the sound of splintering glass. He stumbled away, tears of rage in his eyes.

Gallagher and Kit walked slowly after him. They positioned themselves on either side of him, sitting on the waist-high balustrade, their backs to the street. 'Cheer up, Durkin,' Kit Byrne said, enjoying his misery, 'yeh can always buy another one. If we let you get out alive.'

Durkin did not say anything. He stood with both hands in his jacket pockets, staring into the distance. Mercifully the barricade was now hidden from his view by the tall thick column of Nelson Pillar. Suddenly he jumped as a shot rang out only a few feet away.

Gallagher twisted sideways to see the young Citizen Army man beside him lowering his smoking rifle. Gallagher grabbed him by the collar and swung him around to face him. 'What the hell were you firing at?' he demanded.

A grinning gamin's face stared into his. He was about sixteen, his pale skin marred by acne. Two front teeth were missing. He jerked a thumb up over his shoulder. 'I chipped the Admiral's nose – blew the snot off oul Nelson.'

Gallagher shook him by the collar. 'You fire again without orders,' he shouted, 'and I'll throw you down into the bloody street!'

The youth was undismayed. 'Ah shure, what else were we given rifles for only to fire them,' he protested.

Gallagher shook him again. 'Did you hear what I said? No more firing without orders!' He released his grip and the youth turned away, giving an indifferent shrug. He immediately gave a yell and pointed a finger. 'Lancers!'

There were more shouts of warning from the street below. The crowd

434

scattered in panic, some darting down side streets, the majority running southwards towards the bridge. Gallagher and the youth went down on one knee, the barrels of their rifles resting on the stone balustrade. Kit Byrne did the same, dragging down Durkin beside him. From here, on the northern side of the building, they could see the mounted khaki-clad figures stretched across the wide width of Sackville Street, tall, slim pennanted lances upright.

'You men. . . !'

Everyone turned. A tall Volunteer officer stood panting after his mad dash up the stairs. 'Orders from below. If they charge, no one is to fire until they gallop past the front of the building. Is that understood?'

Gallagher waved a hand. 'Understood,' he shouted, then turned to the youth beside him. 'And make sure *you* understand, Buffalo Bill.'

But the youth was concentrating on the horsemen in the distance. Resting his weight on one knee, rifle at the ready, he squinted along the long barrel of the Mauser. 'Come on,' he cried impatiently, 'what are yez waitin' for?'

Gallagher tensed as the Lancers started to move forward. He shouted a warning to the other men on the roof. He dug the butt of the rifle deeper into the hollow of his shoulder. These old Mausers had a vicious kick when discharged.

On they came at a trot. The troopers sat ramrod-stiff in the saddles, lances held firmly upright, pennants streaming. The horses, high-spirited, silken-coated, trotted forward in an even line. The officer leading them looked calm and self-possessed as if he were on the parade ground.

Kit Byrne broke the tense silence. 'What does the stupid bastard think he's doin'? Leadin' the Charge of the Light Brigade?'

The military mind, thought Gallagher, his sights on the tall arrogant figure in front, the sun gleaming on the naked blade of his upright sword. Incredible he should assume that, by simply leading his men past the rebel headquarters at a smart trot, the garrison would become so demoralised as to abandon the building and surrender.

The jingle of harness and the clatter of hooves against the flinty square setts were clearly audible now. Gallagher's mouth was dry: he was about to kill a man. He felt pity and admiration for the oncoming troopers. They would all be annihilated by the fire of a hundred rifles the moment they trotted past the front of the building, yet not one faltered even though they knew they were riding to their deaths. They were coming nearer. Ten yards; eight . . . Suddenly the youth beside him fired, knocking a trooper out of the saddle. Immediately the

435

excited and inexperienced men at the side windows below opened up with a ragged volley.

Gallagher shouted a curse and fired at the man he was aiming at – and missed. He could see his bullet striking the road two feet in front of the rearing horse. He fumbled frantically in the pocket of his bandolier for another.

'Damn these bloody single-shots!' he snarled. But by the time he had reloaded the Lancers had wheeled about and had gone galloping back up the street, all discipline thrown to the winds. He fired a shot after them, but they were out of range. On the road below, four troopers lay sprawled and a horse was lying on its side kicking its life away.

The youth beside him gave a wild yell of triumph. 'We got four of them!'

Furious, Gallagher spun around and cuffed him across the ear. 'You trigger-happy little bastard,' he roared, 'only for you we could have got all of them!'

Then he marched away. He was in command of the men on the roof and now he would have to face the wrath of his superiors below. Kit hesitated for a second or two, then followed him.

Durkin raised himself from his knees and stood, trembling from shock, his eyes on the bodies below. A few feet away to his right the youth was reloading his rifle, whistling merrily, unconcerned and unrepentant. The long stretch of Sackville Street was deserted now, except for a riderless horse limping back looking for its master. Durkin could see the sheen of blood on its flank where a bullet had nicked it. He then felt something he never felt for a human being – compassion. There were tears in his eyes as he watched it nudging its nasal peak against one of the bodies on the ground. 'Poor thing,' he whispered, 'poor, poor thing.'

He leaped as the rifle exploded beside him. He staggered back a little, then stood blinking, his ears ringing. The youth lowered his rifle and turned a grinning face to him. 'Had to put the poor oul beast out of its misery,' he said cheerfully.

Durkin looked down. The horse was sinking to its knees. Then he closed his eyes and turned his head away as it rolled slowly over on top of the dead trooper's body.

Carew signed the hotel register under the curious stare of the proprietress, a tall angular woman with iron-grey hair. He hesitated a second before writing his old address at Wilton Place. He noticed with satisfaction that the names immediately above his had been entered more than five weeks ago.

'We seem to have the place to ourselves,' he said.

The proprietress sighed. 'Indeed ye have, sir. Up to a few years ago there never was a shortage of English tourists at this time of year. Mostly anglers, ye know. Good trout fishin' around here. But since the war . . .'

Carew nodded in sympathy.

Miriam stood a distance away looking out of the window. She wanted to avoid meeting the proprietress, afraid that she might remember her.

The woman handed Carew the keys. 'I'll have someone bring up your luggage,' she said and turned her head round towards an open doorway behind her. 'Fintan,' she called.

Carew walked over to Miriam and picked up the travelling-bag on the ground beside her. Then he took her by the arm, giving her a reassuring smile, trying to allay her nervousness.

They followed the man carrying the luggage up the stairs. When he had placed the two heavy suitcases down on the floor of the room, Carew gave him a generous tip, then closed the door after him. 'Rather a doleful-looking individual, don't you think?' he said, laughing, turning round.

She stood by the double bed, her face pale, staring at the closed door.

'What's the matter?'

'That man,' she whispered, 'I've seen him before.'

'Of course you have,' he said lightly, walking over to her and placing his hands on her frail shoulders, 'when you were here with Durkin. But he wouldn't remember you after such a long time.'

'No, no,' she said, shaking her head, 'it was not here. It was in Dublin. And he recognised me. Didn't you notice the way he stared?' She lowered her head, frowning. 'If only I could remember . . . I'm trying to visualise him without the moustache.'

He laughed again and kissed her. 'You're overwrought and beginning to imagine things. He simply *looks* like someone you once knew. And as for him staring at you . . .' He placed a finger under her chin and raised it a little. 'Another woman would take that as a compliment.'

She smiled and he said: 'There now, that's more like it. Tired?'
She shook her head.

'Then show me around this place you've chosen. I want to get out of
this strait-jacket of a uniform. I want to dress like a beachcomber and
feel the sea breeze against my face.'

They walked up the village street, holding hands. Rathmore
consisted of about two dozen white-washed cottages, a pub, a post
office, two small shops and the hotel. An elderly man was leaning over
the half-door of his cottage smoking a clay pipe and two shawled women
standing outside a shop stared at them with open curiosity. They
walked on, leaving the village behind them. Away to the west, the
sinking sun was touching the rim of the Wicklow Hills.

'You know,' he said, 'I like this place. The beautiful scenery, the
tranquillity . . .'

'William and I used to come down here from the Leopardstown
races. Sometimes his friends from the racetrack came with us.
Bookmakers, tick-tack men and the like. I never cared for them. I
would go to bed early and leave William and his friends drinking in the
hotel bar. They usually stayed there until the early hours. After a while
I stopped coming. William was relieved. "I like to cut the knot now and
then," he told me, "and enjoy myself with my pals." '

They came to a narrow winding track which led down to the beach.
They descended slowly between high grassy banks, Alec leading the
way. The long stretch of beach was deserted. Waves drove up the long
pebbly incline and withdrew lazily with a rattling sound. They found a
large smooth rock against a sandbank and sat down on it. Carew lit a
cigarette and put his arm round her waist. She leaned back, resting her
head against his shoulder. They sat for a while, not talking, listening to
the sounds the waves were making.

'So peaceful,' she whispered.

'Yes,' he said and sighed. 'Hard to believe that at this very moment
men are dying in thousands in that hell called Verdun.'

'Will this horrible war ever end?' she asked in a voice a little above a
whisper.

'Who can tell. There's talk of a big push this coming summer.' There
had been so many big pushes in the past year, he thought, all ending in
disaster. Neuve Chapelle, Loos. . . .

Loos. He grimaced. The net result was the gain of a salient driven
into the enemy front at the cost of sixty thousand men. Whole
regiments had been wiped out, including the King's Own Scottish
Borderers. Major Craig and all those young subalterns he had dined and

438

wined with were dead, their corpses festooning the barbed wire in front of the German trenches.

He flicked away the cigarette. You poor devils, he thought, you've paid for what you did at Bachelor's Walk . . .

'Alec.'

'Yes?'

'I'm going to have a baby. *Your* baby.'

He rose slowly to his feet, then stared down at her bowed head. 'Are you sure?'

She looked up into his face. 'Of course I'm sure. I've been attending a doctor for the past six weeks.'

'What I meant . . .' he hesitated, then said: 'Are you sure it's mine?' He regretted the words immediately. He sat down beside her and put his arm round her shoulders. 'That was a beastly thing to say. I'm sorry.'

A flush spread over her pale face. 'William and I have not . . .' She stopped, unable to find the right words. She shook her head in exasperation. 'For nearly a year now,' she said in a hard voice. 'Does that answer your question?'

He squeezed her shoulder. 'I've upset you. I didn't mean to. I was taken completely by surprise by what you said. I just wasn't thinking clearly.' She sat stiffly, staring at the sea. He knew he had hurt her; she had been expecting a different reaction – a more tender one.

'I was not going to tell you,' she said in that same hard voice. 'I was going to stay with my sister in England until after the baby was born. I was going to write to William, telling him all, but not mentioning you – '

'Stop this!' he interrupted harshly. Then he relented, placing his hand over hers. 'I want children,' he said softly, 'you know that. And I'm glad this has happened. No more deceit; no more furtive meetings. I'll tell Durkin myself when I get back to Dublin. With you expecting my child, he'll have to give you a divorce. It will be easier with you in England, far away from the unpleasantness.'

How will Durkin take it? he wondered. In his heart he knew the answer. Durkin had confessed to him his deep love for Miriam. And he regards me as his only true friend, he told himself. He sighed inwardly. Poor beggar, he'd been doubly betrayed.

# III

Durkin sat huddled in the corner of the post office basement. Darkness had fallen and the only illumination came from several candles. Nearby, six British soldiers were sitting in a circle playing cards. They had been guarding the telegraph instrument room when the rebels seized the building and now they were prisoners like himself.

One of them slapped his cards down on the concrete floor. 'Full house!' he declared.

''Ere!' another exclaimed, 'that's two Kings and a Jack. Wotcher tryin' to pull, yer white-arsed bugger?'

'Sorry. It's this bleedin' candlelight. Can't see a thing.'

'Then get yerself a pair of bleedin' glasses.'

Suddenly there was a rattle of rifle-fire from the floor above and all talking ceased. Durkin sat up, tense and alert, heart beginning to beat faster. When the firing died away, he slumped back against the wall, breathing harshly through his nose. The soldiers started to talk among themselves again as they resumed their game.

Durkin passed a shaking hand across his forehead. Despite the cold he was sweating profusely. I've paid a high price for my inquisitiveness, he told himself bitterly. Only this morning he had been sitting in the Shelbourne sipping coffee and listening to the cultured accents around him. The two main topics of conversation had been the Fairyhouse races and the D'Oyly Carte Opera Company who were about to open a season at the Gaiety. And now here he was . . . He gave a moan of despair.

One of the soldiers heard him and turned around. 'Care to join us, mate?'

Durkin shook his head; he wanted to be alone with his misery.

'No sense sittin' by yerself and broodin',' the soldier said lightly, 'we'll all be dead by tomorrer.'

The perky Cockney voice with its cheerful message of doom scratched at his nerves.

'Piss off!' he snarled and turned his head away. He was aware of their aggrieved silence, but he didn't care. How can anyone play cards at a time like this? Don't they know the danger we're all in? They joke about death on the morrow, not really believing it will happen. He closed his eyes. His mind was beginning to ramble. The terrible events of the day had completely exhausted him. Try and get some sleep, he told himself, some sleep. . . .

440

He dreamt he was in a vast hall surrounded by the nobility of the land. The walls were lined with full length mirrors which reflected the light from the chandeliers overhead. The men were in evening dress like himself and the ladies were dressed in long white gowns and wore tiaras on their heads. Names were being called and he watched those summoned walk the length of the red carpet to where the royal personage sat in all his splendour. Soon it would be his turn. He could see himself kneeling on one knee before the King – could feel the touch of the sword-blade on his shoulder.

'Arise, Sir William.'

He could hardly breathe from the excitement. He knew all the correct procedures; he rehearsed to himself the proper responses like an acolyte about to serve his first Mass. He waited, trembling a little.

He felt a quick beat of the heart as his name was called. He walked slowly towards the seated figure in the distance with immense pride, now and then glancing at the people lining the red-carpeted aisle on both sides. But something was wrong – he could see it in their horrified stares. A woman was giggling furiously and covered her face with her hand. He began to perspire. Was something wrong about the way he was dressed? He moved his hand down over his chest, stomach, groin. Jesus! His heart leaped. His flies were open.

Durkin's sudden shout startled the soldiers. They whirled around to see him kicking and writhing like a man in an epileptic fit. One of the soldiers walked over and grabbed his shoulder and shook him awake. 'Easy, chum,' he said softly, 'it was just a nightmare you were having.'

Durkin struggled up into a sitting position, wiping the sweat from his face. He looked slowly about him, not quite sure which nightmare was the worst, this or the one his subconscious had conjured up.

There was a burst of firing from above. As usual the chatter of the soldiers ceased and they all sat listening in tense silence. Then the door was pushed open and the noise of the rifle-fire came loudly into the room. Three women of the rebel army entered with trays of tea and buttered bread. The soldiers stirred themselves as the women came towards them with the trays. Durkin gratefully accepted one of the mugs. His mouth was dry and tasted of copper. He drank greedily. The firing from above had died down. Then a new sound entered the room. It was as if someone was using a typewriter a long distance away.

Durkin placed the empty mug down on the floor beside him. Machine-guns. The British had reacted at last. There was a sickish feeling in his stomach. Next would come the artillery.

He shifted restlessly about. If only that crowd upstairs would see

441

reason; if only they realised the futility of fighting the British Army with a couple of thousand antiquated rifles. But he had observed the leaders at close quarters. Poets, schoolmasters, intellectuals, dreamers, men who wanted to sacrifice themselves so that their country might be reborn. And they'll sacrifice me along with them! he wailed to himself, his nerves snapping.

'Bloody lunatics!' he shouted, giving vent to his anger and despair.

One of the soldiers winked at his comrades and tapped a forefinger against his temple. 'Barmy,' he whispered.

The women turned their backs, ashamed to see one of their countrymen behaving in such a manner: weeping to himself and knocking his head against the wall.

# Chapter Nineteen

## I

'Can this thing go any faster?' Carew shouted, trying to make himself heard above the clatter of the engine.

The driver, crouched over the steering-wheel and trying to see through the steam blowing back from the engine, shook his head. 'If I don't get water for this radiator soon,' he shouted back, 'the bloody engine will pack up altogether. But don't worry,' he added, 'there's a farmhouse at the bottom of the hill we're comin' to.'

The ground dipped out of sight twenty yards ahead. As the lorry moved over the crest and down, the driver cut off the engine. Immediately the vehicle, loaded high with vegetables at the back, began to pick up speed. The hill was steep and descended in sharp corkscrew bends. Carew braced himself as the lorry began to shudder and shake violently. Jesus, the whole damn thing is coming apart, he thought. He closed his eyes as they plunged towards a sharp bend, hearing the wind whistling past the open window beside him, wondering if they were going to hit the high grassy bank and overturn. But the driver took the curve with ease. Carew opened his eyes as they rocked and rattled at high speed towards another bend fifteen yards away. He shot a look at the driver. He appeared unperturbed. Perhaps he drives down this hill every day, he thought. Nevertheless he braced himself again as they swept round the bend. He did not relax until they came to the bottom of the hill. The momentum of their descent carried them along the road for a good thirty yards; gravel and stones crunched under the wheels as the lorry wobbled to a stop almost outside the farmhouse.

The driver turned to Carew and grinned. 'Well trained by owner,' he chuckled and opened the door. Carew got out. 'Ye may as well stretch yer legs for awhile,' the driver said, pushing open the gate of the farmhouse, 'till that oul bitch of an engine cools.'

Carew watched him stumping up the drive; only then did he notice that the man was bow-legged. He walked up the narrow hedge-lined

443

road towards a small bridge in the distance. When he came to it he lit a cigarette, and leaned over. His shadow disturbed a trout in the stream below; it darted out of sight under the bridge. He inhaled deeply, staring down at the smooth clear water, watching a school of minnows weaving in and out through the reeds. She has read the letter by now, he told himself. How did she react? With anger? Dismay?

Less than two hours ago he had walked down to the lounge for the morning paper, leaving Miriam upstairs asleep. He had found Mrs Kavanagh, the proprietress, talking to the man who worked for her. Seeing them together for the first time, he had been struck by the remarkable resemblance to each other. Mother and son? he wondered, or aunt and nephew?

'No newspapers this morning, Mrs Kavanagh?'

'No, sir. No newspapers, no mail, no trains. The postman just told me the news. A revolution, sir, in Dublin. Christ between us and all harm – they're slaughterin' each other in the streets. Hundreds dead . . .'

He had raced upstairs and swiftly changed into his uniform. Miriam was still asleep, dark hair spread all over the pillow. He was tempted to wake her, but decided not to: he hated tearful goodbyes. Besides, he told himself, when this trouble is over we'll be together for the rest of our lives. He hastily wrote a letter, then propped it up against a jar of face-cream where she would find it. It was an abrupt end to two days of glorious happiness.

Downstairs he settled the bill with Mrs Kavanagh. 'I need some kind of vehicle to take me to Dublin, Mrs Kavanagh. Is there a motor car in the village?'

But there was only a horse and cart, and she was not quite sure if the owner would . . . He decided not to waste precious time. There was a constabulary barracks in the next village three miles away. There he would find something. Even a bicycle would do.

He felt conspicuous striding along the dusty road in his uniform. One never knew what hostilities the rebellion had aroused in the local populace. Once he encountered a man on the road. Instead of giving the customary greeting, the man had glared at him as he walked past. He had continued, feeling like an invader in a hostile country, defenceless without any weapon.

As he strode towards the crossroads, an ancient battered Ford lorry came chugging into view from the west. He ran towards it. It was loaded at the back with a mountain of vegetables covered by a tarpaulin.

The driver was reluctant to take a passenger. 'I'm overloaded as it is,' he protested. He quickly relented when a five-pound note was waved under his nose. 'Hop in!'

The engine began to overheat as they headed northward up the road. 'Going to market?' Carew inquired.

The man gave a hoarse laugh. 'Market be damned! A fella told me the people are starvin' in Dublin. No supplies gettin' in with all this trouble goin' on. They're payin' up to three shillings for a head of cabbage. Three shillings! Man alive – I'll make a bloody fortune!'

The sound of the motor-horn shattered his reverie. He straightened up and walked back. The driver was sitting behind the wheel, impatient to be gone. Perhaps, Carew thought, he's afraid the rebellion will be over in Dublin before he gets there. Every revolution produced its profiteers, he told himself, climbing into the cab.

The lorry moved off slowly. The driver avoided the hilly country and turned east towards the coastal road. They came on to it near Newcastle, then headed north towards Dublin, crawling along at fifteen miles an hour.

The sun blazed from a cloudless sky and the cab was uncomfortably hot despite the open windows. Carew wrinkled up his nose at the earthy smell coming from the driver's clothes. He must have spent the whole night digging up his fields, he thought, his eyes on the road ahead.

He stared out in amazement as they drove through the seaside town of Bray. The main street was crammed with shoppers and people who looked as though they were on holiday. Excited children were being led towards the beach carrying sandbuckets and spades. It was hard to believe that men were fighting and dying on the streets of Dublin twelve miles away.

They motored on, through Killiney, through Dalkey, up the long narrow main street of Kingstown. A group of soldiers stood with fixed bayonets at the top of the long hill leading down to the harbour. The driver slowed to a stop and Carew opened the door and jumped down as an officer approached. The officer gave a languid salute. He was tall and thin and had a casual air about him. He cast an amused glance at the battered lorry with its cargo of vegetables. 'Nothing like travelling in style, sir,' he remarked dryly.

Carew tried to keep the impatience out of his voice. 'What's happening in the city, Lieutenant?'

The officer gave a shrug. 'The rebels seized most of the principal buildings. But we're closing in on the beggars. Two battalions landed here from England this morning and moved off less than two hours ago. We heard they encountered some opposition at the canal bridge.'

445

'And Dublin Castle? Have the rebels seized Dublin Castle?'

Again the casual shrug. 'Can't say for certain. All telephone and telegraphic communications have been cut by the rebels. We have to rely on dispatch riders till things get fixed up.'

Carew nodded and returned his salute, then climbed back into the cab. The driver had kept the engine running. They drove away. On the outskirts of the town, Carew had a brief uninterrupted view of the harbour. Two destroyers lay at anchor just outside the harbour-mouth.

The long stretch of coastal road before them was completely deserted. Carew gate a satirical grunt. 'No sign of the starving multitude clamouring to buy your vegetables.'

But the driver was not listening; all his attention was concentrated on the dense cloud of black smoke drifting over the city five miles away. When they reached the outer suburbs, he pulled over to the side of the road and cut off the engine. They sat in silence then, watching the smoke, listening to the continuous rattle of rifle-fire in the distance.


## II


The shrill blast of a whistle and fifty men of the Sherwood Foresters jumped to their feet and charged towards the bridge with fixed bayonets. Attending to some wounded from the previous attack, Carew raised his head above the front-garden hedge to spurts of flame coming from the barricaded windows of the tall three-storeyed house overlooking the bridge on the far side of the canal.

Half of the attacking force were hit before they had covered thirty yards, their screams drowned by the ear-splitting noise of rapid gun-fire. The survivors staggered on, stumbling over the dead and wounded. About fifteen of them managed to reach the narrow hump-backed bridge. They collapsed in a heap under a hail of bullets half-way across.

Carew lowered his head and went down on one knee, sweat running down his face, a sick feeling in his stomach. That had been the fifth attack on the house, and it had ended in bloody carnage like the others. The whole battalion was being wiped out piecemeal. That damned bridge! he swore to himself. The firing ceased abruptly. One of the wounded on the ground beside him started to whimper. A heavy

Mauser bullet had mangled his forearm. Carew placed a hand on his burning forehead.

'Easy now, easy . . .' he murmured. He had tied a rather clumsy tourniquet to stop the bleeding. He glanced at the other two. One had a shattered shoulder and was staring upward, eyes blank with shock. The third had lost consciousness: he had been shot in the stomach. All three looked about eighteen.

It was quiet now, except for the moans of the wounded. The rebels were withholding their fire to allow the military to take away their dead and wounded. A group of doctors and nurses from the nearby hospital approached the body-choked bridge under a Red Cross flag. There were not enough stretchers; sheets and blankets had been taken from the houses about and used to carry away the bullet-torn bodies. They were soaked with blood from constant use.

Carew called to two stretcher-bearers running past. 'You men . . .' The young soldier with the mangled arm cried out in agony as he was lifted on to the stretcher. 'Jesus! Oh mother . . .' Carew helped the one with the wounded shoulder to his feet as another soldier came rushing over to assist. 'See to him, will you,' Carew said, nodding down towards the boy lying unconscious on the ground.

The soldier bent over and felt his pulse, then straightened up. 'He's dead, sir.'

'Leave him,' Carew said curtly. He followed the stretcher-bearers across the road, his arm around the waist of the wounded soldier. They turned the corner into a long avenue stretching east. Carew stood appalled as two medical orderlies relieved him of the wounded man. The pavements on both sides of the road and the long front gardens of the houses were covered with dead and wounded. Further down on the right, the small military barracks was under sniper fire from the railway bridge, its tiny garrison hemmed in.

'Sir . . .'

Carew turned round. The Colonel's Adjutant saluted. 'The Colonel is having a conference with all officers. Follow me, please.'

Carew walked after him up a narrow passageway between two houses. They entered a garden, well screened from sniper fire by high walls and apple trees. The Colonel was holding his conference in a potting-shed. He sat on the edge of a small wooden table, one foot dangling. His right arm was in a sling and his face was white and drawn. He had been one of the first casualties when the battalion marched into the ambush at the bridge. Standing beside the open door, Carew looked about him. Besides the Colonel and his Adjutant, there were only two

447

officers and a Sergeant-Major. Christ, he thought, are these all the officers that are left?

'Smoke, gentlemen, if you wish,' the Colonel said, then turned his head to his Adjutant. 'Light one for me, will you, Jimmy.'

Major Smith opened his cigarette-case and held it out to the men standing beside him. The Sergeant-Major was the only one who refused. Despite an order to stand at ease, he still stood rigidly at attention. He was bare-headed. There was a crust of dried blood on his forehead where a bullet had nicked.

The young Second-Lieutenant standing beside Carew struck a match. Carew gripped his wrist as his hand began to shake, then bent his head to the flame, the cigarette between his lips. When he raised his head he released his grip and gave him a reassuring wink. Two wide frightened eyes stared into his.

'Well now, gentlemen,' the Colonel began, taking a quick pull of the cigarette, 'I informed Brigade of the difficulties we're having in trying to take the bridge and the house overlooking it. They've also been informed of the heavy casualties we've suffered.' He turned his head a little. 'How many to date, Jimmy?'

'About two hundred, sir, including the casualties from the last attack.'

A spasm of pain flickered across the Colonel's face. Whether it was caused by his wound or the Adjutant's bald statement Carew could not judge. The Colonel lowered his head and stared at the ground, the cigarette burning away between his fingers.

'Brigade,' he said quietly, 'on receipt of the information, decided to send two companies across the bridges east and west of our present position. Their orders were to root out the snipers and attack the house on both flanks . . .' He paused. 'However, that decision has been quashed by HQ. The GOC has the impression that the Robin Hoods are making surprisingly heavy weather of what he describes as a handful of rebel riflemen. Apparently he has overlooked the fact,' he went on, bitterness creeping into his voice, 'that it has taken hours of heavy fighting and the lives of seventy men just to capture two rebel outposts this side of the canal.' He took a long deep pull of the cigarette. 'The GOC wants no diversionary tactics. The Sherwoods must press the matter frontally. His view is that the situation is sufficiently serious to demand the taking of the rebel position at all costs. At all costs,' he emphasised, then paused to let what he had just said sink in. 'Any questions?'

There was silence for a few seconds. Then the young Second-

Lieutenant standing beside Carew cleared his throat. 'Would it not be best . . .' he croaked, then cleared his throat again before continuing '. . . to postpone the attack till dark? Under cover of darkness we could crawl across the bridge and take the rebels by surprise. Casualties could be kept down to the minimum . . .' His voice tailed away and an awkward silence followed.

The Colonel lowered his head and pursed his lips thoughtfully. 'Yes, that would be the sensible thing to do. But our orders are specific: the bridge and the house must be taken as quickly as possible. And I agree. The rebels are turning this particular fight into an Irish Thermopylae. Perhaps,' he said, giving a slight satirical smile, 'whoever is in command imagines he's another Leonidas. If they can hold out long enough, then the waverers in the rural parts might make up their minds and take to the hills with whatever weapons they possess. In no time at all we could have a full-scale guerrilla war on our hands.' He lapsed into a brief silence, then said: 'Any more questions?'

No one said anything. In the silence they could hear the distant boom, boom, boom of the heavy Mausers the rebels were using as they sniped away at the barracks.

'Right, then,' the Colonel said crisply, giving a curt nod of the head. 'The attack will take place at exactly six forty-five. Regulate your watches with mine. I make it . . . fifty-fifty.'

He frowned a little at the way Second-Lieutenant Hunter's hand was trembling. 'This time we'll attack with three full platoons. Major Smith will lead with his platoon and Captain . . . er . . . Carew, isn't it?' Alec nodded. '. . . will follow with his in support. Lieutenant Hunter will bring his men across the bridge west of here, then will lead them down the far bank of the canal to attack the side of the building facing the main road. The door is undoubtedly heavily barricaded. It will have to be destroyed. That will be your job, Sergeant-Major. Take command of the bombing section. You and your men will have to place slabs of gun-cotton against the door and blow it to smithereens.'

He took a quick pull of his cigarette. 'Now, as regards covering fire. Jimmy, you will take as many men as you need and occupy the school. There's a low wall facing the canal. From behind it your men can keep up a steady fire on the ground-floor windows of the house. Order them to distribute their fire, two or three selecting a particular window as their target. We've got to keep the rebels pinned down behind their barricades to allow the Sergeant-Major and his bombing section to reach the door. Clear?'

'Perfectly, sir.'

'Good. Now, Brigade have sent us a machine-gun. The ideal place for it is the belfry of the Catholic church, five hundred yards away to our left. From there, they will be able to rake the upper-floor windows and the windows directly beneath. They will open fire exactly one minute before the attack begins.' He paused for a few seconds. 'Well, that's it, gentlemen. Anyone anything to ask me?'

Silence answered him. The sniper fire continued in the distance. Boom, boom, boom . . .

'Very well, then. The best of luck to all of you.'

Carew was the last to leave. As he walked through the open doorway the Colonel called him back, and smiled wryly. 'I imagine you're now sorry you blundered into us.'

'Not at all, sir. Glad to be of service.'

'I regret having to drag you into this awful mess. But I've no choice. Most of my officers have been killed or wounded. Staff wallah, aren't you?'

'Yes, sir. Military Intelligence.'

'Oh, really?' The Colonel eased himself off the table. He stood with his back to Carew, looking out, now and then raising the cigarette to his lips. 'Forgive me,' he said after a while, 'but I have to voice my opinion. I can't help feeling that if you chaps had done your job properly this damned rebellion would never have happened. Surely it must have been obvious that trouble was brewing?'

He has good reason to be bitter, Carew told himself, after losing two hundred men in five futile attacks.

'Someone underestimated the seriousness of the situation,' he said with a trace of weariness in his voice, 'it's as simple as that.'

The Colonel turned slowly round to face him. 'You mean someone made a stupid mistake,' he snapped, 'a mistake those poor kids out there are paying for with their lives. And God only knows,' he added, his face showing emotion for the first time, 'how many more will have to pay the same price before this day is over.'


III


They stood and waited to the left of the tree-lined road, rifles held at port. Ahead, round the bend, two hundred yards of straight roadway ran up to the bridge.

Carew glanced at his watch. Seven minutes to go. His hands were slippery with sweat and he was aware of the nervous movements of the men behind him. He looked over his shoulder, then turned his head away, feeling pity for the youngsters under his command, their faces pale and tense under the peaks of the caps. Not one of them looked more than twenty-one. Only two days ago they were probably sampling their first drink in the pubs of Watford or courting their girls in Cassiobury Park or watching the antics of Charlie Chaplin in the cinema. Now here they were, in a strange city in a hostile country, gripping their rifles and fighting down their fear, waiting to be butchered on that damned hump-backed bridge.

He glanced at his watch again. Four more minutes. Nausea gripped his stomach. This was the worst time of all – the waiting. Less than twenty yards separated himself and his men from Major Smith's platoon. Sergeant-Major Bufton and his bombing section were at the rear with their haversacks containing slabs of gun-cotton. His knowledge of explosives was limited, but he had read in some manual or other that gun-cotton is very sensitive to friction and percussion and must be handled with great care. If a stray bullet were to strike . . . He pushed away the terrible vision that flashed into his mind and tried to think of something else.

The heat had gone from the day. The evening sun was changing the dull red brick of the houses on the far side of the road to the colour of rose. A maid in an upstairs window peeped at them from behind lace curtains. This could be any quiet, elegant road in Kensington, he thought. One expected to see couples out for an evening stroll and elderly gentlemen with dogs on leads. He unbuttoned the flap of the holster and drew out the revolver; it felt heavy and awkward in his hand. Wartime regulations demanded that all Staff and non-combatant officers attend the firing-range for practice with rifle and revolver, but Major Calder had considered such regulations a waste of time and never enforced them.

Calder, Carew mused, I wonder whether he is now. Perhaps he's –

Suddenly the machine-gun opened fire from the belfry of the Catholic church. Rat, tat, tat, tat. Carew jerked at the sound. Then came the rattle of musketry as the Adjutant and his men commenced firing from the school-house. Mouth dry, he began to count the seconds. He knew Major Smith would be the first to die. In every attack so far, the rebels had picked of the officers and non-commissioned officers first before concentrating their fire on those following behind. Fifty-eight, fifty-nine . . .

The shrill blast of a whistle pierced the noise of machine-gun and rifle-fire and Major Smith's platoon moved off at the double.

Someone shouted, 'Good old Notts! Come on the Robin Hoods!'

Carew had a brief glimpse of the burly figure of Major Smith as he reached the bend in the road. He saw him wave his revolver and break into a charge, his men following four abreast. Then came the familiar boom, boom, boom of the rebel Mausers.

Carew glanced at his watch again, the sweat breaking out on his skin, the bitter taste of bile in his mouth. The second wave was to follow the first after a one-minute interval. He had a lanyard around his neck with a whistle attached. He placed the whistle between his lips, watching the minute-hand moving inexorably round, trying to ignore the mounting crescendo of rifle and machine-gun fire. Six forty-six. He blew furiously on the whistle and lumbered forward, remembering the encouraging cry of a minute ago.

'Come on the Robin Hoods!' he shouted hoarsely.

He set the pace, keeping his men at a trot, conserving their energy for the final, desperate charge up the two hundred yard stretch of road leading to the bridge. The clatter of heavy boots behind him almost drowned the noise of gunfire. The machine-gun was firing continuously from the belfry of the church and he could see the flash of tracer slanting down over the rooftops. Suddenly thick black smoke began to boil up against the washed-out blue of the evening sky. The house they were attacking was on fire! He gave an exultant shout, 'Come on, men!' and sprinted forward, waving the revolver.

He raced around the bend. Major Smith lay on his face in a pool of blood twenty yards away, spreadeagled between the tramlines. The roadway was littered with dead and wounded and in the distance he could see the bridge and its approaches choked with twisting, struggling khaki-clad figures. The din of battle was deafening.

He charged on, trying to avoid the dead and wounded. He was forced to leap over some and looked back to see his men having the same difficulty, shying away like horses, trying to prevent themselves from trampling on the wriggling and inert bodies of their comrades. Some were jumping to the footpaths on both sides of the road. The entire formation was splitting up and becoming disorganised, the momentum of the charge drastically slowing down. 'Come on, men. Come on!' he bawled, and stumbled on.

A long tongue of flame shot up through the smoke coming from the shattered roof of the house they were trying to take. But the rebel fire never slackened. Continuous volleys mowed down the attackers as they tried to cross the bridge. Suddenly the rear sections fell back in confusion. Panic set in as they turned about and rushed away, full tilt towards Carew and his men charging up the road.

Carew suddenly found himself in the middle of a scrum. He lashed furiously about with the revolver. 'Get back! Get back!' Then the rebel fire lifted and three men fell in a clump inches away to his right and he heard a thud as a heavy bullet struck a man at his elbow. He threw himself flat with everyone else, then began to crawl forward, making for the low stone parapet of the bridge.

A bullet tore up a piece of the road three feet in front of him. When another whizzed over his head, he rolled over to one side behind the only cover available, the dead body of a soldier. More bullets followed, one striking the ground at his foot. A rebel sharpshooter had spotted his officer's uniform and had selected him as a target. He lay still, playing possum, his left cheek against the ground. He had a snail's-eye view of the Adjutant's men firing steadily across the canal from behind the low wall of the school-house twelve yards away. His ears ached from the continuous racket of gunfire.

He braced himself, holding his breath, then jumped to his feet and raced towards the parapet on the east side of the bridge. A bullet whipped away his cap as he dived for cover, ending up sprawled across the footpath, winded, his revolver in the gutter. He crawled quickly forward and huddled against the low parapet of the bridge where it curved round on to canal bank. From here he had a clear view of the body-strewn road they had charged up. His entire platoon had gone to ground and were now advancing on their bellies along the gutters and footpaths on both sides of the road. It was like watching four giant caterpillars coming slowly towards him. He reached out and grabbed the revolver and crawled on his belly round the curve and on to the bridge.

None of Major Smith's platoon had succeeded in reaching the other side: the dead and wounded lay in heaps. Some of the survivors were trying to find cover behind the fallen bodies of their comrades and bullets were still slamming into them, although most of the rebel fire was being directed towards his own platoon creeping up the road.

He wriggled over one dead body and pushed another aside who had a haversack at his hip. One of Sergeant-Major Bufton's bombing section nearly made it, he thought, coming to rest beside the Sergeant-Major himself who was sitting with his legs drawn in, his back jammed against the stonework, the strap of the haversack wound tightly round his hand. He looked over his shoulder to see who was beside him, his face grim and covered in sweat, then looked away again.

The roof and upper storey of the house overlooking them was now fully ablaze and the machine-gun was concentrating on the windows underneath. Carew raised his head a little to see bullets whipping along over wall and windows. Pieces of brick were showering down like confetti. The house stood at the end of a long terrace facing the canal. The windows at the side of the building not only overlooked the main road leading into the city, but also commanded a view of the far side of the canal bank stretching westward. He could see flashes of gunfire as the rebels blazed away at Hunter's platoon as they charged down for a flanking attack.

He looked back. His men were still crawling up the road, and he was near enough to see them being picked off, one by one. He beckoned furiously several times with the revolver. After a few seconds hesitation, a group of men scrambled to their feet and raced towards him. He winced as one suddenly leaped and twisted as he was hit.

Five men led by a lance-corporal struggled up the footpath on their bellies. Carew leaned forward as the lance-corporal reached him. 'The Sergeant-Major will have to make a dash for the halldoor and blow it in,' he shouted, trying to make himself heard above the din. 'When he does, he'll come under fire from the ground-floor windows. Although our chaps across the canal are firing at them, we'll have to join in to give the Sergeant-Major a chance. Concentrate on the two windows to the left of the door. You'll have to fire over the top of the parapet. That means having to expose yourselves, but there's no other way. Understand?'

The lance-corporal nodded: the heavy moustache could not disguise the youthfulness of the face.

'No one is to fire till I give the signal. Pass the word along.'

He had a plan. The extra firepower they would provide would enable the Sergeant-Major to crawl round the corner of the bridge and roll down the canal bank and into the water. It was only about two feet deep at the side. He would be able to wade forward through the reeds unobserved until he reached a point opposite the door. Then one mad dash across twelve feet of roadway. . . .

He was about to tap the Sergeant-Major on the shoulder and bawl instructions in his ear when the top of the house and most of the roof flew skywards in a tremendous explosion.

He pressed against the parapet with the others as debris rained down. Obviously the flames had reached explosives and ammunition stored on the top floor. Heavy black smoke obscured the building and rolled over bridge and stagnant canal water. For an instant all firing ceased.

It was the chance the Sergeant-Major had been waiting for. He jumped to his feet, paused for a second, then ran round the corner of the bridge and charged diagonally across the road, the haversack swinging from his hand. Carew moved quickly forward, crouched, to the corner of the bridge, recklessly exposing himself. Through the veils of smoke he could see the Sergeant-Major kicking open the low gate of the front lawn. Then he sprinted up the narrow path and flung himself against the door.

A bullet chipped the stonework above Carew's head and he hurriedly drew back. He twisted round to the men behind him. 'Commence firing!'

He joined in, right arm resting on top of the parapet, finger feverishly jerking on the trigger, aiming at the window on the extreme left. Then the Adjutant's men opened up and he could hear the swish of bullets overhead as the machine-gun began firing again.

But there was no returning fire coming from the first-floor windows. The house was being vacated floor by floor as the fire gained control. The upper part was now a mass of flames and the roof of the adjoining house had caught fire. Still rebel resistance continued. A bullet sped past his ear and struck someone behind him; he could hear the scream of pain above the noise of gunfire.

He went down on one knee and reloaded the revolver, hands shaking. Then he wriggled forward on his belly towards the corner of the bridge, expecting to be fired at the instant he showed himself.

But bullets were pouring into all four ground-floor windows, ripping the barricades apart. Through the thinning smoke he could see the Sergeant-Major twenty yards away standing with his back to the door, bracing himself for a frantic dash to safety before the door blew. He was in full view of the Adjutant's men across the canal who were peppering the windows each side of him, leaving a narrow fire-free corridor of escape. Suddenly the Sergeant-Major darted forward—then leaped and fell as a bullet hit him. Rapid flashes spurted from the window to the right of the door, stabbing down through a narrow gap at the side of the barricade at the Sergeant-Major squirming on the ground.

Carew rose swiftly to one knee and fired furiously at the flashes. Then he chucked the empty revolver away and threw himself flat and started to crawl across the road. Bullets aimed at the windows zipped over his head. He reached the gutter and inched along it. He caught a glimpse of the Sergeant-Major dragging himself forward on his belly, legs shattered, trying to get away before the door exploded.

Carew jumped to his feet when he reached the spot opposite the door. The bullets from across the canal were no longer flying over his head but were whizzing past on both sides towards the windows. The Sergeant-Major was lying on the path just inside the gateway, his face twisted with pain and desperation.

Carew straddled him and bent down, grabbing him under the armpits. He would have to half-drag, half-carry him across the road to the canal. He sucked in his breath and lifted—

Then the door disappeared in a vivid flash. A scorching blast hit him and flung him six feet out on to the road. He lay there stunned, choking on acrid fumes, ears ringing. He could taste blood in his mouth and there was a burning smell in his nostrils. He tried to rise, pressing the palms of his hands against the square-setts. He managed to lift himself until his knees were off the ground, then his strength gave way. His body hit the ground. The last things he heard before he lost consciousness were the triumphant yells of his men and the thunderous sounds of racing, booted feet.

# Chapter Twenty

I

Unkempt, unshaven, hollow-eyed from lack of sleep, the men on the roof of the General Post Office, rebel Headquarters, watched the morning sun rising slowly above the rooftops. Already they could feel its warmth. It was going to be another cloudless, scorching day. A mile away to the west, smoke was still rising from the building which had gone up in flames the evening before. At dusk they had watched burning drums of oil shooting up into the air and exploding. More buildings were burning to the north and south-east.

They crouched behind the stone balustrade, squinting against the mounting sun, their eyes searching the rooftops for snipers. Every building in the long wide street – the principal street of the city – had been evacuated. The street itself was deserted, except for the two dead Lancers' horses at the base of Nelson Pillar. The carcasses were bloated now and the stench of corruption was becoming unbearable.

With the coming of daylight, the machine-guns began to open up on the other rebel positions south of the river. The men on the roof gripped their rifles tightly. One man turned to his companion. 'It will be our turn next,' he whispered, then switched his gaze southwards towards the bridge three hundred yards away. Suddenly he gave a startled yell and jumped to his feet, pointing. Two field-guns were being un-limbered on the south quay, using the river wall for protection. An officer rushed below with the news.

Ten minutes later the guns opened fire on two rebel posts overlooking the river, east and west of the bridge. The bombardment lasted for nearly half an hour, then ceased. The building to the west lay in ruins; the other was engulfed in flames. Then both guns opened fire again, concentrating on the buildings on the east side of the street.

The first two shells crashed through the roof of a newspaper warehouse and exploded, setting fire to giant rolls of newsprint. Immediately flames and thick black smoke shot up through the

457

shattered roof. More shells landed on the buildings about, setting fire to a bank, two hotels, a restaurant and an art academy.

From the high tower of the Fire Station south of the river, the Chief of the Dublin Fire Brigade watched the fire spreading, powerless to do anything about it. Ordered by the military authorities not to interfere, he looked on in anger and frustration at the deliberate destruction of the heart of the capital. He stood there till late afternoon. By that time an entire block east of the bridge was one vast sea of flame.

As night began to fall, a stiff breeze blew up from the south, driving long fiery tentacles across an intervening street, igniting one building after another. Then the flames reached an oil works opposite the General Post Office. The building exploded in a glaring white ball; flames shot hundreds of feet into the air. The blast blew in the side wall of a large department store on the other side of a laneway in between. Sheets of blazing oil splashed down on the roof and on that of an adjoining hotel. Twenty minutes later both buildings were raging infernos. The huge glass windows of the department store bubbled and burst apart, then flowed in molten streams across the road.

The fierce heat drove back the defenders of the Post Office from their barricaded windows. The barricades, composed of mail-bags and ledgers, began to smoulder. Hoses were turned on; the water at once turned to steam. One young officer mopped his perspiring face, then extended his arms wide in perplexity. 'Why?' he gasped. 'Why did they do it?'

'So they'll have a clear field of fire for their artillery and blast us to hell!' a man beside him growled.

By midnight, the entire east side of Lower Sackville Street and the streets behind it was a solid mass of leaping, roaring flames. On the slopes of the Dublin Hills the people stood looking down at the burning city twenty miles away. Even at that distance they could clearly see the Nelson Pillar silhouetted against the flames.

In a hospital bed, a sedated Alec Carew stared up at the glow of the fires on the ceiling.

In North King Street, Myles Burke and the men at the barricades heard a distant rumble as a building collapsed and saw a million sparks spewing up as though from a volcano.

Father Poole watched from a window on the top floor of the presbytery, then lowered himself to his knees and started to pray for the men trapped in the flames.

In the Vice-Regal Lodge in the Phoenix Park, the Under-Secretary turned away from the sight of the blood-red sky over the city and wept.

Durkin awoke from a troubled sleep in the basement of the General Post Office and, sniffing smoke like an animal, suddenly went berserk. He had to be held down by several soldiers, his fellow prisoners.

On the floor above, Con Gallagher was receiving final instructions from an officer.

'Communication has broken down between ourselves and the Four Courts garrison. The two men we sent have not returned. It's vital we know what's happening.' He paused, then said: 'We may have to vacate this building and retreat westward and link up with them. Bring back information regarding troop strengths and dispositions . . .'

Gallagher nodded, pulling off his heavy boots and putting on a pair of rubber-soled tennis shoes he had found in a cupboard upstairs. He had dyed them with dark-blue ink. His face and hands were daubed with dirt, and the buttons of his uniform were smeared with boot polish. If he was to get through safely, he would have to be not only silent but almost invisible as well. He glanced at the Mauser rifle lying against the wall.

'I don't want that bloody cumbersome thing. I'll take the carbine you took from the dead Lancer.'

The officer sighed. 'I can only give you twenty rounds. We're desperately short of three-o-three stuff.'

'I hope to Christ I can get through without having to fire a shot.'

They walked down a corridor leading to the side of the building. There was a tangy smell of smoke and they could hear muffled shouts on the other side of the wall.

'The roof must be on fire,' the officer said.

Six men were guarding the side-door. Gallagher and the officer waited while the flimsy barricade was removed. A candle stuck in a bottle provided a little light.

'Take care,' the officer murmured. 'The British have a barricade at the top of Moore Street. There's a machine-gun. Maybe two.'

The door was opened. Smoke from the fires in Sackville Street poured in. The officer coughed and spluttered, then clapped Gallagher on the shoulder. 'Good luck.'

Stooping, Gallagher raced across the road into a laneway opposite. He continued for about fifteen yards, then turned left. A few more yards brought him to the mouth of the lane.

He halted then, standing with his back against a wall. Then he peered cautiously round the corner. All the street-lamps had been extinguished but he could dimly make out the barricade at the top of the street fifty yards away. The upper parts of the buildings opposite were aglow with the reflection of the fires, but the lower parts were in shadow. He went down on his belly, cradling the carbine in his arms, crawled slowly forward on to the road. The roar of the fires drowned all noise. Nevertheless he paused when he reached the middle of the road. He could imagine the Tommies at the barricade with fingers on the triggers, eyes straining for the slightest movement.

He started crawling again. There was an overpowering stench of rotting fruit. The street was famous for its open-air stalls and the refuse had remained uncollected for days. As he reached the footpath his nose picked up another, stronger smell: sickly sweet. Animal, he thought, not vegetable. He turned his head to the right. The body of a man lay sprawled in the gutter ten yards away.

His mouth tightened. Now I know what happened to at least one of the two messengers Headquarters sent. He crawled over the footpath, then stretched himself full length against a shop-front. His mouth was dry and his body drenched in sweat.

There was a laneway about fifteen yards away. He waited for a full minute, then started to inch forward towards it on his belly. His eyes were accustomed to the dark now and he could see the barricade more clearly. He continued, pausing every few seconds, watching for the slightest movement, preparing himself for the first flurry of shots.

He managed to reach the mouth of the laneway without incident, wriggling snake-like round the corner. Then he straightened up against a wall, breathing deeply, feeling the tension slowly draining from him. He was at the edge of the markets, a maze of narrow alleyways stretching westward.

He moved off, moving through the labyrinth silently and swiftly, pausing now and then at corners to watch and listen. He knew every inch of this area; it was familiar as the back of his hand. He knew every short-cut, knew which alleys were blind and those that were not. All the street-lamps were out and the moon was just a misty blur in the sky.

He had covered about half a mile when he was forced to halt. He squatted on his heels, panting, his back against the blank wall of a warehouse. It was a little side street and facing him was an acre of waste ground. I'm more than half-way there, he told himself, wondering for how long his luck would last. Then he heard it – the distant tramp, tramp, tramp of booted feet. He rose up quickly and darted across to the waste ground. The only cover he could find was a heap of rubble and he threw himself flat behind it. He waited, clutching the carbine tightly, listening to the rhythmical beating of feet coming nearer.

He was between two streets and they were marching down on both sides in two parallel columns. He hugged the ground. The pile of rubble

460

on his right hid him from view, but he was completely exposed on the left. He drew in his breath as they came nearer.

Then they were marching past, heavy boots rapping against the cobbles, equipment clinking. Many soldiers, he thought, possibly two platoons. Suddenly someone switched on a torch. Gallagher tensed as the beam swept towards him.

'Turn off that bloody light!' someone shouted. 'Don't you know there are snipers about.'

The light was switched off immediately and Gallagher breathed a silent sigh of relief. He lay still, not moving a muscle. He did not relax until they had all marched past. Reinforcements were coming in. They were sealing off the area around the Post Office and the other rebel positions. It was as dangerous now to go back as it was to go forward. He had no choice. He rose to his feet and padded forward on his rubber-soled shoes, senses alert.

He found himself in the centre of a maze of narrow slum streets. Some were in ruins. He stole along cat-like behind a long line of half-demolished cottages, careful lest he make any noise. He had memorised the rough plan of the rebel positions drawn for him by an officer. Directly ahead was a long narrow laneway flanked on both sides by blank walls. There was a rebel barricade at the top. The British would never launch an attack up there: it was far too narrow and completely devoid of cover. He could only assume that the entrance to it was lightly guarded.

Before communication had broken down, Headquarters had been informed that the British had hastily thrown the equivalent of two platoons all around the rebel defensive position. They were stretched to the extreme: a few men here, a few men there; a lone machine-gun covering a key point. But the information they had received was now more than two days old. Reinforcements were coming in all the time. I hope to hell they haven't reached this area yet, he thought.

Suddenly he stopped, hearing voices and the slow beat of heavy boots against cobbles. Soldiers were walking down the street towards him. Only a few feet of rubble-strewn ground and a crumbling wall separated him from them. They were coming nearer. Two, he thought, maybe three. One was pleading.

'Cum on, Slogger, give's a bloody Woodbine. Aw'n dyin' for a smoke.'

'Ah've nowt, lad, nowt.'

'Stingy beggor!'

Another man laughed softly as they walked by.

Gallagher waited, listening to their receding footsteps. He recognised the accents. North of England. They brought back memories of slag heaps, tall factory chimneys belching smoke, rows and rows of grimy miners' houses . . . He knew these men; knew their language. He had worked side by side with them; he had drunk with them and sometimes had fought with them whenever he had been called a red-headed Irish bastard . . .

The ruins gave way to open waste ground. Rubbish everywhere; the whole place was being used as a refuse dump. He nearly stumbled over a sheet of corrugated tin. He hesitated. It was impossible to continue along here without making some noise.

He picked his way down a slope to the street. When he reached the footpath he crouched, cocking his head to one side, listening. In the silence he could hear the slow measured tread of footsteps not too far ahead, moving back and forth, back and forth. A lone sentry on his beat. He started to creep forward.

He felt naked and exposed in the moonlight with nothing but open waste ground on either side. But there was a wall up ahead which provided some shadow. He made for it, treading carefully. A great deal of rubbish had overflowed on to the footpath.

He did not see the tin can; it lay hidden under a heap of trash. His foot kicked against it and sent it rolling out into the middle of the road. He ran for the shadow of the wall, then crouched, heart thumping.

'Who goes there?' The voice was young and frightened.

Answer him quick, Gallagher told himself. 'Joe,' he replied. There's always a Joe or a Sam, he thought. 'Who's that?'

A pause. 'Harry,' the sentry answered, a note of suspicion in his voice.

Another pause. 'How, then, Joe?' The idiomatic greeting was like a password. Many's the time I heard that, thought Gallagher, when walking to work in the early morning through the streets of Newcastle. He could imagine the sentry anxiously awaiting the proper response, rifle at the ready.

'How, again, Harry.'

He could sense the feeling of relief. Then he heard the sentry walking towards him. He placed the carbine on the ground and waited, body taut as a spring.

The soldier strolled into a patch of moonlight, slinging his rifle. He stepped on to the footpath. 'Where are you, Joe?'

Gallagher leaped up from the shadows. His hands were around the man's throat before he could cry out, thumbs digging into his

462

windpipe. He swung the squirming body against the wall, throwing back his head as hands frantically clawed for his face. The soldier kicked out and Gallagher winced as the heavy boot grazed his shin. He exerted the pressure with all his might.

Suddenly the body gave a violent jerk, then went limp. Gallagher retained his fierce grip for several seconds as the soldier's knees sagged against his. Then, gently, he lowered the body to the ground. He stood over it, breathing heavily.

A shuddering sigh escaped him. He had killed a man with his bare hands. He was grateful for the dark – grateful he could not see the face. 'Poor kid,' he whispered, 'poor kid . . .' He stooped and picked up the carbine. He was not out of the woods yet; there could be another sentry up ahead. He stepped carefully over the body and pressed on.

But the barricade blocking the entrance of the lane was unguarded. He lowered himself to his hunkers before it, listening. He could hear the footsteps of another sentry coming towards him. He squeezed through a gap at the side and ran, keeping to the left of the laneway, his rubber-soled shoes making no noise. He halted half-way up and dropped on his belly. Somewhere ahead was the rebel barricade. The last obstacle, and the most dangerous. The men behind it would be on the alert and on the defensive.

He started to crawl forward, the carbine cradled in his arms. Once he stopped and looked behind, thinking he had heard a shout in the distance. Perhaps they found the body of the sentry, he thought. The eastern sky throbbed and glowed from the fires in Sackville Street. He crawled on. He had covered a distance of about thirty yards when he stopped, hearing the murmur of voices. The barricade was only a short distance away. He inched forward a few more yards, then stopped again. The murmuring continued. They had not seen or heard him. He realised now how right he had been in blackening his face and hands. With his dark-green uniform and blue-dyed rubber-soled tennis shoes he had managed to slip through this far without being detected.

He lay flat, left hip against the wall, wondering what to do next. To stand up and walk slowly forward would be asking for a bullet through the head. He decided to announce himself.

'Hey,' he called softly. 'Hey there.'

The murmurings ceased abruptly.

'A friend,' he called again. 'A friend.'

He was about to rise to his feet when a stabbing flame tore the darkness apart. He threw himself flat as the bullet glanced off the wall and went singing away into space. A ragged volley immediately followed. The men behind the barricade had fired directly up the lane, thinking they were being attacked.

Cursing and swearing followed as they fumbled feverishly with their weapons. They were using single-shot Mauser rifles. Gallagher did not wait for them to reload. He jumped to his feet and charged.

The barricade jumped into sight out from the darkness. He caught a quick glimpse of several figures behind it and threw the carbine sideways at them. Then he dived after it, colliding with one man who squealed like a rabbit. The man's body cushioned his fall as they both hit the ground. Gallagher rolled free. He was about to struggle to his feet when he saw the figure standing over him with rifle raised, in the act of clubbing him with the butt. He threw his hands over his face and started to yell at the top of his voice, crying out that he was a runner from Headquarters and to wait, wait, wait . . .

## II

Gallagher sat with his back against the barricade, chewing a thick slice of buttered bread. The bread was stale and the butter rancid. Breakfast how are ye, he thought sourly, washing the soggy mass down with a mouthful of tea. He placed the mug down beside him and fished in the breast-pocket of his tunic for his one remaining cigarette. Everything was in short supply: tobacco, food, ammunition . . . Men too, he thought, glancing sideways at the group beside him.

They were crouched behind the barricade, staring tensely at the heavy black smoke rolling across the blue morning sky. We are not a people, he reflected, who can endure being besieged for very long. Too emotional; too highly strung. He lit the cigarette and inhaled deeply, holding the smoke in his mouth, enjoying the flavour. God alone knew when he would have another.

There was a barricade thirty yards away, facing west. Two more blocked the entrances to two side streets running north. Four yards away from where he was sitting was the entrance to a long street which stretched southwards towards the quays and the Four Courts. Situated half-way down it was a convent which was being used as a headquarters and a casualty station. The whole position is so lightly defended, he thought, lapsing into a sudden mood of despondency, the British will have no difficulty in overrunning us. He could see wave after wave of yelling Tommies swarming over the barricades, stabbing and slashing with their bayonets . . .

A cold feeling of fear gathered in the pit of his stomach; instinctively his hand reached down and touched the pocket containing Una's letter. She wrote to him every week from Carewstown. News of her father's poor health; the baby . . . He closed his eyes. The baby was more than six months old now. If I could only see him . . . He could feel the tears beginning to well up behind the closed eyelids. Sweet God . . . why didn't I go back with her when I had the chance? But he knew the answer to that. Going back to Carewstown meant having to face charges for assault. It was ironic. Fear of imprisonment had made him stay in Dublin. Now here he was: trapped – condemned to die in a rebellion that was already lost.

And if there should be a surrender? He tossed the butt away with an angry gesture. Surrender meant either the firing squad or years behind bars in an English prison.

A field-gun barked in the distance. Then another joined in. The bombardment of the Post Office had started. The men peered cautiously over the top of the barricade, listening. Gallagher remained seated, wishing he had another cigarette.

Both guns fired again, one after the other. Lieutenant Skerritt straightened up slowly and stood, staring at the smoke blackened sky, his face grim. Field-glasses hung at his chest, suspended by a strap round his neck. Gallagher looked up at him. Walter Carew's steward of all people, he thought.

After reaching the barricade the night before, he had been brought to headquarters to make his report. Later he had been assigned to this, the North King Street barricade. In the darkness his ears had picked out the Connacht accent from among the flat, nasal Dublin drawls. Then daylight arrived, and what had been mere voices became faces. The shock of recognition had been mutual.

The first thing Gallagher wanted to ask him was why he was with a Dublin battalion instead of serving with one in the west of Ireland. But he never got the opportunity. At that moment a messenger arrived from nearby headquarters with a request that Lieutenant Skerritt attend an officers' conference at once. The conference had lasted all morning. Only when Gallagher was starting his breakfast did Skerritt rejoin them. Has he been back to Carewstown recently? Gallagher wondered. Perhaps he saw Una. I must ask him. But later, he decided. Skerritt was too engrossed in what was happening a mile away to the east.

Skerritt raised the field-glasses and surveyed the narrow street in front of him. It curved out of sight to the left, two hundred yards away. They're around that bend, he thought, waiting the same as we are. When will they attack? During the daylight hours? Or will they wait for nightfall? He shifted his gaze upward. Suddenly he stiffened. 'Halloo . . .'

Curious to know what it was that had attracted his attention, Gallagher raised himself to his knees and peered over the top of the barricade. All he could see was a two hundred yard stretch of cobbled roadway, flanked on both sides by drab tenement houses. Then, from out of the dull brownish grey in the distance, came a vivid spurt of flame. The bullet whizzed past Gallagher's head. He heard Skerritt cry out as he ducked with the others, feeling the impact as another bullet smacked into the barricade.

Then he turned slowly around.

Tim Skerritt lay on his face a few feet away, squirming, one foot beating a rapid tattoo against the ground. Suddenly he gave a violent jerk as two more bullets struck him between the shoulder blades.

Gallagher stared at the still quivering body in stunned disbelief, his face grey with shock. There were so many questions I wanted to ask him, was all his numbed brain could think, now I'll never know the answers to any of them. He flinched as a bullet thudded into the barricade behind him. Another followed, then another . . . The fire was becoming more rapid and concentrated. The bullets were coming at a steep angle, striking the top of the barricade and zipping over their heads and ricocheting off the cobbles with ear-splitting yowls. Skerritt's lifeless body was hit again and again. Fortunately the barricade was strong; mostly porter barrels filled with sawdust with thick mattresses covering them for added protection.

Nevertheless Gallagher rolled himself up into a foetus-like position and gritted his teeth. A boy next to him started to whimper and over his shoulder he could see the rest of the men cowering like himself, nerves at snapping point.

After this comes the attack, he told himself despairingly. With all the fight driven out of us, they'll take the barricade with no trouble, then use us for bayonet practice.

'Get up, you chicken-livered swine! Get up and fight back!'

Everyone turned their heads.

A tall, ancient figure with a sword in his hand stood over Skerritt's body, glaring at them. 'Cowardly scum!' he shouted.

A bullet tore up a piece of the road beside him and Gallagher saw the

466

sword-arm twitch as another either hit or grazed it. 'Get down!' he roared. 'For Christ's sake. . . !'

The man looked at him with open contempt. 'Get up,' he croaked, pointing with the sword. 'Get up, or by the Lord God I'll run you through with this!' Suddenly a hot wave of shame and anger swept over Gallagher, washing away all his fear. He whirled around, bringing the carbine up to his shoulder. He was fired at the instant he showed himself: the bullet whizzed past his head like an angry hornet. But he had seen the flashes coming from behind two chimneys in the distance. He fired back furiously, giving vent to his rage and humiliation. Above the noise of gunfire he could hear the hoarse voice behind him urging him on.

'That's it – shoot back. Give them a taste of their own medicine!'

Gallagher reloaded the carbine, hesitating as he realised he had used up half his ammunition. But he had silenced the snipers for the time being. He turned to the men beside him. Some were lifting their heads cautiously.

'The house on the right at the end of the curve!' he shouted. 'There are snipers behind the chimneys. Let them have it!'

The roar of the Mausers in the confined space of the narrow street was deafening. Myles Burke sheathed his sword. Stooping stiffly, he removed the strap of the field-glasses from around Skerritt's neck. He straightened up slowly and raised them to his eyes. He could see the heavy bullets tearing huge chunks away from the crumbling brickwork. A chimney pot disintegrated and a bullet skidded off the roof, sending pieces of slate flying in all directions. A chimney stack collapsed and someone gave a howl of triumph as three khaki figures scrambled for safety. They disappeared over the skyline, jumping down into the valley between the roofs.

Myles lowered the glasses. 'Cease firing!' he bawled, coughing, breathing in thick clouds of cordite.

The men sat down heavily and wearily. Some started to rub their shoulders tenderly. Myles carefully placed the strap of the field-glasses around his neck, studying their pale, strained faces. All, he could see, were suffering from exhaustion. Days of inactivity, waiting for an attack that never came, had worn them down. The thing to do was to keep them busy – snap them out of their inertia.

He pointed at two men sitting in front of him. 'You two, pick up Lieutenant Skerritt's body and carry it away out of sight.'

They looked at him dumbly, not moving.

'On the double, damn you!'

They rose quickly to their feet.

'First remove his bandolier,' he ordered. He turned his head to where Skerritt's carbine lay against the wall. 'And you,' addressing a man sitting beside it, 'take Lieutenant Skerritt's carbine and bandolier. Empty two of the pockets and hand the ammunition to the Sergeant there,' pointing to Gallagher. The men stared in amazement. This ancient, stumbling, bumbling, ridiculous figure in an ill-fitting uniform was in command; alert, decisive, arrogant, abusive.

'Get up off your arses the lot of you and face the street! Check your weapons.'

The old bastard is enjoying all of this, Gallagher thought resentfully, stuffing clips of ammunition into the pockets of the bandolier. He looked at the gaunt, quixotic figure standing behind him.

Myles Burke had adopted a relaxed stance as though his portrait were being painted. One hand languidly held the field-glasses to his eyes while the other rested lightly on the hilt of the sword. The affected pose irritated Gallagher. He was reminded of one of those old prints of the Napoleonic Wars; Marshal Ney on the field of battle, calmly awaiting the oncoming enemy.

Myles lowered the glasses and beckoned. 'Sergeant . . .'

Gallagher rose, carrying the carbine by his side.

Myles indicated with a nod of the head. 'That side street twenty yards down . . . There are six men among the ruins to the west of it. Opposite is a Malt House. Take two men and occupy it. Position the men on the roof. There's an outside stairway with an iron platform on top. From there you'll be able to use that carbine to good effect.'

Gallagher picked the two men nearest to him, and led them away.

'Sergeant . . .'

Gallagher turned around.

'This time,' Myles said in a flat voice, staring straight ahead, 'show a better example.'

He raised the field-glasses to his eyes again, pretending not to hear the smothered curse. Only when the footsteps had faded away did he permit himself a wry smile. Make them angry, he thought, then they'll fight all the better.

The field-guns continued to bark at regular intervals. The smoke still rose thick and heavy over the centre of the city, blotting out the pale sun. He studied the street in front of him, pursing his lips thoughtfully. They'll come charging round that bend, no more than six abreast, hemmed in by the narrow street. I'll allow them to reach half-way before giving the order to fire. One good volley will mow down those in

468

front – that will break the momentum of the attack and give the men with the single-shot Mausers time to reload. He lowered his gaze to the men before him. Only twelve of us now – and only one modern weapon between us. Apart from that, we need more elbow-room.

One end of the barricade rested against the side wall of a public house jutting out on to the road. The windows facing the street in front had been loopholed with sacks of maize and flour.

'The first three men on the right . . . Occupy the pub and position yourselves at the windows. The rest of you – spread out.'

They made room for him as he walked to the centre of the barricade. They looked at him with animosity and awe. A youth beside him noticed a tear in his sleeve, and saw the trickle of blood flowing down over wrist and hand.

'You're wounded!' he said.

Myles waved him down. 'Shush, boy. A mere scratch. Of no consequence.' He held himself erect, feet planted wide apart, head proudly uplifted. He felt rejuvenated. The years of humiliation and despair, of hunger and destitution, had all been worthwhile for this brief spell of glory. He was not going to die in some grim workhouse after all, alone and forgotten, but with his sword in his hand facing the enemy, earning for himself a place in the sagas.

The distant cannonade continued. He could sense the nervousness of the men. After their moment of fury had passed, apprehension was setting in. Waiting was always the worst: even his own enthusiasm might wane in time, but there was nothing he could do. Or could he? The British were very sensitive when it came to pride. They could easily be provoked.

He unsheathed his sword, placing it on top of the barricade. He unbuttoned his holster and drew out his revolver. Despite being heavy and awkward to handle, it could outrange all other weapons of its kind. He raised his voice.

'Perhaps they can't decide whether to attack us or not. Let's make up their minds for them. A good, rousing rebel song – that ought to raise the hackles.'

They stared in open-mouthed amazement.

'Let's see now, something we all know. How about *God save Ireland* – all of you should know that.'

The men looked at each other. One shook his head.

'Come on, now,' Myles shouted, 'give it all you've got!' and he started to sing in his high, cracked voice.

469

> "God save Ireland" said the heroes;
> "God save Ireland" said they all . . .

Their silence made him stop. 'Sing!' he roared, raising his revolver. He started to sing again. This time the youth beside him joined in; another man followed suit, then another . . .

> "God save Ireland" said the heroes;
> "God save Ireland" said they all;
> "Whether on the scaffold high
> Or the battle-field we die,
> Oh, what matter, when for Erin dear we fall."

A block away, on an iron platform at the top of an outside stairway, Gallagher listened to the singing and groaned. That romantic old fool is going to get us all killed, he fumed. He looked up at the men on the roof.

'Get ready. They'll attack now for sure.'

Below, on the other side of the street, six men were crouched behind some ruins. Three were armed with revolvers; the other three with Martini-Henry single-shot rifles. Gallagher brought his carbine up to his shoulder, his eyes on the mouth of the street.

'Christ help all of us,' he whispered.


III


A whistle blast split the air, and they came charging round the bend, cheering, bayonets flashing.

'No one is to fire till I do!' Myles shouted, going down on one knee, and resting the long barrel of the revolver on the top of the barricade. He aimed at the leading officer. He aimed low, allowing for the vicious kick of the weapon and fired.

The officer leapt, and his men behind went down in a tumbling tangle as the heavy Mauser bullets tore into them. Those bringing up the rear tripped and stumbled over the bodies, breaking up the momentum of the attack. Myles continued firing while the men with the Mausers reloaded. It was impossible to miss. The street was too narrow and without cover and the soldiers were hopelessly bunched together. Their Mausers reloaded, the men took quick aim and let loose another deadly volley into the packed and struggling mass.

470

Gallagher and his men were waiting for them. As they raced past the waste ground, the men behind the ruins opened up at point-blank range. The leading four staggered and fell and Gallagher and the men on the roof sent the three at the rear spinning to the ground with one volley. The remaining seven, confused and panic-stricken and unaware of the men above them, huddled against the blank wall of the Malt House and tried to fight it out with the men behind the ruins. They managed to let off a ragged volley, then collapsed in a heap under a hail of bullets, Gallagher picking off three one after another with his carbine.

The echoes of the final fusillade died away slowly. No one stirred. All stared at the body-strewn street, numb with shock. In the distance the artillery continued its leisurely pounding of the Post Office. Boom, boom, boom . . .

Gallagher was the first to move. He rose slowly to his feet, wiping the sweat from his forehead with the back of his hand. 'Come on,' he said curtly, 'let's go down and get those rifles and ammunition.' He went swaying down the iron stairway, the two men lowering themselves down from the roof and following him. As he reached the street, the men from the ruins came running over to meet him.

They moved carefully among the bodies. Eight were still alive. One young soldier was whimpering for his mother. Gallagher went down on one knee beside him. 'Easy, son, easy,' he said soothingly, laying a hand gently on his shoulder.

The boy looked up at him, tears running down his face. He was lying on his side, legs drawn up, his hands over his stomach. Blood was trickling out between his fingers. He opened his mouth, trying to say something, but all that emerged was an unintelligible whisper.

Gallagher forced a smile. 'All right, son . . . We'll have you attended to very soon. Don't worry,' he added, and thought: It's like comforting a child who's just woken up from a bad dream. He turned his head and looked at the carnage about him. Jesus, he thought, is any cause . . . any country worth this? Then, from the barricade a block away, the singing started again.

> Wrap the Green Flag round me, boys,
> To die were far more sweet.
> With Erin's noble emblem, boys,
> To be my winding sheet . . .

# Chapter Twenty-One

## I

The Adjutant knocked, and opened the door. Carew put down the book he was reading and raised himself up in the bed.

'I thought I'd need the aid of a bloodhound to find you,' the Adjutant said smiling, closing the door. 'The hospital people seem determined to keep you hidden from troublesome visitors like myself.' He drew up a chair and sat down.

'I wish you could persuade them to let me out of here,' Carew grumbled. 'They insist in treating me like an invalid.'

The Adjutant chuckled. 'Tomorrow morning, I've been told. They're keeping you in for further observation. So relax and take it easy. You'll be on active service soon enough.'

Carew raised an inquiring eyebrow.

'You're still attached to Brigade,' the Adjutant said, 'you and any other stray officer we can lay our hands on. There are quite a few. Many were returning from leave when this damn rebellion broke out.'

'How many officers did we lose?'

The Adjutant paused before answering. 'Eighteen,' he said, 'and two hundred and sixteen other ranks either killed or wounded.'

'Jesus Christ,' Carew breathed.

The Adjutant sighed. 'Amen to that. The Sherwoods and Notts are being withdrawn for a rest. You'll be joining the South Staffs till this is all over. They landed only yesterday and need an officer who knows the city to act as guide.' He smiled. 'The Colonel has recommended you for a DSO. Singing your praises since he heard how you rescued the Sergeant-Major before the explosive charge went off. You've restored his faith in desk wallahs. He thought you chaps did nothing but chinwag and swill whiskey all day long.'

'How is the Sergeant-Major?'

'Got it in both legs. The left leg is in a bit of a mess, but the surgeons think they can save it.'

'And the young Second-Lieutenant, the one who led the attack down the canal?'

'You mean Eric Hunter? Unfortunate little wretch.'

'Killed? Wounded?'

'Wounded, yes. But not physically.'

He told how Hunter had panicked when the first rebel volley killed his sergeant and two of his men. Hunter had thrown himself to the ground, his men following suit, and crawled for the shelter of a nearby pillarbox, leaving his inexperienced troops stretched flat in the open. They remained there, hugging the ground, bullets whizzing over their heads, waiting for their officer to get up and lead them in a charge, but Hunter never moved. The rebels, having got the exact range and presented with an unmoving target, picked them off one by one . . . They found Hunter sitting on the gravel track at the edge of the canal, sobbing like a child and tossing pebbles into the water.

'Poor little devil,' Carew murmured after a while.

'Yes,' said the Adjutant, 'yes . . .'

Silence fell between them. In the distance a field-gun barked and the windows rattled.

'What's happening in the city?' Carew inquired. 'I've been listening to that bombardment all morning.'

'They're shelling the rebel Headquarters. Over open sights, I believe. But first they had to burn the east side of Lower Sackville Street to the ground to do it. Now I hear the west side is on fire. Time is running out for those blighters in the Post Office.'

Carew was silent. It was hard to imagine Lower Sackville Street in ruins. The Imperial Hotel gone, and the DBC Restaurant. Miriam and he used to meet there in the old days whenever Durkin was out of town.

The Adjutant rose to his feet. 'Duty calls, I'm afraid. Glad to see you looking so well.' He paused in the doorway and turned. 'By the way, your friend Major Calder is alive and well. A little shook up, though. He was attending a conference in the Under-Secretary's office in the Castle when the rebels attacked. Had to hold them off with his revolver.' He grinned. 'Chap in Irish Command told me all about it. The Castle officials in the room were in a blue funk. Crawled under the table while the Major stood at the window blazing away at the rebels below. Jolly good, what?'

He closed the door and Carew sank back against the pillow. I wonder, he mused, if they are the same officials who scoffed and sneered at Ian Calder and myself all those years ago when we tried to warn them of the growing menace of the IRB?

473

He smiled wryly. They were not scoffing or sneering now. Neither was that pusillanimous Under-Secretary. When this is all over and the inquiry begins, his head will be the first to roll.


## II


The grounds and buildings of a tennis club near the sea had been commandeered by the Brigade as a temporary headquarters. Tents had been erected on the lawn as there was not sufficient room for all the Brigade staff. In the clubhouse, the Lieutenant-Colonel, his staff and the officers from the four battalions sat in groups waiting the arrival of the new Commander-in-Chief who had been sent from England to take supreme command.

Carew sat with Captain Spires of A Company. He was about to draw out his cigarette-case when Spires forestalled him.

'I wouldn't if I were you, old man. This bigwig dislikes smoking intensely.'

Carew sighed. 'You seem to know a lot about him.'

'Just from barrack-room gossip. He was C-in-C in Egypt. Checked Johnny Turk in his advance into the Delta, but he was made the scapegoat for the Gallipoli affair. Distrusts politicians ever since.'

Carew gave a mild snort. 'He's not the only one.'

'Nevertheless they've given him this chance to redeem himself. If he can clean up – '

The door opened and the Commander-in-Chief strode in, followed by his staff. The Lieutenant-Colonel and several senior officers advanced to meet him. Carew looked idly on. One of the C-in-C's staff officers, a tall aristocratic-looking figure, seemed vaguely familiar. He turned towards Spires.

'That officer being introduced to the Lieutenant-Colonel,' he whispered. 'I've seen his photograph in some society magazine or other. Know who he is?'

'Prince Alexander of Battenberg,' Spires whispered back.

Introductions over, the C-in-C mounted the rostrum and faced them. He carried a swagger cane, which he tapped impatiently against his thigh, giving an impression of restless energy. His face was strong and wide, and he had a square determined chin. On the wall behind him was a large map of the city. Someone had shaded the areas held by the rebels with red crayon.

'Now, gentlemen, I will be as brief as I can,' the C-in-C began, standing with booted legs apart, grasping the swagger cane with both hands and holding it level against his stomach. 'The Government is gravely concerned about this situation, and they have given me orders which are simple and specific.' He paused. 'My orders are to crush this rebellion as quickly as I know how, using whatever methods I choose to employ.' He stared at the upturned, expressionless faces. 'I have no intention of sparing the city, gentlemen. If necessary I shall not hesitate to destroy all buildings within any area occupied by the rebels. Drastic measures, I admit, but I have no other choice. The rebels intend to hold out as long as they can, in the hope that the rest of the country will rise with them. Fortunately there have been only a few sporadic attempts at insurrection in the rural parts, all which have been stamped out.

'This does not mean that the danger is over,' he continued. 'Far from it. The longer the Dublin rebels hold out, the greater the chance of the trouble flaring up again. We must not let that happen,' he emphasised, turning round to the map on the wall. He studied it for a moment before speaking. 'The shaded areas south of the river,' indicating them one by one with the tip of the cane, 'are buildings occupied by the insurgents. The College of Surgeons, the biscuit factory . . . It may be necessary to raze to the ground the areas surrounding them before bringing up the artillery.' He raised his cane higher up the map. 'The Post Office, the rebel headquarters . . . the roof and upper stories are now fully ablaze. Soon the rebels will have to evacuate. They may hope to link up with the Four Courts garrison, but that's impossible as the streets between have been barricaded by our forces and covered by rifles and machine-guns.'

He tapped his cane against a spot north of the river. 'Lastly, the Four Courts and the streets behind it. Our men are finding it a tough nut to crack. Yesterday, nearly a full platoon was wiped out in one attack.' He turned and faced them. 'I'm sending a battalion from this Brigade to reinforce them,' he said. 'You can expect fierce resistance, gentlemen. The rebels are making a last ditch stand and are determined to make us pay dearly.'

It was late afternoon when they crossed the bridge over the Liffey, A Company leading. They continued northwards for nearly half a mile until they reached the corner of Great Britain Street, then wheeled left and headed west through the deserted streets. The bombardment had ceased and an ominous quiet lay over the city.

Lieutenant-Colonel Gutridge marched at the head of the battalion along with Alec Carew and Captain Spires. A newcomer like his men, he was glad of Carew's presence. With him as guide, it had not been necessary to halt every so often along the route to consult maps.

He marched on, his eyes searching the windows of the houses on both sides of the street. He had heard how the Sherwoods had been raked by automatic fire from a house as they went swinging past towards the bridge. He was not going to make a blunder like that. He was not going to lead his men straight into an ambush. He blew furiously on the whistle suspended by a lanyard around his neck and raised his arm. He could hear boots crashing to a halt all the way down the line as he turned to Carew.

'Form an advance guard, Captain, and go on ahead. We'll follow at a distance of three hundred yards. Signal if you see anything suspicious.' Carew nodded and unbuttoned the flap of his holster. Three minutes later he was leading six men in Indian file up the footpath on the north side of the street. Opposite, five men led by a sergeant advanced in similar fashion. The street swerved to the left ahead. As they came round the bend they saw a manned barricade at the top of Sackville Street. They continued towards it.

There were about fifty soldiers at the barricade, their rifles trained on the burning Post Office building midway down the street. Two machine-guns were in the centre, one on each side of the Parnell Monument. As he led his men past, Carew could see the distant smoking ruins of what had been the east side of Lower Sackville Street. Here and there, smoke-blackened skeletons of buildings stood forlornly amidst acres of rubble. Debris lay scattered all over the street. He was reminded of recent newspaper photographs of Ypres. They passed another manned barricade at the entrance to a street a hundred yards further up. The soldiers had the tensed expectancy of a firing squad. He felt a twinge of pity for the rebels trapped in the Post Office. They had no choice but to make a dash for it, and the result would be bloody slaughter.

They pressed on, watching the rooftops for snipers. Their destination was the Technical School which was situated less than four hundred yards from the rebel defensive position. They reached it without incident, and waited for the main body to arrive. The Technical School was being used as a base of operations. In a room off the main hall, a Colonel from Irish Command explained the situation to Lieutenant-Colonel Gutridge. A crude map of the area held by the rebels had been drawn on a blackboard.

'Our chaps have managed to contain the rebels since the beginning of the week. And with only a hundred and fifty men, I might add. Now with the South Staffs reinforcing them, we can launch a full-scale assault from all quarters. But it will not be as easy as it sounds, gentlemen. Yesterday we lost a third of our force in an attack up North King Street. Here,' he said, turning to the blackboard and indicating the spot with a ruler. 'The street is two hundred yards long. It's extremely narrow and without any cover. I do not intend to launch another suicidal attack up it trying to take that damned barricade at the top.' He turned to face them. 'However, there is another way it can be taken and with the minimum of casualties. An armoured lorry. At this moment a vehicle is being improvised at the railway works. It will arrive sometime tomorrow. It's simply a large boiler mounted on a chassis with slits in the sides through which troops can fire. It can accommodate eighteen to twenty men.' He paused. 'Now, here's the plan. The lorry proceeds up the street towards the barricade with men inside the boiler, armed with rifles, grenades and picks. It stops half-way, turns and backs up against the door of one of the houses on the south side of the street. The door is smashed down and the men enter. Once inside, they start to tunnel through the houses.

'Twenty minutes later the action is repeated. This time our men break into a house on the north side of the street, then start to tunnel their way forward. By nightfall they should be near enough to the barricade to lob hand grenades down from the rooftops. By that time our men on the south side of the street will have reached the Malt House in the side street below the barricade. That's it there,' he said, pointing at the blackboard. 'From it they will be able to infiltrate through the ruins opposite and outflank the beggars.

'Ten minutes after the action starts a flare will be the signal for an all out attack.'

'Are there any civilians in the area, sir?' an officer inquired.

'Some. We don't know how many. Most of them left when the trouble started at the beginning of the week.'

A short while later, Alec went searching for A Company – or what was left of it. The battalion had been broken up into platoons and deployed round the rebel position. It was twilight and the end of another scorching day. He screwed up his eyes against the rays of the setting sun.

He turned a corner and found himself at the edge of a wasteland. Whole streets lay in ruins. He walked between two long rows of half-demolished cottages. In the roofless shells and on patches of waste ground, soldiers were settling down, gathering round crackling fires, brewing tea. The tangy smell of woodsmoke filled the air. He paused for a moment in the centre of the narrow cobbled roadway listening to the voices. Gruff northern and midland accents. Men from the Black Country, he thought, and from Newcastle-on-Tyne . . . He continued on up the street. There was an entrance to a lane near the top. As he passed he heard a sharp yelp of pain. He turned round. A group of soldiers were standing in the doorway of a crumbling building. He heard a thud followed by another cry of pain and he marched down towards them.

'What the hell is going on here?' he snapped.

They whirled around. There were five privates and a sergeant. The sergeant had a civilian pressed against the door, his left hand gripping the man's shirt collar. His right fist was drawn back, ready to deliver another blow. His victim was on the verge of collapse; his eyes were closed and blood was pouring out of his shattered mouth. Then Carew noticed another man on the ground in the far corner. His hands were clutching his stomach and his face was covered in blood.

'What's the meaning of this?' he demanded.

'We found these two hiding here, sir,' the sergeant replied, lowering his fist.

'Is that any reason to ill-treat them?'

'One of my men was found strangled near here two nights ago. It could have been one of these two bastards that did it.'

Carew turned to the soldiers behind him. 'Take these two men away and have them attended to immediately. Then hand them over for interrogation.'

The man on the ground moaned with pain as he was being lifted. Both were young and shabbily dressed. Just a couple of down and outs, thought Carew. As the soldiers led them away, the sergeant started to follow.

'Not you, sergeant,' Carew said harshly. 'I want a word with you.' He waited until the soldiers were out of earshot. 'I could have you up on a charge for this.'

The man stared impassively at him. He was of medium height, stocky, with a heavy black moustache and thick eyebrows which almost met above his nose. There was a cold viciousness about him. Carew could see it in the flat soulless eyes and the cruel lines about the mouth. The perfect fighting animal, he thought.

'What's your name?'

'Turnbull, sir. Sergeant Turnbull.'

'I don't condone brutality, sergeant. I could see to it that you lose those stripes.'

'Yes, sir,' the sergeant said slowly, his mouth twisting a little into what was almost a sneer, 'I suppose you could.'

'There's no supposing about it!' Carew drew a deep breath. 'Just make sure that this sort of thing never happens again. Understand?'

He spun on his heel and strode away.

# Chapter Twenty-Two

## I

They pounded with their fists on the heavy door, yelling at the top of their voices, trying to make themselves heard above the general uproar overhead. From the frantic shouts they knew that the fire was out of control and that the Post Office was being evacuated. Smoke was snaking under the door. It stung their eyes, and clogged their throats, making them cough and wheeze.

Suddenly there was a thunderous crash from above; they could feel the walls shaking from the impact. They fell silent, turning to each other in the candlelit darkness.

'Jesus,' a young soldier whispered, 'the roof's cavin' in.' A sob escaped him, and he started to beat at the door again. 'Help!' he screamed. 'For Christ's sake help!'

The Lance-Corporal in charge placed a hand on his shoulder. 'Stop it,' he said wearily, 'they can't hear you. They've forgotten us.' He shrugged despairingly. 'It's no use. We're finished, finished.' His pronouncement of doom descended on them like a weight too heavy to bear. They sank to the ground, drained and spent, the young soldier weeping uncontrollably.

Durkin staggered towards a corner and slid to the ground. His hands were numb from constant pummelling. Like the others he had screamed himself hoarse and had driven himself into a state of wild hysteria. He was limp with exhaustion. His clothes were filthy with dust and dirt and thick stubble covered the lower half of his face. He did not care. This was the end.

He raised his head and looked round him in the flickering half-light provided by two guttering candles. It was like a foretaste of Hell: the gloom, the suffocating heat, the smoke rising like clouds of sulphur . . . He closed his eyes and leaned his head against the wall. He was reminded of another place, dark and hollow-sounding, where a tall terrifying figure towered over an open Bible, his shadow thrown against

480

the wall by two tall smoking candles. A high-pitched fanatical voice came booming up the long corridor of memory.

'Do you repudiate the Scarlet Whore of Rome now, brother? Dost thou renounce its idolatry and pomp? Take the oath now, brother. Cast aside all those popish superstitions and beliefs. Recant now, I say. Recant, recant, recant!'

Why did he do it? Durkin asked himself, tears streaming down his stubbly cheeks, remembering his father's whine of protest as the ranting went on and on.

'For pity's sake, sir, enough. Have done with it. I'll conform.'

Why, why, why? he groaned silently, beating his fist against his knee. But he knew why. His parents had apostatised for food, clothes, money . . . Most of all they had done it for him. And he had prospered on the fruits of their apostasy: a good education, a place in society, wealth . . . Lucky Durkin, he thought bitterly, and now my luck has run out . . .

He coughed as the smoke clogged his throat. He was going to die, and in a most horrible way. *Unshriven.* The thought filled him with terror. If only he had a priest to confess to. All those sins, the deceits, the slanders, the petty blackmails. The lives I've ruined, he thought, remembering Andy Kinsella. He began to whisper an Act of Contrition. The words came drifting back along with other boyhood memories: the musty dark of the confessional; the smell of incense; lamps burning at the feet of statues.

'O my God, I am heartily sorry for having offended Thee.' His voice rose to fever pitch. 'Merciful Christ, look down on your unworthy servants. Save us from hellfire and eternal damnation.'

The nerve of one of the soldiers suddenly snapped. 'Shut up!' he screamed hysterically. 'Shut yer bloody mouth, ye psalm-spoutin' bleeder!'

Durkin ignored him. He heaved himself off the ground and went down on his knees. 'Have compassion, dear Jesus,' he cried, joining his hands, 'and save us all from a fiery death. . . !'

The soldiers scrambled to his feet. 'Shut up, ye stinkin' lump of shit!' he shouted. As Durkin opened his mouth again, he cuffed him across the face. 'Hypocrite! Sanctimonious pig!' he roared, striking his head with his open hand.

Durkin accepted the blows with the noble indifference of a martyr: redemption through fire and pain and the foul mouthings of Satan. He was appalled that anyone should blaspheme, here, on the very brink of eternity.

'Father,' he entreated, stretching out his arms in the shape of a cross, 'forgive him, for he knows not – '

The blow struck him on the cheekbone and sent him sprawling on his back. He lay there stunned. He could hear the soldier being dragged away by his companions. A little sanity returned and he began to pray quietly and fervently.

'O God, get me out of this, please, God. I'll mend my ways, I'll be good. Please God, please, please, please.'

He had never believed in miracles – they were for the innocent and the simple-minded. Even as he mouthed the words he had no faith. He sat up with a feeling of incredulity when he heard the bolt being pulled back.

The door was flung open and a voice bawled: 'Come out the lot of yez, quick. The place is being evacuated!'


II


Durkin clambered up the stairway through a fog of smoke, coughing violently. Half-way up he halted to catch his breath. Two soldiers came rushing up from behind and roughly elbowed him aside. He clutched the handrail for support, breathing heavily.

He continued after a minute. When he reached the ground-floor he drew back in terror and confusion. There were flames everywhere. Cursing, sweating men were trying to douse the fires. Officers bellowed orders and great hoses wriggled over the floor like gigantic boa constrictors. Above the tumult and the roar of the flames he could hear another sound – a distant rat, tat, tat, tatting. Machine-guns were raking the front of the building. He became aware of zipping noises above his head as bullets tore through the shattered windows. A burst of fire struck a pillar and plaster showered down like hail.

He crouched, not knowing which way to go. Four men staggered past carrying a wounded comrade on a stretcher. Durkin stumbled after them. Pieces of burning debris fell all round him. He tried to hurry, but in his haste he tripped over a hose and landed on all fours. The fall winded him. He rested on his hands and knees, his breath coming in great convulsive sobs. He felt drained of strength and his heart was pounding madly.

Someone near him was shouting at the top of his voice. The words penetrated his dulled senses.

'Abandon everything! Make for the corridor at the rear!'

The thought of being left behind in the blazing building made him rise groggily to his feet. He stood swaying, as men pushed hurriedly past him.

'For Christ's sake get a move on!' someone shouted, and punched him between the shoulder blades. The blow sent him staggering forward. He was caught up in the middle of the stampede, swept along like a leaf on the surface of a rushing stream. The shock cleared his head. He clutched at the shoulder of the man in front, terrified of being trampled underfoot.

The headlong, panic-stricken dash ended abruptly as it surged against a solid mass of tightly packed, smoke-begrimed men and women standing patiently in the long corridor leading to the side entrance. Durkin was trembling from head to foot. The corridor was full of smoke and hot as the inside of an oven.

A grim-faced officer stood by the open doorway leading to the street, a Mauser pistol in his hand. His eyes roved over the haggard, smoke-blackened faces of the advance guard standing in front of him.

'Our objective is the factory in Great Britain Street,' he declared. 'A new Headquarters will be established there. But first we'll have to clear the way for the rest of the garrison. That means having to take the barricade at the top of Moore Street — '

The rest of his words were drowned by a loud explosion that rocked the building. Another immediately followed.

'They're shelling us again!' someone shouted, panic in his voice.

The officer waved the pistol over his head. 'Come on, boys,' he cried, 'follow me!'

Two more shells landed in quick succession several stories above and everyone crouched instinctively as a floor collapsed in a thunderous roar. The entire corridor shook and rocked as though from an earthquake.

Panic-stricken, Durkin began to beat his way frantically forward. Fear gave him added strength. He punched and kicked aside anyone who impeded him. He could see men dashing out through the doorway and he struggled towards them. An officer grabbed at his sleeve but he tore himself free.

'Come back you bloody fool,' the man screamed, 'that's the advance guard!' But Durkin did not hear him. He followed the men into the smoke-filled street, sobbing with relief.

The officer in charge threw up his arm as he reached the mouth of the laneway leading into Moore Street. He turned to his second-in-command.

'It's a fifty-yard dash from here to the barricade at the top of the street. We'll split into two sections. I'll lead my section up along the right-hand pavement. You and your men make a run for it across the street and advance at the double up along the left. Attack when I give the word.'

An exhausted Durkin joined the men forming up on the left. He rested his back against the wall, panting a little. He was glad they had stopped and that he had been able to catch up with them. There was safety in numbers.

He jerked as another shell hit the Post Office a block away. Thank God I got out of that place, he thought, his eyes on the officer standing at the mouth of the lane checking his pistol. The officer rapped out an order, braced himself, and darted round the corner, his men following at the double.

The men in front of Durkin suddenly rushed forward. The abrupt movement took him by surprise and he stumbled after them. They were half-way across the road when the machine-gun opened fire.

Men twisted and fell. He threw himself flat as bullets tore up the ground around him. He lay spread-eagled, stunned with shock. He could feel something warm trickling down his leg.

'Oh, Christ, I've been hit,' he whimpered, but there was no pain. His bladder had failed.

Machine-gun and rifle-fire swept the street. The barricade was hidden by the bodies in front of it, but Durkin had a partial view of the eastern side of the street. He could see members of the advance guard being picked off in ones and twos as they charged along the pavement. He closed his eyes, unable to watch. He could hear the bullets thudding into the bodies in front of him.

'Enough, enough,' he moaned, hugging the ground, but the firing went on. He clawed at the cobbles, trying to hold on to his nerve, trying to hold on to his sanity, praying for darkness to fall.

# III

Clouds drifted slowly across the bright face of the new moon, shrouding the corpse-strewn street in funereal darkness. Durkin breathed a sigh of relief and shifted his leg slightly, stifling a groan. His body was as stiff as a board. He had lain like this for nearly three hours, not daring to move an inch. At the barricade ahead, the soldiers were on the alert for the slightest sound and the slightest movement. As night fell, the fighting had flared up again all round him as the rest of the Post Office garrison tried to break through the cordon. The rifles and machine-gun had opened fire, blasting away at them in the bright moonlight. He had seen some of the survivors breaking into the houses, carrying wounded with them. They were there now, waiting for daylight, waiting for the British to root them out with bomb and bayonet.

He gritted his teeth. Every muscle ached and there was a tight band of pain around his middle. His bladder was full again. If only he had the courage to take advantage of the darkness and sit up and unbutton his trousers and relieve himself. But that would be inviting a bullet through the head. He squirmed a little, trying to hold it. But the agony was too great. Ah, to hell with it, he told himself resignedly, I've pissed in my trousers once already.

Nevertheless he was overcome by a feeling of self-disgust as he eased himself, as the acrid smell of urine filled his nostrils. One more humiliation. He had experienced his moment of truth. In the face of danger he had conducted himself in a despicable, cowardly manner. He felt naked, stripped of all the bravado he had clothed himself with over the years.

It was warm and close and he rested his hot, sweaty forehead against a cool cobblestone. Miriam saw through me, he told himself. She could see what lay under all the veneer. Now he knew the reason for her coldness, the flinching away whenever he touched her, the look of disdain in her eyes. He wept softly. He felt so tired. All those nights with hardly any sleep. He dozed off.

He awoke with a start, wondering for how long he had slept. What the hell am I doing just lying here, wallowing in self-pity? he asked himself with sudden irritation. I'm alive, and if I want to stay alive, I'll need all my wits about me.

'Come on, Billy Boy,' he whispered, 'you've been in tight spots before.'

He considered various ways of getting out of his predicament. To

485

crawl back to the south end of the street in the direction of the Post Office was too risky. British patrols were certainly all around that area now, ready to shoot on sight.

Two alternative routes of escape were the laneways each side of him, but some of the survivors of the Post Office garrison were lurking there, ready to fight it out when daylight arrived. If he stayed where he was, he would be caught between two fires when the action started. He ran his tongue over his cracked, parched lips. He had no alternative but to make his way towards the barricade.

The thought of what he must do filled him with dread. He hesitated for a moment, praying that the moon would remain hidden, praying that his extraordinary luck would hold. He took a deep breath, and started to move slowly forward on his belly, trying not to make any noise. He had to make a detour round the bodies in front. They lay in a heap on top of each other. Already they were beginning to smell in the heat. As he inched past, his leg touched an outstretched lifeless hand. He gave a twitch of revulsion and crawled on as quickly and as noiselessly as he could, thankful he could not see the mutilations in the dark.

He expected the machine-gun to open fire at any second. Each movement forward demanded all his courage he could muster: it was like experiencing a succession of little deaths. He stopped after covering several yards, breathing heavily. Sweat was running down his face and into his eyes and he wiped it away with the cuff of his sleeve. He rested, unwilling to go any further.

He sighed. His mind was starting to wander again. Do you intend to remain here till daybreak? he asked himself angrily. There were no bodies to hide behind now he was nearer the barricade. He began crawling again, dragging himself along between the dead, wrinkling up his nose against the stench of blood and shit.

The moon appeared through a gap in the clouds, bathing everything in a bright silvery light. Durkin froze, heart thumping painfully, waiting for the flurry of shots which must surely come. But nothing happened. He lay, his right cheek pressed against the ground, staring into the blank dead eyes of a young girl three feet away. He closed his eyes, shutting out the sight, trying to shut out the memory.

It had happened at dusk, after the attack had collapsed and the firing had died down. Lying in the centre of the road, thankful for the darkness cloaking the street, his attention had been attracted by a movement further up. The door of a shop had been cautiously opened and the shopkeeper appeared in the doorway, holding a stick with a white pillowcase tied to it. He had been near enough to see the man's wife and golden-haired daughter behind him, urging him on.

Suddenly all three burst out on to the pavement, the man frantically waving his improvised white flag, the women screaming hysterically at the soldiers to hold their fire. Then the rifles and machine-guns opened up. Once again he could hear the screams, could see the figures madly pirouetting in a wild dance of death. He shuddered and opened his eyes as clouds stole across the face of the moon. The white face with its dead staring eyes and open mouth merged into the shadows. He crawled forward again.

The barricade loomed up in front of him. Now that he had reached his destination he was undecided what to do next. To stand up was to risk being shot by some trigger-happy soldier. The only other way was to proclaim his presence. He swallowed with difficulty: the inside of his mouth was as dry as a bone.

'Help,' he croaked. 'Help me.' The mumblings ceased abruptly. He could hear a bolt being drawn back. 'Don't shoot, for God's sake,' he pleaded. 'I'm a civilian. Don't shoot!' Seconds dragged by. Then a harsh voice broke the silence.

'Stand up and put your hands on your head.'

Durkin obeyed immediately, scrambling clumsily to his feet.

'Now, advance slowly.'

He stumbled forward. He could see the shadowy outlines of the soldiers and the gleam of bayonets. Suddenly hands reached out and grabbed the lapels of his jacket. He was hauled over the top of the barricade. Two soldiers took a firm grip on each arm and half-carried, half-dragged him away.

'What are you going to do with me?' he whimpered as they shoved him against a wall. The tip of a bayonet prodded his chest. He hiccuped with fear. A torch was switched on in front of his face.

'Is this the man?'

'Yes, sir.'

'What's your name?'

Durkin screwed up his eyes against the light shining in his face. 'William Durkin. I'm a civilian.' Panic crept into his voice.

'There are many rebels wearing civilian clothes.'

'I'm a journalist.'

The muzzle of a revolver was pressed against his teeth, and he could taste the metal.

'Liar! You were with those bastards who launched the attack on the barricade.'

Durkin shook his head wildly. 'No, no, I'm a journalist, I tell you. I'm well known in the Castle. I've done valuable work for military intelligence. Ask Captain Carew. He's a personal friend of mine.' He was fluent now, unaware that his hiccups had ceased. The tension in the voice of the officer worried him. This bastard is likely to blow my head off if I make the wrong move or give the wrong answer, he thought.

'For God's sake, Captain,' he pleaded desperately, 'don't do anything rash. You'll need me when this is all over. I've seen things. I can point out the leaders. I'll do anything you ask.' The revolver was lowered and the light switched off.

'Take him away for interrogation,' the officer said, not bothering to conceal his contempt.

# Chapter Twenty-Three

I

The armoured lorry rolled slowly towards the rebel barricade. It was a makeshift affair: a huge boiler with fifteen men inside, mounted on a chassis with slits in the sides through which troops could fire.

Gallagher and his men opened fire at the ungainly monster. With dismay they saw their bullets bounce harmlessly off the steel-plated front. Myles Burke lowered himself stiffly and rested his weight on one knee. Holding his heavy long-barrelled revolver with both hands, he squeezed the trigger, aiming carefully at the narrow slit, hoping to hit the driver.

The lorry stopped half-way up the street. Its engine revved madly, as it turned sideways. As the rebel defensive position swung into view, the soldiers unloosed a volley.

Gallagher and his men ducked as a broadside struck the barricade. Myles Burke calmly reloaded his revolver. He was unafraid – happy even. This was the way he had always wanted to die.

> And how can man die better
> Than facing fearful odds . . .

The lorry reversed and mounted the footpath, backing up against a tenement door. Sergeant Turnbull jumped out, his rifle slung across his back. He was carrying a pick. He smashed down the doorpanel with two swift blows, and thrust his hand through the opening. Finding the bolt, he pulled it back and kicked in the door. His men jumped out in ones and twos and followed him into the long narrow hall. All were loaded down with rifles, grenades, picks and crowbars.

The sergeant's orders were to tunnel through the houses towards the Malt House overlooking the rebel defences. Having captured it, he was to wait till nightfall when a star-shell would announced the commencement of an all out attack. He was then to lead his men through ruins opposite and outflank the barricade.

489

'Corporal, take five men and search the ground-floor rooms and cellar. The rest of you, follow me,' the sergeant ordered the men.

Rifle in one hand and pick in the other, he mounted the rickety stairs, his men behind him. The upstairs rooms were empty, clothing strewn all over the floors. The occupants had obviously departed in a great hurry.

They climbed the stairs to the rooms above. The doors were closed but unlocked, empty like the ones underneath. The sergeant stood in the centre of the floor looking at the few miserable pieces of furniture, a table, three chairs, an old chest of drawers. His eyes came to rest on a kitchen dresser standing against the far wall. It was scrubbed almost white. The pride and joy of the household, he thought, gazing at the set of willow pattern delft-ware on the shelves. The ostentatious display in the midst of so much poverty offended him. He leant his rifle against the wall and handed the pick to the soldier behind him. Then he walked forward, took hold of the dresser with both hands and pulled. It toppled to the floor with a crash of splintering wood and breaking crockery. A cup rolled free, undamaged. The sergeant crushed it to powder with his heavy boot.

His men looked on in silence. Not one questioned the senseless act of destruction. They revered and feared him; revered him for his courage and utter disregard for danger; feared him for his viciousness and mindless brutality. There were some who thought him mad. He jerked his thumb towards the blank space where the dresser had stood.

'Right – break through.'

The soldiers attacked the wall in turns, using pickaxes. The noise was drowned by the roar of the lorry engine and the sound of firing in the street below. Sergeant Turnbull walked to the window and looked down. The lorry was backing slowly towards an open doorway on the opposite side of the street. It stopped in front of the doorway. Soldiers jumped out and dashed into the hall, two of them carrying a box of grenades between them. The sergeant gave a grunt of satisfaction and turned away. Now they'll start to tunnel their way forward like ourselves, he told himself. By nightfall they should be within grenade throwing distance of the barricade. His men continued to wield their pickaxes against the wall. Ten minutes later there was a jagged hole big enough for a man to wriggle through. The sergeant went first and his men followed, one after another.

The rancid heavy smell of sweat and sour wine hit his senses. Two empty wine bottles stood in a corner. The room was almost bare. There was a small rickety table in front of the fireplace and three filthy,

490

verminous-looking mattresses on the floor. The sergeant turned his head. Four soldiers were standing behind him and another was emerging from the hole in the wall.

'You lot search underneath,' he ordered. As the soldiers went clattering down the stairs he walked to the window and drove the butt of his rifle through a window-pane to let in some air. More soldiers came struggling into the room. He walked out to the landing. The door of the back room was closed. He tried the doorknob, but the door was locked. He could hear a scuffling noise on the other side. He turned to a soldier beside him who was holding a pickaxe. 'Break it down,' he told him, then moved to one side and he reached for his bayonet, attaching it to his rifle as the soldier raised the pickaxe.

As the door flew inward after the third blow, hanging on one hinge, the sergeant marched in, finger on trigger. Two men were sitting on the floor, under a window. Another was curled up in a corner.

Sergeant Turnbull stood facing them. 'Stand up!' he snapped.

They rose slowly to their feet. One, a youth of about seventeen, was shaking with fear. His companion was small and middle-aged. He wore a cap and thick grey stubble covered his face. The third man staggered against the wall. He was drunk. The wine drinker, the sergeant thought, remembering the empty wine bottles in the other room.

'Search them,' the sergeant growled to his soldiers.

They ran their hands down their bodies, and made them empty their pockets. A soldier laid the contents on a chair. A penknife, rosary beads, a few coppers and a photograph. The sergeant stretched out his hand for the photograph and the soldier handed it to him. It was cracked and faded. It showed a young soldier standing stiffly to attention, a pith helmet under his arm.

'That was me,' a voice croaked, and the drunk staggered out of the corner. 'That was me before they sent me off to fight oul Billy Kruger.'

The sergeant turned to face him as he collapsed against the wall, a scarecrow of a man in ragged trousers and a torn overbig jacket which reached almost to his knees. The left side of his face was hideously disfigured. From eyebrow to chin, the flesh was deeply scarred and puckered. The left eye was missing.

'That was me,' he croaked again, 'an' I served with better men than youse pack of lousers.'

'Aisy, Whacker,' the middle-aged man warned nervously, 'aisy now.'

But the One-Eyed man was too drunk to care. 'I don't give two shits for any of these whures' melts!'

491

The sergeant stared steadily at him and, slowly and deliberately, crushed the photograph into a tiny crumpled ball and dropped it to the floor. The One-Eyed man's mouth fell open in disbelief. A vein stood out in his neck and a bubble of spittle formed on his lower lip.

'Yeh vindictive bastard!' he howled, raising his fist.

The sergeant stepped back, holding the rifle steady and straight before him. Then he lunged, plunging his bayonet into the man's belly, pinning him to the wall like a fly.

The youth screamed and clapped his hands to his eyes, unable to watch the skewered, squirming body of his companion, his hands tightly gripping the bayonet hilt. He continued to scream until a soldier cuffed him across the mouth.

The sergeant withdrew his bayonet in one swift, smooth movement. The One-Eyed man's body flopped to the floor. It wriggled and lay still, the eye popping, the mouth drawn back in an agonised snarl.

No one moved; all stood looking down at the body in silence. Then the youth started to weep and the middle-aged man crossed himself and began to pray.

'Give him eternal rest, O Lord, and let perpetual light shine upon him –'

'Knock off that bleedin' bullshit!' Turnbull rapped, nudging the body with the toe of his boot. 'Come on, lift this heap of garbage and carry it downstairs.'

The youth had to be pushed forward. Sobbing, he lifted the legs while his companion took a firm grip under the arms. They lifted the body and staggered forward with it through the open doorway. The sergeant and his men followed them down the stairs. As they reached the hall, he prodded the middle-aged man in the back with the tip of the gory bayonet.

'Down to the cellar.'

The soldiers who had been searching the lower part of the house were standing in the hall, silently looking on. One of them ran down the short flight of stairs leading to the cellar and opened the door. The two men descended the steep stairs awkwardly with the body. The sergeant stood wide-legged in the doorway and watched them disappearing into the darkness below. He could hear them whispering to each other.

'Come up!' the sergeant barked.

The youth came first, blinking against the light, his face tear-stained. The middle-aged man climbed laboriously after him. His head was bowed and the peak of the shabby cap hid his face. The sergeant waited until he was half-way up, then raised the rifle to his shoulder, aimed at the cap and squeezed the trigger.

492

A vivid finger of flame slashed through the gloom and the man tumbled head over heels down the stairs. The crack of the rifle reverberated throughout the cellar with the sound of a thunderclap. The youth stood motionless, paralysed with shock. He stared blankly up at the sergeant as he eased back the bolt and brought the rifle up to his shoulder again. He screamed.

The sergeant aimed deliberately at the wide-open mouth and fired.

## II

They crouched behind the barricade, alert for the slightest sound or movement. All through the afternoon and evening they had been listening to the British tunnelling through the houses on both sides of the street. At nightfall there had been an outbreak of firing as they captured the Malt House. Now there was silence, broken only by the leisurely footsteps of Myles Burke as he paced slowly back and forth, back and forth, the metal tip of the scabbard scraping against the ground. Clink, clink, clink . . .

The sounds scratched at Gallagher's taut nerves. He held the carbine tightly to his chest. There was hardly any ammunition left. All those precious rounds wasted on that damned armoured lorry, he thought. When the attack starts, there will be enough to hold them off for ten minutes or so, then that will be that.

The man beside him clutched at his sleeve. 'What was that?' he whispered.

Gallagher raised himself cautiously and peered over the top of the barricade, senses fully alert. 'I don't hear anything,' he murmured after a while.

The man sighed. 'I could have sworn I heard something. To the left. From the rooftops . . .'

Something hit the ground with a thud in front of them.

'Everyone down!' yelled Gallagher and ducked.

A vivid flash tore the darkness apart as the grenade exploded. The blast flung Myles Burke to the ground. He lay on his side, stunned and dazed, the hard cobbles cutting into his ribs. Two more grenades exploded simultaneously and a splinter tore its way through over Gallagher's head. More grenades followed in quick succession, bursting with deafening bangs, sending jagged fragments flying. But they were being thrown from too great a distance, falling short of their target by several yards. Nevertheless they kept the men cowering behind their flimsy shelter, playing havoc with their exhausted nerves.

Gallagher winced as another grenade exploded. It seemed to him that that one had landed nearer than the others. He imagined the soldiers crawling along the roofs from chimney stack to chimney stack. In another minute or two, he thought, gripping his carbine fiercely, they'll be near enough to lob grenades right down on top of us. He closed his eyes and gritted his teeth, trying to fight down a rising panic, trying to fight the urge to jump to his feet and run away.

Suddenly the men inside the public house opened fire. Protected by heavy sacks of maize and flour, and firing through loopholes, they raked the roofs of the houses on the north side of the street. Like the men at the barricade they were armed with Lee-Enfields they had captured after the disastrous British attack two days before.

A lull descended on the street, and Myles Burke rose groggily to his feet. The fall had badly shaken him. He stood on trembling legs, his senses reeling. He shook his head slowly, trying to clear his befuddled mind. They'll attack soon, he told himself. That grenade assault was intended to soften us up. He reached for his sword. His hand closed around the hilt, but he had no strength to draw it out. He was grateful for the dark, thankful the men could not see him. He knew what they would say. A pathetic old man, so old and feeble.

He could feel the full weight of his years now. He felt betrayed by the ancient rebellious body which defied him. Anger gave him strength. He took a firmer grip and jerked the sword out with a rasp of steel. The effort caused him to fall sideways. He straightened himself, setting his feet wide apart, trying to maintain his balance. He walked slowly forward, putting firmness into each step. He stopped short of the men slouched on the ground, their backs against the barricade. He could barely see them in the dark. A man was weeping.

'Stop snivelling!' he snarled.

The sound ceased abruptly.

That's the way, he thought, let them know you're still in command. 'The rest of you, get up and face the street in front. Check your weapons. See how much ammunition you have left.'

They obeyed reluctantly. Gallagher knelt on one knee and laid the carbine on top of the barricade. Then he searched the pockets of his bandolier. A loaded carbine and a few rounds in reserve, he thought. No more, no less than the rest of the men. A few quick volleys and then it will be every man for himself.

494

There was a rushing, whooshing sound and a star-shell exploded in the night sky. The street before them opened out in a harsh blue light. A tense silence followed. Then a whistle blew.

'Jasus help us,' the man next to Gallagher whispered and crossed himself.

Gallagher dug the butt of the carbine into the hollow of his shoulder as the soldiers came charging round the bend two hundred yards away. Just the same as the last attack, he thought, only this time they're not cheering.

'No one is to fire till they reach half-way!' Myles Burke shouted hoarsely.

One man ignored him and opened a rapid fire. The rest of the men followed suit. A hurricane of lead swept into the leading wave at a range of a hundred and eighty yards. Gallagher emptied the carbine into the packed struggling mass, then reloaded with the last of his ammunition. Already the light was beginning to fade as the star-shell fizzled out. The men continued firing, using up their ammunition recklessly. The last shot rang out as darkness closed in. In the sudden silence they could hear the cries and moans of the wounded.

A man started to slink away, and two more followed. Myles Burke stood in the middle of the road and raised his sword threateningly.

'Get back!' he barked.

'We've no more ammunition,' one whined as the other two sneaked past him.

'Use your bayonets!' He barred the way of another man in the act of running away. 'Back to your post!'

'Get outa me way, yeh crazy oul bastard!' the man snarled, holding his empty rifle in front of him. He dodged sideways and Myles made a swipe at him with the flat of the sword. The man ducked and drove the butt of the rifle into his ribs.

Myles dropped the sword and sagged to his knees, gasping, his hand pressed against his side. Men fled past him.

Gallagher was the last to leave. He could hear shouts and curses as the soldiers stumbled over the bodies of their fallen comrades. Then came the rush of booted feet. 'Come on the Staffs!' a voice screamed. Gallagher threw his empty carbine aside. In the failing light he saw the white-haired figure kneeling in the centre of the road. He looked so frail and helpless. They'll use him for bayonet practice, he thought. He couldn't leave him to die like that.

He ran forward and lifted him quickly to his feet, throwing him over his shoulder like a sack of coal. Shots were fired as he staggered forward with his burden. Terror spurred him into a run. He turned the corner on his left and headed south towards the river as darkness closed in.

The roar of gunfire came rushing towards him: vivid flashes ripped the night apart. Gallagher stumbled to a halt, panting. He could hear the soldiers crashing through the barricade. Suddenly their shouts and triumphant howls were drowned by gunfire. He remembered the handful of men at the barricades north and west of the street, now being attacked front and rear.

'Let me down,' a voice groaned against his ear. 'Leave me.'

'Shut up,' Gallagher hissed. He knew there was a side street on the right nearby. He picked his way across the road and mounted the footpath. After a few paces his left arm brushed against a lamp-post. He remembered it stood at the entrance of the street. He turned the corner and broke into a trot, his right arm around the legs of the man lying across his shoulder. He could feel the scabbard cutting into the flesh of his arm.

Suddenly another star-shell burst high above, turning night into day. Ruins shot into view all round him. There was a vast tract of waste ground directly ahead and he ran towards it. Shots were fired at him as he scrambled up the slope. A bullet thudded into the ground near his foot and another went singing past his head. He stumbled over the rubble-strewn ground. The only cover he could see was the jagged remains of a low wall about thirty yards away. He forced himself to go faster, heart thumping, his tortured breathing mingling with that of the man he was carrying. Already the light was beginning to fade when he reached the wall. He fell to his knees behind it and lowered Myles Burke to the ground. He sat him up against the wall and then peered over the top of it, panting, the blood pounding in his ears. Any minute now, he told himself, they'll come charging up the slope. He struck the top of the wall with his fist.

'If only I had a weapon,' he groaned aloud.

The man beside him stirred. 'My revolver,' he whispered. 'It's loaded, but there's no more ammunition.'

Gallagher unbuttoned the flap of the holster. The revolver felt unusually heavy. Better than nothing, he thought, holding it with both hands, resting the long barrel on top of the wall. The light was dying; he could not see beyond a distance of ten feet. There was spasmodic firing away to the south and behind him to the west. The rebellion was coming to an end in a series of isolated gun battles all over this vast wasteland of ruins and crumbling tenements.

He looked behind him. Although he could not see them, he knew there was a row of tenement houses about fifty yards away. He should be able to steal away with his companion and find refuge in some cellar or other. There they would hide and wait until it was all over.

Suddenly the sounds came towards him from out of the darkness ahead; the sound of boots crunching over rubble; the clinking of equipment. He drew back the safety catch with his thumb. If I can make them dive for cover and stay there long enough for the two of us to get away, he thought, his finger tightening on the trigger.

### III

Nine men followed Carew up the slope in the failing light, all that was left of a platoon section after the attack on the barricade. Carew scrambled up, holding his revolver tightly. This was like going over the top into no-man's-land. When he reached the crest he crouched instinctively, picking his way through the rubble. Somewhere in the darkness ahead was the man they were pursuing, the man he had fired at as he struggled up the slope carrying a comrade over his shoulder. His men stumbled noisily after him. He looked over his shoulder to see them advancing upright, dangerously bunched together. 'Spread out –'

A bullet grazed his shoulder. He threw himself flat, seeing the flashes ahead as he fell, hearing the bullets thumping into the bodies behind. He fired from the ground, the revolver bucking in his hand. Then the light finally died. He reloaded in the dark, his hand shaking. If he had been advancing upright like the others, he would have caught that bullet. He felt his right shoulder with the fingers of his left hand. The bullet had sliced an epaulette in two.

There was fighting going on south of them and he could see flashes of gunfire in front of him about half a mile away. He waited for more shots to come whining out of the dark. Behind him a soldier was moaning in pain. He turned his head around. 'Who's hit?' he whispered.

Just then a star-shell burst to the south where the fighting was heaviest and he flattened to the ground again as the harsh blue light spread out over the rubble-strewn ground. The jagged remains of a low wall appeared before him thirty yards away. So that's where the firing came from. He raised the revolver in readiness. He'll show himself now

497

and open fire, he thought, now that we're lying here exposed in this damned light.

But nothing happened. He wondered if the man was out of ammunition. Only a single weapon had been used. A revolver by the sound of it. He gritted his teeth in fury. One man and a maimed companion and only one bloody revolver between them, holding up almost a whole section. Then he heard the sounds in the distance. Heavy boots moving hurriedly. And a curious clinking sound. Clink, clink, clink . . . He jumped to his feet. The bastards were getting away! He turned around. His men were lying flat on their bellies, huddled together like sheep. One of them was still groaning, clutching his arm. The man beside him lay in an odd twisted attitude, his arms outflung. Carew knew he was dead. All the same he stopped and placed his hand against the side of his neck. There was no pulse. He straightened up.

'Anyone else hit?'

No one answered. No one moved.

'All of you,' he ordered, 'on your feet.'

Still no one moved or said anything. Even the wounded man had ceased his groaning. Some stared at the ground; others turned their heads away. He knew what they were thinking. The rebellion was almost over. Why take any more risks? Better to be court-martialled than be killed.

His voice shook with anger. 'By God, I could have you shot for this. Every last one of you!'

Suddenly he lost control and kicked out at the soldier nearest to him, striking his shoulder with his foot. The youth gave a yelp, and started to cry. Carew stood breathing deeply, castigating himself. I shouldn't have done that. It was stupid and unnecessary. Another officer would have behaved differently. The anger drained out of him as he stared at the men at his feet.

He started to make his way alone across the open waste ground. The fighting to the west had died out altogether. Intermittent firing to the south told him that a handful of rebels were still holding out. Diehards, he thought, like the two I'm hunting. He had a duty to kill or capture them. A rebel's life was always forfeit, especially in wartime. Besides, he owed it to that poor dead kid back there.

He slithered down a slope to the street below and crossed the narrow cobbled roadway. Dimly he could make out a row of tenement houses. He walked along the footpath towards them, revolver at the ready. It was the obvious place for the rebels to hide.

Directly ahead he heard the noise again. Clink, clink, clink. One of them must be wearing spurs – for a sword. Carew aimed his revolver and fired, slowly and deliberately, towards the noise, as though he were on the firing range.

Dazzled by the gunflashes, he had to reload by touch. He rose to his feet. He could hear nothing now except the distant sound of firing. When he reached the tenements he expected to see two bodies sprawled across his path, but the stretch of pavement before him was deserted. Nevertheless he had hit one of them – possibly both, judging from the amount of blood on the ground. There was light enough to see dark splotches of it leading away into the darkness.

He pressed on. He was reminded of one of those adventure stories he had read as a boy. The lone hunter following the spoor of a wild animal, but he was on the trail of the human species, the most dangerous of them all. He stopped at the foot of a flight of broken steps. There was blood on them.

He hesitated. Let them be, a gentle voice whispered in his head. You've wounded one, maybe both. What harm can they do now? Let them be. It was the voice of compassion; it belonged to the pulpit. It was the voice of his father. Another voice intervened, harsh and insistent, ordering him to carry on and do his duty.

Carew mounted the steps slowly, gripping the revolver. Drunken voices bawled uproariously in his head. One voice rose to a triumphant pitch.

'I have blooded my son! I have fleshed my bloodhound!'

# Chapter Twenty-Four

## I

Carew stood in the hallway, his back against the wall, eyes trying to pierce the dark, ears straining for the slightest sound. He knew they were here, hiding somewhere in this stinking ruin. He wrinkled his nose at the stench of poverty and overcrowding. It was hard to imagine that only a week ago the houses had been alive with the shrieks of children and squabbling housewives. Now it was dead and still, the army of slum dwellers all gone.

He inched along the hall, and stopped. He could hear noises underneath. The movements caused the rotting floorboards to tremble beneath his feet. He put one foot carefully before the other. His hand touched a banister rail. He halted and searched about with his foot. There were stairs on the left, leading to the bottom of the house. He moved to the top of the stairway, staring down into the blackness. His quarry had gone to earth.

There were basement rooms in these old houses which had once been the servants' quarters. He walked slowly down, left hand holding the banister, right hand gripping the revolver, ready to fire.

At the bottom he paused, standing absolutely still in the foul-smelling dark. He knew there was a closed door in front of him, as the sounds he could hear were muffled. Someone was fumbling about on the other side. Then a light suddenly appeared from under the door.

A stupid thing to do, Carew thought. Maybe they think they're safe. But then one or both are wounded and need light to tend their wounds. He stepped forward softly. His fingertips touched the wood of the door. Then he lowered his hand, searching for the doorknob. He closed his hand around it and turned it gently, wincing as it squeaked a little. He held his breath, then pushed the door inward and jumped to one side, expecting a burst of gunfire to greet him, but there was only the sound of a chair toppling over, and someone's heavy, rapid breathing.

Carew raised his revolver. 'Throw out your weapons!' he shouted.

'Throw them out,' he shouted again, 'or I'll toss in a grenade!' He wondered if the bluff would work. He could sense the fear and indecision going on in the mind of whoever it was in the room. 'I'll give you three seconds,' he snapped, then started to count. 'One, two –'

'Wait,' a voice croaked. 'Please wait. There's a badly wounded man in here.' There was a pause. 'There are no weapons. None.'

'You lie! You opened fire and killed one of my men!'

A sigh drifted out towards him – a sigh of weariness and despondency. 'One revolver between two of us. It was thrown away. No more ammunition.'

Carew nodded to himself. He had thought as much, but he was not going to take any chances. 'Stand beside the light where I can see you. And put your hands on your head.' He moved away from the wall and went round into the light, standing in the doorway, his revolver held high and ready.

A tall, gaunt, ancient figure faced him with his hands on his head. The light from the oil-lamp on the table beside him rested on the bony protuberances of the face, leaving the sunken cheeks and deep eye-sockets in shadow. Carew stared in amazement. He became aware of the heavy, agonised breathing and turned to the man lying on the floor.

He lay on his side, one hand resting on his stomach. Carew's eyes searched for weapons, but there was nowhere to hide any. There was only a table, an upturned chair, a mattress on the floor in the far corner . . .

The man on the floor twisted a little and moaned.

'Attend to your friend,' Carew said, addressing the old man. He noticed that the holster at his side was empty.

The man lowered his hands from his head. His right arm accidentally knocked against the side of the table and Carew saw him wince.

'Are you wounded?'

The man shrugged. 'A scratch. Nothing more.' He took a few steps towards his wounded companion, the metal tip of the empty scabbard scraping against the floor. Clink, clink.

So it was that I heard, Carew thought, watching him as he sank stiffly to his knees beside his friend. He leaned over the wounded man without touching him, hesitating, clearly at a loss. After a moment he placed his hands on the man's shoulders and turned him awkwardly over on his back. The wounded man cried out in agony as the old man ran his hand down his side.

'Where's he hit?' Carew asked. The wounded man again cried out, and it seemed to Carew that the old fool was causing more pain with his clumsy attempts at first aid.

The man sighed. 'There's a wound just above the hip-bone. A bullet is lodged in his stomach. He's lost a lot of blood.' The wounded man gave a gasp and uttered something Carew could not hear. The old man straightened up and lifted the strap of the water-bottle over his head.

'What are you doing?' Carew asked.

'He's asking for water,' the man replied, in the act of removing the top.

'For Christ's sake!' Carew's voice exploded in anger and irritation. He stepped swiftly forward, placing the revolver on the table as he passed. 'Don't you know better than to give water to a man with a stomach wound!' He snatched the water-bottle and flung it to the ground. He bent over the wounded man.

He stared at the grimy, broken-nosed face. The eyes were closed and the mouth had dropped open. Red stubble covered the cheeks and jaws. Carew knew by the shallow breathing and the deathly pallor that the man was probably dying. He did not think there was much he could do.

'He's going,' he said to the man behind him. 'I suppose both of you are Catholics. Shouldn't you say a prayer? An Act of Contrition – isn't that what you call it?'

The wounded man croaked. The water-bottle was lying on the floor close by. Carew stretched out, grabbed the strap and pulled it to him. He removed the top. He unbuttoned the flap of his tunic pocket and took out a handkerchief and rolled it into a ball. Holding it in his left hand, he dipped the waterbottle with his right and soaked it with water.

Carew leaned forward. The man's breath was stale against his face. Holding the wet wad of handkerchief in his hand, he squeezed gently, releasing just enough water to moisten the man's mouth and tongue. He paused every few seconds, then squeezed again. All the time the man's eyes stared up into his. Carew did not stop until he had squeezed the handkerchief almost dry.

He leaned his face closer. 'That's all I can do for you, old man,' he whispered, wondering if the man could still hear.

He was about to straighten up when the hand grasped his. He stiffened.

An act of gratitude? Or was it a desire for one last physical contact before dying? It was a workman's hand; big, hard, callused and terribly scarred. He made no attempt to withdraw from the grip. I owe him this much at least, he thought as the seconds passed. He turned to face the old man, who was standing with his back against the table pointing the Webley at him.

'Don't be stupid!' Carew said harshly. But I'm the stupid one, he told himself, leaving that damned revolver on the table. He had misjudged this Methuselah in his filthy, ill-fitting uniform. He had thought him senile and feeble-minded. 'Give it here to me,' he said as if he were speaking to a child, requesting him to hand over a toy that might do him harm.

The man raised the revolver threateningly as Carew took a step forward. 'Don't come any closer!' he warned.

'This will not gain you anything,' Carew said, backing towards the door, blocking the way of escape. 'You've lost, you know. The rebellion is over. May as well give me that revolver and surrender.'

'Surrender is it!' The revolver wobbled dangerously. 'I know what surrender means. To dangle at the end of a rope like a common murderer. To be buried in a grave of quicklime! I wanted to die at the barricade!' he shouted. 'I wanted to die with my sword in my hand facing the enemy! I wanted to make my mark on history! But he,' he pointed at Gallagher's inert body, 'he robbed me of all that. Stupid fool – he had to be humane. Throwing me over his shoulder like . . . like . . .' A spasm of rage shook him. 'God – the humiliation of it!'

Mad, thought Carew, quite mad. He felt so tired. His nerves were close to snapping point. 'Enough of this nonsense,' he groaned wearily. 'Hand me that revolver.'

The man stepped back and aimed it at Carew's chest, but he had not got the strength to hold it steady. The arm sagged from age and weariness, the revolver slowly sinking downwards.

'Give it to me,' Carew said. He stretched out his hand. 'Give it to me,' he repeated.

The man took another step back. 'I'll not surrender!'

Suddenly Carew lost his patience. 'You stupid old bastard!' he shouted. 'Don't you understand? The rebellion is over. You've lost. Now give me that revolver, God damn you!' It was a relief to let off steam. He felt a need to wreak his wrath on someone. He glared venomously at the man facing him, this half-crazed old fool who had outwitted him and was now holding him at bay with his own revolver.

'So you don't intend to surrender, eh? Want to be a dead hero, is that it?' His lip curled with contempt. 'Why you doddery old fool, do you think they'll bother executing you?'

Careful, careful, an inner voice cautioned, this is not the way to handle it. He dismissed the warning and went recklessly on. 'They'll throw you into prison and let you rot there for the rest of your miserable life! They'll throw you into a dark underground cell,' he continued recklessly, working on the man's imagination, taking sadistic pleasure

503

in watching sweat breaking out on the high bony forehead. 'You won't be able to breathe! You'll suffocate!'

The man shook his head as if trying to banish the image. 'No, no!'

'Yes!' Carew shouted. 'Now give me that revolver, blast you!' and stepped towards him.

The bullet struck him low in the stomach and sent him staggering back. His cap fell off as he collapsed against the wall. He stared stupidly at the man facing him. He felt no pain. His legs buckled and he slid slowly to the floor. He sat with his legs outspread, his back against the wall. A thin veil of smoke hung motionless in the dull light of the lamp and the smell of cordite filled the room. The old man stood still, his arms hanging down by his sides, the revolver dangling from his right hand. He looked bewildered.

Carew wondered what was going on inside the narrow skull. He can get away now without hindrance, he told himself, but he can't afford to leave a witness behind. If I'm found and live to testify, I can have him jailed for life for trying to murder an unarmed officer. He tensed as the man came slowly towards him. Now comes the bullet in the head, Carew thought resignedly. A trembling hand touched his shoulder. He opened his eyes and looked up.

'Forgive me,' the man whispered. All the defiance was gone. 'I didn't intend to harm you. You see . . .' He paused, groping for words, trying to explain. He gave a helpless shrug. 'I'm sorry,' he said lamely.

Carew nodded, then jerked, as pain knifed up through him. He bit his lip to prevent himself from crying out. He closed his eyes again, feeling the sweat breaking out on his forehead. He dared not move.

The hand on his shoulder tightened. 'Can I assist in any way?'

Carew shook his head, keeping his eyes closed. His mouth was dry and he moistened his lips with his tongue. 'Get help,' he whispered. 'You're bound to run into one of our patrols.' He winced. 'Please hurry.'

He wanted to be alone with his pain, to give utterance to his agony in private. He could feel the hand being lifted from his shoulder; could hear the man walking away towards the door, the tip of the scabbard scraping against the floor. Clink, clink, clink . . .

Sergeant Turnbull led his men through the ruins and out on to open waste ground. The last vestige of cloud drifted slowly across the face of the moon, and the men crouched instinctively under its harsh silvery-blue light. They were now an easy target for any rebel sniper. Their eyes were on the stocky figure of their sergeant.

Their uniforms were covered in dust. All day they had been tunnelling through the houses, smashing down wall after wall with picks and crowbars, battering their way towards the Malt House. They had left the picks and crowbars behind, together with fourteen dead bodies. In nearly every house there had been men, women and children; poor working class families cowering in terror. Acting on the sergeant's orders, they had massacred every male from the age of sixteen upwards. The sergeant had disposed of half of them with bullet and bayonet, killing with a cold ferocity, indulging himself in an orgy of bloodletting.

A flurry of shots broke out in the distance and the sergeant abruptly changed course, heading southwest towards the sound of battle. His men followed reluctantly, eyeing him with a mixture of hate and fear. Violence drew him like a magnet. He was like a beast of prey with the scent of blood in its nostrils.

Suddenly he stopped and raised his arm for his men to do likewise. He had heard something in the distance. He stood listening, his head cocked to one side. The men remained absolutely still, their eyes searching the area. They wanted to get away from this wide, open, desolate place, back to the shadows of the streets. There were suppressed sighs of relief when the sergeant moved forward and motioned for them to follow. They stumbled after him, bayonets gleaming in the moonlight.

A few moments later they were slithering down the slope to the cobbled roadway below. There was a line of cottages in ruins on the other side. Away to the south they could see the dark bulk of some tenement houses standing high above the surrounding desolation. They gathered in a group on the road, their eyes on the sergeant. He was standing alone in the middle of the road, half-crouched, listening. They all heard it. The slow beat of footsteps and a curious clinking sound. They waited, rifles at the ready. Out of the moonlit darkness, a tall white-haired figure walked slowly towards them, a revolver dangling from his hand. Despite the filthy, ill-fitting uniform there was a certain dignity about him that impressed them. Obviously a senior officer. Perhaps a general in the rebel army.

Sergeant Turnbull slung his rifle from his shoulder, and reached down to pluck the revolver from the unresisting hand.

'A Webley,' he commented, snapping it open. 'British Army issue.' Only one shot had been fired. He sniffed. And fired recently. 'What happened to the officer you took this from?' he demanded, staring into the aged bony face. 'Shot him in the back, I suppose.'

Myles stared back impassively.

'Rebel scum,' the sergeant sniffed derisively. 'Murder one of our officers and take his weapon.' The mouth twisted under the heavy black moustache. 'Then come to us as cool as you please and surrender.' He raised the revolver threateningly. 'Expecting to be treated as a prisoner of war.'

He's trying to goad me into making some kind of protest, Myles thought. That's all the excuse he needs to pull that trigger. He had encountered men like this before. Warfare did something to them – aroused a deep-seated murderous instinct. Now that the rebellion was lost, he wanted to die rather than spend the remaining years of his life in prison. Except for that wounded officer lying back there in the basement, he would tell this mad dog of a sergeant to go to hell and do his worst. But a man's life depends on me remaining cool and calm, he told himself.

Sergeant Turnbull stood, his teeth bared, holding the revolver upright against his cheek. He had expected some sort of reaction, and this silent individual baffled him. He did not know what to do. He knew he intended killing this man from the moment when he had seen him walking out of the darkness. One more victim, he had thought, but unlike the others, this one was not afraid to die. Or was he?

He pressed the revolver against Myles' narrow chest. 'I'm going to blow the heart out of you, you bloody swine!' he growled, waiting for the first sign of fear, the plea for mercy.

The man's eyes stared unwaveringly into his. He stood as still as a statue – even the face looked as if it had been carved out of stone. In the tense silence a soldier shifted uneasily, his heavy boot scraping over the cobbles. The sergeant cocked the revolver. He knew his men were watching him. Indecisiveness was a sign of weakness, and yet he hesitated to pull the trigger. Gone was the fierce sensual pleasure he had experienced when watching the others grovel and whimper before he killed them. Now there was only emptiness. There was grudging admiration for this man facing him. Courage was the only thing the sergeant respected. The old bastard deserves to live, he told himself. He lowered the revolver and took a step back.

Myles did not move. He felt relief, but not for himself. Now he could get on with his mission of mercy. He would not even try to explain what had happened in that basement to this irrational trigger-happy tyke. He needed the hearing of a more disciplined individual. Only an officer would be in a position to organise and promptly dispatch the proper medical assistance.

'Take me to your commanding officer immediately,' he said coldly. The bullying, hard-bitten sergeant, he thought. The man with the empty threats. All piss and wind.

There and then the sergeant condemned him to death. For the first time in his life he had relented, and for that he was being mocked at in front of his men. He would have to kill him now if only to save face.

'Walk ahead of us up that slope,' he ordered.

The man hesitated for a few seconds, before climbing the slope, hunched a little, heels digging into the soft soil. The sergeant motioned to his men not to move. He stood holding the revolver in his right hand, running the fingers of his left hand over it, feeling its newness. One of the latest makes of Webley. It was inconceivable that a British officer would surrender it voluntarily, unless it had been taken from him when he was either dead or badly wounded. There was poetic justice in shooting a man with the same weapon he had used on his victim. He waited until the man almost reached the top, until his tall dark figure appeared just above the skyline, then fired twice in rapid succession.

The man suddenly jerked upright and flung his arms out wide. For a split-second he hung motionless, cruciform against the moonlit sky, then fell back and tumbled over, sliding down on his back in a welter of dust and rubble. He came to rest at the foot of the slope, his two feet on the footpath. One booted foot began to beat a gentle tattoo against the pavement. It sounded like an operator tapping out his signal of distress. Dot, dot, dot, dash . . .

No one moved. The sergeant walked forward, the revolver dangling from his hand. He came to a halt in front of the dying man, looking down at him. Then he raised the revolver and emptied it into the quivering body. He threw the revolver away with an indifferent gesture.

Far away to the south a rebel Mauser boomed like a distant peal of thunder.

The sergeant turned his head. Even at this distance he could see the flashes of gunfire. He unslung his rifle. 'Come on,' he said brusquely. His men shuffled after him in a ragged file.

One man dawdled, pretending to adjust his puttees. He looked down at the body. 'Poor old beggor,' he said. 'Anyroad, he died . . .' and paused, searching in his mind for the right word '. . . *nobly*.'


## III


Carew released a shuddering sigh of relief as the pain finally eased. He remained absolutely still with his eyes closed, breathing deeply, preparing himself for another attack. Beads of sweat stood out on his forehead. 'Where is he?' he whispered and opened his eyes. His vision was blurred and the oil-lamp on the table a few feet away shimmered like something seen underwater. 'Where is he?' he whispered again. For how long had he been gone? A half-hour? An hour?

His belt was unbuckled and his tunic undone. In an attempt to staunch the flow of blood, he had pushed a handkerchief down inside his shirt to where the wound was just below the navel. Surprisingly there had been very little blood. It was then he realised that he was bleeding internally. If help did not come soon he was going to die.

'He wouldn't abandon me,' he moaned, trying to fight off the feeling of despair. But he knew in his heart that self-preservation was stronger than any solemn promise made. He could not blame the old man. Securing help meant capture and life imprisonment for him.

He felt himself sinking into apathy. He was becoming resigned to his fate. But the will to survive was greater. He tried to struggle to his feet, pushing his elbows against the wall, managing to raise himself more than a foot off the floor. Then the pain gripped him like a vice. He flopped down, gasping, the salt taste of blood in his mouth. He could feel all his strength ebbing away. Even trying to keep his eyes open was an effort. From a long way away, he heard voices, murmuring, saw movements close by. His mouth was parched and he craved for water to drink. But the water-bottle was out of reach. Thirst was his only discomfort. Even when he was picked up, he felt no pain. He was glad not to die alone and uncomforted. Then the dark pressed against his face like a blanket. . . .

# Chapter Twenty-Five

## I

Father Devlin pulled hard on the reins, bringing the trap to a halt on the dusty road. Through a wide gap in the demesne wall, he had a clear view of the smoke-blackened ruin of Carewscourt, sharply outlined against the pale evening sky.

'Another victory for old Ireland,' he commented with heavy sarcasm to Malachi Drennan, sitting opposite him.

'Hard to believe that it's gone,' Malachi said in his mournful voice, 'and the last of the Carews with it.' He rubbed his long pointed chin. 'Have they found the men who burnt it down?'

Father Devlin shook his head. 'No, and I doubt if they ever will.'

Malachi chewed reflectively on his upper lip. 'Still,' he said, 'the Carews lived off the sweat of the people for long enough. For more than two hundred and fifty years.'

'Ach!' Father Devlin exclaimed irritably. 'Ancient history, ancient history. Captain Carew would have made up for all the wrongs of his ancestors if he had had time. He spent every penny he possessed trying to improve his property. The estate would have been a model of its kind. Think of all the employment it would have given. Now look at it. Everything gone in a single night.' He gazed at the ruin. Dark specks hovered over it. Already the rooks were settling in. He shook his head in perplexity. 'Why?' he asked himself. 'Why?'

The mare broke into a trot down the road towards the O'Malley farm, kicking up the dust, but she was an old horse, and could not keep it up. Father Devlin did not urge her on. He held the reins lightly, rocking with the gentle motion of the trap. Malachi lapsed into a comfortable doze, feeling the evening sun warming his back. It was mild and pleasant now after the fierce heat of the day. Away to the west they were still cutting turf on the bog, taking advantage of the good weather. Father Devlin screwed up his eyes against the sun.

One of the turf-cutters was coming up the road on his way to the village. He was leading a donkey which had turf-filled creels hanging at each side. As they passed, the man touched the peak of his cap in deference, but deliberately turned his head away.

Father Devlin did not acknowledge the salute. His eyes were on the road ahead, his face grim, feeling the bitter loneliness of the excommunicated. His whole world was falling apart. And yet up to a very short while ago he still had ruled this little Eden he had created with a rod of iron.

When the news of the Dublin rebellion reached Carewstown he had immediately condemned it from the pulpit, calling it an act of madness. The rebel leaders, he had told the congregation, were criminals and traitors to the Crown. The law of the land had to be upheld and enforced. Then came the news of the unconditional surrender. Five days later the executions began. Day after day the rebel leaders died before the firing squads. Some died alone; others in batches of three or four. It was said that the British Commander-in-Chief had ordered a grave large enough to hold a hundred to be dug in the yard of the military prison at Arbour Hill.

He had seen the mood of the people of the parish slowly changing. First the bewilderment, then the anger, finally the open hostility against those in authority and the supporters of the regime. He had found himself classed among the latter.

One Sunday morning he found himself celebrating Mass in an almost empty church. He was profoundly shocked. The Catholic population of Carewstown were simple godfearing people. Never would they abstain from their religious duties, no matter how much they disagreed with his political views. He had retired to his study after Mass and had poured a large measure of whiskey for himself to restore his shaken nerves. He was about to gulp it down when his curate came bursting into the room, consternation written all over his face, braying out the news that nearly all the parishioners except the old and infirm had gone to the next parish to worship in the church there.

A wheel struck a pothole and Malachi awoke with a jerk.

'Welcome back, Malachi,' Father Devlin said.

Malachi passed a hand over his eyes. 'Forgive me, Father. I must have dozed off.' He looked about him. 'Are we near the O'Malleys' yet?'

'Half-way there,' Father Devlin said. He leaned forward and slapped the mare's rump. 'Get along there, ye lazy oul bitch!'

Malachi raised his voice above the clatter of the wheels. 'The Merricks are sellin' out and goin' to England.'

510

It took a few seconds for Father Devlin to bring his thoughts back to the present. He turned a shocked face to Malachi. 'No! Why, they have been in Ireland as long as the Carews. They and the Townshends and the Brisketts.'

Malachi shrugged. 'They're afraid, afraid they're goin' to be burnt out like the Carews. Aye, and it won't be long before the Townshends and the Brisketts follow them.'

Father Devlin shook his head. He felt more isolated than ever. Once he knew everything that was going on in the parish. Now he was enclosed by a wall of silence. The only one who kept him informed was Malachi.

They swayed with the motions of the trap, their knees almost touching. Malachi kept his gaze steadily fixed on the road ahead. He could see the roof of the O'Malley farm-house in the distance.

'When is Bull O'Malley goin' to Dublin?' he shouted, trying to make himself heard above the noise of the wheels.

'The day after tomorrow,' Father Devlin shouted back.

'Where to?'

'The Hospital of the Incurables.'

Malachi crossed himself reverently. 'Jesus, Mary and Joseph preserve us.' He shook his head sorrowfully. 'Did ye ever see a man to fail so? The livin' flesh just walked off him. The man's a fright to behold.'

'Take your last look at him, Malachi,' Father Devlin shouted. 'You won't be seein' him again. Not in this world anyway.'

Malachi was silent for nearly a minute. He leaned across to Father Devlin and touched his shoulder. 'All the same,' he hollered into his hear, 'isn't it a blessin' that he has his only daughter takin' care of him. Shure, when there's sickness about, there's nothin' like a woman to take care of a man.'

Father Devlin grimaced. So that's it. Pretending he wanted to go along with me just to see Bull O'Malley. He still has that lassie on his mind. He glanced at him. If you think you're going to use me as a matchmaker again, bucko, you have another think coming. He gave a contemptuous grunt. Marriage at his age. 'There's no fool like an old fool.'

Malachi turned his head. 'Did you say something, Father?'

'Nothing worth repeating.'

A dog, tail wagging, greeted them outside the O'Malley farmhouse. Father Devlin walked up the short drive to the door, Malachi following a few steps behind.

The door was opened by Una Gallagher. Father Devlin forced a smile on his face. 'Good evening, Mrs Gallagher. How is himself?'

She opened the door wider without speaking and pointed towards the kitchen at the rear. Father Devlin removed his tall silk hat and walked in, Malachi at his heels. He tried not to let the shock he felt show on his face on seeing the gaunt figure sitting on the settee by the fire. Only a month had passed since he had last seen Bull O'Malley, and he had deteriorated rapidly in that short space of time. My God, he thought, the man is wasting away to nothing. He gave a false hearty laugh as he walked towards him. 'Mr O'Malley – and how are ye?'

'Poorly, Father, poorly,' Bull O'Malley whispered and tried to rise to his feet.

Father Devlin placed a heavy hand on his shoulder, restraining him. 'Save your strength, Mr O'Malley.' He turned around and beckoned to Malachi. 'And here's your old friend Malachi to see you.'

Malachi shuffled forward with his hand outstretched. Bull O'Malley placed a trembling bony hand in his and Malachi grasped it and shook it warmly. Bull O'Malley winced with pain. Then he began to weep. 'Ah, Malachi, Malachi . . . that ye should see me like this.'

'Now, now, now,' Father Devlin said soothingly. He sat down on a chair opposite the settee and Malachi sat on another one beside him. They both stared in awe, remembering the Bull O'Malley of old, trying to compare the image with this sad emaciated creature sitting before them. The once fleshy heavy-boned face had shrunk, the yellow blotched skin hanging loosely about the jaws. I'll give him two weeks, Father Devlin thought, three at the most.

'A long illness doesn't tell a lie, Father,' Bull O'Malley whimpered, 'it kills at last.'

'Poppycock!' Father Devlin snorted. 'Why ye'll be back with us in no time, hale and hearty as ever.'

'Ah, Father,' Bull O'Malley said, looking slyly at him, 'an old bird is not caught with chaff. I know I'm finished, and so do you.'

Father Devlin raised his hands in protest, then let them fall again, not knowing what to say.

Bull O'Malley sighed wearily. 'I'm resigned to God's holy will, Father,' he whispered brokenly, and started to weep again.

Father Devlin and Malachi sat in silent embarrassment. Father Devlin placed both hands on top of his tall silk hat which rested on his knees and focused his gaze on a picture on the wall facing him. Malachi continued to stare at the man they had nicknamed 'Bull' because of his vitality and strength. Then he turned his head away and sighed. It's not the tree that is a long time shaking that is the first to fall, he told himself.

There was the sound of running water and the clink of delft behind them as Una Gallagher busied herself with the washing up. They knew she was listening to every word.

Bull O'Malley dried his eyes with the cuff of his sleeve. 'Ah well,' he sniffed, 'at least I lived long enough to see my grandchild.'

'Ah,' Father Devlin said, glad of something else to talk about, 'and where is the little chap?'

'Fast asleep in the next room,' Bull O'Malley answered. 'Faith, it won't be long till he's walkin'.' For the first time since they arrived, Bull O'Malley smiled. 'Oh, a hardy little snipe,' he enthused. 'And hair – hair as red as a flame.'

Father Devlin nodded and smiled. 'And your two lads, Mr O'Malley. Where are they now? Have ye heard from them lately?' He immediately regretted having asked the question when he saw the pain in Bull O'Malley's eyes.

Bull O'Malley turned his head away. He did not speak for a while. 'Sonny is in Boston,' he mumbled. 'And Luke . . .' He shrugged. 'Somewhere in South America. Argentina, I think. I haven't heard from him since before the war.' Father Devlin's face was grim. He lifted his hat from his knees and placed it down on the floor beside him. It was a waste of time reminiscing when there were important things to discuss. It was surprising how neglectful some people were when it came to the simple matter of drawing up a will, especially if there was land and a lot of money involved. He considered it his duty as parish priest to ensure that some money was donated for the upkeep of the church. And, perhaps, some for himself. He was a poor enough man, and had to depend on the generosity of the people for the few comforts he enjoyed. He joined his hands and leaned forward, his elbows resting on his knees. He decided not to beat around the bush but to come directly to the point.

'Ye know, Mr O'Malley,' he said, 'it's always sensible to have your affairs in order at a time like this. Ye understand me, now? One has to be realistic. It's only fair to your family.' He raised his hands in mock horror. 'If ye only knew the amount of times I've been called to settle family disputes over who should get what –'

'There's no need to concern yourself, Father Devlin,' Una Gallagher cut in. 'All that has been taken care of.' She walked forward and then turned to face him, standing behind the settee, placing her hand on her father's shoulder. 'A new will was drawn up several days ago.'

'I'm glad to hear –' Father Devlin began, then suddenly checked himself. 'A *new* will, did ye say?'

'Yes. On my insistence. Under the new terms, Luke and Sonny get three hundred pounds each, and my mother and I take everything else.'

Father Devlin's mouth dropped open. 'Everything?'

'Everything.'

Father Devlin cleared his throat, then looked across at Bull O'Malley who was staring at the floor, deliberately dissociating himself from what was going on. 'If you don't mind me saying so, Mr O'Malley,' he said, 'I can forsee trouble arising over a will like that.'

'You can leave my father out of this,' Una Gallagher said coldly.

Father Devlin thought. 'I beg your pardon, Mrs Gallagher,' he said politely, 'I don't wish to pry, but your mother. . . ?'

'My mother is upstairs, Father. She is tending my husband.'

Father Devlin jerked upright. 'Your *husband*. . . ?'

'He arrived home yesterday. He has been injured, but he will recover. A priest, ministering to the dead and dying, found him, tended him, and arranged for him to be returned. He travelled in a brewery barge! They were kind men, Father Devlin. The priest saved Con and a soldier, both wounded and left to die. A good man, Father Kinsella. Not a hypocrite like you!'

'Una!' Bull O'Malley glared up at her, showing a little of his old fire. 'It's the priest yer talkin' to!'

'I'm well aware of who I'm talking to,' she retorted. 'I'm talking to the man who tried to ruin my life and that of my husband!'

Father Devlin jerked upright on the chair. 'That's a monstrous thing to say!' he bellowed, face blazing with fury.

'Is it?' She looked about her. 'This is where it all started. Right here in this kitchen all those years ago, when you tried to arrange a marriage between me and that man sitting beside you.'

Malachi looked down at his boots, his hands fiddling with the brim of his hat which rested on his knees.

'I was being bartered for seventy acres of land!'

'Please, Una,' Bull O'Malley begged, 'don't start that all over again. I haven't the strength.'

Father Devlin turned his head away, avoiding her eyes.

'You started a chain of events which nearly ended in tragedy for all of us, Father Devlin,' she said in a hard voice. 'But your interfering in my life, and my husband's, is over. We, Con and I, will run this farm together. My mother will have enough comfort in her life and will answer to no one. My son will grow up proud of his father, and he'll hold his head up high. He will bow to no man, Father Devlin, to no man.'

Father Devlin sagged in his chair. And what of me? he wondered. Growing older and becoming more isolated in my own parish, mistrusted and ostracised. Black despair filled his heart. He raised a despondent face and caught Una Gallagher smiling at him.

## II

'What happened then?' Freddy Mulligan asked.

'Oh, I had to slap him across the face to bring him to his senses,' Durkin said. 'What else could I do? The main thing was to calm him down. I had to calm *all* of them down in fact. Their nerves had gone completely. Imagine soldiers behaving like a crowd of hysterical schoolgirls. One expected them to react in a disciplined manner during a moment of crisis. But the minute they saw the smoke coming from underneath the door and heard the roof caving in, there was bloody pandemonium. I can tell you I had a job trying to restore order.'

He sipped his whiskey, eyeing them over the rim of the glass. 'The Lads'. Freddy Mulligan, the tick-tack man, Jack Mooney and Benny Moran, bookmakers, and Pee-Wee Whelan, the jockey, with his check cap, yellow waistcoat and jodhpurs. Well-known figures at the race-meetings of the Curragh, Punchestown and Fairyhouse. Men of the world, sharp-witted, not easily fooled, they stared at him with interest and respect, no sneer of disbelief on their faces. After all, he had not been just a mere spectator – no idle bystander. He had been in the very centre of things, the rebel Headquarters itself.

'Then what happened?' Mulligan asked.

'Oh, we were released eventually. Just in the nick of time. The whole bloody place was tumbling down around our ears. Fires every-where . . .'

Mrs Kavanagh paused in the act of pulling a pint, listening intently. Durkin wished he had a larger audience, but there were only two other bona fide customers besides themselves in the hotel bar, a middle-aged couple sitting near the window.

'I found myself caught up in the middle of a stampede as everyone rushed towards the corridor at the rear. The corridor was full of smoke and hot as the inside of an oven. Shells were crashing down on the roof high above our heads.' He took another sip of whiskey as they waited, hanging on to his every word.

'The whole garrison was in that corridor, waiting to make a dash for it. I forced my way through to the top where an officer was standing at an open doorway leading to the street. With him was the advance guard, checking their rifles.

' "Where the hell are you going?" he demanded.

' "With them," I replied.

' "They are about to launch an attack on the British barricade," he said.

' "I guessed that," I told him. "But I would rather go with them than to be fried alive here."

' "It's a no-come-back job," he warned me.

' "We all have to die sooner or later," I told him.

'He looked at me. "By God," he said, "you're a cool customer, and no mistake." He held out his hand. "Shake," he said. "I wish I had more like you. Go now, and the best of luck." '

He swallowed the last of the whiskey and was at once handed another. He smacked his lips. 'Well, it was a bloody massacre,' he continued. 'It was a fifty yard dash up the street towards the barricade without any cover. The rebels were picked off one by one. I had to take cover behind the bodies of three dead men in the middle of the road. In the *middle of the road*, mind. And all the time machine-gun bullets were flying just a few inches above my head.'

'Jays,' Pee-Wee Whelan whispered reverently.

'When darkness came I had to crawl on my belly towards the barricade.

' "Who goes there?" a sentry shouted.

' "Friend," I answered.

' "Advance, friend, and be recognised."

'I stood up and walked forward with my hands over my head and climbed over the barricade. Then this bloody officer comes up to me and threatens me with a revolver. "You were with the attacking force!" he roars. "You're one of them!"

'I could see he was as jumpy as hell. Keep a cool head, Billy Boy, I told myself. He squeezed the trigger a little. "How would you like the contents of this?" he snarled.

'I looked him straight in the eye. "Well," I replied calmly, "I don't think I would feel the last five bullets." '

'By God,' Jack Mooney breathed, 'that was a right smart answer.'

Durkin nodded. 'It did the trick all right. He lowered the revolver, shame-faced. He apologised afterwards.'

Then Benny Moran began to tell of his experiences. Nothing as dramatic as Billy Durkin's of course, but thrilling nevertheless. At least he thought so.

Durkin sipped his whiskey, uninterested. He looked about him. This place held so many memories. Miriam and himself used to stay here in the old days. He furrowed his brow. I wonder why she hasn't answered my letter? He had written to her two weeks ago, telling her of Alec Carew leaving for England. Probably too upset, he thought. They had been such good friends.

'How's the oul sparring partner, Billy?' Jack Mooney asked, after Benny Moran had finished.

Durkin stared at him in surprise. It was as if he had been reading his thoughts. 'I expect to be hearing from her any day now, Jack. She's in England, ye know. Her sister's husband was killed in France and Miriam decided to go across and stay with her for a while. Anyway, I'll be joining her shortly.' And staying in England for good, he thought. Dublin was no longer a safe place for him to live in.

The Castle authorities had forced him to accompany Major Calder and the detectives of G Division to Richmond Military Barracks to assist them at the identity parade. He had protested at first. Then Major Calder had reminded him of his duty as a loyal subject. Besides, refusal meant jeopardising his knighthood. He had acquiesced readily enough when he had been told that.

But it had been a nightmarish experience walking down that long line of dirty and dishevelled rebel prisoners with Major Calder and the detectives by his side. He had felt himself wilting under the fierce hostile stares. Many seemed to recognise him; men who might have been members of the Post Office garrison. Now and then a detective would halt, peer into a man's face, then pick him out for the firing-squad. He had walked on, sensing the Major's disappointment at his failure to identify anyone.

Then they came to the last man at the end of the line. He had halted before him, experiencing the sweet taste of revenge. Now it's my turn, you little slum rat! he had thought. He had placed a heavy hand on the man's shoulder. 'This one. He and another held me prisoner against my will. His name is Byrne – Kit Byrne . . .'

'Now that you're going to settle permanently in England, Billy,' Benny Moran said. 'Does that mean there will be no more issues of the *Eye-Witness*?'

517

'Not at all,' Durkin replied. 'I've sold it to another publisher.'

'Ah, it will be only a pale imitation,' Jack Mooney said, smirking. 'It will lack that special Durkin touch.'

Durkin chuckled. 'All but the next one, Jack. My last. But I need something sensational for the front page. Any of you bastards heard of anything spicy lately – I don't want more on the rebellion . . .'

'How about the vicar and the choirboy?' Benny Moran asked with a laugh.

'That was in the February issue, Benny. He was unfrocked as a result.'

Everyone laughed and Durkin gulped down a mouthful of whiskey. He accepted another glass with reluctance. He had to drive them all back to Dublin in his new car and wanted to have a clear head.

As usual after a few whiskeys, Jack Mooney suggested they all have a sing-song just to liven things up a bit. 'Something cheerful. Something frisky. Not some oul melancholy come-all-ye.'

Mrs Kavangh shot a disapproving glance at him. 'No singing allowed,' she said sternly.

But Jack ignored her. 'How about *The Wake at Kildare*? All of you should know that.' Leaning against the bar, he threw back his head and began to sing in a hoarse tipsy voice.

O mother, darling mother, there's a wake at Kildare,
You know my darling Roger, he's promised to be there;
He loves me, O he loves me, O he loves me for my sake,
O mother, darling mother, may I go to the wake?

Mrs Kavanagh's mouth tightened. She knew the song to be a bawdy one. Already the middle-aged couple sitting near the window were preparing to leave, sensing trouble. Mrs Kavanagh's face turned a brick-red. 'I must ask you to stop singing at once!' she shouted. But her cry of protest was drowned by loud raucous voices as the rest of the company joined in.

To hell with it, Durkin thought, why be the odd one out? Let's celebrate. After all I'm lucky to be alive. He swallowed off his whiskey in one gulp, then added his voice to the chorus.

O Nellie, darling Nellie, beware of Kildare,
I know your darling Roger has promised to be there;
He loves you and he loves you, O he loves you for his sake,
But keep your legs together coming home from the wake.

518

Mrs Kavanagh fled through the open doorway with her hands covering her ears. 'Fintan!'

Durkin stood in front of the group, beating time with his hands. Then Pee-Wee placed a pint of stout on his head and started to dance a jig, his hands on his hips. The voices rose higher.

Our wee Nellie, as proud as any queen,
She dressed herself in petticoats and drawers so neat and clean;
He stuffed her up with whiskey and he stuffed her up with cake,
And he stuffed it up wee Nellie coming home from the wake.

A thin man came striding through the doorway from the kitchen, his face flushed with anger. He almost collided with Pee-Wee who was still performing his little jig with the pint of stout balanced on his head.

'Stop this,' he shouted. 'Stop this at once!'

The singing ceased abruptly. Pee-Wee stood still. Then he carefully raised both hands and slowly removed the pint glass from his head, the contents unspilled.

The man faced the four of them, his back to Durkin. His voice shook with wrathful indignation. 'This sort of behaviour will not be tolerated here! Kindly finish your drinks and leave!' Then he turned around to face Durkin.

His face suddenly went blank with shock.

Durkin stared at him, puzzled. He looked vaguely familiar. The falcon nose; the sensitive mouth; the dark hair turning grey at the temples. Where had he seen. . . ? Then it dawned on him. It was the heavy black moustache that had confused him. 'Jesus Christ,' he gasped, 'it's Fintan Butler!'

Butler's face was the colour of putty. Beads of sweat started to stand out on his forehead.

Durkin's loud guffaw cut his feeble protest short. 'Oh, give over, Butler. Who the hell do you think yer foolin'? I'd recognise you anywhere, even with that snot-stopper under yer nose!'

The Lads gathered round. 'Who is he, Billy? A friend of yours?'

Durkin threw back his head and crowed with delight. 'Oh sweet God above, this is too good to be true.' He pretended to be shocked. 'Who is he, you ask? Boys, you surprise me. Have you not heard of that noblest of patriots, Fintan Butler? The man who encouraged the youth of Ireland to stand with gun in hand and defy the might of the British Empire. The man who delivered that oft-quoted oration at the graveside of that warrior of battlefield and boudoir, Garret Lysaght.

519

The man who – but enough!' He looked sternly at them. 'I can see by the puzzled look on your faces that you don't know. For shame!'

Butler tried to move away but Durkin grabbed him by the arm and held him. By God, he thought, I was looking for a sensational article for the front page and now I have it. He could not resist a gleeful chuckle. Lucky Durkin. Always in the right place at the right time.

'Tell us, Butler,' he said with a mischievous grin, 'how come we find you of all people living in an out-of-the-way place like this when your comrades were fighting and dying in Dublin? Hmmm? Tell us, now. You know, when I was being held prisoner in the Post Office I made inquiries about you. "Where, oh where is Fintan Butler?" I asked. "Is he perchance on the roof, sword in hand, defying shot and shell, hurling insults at the enemy to do his worst? Or maybe he's leading a charge against a barricade, urging his men on to greater efforts." ' Durkin placed his hand over his heart and stared mournfully at the ground, shaking his head sadly. ' "Alas," ' they said, ' "Fintan has fled to where the enemy can't find him. Come to that, we can't find him either." ' Freddy Mulligan and Jack Mooney snickered as Durkin staggered back as though from shock. 'What? Fintan has skedaddled? The man who plotted and planned for his rebellion, and now that the great day is at hand, flees? Horror of horrors!'

Fintan Butler began to cry silently, the tears running down his cheeks, a look of appeal on his face. Freddy Mulligan and Jack Mooney had him wedged between them so that he could not move.

The sight of Butler's tears goaded Durkin into persecuting him further. 'Did you know that Fintan here visualised himself as another Brian Boru? Believed he was a reincarnation of that oul warrior. Saviour of our country and all that. Even wrote a book about him.' He sighed and shook his head. 'But he does not tell the whole story. Omits any mention of his sexual activities. Nothing about randy oul Brian ravishing his women in the heather.'

'You should have written it, Billy,' Jack Mooney said with a laugh.

'I wrote a little something, Jack, but only in verse.' Durkin looked at Fintan Butler with an apologetic expression on his face.

> Ah, me mind wanders back o'er the ages,
> To the days of that horny ould Celt.
> I can see Queen Maeve in her nightdress,
> And Brian Boru in his pelt.
> And I can hear that sturdy oul warrior saying,
> Through teeth that were gnashed and clenched tight,

'Ye had yer way last night, love,
But it's the hairy side out tonight!'

There was another explosion of laughter. A flushed and grinning
Durkin pointed a finger at Butler's woeful, tear-stained face. 'Lads,
lads,' he shouted above the uproar, 'I'm afraid Fintan does not share
your amusement.'

'All right, Durkin,' Butler said, releasing his arm from Mulligan's
grip, 'you've had your fun.' He tried to walk away but Durkin placed a
brawny hand on his chest and pushed him back against the bar. 'Stay
awhile. The fun, as you call it, is only beginning.'

'Let me go, Durkin, or you'll be sorry.'

Durkin guffawed. 'Is that a warning?'

'Yes.'

Durkin's good-humour vanished. 'Listen, you windy bastard,' he
growled. 'For years you've been looking down your supercilious hook
nose at me as if I were something that had just crawled out from under a
stone. Well, understand this. No one humiliates Billy Durkin and gets
away with it.'

Fintan Butler was fully composed now. He looked at Durkin with
undisguised contempt.

Durkin clenched his fist. He thrust his head forward aggressively,
conscious of his four companions watching him. If he lost the initiative
to Butler, if he allowed him to turn the tables on him, the news would be
around every pub in the city. Mulligan was a notorious gossip and the
other three no better.

'Butler,' he hissed, 'you are going to find out how vindictive I can be.
Just you wait. I'm going to spread your story all over the front page of
the *Eye-Witness*. By the time I'm finished with you, the only place you'll
be safe will be inside a monastery.'

Butler's eyes widened. 'Durkin, you amaze me with your remarkable
insight. For that's the very place I intend to enter. But of my own
accord.' He sighed. 'Fate really. I realise now I was meant to serve God
rather than my country. I was never a success as a revolutionary.'

Durkin tried not to let the frustration he felt show on his face.
'Nevertheless –'

'Nevertheless nothing, Durkin,' Butler said. 'No one is interested in
me. The men who were executed – they're the ones the people want to
read about.' He reached into his pocket and drew out a packet of
cigarettes. He lit one and leaned casually back against the bar. The
weeping, pathetic creature of a moment ago had vanished. Butler was

521

now confident and relaxed. He took a long pull of the cigarette and blew a stream of smoke into Durkin's face. 'I'm afraid you'll have to entertain your readers with something else, Durkin. Something salacious. Adultery for instance. That always appeals to you and the depraved morons who read your filthy rag.' He took another pull of the cigarette and viewed Durkin through a haze of tobacco smoke. 'I may be of help to you in your search for copy, Durkin. After all, an out-of-the-way hotel like this is the ideal place for what you would call a dirty weekend. Let me see now . . .' He raised his eyes, watching the smoke curling upwards towards the ceiling.

'Ah yes,' he said after a few seconds, 'I remember now. A few weeks ago, just before the outbreak of the rebellion, we had an army Captain and his . . . er . . . wife staying here. A Captain Alexander Carew. At least that's the name he entered in the register. A friend of yours, Durkin, I believe. And the lady . . . At first I could not recall where I had seen her before. Then I remembered. It was at a reception my publisher gave years ago. She presented me with one of the original illustrations which she did for my book.' He paused.

'It was your wife, Durkin.'

There was a sharp hiss as Freddy Mulligan drew in his breath. It was the only sound in the stunned silence. Then Durkin's face swelled with fury.

'Why ye lyin' bastard!' he snarled and took a step forward, raising his fist. Butler straightened up, on the defensive. He was taller by more than a foot and had a longer reach. Durkin halted, not sure what to do next.

Then Butler reached into his inside pocket and drew out a crumpled piece of notepaper. 'Of course you need proof, Durkin. Here it is. Amazing the things one finds in a wastepaper basket.' He opened it out and began to read.

Miriam dearest.
   By the time you read this I shall be on my back to Dublin. Some trouble has broken out there. But you are not to worry. It won't last long, and besides I'll be attached to the Staff and out of danger.
   I wanted to wake you and tell you, but you looked so peaceful lying there I decided not to. Anyway I hate goodbyes. Aren't you glad your sailing was postponed, giving us the opportunity of spending two glorious days and nights together –'

Durkin snatched the letter from his hand and looked at it. His heart gave a sickening lurch. But it was not the contents that made the colour drain from his face, it was the unmistakable handwriting of Alec Carew, that peculiar backhanded scrawl which no one could imitate no matter how hard they tried. He read the rest of the letter in a daze, wincing when he came to an intimate passage at the foot of the page. There was more writing on the other side and he turned it over.

No more furtive weekends like this. When this trouble in the city is over, I'll tell Billy about us. He'll have to give you a divorce when he hears that you are expecting my baby. It will be easier with you in England, far away from any unpleasantness that may occur . . .

He crumpled the letter into a ball, tears in his eyes. His wife and his best friend. He raised his head to see his four companions staring at him, carefully watching his reaction. Then Freddy Mulligan turned his head away, his hand covering his mouth, trying to stifle the laughter.

Durkin groaned. The news of his betrayal would be all over town tomorrow. Mulligan and the rest of them would see to that.

Then Butler began to laugh. 'Why don't you print that on the front page of the *Eye-Witness*, Durkin? The scoop of the year! Billy Durkin – tracking down every case of infidelity that comes his way. Peeping through the keyholes of bedrooms in every little seedy hotel in Dublin. And while he's away gathering more dirt for that rag of his, his wife is jumping into bed with another man!' He laughter rose higher. 'There was a cuckoo in the nest, Billy Boy,' he howled, 'a cuckoo in the nest!'

## III

Father Poole drew the curtains aside and peeped out at the dark, wet, wind-fretted street. The glorious sunny weather – 'rebellion weather' they were now calling it – had finally ended. For two days now fierce storms had swept the country. The temperature had dropped so that it had been necessary to keep a fire going all day in the study. He could see the reflection of the flames on the window pane and could feel the heat of them against his back. The worst of the storm is over, he told himself. The rain was coming in fitful showers and the wind had fallen to a banshee whine. He could feel the damp icy touch of it caressing his cheek as it snaked through a crack in the corner of the window. He

523

shivered a little and shuffled back towards the fire in his carpet slippers.

He was eighty-seven years of age now. At times it seemed to him that it was a perversion of nature that one should live so long. He lowered himself into the armchair, groaning at the stiffness of his limbs. His spectacles and the newspaper were on the coffee-table in front of him and he reached out for them. He had read the paper just after supper, but already he had forgotten what it contained. His memory was failing rapidly. It was as if his brain was a cracked and leaking vessel through which memory continuously dripped, leaving a residue of sensations, pleasant and unpleasant, adhering to the sides. He brought the paper close to his face and started to read slowly, his lips moving soundlessly.

*The Prime Minister, Mr Asquith, accompanied by his private secretary, arrived at Kingstown this morning. While motoring through the city, Mr Asquith had pointed out to him the places where there had been fighting. Instead of adopting the direct route to the Viceregal Lodge, a detour was made and the Prime Minister . . .*

Father Poole gave a low grunt. A bit late in the day, he thought, for the Prime Minister to be rushing across to Dublin to try and calm things down. The executions had caused revulsion both in Ireland and America. Even the newspapers, which only a short time ago were condemning the rebels as criminal lunatics, were now clamouring for a cessation of any more acts of revenge. His eyes moved down the narrow column of the editorial.

*The striking feature about the present situation in Ireland is that we are virtually living under a military despotism. As a result of secret military trials, executions have been carried out. Not only is the country under martial law, but searches and arrests are being made all over Ireland. Many of those arrested have no connection or sympathy with the rebellion. It would be strange indeed if disaffection would not be fostered by such proceedings.*

*The policy which is being pursued is in effect a policy of exasperation which must leave behind it feelings of racial hatred and ill-will which it may take many years to obliterate.*

Father Poole heaved a sigh. It had been stupid of the Government to put a military man in charge. He had made martyrs of the executed rebels. He had played right into the hands of the wild men, the advocates of physical force. These men now had the support of the people, something they never had before. Perhaps in time they would free Ireland from her seven centuries of bondage, but she would have to go through hell first. Thank God I won't be alive to see it, he thought as he turned the page.

The agony at Verdun was continuing.

The door was gently pushed open and Father Kinsella came carrying in a loaded tray. The housekeeper had been called away and in the meanwhile they would have to fend for themselves. Father Kinsella placed the tray on the coffee-table.

'I wish you would not sit with your back to the window, Father,' he said. 'There's a draught.' He removed the cosy, lifted the teapot and poured the tea. Father Poole winced. It was almost black.

'One or two spoonfuls of sugar, Father?'

'Three, if you please,' Father Poole said. It would need a pound of the stuff to kill the taste of that concoction, he thought. The sooner Mrs Dillon returns the better. He broke off a morsel of soda bread, chewed it with his few remaining teeth. He picked up the newspaper from his lap.

Father Kinsella stood. 'Father Poole . . .'

'Hmmm?'

'Promise me you will go straight to bed as soon as you have finished your supper.'

'Yes, yes,' Father Poole said, holding the newspaper close to his face.

Father Kinsella shook his head resignedly and walked towards the open door. He had almost reached it when Father Poole gave a low moan of distress. 'What's the matter, Father?'

Father Poole lowered the paper, sadness written all over his face. 'A paragraph here about a man who committed suicide. Suicide,' he repeated with a sorrowful shake of the head. 'Do yeh know, Robert, the thought of it never fails to horrify me. How can a man deliberately put himself beyond the reach of God – to wander in darkness for all eternity? Of course,' he said hopefully, 'it may have been temporary insanity. In which case . . .' He raised the paper in front of his face. '*Shocking discovery in house in Rathgar*,' he said, reading the headline. '*Suicide whilst the state of the mind was unbalanced was the verdict at an inquest in the City Morgue today on the death of William Durkin, publisher and –*'

'William Durkin!' Father Kinsella asked. 'Did you say William Durkin?'

'Yes,' Father Poole said, peering closely at the small type. 'William Durkin, publisher and editor of the *Eye-Witness* and *Society Life*.'

'Durkin dead,' Father Kinsella said. He gave a slow grim nod. When he reached the doorway he paused, pondering, his hand on the doorknob. 'How did he die?' he asked.

Father Poole hesitated before replying. 'He hanged himself.'

Father Kinsella gave a smile of satisfaction. 'So did Judas,' he said and closed the door.

Father Poole stifled a groan. It would be best if Father Kinsella was transferred to another parish. Someplace in the country, far away from the city and its bitter memories. He would write first thing in the morning, recommending the transfer and stating his reasons for it. Whether they would heed him or not was another matter. He was officially retired, but he had persistently refused to go to a home for aged priests. 'It's a silly notion to judge a man by the number of his years,' he had argued. 'I'm still active, still have all my facilities. A little slower than I used to be, I'll admit, but . . .'

He lay back in his chair, his supper untouched and forgotten. He could feel the burden of his years now; the body no longer responded to his dictates, and he could not even remember the words of the Mass. 'I'm just an encumbrance,' he said, addressing the empty room. It was unfair to the other priests to have to look after him and attend to their duties as well.

He had made up his mind to be transferred to a home for retired priests as soon as possible. He removed his spectacles, and placed them in their case. There I'll just dodder around, he told himself, reading my breviary and wait for death to claim me. Rain tapped against the window panes and he could hear the wind moaning along the deserted street outside. The heat from the fire was making him drowsy. His eyelids drooped. The clock ticked away with monotonous regularity.

Eighty-seven years, he mused. He was a part of history, a link with the past. He conjured up faces and images from bygone days.

The face of a professor of moral theology at the seminary, who had witnessed the storming of the Bastille. The image of an old man dying on a filthy bed of straw in a hovel off Newmarket, a veteran of Waterloo . . . How strange, he thought, I have difficulty remembering things which happened yesterday or the day before, yet the events of seventy or more years ago are still fresh in my mind. He could remember Dan O'Connell speaking at a monster rally in Dublin; could remember the Young Irelanders being conveyed through the streets under cavalry escort on their way to life imprisonment in Van Diemen's Land. Mitchel, Smith O'Brien, Meagher of the Sword . . . Names which had passed into history. He had seen them all; had heard them speak. They were not mere names to him, but creatures of flesh and blood.

He lay with his hands joined across his chest, his eyes half-closed. Eighty-seven years. It had been a long and fruitful life. He had no regrets. He dozed off, snoring gently.

The sound of shots jerked him awake. Had he actually heard shots or had he dreamt he had heard them? He waited, tense, but all he could hear was the mournful sigh of the wind. He shook his head. He must have been dreaming. What veterans we Dubliners have become, he thought. We are as familiar with the sounds of rifle and artillery fire as the people of France and Flanders.

Crackooomm! The single report echoed and re-echoed along the narrow side-street. His first instinct was to go to the window and look out. He half-rose from the chair, then checked himself. A figure in a lighted window would be an inviting target for any trigger-happy soldier. He lowered himself to the chair again. There was nothing he could do but wait.

A minute passed. The thunderous knocking startled him. He hesitated for a second, then rose slowly and padded across to the door. The corridor was cold and draughty and illuminated by only a single gas-jet. The jet had been lowered, leaving most of the corridor in darkness. He had to feel his way along the wall towards the front door. He fumbled for the bolt in the semi-dark and opened the door. A gust of wind tossed his thick white hair and flattened the lower part of his cassock against his legs.

The tall figure of an officer confronted him, holding a revolver in his hand. His cap was pulled over his eyes against the whipping wind and the collar of his trench-coat was up around his neck and throat. Behind him, six soldiers bunched together, their rifles held at port, bayonets gleaming in the lamplight.

'Your pardon, Padre,' the officer said, his voice a little breathless as though he had been running. 'We're looking for a man. He ran in this direction.'

Father Poole held the door half-open. 'Well, he's not in here.'

'He may have forced his way in somehow without your knowledge. He's armed, Padre. When we called on him to halt, he fired at us.'

Father Poole shivered as the cold pierced his clothes. He pulled the door wide open and stood aside. 'Come in and search if you must,' he said, 'but I assure you it's a waste of time.'

The officer hesitated.

Father Poole said with irritation: 'For heaven's sake, Lieutenant, do one thing or the other. I'm freezing to death standing here!'

'I'll give you the benefit of the doubt, Padre. I advise you to bolt the door and ensure all windows are fastened. This man is desperate and dangerous.'

Father Poole nodded. 'I'll do as you say, Lieutenant. Good-night.'

The officer gave a casual salute. 'Good-night, Padre. Sorry for the disturbance.'

Father Poole closed the door and shot the bolt home. He shuffled back up the ill-lit corridor. He was conscious of a strong draught against his face and in the silence he could hear the pat, pat, pat of rain on the linoleum covered floor. He groaned with vexation. Someone had left a window open in the passage-way between the church and the presbytery. His right shoulder brushed against the wall.

The bottom half of the window was open. He tried to pull it down, but it was too stiff. He tried harder, pulling it down by degrees. The effort left him exhausted and he rebuked himself for being a stupid old fool. Any kind of exertion at his age was dangerous. He felt light-headed, and he was gasping and wheezing like an old bellows. What I need now is a stiff swig of brandy, he told himself, shuffling back down the corridor to his study.

He paused before the closed door. Odd . . . he was sure he had left it open. He shrugged. Probably the wind. He opened it and walked into the welcoming warmth of the room, closing the door behind him. He was frozen to the marrow. A rustling sound brought him to a halt. It had come from behind. He turned slowly round.

A man was standing with his back to the wall between the door and the sideboard. He raised his arm and pointed a revolver at the old priest.

'Put that down!' Father Poole ordered harshly. He deliberately turned his back and took a few steps towards the chair and lowered himself into it, facing him. He screwed up his eyes. He could vaguely make out the jacket and trousers but, without his glasses, the face was just a blur. 'Are you hungry?' he asked. He looked down at the untouched supper on the small table before him. He had not even drunk the tea.

'This is the best I can offer,' he said offhandedly, and sat back in the chair, joining his hands.

The man did not move. Father Poole could sense his fear and mistrust. 'Come forward,' he said. 'Surely you're not afraid of an old man like me.'

The man hesitated still, holding the revolver out in front of him.

'For God's sake,' Father Poole exclaimed testily, 'put that damned thing away. This is the second time within the past ten minutes I've had someone point a revolver in my face.' He pointed to the chair on the other side of the table. 'Sit down and eat,' he said.

The man gestured upwards. 'Who else?'

'Upstairs? Only Father Kinsella and Father Murphy. Both fast

528

asleep. If that hammering at the front door didn't wake them, nothing will. Now please . . .' pointing again to the chair.

The man sat down facing him, placing the revolver on the table within reach of his hand.

Father Poole went stiff with shock. It was not a man who sat opposite him, but a youth of about sixteen. 'God preserve us,' he gasped, 'you're just a child!'

The youth flushed. 'I'm seventeen!' he snapped. He had a long thin face covered in freckles. The rain had darkened his red hair and had flattened it close to his skull. Then he began to eat, wolfing down the chunks of soda bread, hardly chewing, washing down each slice with a mouthful of tepid tea.

'When did you eat last?' Father Poole asked as the last slice vanished into his mouth.

The youth drained the cup. 'The day before yesterday,' he replied.

Father Poole leaned forward and twisted his head sideways like a bird. 'You're not a Dubliner, that's for sure. West of Ireland. Am I right?'

The youth looked at him with narrow, suspicious eyes. Then he nodded.

'What part?'

The youth hesitated before replying. 'Connemara.'

Father Poole sighed and shook his head. 'Oh child, child . . . yer a long way from home.' He lay back in the chair. 'What's your name?'

Again the hesitation; again the narrow-eyed suspicious look. 'Donal . . .' The surname trembled on his lips. Then he closed his mouth firmly. 'That's all you need to know,' he said curtly.

'That's all I want to know,' Father Poole said. 'I suppose with that red thatch of yours, they call you Red Donal? Or is it Donal Ruadh? Ah . . .' He gave a triumphant smile. 'I can see by that look on your face I'm right.' He raised both hands then lowered them gently to his knees. 'Well now, Donal Ruadh, what am I going to do with you at all, at all? For obviously you're destined to die by the bullet or rope, and you're too young for either.'

'I'll go as soon as the coast is clear.'

'Do you know the city?'

The youth shook his head.

Father Poole sighed. 'No, you're used to the wide-open spaces. The heather covered hills; lakes; bogs . . . After that, a city can be a strange and frightening place.' He studied the tall tense figure facing him. He noticed the dark circles under the eyes and the nervous tic under the

529

cheekbone. Poor kid, he thought. Hunted like a wild animal; without food; seeking shelter in anyplace he can find. 'I suppose you were involved in this recent madness?'

The youth nodded.

'And now you're on the run.' He pressed his thumb and forefinger against his closed eyelids. 'So young,' he moaned, 'so young.' A spasm of anger shook his tiny frame. 'Child, child, who was the fanatic that poisoned your mind? Who was he that made you take a gun in your hand?' He was startled by the youth's passionate outburst.

'It's not over yet! Next time we'll take to the hills and fight them from there! There'll be no surrender, no layin' down of arms. We've learnt our lesson. Next time we'll drive the British out for good!'

Father Poole put a warning finger to his lips. 'Shh, do you want the two upstairs to hear you? Quiet now, in God's name.' They sat in silence, listening, expecting to hear a call from above, expecting to hear a rush of feet down the stairs, but nothing happened.

Then they heard it; the distant shout of command carried on the wind. Then came the sound of booted feet. The patrol was returning. Donal reached for his revolver.

'Don't touch that!' Father Poole hissed sharply. 'Quick, dim the light.'

Donal obeyed silently, twisting the key until only a little light showed. He remained standing.

'Sit down,' Father Poole whispered. There was sufficient light from the fire.

The boy moved back to the chair and sat down. Firelight rested on one side of his face, leaving the rest in shadow. A sudden shout made him jump to his feet and grab for the revolver.

'No!' Father Poole clutched his sleeve. 'In God's name,' he begged, 'don't do anything rash.'

Donal trembled.

Father Poole tightened his grip. In the darkness they listened to the tramp of heavy boots coming nearer. Please, God, Father Poole appealed, let them pass. He closed his eyes, and his lips moved in silent prayer. He expected to hear a command to halt; expected to hear the dash of booted feet and the crash of rifle butts against the door. He could hear the youth in front of him sucking in his breath. Tension drained out of them as the last man went pounding past. Still they waited for the sounds to recede. Then Father Poole released his grip on the youth's sleeve.

'Thanks be to God and his everlasting mercy,' he whispered. 'You can put that revolver back on the table,' he said. 'You won't need it now.'

They sat in the dark listening to the wind and the rain lashing against the window panes.

Father Poole pondered for a moment. 'Tell me, Donal Ruadh, if you manage to escape from the city and into the hills, what will you do?'

'There will be others like me. Men on the run. We'll organise into bands, then strike!'

Father Poole emitted a grunt. 'Have you ever killed anyone?' he asked.

'Not yet.'

'But you will if you have to?'

'Oh yes. A country's freedom cannot be achieved without blood being shed.'

'Whose, I wonder,' asked the priest.

'I don't understand,' the youth said after a short pause.

'I was thinking of all the innocent civilians killed. Those that were murdered in the tenements in North King Street.'

'In war there are always civilian casualties.'

He's too young to have an answer for everything, Father Poole thought. His mentor did his work well, but God forgive him whoever he was, for I find it hard to.

A curious excitement grew within him. God had answered his prayer in the closing years of his life by sending him this youth who had embarked on the path of violence; this child who was willing to perpetrate a massacre in the name of patriotism.

'I asked for the unrepentant sinner, but He sent me the unrepentant rebel instead. Tell me, Donal Ruadh. Do you have a family? Father, mother?' The boy nodded. 'Brothers, sisters?'

'All my brothers and sisters are in America.'

'Ahhh,' Father Poole said softly. 'And now you're the only one left. The only comfort your poor parents have. Tell me, did they object to you joining the Volunteers?'

The youth shrugged. 'They were against it. Particularly my mother.'

'But you would not listen. You ran away from home. Is that it?'

The youth turned his head away. 'Yes,' he said, addressing the fire.

'And now your poor mother must be out of her mind with worry. At this very moment she's probably scanning the newspapers, looking for your name, trying to discover if you are among the dead or being marched down to the docks, on the way to prison in England.'

The youth closed his eyes, both hands gripping his knees.

531

'She probably thinks you're lying in the gutter of some Dublin slum street with a bullet in your body. The agony she must be goin' through, not knowin' if you're dead or alive. Think of the torment she's undergoing at the moment, Donal, not knowing if you're dead or alive. You surely don't want to torture her like that, do you now?'

There was a stifled sob as the youth clapped his hand to his mouth. He turned swiftly away, shoulders shaking. There was nothing of the fierce gunman of ten minutes ago; now there was only a frightened, homesick child.

Father Poole waited until the sobbing had ceased. Then he rose slowly to his feet and moved around to the other side of the small table. He placed a comforting hand on his shoulder and lowered his head. 'Do you want me to help you, Donal?' he asked, speaking softly into his ear. 'I can get you out of the city . . . I can get you home.'

The youth wiped his eyes with the cuff of his sleeve, but said nothing. Father Poole waited patiently. Then he said, 'If you want me to help you, just say so. If you refuse my help, Donal, then you can go out into those streets with your gun in your hand. Sooner or later you'll blunder into a patrol . . . a few shots exchanged . . . then your bullet-riddled body left sprawled in the gutter.' He paused for a few seconds. 'Is that what you want? Another martyr for old Ireland? God knows,' he added bitterly, 'there have been enough of those in the past few weeks.'

He waited for some kind of response while the clock on the mantelshelf ticked away the seconds.

Then the youth lifted his head slowly. The tears had left long dirty streaks down his face. 'Help me, Father.'

Father Poole sighed with relief. 'I'll help you, Donal. But first you must promise me something. Promise me you'll give up this madness. This sort of life is not for you. Forget all thoughts of revenge and killing. Leave that to men older than yourself.' He meditated for a moment. 'How do you and your parents exist, Donal Ruadh?'

'My father has a small farm.'

'Which will be yours some day.'

''Tis only seventeen acres of poor land.'

'Many men have to live off less.'

Father Poole raised his hand from the youth's shoulder and tweaked his ear. 'Yer a fine handsome lad. There's a girl, I suppose. Hmmm?'

'Yes,' the youth said reluctantly.

'Your future wife?'

There was a helpless shrug. 'She runs away whenever she meets me.'

'Then why don't you run after her? Faint heart never won fair maiden.'

The youth straightened up a little. 'Do you think I should?' he asked.

Father Poole experienced an inner glow of satisfaction. The lad's thoughts of violence and bloodshed were veering away towards the happy pursuits of youth. He laid a reassuring hand on his shoulder. 'Of course I do.' Then he became serious. 'There are two paths before you, Donal Ruadh,' he said. 'One leads to happiness. The other one can only lead to destruction and death.' He paused. 'Which one will you take?' He waited anxiously for the answer.

Several seconds passed. Then the youth released his breath in one long weary sigh. 'I just want to go home, Father,' he said.

Father Poole offered silent thanks. 'Then promise me you will abandon all your violent ways. Promise me you'll cleanse your heart and mind of all thoughts of revenge. Promise!' he whispered fiercely, digging his fingernails into the youth's shoulder, making him wince.

'I promise,' the youth murmured.

Father Poole patted his shoulder. Already his thoughts were on what lay ahead. He waddled over to the writing-desk and drew up a chair and sat down. Then he reached into his inside pocket and took out his spectacle case. There was a pad and pencil on the desk in front of him. He put on his spectacles and picked up the pencil, then began to scribble a note. Suddenly he paused. If the youth were to be captured and the note found on him, it would undoubtedly cause trouble for himself and the other two priests. He shrugged. It was a risk he would have to take. He continued on writing and then signed his name in full.

He folded the note. 'Come here to me, Donal Ruadh,' he said, standing up. The youth walked over to him. Father Poole stuffed the folded note into his breast-pocket. Then he placed both hands on his shoulders. 'Now listen carefully to me . . .'

They were dimly aware of the rain, tap, tap, tapping against the window panes. It was no longer coming down heavy and the wind had dwindled to a whisper. 'There's a side street almost opposite the church. It runs west and leads directly to the canal basin. There's a small house at the end – number eighteen. Give that note to the man who opens the door.' God alone knows what Noel Dunne will think, he thought, when he hears someone banging on his door at this time of night. 'He'll smuggle you on to one of the brewery barges. It will be an uncomfortable journey, wedged between porter barrels and covered by a tarpaulin, but you'll be alive and safe. He's done it many times before. In a few days you'll be in Tullamore – nearly half-way home.' He lowered his hand from the youth's shouldes and led him by the arm to the door. As he opened it, the youth looked back at the revolver lying on the table. 'Forget about that,' Father Poole said. 'It's too dangerous a toy for a youngster like you to be playin' with. Come now, and for heaven's sake try not to make any noise.'

They crept down the corridor. As they passed under the gas-jet Father Poole whispered, 'Put that out. I have no wish to be silhouetted in the doorway with the light behind me.' He had to feel for the bolt in the dark, and eased it back gently. The youth stood behind him. 'Go back a little,' he whispered. 'If it's safe to come out, I'll beckon.'

He opened the door slowly. A light rain was falling and the wind had dwindled to a damp breeze. He pulled the collar of his jacket up about his neck and throat and descended the steps. The gate was open and he stood in the gateway looking up and down the street, ears cocked for the slightest sound. The street was deserted and he could not hear a thing. He turned around and beckoned.

The youth emerged from the doorway and tripped lightly down the steps. Father Poole gripped his arm and pointed to the entrance of a street on the other side of the road. 'Keep to the shadows,' he cautioned. 'And if you run into a patrol, surrender. Don't try and run for it, or they'll shoot you down.' He released his grip. 'Away with you now, Donal Ruadh, and God go with you.'

The youth moved away without a word. He halted at the edge of the footpath, looked swiftly to the left and right, then ran across the road. He halted again at the entrance to the street and peered around the corner. Then he turned around, waved and disappeared from sight.

Father Poole remained standing in the gateway, listening, oblivious of the rain soaking through his thin clerical jacket. This was the moment he had been dreading. He dug his fingernails into the palms of his hands, expecting to hear a challenging shout to halt followed by a burst of gunfire. Please, God, he prayed, don't let it happen. Let him get away. Show your infinite mercy.

He stood shivering in the drizzling rain, unwilling to go inside, waiting and listening. Minutes dragged by. But the only sounds he could hear were the hissing of the rain and the beating of his heart. He heaved a thankful sigh. The youth had reached his destination safely. 'All praise to you, O God, and your everlasting mercy,' he whispered.

Then he turned around and mounted the steps and closed the door on the night.